David Wedderburn, Luisa J. W. Percival

Life of Sir David Wedderburn, bart., M.P.

David Wedderburn, Luisa J. W. Percival

Life of Sir David Wedderburn, bart., M.P.

ISBN/EAN: 9783337332648

Printed in Europe, USA, Canada, Australia, Japan

Cover: Foto ©Andreas Hilbeck / pixelio.de

More available books at **www.hansebooks.com**

LIFE

OF

SIR DAVID WEDDERBURN

BART., M.P.

COMPILED FROM HIS JOURNALS AND WRITINGS

BY HIS SISTER

MRS. E. H. PERCIVAL

.

LONDON

KEGAN PAUL, TRENCH & CO., 1, PATERNOSTER SQUARE

1884

PREFACE.

TIIIS volume has been a labour of love on the part of
my youngest sister, assisted by her husband. In her
childhood she was the special plaything of my brother
David, who, as a boy, found never-ending pleasure in
petting or tormenting her. She, on her part, returned his
affection with a child's devotion. And these relations
continued with little alteration in after years, until her
children came to fill her place, and in their turn became
to him, even in infancy, the objects of absorbing attention:
teaching them, teasing them, never tired of sharing in
their games; a certain ally in every trouble and difficulty,
he found constant interest in drawing out their character
and stimulating their intelligence. This youthfulness of
disposition was one of my brother's most striking characteristics. Ever young and bright, in the home circle he
seemed almost a playmate of the boys. His relations to
my sister seemed thus gradually to be reversed as years
passed on. Almost unconsciously she came to watch him
with a sort of motherly care. And this feeling became
confirmed after my mother's death, when he began to
show symptoms of failing health. Thus it seemed to us
natural that she should now undertake this record of his

life. The work has proved a solace to her in distress;
and it has been carried out in a way that must, I think,
approve itself to all my brother's friends. It is the record
of a happy life—happy from good health and a joyous
temperament, and from the surroundings of both his
private and public life, throughout which he enjoyed complete freedom of action, together with the opportunity of
much public usefulness.

With regard to the form of the book, I may mention
that it was originally intended to draw up only a brief
memoir of a life that was very dear to us, to preserve
as far as might be the features of a character which we
regarded with affectionate pride. This plan would have
included only a collected reprint of articles, lectures, and
speeches already published by him, and would have been
intended for only a limited circle of private friends. But
as the materials came to be opened out, so much was found
that was both new and interesting, that we determined to
alter the original plan, and to make the present memoir
consist mostly of fresh matter, only reproducing some
striking passages from what has been already published.
My brother had, even from boyhood, been in the habit
of keeping elaborate journals when on the travels which
occupied so large a portion of his time. These journals,
neatly written in a series of large note-books, not only contained facts, figures, and descriptions, but also the reflections
suggested by what he saw, and the mature conclusions
drawn from his experience of other countries. They thus
formed a storehouse from which he was accustomed to
draw materials for lectures, for political speeches, and for
magazine articles, such as those on Java, Japan, India,
and Australia, which he published from time to time in

the *Fortnightly Review* and the *Nineteenth Century.* And so carefully were these journals worked up at the time, that the materials now extracted have needed but little alteration to make them suited for public use.

To make now a judicious selection from this great mass of material has involved much labour, in which I would have gladly taken a part. This, unfortunately, I was unable to do, owing to my absence in India. But I feel that the work has been done much better than I could have hoped to do it among the preoccupations of official duties. It will be noticed that there is in this memoir an absence of letters from my brother's friends and acquaintances; and it may be mentioned that this is accounted for by his habit of never keeping letters, but destroying all correspondence as soon as disposed of. He did not, in fact, keep up any correspondence of a continuous or elaborate kind, and his own letters were seldom more than mere notes, disposing of the matter immediately in hand. When abroad, the place of letters was entirely taken by the journals, and while in England he kept no record of his life and occupations. This gives what may —at first—appear undue prominence in this book to the accounts of foreign travel.

The illustrations are selected from his own pencil sketches, which always formed a sort of running commentary upon the contents of journals.

W. WEDDERBURN.

MEREDITH, GLOUCESTER,
December, 1883.

CONTENTS.

—•◦•—

CHAPTER I.
1835-1854.

CHAPTER II.
1854-1863.

CHAPTER III.
1863.

CHAPTER IV.
1864-1866.

CHAPTER V.
1866.

CHAPTER VI.
1867-1869.

CHAPTER XXIII.

1881–1882.

CHAPTER XXIV.

1882.

SIR DAVID WEDDERBURN'S LIFE.

"The Ancient House of Keith".

CHAPTER I.

1835-1854.

PARENTAGE—CHILDHOOD—AT SCHOOL—EDINBURGH UNIVERSITY.

DAVID WEDDERBURN was born at Bombay on the 20th of December, 1835.

The Wedderburn family is of ancient descent on the Scottish Border, and the name is believed to have been taken from lands in Berwickshire. In 1296 Walter de Wedderburne was one of the barons who swore fealty to Edward I. at "Berewyk sur Twed." And the "seven spears of Wedderburn" are well known in Border minstrelsy. The immediate ancestors of the present family were settled in Forfarshire during the fifteenth century, and obtained charters for the lands of Tofts in that county. John Wedderburn of Tofts is described as "a person of fine

accomplishments, and much in favour with King James V."
And the historian Pitscothy relates that in 1530, when Lord
William Howard came as ambassador from Henry VIII.,
King James selected Mr. Wedderburn as one of three
landed gentlemen to represent Scotland in a friendly
archery tournament against England. The prize to the
victors was a hundred crowns and a tun of wine. "They
contended at St. Andrew's, and although the English
acquitted themselves. as excellent archers, the Scotch
carried away the prize."

His grandson Alexander is described as "a man of excellent parts, who employed much of his time in making
up differences among his neighbours, in which good office
he was so dexterous and impartial that he generally gave
satisfaction to all parties. As he was trusted by the town
of Dundee in all their affairs, he had frequent opportunities
of seeing King James VI., with whom he was in great
favour ; he accompanied him to England anno 1603, and
when he was about to return to Scotland, His Majesty took
a diamond ring off his finger, and gave him as a token of
friendship, which is still preserved in the family." His heir,
Sir Alexander, known as the Knight of Ripon, was one of
the Commissioners appointed by the Parliament of Scotland
to negotiate the union between England and Scotland.

A baronetcy of Nova Scotia was conferred by Queen
Anne on Sir John Wedderburn of Blackness in Forfarshire ; but it was attainted in 1746, when the fifth baronet
embraced the cause of Charles Edward. He served as a
volunteer at the battle of Culloden ; was taken prisoner,
and executed on Kennington Common. His son John,
grandfather of David the subject of the present memoir,
was then only a lad of sixteen. But he also fought at the
battle of Culloden, holding a commission as cornet in Lord
Ogilvy's regiment. After various adventures he succeeded
in effecting his escape from the country, and resided in

Jamaica till he was able to return to Scotland. He purchased the estate of Balindean in Perthshire, continuing
to assume the title ; and in 1803 a new patent was issued
to his eldest son, Sir David Wedderburn of Balindean.

In 1858 Sir David was succeeded by his brother John,
who had entered the Bombay Civil Service in 1806, and
remained in India for thirty years. During that time he
filled various important offices, and was a trusted friend of
Mr. Mountstuart Elphinstone, then Governor of Bombay.
In 1822 he married Henrietta Louisa, daughter of William
Milburn, Esq., by whom he had three sons and four
daughters.

ALICIA HENRIETTA, *m.* 1862, Colonel W. Hope, C.B.

JOHN, *b.* 1825, *m.* 1856, Alice, d. of D. C. Bell, Esq., *d.* 1857.

ELIZABETH, *d.* 1876.

MARGARET, *d.* 1874.

DAVID, *b.* 1835, *d.* 1882.

WILLIAM, *b.* 1838, *m.* 1878, Mary Blanche, d. of H. W.
Hoskyns, Esq.

LOUISA JANE, *m.* 1869, E. H. Percival, Bombay Civil Service.

The facts connected with David's early childhood are
supplied by his eldest sister, the only one of the family now
left who remembers that time.

At the end of 1836, when David was a year old, Mr.
John Wedderburn resigned the Service, and started for
England, with his wife, mother-in-law, and the baby, by the
overland route, being one of the first families to undertake
the then difficult journey. The old *Hugh Lindsay*, the first
steamer on that line, with poor accommodation and worse
fare, steamed slowly with them to Cosseir, where they took
camel caravan four days across the desert to Thebes. The
temples of Carnac were visited, and even the baby is said
to have lifted his little hands and eyes in the temple of
Dendera, saying, *Burra, burra,* " Large, large." A slow and
pleasant sail down the Nile brought them in time for the

next monthly mail to England, and after a tedious deten-
tion in quarantine at Malta, they landed at Falmouth. A
weary posting journey, from the extremity of England to
Edinburgh, changing horses every ten miles, at last brought
them, in May, 1837, to Inveresk Lodge, Musselburgh, where
the four elder children, who had been sent home some time
before to the care of their uncle and aunt, were waiting to
welcome them.

At two years old, David knew his letters and was trying
to read, but by the doctor's order all teaching was forbidden
till the mature age of four was reached.   The family settled
for a time in Charlotte Square, Edinburgh, but in 1841
moved to Keith House, East Lothian, the property of Mr.
Wedderburn's nephew, Lord Hopetoun.   There David, and
his little brother Willie, ran wild among the bonnie banks
and braes, learning to know and love every beast, bird, and
flower, with other woodcraft from the young keeper, who
was courting their nurse, and found his best method was to
win her boys, who knew no greater hero than Sandy, and
longed to follow his noble profession.   Many and ingenious
were the home games too, David especially delighting in
acting historical scenes of which he had read.   On one
occasion a heavy thud and bitter cry were heard from a
corner where the boys were playing, and the sisters rushed
to the rescue.   "How could you give him such a blow, you
naughty boy!"   "But," said David, half sobbing, "it was
Robert Bruce breaking his battle-axe on the head of Henry
de Bohun."   "Oh, was it in the battle?" cried Willie,
rubbing his head very hard; "then I don't mind it at all."
Such vivid illustrations of history were forbidden in
future.

In 1844, when the family moved abroad, the education
of the boys became a serious matter, but steady lessons
were carried on by their sisters, who found them, on the
whole, quick and willing pupils.   Even when travelling

through lovely scenery, after a four-hour's drive in the early morning, the lessons went on during the midday rest in some quaint town or village, although there was usually another long drive to the night's halt. This would be continued for weeks together, varied by a few days among the picture galleries or ruins of some historic town, where the little students were as eager with their catalogues and guide-books as their elders. In Florence especially, where two winters were passed, the boys were well-known devotees among the statues, antiques, and picture treasures of the old palaces. They soon learnt to chatter Italian with old and young, with artists and connoisseurs in the galleries, and in frequent international contests with Italian boys in the back streets.

When, in 1847, the family turned homewards, the boys were left at school near Bern. The head-master asked as to their attainments. "Ah! home teaching; we must not expect much;" but to his surprise he found them thoroughly well grounded, and in all points above the average of his own pupils. "Brain of elder boy rather overworked," he said; "too much excitement of sorts." So all studies were stopped, except learning German orally, and steady work in the carpenter's shop. The last sight the family had of the boys was starting with some twenty others in linen blouses, with little knapsacks and alpenstocks, for a walking tour in the mountains.

An old family friend, the Rev. James Dodds, thus records his early impressions of the boy :—

"In 1841 and 1842 I frequently saw, at Keith House, East Lothian, David Wedderburn, a boy of quick parts and singular promise. As minister at that time of the parish in which his home was situated, I was well acquainted with his parents, the late Sir John and Lady Wedderburn, and with the various members of their family. Among a group of intelligent brothers and sisters, David was con-

spicuous for quickness of observation, and a thoughtfulness
beyond his years. He had many characteristics of a pre-
cocious boy, but he early showed a solidity of understanding, which, joined to what I sometimes called a hereditary
strength of memory, raised him above the level of prema-
turely clever children, and gave promise of high intellectual
attainments. He owed much to the fostering and judicious
care of his parents, who wisely restrained, while they guided
the development of his mental powers. In forming plans
for his education they uniformly kept in view the peculiarities of his temperament, and felt the necessity of holding
him back, rather than pushing him forward in the different
branches of school learning.

"He was never, with all his mental superiority, a forward
or assuming boy. On the contrary, modesty and a delicate
sensitiveness were among his most striking characteristics.
While excelling in many things, he never seemed to delight
to excel. He also early showed a regard for the feelings
of others, which doubtless lay at the foundation of the
chivalrous spirit which afterwards distinguished him both
in private and in public life.

"I must always associate David Wedderburn especially
with that kind and excellent mother, who reared him with
a tenderness and a judgment peculiarly her own, and whose
love he returned all his life long with an ardour never surpassed by the most devoted of sons. He was blessed with
an admirable father, a man of distinguished attainments
and truly noble character, who did ample justice to all his
children, and left them the precious legacy of a bright
example. But it was his mother who had the chief share
of the work of training the mind and forming the character
of David Wedderburn. The occasional delicacy of the
boy's health called forth special maternal solicitude, and
furnished peculiar opportunities for the exercise of a wholesome maternal influence. Thus there arose between mother

and son a bond of affection stronger and deeper than is often met with even in the happiest families."

The following sketch of their early life together is given by his brother William :—

" In looking back to early years when, in childhood and boyhood, I was brought up with my brother David, I find that my impressions regarding him remain very clear, and his originality of character stands out with surprising dis-' tinctness. The influence of his father and mother in respect of transmitted qualities, as well as the effect of their example and training, may be traced from an early period. With regard to hereditary transmission of character, I always thought that in temperament my brother had little in common with my father, who was remarkable for his calm disposition, and who after his retirement from India took little active part in public affairs : benevolently contented with the happy family group which surrounded him, and especially devoted to my youngest sister, he occupied himself in directing our education, and employed most of his leisure time in the quiet pursuits of an English country gentleman. The eager questioning spirit and restlessness which distinguished my brother David must have come from some remoter ancestor, or more likely from my mother, who was remarkable for her quick active mind, and who specially sympathized with him, watching him through life with an ever-anxious thought for his welfare. As regards home training, my father rarely made use of direct precept. But his character and imposing presence had a great influence over us : he seemed to us the embodiment of justice combined with power ; and until later, when we realized how very gentle his disposition really was, our affection was largely mingled with awe. Unlike the previous generation, my father was in politics a liberal. But he was singularly impartial, and took no steps to create in us any party preference. In him we saw the 'constans et perpetua

voluntas jus suum cuique tribuendi,' and we knew that
his approval would be secured when in practical matters,
however trifling, we showed a just and liberal sense of the
rights of others.

"More than two years older than me in age, and with
a still greater superiority in development of intelligence,
David entirely dominated me by his will and opinions.
'The Boys,' as we were called in the family, seemed to be
a sort of joint entity of which he was the ruling mind: our
pursuits were dictated by his choice, we liked or disliked
people and things much according to his judgment; and I
was only too proud to be his faithful follower in all childish
adventure, although in my secret soul I did not invariably
relish the entertainment provided. The leading impression
which these memories produce on my mind is that my
brother's character was formed very early; and that it
changed very little in the course of his life. This impression is confirmed by the fact that as a boy he was always
regarded as very forward and original for his age, while in
later years he seemed so much younger than his contemporaries in his ways and disposition. Thus I remember that
as a boy he showed in a marked degree many of the characteristics of a grown man: self-reliance and absolute
independence of judgment; love of scientific research; and
an interest in political struggles. On the other hand, in
mature life, while developing these characteristics in a
wider field, he retained a certain boyish impatience of control, together with all his fresh gaiety and an undiminished
delight in small innocent pleasures. These peculiarities
were quite recognized in the family; often we laughed,
partly annoyed and partly pleased, at instances of what we
called his 'boy-ways;' and we were amused when the
sketch of his character was received from a professional
expert in handwriting, and the first remark was, 'The
writer is very young.' This struck us as a remarkable

point in the delineation of character, for in years he was
then no longer young.   The truth here indicated seems the
key to a good deal that was peculiar both in his public and
private life, as evidenced by a certain unworldliness in his
ways and by the uncompromising attitude he was apt to
assume when his principles or feelings were concerned.

"It must have been about 1843, when we lived at Keith
House, that I can first recollect anything.   Even in those
early days William Wallace and Robert the Bruce, the
Duke of Wellington, Napoleon, and Blucher, were realities
to me from the scenes we represented and the battles we
fought in their names.   Some of our child games, all
originating with him, were elaborate and ingenious.   For
example, before we had reached the stage of tin soldiers we
carried on historical battles with armies of coloured beads,
which were marshalled and marched about in proper array.
Additional life was given to all such games of imagination
when we became possessed of beautifully finished little tin
soldiers, horse, foot, and artillery ; as well as complete sets
representing a forest full of game, and all the trees, animals,
and birds of the garden of Eden.

"In the spring of 1844, the family left England to spend
several years on the Continent, and there is no doubt that
the novelty of his experiences during this period had an
important influence on my brother's character, giving scope
to his love of travel, and stimulating his sympathy for other
nations and races.   He began early to illustrate his travels,
and I can recall sketches of Schlangenbad and of Godes-
berg on the Rhine which impressed my early fancy ; also
coloured costumes of peasants of Antwerp and Louvain,
which must have been done when he was only eight years
old.   After a year spent in Switzerland, chiefly near Thun
and at Geneva, we all went on to Italy over the Mont Cenis
Pass, travelling *vetturino* through the pleasant old towns
of Northern Italy.   We ultimately settled for the summer

at the Baths of Lucca, going for the winter to Florence ; and this arrangement was repeated the following year, the family afterwards proceeding to Naples and Rome. It was about this time that he began to keep a regular journal of his travels, a practice which he never discontinued. In this journal he not only noted the ordinary incidents and accidents of the daily progress, and described the objects of interest and works of art, but also recorded his own opinions as to their relative merits, with historical allusions, quotations, and reflections very remarkable in a boy of his age. Only a fragment of this early journal has been preserved, from which the accounts of two days, one at Naples and one at Rome, have been selected :—

March 19, 1847, *Naples.*—We started early for Baia, got our nice old guide Pietro Rocco, two torches, and a most nefarious ass for Mama, and proceeded to Lake Lucrino passing Monte Nuovo, which was raised in thirty-six hours by an eruption. We walked to Lake Avernus, which means "without birds," as it was said birds died in flying over it ; and to the Sybil's bath, where the torches were lighted, and we went into a long cave and came to a little hole, the men were to carry us through some water to which this door led, but Papa said it was all hocus-pocus nonsense to get money out of people and would go no further. We met the carriage at Arco Felice and passed through the ancient town of Cuma ; it was curious to see the mixture of Grecian and Roman walls, the former being of large blocks, and the latter of little diamond-shaped stones ; we walked to the Sybil's grotto, and saw a beautiful view from the place where Apollo's temple was, with the entrance at this end to the passage that leads to the Sybil's bath. We then went upstairs to the place where she gave her oracles, also in a cavern ; the smoke of the torches was quite suffocating. The Amphitheatre of Cuma is still to be seen, but is turned into a vineyard, we drove to Fusaro, the ancient Acheron, near which was Tartarus ; this lake is very celebrated for its oysters and eels of which we took a number to dine on at Baia where we next went, and were nearly upset on the way. We entered the "cento camerelle" or prisons of Nero, creeping through low doors into

little rooms, numbers of which are in every direction ; also the
" Piscina mirabile " built by Lucullus for fresh fish or (more probably) to supply the Roman fleet with water, it was filled with
rain and has forty-eight arches, on the pillars a petrifaction has
formed which polishes very easily.   We then proceeded through
the Elysian fields to the temple of Bacchus, as our guide called
it, or in other words our dining house, where we had a good
dinner off our eels and oysters.   We saw the temple of Venus,
a fine old building of brick formerly encased inside with marble,
we went into the chamber of Venus as it is called all stuccoed in
basso-relievo, then to the temple of Mercury, the dome of which
has a very good echo, if you stamp with your foot, it seems as if
people were stamping above and if one person whisper at this
side of the building, another at that side will hear, though one in
the middle will not.   There is here a temple of Diana in the
same style as in the other two.   We then drove home and had a
good supper of crayfish.   As we passed Pozzuoli we saw the
place where St. Paul landed, and walked to Rome.

April 20th, Rome.—Having arranged with the guide and a lady,
Miss Plummer, we and the Nisbets drove to the catacombs of St.
Agnes, we had a number of candles, and went down some steps
into long passages, full of large and small niches for children and
men ; those of martyrs are known by two plates full of their
blood, these have been carried away, but the marks are there and
in some places are holes for lamps, these niches fit exactly to the
form of the body small at the feet, they were the burying places
of the Christians in the times of persecutions, their extent is not
known : in excavating one gallery they fill up another, the expense
being too great to carry out the earth.   We saw some chapels,
one where it is supposed the catechists catechised catechumens on
their catechism in the catacombs ; others with frescoes, as Moses
striking the rock, and the Good Shepherd, which are interesting
as being done in the second century.   By this time Mama felt
rather faint, so having thanked Miss Plummer we came away, I
noticed some marks on the walls by which the guide may know
his way.   We next drove to the Villa Albani a very good specimen of an Italian Villa, the view of the distant hills is beautiful
there is a fine verandah full of statues and the stairs are adorned
with bas-reliefs and flowers, the finest is Hercules in the garden
of the Hesperides, also the Antinous found in Hadrian's villa, so

white you might think it was done yesterday. The room where it is and the next are such comfortable little sitting-rooms all scented with flowers, then we went along colonnades full of statues and beautiful pillars of oriental alabaster, and numbers of mosaics, busts, etc.   In the afternoon we went to Santa Maria degli Angeli where are fine pictures, Papa and we two went into the cloisters but ladies cannot enter, they are the largest I ever saw, with four cypresses in the middle planted by the hand of Michael Angelo ; the monuments of Salvator Rosa and Carlo Maratta are there. At San Pietro in Vincoli we saw Michael Angelo's Moses, he is seated and has a long beard and flowing robes cut so deep you cannot reach with your hand to the end, he looks as if he were just going to speak.   In the vestry is Guido's Hope, her hands are clasped in prayer, her eyes raised to heaven, and a green drapery is thrown over her shoulders, it is a beautiful thing. Then we saw the temple of Minerva a pretty old ruin with a bas-relief of Minerva at the top, the capitals of the pillars and other parts are beautifully carved, also the temple of Nerva, three fine pillars strengthened with iron.

" During all this time, our education was proceeding by the unwearied exertions of our elder sisters, who passed on to us the results of their own studies in languages, history, and literature.   By their help and with the facilities of the Hamiltonian system, David worked through quite a number of Latin authors, and even penetrated as far as the Greek Testament.   And while thus obtaining his first glimpses of the Romans, and seeing around him the vestiges of their political greatness, he was at the same time gaining a prac- tical knowledge of the language and character of their modern descendants, for whom he ever afterwards retained the strongest feeling of respect and regard.   It was an almost unconscious education in history and politics.   For in those years Italy lay in the grasp of Austria, the Bour- bons, and the Pope ; and though all seemed quiet on the surface, the people were preparing themselves for the national struggle under King Charles Albert.   We studied Silvio Pellico's picture of Austrian dungeons, and heard from

Signor Tolomei, our friend and teacher, personal narratives of similar wrongs and suffering ; and it is easy to understand how an imaginative boy would become filled with sympathy for the national aspirations, and with an abiding hatred of arbitrary power and foreign oppression. But although at this period his surroundings gave force to such feelings, his sympathies were already with the free democratic races, especially the Athenians and the Romans of the Republican period. This had made an impression upon me, because my boyish partiality was rather for the kings : it seemed to me disorderly and contrary to nature that a State should be without a hereditary ruler, like a family without a father. Hector and Hannibal were among his favourite heroes, on account of their brave struggle against an overwhelming fate.

"He was very fond of Macaulay's 'Lays of Ancient Rome,' and it was always a delight to him to recite the sounding lines of ' Horatius Cocles ' and the ' Battle of Lake Regillus.' Poetry he seemed to get by heart as he read it, without an effort, and anything once learnt never seemed to fade from his memory, but remained a possession for life. The amount which he knew was something quite surprising ; he could repeat a large portion of Scott's ' Lady of the Lake,' and long passages from Tasso's ' Gierusalemme Liberata.' It used to be the habit for us as children to learn portions of the Bible, and repeat them aloud on Sunday evenings. In this way he gradually learnt the whole of Matthew's Gospel, which he could repeat with hardly a mistake ; similarly he knew all the Scottish Paraphrases.

"One other characteristic was his love of natural history, especially all relating to animals, birds, and insects. In our garden at the Baths of Lucca we used carefully, from day to day, to watch the proceedings of the various tribes of ants, noting the progress of their operations whether of war or engineering. We had books to help us in this study, and invented new names according to their colour and habits for those varieties which we were not able to identify. The feeling of being in a foreign land gave zest to our research, and I can recall the pride with which we first discovered the ant-lion and the praying mantis.

"In the summer of 1847 the rest of the family returned to England, leaving David and me at the Pestalozzian school of Hofwyl near Bern, under M. de Fellenberg. Here our life was a very pleasant one indeed, the school work being light, while much time was given to the carpenter's shop, the gymnasium, and the playground. Gardening was also a regular occupation. We were taught to swim in summer, and in the winter learnt skating and toboganing. The month of August was given up to the pleasant duty of voyages *en zig-zag*, the school being divided into small parties under the different masters. David and I with the smaller boys visited the Lake of Bienne and the valley of the Grindelwald, passing over the Wengern Alp. Our longest day's march was twenty-one miles.

"The following description of Hofwyl was written by David himself at the time :—

Hofwyl is situated about seven or eight miles from Berne. Papa and mama came with us and arranged all our affairs with M. de Fellenberg; they remained a day or two at the hotel, to see us comfortably settled. We soon began to feel at home, as we made little acquaintances with boys of our own age, who helped us and told us the ways of the school. Our daily routine is this : we get up at five o'clock, and M. de Fellenberg reads prayers ; we breakfast at six upon milk and bread, together with any fruit we may have bought during the preceding day; then we go to our lesson. We have carpentering, study gymnastics and German. At nine we get a lunch of bread, and are allowed to play for a quarter of an hour as we are eating it ; at twelve we dine, and then have play till two; we then have drawing, writing, etc.; at four we again get bread and at five bathing—there is a pond for the purpose.

Mr. Marti, who teaches us how to swim, puts a rope round us

which is attached to a stick something like a fishing-rod; we jump
in, and he shows us how to use our feet and hands. At six we
have supper, and on alternate nights we either work in our gardens
and play till nine, or else we have study at seven. Our days are
thus employed, and we are very happy at our different occupations.
My favourite master is Mr. Marti, for several reasons : one is that
I like him himself very much, and because I like the lessons he
teaches,—he teaches drawing, bathing, and gymnastics; he also
takes us to walk and upon excursions, and goes with us in the
boat on Saturday, which is a half holiday. There is a pretty little
lake not far off where we go in boats; it has trout and perch in it,
and the shores are bordered with white and yellow water-lilies.

The number of boys is upwards of thirty; sometimes we play
all together at shinty ball, and great fun it is. Gardening, too, is
a great amusement; we have each a little bit of ground in which
are vegetables such as carrots, turnips, etc., and when we have
bread we run, pluck up some radishes and eat them with it.
Opposite the house is a nice little bosquet where we walk in
during our play-time; here we either play hide-and-seek or walk
on stilts. In August we are to go on a journey among the Alps;
I am greatly looking forward to this excursion.

" In the early part of 1848 the revolutionary disturbances
broke out over Europe, and it was understood that the school
was to be broken up and the boys sent home. In Switzerland itself the war of the Sonderbund was going on, and we
watched the progress of events with the keenest interest,
our sympathies being with the Federal cause. In our walks
we used to meet the troops of the different cantons upon
the march, and from the school could hear the sound of the
bombardment of Freiberg. It was with much regret we
left Hofwyl. We were put in charge of a young Swiss
tutor for our journey to England, going by way of the
Rhine and crossing from Ostend. At Mannheim we saw a
little fighting. While the steamer stopped we had gone
into the town, and were there when the disturbance broke
out, and had to run for the bridge where the steamer was
moored. The insurgents had assembled there, and after

we got on board, wanted to take the steamer to break the bridge, pointing their guns and threatening to fire on the man at the helm. Our tutor was naturally alarmed, and entreated us to lie down under the saloon benches below water-mark, showing us, in fact, the example. David, however, could not be persuaded to do this, so we remained on deck watching the proceedings. As a matter of fact the steamer was not fired on, and we got safely away. As we passed out of sight down the river, we could see the Bavarian troops crossing the bridge and exchanging shots with the insurgents. In candour I must admit that, on this occasion, if left to myself, I should probably have yielded to the entreaties of our worthy tutor.

"After a holiday in London with my father and mother, and a short tour with them to some of the cathedral towns in the south of England, we were sent to M. Heldenmaier's school at Worksop in Nottinghamshire. This school, though not strictly Pestalozzian, was conducted on continental principles—the study of modern languages, science, drawing, and music being much encouraged ; indeed French was the language always required by school discipline to be spoken, even in play-time. Though younger than many of the boys, of whom there were sixty or seventy, David at once went to the top of the school, being in a class with two or three other boys much older than himself. His knowledge of French, German, and Italian was of course a great help to him, and he was also a capital Latin scholar, thanks in part to the good grounding he had received from my sisters. As the system followed did not admit of prizes, his position in the school involved no special recognition. After being at Worksop for eighteen months, he was removed to Loretto House, Musselburgh, under the Rev. Thomas Langhorne. I remained for some time longer at Worksop, and did not go to Loretto until after he had left."

On their return from the Continent the family had resettled themselves in their old home at Keith House, where the boys delighted to spend their holidays. They revived their love of country life, and made various collections after the manner of boys of their age, such as minerals, coins, seals, and objects of natural history. The one that interested David most was a collection of birds' eggs ; many of them he found himself, but those that were beyond his reach he obtained by barter and an expenditure of pocket-money, and the eggs, carefully arranged in trays of the boys' own making, have been preserved to delight the next generation.

At Loretto he quickly rose to the top of the school, taking five first-class prizes in July, 1850. An old school-fellow says, " He was always a leading authority among the boys and dux of his class, in fact the pride of the school ; not only looked upon by both masters and boys as the cleverest boy, but as the fairest referee in any dispute, as he always took an impartial view of things, and insisted on fair play being carried out." The Rev. W. H. Langhorne has kindly written the following account of his recollections of him while at the school :—

" I knew Sir David Wedderburn from early childhood ; and later, when he was about fourteen years of age, he became a pupil of my brother and myself at Loretto, in January, 1850. I remember him at Keith as a sharp intelligent little boy of a somewhat delicate temperament, and as he took kindly to me, I had all the more pleasure in having him afterwards as a pupil.

" I believe he began mathematical studies with me, and in these, as well as in his other classes, he was remarkable for his diligence, perseverance, and conscientiousness, being generally at the head of his class. One conspicuous characteristic of his mind was an innate or ingrained spirit of independent inquiry, which would never allow him to take anything for granted, however high the authority

C

might be that claimed his allegiance or demanded his
assent. This not unfrequently led to arguments in the
open class, which had to be put aside until the end of the
lesson, and it perhaps somewhat delayed his apparent pro
gress, because he could never be got to proceed beyond a
point about which he had not entirely satisfied his own
mind. It was no use saying that the matter in doub
would be made clear to him after a while, when his mind
had accustomed itself to the steps of the process—he would
simply decline to proceed.

"In the result, however, he made himself thoroughly
master of the subjects in hand, and was ready, therefore, to
enter upon the more difficult departments of mathematica
science with confidence and assurance; so that he wa
perhaps the only boy who never sent up wrong answers
and if he could not work out the whole paper at a sitting
he would worry out the problems he had left unfinished a
some later time.

"With all this aptitude for study he had a very keen
sense of the ludicrous, and only laughed with full heartines
at what was really absurd and ridiculous, not seeing an
particular fun in what generally amuses young peopl
For example, in the Greek class, a boy was asked wha
obeliskos meant, and not knowing what to reply, got h
next neighbour to prompt him; the latter whispered, '.
toasting-fork,' which the first repeated with all gravity; n
one relished the joke more than David, and it tickled h
fancy for a long time.

"I recollect I had a class on Sunday evenings for Paley
'Evidences:' in this David was a kind of terror to me.
had always encouraged the boys to speak out and giv
utterance to any difficulties they might have, in order
exercise their intelligence and see how far they were follov
ing the argument; but I never bargained for David Wea
derburn's fire of inquiries, which, however, I made the be

of that I could, sometimes concluding by saying that there were many questions with which a child might puzzle the wisest of men. But not always wishing to own that I was not wise myself, I dare say I had to find refuge when pressed in a quibble, which I passed off as a sufficient answer. The class not being so inquisitive, generally accepted the explanation ; but David looked grave, as if saying to himself, ' That is no answer.' He wanted, in fact, to get to the bottom and foundation of the subject, which few men, if any, had ever reached, and to this he was impelled by the inward truthfulness and accuracy of his mental constitution. This was all very well in abstract mathematics, where quantitative truth is attainable by processes of reasoning, but he would have puzzled Paley himself, had Paley been his instructor in moral philosophy and his own ' Christian Evidences.'

"As to character, he was very much respected, having a naturally high standard of morals, and being quite incapable of any conduct unbecoming a Christian and a gentleman. His intimate associates were few, as may be conceived from what has been already said, for his tastes and the qualities of his mind and disposition were quite out of the common order. He was a great reader, and what he read he formed a good judgment upon as he went along, and his retentive memory enabled him to reproduce his knowledge, although not always with ease ; for here again his critical faculty manifested itself, so that he could not give out as knowledge what he had any doubt about. The result was that he held many things in suspense that ordinary people accept without inquiry or question, and as he grew older this habit of mind became more confirmed. On entering public life, he naturally found much that could not stand the test of inquiry, and having an ideal of his own strongly formed in his mind, he could ill reconcile himself to things as they are."

In the summer of 1851, Mr. Wedderburn took his whole family to London, by sea, to visit the Great Exhibition, and the boys examined every part of the wonderful palace, to which they went daily, often by themselves.

At each school that he attended David rapidly took a high place, although never pressed to work by his father, whose parting injunction at the end of the holidays generally was, "Don't make an idiot of yourself, my boy, by overwork." Their father always placed great confidence in the boys, consulting their tastes and wishes to an unusual extent, as to the course their education should take. The Scotch system, under which mere boys attend the University and select their own subjects for study, commended itself to him, rather than the rigid routine and discipline of an English public school.

Accordingly David was sent at an early age, in the autumn of 1851, to the Edinburgh University, and although the youngest but one in the large Humanity (Latin) class of Professor Pillans, he was second in the examination for the gold medal. At the same time, he distinguished himself in the mathematical class of Professor Kelland, and obtained prizes two years in succession. He boarded, during the three winters that he was in Edinburgh, in Hill Street, with Mr. and Mrs. Stirling; she was a remarkably clever woman, a sister of John Hunter of Craigcrook and a niece of Lord Jeffrey. He greatly endeared himself to the old couple, and Mrs. Stirling used frankly to tell the others that she cared more for him than for all of them put together. Residence in their house was made pleasant and beneficial by the society they gathered round them; many small parties for games, acting, or dancing, kept the young men at home by the attraction of cheerful evenings, whilst an intellectual tone was given by the presence of such men as Dr. John Brown, Professor Blackie, and Mr. Lorimer.

He attended lectures on logic and metaphysics by Sir

William Hamilton, on rhetoric by Professor Aytoun, and
on Greek by Dunbar and Blackie.   From each of these
distinguished men he received certificates as to his ability
and the steady interest he took in their particular subject.
The first summer after he entered the University he
remained in Edinburgh in order to attend the botany
lectures by Professor Balfour, but the confinement to
town in summer seemed to try his health and brought on
a cough, which induced his parents to take him away to
the Isle of Arran for change of air and scene.   They never
afterwards allowed him to stay in Edinburgh through the
summer session ; so that in future he spent half the year in
the country, and was able to indulge his taste for walking
and driving excursions.   On one of these occasions, in the
autumn of 1852, he and his brother William made a tour
together in the Highlands, visiting Staffa and Iona, and
going as far north as Inverness.

Early in the summer of 1854, Mr. Wedderburn again
left home, taking the whole family with him for a tour in
England.   They spent three weeks in London, making
excursions to Cambridge and Windsor, and then went to
Leamington, from which they visited all the places which
make that neighbourhood so interesting, Warwick Castle,
Kenilworth, and Stratford-on-Avon.   After two days of
sight-seeing at Oxford, they made a driving tour through
Berkshire and Wiltshire.   At Gloucester they halted, in
order to see the small property, where " Meredith," the
house which was to be their home for many years, was
afterwards built.

They went on to Tintern Abbey and Raglan Castle on
the Wye, and thence drove all through Wales ; stopping at
Pembroke to see the dockyards, and staying a few days at
Aberystwith for the sake of sea-bathing, to which David
was always much addicted.   They ascended Snowdon, and
at Bangor the brothers enjoyed sea-fishing and boating ;

all were sorry to leave Wales and take the railway to
Chester.

They crossed from Liverpool to the Isle of Man, of
which, at that time, Mr. Wedderburn's nephew, the Hon.
Charles Hope, was Governor, and the two large families
enjoyed a week together thoroughly, visiting all parts of
the island.

Of these tours David, as usual, kept a detailed journal,
showing how accurate, even then, were his powers of
observation and description, and how strong was the love
of nature, which characterized him all through life.   They
returned by Morecambe Bay, reaching Keith House at the
end of July.

CHAPTER II.

CAMBRIDGE—HEIDELBERG UNIVERSITY—CALLED TO THE SCOTCH BAR—
DEATH OF HIS FATHER—ESSAY ON LUCRETIUS.

IN the autumn of 1854 he matriculated at Trinity College, Cambridge. While there he appeared to be singularly free from ambition for university distinction, and rather eschewed the society of so-called reading men, never allowing work to interfere with anything else that he wished to do. He belonged to cricket, boating, and archery clubs, but was not especially devoted to any of them ; he was then and always a keen chess player, and was a member of a small chess club, which often met at his rooms, and gave an excuse for jovial gatherings and a supper to which other than members were invited. He attended the Union Debating Society, and took a lively interest in the discussions, although not himself a frequent speaker.

In spite of seeming idleness, when it came to examinations his natural ability stood him in good stead, and he passed first class in the examination of Freshmen in June, 1855. The prize he selected on this occasion was a fine edition of the " Poetical Works " of Milton, of whom he was a great admirer : he could repeat by heart long passages from " Paradise Lost." He also gained a Trinity Scholarship in 1857, but did not compete for a Fellowship, as some of his friends wished him to do. Before going up for the

Mathematical Tripos, his private tutors were Mr. Walton and Mr. Percy Hudson ; but he had no great love for mathematics, which, as he said in a letter home, "will neither enter my head themselves, nor suffer anything else to do so." However, when he took his degree in January, 1858, he passed out high among the Senior Optimes, his name standing between those of Lord Frederick Cavendish and Mr. Campbell-Bannermann, M.P. ; the latter was then and afterwards one of his most intimate friends. His attachment to Cambridge induced him to stay on till the summer, the scholarship enabling him to keep his rooms, and he at one time thought of going up for the Classical Tripos. But as the names in the third class, which was all he hoped to attain to, were arranged alphabetically, the fear that his name would appear as "wooden spoon" made him turn to Natural Science, instead of Classics, and he took a second class in that subject.

The vacations were generally spent with the family at Keith House, but in the summer of 1856 he made his first independent run abroad, joining in Paris his brother William, who was studying there with a view to passing for the Indian Civil Service. Mr. D. Home, who has since become so well known as a spiritualist, happened to be boarding in the same house, and an acquaintance sprang up between them, which was afterwards renewed in England. When the weather became too warm to be pleasant in Paris, the brothers went to Normandy for a month, taking Dieppe as their head-quarters, but making walking excursions through the pretty villages along the coast. At Dieppe they met Mr. Catlin, of North American Indian fame, and found him a most amusing companion.

In December, 1854, his brother John came home from India, after ten years' absence. He had entered the Bengal Civil Service in 1844, and was one of those first selected to serve under Sir John Lawrence in the settlement of the newly annexed province of the Punjab. He was for some time Deputy Commissioner at Mooltan, and was very highly thought of by those under whom he served. John's return was a great event in the family, and to David, who had been a child when he left England, it was a great pleasure to have the society of his clever elder brother.

John married whilst at home, and returned to India with his young wife and child in the spring of 1857. He had just taken up his appointment as Deputy Commissioner at Hissar, when the outbreak of the Indian Mutiny at Meerut took place. He refused to leave his post, though fully aware of the danger from the first. In the one letter received from him during that time, he wrote, " The fate of our Indian Empire and the life of every European here is at stake." Very shortly after this, on the 29th of May, the wave of mutiny reached Hissar, and they, with all the Europeans in the station, were murdered, John himself being shot down by his own sentry at the door of his office. For those at home this was a time of terrible suspense, as the dreadful news was not fully confirmed till July. Such an event was enough to sadden any young life, and it was long before David's affectionate and sensitive nature recovered from the shock ; his own changed position and increased responsibilities as an eldest son were distinctly painful to him.

In the spring of the following year his old uncle and aunt, Sir David and Miss Wedderburn, who had so long made Inveresk Lodge a happy home to their many nephews and nieces, died within a few days of each other, and the title, with the old house, fell to David's father, now Sir John Wedderburn.

For the sake of change after these sad events, Sir John took his family again abroad, and they went by Ghent and Cologne to Dresden, where they took a house and stayed for three or four months. David revived his knowledge of

German, and was constantly in the glorious picture galleries and art collections for which that town is so famous ; they made excursions up and down the Elbe, and spent a week in beautiful Saxon Switzerland. The two brothers made more than one pedestrian trip into the mountains, which enabled them to see something of the life of the poorer classes ; a peasant wedding near Teplitz, in Bohemia, where they were welcome guests and invited to dance with the bride, was an episode such as David delighted in. Besides a visit to the interesting old town of Prague, the family on their homeward way stopped at Nuremburg, Augsburg, and for some days at Munich ; they went also to Heidelberg, and at Epernay inspected the champagne cellars. The brothers stayed in Paris when the others returned to England.

Sir John decided to spend the winter of 1858–59 at Inveresk Lodge, in order that his two sons might live at home while attending the lectures at the Edinburgh University ; David to begin his law studies, and William to prepare for the Competitive Examination of the Indian Civil Service, in which he passed third the following summer.

At Easter the family collected for some weeks at Gloucester, while Sir John superintended the building of the new house, which he called " Meredith," and from that time the spring months were spent there, to avoid the cold time of the year in Scotland for Lady Wedderburn. In the winter of 1859 David settled in lodgings in Hanover Street, Edinburgh, and for a short time entered the office of a Writer to the Signet ; but the work of this office was little to his taste, and it is to be feared that his services were not of much value.

Although he had the strongest aversion to military life as represented by a standing army, and frequently quoted Thackeray's line, " the noble art of murdering," yet he was one of the most consistent supporters with sword and pen of the auxiliary forces. He joined the Midlothian

Yeomanry Cavalry in 1859, and continued in it till 1869,
a short time before it was disbanded ; he was attached to
the Dalkeith Squadron, and was very regular in his attendance at the annual periods of drill : one of his superior
officers says, "I always found him most attentive and
willing to help in every way"; he was uniformly kind and
genial with all." The Advocates' Company was the first
Volunteer Corps raised in Scotland, and he was one of the
original members and remained in it until, owing to the
limited numbers, it was found necessary to merge it in
the general force.   He was present with it at the first great
Volunteer Review in Scotland, which was held by Her
Majesty in Holyrood Park, in August, 1860.

In this year he was fortunate enough to obtain chambers next door to the New Club, of which he was a member,
and he occupied them during the rest of his residence in
Edinburgh.   The Speculative Society, founded by Lord
Brougham, was a well-known debating club in Edinburgh
at that time, and he was admitted a member in December,
1859.   He became one of its chief supporters, and was
elected president in two successive winters, 1863–64 and
1864–65.   He read before it essays on "Louis Napoleon,"
on "Competitive Examinations," and on "Lucretius and
the Epicurean Philosophy."   The last was a subject which
ever so greatly interested him, that some extracts from
the essay are given at the end of this chapter.

Sir John Wedderburn was anxious that his son, before
being called to the Scotch bar, should study the Roman
law at Heidelberg, under Vangerow, then its best teacher ;
David went there in April, 1861, and spent most of the
summer attending the lectures on Roman law, and also a
course on chemistry by Bunsen.   He mixed to a certain
extent in the society of the German students, and saw a
good deal of their life, with its peculiar customs of beer-
drinking, part-singing, and duelling.   His friendship with

Donald Crawford dates from this time, and the latter thus describes their meeting and life together there :—

"My first distinct picture of him was our meeting at Heidelberg. As we walked along the street together, I told him I had just come from Oxford, where I had got my fellowship. With a characteristic gesture and smile he took off his cap, and we began talking on university subjects and our own plans. We hoped that seats in Parliament would soon be given to the Scotch universities, and he told me that nothing would gratify his ambition so much as to sit in Parliament for a Scotch university.

"At Heidelberg he lodged with a landscape painter named Eckert, who lived in a detached house in a garden on the outskirts of the town ; he had a wife and one child, 'der kleine Joseph.' Eckert was a very good fellow and quite a character, and his perpetual flow of racy conversation on all subjects, social, political, religious and artistic, supplied the best lessons in German which could be imagined. L. M. Carmichael lodged in the same house. Before I came they had had at least one long expedition with Eckert, and we made another together, going up the Neckar a certain distance, and then walking through the Odenwald. We came out on the plain, I think about Darmstadt ; we were a very jolly party, and Eckert recounted our adventures in a poem, which he composed as we went along. Years afterwards David used to repeat many stanzas of it. Even at this time he had all the qualities which on many future expeditions in after years made him a delightful companion. He entered into everything with so much spirit, his gaiety was catching, although his mood was not always equable. Full of observation and illustration, he beguiled the way with his talk and snatches of song and stories. As the summer advanced, he and I used to stroll up to the Castle in the evening, and sup on what he called a 'filled dove' (*gefüllte Taube*), and watch the fireflies.

"His temperament was singularly averse to the plod-
ding and pushing which are in some degree necessary in
every line of life. I remember once—it was on a riding
tour—we were talking of hard work and want of work :
some one said, that although always tempted to be
indolent, he felt an Anglo-Saxon *malaise* when not busy.
David said he never felt the slightest desire for work,
or the slightest discomfort at not having any to do. He
never did seem to work very hard at anything, yet in
truth his mind was so quick and active, his observation so keen and interests so universal, that he was never
idle. He was always learning, and his powerful memory
made him remember all that he learnt. This, with his
natural vein of humour, so much enjoyed by those who
knew him and cared for him, gave his conversation a great
interest and charm. It was never commonplace. Fond of
discussion, sometimes of paradox, he always put his views
in a striking and ingenious light, and instead of arguing
from vague generalities he always had his reasons vividly
in view, backed with plenty of illustration from his accurate
knowledge."

In December, 1861, he was called to the Scotch bar, and
although he had apparently devoted himself but little to
the study of law, the examiners remarked that they had
rarely passed any one so well prepared. His active mind
and clearness of apprehension enabled him not only to
acquire knowledge rapidly, but to make the best use of all
he knew when occasion required.

Up to this time, one of his greatest pleasures had been
to come out by coach or rail to Keith from Saturday to
Monday, or on any other holiday, frequently accompanied
by one or other of his many friends. Keith is a quaint old
house with two projecting wings, once joined by a wall and
forming a courtyard, but this wall has long vanished, and a
projection in the centre containing hall and staircase adds

to the comfort, at least, of the place. Nearly all the windows look on the fruit and flower gardens behind ; and the green park beyond, with fine limes and beeches, bounded by the flowing outline of the blue Lammermoor Hills, forms a lovely view. Sir John, known as Benevolus, delighted in seeing young people enjoy life, and encouraged all their merry devices ; it is difficult to say whether the gatherings were more cheerful in summer or winter. The charms of the four gardens, famous for their unlimited supply of gooseberries, strawberries and roses, were fully appreciated, while there were many tempting spots for picnics in the neighbourhood : the top of Lammerlaw, or the grand ruined castles of Crichton and Borthwick. At home archery and croquet were zealously entered into by all the family. David was a fair shot, and a proficient at croquet, a game for which he retained his liking long after it had gone out of fashion. The idea that anything good in itself should be " in or out of fashion " always roused his indignation. In winter there was plenty of old-fashioned shooting for the young men, and at New Year especially the house was filled to overflowing, the hall and staircase were a mass of evergreens, and the evenings were devoted to charades, tableaux, and dancing.

Towards the end of 1861 the war in America, and the imminent risk of a collision with this country, caused great anxiety to all who had money in American securities. Sir John had invested the bulk of his property in State bonds, and not only did the interest on this actually fall to one-third, but there was considerable fear of repudiation. This fact, and his own serious illness in January, 1862, led to the breaking up of the happy home at Keith House ; his eldest daughter was married to Colonel Hope, C.B., and went to India, and the family moved south, to make their home in future at Meredith, in Gloucestershire. In July, Sir John, who had never quite recovered, became rapidly worse, and

David arrived from Edinburgh only in time to be with him for a few days before his death.

Sir John's Indian pension ceased with his life, and the value of the American securities was so very uncertain that he thought it necessary to leave all that he had to his widow, and David found himself in no way in the position of an eldest son, but dependent almost entirely on his mother, who for some years could give him but a small allowance. Through his school and college days it had been an annoyance to his father, who retained his business habits, that David never could keep any accounts of his own money. The question every vacation, "Well, my boy, have you any accounts to show me this time?" was always met by the same response, and in after life he used to regret that he had vexed his kind father by such a trifle. He never did, however, mend his ways in that particular, but in his case it led to no evil results ; thanks to his good memory, he knew what he was spending, and his simple tastes made him content with what he received ; he never exceeded a moderate allowance, and seemed always to have money when he wanted it. He now assured his mother that whatever she could spare him would be enough for his wants ; and his position, which in some cases might have caused unpleasant feeling, seemed only to increase his affection for every member of the family. It had not even the effect of making him wish to earn money ; when at one time it was proposed, and even urged by his brother, that he should join the Bombay bar, in which there seemed to be a good opening, it was no temptation to him, and he said that he far preferred £300 a year in England to £3000 anywhere else.

The fact that his mother and sisters had left Scotland greatly lessened the pleasure of his life in Edinburgh, and he took every opportunity of being with them in England ; perhaps his most striking characteristic all through life was tender devotion to his mother, and strong attachment to every member of the home circle.

A description of his life in Edinburgh for the next few years has been written by Charles Stewart, who was then much with him :—

"During that time he certainly had plenty of leisure, and he took advantage of it to acquire a great deal of knowledge by reading. It was, and still is, the custom for the members of the bar to spend a considerable portion of the day at the Parliament House, whether they had business to take them there or not, and even those advocates who had the least practice or even none at all, habitually spent several hours of the day in the purlieus of the Court. These hours were spent partly in walking up and down the old Parliament Hall, which like Westminster Hall constitutes the centre or antechamber of the Law Courts, and partly in the quiet nooks of the library or the writing-rooms. If there were cases of interest going on, half-hours would be spent in listening to them in the Courts. The centre of the Parliament House life was the huge fire-place in the old hall and the benches adjoining it. Here the news of the day, political, legal, and literary, was freely discussed ; and those whose bags were full of briefs, as well as those who had no bags at all, met there many times in the day and spent a passing five minutes in fun and merriment. Sometimes, when graver subjects were prominent, an hour or more would be spent in serious conversation or exhaustive discussion. Here practical politics and theoretical philosophy were discussed by this peripatetic school at ample leisure. Two friends, robed and wigged, arm-in-arm would pace the boards by the hour, and there were few topics under the sun which were not dealt with in one mood or another. In times of public crisis, politics were of course prominent, and here political plans would be made and party battles fought.

" The more serious and stable work of the day was done in the reading-rooms and writing-rooms of the Advocates' Library. Probably there do not exist in the world more convenient and agreeable retreats for the legal or literary student than this splendid institution affords. A library inferior only to that of the British Museum and the Bodleian, quiet rooms and solitary bays, and all under the same roof as the busiest interests of life. All this afforded opportunities for a life, which in many, if not in all respects, was delightful to David Wedderburn. The unbounded facilities for mixed reading, the constant and sociable meeting with his intimate friends, and the unrestrained discussion were all exactly to his taste. Here, every day and almost at every hour, if he was in the mood for conversation, he could have half an hour's talk with allies, such as J. F. McLennan, Alexander Sellar, Stair Agnew, Æneas Mackay, Archibald Anderson, or Henry Moncrieff, and with each of these and many more he had always topics closely in common.

"The strictly legal life of the place, the gossip of the Law Courts, did not interest him. He never cared who was to be the new judge, or the next solicitor-general ; and he was indifferent as to the working of any new rules of procedure. Still less would he concern himself about the scandalous *causes célèbres* that might chance to be proceeding, or the social tattle that was not always excluded from legal circles. For gossipy quidnuncs he had a special disdain ; about personal scandal, a splendid unconcern. It was what may be called the higher life of the Parliament House, if it is proper to apply such a word to interests which were other than legal, which interested him and in which he took delight. During the early part of his life in Edinburgh the Law Courts met at nine o'clock in the morning. From this hour till one or two o'clock it was his almost invariable practice to be in the Parliament

D

House engaged in such occupations as I have described. The busier lawyers would remain till the Courts closed, but he and others like himself whose legal avocations were almost nominal would leave at luncheon-time. The rest of the day with him was absolute leisure, leisure well employed, the very reverse of absolute idleness. Two or three hours in the afternoon would be devoted to a country ride or to a game of golf on the links at Musselburgh. He was not so addicted to golf, however, as were many of his compeers. Directly it was taken too seriously, it ceased to amuse him. In this, as in all other sports, he was pleased to be a participator, but he was never an enthusiast; he enjoyed sport if it was carried on in moderation, but "a keen sportsman" was apt to bore him. He despised the excessive addiction to sport and the immoderate indulgence in it, which was common among his contemporaries; he had none such among his most intimate friends. He had a constant sense of the justness of the Frenchman's reproach of the English love of killing something. It was generally on his lips at the beginning of a day's shooting, and though he never actually gave up sport on grounds of principle, he was, I believe, on more than one occasion very near to doing so. He liked the exercise, the fresh air and the companionship, but he liked a small bag better than a big one. He was a good shot, but he was almost as well pleased if he missed a bird as if he hit it. I never heard him laugh more cheerily than when out on a day's shooting in Ireland a snipe escaped six successive shots from his gun and my own. He never cared to join in exclusively sporting expeditions, either for fishing in the lochs or rivers of Scotland or in search of bigger game in India, Africa, or America. There were always more important things to be done which interested him more. In Norway it seemed to him waste of time to fish for salmon while there were *kiökken mödens* to explore, and he probably regarded the chase of bears in

America, or tigers in India, as only worth engaging in if it was one of the established institutions of the country.

"The riding expeditions round Edinburgh in company with a couple of his friends, were thoroughly to his mind. The counties in the south and centre of Scotland are admirable ground for excursions of this kind. The valleys of the Tweed and its tributaries, the moors and uplands of Lanarkshire, Dumfrieshire and Peebleshire, the Ochils, the Lammermoors and the Pentlands are just the country for riding expeditions. The distances are not too great to cover in an absence of two or three nights from Edinburgh, and the country which can be visited in this manner is among the most beautiful and diversified in the world. He thoroughly enjoyed these outings, and to his most frequent companions, Alexander Sellar, Donald Crawford, and myself, they are memories of innocent pleasure and thorough friendship, which it is vain to hope that later life can reproduce. The rides of thirty miles down valley and over moor, the rough meals, the evening ramble on the grassy hills, the homely and comfortable 'howf,' the 'plain living and high thinking,' and the return to work invigorated and refreshed are memories which a man is fortunate to possess. David Wedderburn enjoyed them at the time with all the strong power of present enjoyment, which was one of the happiest gifts of his nature, and in later days it was an almost equal pleasure to him to recall them.

"In the general society of Edinburgh he took only a moderate share. A wide circle of acquaintances was a thing he never aimed at, and distinctly disliked. He liked intimate friendships and opportunities for enjoying them, but he dreaded anything like a visiting list, and was averse to going to any house where he was not well known. No man could enjoy a ball more than he, but his tastes prevented him from frequently attending them. At the social festivities of Edinburgh no one could be a more welcome guest, but he was satisfied with a very little in that way, and on most occasions was better pleased to spend the evening in the Club Library, or in an easy-chair over his own fire. A friendly dinner-party always suited him, and he could spend half the night in dancing now and then, but a conversazione or a rout was 'not in his line.' The finely marked grades of society which to many young men make one house more desirable than another, were absolutely unheeded by him. If he was cognizant of them at all, he would pretend not to be so ; and so long as a friend's roof covered honest hearts and refined thoughts, he would as soon, nay sooner, enter it than though it were a lordly mansion."

The above remarks as to Sir David's views upon sports really applied to almost all pursuits, however harmless and even good in themselves. He had a horror of being, what he called, a slave to anything, be it work, pleasure, or a habit. He joined gladly in any amusement ; was a member of the St. Andrew's boat club, and won pewter pots in the races, but most enjoyed the picnic spreads in the boat-house afterwards ; he was also active in getting up the fancy balls given by the club, at one of which he appeared singularly well disguised as an Egyptian. When at all in the position of a host at a dance, he would exert himself the whole evening, and generally chose as his partners the younger and shyer girls rather than the belles of the ball.

The interest and spirit which he threw into anything of the nature of charades or private theatricals made him invaluable as an amateur actor. For several successive winters he assisted at the house of his friend Donald Crawford in getting up little plays, such as " The Rose of Amiens " and " Ici on parle Français." Although he never learnt music, his ear was good, and he was always willing to enliven an evening by cheerily singing some of the many Scotch and German songs with which he was familiar from boyhood. Early in life he showed a taste for drawing, and used to make little illustrations of incidents in the books he read ; later on he took scenes from real life, and any misfortune to himself or his friends, which struck him, if not them, in a ludicrous light, was made the subject of a spirited pencil sketch.

He was fond of organizing small yachting expeditions on the Firth of Forth, to Inch Comb or the Isle of May, in some of which the Vikings, as they called themselves, had a roughish time of it. When they came within reach, he would have a day with Mr. Hill's otter hounds ; the going on foot, the sagacity of the dogs, and the picturesque streams which they followed were all attractions to him. For about ten years he had a handsome horse—" Sunbeam "—the only animal he ever really cared for ; he was proud of its spirit and gentleness, and liked a day's hunting on it. After the death of this horse, in 1869, he never took kindly to any other or cared much about riding.

While in Edinburgh he joined the St. Luke's Lodge of Freemasons, having an idea that it might be useful to him in foreign travel : but he did not take much interest in masonic matters, nor did he care to rise in the order beyond the rank of a master mason. As he said soon after joining, " One advantage of Freemasonry is, that you can have as much or as little of it as you like, and in my case it will be very little."

Many of his friends believed at this time that his prospects as a lawyer were good, always supposing that he diligently pursued his studies and had the patience to wait for practice. With his fine talents improved by a first-rate education, he had every reason to expect success in a profession which, in spite of all that is said to the contrary, seldom fails to reward in the end its worthy votaries. But he never really felt law to be his vocation, and gradually the love of that mistress, which was small at the beginning, like Slender's, diminished on further acquaintance. Politics became more and more his favourite study, and he formed earnest views on the leading questions of the day ; it was soon evident that he preferred to apply his abilities to public life rather than to professional business of any sort. Though nominally practising at the bar in Edinburgh, the time there was constantly broken into by lengthened tours abroad, even extending as far as India and America, which enabled him to study the larger questions of politics, especially those connected with the colonies.

Extract from the Essay on " Lucretius and the Epicurean Philosophy," read before the Speculative Society on the 9th of December, 1862 :—

It would be difficult to find a more striking instance of the power exercised by a name over the minds of the vulgar, than in the case of "epicure" or "epicurean." This combination of letters has gradually come to denote something little better than a selfish, indolent gourmand, sunk in sensual enjoyments, and without belief in a God, or hope of a future existence. Hence the name of Epicurean has become a term of reproach in the mouths of men, ignorant alike of the character and tenets of the wise and good philosopher of the Garden. Epicurus applied himself to philosophical studies from his earliest youth, and established himself as a teacher at Athens. He silently lived down all calumnies by a life so temperate and virtuous that the baffled malice of his enemies could only account for it by supposing him to be altogether devoid of the ordinary passions of human nature.

Epicurus divided all knowledge into three branches : Canonics, Physics, and Ethics ; Canonics being the introductory branch, in which he treats of the criteria of truth. He asserts that there are three ways by which we acquire knowledge—$\alpha i\sigma\theta\acute{\eta}\sigma\epsilon\iota\varsigma$, sensations, $\pi\rho o\lambda\acute{\eta}\psi\epsilon\iota\varsigma$, ideas, and $\pi\acute{\alpha}\theta\eta$, affections. He thus appears to admit a source of human knowledge, which has been pretty generally rejected by modern philosophers,—that of innate ideas, but he appears also to lay but little stress upon the point, and, in fact, to refer all ideas, almost as completely as Locke or Hume have done, either to outward impressions on the senses, or to the inward passions and affections. Thus he admits the existence of the gods, because of the universal prevalence of human belief in their exist- ence, and as a cause must exist for every effect, he supposes these ideas of divine beings to be derived through the senses, from emanations of the immortals themselves. And thus, although the gods "lie beside their nectar" and have no part, either as creators or preservers, in his theory of the universe, he does not attempt to resist the force of so powerful an argument for their existence, but consistently follows out the principles he has laid down. Epicurus fails to discover in nature any evidence what- ever of Divine interference; all appears to him the work of blind necessity, which man in his ignorance calls chance; he cannot see any Providence shaping human ends, or discern any proofs of an intelligent Creator of the universe.

> " He finds Him not in world or sun,
> In eagle's wing or insect's eye."

Nevertheless he feels the blind, indefinite, but eager yearning of the human heart after an ideal nature, infinitely wiser, better, and mightier than our own; he therefore believes such a nature must exist; and if the gods of Epicurus appear but mean and selfish beings, when contrasted with the ideas formed of the Supreme Being by the Christian or Mussulman, still we must admit that in their calm impartial serenity they show well by the side of the capricious, deceitful, licentious deities of Olympus. In Physics Epicurus followed the atomic cosmology of Democritus, as we have it carefully elaborated in the two first books of Lucretius.

It is, however, to his system of Ethics that Epicurus owes most of his fame, and indeed his ethical principles are much more easily reviled than refuted. Nothing can well be more simple, logical, and consistent, while the ultimate results arrived at claim the admiration of those even who are most shocked by the general principles. The end of our being is to increase to the utmost the sum of human happiness. Man is a creature susceptible of pleasure and pain; he seeks the former and avoids the latter: our duty then is to seek to increase as much as possible the aggregate of pleasures, and to diminish that of pains, both in our own case and in that of others. Good and evil, or virtue and vice, are thus determined respectively by their tendency to in- crease or diminish the sum total of happiness, which depends upon freedom from pain, and the enjoyment of pleasure, mental and bodily. Moreover, the pleasures and pains of the mind are incomparably greater than those of the body, and must therefore be always sought in preference to them. Upon these principles may be discovered, by gradual inquiry and investigation, what are really virtues to be inculcated, and vices to be denounced; and this is in effect pretty nearly the course followed by Dr. Paley, who builds up the whole system of Christian morality upon foundations very similar to those laid down by Epicurus.

Such is a general outline of the doctrines of that " Glory of the Grecian race," whose admiring follower and imitator Lucretius proclaims himself to be ; in whose footsteps he desires to tread, as a kid in those of a warhorse, and with whom he no more aspires to equality, than would swallows compete with swans. Nothing can be more magnificent than the panegyric passed by Lucretius at the beginning of his poem on that "Grecian man who first dared to raise mortal eyes against the towering form of Superstition, and to withstand her crushing influence ; whom neither the thunderbolts nor threatening murmur of the heavens restrained, but rather incited the more, with eager courage to burst the closed gates of nature, and to travel far beyond the flaming walls of the world. Having traversed in spirit the immeasurable universe, he returns as a conqueror, to tell us what can and what cannot exist; while Superstition in her turn lies crushed beneath his feet, and by his victory we are exalted to the skies." Lucretius clearly foresees that he is subjecting himself to a charge of impiety and wickedness, but from this he does not shrink ; he boldly proceeds to point out some of the horrors and cruelties entailed by Superstition upon men, and winds up with the famous line, "Tantum Relligio potuit suadere malorum." Here we have the clue to much of the unjust obloquy which has been cast upon the Epicurean philosophy. It is perhaps needless to say that *Relligio* here must be translated " superstition," in order to convey the true meaning, but unfortunately in many ages and countries religion and superstition are one and the same thing. Besides, the lofty generalizations of the Epicurean philosophy are far beyond the comprehension of the vulgar ; they are utterly unable to follow out such purely abstract principles to their just conclusion, either in ethics or physics ; with them freedom from superstition means also freedom from all moral law and restraint, and we can hardly wonder if the corollary which they draw for themselves from such doctrines is simply this : " Let us eat and drink, for to-morrow we die."

The whole argument of Lucretius is interspersed with images and illustrations of such extreme beauty, that we can only regret their comparative rarity, and wish that the subject had afforded greater scope for the poet to display his genius in the treatment of human passions and in depicting the aspects of external nature. The opening address to Venus, his frequent bursts of affectionate admiration towards his great father and teacher, his description of the nature of the gods, the pictorial scenes from pastoral or martial life, are all gems of the purest water; while the beauty and richness of his imagery have afforded an inexhaustible mine of wealth to his countrymen, most of whom—from his immediate successors, Virgil, Horace and Ovid, down to Torquato Tasso—have borrowed largely from Lucretius, the first, if not the greatest, of Italian poets.

"O wretched human minds! O blinded souls! In what darkness and danger is passed this existence, whatever it may be! Can you not see that all which Nature craves for herself is absence of bodily pain, and mental enjoyment of serene happiness, free from care and fear? Little indeed is necessary to our bodily comfort; our pleasure is as great, when stretched in summer on the flowery grass, beside a stream, beneath some spreading tree, as when surrounded by all the magnificence that wealth and art can furnish; and burning fever does not leave us sooner because the couch on which we toss is hung with tapestry and purple. Neither can wealth and power in any degree relieve our minds from superstition and the fear of death, nor dispel the thick darkness in which our life is shrouded; this result can only be accomplished by the study of nature, and by the light of reason."

The doctrines taught by Epicurus, as we learn them from the greatest of his disciples, appear to me sounder and more practical than those of any other among the Grecian philosophers. They certainly, both in physics and ethics, approximate most remarkably to the views generally entertained by modern English thinkers. Of the atomic theory enough has been said, but we must not fail to point out what may be called the great doctrine of "Non-Intervention," or the mechanical uniformity of secondary causes, as to which almost all philosophers are now at one. Special providences and miraculous interventions form no part of modern science; we are now beginning to trace the working of immutable, uniform laws, even in the most obscure classes of phenomena;

one by one these phenomena pass from the regions of mystery, confusion, and darkness to those of reason, order, and light. As we can now calculate eclipses, and describe the exact orbit of a comet in space, so shall we be able ere long to foretell and trace the path of the waterspout, hurricane, and typhoon. The most recent geological theory rejects the idea of sudden and mighty convulsions, and teaches us that the forces now at work around us are sufficiently powerful to have produced, in the lapse of by-gone ages, all the results we see on the earth's surface. A still bolder philosopher maintains, and very nearly proves, that in like manner, by simple secondary causes, working throughout count-less æons, all the various races of organisms may have been produced. Now what does all this come to, but pretty much what Epicurus means by saying, " The blessed gods are to be worshipped on account of the excellence of their nature, but they do not concern themselves with the scheme of the universe, nor with the affairs of men"? The path of progress of human knowledge has been compared to a circle : a more appropriate simile would perhaps be that of a spiral having truth as the origin and centre. After long investigation and toil, and the lapse of many centuries, we may find ourselves once more very near the point from which we set out ; but we have not described a circle, we are nearer the centre, and to that centre we may in time approach indefinitely near, although absolute truth may never be attainable by human faculties. " Our little systems have their day, they have their day and cease to be ; " neither forms of religion nor schools of philosophy can hope for im-mortality, they must adapt themselves to the progress of the human mind; and the most boasted of our discoveries and theories must eventually be swallowed up by a wider and higher generalization. It is not the less interesting on that account to examine what the great and wise of old have done for the common cause. Among these Epicurus appears entitled to take a very high position; unfortunately we know him at second hand, and from the works of his Latin admirers. Excellent as they are, they cannot altogether compensate the loss of the Greek originals, which, had they survived to justify the admiration of Lucretius, himself so great a genius, must have placed their author in that foremost rank which has been reserved for Plato and Aristotle alone among ancient philosophers.

CHAPTER III.

1863.

TOUR IN DENMARK, SWEDEN AND NORWAY—"OUR SCANDINAVIAN
COUSINS "—" DANISH BALLAD POETRY."

WITH the view of a trip to Scandinavia, Sir David and
two friends, Donald Crawford and Charles Stewart, took
lessons in Danish during the spring of 1863. In July they
started together from Leith to Hamburg. The Slesvig-
Holstein question was then a burning topic, and they
found opinions running high. He had a strong predilec-
tion for the Danes, and even held the view that, in the war
which ensued between Denmark and Germany, England
did not redeem her pledges to support the weaker country.
They went by Kiel to Copenhagen, and enjoyed their stay
in that charming city, the principal attraction being the
wonderful collection in the Thorvaldsen Museum of all his
works. They visited Stockholm and Upsala, and returning to Christiania hired three carioles to drive over the
Dovre Fell to Trondhjem. On the way a day was devoted
to the ascent of Snæhætten.

From Trondhjem they made their way by the Romsdal
valley, with its grand and rugged scenery, to Bergen. They
spent three days at that pretty and cheerful town, and then
steamed up the Hardanger Fiord to Vik, from which they
walked to the Vöringsfos, in some respects the finest waterfall in Europe—a great body of water falling five hundred

feet. They descended the splendid Nærodal, and took
boat to Lærdal, an eight and a half hours' row in an eight-
oared boat, the magnificent scenery and the endurance of
the rowers both exciting their wonder and admiration.
Four days' driving by the fine road over the Fille Field, so
costly a work for a poor country, brought them back to
Christiania, and they sailed for Hull, having an unusually
rough passage.

Sir David did not keep any journal of this tour, and the
only record of it from his own pen is a vivid account of an
accident, which happened to himself in the ascent of
Snæhætten. This was written in 1881, eighteen years
after the event, and shows how clear every incident of
travel remained in his mind. It was published under the
title "An Adventure on the Dovre Fell," in the *Every
Girl's Annual*, a magazine in which he took great interest,
giving many copies of it as presents to his little girl friends.

He always retained a lively interest in all connected
with Scandinavia, its people, and literature. He kept up
his knowledge of the Danish language by reading and
translating, and several years after this tour he gave his
impressions of the country in a lecture before the Ayr
Young Men's Association :—

OUR SCANDINAVIAN COUSINS.

Of all the races inhabiting Europe, that with which we are
most closely connected is undoubtedly the Scandinavian. The
history, language, and institutions, as well as the character and
personal appearance of this people, alike indicate the closeness of
the relationship which exists between us ; and nowhere in Europe,
beyond the limits of his own land, does the wandering Briton feel
so thoroughly at home as among the hardy Norsemen. The
national characteristics of which we are proudest have been transmitted to us by our Scandinavian forefathers : love of liberty, intense national feeling, strong domestic affections, together with
that restless spirit of enterprise and adventure which has carried
Englishmen, as conquerors and colonists, into every quarter of the

globe. We have only imitated, on a somewhat wider area, the feats of the Northmen about one thousand years ago, when their name was a terror throughout the whole of Europe, and when they discovered and colonized Iceland, Greenland, and America (A.D. 1000).

If the smallness of their numbers be taken into account, no race has ever played a more brilliant part on the world's stage, except indeed the Greeks. A mere handful of warriors from the narrow valleys of Norway and the scattered islands of Denmark, no nation was able to stand before them. "A furiâ Normannorum, libera nos, Domine !" was the prayer of all Christendom, helpless to defend itself. Normandy and Brittany were torn from the successors of Charlemagne ; Alfred the Great, of England, was driven from his throne ; independent principalities were established in Scotland, Ireland, and the Orkneys ; the Mussulmans of Cordova gave way before the followers of Odin ; even the Emperors of the East found no protection against the fair-haired pirates save in the swords of the Varangians, their Scandinavian guards. In Constantinople (Micklegaard) the two streams of conquest met, and when the Norman chivalry (who already held the fairest provinces of France and Italy) encamped at last before the walls of that imperial city, they found themselves confronted by men of their own race, who had followed a more easterly route, conquering Russia by the way, and founding there a dynasty which subsisted for seven hundred years. It may be said of the Scandinavians that they furnished kings and nobles to Europe, but the free Vikings themselves were not fond of such grandees, and their highest praise of Iceland was, "A place where men may live in freedom, far away from kings and jarls." It was in search of similar freedom that the rocky shores of New England were peopled, and Britain has certainly no less reason to be proud of her children, than of her warlike kinsfolk—the Northmen. These last are said to have "left the sceptre of the main" to us, their posterity, and it seems likely to be a hereditary possession in the hands of our race for ever.

Scandinavia has fallen out of the first rank, owing to the more rapid growth of other nations in modern times. However brave and energetic a scanty race may be, they must in time be outstripped by others possessing wider and more fertile territories. Man for man, the Slavonian is no match for the Scandinavian, but the predominance of the latter is gone for ever, while the Russian Empire continues to grow vaster and mightier day by day, overshadowing Europe and Asia.   The utmost number at which the pure Scandinavians can be estimated is less than seven millions, and this can scarcely be much exceeded in the future, so limited is the extent of fertile land in their wide territory.   Moreover they are not united under one government, Denmark and Sweden being kept apart by the remnants of that jealous rivalrȳ which has caused so many calamities to both nations.   At the present day, when the larger nationalities of Europe are consolidating into huge military monarchies, it is indeed much to be regretted that small constitutional countries, as in the Netherlands and in Scandinavia, should hold aloof from their kindred and neighbours. The force which draws together the different branches of a race appears to vary, like gravity, directly as the mass, and half a dozen nations may ere long embrace the whole of Europe.   When Panslavism is triumphant, and German and Italian unity are complete, it will be difficult for lesser nations to maintain their places in the system; but if they aspire to independent life, they must have no divisions among themselves.   Probably the fairest possible prospect for Europe lies in her becoming a federation of great States, whose political boundaries would be coextensive with the natural limits of language and race.   The sole chance for Denmark and Sweden to escape ultimate absorption by Germany and Russia, lies in a close and hearty union.   Forgetting ancient feuds and jealousies, and acknowledging the ties of blood, language, and religion, the three Scandinavian kingdoms must become one indivisible State, and this without delay.   Failing the adoption of such a course, with the protection of the Western Powers, it is greatly to be feared that these free and prosperous countries may be partitioned, like unhappy Poland, simply because they are weak and their neighbours are strong.

The admiration and regard still cherished by Scandinavians, and especially by Danes, for England appear somewhat unaccountable, when we recall the part played by her in the recent history of Denmark.   Within the present century, the tyrant's plea of necessity has been twice put forward by English statesmen to justify a destructive attack on the fleet, and even on the capital of Denmark.   As for the bombardment of Copenhagen in 1807, without even a declaration of war, it would be difficult in modern history to find a parallel to so cruel and selfish an act of aggression. In 1814 England took an active part in the severance of Norway from Denmark after many centuries of union. The Danes, however, have long ceased to show any resentment for these repeated injuries, and in their unequal contest with Germany they looked to their British cousins with the warmest confidence· of succour. The sympathies and moral support of the British people were, however, all that they received, notwithstanding the treaty of 1852. It is scarcely too much to say that open hostility would have proved less fatal to Denmark than the half-hearted friendship of the English Government. Had the Danes not been simple enough to put faith in the assurance that " they should not stand alone " in resisting the aggressive policy of Prussia, they would doubtless have seen the necessity of yielding to overwhelming odds. Denmark's many friends all failed her in the hour of need—even England, in whom she chiefly trusted, and her closer kindred on the other side of the Sound; she thus found herself alone face to face with two great military powers and the whole German nation.

The odds can hardly be exaggerated, they were about forty to one, with the needle-rifle against muzzle-loading smooth-bores; unconditional surrender, without even firing a shot, could scarcely have been deemed disgraceful. Fairly brought to bay, the Danes fought without hope of victory, but with the indomitable courage of their race, returning as they best might the withering fire of their assailants, and calmly awaiting the assault, which they knew must sweep them from their shattered works. Duppel, like Thermopylæ, was a hopeless fight, in which the conquered reaped the chief glory; and Denmark may boast that she resisted for months the same splendidly appointed troops which crushed the Austrian Empire in as many weeks, while the honour of the Dannebrog, and the ancient renown of Danish seamen, were triumphantly maintained off Heligoland against the same navy which destroyed the Italian ironclads in the most brilliant naval action of recent times.

It would be unjust to maintain, in our admiration of Danish pluck, that the weaker party was entirely in the right. We must admit that the Slesvig-Holsteiners were not without substantial grievances, and that the sympathy felt for them in Germany was genuine and sincere, while the conduct of the Danish Government was injudicious throughout. On the other hand, the policy of

Prussia, by which the entire spoils of the war were secured to herself, while the wishes of the Slesvig-Holsteiners and the rights of the various princes were ignored, the German Confederation was humiliated, and Austria was used as an instrument for her own ultimate destruction, will command the admiration of those who regard success as the sole test of merit. Let us hope that blood will prove thicker than water, and that the Danes will come once more to feel their old regard for England, and to take that pride in her greatness and prosperity which appears peculiar to the Scandinavians alone among the nations of Europe.

In reviewing the early history of the Northmen, we are constantly reminded of another race, inhabiting the opposite extremity of Europe, to whom they present many points of resemblance, as well as of glaring contrast. It is at least clear from the history of the Greeks and Scandinavians, that no race, however brave, enterprising, and intellectual, can found or maintain an extensive and permanent empire without acknowledging a vigorous central authority, such as cannot exist in a country divided into small oligarchical communities or feudal principalities. Unconquerable when united, each of these famous nations has experienced the fatal effects of dissension. Russia has played the part of a modern Macedonia, and those heathen barbarians, among whom the Northmen conquered and colonized, have now consolidated a power before which Sweden and Denmark were helpless, as were the Thebans and Athenians at Chæronea.

Even in heroic times the Greek and Goth had very different codes of honour and morality. The genuine type of a Grecian hero is Ulysses—wise and brave, but ever suspicious, and watchful to take advantage of an adversary. The champions of whom we read in Northern sagas, like Hamlet, are "remiss, most generous, and free from all contriving." They scorn to strike an unarmed foe, whom they will defend even against their own allies; to treachery they fall easy victims, regarding suspicion as base and dishonourable ; they are slow to wrath, but when roused become reckless of consequences, and are in their Berserk fury destructive even to themselves. The ancient Greek would have regarded the Viking as a wrong-headed barbarian, with no admirable qualities except physical strength and courage, who threw away the fair chances of his own game by mere obstinate stupidity ; and who deserved to fall as the wild beast succumbs to the

superior sagacity of man.   The Northman would, in his turn, have
cordially reciprocated the contempt of the Greek, regarding him
as treacherous, pusillanimous, and base.

Similar differences of opinion exist in Europe at the present
day, and seem to be very much a matter of climate and latitude.
We of the Northern faction bestow upon treachery, dissimulation,
and fraud, the dislike which a Southerner reserves for violence,
rudeness, and intemperance.   It must be indeed admitted that,
along with the virtues, we have inherited many of the failings of
our Scandinavian forefathers.   The two chief blots on the character of the Northmen are intemperance and religious intolerance :
and these same reproaches may be cast, with only too much
justice, upon our own prosperous and enlightened nation.

In this country it would be strange if our hearts did not warm
towards our Scandinavian cousins, with whom, indeed, we are not
on the most intimate terms, thanks to the stormy North Sea rolling between us, but whom the more we know the better we like.
For honesty, courage, good temper, and manly independence, it
would be hard to find their equals among the nations of the globe.

The following lecture on " Danish Ballad Poetry " was
delivered in January, 1871, under the auspices of the Glasgow Athenæum; and later, in London, he attended meetings of the British Scandinavian Society, and read a paper
on the same subject before it.   The ballads introduced into
the lecture are taken from a number of translations made by
Sir David himself : to those who know Danish, they are at
once stirring and pathetic ; along with a very close translation
of the words, he has succeeded in retaining much of the metre
and ring which make them so dear to a ballad-loving people :—

DANISH BALLAD POETRY.

A very moderate amount of study is sufficient to enable a
Scotchman to understand the simple and vigorous dialect now
spoken throughout Denmark and Norway, which in its idioms, as
well as words, continually reminds us of the close relationship
subsisting between the Scandinavian and the Lowland Scot.   The
Danish or Norse language, for it is known by both names, has a
character which fits it peculiarly well for being the vehicle of

ballad poetry, being direct and simple in grammatical structure, with few inflexions, and great terseness of expression. It is a very pure Gothic dialect, with little admixture of any foreign element, but with one or two marked peculiarities, distinguishing it from other modern European languages.

Sir Walter Scott tells us that in April, 1788, "the literary persons of Edinburgh were first made aware of the existence of works of genius in a language cognate with the English, and possessed of the same manly force of expression." It was Henry Mackenzie, author of "The Man of Feeling," who introduced his countrymen to this new national literature, in an essay read before the Royal Society; and the study of German was soon afterwards commenced in Edinburgh by a small class of six or seven young men, among whom was Walter Scott. The words which he uses in speaking of German ballads and legendary poetry, their close resemblance in style and character to our own, the remarkable coincidence—as he terms it—between the German language and that of the Lowland Scottish, all apply with far greater force to the language and literature of the North. Among the various dialects of Gothic or Teutonic origin now spoken or written in Europe, modern German, or "High Dutch," although the best known in this country, is the least closely related to English, and we must look for our nearest kindred in language, as well as blood, on the opposite coasts of the North Sea, among the Norwegians, Danes, and Low Dutch, in Slesvig-Holstein, as well as in the Netherlands. It is, indeed, remarkable how closely akin in race and speech are the inhabitants of Great Britain with their opposite continental neighbours, the same people cropping up on either shore of the North Sea, just as the chalk cliffs do on each side of the Channel. The resemblance does not diminish, but increases with the breadth of intervening salt water, as we proceed northward. The Border land is *par excellence* the home of ballad poetry, and it is here that local names and dialects, as well as character and feature, declare the Scandinavian origin of the people. It need not then excite surprise if a strong resemblance shows itself between Scottish Border ballads and the Kæmpeviser of the North.

If it be true that they who write the ballads of a nation exercise over it a more powerful influence than those who make its laws, it follows that the character of a people may be better under-

stood from a study of popular poetry than from that of political
institutions. From songs and ballads may be gathered a certain
knowledge as to what virtues are loved and admired, what vices
are hated and despised, in any age or country; and the hero of a
popular poem usually possesses those qualities that his countrymen take pride in attributing to themselves. In Danish poetry
the quality which seems to be preferred above all others is " Tro-
fasthed "—faithfulness to oath and allegiance, to friend and lover.
Fearless, faithful, and single-hearted—"fair, gentle, and strong "
—the ideal Dane presents a most attractive national character;
and making allowance for idealization, this is in truth the character
of the Danish people.

A good illustration of this temperament is furnished by the
ballad of the Danish soldier, who, exhausted and parched with
thirst, finds on the field of battle a well-filled flask; just as he
raises it to his lips he hears a groan, and looking round sees a
desperately wounded foeman, who prays for a drink. The Dane
stoops down and puts his flask to the mouth of the wounded man,
who instantly fires a pistol at his heart. Startled, but not wounded,
the honest soldier drinks off half the contents, and once more
hands the flask to his enemy, merely saying with a smile, " You
scoundrel, I meant to have given you the whole, but now, as a
punishment,you shall only have the half." The king, hearing of
the occurrence, sends for the soldier, and says, " You have a noble
heart—you must have the shield of a noble: a half-empty flask
shall be your crest." The descendants of the chivalrous yeoman
are said to be still at Flensborg, and to hold in high honour the
founder of their race.

The sterner features of the same loyal nature are shown in the
legend of the " Armour-Bearer's Oath." A great chief of Fyen
dies an outlaw, *Fredlös.* His last wish is to be buried in Danish
soil, but his hereditary foes will allow no rest to his bones; his
friends and brothers-in-arms are few but faithful.

His weapon-brothers trusty
 Stood round him at the close;
Where, then, can he be buried,
 That he may find repose?
Not many friends remaining
 Has he, to guard his bed;
Long are the arms of vengeance,
 And hate survives the dead.

Few friends has he to mourn him;
 An outlaw in the land;
Against the Danish monarch
 He raised rebellious hand.
But now his heart would slumber
 On Denmark's gentle breast,
If there prepared in secret
 Might be his couch of rest.

Around the bier they gather,
  And kneeling humbly there,
With lifted hand and weapon,
  By Christ's dear blood they swear;
In spite of fame or favour,
  In spite of love or gold,
Their hearts that fatal secret
  Shall true and silent hold.

At Stubberup in Fyen,
  On Hirtsholm's level strand
The village calmly slumbers,
  And dark are sea and land.
A single light still twinkles
  Where lonely in her room '
A peasant maid is seated,
  And plies her busy loom.

While slowly heaves her bosom
  She gently lifts her eyes
And gazes through the window,—
  No more the shuttle flies !
For in the gloomy distance
  She sees a gleaming light :—
No star is it that twinkles
  Amid the clouds of night.

The church upon the hillock
  Sends forth that ruddy glow ;
Though at the thought she shudders,
  She cannot choose but go ;
With noiseless footstep gliding
  Up to the churchyard gate,
Behind a granite pillar
  She trembling lies in wait.

Up from the beach there passes,
  With swift yet quiet tread,
Close by, a dark procession
  Of mourners for the dead ;
Into the church more slowly
  The bier is borne along,
With ruddy gleam of torches
  Amid a silent throng.

The body deep they bury,
  The grave they close apace,
And of that night's sad labour
  They clear away all trace.
With folded arms they linger,
  Their eyes bespeak their woe ;
Loud crows the bird of morning,
  And summons them to go.

Straight was each torch extinguished
  The night grew doubly black,
The heavy door was fastened,
  And swift they hastened back ;
Among the rocks they vanished,
  Beside the dark sea stream :
Alone was left the maiden,
  And all was like a dream.

Then from her place of hiding
  She hastened, nothing loth,
But felt her foot entangled,
  In folds of heavy cloth ;
She seized it and she bore it,
  As home she fled away,
And when she looked—behold there
  A silken banner gay :

Blue as the early violet,
  As ocean's mighty flood,
Seven pointed, in the centre,
  A star of silver stood !
She laid it, deeply pensive
  Within an oaken chest,—
Then all that night of terrors
  Forgot in peaceful rest.—

Bright was the winter morning,
  The bells rang out amain ;
Across the snow right gaily
  Came home a bridal train :
Young Iver with his chosen
  Came, followed by a throng
Of village lads and maidens,
  With ribbon, wreath, and song.

The bride was there surrounded
  With guard of maidens gay,
But soon the band of matrons
  Danced her from them away.
The bridal crown of silver
  Forsook her golden hair ;
She stood in cap and 'kerchief,
  A wedded woman there.

The bridegroom with his darling
  Is scarcely yet alone,
When, death-like in his colour,
  He stands as turned to stone ;
For seized with fear and anguish
  He stares in speechless dread
Upon the splendid curtain,
  That decked the bridal bed ;

Of silk, like azure violets,
  Like ocean's mighty flood,
A seven-rayed star of silver
  Right in the centre stood !—
"Where got you this, my darling?"
  In sorrow and in fear,
With trembling voice he questions :
  "Oh say how came it here ?"

"This velvet was not stolen,
  For gold it was not bought ;
I asked for no such favour,—
  It came to me unsought,
For in the dark I found it,
  Beside the church, at night,
Wherein I lately witnessed
  A strange and solemn sight !"

Thus spoke she, sweetly smiling,
  He smiled but did not speak,
Unseen the big tear trickled
  Upon the sunburnt cheek ;
His arms were folded tightly ;
  Strange fire was in his eye ;
Then, bending o'er her lightly,
  He whispered with a sigh :

"Thou purest lily blossom
  That now must broken be,
The fierce avenging angel
  Aims e'en his shaft at thee !

Accursèd and forsaken
  Alike of God and men, *
I must, I dare not waver :—
  Sweet bride, forgive me then !"

The rosy streaks of morning
  Spread out both broad and long.
Then drum and fife resounded
  With joyous festal song ;
A swarm of merry jesters
  The chamber door without,
The bridal pair to waken,
  Raised music, noise, and shout.

But long they would not tarry,
  They open forcèd the door ;
And burst into the chamber
  With clamour and uproar ;
But thunderstruck, with horror
  They started all aside,—
For cold and pale and gory
  There lay the gentle bride.

But vanished was the bridegroom!
  For him that mighty oath
Had proved a bond more holy
  Than vows of loving troth ;
With blood of her, his darling,
  He stained his cruel sword,
And proudly kept untarnished
  The faith he owed his lord.

Nor till the hour of judgment
  Shall e'er be brought to light,
Where true-fast hands have buried
  The bones of Stig the White.

        (CHRISTIAN WINTHER.)

A special tone and colouring is given to Northern poetry by the picturesque mythology of Scandinavia, as complete and characteristic as that of Greece. In the early sagas Odin, Thor, Freya, Baldur, and Tir are personal existing divinities, as are Zeus, Ares, Aphrodité, Apollo, and Hermes, in the poetry of Homer and Hesiod. In the more modern ballads they no longer have any real existence, but their names and attributes are assigned to the powers and phenomena of nature. The ocean is Ægir, and Hertha is the land, Gefion's Isle is Sjœlland, the heart or literally the soul of Denmark; Thor's hammer is the lightning, the sun is Baldur the Good, while Odin is the great Alfader—the Providence whose sleepless eye watches over the world.

The ideas evoked by these grand old names are thoroughly in harmony with the language, the scenery, the character, and incidents of the ballads, and distinguish Scandinavian poetry from that of most European nations, who are usually compelled to borrow classical or other foreign imagery and names. It cannot be disputed that the gods of Asgaard, though rather a rough lot, stand far higher as to moral character than the gods of Olympus; warlike, adventurous, good-natured, and simple-minded, they are Norse rovers and sea-kings on a large scale. Valhalla, like the Paradise of Mahomet, is open to the spirits of all the faithful who fall in fight, but to them alone; perpetual fighting and feasting, not voluptuous repose, supply the joys of that heaven to which the restless soul of the Northman aspired, when the welcome hour should arrive for the Valkyries to invite him to their halls.

But even over such rude revels is thrown an atmosphere of sublimity, from the grandeur of the impending catastrophe. Although prolonged, these revels are not to be eternal: the hand-writing is on the wall, and the fatal hour of Ragnarok approaches, when Aser and Einherier (gods and heroes) shall fight their last fight, and perish along with all their enemies, amid the destruction of existing nature. In no mythology is there found a more awful and magnificent conception than this "twilight of the gods," this breaking loose of the powers of darkness, this sudden destruction of all things visible, to be replaced by a new heaven and a new earth. It is only natural that the existence of such grand myths and legends should have tinged the whole of Northern poetry.

A very conspicuous part is played in Danish legends by mermaids and mermen, as is indeed natural among a maritime people, inhabiting an archipelago of islands and peninsulas. The Havfru, or Havmand, although sometimes cruel and vindictive, luring mortals to destruction, like the Greek Syrens, is frequently of an entirely different character, full of tenderness, gratitude, and affection. Take as an example Agnete of Holmgaard, who listens to the promises of a merman, which promises he appears to have loyally fulfilled, and springs into the ocean to become his bride.

> They lived there together eight long years and more,
> And seven fair sons to the merman she bore.

Under tangle and seaweed she sat in her bower ;
She hears the bells ringing high in the church tower.

Agnete goes in by her husband to stand—
" To visit God's table I long for the land ! "

" Now, hear thou, Agnete, what I to thee say,
In twenty-four hours thou must leave me for aye ! "

Agnete she kissed all her children so bright,
She wished them a thousand times loving good night.

Then loud wept the great ones, and loud wept the small—
The babe in the cradle wept loudest of all.

Once more under heaven she stands on the shore,
She had not seen sunlight for eight years and more.

In the house of her kinsfolk she stands by the door—
" Thou heathenish woman, we know thee no more."

Agnete she enters the church door to pray,
But all the small images turned them away.

Of the cup at the altar she fain would then drink,
But she seemed as if standing on ocean's dark brink.

She trembled so sorely, she spake not a word,
She spilled on the pavement the wine of the Lord.

When the mist and the darkness were closing around,
Agnete again on the sea-shore was found.

She folded her hands, that most sorrowful wife—
" May God now forgive me, and take my young life ! "

She sank on the grass among violets blue ;
I tell you the blossoms seemed withering too.

The chaffinches twittered on green branches high :
" In truth now, Agnete, we know thou must die."

When the sun set at evening behind the green hill,
The suffering heart of Agnete grew still.

The tide rises slowly, with sorrowful moan—
In the depths of the ocean she sank like a stone.

Three days in the deep of the sea she had lain,
When the waves cast her up to the surface again.

The boys, who so early were watching their geese,
Found Agnete stretch'd on the sea-shore in peace.

In the sand was she buried, beneath weed-clad stones,
From the wash of the billows these shelter her bones.

Each morn and each eve they are wet with the tide ;
But girls say, " The merman still weeps for his bride."

(ŒHLENSCHLÄGER.)

More elaborate in style and metre is the story of " King Valdemar," by the same author, embodying more than one popular
superstition. Valdemar the Fourth of Denmark, surnamed Atter-
dag, from the cheery proverb he was fond of quoting in gloomy
times, " I Morgen er atter Dag" ("To-morrow it is again Day "),
flourished at the end of the fourteenth century, and was the
father of Margaret, the Semiramis of the North, who wore the three
crowns of Denmark, Sweden, and Norway, and ruled over a
united Scandinavia. In most European countries there exists in
some shape or other the legend of the " Wild Huntsman," and in
Sjœlland the hero of this legend is Valdemar. So strong was his
love for his favourite hunting seat, where he settled after his
foreign wanderings, that he is alleged to have said—"Give me
Gurre, and let who will have Paradise." To expiate these words
he must hunt there nightly until the day of doom. The incident
of the ring, and the king's conduct regarding it, remind us of
Charlemagne and the magic ring of Fastrada, which is said to
have caused the foundation of Aix-la-Chapelle.

> King Valdemar of Denmark passed over land and sea
> Unto the Holy Sepulchre, a pilgrim bold and free ;
>   There slaked he his thirst
> In Kedron, then became he a true crusader first.
>
> And like a true crusader, with helmet, lance, and sword,
> He sought in love and beauty, his valour's just reward.
>   On Rygen's neighbour isle
> He found the love he sought for in Tovelide's smile.
>
> When he sat not in council, nor wielded battle-spear,
> In Gurre's verdant forest he rode to hunt the deer.
>   When wearied by the chase,
> So lovingly he rested in Tovelide's embrace.
>
> But often, e'en in summer, with thunder falls the snow ;
> And Death, the fatal mower, approached with sudden blow ;
>   He marked her for his prey,
> Nought recked of youth and beauty,—the roses fade away.
>
> But still she smiled so kindly, e'en in her winding-sheet
> A lily fair and graceful, a blossom pale and sweet.
>   The rosy purple flood
> Glowed in her cheek no longer—cold, ice-cold was her blood ;
>
> Her eyes so blue and loving were veiled with eyelids white ;
> She seemed a statue carven of alabaster bright.
>   In many a silky coil
> Her golden locks were woven, her fingers' latest toil.

Where'er the king now journeyed her coffin too was borne ;
Beside his couch he placed it to gaze at eve and morn ;
      That face so cold and white
He kissed before he slumbered, and said to it "Good night."

But ah ! one morning early, in sorrow and despair
He gazed upon her features—destruction's hand was there ;
      Her beauty passed away :
He saw no more his darling snatched from him by decay.

Then from the dead one's finger the monarch drew his ring ;
He cried, "Below on earth here fades every mortal thing !
      Nature alone is there,
That still remains eternal, so joyous and so fair.

"No more is Tovelide on earth.   Now from the dead
I take the ring of marriage, her spirit now I wed
      With mine, where well I know
She oft from heaven descending will visit me below.

"Yes ! in that lovely Gurre, where under beech and lime
Enraptured with each other we sat so many a time,
      Her spirit floats above,
And I once more will offer the hand of truth and love.

"Deep in the earth I bury now this her ring of gold,
Where moss-grown Runic pillars tell of the Kings of old ;
      There shall I still in May
Behold her when the forest is decked with blossoms gay.

"There seated, sad and thoughtful, beneath the beech tree's shade,
So often as the nightingale within the leafy glade
      Sings sweet my soul to cheer,
My well-loved Tovelide, thy voice I then shall hear.

"The corn shall wave before me gold-yellow as her hair,
Her eye the blue forget-me-not, the rose her cheek so fair ;
      In Zephyr's gentle breath
Her soul shall hover round me, with love that conquers death."

Now from the corpse was turned the Danish monarch's love,
Within the grave they laid it, and flowers grew fair above ;
      But when the sun had set,
In spring-time and in harvest, again his love he met.

They say that still he dwells there until this very day,
Nor yet from brave old Denmark can turn his heart away,
      That still with horse and hound
He passes, when at midnight the tossing woods resound.

                (ŒHLENSCHLÄGER.)

The story of "Svend Forkbeard," his treacherous capture by
Sigbald, the Jomsborg Viking, and the part played by the Danish

ladies in his release, seem to be historically true.   In gratitude,
King Svend conferred upon women in Denmark certain rights
of succession to lands, which, meagre as they were, certainly in
that age and country amounted to considerable concessions from
the sword to the distaff.   King Svend is feasting with his warriors
in his palace hall, and listening to the song of his Skjald—

> When to the hall there enters
> A Viking free and bold.

The aged bard has ended ;
  The Viking flings aside
His cloak, and straight approaches
  The king with fearless stride :
" All hail, King Svend ! thou sittest
  In peace and plenty there.
By me to-day Jarl Sigbald
  Sends thee his greeting fair.

" His long ship here is anchored ;
  He fain would speak a word
With thee on sundry matters,
  But sick he lies on board.
If, therefore, thou wilt listen
  To what he now would say,
A hearing thou must grant him,
  And visit him to-day."

Then cried an aged warrior :
  " The bard a warning spake,
And sore my heart misgives me ;
  Do thou that warning take !
Jarl Sigbald thinks of treason,
  He speaks no honest word ;
His wiles can make me tremble,
  Though not his naked sword."

" The Viking's heart is falser
  Then foam upon the tide,
And him thou shalt not follow !"
  Was heard on every side.
Then rose King Svend full proudly ;
  Across the hall he strode ;
The glance he cast around him
  With scorn and anger glowed. ·

" Hath honour then her dwelling
  No more on earth below ?
Shall even we, the Northmen,
  Her voice no longer know ?

Doth this beseem a monarch,
  To fear lest men betray ?
Base is the soul that dreameth
  Of guile by night or day ! "

Down to the beach he marches,
  His champions with him go,
So bold and free his bearing,
  He fears nor friend, nor foe.
Across the gleaming water
  His barge conveys him then,
Of all that seek to follow
  There is but room for ten.

The barge glides like an arrow
  Towards the Viking's home :
" Say now, the Jarl, how fares he ?
  A friendly guest I come."
Upon his couch lies Sigbald,
  But strong in health the while,
He rises quick, and welcomes
  The king with traitor's smile.

" Ha ! Sigbald, wilt thou basely
  Thy king and lord betray ?"
" Not so, but we from Denmark
  To Jomsborg must away."
Svend's eye gleamed deadly lightning,
  Forth leapt his trusty blade,
But still with mocking laughter
  The Jarl stood undismayed :

" How now, my liege ! so slightly
  Thy worth thou canst not feel,
That thou should'st think in earnest
  To buy thyself with steel !
Such price indeed were paltry,
  Unheard of yet before,
A king must not be cheapened,
  Now thus I swear by Thor :

" That if perchance thy kingdom
  So much of riches hold
As fairly may o'erbalance
  Thy body's weight in gold,
So highly do I prize thee
  That nothing less can bring
To me a worthy ransom,
  To thee release, my king ! "

Soon of the Viking's treason
  Was widely spread the fame,
And grievous was the sorrow
  Where'er the tidings came ;
In lowly hut of peasant,
  In lordly hall of chief,
Still shares the faithful Danesman
  His monarch's joy and grief !

It was the end of harvest.
  When red the sunset shone,
No music filled the copses,
  The nightingale was gone ;
The birds upon the branches
  Were silent far and near,—
As if they knew, and sorrowed
  For sorrow reigning here.

No longer smiled the forest,
  That late was summer green,
For Denmark's hope had vanished,
  And faded now unseen ;
The flower that waved so graceful
  In balmy summer air
Now lost its scented glory,
  And withered in despair.

Thus slowly comes the winter ;
  King Svend to Denmark's shore,
Though hours and days are passing,
  Returns again no more ;—
For in the Danesman's bosom
  Dwell truth and honour free,
With might in every sinew—
  But little gold has he.

Thanks to our Danish ladies !
  Each fair and bright-haired maid !
While lives the name of Denmark
  Their glory cannot fade !
They gave the jewelled girdle,
  With clasp and golden gear,
The ring e'en of betrothal,
  In faith it cost them dear.

Once more the spring-time blossomed
  On Hertha's mother breast,
King Svend returned to Denmark,
  And every heart was blessed.
The beechen grove breathed fragrance,
  Sweet sang the nightingale,
At once the cloud of sorrow
  Was gone from hill and dale.

And still when Denmark's islands
  Are green with vernal shades,
Each season brings fresh beauty
  To deck the Danish maids.
As though a summer garland
  The blooming South gave forth
To crown with golden glories
  Our maidens in the North.

(H. P. Hölst.)

No such mighty genius as Dante or Goethe adorns the literature of the Scandinavians, but small as are their numbers they
can boast of many worthy names—Œhlenschläger, Ingemann,
Andersen, are poets of whom any people may well be proud. The
lovers of ballads and lyrical romances would be well repaid for
the slight trouble of acquiring a competent knowledge of Danish,
in order to enjoy these and many other less-known authors, as
Hölst, Möller, Winther. A language which has long been the
vehicle of thought and poetry to such a race as the Northmen will
certainly die hard, but as a literary language that of Denmark
cannot survive the loss of political independence. The number

of written languages is steadily on the decline, and Hoch-Deutsch threatens with literary as well as political extinction all other branches of the pure Teutonic family, including the Scandinavian. Platt-Deutsch in Germany is now a mere *patois*, although in Holland national independence and colonial possessions still give to Low Dutch the dignity of an imperial language.

If the time must come when Danish shall cease to be the language of statesmen and philosophers, it will still remain, like the classics and like its kindred Icelandic, enshrined and crystallized in the verses of its bards, whose trumpet notes will stir the blood of future generations, as the gallant heart of Sir Philip Sydney was stirred by the grand old ballad of " Chevy Chase."

Retrieving.

CHAPTER IV.

1864–1866.

PYRENEES AND NORTH SPAIN—EGYPT AND INDIA—FIRST VISIT TO IRELAND
—CRITICAL NOTICES OF BOOKS.

IN April, 1864, Sir David started with his cousin, Mr. Hope
Wallace, for the Pyrenees and the North of Spain. They
went from Paris to Bayonne, and took a special interest in
visiting some of the scenes of the Peninsular War, in which
their near relative, Sir John Hope, had distinguished
himself. They penetrated into Spain by St. Sebastian as
far as Burgos, in order to see the wonderful and splendid
alabaster tombs of the Castilian sovereigns at the Great
Cartuja of Mira Flores ; and the famous cathedral, which
he thus minutely describes :—

The cathedral of Burgos is certainly one of the most magnificent I have ever seen, the richness of the carving and sculpture,
both inside and outside, has never been defaced by sacrilegious
hands, and it may be compared to embroidery and crochet work,
being so light and yet so elaborate, especially the twin spires,

which resemble, on a smaller scale, those of Friburg in Breisgau. The central lantern, the constable's chapel, the numerous doorways, and in fact the whole building, are covered with statues and finely carved pinnacles outside, while inside the columns and screens are a marvel of sculpture in stone and in wood. There are a number of large and beautiful chapels all round the cathedral, which is in fact a cluster of churches, the choir being the central one, with very fine oak stalls, carved and inlaid, and a lot of old tapestry representing the creation.

In one transept there is a remarkable iron staircase, leading to what must have been once an immense pulpit. Perhaps the general effect of the cathedral is somewhat injured by its being so much divided by the screens and reredos, but the details are so rich and varied, and the absence of tawdry decoration so marked, that altogether I know no church to surpass, or perhaps to equal it. One chapel is very remarkable, the whole roof being encrusted with coloured pottery, as brilliant and elaborate as a Dresden china vase; the beautiful rose windows are filled with stained glass, so that colour is not wanting, nor are incense and music, the latter being, however, such as seems more suitable to a ball-room than a cathedral. There is a similar difficulty in getting a good general view of the exterior as of the interior, owing to the houses close around, and to the way in which the cathedral has been built against the hill, on which stands the citadel.

Burgos is certainly, with its old gateways, walls, arcades, churches, and houses, a most interesting place, worthy of its fame as the ancient capital of Castile.

They did not proceed further into Spain, but returned to the South of France, and devoted a short time to visiting some of the picturesque valleys of the Pyrenees.

In the summer of 1864 he accompanied his mother and sisters to pay some visits in Scotland, going to Mull and the West Highlands. At Ardgour he had his first experience of deer-stalking; his want of success on that occasion he was wont to put down to the midges. He used often to complain of their rapacity in the Highlands, and say, " I wonder what they live on when I am not there."

His brother in India having written to say that he could

obtain leave of absence for three or four months, to 'make a tour, in the cold season, round India, he at once decided to go out and join him. The short time left for preparation was rather an advantage in his eyes, for he always disliked making plans long before, and his travelling equipments were of the simplest description. He left England in November, and sailed from Marseilles in the S.S. *Ellora* for Alexandria, seeing Malta for a few hours of a bright moonlight night, when it looked very picturesque. He was ten days in Egypt, and, like all travellers from the West, was much struck by the first view of a great Oriental town.

November 20th, Cairo.—The streets of Cairo are perhaps the great sight of the place, and are unsurpassed in the interest and amusement of the pictures they present; you feel yourself among the very scenes and characters of the "Arabian Nights," the buildings, dresses, and names are the same as in the days of Haroun-al-Raschid; the groups and processions, weddings, funerals, crowds on foot, walking, or seated by the side of the narrow street, calmly pursuing their avocations; riders on horses, donkeys, or camels; carriages preceded by running footmen shouting "Guarda!" "O-ah!" Turks, Arabs, negroes, veiled women, Englishmen with muslin scarfs round their hats, all mixed up together in a thoroughfare not much wider than Burlington Arcade, present a series of pictures as brilliant, varied, and shifting as those of a kaleidoscope. The Italian Bazar exhibits all this to great advantage, and, owing to the height of the houses and narrowness of the streets, there is almost always shade, even where the bazar is not roofed over. The Turkish Bazar is perhaps even more striking. You ride through a perfect sea of turbans, apparently impenetrable, and turning into narrow, covered side streets, you find the Eastern merchants calmly seated by their costly wares, smoking or dozing, and apparently quite indifferent as to whether a customer comes or not. Every trade is carried on in the open thoroughfare, each one in its own district, dozens of shoemakers, armourers, or coppersmiths working away side by side. We were never tired of strolling about the city, and observing something new at every turn.

We visited a number of the chief mosques : Sultan Hassan, Tayloon, and the Grand Mosque in the citadel, built by Mehemet Ali, and containing his tomb. The buildings of Cairo, although many of them possessing much grace and beauty, are of such perishable materials, that the whole city and especially the mosques appear to be in a state of ruin and neglect, the wonder being that they do not come down with a run. Very little stone is used, ill-baked, or sun-dried bricks are the principal material, except in the case of Mehemet Ali's mosque, which is built of large blocks of Oriental alabaster, while the floor inside is covered with the richest Turkey carpets. There is much richness, as well as simplicity, about this building, which is in shape more like a church than a mosque, internally at least. In the Citadel we saw Joseph's well, where water is drawn up by bullocks from the Nile ; the Pasha's palace fitted up in Oriento-Parisian style, and the Mameluke's Leap, whence there is a grand view of Cairo with its countless minarets and flat-topped houses, and the Nile valley beyond, with the pyramids of Gizeh and Sakkara on the horizon. One evening Lees and I having gone alone to admire this view at sunset, were of course benighted on our way home, and lost our way in the labyrinths of the city. At that hour no donkeys were to be seen ; moreover Cairo is not lighted with gas. It was not very pleasant groping one's way along through the Arab quarter, thinking of fanatics, and tumbling over vicious dogs, lying as usual in the middle of the path. One of these amiable animals fastened his teeth in the unbelieving flesh of poor Lees, whereat I could not help laughing consumedly, although in momentary expectation of a similar fate ; however, by using the word " Uzbekeh " we reached home without further misadventure.

S.S. "Malta."—I do not pine much after the fleshpots of Egypt, having only twice been well fed while in that ancient land. For several days the heat was very oppressive, so that the exertion of putting on a clean collar was of itself sufficient to render the operation nugatory ; I accordingly abandoned that superfluous and conventional article of dress. On the night of the 11th of December, as we stood on the forecastle, the outer light of Bombay was distinctly visible ; a number of us stood there watching it for a long time before turning in, and with very varied feelings. I believe that I was the only one on board who regarded it with unmixed satisfaction, as the first signal of my native land, where

I hoped to find so many old friends, and to see so many new sights.

December 12th, Bombay.—At sunrise, when standing on deck admiring the fair harbour of Bombay, the well-known face of H. Birdwood appeared amid the bustle and confusion, and we went on shore at once. He was living in tents on the Esplanade, and one was ready for me with every luxury, of which perhaps a cold bath was the greatest. The pomflets and prawn curry, with good tea and iced water, were simply nectar and ambrosia after the fare of the P. and O. steamer. In the evening Willie arrived from Ahmedabad—Hooray! Haven't we just nicked it off?

December 13th.—Houses, servants, horses, are all at famine prices in Bombay, and the great Parsee and Hindoo merchants rule the roast, not caring what they pay for anything. I attended a remarkable meeting, held with the view of doing honour to the memory of David Sassoon, a mighty Jew, lately deceased ; all the most influential citizens, native and European, were present in the Town Hall, the Governor, Sir B. Frere, presiding. The Parsees took a special and active share in the proceedings, moving and seconding resolutions, among others Sir J. Jeejeebhoy read a speech of some length. In liberality and public spirit the mercantile community of Bombay are almost unrivalled, and although some portion of their apparent wealth is due to an inflated credit system, many of them have really amassed colossal fortunes, chiefly by cotton since the outbreak of the American War. We went to a reception of Lady Frere's at Parell ; it was very pleasant, the band playing under the beautiful old mango trees, sun setting and moon rising, while we sauntered about the garden. Bombay is certainly a very striking place : you pass suddenly from a crowded bazar into a forest of palms, and come out under a rocky hill, covered with villas and gardens ; when you least expect it, you find yourself on the sea-shore, and you step at once out of the narrow streets of the Fort upon an open grassy plain, dotted with tents.

S.S. "Euphrates."—The steamer was comfortable, and we were a very pleasant party. It was a charming sail down the coast. The first point at which we touched was Carwar; it is the only good harbour except Bombay on the west coast, or indeed in all India, and is, besides, very picturesque.

December 18th, Calicut.—They ran us up dexterously, in most

F

disagreeably narrow boats, on to the sandy beach, where Vasco de Gama landed nearly four centuries ago. The costume of the natives of Malabar is striking, being chiefly conspicuous by its absence, as they wear very little, except an enormous round hat made of palm leaves, or an umbrella of the same. Through groves of cocoanut and areca palms we found our way to the hotel, where we refreshed the outer and inner man, and enjoyed the performances of jugglers and snake charmers in the verandah.

December 20th, Nilgherry Hills.—The scenery is charming the whole way, and I was especially struck with the variety and luxuriance of the vegetation, all new to me, except as seen in a conservatory, in particular the graceful, feathery bamboo. High up on some of the steepest slopes are coffee plantations, the glossy green leaves and red berries of which have a bright effect. A very pleasant place is Ooty, a great collection of comfortable villas, scattered over a large extent of undulating country, nestled among trees on the slopes and in the hollows, sheltered on every side by high hills, and enjoying a climate which probably comes as near perfection as any on this globe. In the gardens flourish all kinds of delicate and beautiful flowers, heliotrope growing into bushes eight feet high, and geraniums forming regular bullfinches. The fact is that on some part or other of the Nilgherries will grow any plant whatever that is a native of the torrid or temperate zones; snow never falls, even on their summits, except a few flakes at long intervals of years; and except a little hoar-frost in the hollows, from which the verbenas occasionally require shelter, frost also is unknown. The public gardens are beautifully laid out with terraces and fountains on a steep slope, and the naturalization of useful and ornamental plants is most successfully carried out by Mr. McIvor, especially the tea-plant and cinchona.

January 7, 1865, Madras.—The whole aspect of Madras is that of an old, well-established English settlement, with their comforts about them; a Saheb is an object of respect in virtue of his race, all the servants speak English, and the official nobility are not overshadowed, as at Bombay, by the wealth and influence of the native merchants and bankers. It may be called the benighted Presidency, but is by far the pleasantest to live in; Madras itself is remarkably healthy, for an Indian native city; while the constant sea breeze, and the neighbourhood of the Nilgherry and Shevaroy Hills, accessible by railway in a few hours, more than compensate to Europeans for its low latitude, as compared with Bombay and Calcutta.

At Calcutta they were hospitably entertained by Mr. (now Sir George) Campbell, then Judge of the High Court, who most kindly devoted himself to showing them all that was interesting. At the Botanic Gardens, and at Barrackpore, they saw sad signs of the cyclone which had recently done so much damage. ' They went to Chinsura to meet their sister and Colonel Hope, C.B., commanding the 71st Highlanders, who were about to embark for England with the regiment. After about ten days in Calcutta, they started up country by railway, stopping to visit the Opium Factory at Patna.

January 24th, Bankipore.—The Dak bungalow was as full as an egg; after dinner we were obliged to compose ourselves to rest, one on a bedstead in the verandah, the other two doubled up in palkees outside. Even here, however, there was no rest for us; an unprotected British female, with lots of children, arrived in the middle of the night, and boldly demanded palkees and coolies for self and offspring. It is almost needless to say that she turned us out of our temporary refuge, and went off in triumph, leaving us trembling and astonished. For this luxurious accommodation we were only charged two rupees a head by a paternal Government.

January 31st, Lucknow.—We were taken to see the places whose names we knew so well: Kaiser Bagh, Chutter Munzil, Residency, Imambarrah, etc., buildings interesting for their size and architecture, but far more so from the events of 1857. Above all, the Baileyguard Gate, and the other shattered buildings within that famous enclosure, which still bears witness to the most gallant defence on record. Commanded on all sides by powerful batteries, the clay walls are riddled with round shot in every direction, had they been of harder material they must have been levelled, as it is they look a little like the ruins on the Palatine Hill. From the top of the Chuttur Munzil the view is very striking, of palaces, mosques, tombs, bridges, minarets, and spires rising on all sides, interspersed with trees and gardens; while

every building and every garden is memorable as the scene of a
fierce struggle in that " crowning fight," which crushed the great
Indian Mutiny.

February 3rd, Agra.—The Taj surpasses in grandeur and beauty
all description : it is " a sight to dream of, not to tell ; " passing
through the splendid gateway, you enter a well-kept garden, and
there, above the dark-green foliage of mangoes and cypresses, the
glittering domes and minarets rise like an exhalation into the clear
blue sky : *vedi e muori !* The interior is in keeping and, if
possible, more highly and perfectly finished in every detail of
carving and pietra dura ; design and architecture Saracenic with
the finish of Florentine jewelry.

At Delhi, as at Lucknow, the chief interest centred in
the marks of the great siege, still a matter of recent history,
and under the guidance of Colonel Hamilton, the commissioner, with whom they stayed, they traced the military
operations from the famous Ridge to the storming of the
Cashmere Gate. Of the endless architectural remains of old
and new Delhi, Sir David seems to have been most struck
by the Great Mosque.

February 8th, Delhi.—Among the lions of modern Delhi the
Jumma Musjid stands pre-eminent in every sense, its snow-white
domes and minarets gleaming brightly above the city. The main
mass of the building is composed of sandstone, whose rich red contrasts so beautifully with the white marble of the upper portions.
It consists of a vast courtyard, approached by flights of steps like
the base of a pyramid, and surrounded by a screen on three sides,
each of which has a lofty gateway in the centre. The mosque itself
is on the fourth side, that nearest to Mecca, and is a glorious
specimen of the Mogul architecture in its prime, rich and yet
simple, graceful and yet massive, perfectly finished, without any
superfluous ornament, and in complete preservation owing to the
excellent quality of the materials. The red hair of the Prophet's
beard, his shoe, and various renowned autographs were duly
inspected.

February 13th, Hurdwar.—Mr. Williams equipped us with gun
and rifles, two elephants, and sent us into the Doon forest to
shoot. Saw lots of game : spotted deer, hog deer, hare, peafowl,

and jungle fowl, besides hosts of monkeys and great variety of birds. Did not fire with very deadly effect, never having shot out of a howdah, but bagged an enormous peacock. Elephants behaved beautifully, beating the cover with their trunks, breaking down trees to make a way through the jungle, and picking up plaid, and stick, which had been dropped. Forest like an English nobleman's park, well stocked with deer and peacocks, but with a background of mountains, such as no English park possesses : the outlying bastions of the Himalayas themselves, and topped here and there with snow. At a most picturesque camping ground in the jungle, we found a large tent pitched, servants in atten-dance, and every luxury of the season provided for us by the kindness and forethought of Mr. Williams.

February 14*th.*—We turned out early on foot to circumvent, if possible, the jungle-fowl, which were crowing and clucking all round, as if the forest were a barnyard. We found soon that there were pigs, as well as poultry, for a big wild boar trotted across the road just in front of us, taking us so completely by surprise, that he departed unassailed, which was perhaps as well for all parties under the circumstances. We were here deprived of our howdah elephant by the rightful owner, but we pursued our way on the pad elephant, and succeeded in bagging a deer, besides losing another, and a peafowl for want of a retriever; the old elephant did his best, but speed is scarcely one of the many valuable qualifications of that noble animal.

They made a run up to Mussoorie, and were fortunate enough to have perfectly clear views of Jumnotri, Gangotri, and the other distant peaks of the Himalayas; there was much ice and snow about at that time of year, and the change of temperature between there and Umballa was considerable. They drove on to Umritsur, and, after seeing the Golden Temple, took train to Lahore. Heavy rain set in, but nothing daunted they set off to drive to Peshawur. Near Wujeerabad the road abruptly terminated in a broken bridge and red rushing stream, the Chenab having the previous night carried away its eight bridges. As neither boats nor fords were available at this unforeseen and almost unprecedented conjuncture, they were forced to turn their backs on Peshawur. On their return journey to Delhi they diverged to Putiala, in order to be present at the wedding of the young raja.

March 3rd, Putiala.—The maharaja came to call on the commissioner, at whose tents we all met him, and soon afterwards, climbing on to the numerous elephants in attendance, we proceeded to the palace, a large and handsome building in the middle of the city. Here the little maharaja received us in state, and we were ushered into the grand reception hall, crowded with gorgeously dressed rajas, sirdars, and nautch girls. We all squatted on carpets, sahebs on the right, rajas on the left; presents were made and the nautch girls performed their discordant music and ungraceful dancing. Back through the filthy streets to tiffin, then on fresh and very gorgeous elephants to visit the Raja of Jheend, whose army, camp, dress and appointments are all perfect; a good band, handsome tent, and splendid howdahs of gold and silver." He looked like an Assyrian king; he and his little son, dressed in purple and gold, gave us each a swell turban. Elephants again to the palace, where more Durbar, nautching, athletic feats and fireworks, chiefly smoke and noise, but the great court looked very well, coloured lights and torches, crowds of people on the roofs, elephants below.

Returning to Agra they undertook the fatiguing journey of three hundred and eighty miles by mail cart to Indore, stopping to see the Fort at Gwalior, and passing through the fertile opium-growing plains of Malwa, brilliant with the many-coloured poppy-fields. At Dewas they stayed a short time with the Resident at Indore, Colonel (now Sir Richard) Meade, and then pushed on to the railway at Bhosawul, ascending to the rock fortress of Asseerghur by the way.

His brother's leave of absence being ended, Sir David went with him to his station, Ahmedabad, and spent a fortnight there, seeing the fine old buildings and ruins which abound in and about that city, and joining in the Indian sports of hog-hunting, antelope and nilgau shooting.

On his return to Bombay, he visited the Elephanta Caves,
and in spite of the heat of April, made a run by Poona to
the hill station of Mahableshwur. He enjoyed two days
there, but had a very hot ride of seventy-two miles back
to Poona.

April 14th.—Bombay looks very bright and bustling ; view of
the city, bay, hills, and islands really lovely, quite like Naples,
nothing like it at the other Presidencies. Passed the Back Bay
reclamation works ; hard at it emptying the hill into the sea.
Their faith is greater than a grain of mustard seed, but their success is at least doubtful, and meanwhile they are making a horrid
mess.

S.S. "Carnatic."—The weather was magnificent the whole time,
a cool northerly breeze making the temperature seem delightful
after the scorching land wind. The nights were especially charming, "brightest constellations burning, mellow moons and happy
skies."

He returned by Trieste, and, after three days' sight-
seeing at Vienna, ran straight through in fifty-four hours,
without stopping, to Gloucester, reaching home on the 11th
of May.

In the autumn of 1865, he made his first trip to Ireland
with Charles Stewart and two other friends.

September 16th, Dublin.—The International Exhibition reminded me of the one at Manchester in 1857, which it almost
rivals in number, if not in quality, of its art treasures. Sculpture
from Italy well arranged, and many good statues, several remarkable for the care with which dress is done, something new in
marble, especially "Drawing Girl" and "Child with Doll." Paintings from all countries ; Scandinavian remarkable in number and
excellence—a very rising school.

From Athlone they went in search of the "Deserted
Village ;" after a long walk and many inquiries, they found
a ruined house which, as a native informed them, had been
Goldsmith's house, and was almost the only remaining relic
of Lishoy.

October 2nd, Killarney.—Set off in car for the Gap of Dunloe. Long before approaching the fatal spot, we were beset by guides, touters, beggars, and other nuisances to an extent which I never saw equalled (except in Egypt); their numbers and pertinacity were something quite appalling, but we constantly referred them back to another car just behind us, and thus got rid of a great many. When we got down to walk up the steep glen, they still pursued us with bottles of potheen, and lace collars; ambuscades started out from below bridges and behind rocks, hunting us nearly the whole five miles down to our boat on the other side of the Gap, but we hardened our hearts and "always gave them nothing."

October 4th.—A splendid morning determined us to ascend Carrantual, the highest of all Irish mountains; and we had a wonderfully clear and extensive view, embracing all the south of Ireland. I have seen nothing in this country to compare with it, and scarcely anything in Scotland to match it, except Skye; immense precipices of slaty rock, alternately smooth as glass or rugged as the edge of a saw, overhanging and surrounding little tarns.

Mr. Fitzpatrick, M.P., afterwards Lord Castletown, Lord Lieutenant for Queen's County, invited Sir David and Stewart to Lisduff, where they spent nearly a week, shooting and making acquaintance with some of the neighbours. Returning by Milford Haven, the spot was pointed out to him where the *Great Eastern* lay, so near to the shore, that you could walk on board of her : there are not many harbours in the world where such a thing could be done.

As may be seen from the extracts hitherto given from Sir David's journals, he up to this time travelled for pleasure only, enjoying all he saw and did with youthful freshness, noticing the most trivial incidents, and making the very annoyances of travel a source of amusement to himself and his companions. Although he brought a keen power of observation to bear on all external objects, he did not then look much below the surface of things ; as he himself said, " I was a boy till I was thirty."

In June, 1866, he made a cruise on board H.M.S. *Lizard*, with S. Grove, R.N., then captain superintendent of the fisheries on the East Coast of Scotland. He joined the ship at Granton, and they cruised along the coast, touching at the various fishing ports *en route;* he was ready to give a helping hand in anything and everything that took place, and was sorry to be obliged to leave again at Aberdeen.

The first published papers from his pen were some critical notices of books, which appeared in the *Fortnightly Review* in 1866–67. The first was on "The Story of the Bhotan War," by Dr. Rennie. The next, on "Across Mexico in 1864–65," by his friend W. H. Bullock. The others were on the "Romans Nationaux," by Erckmann-Chatrian, for whose writings he always had a great admiration, especially for the earlier ones. He calls them—

a series of pictures, which can scarcely be surpassed for romantic interest, historical accuracy, and photographic minuteness of description. They treat of "fierce wars and faithful loves;" the name has been well chosen, for national feeling gives the key-note to the whole series; the spirit of enthusiastic patriotism, which runs through them all, entitles them most justly to be called "Romans Nationaux."

Going to the Railway Station, Bankipore.

Watervliet, N.Y. October 1866.

CHAPTER V.

1866.

TOUR THROUGH THE UNITED STATES AND CANADA—LECTURES ON
AMERICA.

IN August, 1866, Sir David started for a lengthened tour in America with Baron Mackay, now Lord Reay, and Charles Dalrymple, afterwards M.P. for Bute. They sailed in the *S.S. Scotia*, Captain Judkins.

September 4th, New York.—This huge mass of buildings, although certainly imposing, contrasts unfavourably with the massive grandeur of Liverpool. The most striking objects by far in the whole scene are the huge steam ferries constantly plying in every direction across the broad expanse ; they are simply floating covered streets, and when we drove on board one, there were a lot of other vehicles, and at first I could hardly persuade myself that we were actually afloat, but the vessel glided away smoothly and rapidly, without noise or smoke, and landed us on the opposite side some distance up the river.

September 12th, Providence.—We visited a Primary and Intermediate School, where are children from the age of six and
upwards. Nothing can be prettier than the spectacle of the little
creatures, sitting demurely at their green desks, all pictures of
health and cleanliness, with bright intelligent faces ; at a sign from
the school-mistress they rise with military precision, and then the
ceremony of introducing the illustrious strangers to the lady takes
place. We passed through a number of well lighted and venti-
lated rooms, until we came to a more advanced lot, whose elegant
and accomplished teacher trotted them out in spelling, geography,
and recitation. Nothing can possibly surpass their accuracy and
quickness, none of them probably being much above twelve years
old. We then went on to the Grammar School, for more advanced
pupils, presided over by a master, having female teachers under
him. Here the young people, especially the damsels, were even
prettier and wittier than ever, and really astonished me by their
performances in mental arithmetic and geographical drawing.
Finally the whole lot were assembled in the great school-room,
about five hundred in all, and went through a series of general
performances for our edification : some very pretty singing, calis-
thenic exercises by flugel, and recitations in prose and poetry.
There was a small sprinkling of young darkies, who since the war
have been put on terms of perfect equality with the rest, and who
show no marked symptoms of intellectual inferiority. It may also
be remarked that the girls, who in this department receive exactly
the same instruction as the boys, seem to be fully equal to the
latter, taking rank among them promiscuously, although they do
not generally sit at the same desks, the boys being in front. In
conclusion Mr. Leach said, " My young friends, these gentlemen
from Europe will now kindly tell you something about their own
countries." There was no help for it, and we had to rise and
harangue them in turn, of course laying on the butter pretty thick,
and not without cause ; the speeches seemed to give satisfaction,
but were received in perfect silence. The children then filed out
to their class-rooms in most orderly manner. There is also a
High School; and the cost to Providence, a city of sixty thousand
inhabitants, of this splendid system of free education, is upwards
of one hundred thousand dollars.

September 19th, Toronto.—We first went to the Upper Canada
College, where, for £36 a head, sixty boys get an excellent

education, and are boarded and lodged better than at the most expensive English schools ; they all learn military drill.   We went to see Osgoode Hall, a beautiful building for the use of the Law Courts, quite the best I have ever seen, putting Westminster and Dublin to shame.   Everything is most handsomely finished, and there is none of the dinginess characteristic of the purlieus of the law, all being new.   A case was going on before a vice-chan- cellor, the witness being cross-examined in his presence : this is always done here, and the Equity Judges go on circuit like the rest.   It is needless to enlarge on the advantages of such a system ; one result is that the Courts are very popular, great con- fidence being felt in the rapidity and justice of decisions ; another is that law is the favourite profession among rising young men. The different branches of the profession are not kept strictly apart, the same man being generally barrister and solicitor both, but in practice the two lines are generally followed by different members of the same firm, as in Norway ; they do not wear wigs, even judges have robes only.

September 22nd.—We left behind us the gorgeous towers and cloud-capped palaces of Ottawa, not without the feeling that they are considerably out of keeping with their surroundings of wooden shanties and primeval forest, of which we had a fine view yester- day from the top of the Parliament buildings.   At some future day, when this northern Washington is a provincial town of the Great Republic, this palace may be turned into a college or a lunatic asylum, and be known by the name of the "British Folly"—*absit omen.*

Nothing can be finer than the river St. Lawrence : the banks are well wooded and pretty thickly studded with towns and villages, but it is the stream itself that has all the grandeur, wind- ing in every direction, spreading out to a width of miles, then contracting to a couple of hundred yards ; now tearing along in foaming waves between wooded islands, and now calm and green as an emerald.   The steamers are large and comfortable, food excellent and included in the ridiculously small sum paid for our tickets, which are available either by land or water ; altogether the voyage is exceedingly pleasant.

September 27th, Quebec.—We drove to the Montmorency Falls ; the cascade is very beautiful, falling in splendid shoots of spray, which mix and cross in all directions, right down to the St. Law-

rence ; and from the surrounding scenery, as well as its own height
and volume, it is almost unrivalled in the elements of the picturesque. Standing in the wooden summer-house, you have the
waterfall thundering past you "in clouds of snow-white foam,"
opposite a precipitous wooded cliff, beyond which the spires of
Quebec glitter like silver in the sun, whilst across the wide St.
Lawrence lie the Isle of Orleans and the heights above Point
Levis, fringed with white houses, and crowned with forest, now
beginning to assume the brilliant colours of autumn. We walked
up to the Citadel : the view from the rampart is magnificent, and
the sunset on the river and the forest-clad mountains required
Claude Lorraine to do it justice ; the tin spires and roofs shone
like burnished gold, and the whole scene was like a picture of the
celestial city.

October 6th, Albany.—The famous Penitentiary is in a first-rate
situation, and has nothing of a prison in its appearance; the
superintendent received us very politely, and showed us all over
the place, which he is now enlarging and improving with the funds
which he has accumulated, putting the country to no expense ;
last year he had 21,000 dollars to the good. The ordinary
discipline is very strict, but the prisoners are well fed, have lots of
occupation, fresh air, and light, and are exceedingly healthy. The
walls, by no means very high, are guarded by a few armed sentries
in plain clothes, and they never lose a prisoner; particolored
garments of red and black are worn. All their work is contracted
for and taken by wholesale dealers ; it is wonderful how, by minute
subdivision of labour, men working at even the shortest sentences
can be taught to work efficiently at a new trade. A large proportion are blacks from the District of Columbia, sent here by Federal
Government from Washington, a small allowance being made for
each. A good many are soldiers and sailors convicted by court-
martial, and every variety of felony and misdemeanour is here
represented ; more than two-thirds acknowledge themselves to be
of intemperate habits, only two hundred and eighty claiming to
be temperate. The cells are small, but airy and light, with open
gratings opening on galleries, approached by iron staircases. The
women work in the laundry, and at cane chairs. All is perfectly
orderly, and strict silence is preserved ; when any one has finished
his work, he folds his hands, and looks straight to his front, until
the overseer furnishes him with more. In the yard they march in

close single file, each with his hand on shoulder of man in front, generally very submissive, seldom requiring extra punishment— possibly the large proportion of negroes may have something to do with this,—but the superintendent says they are all thieves by nature.

October 7th.—We drove out to the Shaker settlement of Water-vliet; sounds of revelry guided us to the Meeting-house—a large building rather low in the roof, with an unexceptionable floor, and raised benches for spectators, men left, women right. On the square open space the Shakers were drawn up, the two sexes ranged opposite one another, nearly a hundred altogether, about two-thirds being women. The men wore long drab coats and waistcoats, their hair long behind, short on the forehead; the women maroon coloured dresses, long and plaited like kilts, no crinoline, large white neck-kerchiefs, and close-fitting net caps, everything spotlessly clean. At first they sang various hymns, standing perfectly still; then an old gentleman gave a kind of address in a low voice; then singing again, only accompanied by a swaying motion, until, at a given signal, most of the men proceeded to hang up their coats, the women laid aside their huge pocket-handkerchiefs, and all who were not absolutely incapacitated by age or infirmity went to work in good style. Round they went in admirable time to the vocal accompaniment, backing and filling, poussetting and stamping, all in the most solemn and matter-of-fact way, and apparently so much in earnest, that none of us felt any inclination to laugh; absurd as the scene was, it had a sort of pathos and solemnity. The drill was perfect, the movements not ungraceful, and many of the hymn tunes pretty, resembling Scotch airs; the whole thing something between Petronella and a Nautch, performed by people between seventy and seven. A very aged brother gave us a sermon, chiefly in praise of his own communion, whom he warned, however, against being puffed up by their own superior purity; then one or two sisters hazarded a few almost inaudible remarks, the marching, singing, and clapping of hands was renewed, until the assembly was dismissed, about 11.30 a.m. The Shakers are certainly a peculiar people, keeping themselves to themselves, spending nothing on missions or charity, but managing to recruit their numbers and increase their property; here they own about three thousand acres.

They paid a very enjoyable visit of a week to Mr. Langdon, at his pretty house on the Hudson, near Poughkeepsie. Sir David and his host were daily on the river before breakfast :—

October 11th.—We had our morning row round the island, coming back under sail. Nothing could be brighter or more beautiful, the Catskills perfectly clear, the foliage gleaming in scarlet and gold, the numerous country-houses on both banks, the steamers and sloops on the water contributing greatly to the cheerfulness and animation of the scene. The Hudson is certainly a splendid piece of water, but there is so little current, that it more resembles a lake than a river; it is here three quarters of a mile wide on an average, the tide rises several feet, but the water is quite fresh although muddy. The woods around are by no means devoid of life ; there are lots of red and grey squirrels, chipmunks, jays, kingfishers, robins (rather larger than a thrush), also woodchucks.

October 16th, Philadelphia.—While the indefatigable Baron went off again to hunt for schools, we took a horse-car out to Fairmount Park, where we ate toffy, watched boys playing baseball, and dozed in the shade,—an afternoon of real enjoyment.

October 17th.—We proceeded to the High School, where young women are trained, chiefly for the vocation of teachers. For these there is a great demand in Philadelphia, where 80,000 children study under 1400 female teachers, only thirty or forty men being employed in the boys' High School ; I scarcely know whether to admire or to despise the Philadelphian youth for showing so much docility under petticoat government. As for these young women's power of acquiring and communicating knowledge, no one can have a doubt on the subject who has heard them, without book or notes of any kind, teaching and examining their classes in physical geography, cube roots, chronology, and the constitution of the United States. Each teacher has a special subject of her own, and clearly has it at her finger ends ; sometimes a pupil is turned on to teach, apparently with great success; there was no showing off about the matter, as they merely went on with the lesson or recitation of the day, although no doubt our presence put them upon their mettle.

October 12th, Baltimore.—We came in for regular Indian summer ; in fact, piping hot. Went to Mr. Latrobe's office. He

showed us photographs of Indians with whom he negotiated a
treaty lately; they are dressed like white men, and might easily
pass for such. He says they displayed much good sense and
acumen during the negotiation; they are quite civilized, and have
a form of government resembling that of the United States, with
elective president or chief; their territory is now quite surrounded
by States of the Union, but its boundaries are well defined, and
they are quite independent; perhaps some day they may be
admitted to the great Federation. They are Creeks, Chocktaws,
Chickasaws, Cherokees, and Seminoles; these last have been more
recently imported from Florida to Indian territory, and are less
advanced in civilization.

October 23rd, Petroleum.—We got up early and started for
White Oak oil springs. It was a charming walk through the
forest—bright sun, bracing air, and the path lay through glades
with clearings of small extent, across little creeks, and over steep
hills with splendid tall timber growing all around; occasional
stumps and dead trees, killed by girdling or fire, completing the
picture, which fully realized my idea of American backwoods. A
walk of some three miles brought us to the first well. Here a
steam-engine of simplest construction was pumping oil out of the
ground into a huge vat, containing about six hundred barrels,
in a thick green jet of liquid, resembling turtle soup in colour and
consistency, and smelling by no means nice, from a sickly soupçon
of decayed animal matter. It sells at present for only five or six
dollars a barrel, oil being cheap. This spring gives upwards of
seventy-five barrels a day, and is worked chiefly with the flame of
its own gas. The largest well in West Virginia gives a thousand
barrels in ten hours at present, but of course the yield is precarious
and temporary; owners of land get generally one-third of the oil,
sometimes more. It is a most extraordinary thing to see oil
pouring out of the earth in a continuous spirting stream and filling
vats twenty feet high. Hitherto this district has remained in its
primeval condition, emigrants passing on to richer soils in the
Western free States; now, however, there appears to be a prosperous
future for the new State of West Virginia. Formerly, so great was
the difficulty of obtaining white settlers in slave States, that in
Missouri the finest land was offered at $12\frac{1}{2}$ cents an acre, instead
of $1\frac{1}{4}$ dollars, the regular price.

October 24th, Cincinnati.—The name is derived from a party

of officers of the revolutionary war, who obtained grants of land
in the neighbourhood, and having beaten their swords into plough-
shares, took the title of Cincinnati, which was afterwards given to
the city. We lost no time in calling on Mr. Lars Anderson, who
has a very handsome house in Pike Street. Four of his sons
served in the Federal army, and have now returned to civil life ;
two of them carry on a large business in wine, their grandfather,
Mr. Longworth, having introduced vine-growing into Ohio. We
went over the cellars, which exactly resembled, on a smaller scale,
those of Moët at Epernay ; the workmen employed are Frenchmen,
and all the champagne bottles are imported from France, as they
cannot make them strong enough here to withstand a pressure of
fifteen to twenty-four atmospheres. We tasted the different wines
made here—a still white and a red which resembles Hungarian,
both fair ; the Sparkling Catawba is delicious, tasting strongly
of the grape, and something like St. Péray.

Captain Anderson was on General Sherman's staff, and was
wounded in the arm ; and we got out of him some of his experiences, which were of course most interesting. At the battle of
Kenessaw Mountain his men and the Confederates were intrenched
for days within thirty yards of each other ; except when by mutual
agreement they established a truce, as often happened, not a man
could show on either side without being shot. At this juncture a
Yankee selling "notions" came into camp, with little bits of mirror
an inch and a half square on wire to fasten to the back sight of
rifles. The colonel bought a thousand of them, and served them
out to the men. Sitting with their backs to the enemy, and exposing the thumb only, they were able in a short time to silence
the Confederate fire so completely, that they got out upon the
parapet and chaffed the "rebs" with impunity. The invention
was invaluable, being both simple and efficient, but it was not
adopted, nor even noticed in general despatches. There is red
tape here in this "Great Republic."

October 28th, St. Louis.—In the evening the Baron and I
attended a spiritualist meeting ; the room was very full, and we were
harangued at considerable length by Eliza Doten. Her language
was exceedingly fluent and accurate, occasionally grand and
poetical, as when she compared the myriads of human existences
constantly appearing and disappearing, to corpuscles of blood,
circulating in the grand system of the universe, changing their

appearance, but perpetually renewing themselves afresh.   The immortality of the soul, its intimate relations with the body, upon whose health and well-being all moral happiness and excellence so greatly depend, the duty of being good housekeepers, and maintaining the spirit's tabernacle in repair by fresh air and exercise, were points on which she laid great stress.   Her subject was " Breath, Blood, and Spirit."   On the first two topics her physiology seemed to be correct, and she explained it clearly, saying that at the very moment we were poisoning ourselves in that ill-ventilated room.   At once every window was opened, to my great delight. On the last point she was rather vague, as was to be expected ; but I liked her doctrines, which are eminently practical, "laborare est orare " and "mens sana " found only " in corpore sano."

November 4th, S.S. " Belle Memphis."—The weather was beautiful ; the accommodation and fare on board are wonderfully good, the scenery is pleasing, and altogether I felt so comfortable and jolly that I only wished we were going on to New Orleans. The broad, bright river winds between wooded banks, which here have still at this date the brilliant colouring of the fall.   Few signs of cultivation are seen, but here and there some log houses, with large piles of firewood, and a rough path down the face of the low earthy cliff, mark the spot for a landing.   It is great fun to see the lazy, jovial way in which the negro porters on board go to work, always on the broad grin, chaffing one another, each trying to let his neighbour do the lion's share of work, tumbling about over pigs, or under cotton bales, and never getting hurt.

November 5th, Memphis.—At the Gayoso House we made friends with the landlord's son, who gave us a note to his father, Mr. Cockrell, and we set out in a glass coach for his plantation. We found him at his own gate, surrounded by pointers of all ages.   He received us most hospitably, and gave us lots of champagne.   He gets on very well with his negroes, paying eighteen dollars a month for a strong man, twelve for a woman, besides feeding and lodging them ; this being somewhat above market rates, his niggers naturally stick to him.   He has to pay fourteen dollars for packing a bale of five hundred pounds : one bale per acre is a good crop, half a bale rather middling, one and a half not unknown on very fine land ; at present a bale is worth a hundred and eighty dollars.   He prides himself greatly on the care he always took of his slaves when sick or old, also in keeping

families together. He is a true Southerner, and has many stories
to tell against the Federals for robbery, insult, and above all for
killing his valuable pigs.   We walked with him through his
garden and cotton fields ; frost and hot sun have combined to
ripen and burst the pods, and fields quite lately picked are white
once more to harvest.   The dogs found a fine bevy of quail, and
we found lots of persimmons—a new fruit to me, bright yellow
when tree-ripe, but only good to eat when overripe and frostbitten ;
the flower reminds me very much of fresh dates, which, when ripe,
have a similar harsh astringency.   We saw the negroes picking the
cotton, which comes quite easily out of the dry pod, and is collected
in large baskets.   Before dinner they all came up, one by one—
men, women, and boys—to receive a glass of whisky, which Mr.
Cockrell gives them daily : a bad custom I should say ; they all
tossed it off without winking, and he had a friendly word for each
uncle and aunt.

They went to Kentucky in order to visit the Mammoth
Caves, and then turned south, through Tennessee and
Georgia, as far as Charlestown.   Fort Sumter still lay
almost in ruins, and they saw many other sad marks of the
great war.   By the time they reached Richmond, they had
heard the Confederate views fully and ably expounded, but
Sir David says :—

The arguments of Democrats confirm me in Republicanism,
and I think my gallant Southern friends have pretty well made a
Yankee of me.   The idea of slavery tinges all their thoughts, as
a form of feudal service ; it is the *labour* not the *person* to which
they claim an absolute right, and to sell slaves has long been
looked on as reprehensible, while to illtreat them was placed in the
same category as wife-beating.   Mediæval knights and barons were
not more genuine aristocrats than modern Virginians or South
Carolinians ; Venice was scarcely a more aristocratic republic than
either of their States, in all except name ; it was their own States
and not the great Union that they loved, and still love to a degree
that foreigners can scarcely appreciate.

November 19*th, Washington.*—The Capitol is certainly a grand
building, set on a hill, snowy white, richly adorned with Corinthian
pillars of marble, and crowned in the centre with a lofty dome, on

the top of which stands the Goddess of Liberty, turning her back
upon Washington city. Everything in the building is massive and
handsome—bronze doors, marble staircases ; the Senate hall, and
the hall of Representatives, comfortable and spacious, with lots of
accommodation for the public. Each member has a convenient
desk and armchair, which enable him, by aid of reading and
writing, to endure with equanimity the delivery of long written
speeches. We ascended to the top of the dome, where you find
yourself face to face with mythological and allegorical parties of
large stature, sprawling about on the ceiling in company with
Franklin, Washington, and other respectable American gentlemen.
The view looking down inside gives an idea of height equal to
that of St. Peter's.

Passing through New York again, they spent a most
enjoyable week at Boston, seeing much of interest, and
making the acquaintance of Dr. Howe, the philanthropist,
who showed them over his institutions for the blind and
imbeciles, for whose instruction he has done so much.

November 30th, Boston.—We had the honour of dining with
the "Autocrat of the Breakfast Table," Dr. Holmes, a genial,
pleasant man as ever was, who allowed and even encouraged me
to argue with him as to the merits of Dickens, whom he ranks far
above any modern writer, as having influenced the tone and style
of contemporary literature.

December 1st.—We took a long journey by street cars right
through Boston from end to end, landing in Harvard Square, Cambridge. The University of Harvard College, chief seat of learning
in the United States, is situated here in a number of detached
buildings, convenient no doubt, but not particularly picturesque.
Unitarianism is the ostensible creed, but there is toleration for
every form of faith, as is especially exemplified by the varied religions of the professors. We visited Professor Longfellow, who
opened the door for us himself, and gave us a very kind welcome,
inviting us to stay for tea. Although I had had no dinner, I did
not hesitate to choose the feast of reason, and we spent a most
agreeable evening. We stayed about four hours, Dalrymple and
I being with the poet in his study most of the time, afterwards
joining the rest of the family, one son, three daughters, and gover-

ness, at tea. Longfellow is certainly one of the most agreeable men
I ever met, and shows to great advantage in the domestic circle,
to which we were so kindly admitted. He showed us his books,
including a beautiful new edition of "Hyperion," the work in
which the romance of his own life is told, a romance which had so
happy a dénoûment, but now clouded over by so tragic an event.
We also saw the scrap-book of his Scandinavian tour, and had a
long talk about the countries and literature of the North, on
classical subjects, the merits of English hexameters, our own
travels in America, and the institutions of Harvard College.
Once his gentle manner changed for one instant, when an allusion
was made to secession, and State rights ; " incedis per ignes," when
this subject is brought forward whether in Massachusetts or in
South Carolina. We parted almost like old friends, and he gave
me a packet of Spanish cigarettes ; he told us that his house was
Washington's head-quarters during the siege of Boston, and an
old tree still stands on Cambridge common close by, under which
the general assumed command of the revolutionary army.

December 5th, S.S. "Africa."—At 10 a.m. we moved out of
dock " Tücher wehen in die Luft." There were no handkerchiefs
waving there for us, but I could not help feeling that whereas we
had come to America as utter strangers, we now left a good many
there whom we might fairly count as our friends, and glad as I
was to see the *Africa's* bowsprit coming round to eastward, my
satisfaction was not unmixed with a feeling of regret.

December 12th.—To-day the sea really presented a splendid
sight, and the waves were worthy of the great Atlantic, far larger
than any we have yet seen. The motion imparted by them to
the vessel was, however, by no means disagreeable, their course
being exactly the same as ours, and not a drop of water came
over the decks. It was grand to see the green mountains of
water, crested with foam, bearing down upon us from behind, and
rising high above the stern of the vessel, as if they were going to
sweep right over us. But when they overtook us, they merely
lifted the stern high into the air, the bows going down into the
hollow, to be lifted again in their turn, as the waves passed rapidly
but smoothly beneath. To be pooped by these green monsters
would be destruction, but thanks to the speed at which we were
running there was no danger of that. The horizon all round
seemed fringed by ridges of moving hills, the near waves in

colour and appearance resembling the rapids above Niagara falls,
on a far larger and grander scale, while the foam was blown off
their crests like snow flakes by the force of the gale, which often
caused a whole ridge to break over, as if it had come against a
rock. All the time lots of seagulls were skimming about,
apparently quite at their ease. It was great luck to see such a
scene in safety from a dry deck; occasional scudding drifts of
hail "vexed the dim sea."

He reached home punctual to the day he had named,
the 17th of December, his mother's birthday, which he made
a point of spending with her if possible, "a most successful
journey from beginning to end."

The information obtained in this tour, and the impressions made on him, were summed up in a lecture he gave
before the Literary and Scientific Association at Gloucester,
in November, 1867, as well as in two lectures, delivered
in February, 1868, before the Philosophical Institution in
Edinburgh, and from these the following is taken:—

There exists at the present moment no subject so interesting
and instructive, alike to historian, statesman, or philosopher, as
the great American Republic. All that is grandest and most
promising in the future of the human race, especially of that great
family to which we as Englishmen belong, is bound up in the
fortunes of the youthful giant who already overshadows the entire
New World. Never in history has so vast a political experiment
been attempted; never have so many favourable conditions been
combined for the full development of human prosperity. An
almost unlimited extent of fertile territory, abounding in every
source of material wealth, and enjoying a temperate, invigorating
climate, is now being gradually peopled by a bold, energetic,
freedom-loving race, unshackled by the bonds of feudalism and
immemorial usage, but inheriting, as a natural birthright, the
liberty which cost their ancestors so dear, and the political experience earned by Europe during centuries of barbarism and
tyranny.

With so fair a start, and in so glorious a field, how can limits
be assigned to the progress of our race? It is no mere figure of

speech to call this mighty nation of the future " England's eldest born." England is now at the zenith of her glory and greatness, and she may well feel maternal pride, rather than jealousy, in recognizing the fact that the day will come when she must be overshadowed by her great and glorious offspring. Americans have long complained, not without some reason, that England has shown herself but a jealous stepmother towards their country, and that English writers have done much to foster a feeling of mutual envy and animosity between two nations united by the bonds of blood, language, and tradition. It depends chiefly upon the English to prevent transient causes of irritation from producing a lasting feud between the two great branches of the Anglo-Saxon race. If Englishmen and Americans only knew each other better, all unreasonable rancour would rapidly disappear.

Northerners complained that while they had every reason to expect the support of England in their anti-slavery efforts, the moral support she gave to the slave-owners during the war was worth more than an army of 200,000 men, and cost the Northerners years of additional wasting war. They complained, too, of the peremptory course adopted by England in the "Trent" affair; at the time England rather fancied that she was being bullied, and that she was acting on the defensive; either view doubtless might be held in perfect good faith. Neither Northerners nor Southerners are satisfied with the conduct of the British Government, but all alike vie in showing kindness to individual Englishmen, to whom they gladly discourse of their political troubles and hopes, as to a sympathizing but impartial audience.

In spite of the millions of German and Irish immigrants, and of negro freedmen, the American nation in its collective capacity is essentially English. The Yankee is an Englishman under new conditions of existence. Our colonies lean more or less on Great Britain : the American States have each an independent existence. Their institutions are framed to suit their own peculiar circumstances, and are not imported like costly exotics, or antiquities, from a distant country, or a bygone age. The limbs of the young giant are confined in no swathing bands, and he soon learns to walk without leading strings.

Universal liberty—religious, civil, and social—is the ruling principle in each new settlement; the community makes its own laws, and the individual chooses his own form of faith, and his

own mode of life, with far greater freedom of choice than can be
exercised in older countries as to the cut of his coat or the shape
of his hat. Anomalous as it may seem, the maintenance of
slavery in the Southern States was in a great measure due to this
very principle of liberty on which State sovereignty is founded.
Each State of the Union is sovereign within its own borders, and
is absolutely free to regulate its own domestic economy without
interference from its neighbours. Thus, however distasteful negro
slavery might be to the Northerners, they neither possessed nor
claimed any more right to interfere with that institution in the
Carolinas than in Cuba, nor did they hold themselves responsible
in any way for the delinquencies of their Southern brethren.

Republican and Democrat are the names generally given in
America to the two great parties; the former have always been
the supporters of Federal authority, as opposed to State rights,
and have identified themselves especially with the Union, and
with the triumphant war waged for its preservation. To protect
local independence and self-government against the encroachments
of centralized power is the policy of the Democrats, and until the
war they had been in all respects successful, extending their toleration to the "peculiar domestic institutions" of the South.

However needful in time of war a strong central authority
may be, centralization is fraught with peculiar dangers in a vast
Federation, like the United States, where the only hope of permanent union lies in the practical independence of each community. American citizens will never submit to be governed by men
at a distance, who may possibly mean well by them, but who are
ignorant of their circumstances, wants, and feelings, and who are
apt to think that one set of laws is equally well adapted to every
country, climate, and race.

By a freewill union for common interests and objects only, a
society gains the combined strength of all its members, no force
being expended in coercing the minority. This is the theory of
the United States Constitution, and is, to a certain extent, the
practice in the administration of the British Empire. If it were
possible to carry out the system thoroughly, the British Colonies
might become a source of strength, and not of weakness to the
mother country.

At the time of Mr. Lincoln's election the regular army of the
United States consisted merely of a few thousand troops, em-

ployed in garrisoning the sea-coast and frontier forts. Five years later the Federal States emerged from a terrible civil war the greatest military and naval power in the world. A few months more, and over a million trained soldiers were disbanded, and disappeared from view. In no other country could such forces have been raised, for this vast army was composed of volunteers, many of them foreign immigrants, tempted by high bounties, but by far the greater number native Americans, the flower of the nation, whose motive for enlistment was patriotic love for the Union. Still less could any other country have once more absorbed with such marvellous ease and rapidity an armed force, amounting to one-twentieth of the whole population. As soon as the war came to an end the volunteers, many of them veterans of a hundred fights, eagerly took their discharge, and returned to their former avocations as peaceful citizens.

The world has probably never known a fiercer or more widely extended contest, than that which raged for four years in America. It seemed at the time a cruel, fratricidal war, productive of unmitigated evil. But light has come out of darkness; slavery has perished; the Union is established more firmly than ever. It is not good, either for nations or for individuals, to drift continuously down the stream of prosperity. The noblest qualities of man are displayed in suffering and self-sacrifice, and there are virtues which a struggle with adversity alone can develop. The American people have undergone a baptism of blood and fire; they have shown the world that the almighty dollar is not their god; they have lavished their lives and their wealth alike ungrudgingly at the call of patriotism, and they may now boast—

> " Earth's biggest country's got her soul,
> And risen up earth's greatest nation."

To no one cause do the United States owe more of their prosperity and progress than to the admirable system of education, which prevails throughout the country, varying considerably in different States, and carried to the highest perfection in those of New England. Free schools, supported by the State, are open to the children of rich and poor alike, from the earliest age until they are fitted for the universities, or for active life in the world. All branches of a useful and liberal education are taught in turn, some being optional, others imperative; and if in the Northern States it is possible to find a person unable to read or write, it may at least be confidently asserted that he is not a native American. In all fundamental branches—such as arithmetic, geography, English reading and spelling—the highest degree of accuracy is attained ; and it cannot be denied, paradoxical as it may seem, that the Americans, as a nation, speak better English than we do.

The superiority of American education is, however, by no means so conspicuous in the higher schools and colleges ; that accuracy and depth of research, which European scholars display, will be looked for in vain. Mediocrity has hitherto characterized most of what the New World has produced in art, literature, or science ; and America, with her millions of educated citizens, has given birth as yet to few scholars or philosophers who can take rank with the great men of Europe. But give her time ; in a new country men of action flourish more than men of thought, and nations, like individuals, become philosophical only in their riper years.

In America, as elsewhere, liberty and education go hand in hand. A selfish oligarchy establishes its power on the ignorance of its subjects, and a popular government grudges nothing that will promote the enlightenment of the masses. Such a system of national education, as prevails in the Northern States, if carried out in the United Kingdom, could not cost less than five millions annually. But expense should not be considered for an instant, and is perhaps the least of the difficulties to be encountered in carrying out a scheme involving more than any other the future greatness, if not the safety of this empire. We need not be ashamed of taking in this matter an example from the Yankees, who do not suffer party feeling, class prejudice, or sectarian intolerance to interfere with the training of their future citizens, the rising hope and pride of the Republic.

The question of conceding full political rights to women is beginning to assume some prominence in the United States ; the legislature of Kansas having even decided that the two words " white " and " male " ought to be erased from the State constitution. In some countries such an erasure would amount no doubt to a political and social revolution, but this is hardly the case in the Far West, where, in fact, both women and negroes are so scarce, that it signifies comparatively little whether they have the franchise or not, except as a matter of principle.

The great disparity in numbers between the sexes in America, a disparity which increases with the degrees of west longitude, confers on American women a superior position to that enjoyed by their sisters in other parts of the globe. It gives them, in fact, the control of the matrimonial market, and completely turns the tables on the stronger sex. If a fair test of civilization be the social position of women, in any age or country (and it is not easy to suggest a better), then we have one more proof of the westward march of civilization. From the zenanas of Bengal to the prairies of Kansas the step is a wide one, morally as well as geographically, and Europe lies about half-way between them.

Although women enjoy more of social liberty and equality in America than elsewhere, they are not on that account deprived of the chivalrous consideration which is due to physical weakness. On all occasions they take precedence, when an ugly rush is anticipated; they have their own "ladies' entrance" at hotels and post-offices; while the best cars on railroads, and cabins in steamers are set apart for them, and for such men as are privileged to travel in their company. Altogether the American ladies have a "good time" of it, and display almost as little zeal to acquire political rights as do their British sisters. After all, the matter lies in their own hands; if they really desire to possess the franchise, their power to obtain it, within a very short time, is beyond doubt, even in a conservative country like our own.

The number of religious sects is very great in the United States, all being legally on terms of perfect equality, and existing without assistance or interference from the civil government. The Roman Catholics are the most numerous, including the Irish and many Germans; then come Methodists, Baptists, and Presbyterians—the Episcopalian being the most fashionable Church, favoured by the upper ten thousand. All are alike free and voluntary; there is room enough for all; no political or social pressure is exerted upon any form of belief, and a man may be anything or nothing, just as he pleases.

It was not always so in America, and even now this statement applies more especially to the Western States, Puritan intolerance having long lingered in New England, where the noble little State of Rhode Island became the cradle of religious liberty by affording a refuge to the persecuted Baptists from Massachusetts. The older States indeed retain many special characteristics from the

circumstances of their original foundation.   The Puritan settlers
of Massachusetts and Connecticut, the Cavaliers of Virginia, the
Quakers of Pennsylvania, the Catholics of Maryland, have all,
more or less, stamped their own character on the constitution and
history of their respective States.

Respect for the dead appears to be a national characteristic in
America, where the cemeteries far exceed in beauty anything that
Europe can show.   No trouble or expense was spared to collect
and identify the remains of the Federal dead on Southern battle-
fields, and a grateful country has done all that is possible to confer
immortality on the name even of the humblest private.   The
Southerners, too, have done what they could, but means failed
them, and most of the Confederate slain lie where they fell,
nameless, but not unhonoured.   During the war there was one
spot, in the very hottest of the fight, which was sacred, where
Yankees and rebels met in peace.   It was the grave of Washington
at Mount Vernon.

The United States are not a terrestrial paradise, indeed for the
wealthy and refined there are many pleasanter countries to live in.
But for the man who lives by the sweat of his brow, for him who
has a large family and small means, for him who wishes to work
but cannot find employment, and for him who longs to own the
soil he cultivates, indeed for about nine-tenths of the human race,
America is the best country man has ever yet seen.

Tennessee   Nov. 1866.

CHAPTER VI.

SECOND VISIT TO IRELAND—TRIP TO DEVON AND CORNWALL—ELECTION
AS M.P. FOR SOUTH AYRSHIRE—FIRST SESSION IN PARLIAMENT.

SIR DAVID'S brother William came home from India in
May, 1867, for six months. They were together in Scotland
most of the summer, paying visits, and having three weeks'
grouse shooting with Mr. Sellar, at Rhifail, in Sutherlandshire.

In November he was gazetted as lieutenant in the
Royal South Gloucestershire Militia, and continued to
serve with that regiment to the year of his death. He
proved his desire to thoroughly master any work that he
undertook, by drilling with the recruits before the regular
training; he had a private's uniform served out to him,
joined the ranks, and thereby considerably puzzled the
officer of his company, who at first failed to recognize him.
A brother officer writes of him, " He was a great favourite
with us all, and his genial and cheery prose and song added
much to the sociability of the mess-room—ever giving a
good example to his men, by his willingness to obey his
superiors, and in carrying out the most irksome duties with
alacrity. Although widely differing from many of us in
politics, he never made his views prominent, or antagonis-
tical, but if the subject was touched on, he was remarkable
for placing his views in a sober and pleasant way, while

still holding to them in their entirety. His kindliness of feeling made it impossible for him to give offence."

The lectures on America, which he delivered in Edinburgh in the beginning of 1868, drew public attention to his capacity for political life; and in the summer, when there was a prospect of a general election, he was mentioned as a possible candidate to contest Midlothian in the Liberal interest. His position as an elector and a magistrate for the county, rendered him in many ways a suitable choice, but for that formidable undertaking an older man was selected in Sir Alexander Gibson-Maitland. Although desirous of entering Parliament, Sir David took no steps to bring himself forward for any constituency, but on the contrary, in August, started for a tour in Ireland. At Belfast he met his friend W. E. Price, and after visiting together the Giants' Causeway and Londonderry, they travelled on through the mountains of Donegal.

August 21st, Letterkenny.—The number of " gallant gay policemen " in every little village of this quiet remote district, where a Fenian is known only by report, is a caution, and argues something very rotten in the state of matters, which converts into good-looking loafers the flower of the population. It brings forcibly to our minds the peculiar condition of the country, where no volunteers are permitted, the local militia are not called out for training, the enrolled pensioners are paraded without arms, and every town swarms with soldiers, while crime of every sort, except rioting and its results, is less frequent than in any other community over which the Union Jack flies.

August 25th, Castlebar.—The Irish railways are certainly not up to the mark; slow, unpunctual, dear, scanty as to number of trains and carriages, as well as dividends. The traffic of the country is not developed; the roads are preferred to the rail, cheaper and nearly as expeditious; and the only remedy appears to be the substitution of State management and centralization in place of the fifty-six separate companies which now mismanage Irish railways. To purchase all the railroads, and organize them on a system similar to that of the Post Office, would be a boon for Ireland far greater than the disestablishment of the Church.

In September the Triennial Festival of the three choirs was held at Gloucester, an occasion for social gatherings in the neighbourhood, which he always enjoyed. Soon after, he started with his youngest sister and two friends for a run through Devon and Cornwall.   .

October 5th, Clovelly.—The whole aspect of the place reminds me of Italy, although wanting a little in brilliancy of colouring; the street being a series of steps, the patient ass is the only beast of burden employed. There are lots of pretty children about, indeed the Devonians in general are quite above par in looks.

October 9th, The Lizard.—Nothing can be more beautiful as a marine picture than Kynance Cove. When the tide goes down, a strip of fine smooth sand joins a little cluster of rocky islands with the mainland; huge blocks of serpentine and granitic porphyry are strewed about this isthmus, and fantastic caverns have been hollowed in the cliff by the sea. The rocks are of the richest red and green serpentine, covered in many places with brilliant seaweed, and glittering from the moisture of the spray, while green foam-crested waves come rolling from both sides, and the whole forms a scene worthy of the sea-nymph's haunt.

October 11th, Plymouth.—The key of the grand system of fortification with which the "Three Towns" are surrounded, is a very strong fort constructed on the most approved principles of modern science. No expense has been spared, and the works are Titanic in size, but finished with the care and neatness of jewellers, like the buildings of the Great Moguls. But is the game worth the candle? and is the remote contingency to be guarded against worth the vast outlay on land, labour, and material? Whilst examining the finely fitted brickwork, freestone and granite, and the smooth velvety slopes, I could not help referring to the way in which greatly superior forces had been kept waiting outside the mud breastwork of Lucknow Residency, and the hastily constructed rampart of earth and logs which surrounded the Confederate position before Richmond and Petersburg.

On arriving at Plymouth he found letters, inviting him to stand for the new constituency of South Ayrshire. The circumstances attending the election are given by one of his friends and supporters in that county.

"Prior to the Reform Act of 1868, Ayrshire returned only a single member to Parliament, and for many years the county had been strongly Tory. Up to the passing of the Act which divided the county into North and South, and gave it two members, it had been represented by Sir James Fergusson, a Conservative. The Liberals of South Ayrshire had selected Mr. Oswald of Auchencruive to contest the seat against Colonel Alexander of Ballochmyle, the Conservative candidate. Unfortunately Mr. Oswald was so unwell as to be unable to address the constituency, and he died during the general election. This cast a gloom over the Liberal party, and it was generally felt that his death was likely to be followed by their defeat. The leaders of the party, however, did not lose hope, and various gentlemen were applied to, but all of them wanted courage to fight against what was regarded as a Tory stronghold. Ultimately, at the suggestion of Mr. Russell, of the *Scotsman*, Sir David Wedderburn was approached, and he gallantly intimated that, although it seemed like leading a forlorn hope, he would try to win the seat. His first appearance was at Ayr, and he made a most favourable impression. The election was at hand, and he went rapidly over the division, addressing the electors at every village, and sometimes at three different places in one day. His addresses were tasteful, instructive, and well delivered, and he was everywhere received by his party with the utmost enthusiasm. He objected, however, to personal canvassing, as unfair to the electors, and beneath the dignity of a candidate, and he abstained from it during the election.

"The contest was carried on by Colonel Alexander and Sir David Wedderburn in the most gentlemanly manner. Their allusions to each other were always made in courteous and even complimentary language. In that respect, the election for South Ayrshire in 1868 may be regarded as an example to future candidates. Intelligent and unpretentious, conciliatory and firm in maintaining his opinions, Sir David was the model of a patriotic and upright politician. He was much esteemed throughout South Ayrshire, and many humble Liberal voters speak with pride of their old member. All who remain of those who were engaged with him in the election of 1868, recall his name with feelings of affectionate remembrance."

Another Ayrshire friend writes : " The contest in 1868 was remarkably free from party feeling or bitterness. Sir David was well received everywhere, and earned golden opinions. I believe that his appearance—he was a gentleman in the highest sense of that term—and address created a most favourable impression upon every one. It was reported at the time that one of his most formidable political opponents said, after hearing his address, ' I rather like that chiel's appearance.' "

He was then very young-looking for his age, and he used jokingly to complain that the boys during his canvass whistled after him, " Daintie Davie, wi' the curlie pow." His popularity with the poorer class of the electors was always remarkable, and there was only one point on which he could not meet their wishes—" to take a drap " of whisky. The difficulty of declining their hospitality, when it assumed this form, as it almost always did in Scotland, certainly increased his dislike to personal canvassing, and he invented a compromise by which a scone or a bit of bannock took the place of the obnoxious spirits. His readiness and good humour enabled him to bear cheerfully the ordeal of " heckling," or the Scotch custom of asking the candidate troublesome questions in public. The hustings speech, from which the following extracts are taken, stated in a clear and straightforward manner the principles which he represented :—

I come among you as a stranger, but not uninvited. The time is short and the enemy is very strong. My opponent is an honest

H

and able man, and one who would do honour to the Conservative cause. If it were a mere matter of choosing between individuals, I might as well retire from the field at once; I am quite aware of that. This is no question of men, but of measures; I have nothing to set against the many advantages of my honourable opponent except the Liberal principles, which I trust I share with the majority of the electors of the county. If we turn to the recent Reform Act, to which this constituency owes its existence, we find several amendments necessary to render it a complete and satisfactory measure. Of these the most important are, the assimilation of the franchise in counties to that in boroughs, and redistribution of seats with a full acknowledgment of the claims of Scotland to increased representation. When we consider that in counties rents are lower than in towns ; when we know so well, at least in Scotland, that the intelligence of the population in counties is quite equal to the average intelligence in towns, I think we shall not hesitate in maintaining that those householders in counties are fit and proper persons to have a voice in the administration of the country. The recent extension of the franchise renders more than ever important the subject of popular education ; I would be prepared to vote for any well-considered measure calculated to extend the blessings of education to the people.

One question of the day, perhaps the most important and the most perplexing with which British Statesmen have to grapple, is how to legislate for Ireland so as to efface the traces and memory of centuries of misrepresentation, injustice, and oppression, and so convert the Irishman, from a conquered and struggling subject, into a loyal and contented citizen of the United Kingdom. The policy of England towards Ireland has been hitherto tolerably consistent; it has borne a strong resemblance to that of Russia towards Poland. In every other part of the empire, on which the sun does not set, the complaints of our fellow-subjects have been listened to, and their wrongs have been redressed. In Ireland alone we reply to murmurs of dissatisfaction by increasing our military garrisons and suspending the Habeas Corpus Act. The cry has always been : "The Irish are disaffected; they are of a different race and religion to ourselves ; it is useless to attempt conciliation, nothing will ever content them : " so Ireland is placed in a state of siege. . It is time that this should come to an end ; we must now try the effect of justice and conciliation upon a virtuous, patriotic, and generous-hearted people. The first step in this direction, upon which I think the Liberals throughout Great Britain are thoroughly agreed, is the disestablishment and disendowment of the Irish Church; and though we need not hope at once by such a measure to produce content in Ireland, we may be satisfied that it will be accepted in the spirit in which it is given, as a measure of justice and conciliation.

I consider the true foreign policy of Great Britain to be one of non-intervention in all cases where the honour and interests of this country are not directly involved. I have always felt, and shall continue to feel, the warmest interest in the welfare of our colonies and dependencies, more especially in that of our great Indian Empire. In our Army and Navy various changes are necessary, in order to bring them to that state of efficiency which the vast outlay upon the two services entitle the British nation to expect.

A question in which I know that a great number of the electors in this county are deeply interested, is the Law of Hypothec; it appears to me that it is quite necessary that this law should be totally repealed; the evils it produces were brought out very fully in the report of the commission. Small tenant farmers in particular suffer peculiarly under this law; this hard-working and deserving class is brought into competition with men of no capital; the farms are raised to a rack-rent, and every creditor of the tenants suffers heavily except the landlord.

The effect of the Game Laws is another important question; on behalf of all classes in the community, I am certain a sweeping alteration of the Game Laws is necessary: nothing conduces more to the pleasure of living in the country than friendly feeling and friendly relations between various classes of the community, particularly between landlord and tenant. Now, is it possible that such relations can subsist when an occupier of land sees, throughout the spring and summer, hares and rabbits destroying his young wheat and turnips and then, later in the season, sees the same animals going in cart-loads to the next market town to be sold, after having in effect increased his rent by so much in an unfair and vexatious manner? The most satisfactory remedy seems to me to be that proposed by the Farmers' Club of this county: That the occupiers of land should have a joint and equal right with their landlords, at all times, to destroy hares and rabbits upon arable land.

I come before you as a humble follower of Mr. Gladstone, perhaps the most trusted and popular leader whom the Liberal party in this country has ever possessed. The political programme of this leader and of this party is retrenchment and reform, reform not merely Parliamentary, but social, educational, legal, sanitary, military, and reform of the public services. The constitution of a nation, like that of an individual, must develop with its growth. A truly United Kingdom under leaders alike able and trustworthy, strong in her natural resources and the energy of her people, she need fear the rivalry of none. We have learnt in modern times this political lesson, that the prosperity of our neighbours, instead of being a danger, is the surest source of prosperity to ourselves.

On the 24th of November he was returned at the head of the poll, by the narrow majority of 25, the numbers being 1416 to 1391. The result was all the more gratifying to him from the fact that, when he had originally hesitated to undertake the inevitable cost of a county election, his supporters had most liberally agreed to defray all the expenses beyond a moderate sum which he named as all he would feel justified in spending. One very pleasant effect of the contest was that it led to a lasting friendship between his opponent, Colonel Alexander, and himself.

The pleasure of his own return to Parliament was greatly enhanced by the return at the same time of several of his intimate friends and contemporaries, as well as by the victory of Liberal principles in the country generally. The spirit in which he entered on his new life is shown by a letter to his Cambridge friend, Carmichael, who had just passed high into the Staff College.

Meredith, Gloucester, February 11, 1869.

You certainly have my warmest congratulations on your brilliant success. There is something truly plucky in a fellow, ten years after leaving college, taking up with equal zeal old and new subjects, and working them up, as you have done, in the idle languid atmosphere of Indian military life.

> " Oh, I feel the crescent promise of my spirit hath not set !
> Ancient founts of inspiration well through all my fancy yet."

I believe that you are like myself, and have come slowly to maturity. As for myself, I am now what I ought to have been ten years ago, full of hope and zeal, with a congenial career and eager for work.

I go up to town on Monday, and have taken lodgings at 17, Pall Mall, opposite the Reform Club, along with my friend and neighbour Price, who is now member for Tewkesbury. Henry Campbell is much pleased, as you may suppose, at getting into *the* House, and has been very busy looking out for *a* house. We shall no doubt all meet in London this season. I dined at the Oxford and Cambridge in December with Carter, Crompton, and Campbell, and we were all as jolly and absurd as if we had been so many Freshmen.

I have done a good many Danish translations, but I have taken no steps to have them published. Do you remember Roden Noel in our year? He has come out as a poet lately. In fact it is a very distinguished year altogether !

According to the pledges given at his election, his first utterances in Parliament were on the subjects of the Game Laws and Hypothec. He took greater interest in matters connected with India than in anything else before Parliament. It was a vexation to him that the Indian Budget always came on so late in the session, and was almost invariably brought before a comparatively empty House ; he never failed to be present, and generally took part in the discussion. In his first year the point to which he called attention was the unnecessary retention throughout the year of large bodies of English soldiers at hot and unhealthy stations in the plains, such as Secunderabad, Lucknow, and Peshawur. He said :—

There cannot be a better instance than that of Morar, which has been recently selected as one of our principal military centres, although at that station the 71st Highlanders in a few weeks buried ten per cent. of their strength, 70 out of 700 men. Here large and costly barracks have been built, and here a strong brigade of European' cavalry, artillery, and infantry is to be quartered, besides native troops. But what happened at Kurnaul and elsewhere will doubtless happen here also : deserted barracks and a well-filled graveyard will remain to mark' the site of this great military cantonment. There are throughout India many spots on the mountains or lofty plateaux where, under proper sanitary arrangements, combined with industrial occupation, our troops might be kept in as good health and spirits as they enjoy in this country ; in fact, we are now in a position greatly to diminish the number of our military stations, and to place in healthy localities those which we retain.

In the discussion in Committee on the Scotch Education Bill he proposed to insert a clause authorizing the payment of grants-in-aid to certain classes of evening and adult schools :—

No scheme of education can truly fulfil a claim to be national which does not make some provision for the support of evening schools. The importance of such schools increases as the labour of children becomes more valuable. In America children employed in factories during the day crowd to evening schools. Considerable expense is involved, and there is great risk that voluntary assistance will fail if a national system with compulsory rating is introduced by this bill. The demand for these schools is greatly increasing among the working classes, and the commissioners say "the establishment of night schools is so important that every obstacle in the way of their creation ought to be removed." Sharing fully in this view, I beg to move the insertion of this clause, which is meant to extend to all evening schools under inspection those advantages of State support which a limited class has hitherto enjoyed.

Sir David soon settled down in London to a regular mode of life rather peculiar to himself, and to which he adhered as long as he was in Parliament. He cared little for general society, and seldom attended evening receptions

or balls, but he always liked to eat his dinner in good company ; he objected to solitary meals, and almost invariably
breakfasted with W. E. Price at the Club.   He was very
regular in his attendance at the House, and was glad to
accept an impromptu invitation to go home to dinner with
any Parliamentary friend.   Besides the Reform Club, where
he occupied rooms, he belonged to the New University and
Albemarle Clubs ; the latter he joined principally in order
to be able to give small dinners to his lady friends, generally
combined with taking them to the theatre afterwards.   He
never lost his fondness for a good play, and took every
opportunity of seeing the best of their kind in all countries
that he visited, but nothing pleased him so much as a play
of Shakespeare really well acted.   The occasional dinners
which he gave at the Reform Club were noted for the
pleasant admixture of guests of each political party, as he
never allowed his strong opinions to cause any coolness
between himself and old friends.

There was one point on which he never wavered : he
had an intense dislike to taking advantage of his position
as member of Parliament in any way, and nothing roused
his anger so much as an application for the use of his name
to promote a company or speculation.   It was the only
kind of application to which he would return a refusal more
curt than courteous.

At one time, when in London, finding his friend Maynard Wemyss was taking lessons in painting from David
Cox, junior, he joined him, and derived much pleasure from
the instruction and conversation of so able a master.   He
was in the habit of visiting all the exhibitions of good
pictures in London, and would go to the Academy before
breakfast to avoid the crowd and heat.   Although loyal
in his attachment to the old masters, he had a good knowledge of modern schools of painting, and a wonderful
faculty for recognizing the pictures of the leading artists

by their style, and for identifying the subjects of the pictures, whether taken from nature, history, or fiction.

His love of truth and desire thoroughly to investigate everything induced him at different times, and more particularly whilst living in London, to turn his attention to the phenomena of spiritualism. A friend who joined with him in these inquiries gives Sir David's impressions on the subject.

" Though the bias of his mind was strongly against acceptation of the supernatural, he was too keen an inquirer for physical truth to reject even the improbable stories of the spirit-rappers without a fair investigation. His mind was too open to new facts and too untrammelled by preconceived notions to allow of his being deterred from the inquiry by fear of ridicule. Chance gave him unusually favourable opportunities, and he pushed his way further than most men in this hazardous investigation. There were one or two families among his acquaintance where table-turning and the more occult branches of the mystery were seriously and sedulously pursued, and he thought the pursuit not unworthy of study. In some of these circles there was no room for the imputation of fraud ; the spirit in which the phenomena, whatever be their real nature, were approached, was far removed from the vulgar and idle curiosity which not uncommonly pervades these séances. The search after truth was genuine and unprejudiced, and gradually well-tested facts aroused in his mind a half-formed conviction, long resisted but inevitable, that there was in it more than science can at present explain. There were many stages in the inquiry, and through these, with the aid of one or two intimate friends who viewed the matter in a like spirit, he cautiously and scientifically endeavoured to find his way. He had nothing in common with the silly quidnuncs, who run after the professional mediums ; the charlatans and tricksters of spirit-rapping who abounded at that time found him an impossible

dupe. No man could be less easily befooled, but no man
was less frightened of facing a new truth, even though
it should upset the theories of a lifetime. The belief in
spiritualism, however, never gained great hold of him.
Such truths as could be ascertained he regarded as too
vague and inconclusive for practical use ; the manifesta-
tions, unaided by trickery, could apparently never advance
beyond a certain point, and the road seemed to lead
nowhere. The conviction which he had arrived at was not
deepened, and he found, like many others, that the phenomena were apt to become meaningless. The interest of
the investigation after it reached a certain point diminished,
though it was not lost, and in the later years of his life the
subject was little more to him than an interesting topic
of conversation."

Every year, as the season advanced, he began to tire of
London, and to find the heat and late hours of the House
irksome to him. At first he tried keeping a horse for the
sake of a morning ride ; but the monotonous round of the
Park wearied him, and the horse became an annoyance
rather than a recreation. The only amusement, of which he
himself said that he never had too much, was a good game
at golf ; he belonged to the Golf Club at Wimbledon, and
was always glad of an afternoon on the common with a
Scotch friend. But what he looked forward to most in the
week was a Saturday to Monday outing, to the house of
one or other of his many kind friends within easy reach of
London, such as Mr. Pennington, M.P., or Mr. Bidder, Q.C.,
or Mr. Campbell-Bannerman. His love of natural history
made a day with Mr. Alfred Wallace at Godalming, or Sir
J. Lubbock at High Elms, particularly attractive to him.
He generally contrived to run down to Meredith about once
a month, but although such an inveterate traveller, it is
curious that he always complained of railway journeys,
however short.

At the close of the session he again went to Mr. Sellar at Rhifail, and after shooting there made a run in the following month to the Orkney Islands. He returned to Gloucestershire in time to see his youngest sister and her husband, E. H. Percival, before they started for Bombay, at the end of September.

Constantinople   19ᵗʰ Octʳ 1869

CHAPTER VII.

1869.

TOUR IN HUNGARY—TURKEY—SYRIA AND EGYPT—LECTURES IN AYRSHIRE
ON "THE TURKISH EMPIRE AND THE SUEZ CANAL."

SIR DAVID at one time proposed to accompany the Per-
civals as far as Egypt, to be present at the opening of the
Suez Canal, and to return by Turkey, but owing to the
season of the year he decided to reverse his plan, and take
Egypt last. Accordingly he started for Turkey through
Germany, accompanied by Maynard Wemyss.

October 9th, Ratisbon.—We drove out to see the Valhalla, which
is an imitation of the Parthenon. Vast flights of steps lead up to it,
and somewhat tend to dwarf the main building, which is entirely
of Bavarian marbles. Inside everything is of beautifully coloured
marbles, red, yellow, black, and white ; but the Grecian character
of the building is modified by Scandinavian symbols and Teutonic
names. Busts of great Germans and quasi-Germans, and tablets
inscribed with the names of the more ancient worthies whose

features are not known, are placed around the walls. One or two women only have been admitted, and many great German names are missing, while many whom other countries would justly claim are here as being of Teutonic descent. On the whole, the Valhalla gives a fair idea of what the Parthenon may have been, and only cost a trifle of 14,000,000 gulden. The cathedral at Ratisbon is a most perfect specimen of Gothic architecture, both inside and outside. The stained-glass windows are most beautiful : beside them the best efforts of Munich modern art appear tawdry. The west front, very richly sculptured, is even now being crowned with beautiful twin spires of open-work, like Burgos.

October 14th, Pesth.—We made an excursion to Gödölö, about fifteen miles from Pesth, where the Emperor has a palace and estate. The village is of a thoroughly Oriental type, as unlike as possible to a German Dorf. We delighted one good lady by asking leave to view the interior of her house ; it was a model of cleanliness and comfort, the walls were adorned with bright coloured plates and crockery, and vast heaps of feathered beds proved that there was no risk of our friends suffering from cold ; moreover, the chimney was big enough for a baronial hall, and covered in with a little roof. Fat woolly pigs, fed on maize, abounded on the premises of this well-to-do yeoman farmer. It was vintage day on the Emperor's estate, and we hurried off to the vineyard, about a mile distant. A gipsy band and a lot of "happy peasants," male and female, got up for the occasion to dance, and a lot more engaged in the operations of the vintage, composed the assembly. The young Crown Prince and his sister, two nice-looking children, were already there, and the dancing soon began. All had high boots, including the young women, and very absurd they looked with the short but multitudinous petticoats. The dance was a little in the Shaker style, but with a greater determination to waltzing, and in the intervals the royal children did the civil with grace and affability. The vintage went on merrily, the grapes were very fine, and the must delicious. The whole scene was something quite unique, and was rendered complete when the "Queen" herself rode up on a beautiful horse, looking the very picture of graciousness as well as grace ; the sternest republican might have joined in the "Elje" which greeted her. No wonder she is popular.

October 17th.—At Orsova we quitted the Austrian territory,

now one of the pleasantest in the world for a stranger to visit ;
every one, even officials, polite and agreeable : passports and police-
spies things of the past, it is now a land of liberty. Verily it is a
good thing for a nation to undergo tribulation !

October 19th, Constantinople.—The sail down the Bosphorus is
wonderfully beautiful, and indeed unrivalled. Both shores, Asiatic
as well as European, are thickly studded with palaces, minarets,
kiosks, and elegant houses of every form and colour; dark
cypresses tower above the lighter foliage, sheltered bays succeed
to jutting promontories. A fit close to the glorious panorama
is furnished by the view of Stamboul itself, surpassing in beauty of
situation, as well as apparent size and grandeur, every other city
which I have ever seen.

A remarkable performance, which we saw to-day, was that of
the dancing dervishes. The spectators, faithful and infidel, are
in the galleries round an octagonal mosque ; the dervishes, twenty
in number, occupy the smooth bare floor in the centre. After
many genuflexions and pious exclamations, they all pass round,
bowing twice to each other before the Mihrab, where the chief
Imam, a very old gentleman with a green turban, takes up his
position. Presently the others discard their upper robes of various
colours, and appear in white jackets and skirts, retaining of course
their high felt hats. Some very feeble and discordant music
strikes up, and one by one, after saluting the Imam, they go
twirling off with their arms stretched out and their eyes closed.
Their action is very smooth, and they never jostle one another,
or seem to get giddy, although they always turn the "reverse"
way, and keep it up for a long time. During the pauses an old
boy, whose dancing days were over, carefully cloaked them.
Instead of objecting to spectators they rather encourage their
presence.

October 20th.—The interior of the great mosque of St. Sophia is
magnificent, the great central dome apparently defying the law, of
gravitation, so vast is the open space unbroken by columns or
supports. Splendid marble and porphyry pillars, rich mosaics
bearing evident traces of their Christian origin, and the almost
total absence of tawdry and incongruous objects, combine in producing the highest sense of grandeur. The pulpits and the Sultan's
" Box " inside, and the four minarets outside are the only architectural contributions of the Moslems to this great temple, a model

which they have strictly followed in all the grand mosques of Constantinople.

October 21st.—We crossed over to Scutari in time for the howling dervishes, one of the most extraordinary spectacles which I have ever witnessed. In a small building were seated on the ground a number of old men of reverend but fanatical appearance, singing out at the top of their voices; in front of them was drawn up a line of a dozen individuals swaying from side to side and uttering unearthly howls, "Allah hu !" in unison. The spectators consisted of some merry little girls, and a lot of unbelievers. The howlers wore no uniforms, as the dancers did, and only a few of them were dervishes, the others being apparently casual laymen, from respectable old gentlemen in European trousers to a little boy of six or eight years old ; a couple of niggers took an active part in the proceedings, and if any one tailed off, some one else took his place. They warmed to their work as they went on, and presently a sick man was carried in and laid before the chief Imam, a handsome benevolent looking young man, who proceeded to bless him, and stand upon him, after which he was helped out, evidently thinking himself better. Then came children, old men, all and sundry, to undergo the same ceremony, and all seemed to like it, although some of the little girls must have been almost squashed. He did the whole thing very gently and tenderly, as if he quite believed in its efficacy, and afterwards blessed various articles of dress. Meanwhile the howling and stamping went on, but the numbers diminished gradually, until a faithful and vigorous few only remained to receive the final salutation and blessing. In this as in other similar cases, *e.g.* Shakers, the earnestness of the performers quite eliminates the ridiculous element, the feeling excited being rather one of melancholy; part of the ceremony had certainly a very scriptural appearance.

October 23rd, S.S. " Taurus."—Gradually the many domes and minarets of the glorious city " faded o'er the waters blue." Small blame to the " Dogs of Moscow " for being covetous !

October 29th, Mercina in Cilicia.—About 11 a.m. our whole party, ten in number, guided by the Agent des Postes, started for the ruins of Pompeiopolis, scarcely realizing the work we had before us. We pursued our way gaily, amused with everything we came across, flowers, insects, and human beings. A great and fertile plain extends between the mountains and the sea, partially cultivated, but overgrown with beautiful myrtles, ten or twelve feet high, and covered with blossom. After a long tramp under a blazing sun we reached Pompeiopolis about 2 p.m.; we were repaid for our march : the ruins of a great city, with acropolis and theatre, lie scattered about among the wild myrtles, some built of Roman bricks and cement, but chiefly blocks of limestone or marble. But the columns are the great wonder of the place ; forty stand erect and perfect with Corinthian capitals of "many a woven acanthus wreath divine," others stand mutilated, while numbers are strewn in wreck upon the ground. There must have been a colonnade of a hundred or so in double row, terminating in the portico of a temple ; they are about twenty-seven feet high, ten feet apart, formed of four blocks altogether, chiefly smooth, but a few at the end are fluted. One row is almost perfect, the other nearly all prostrate ; they seemed to have had statues on pedestals at about two-thirds of their height. These beautiful pillars, standing in desolate grandeur by the sea-shore, with a background of wooded mountains, and picturesque brigand-looking goat-herds tending their flocks in the foreground, could hardly be surpassed as a subject for a painter, and we were the more delighted with the place, as we had never heard of it, and felt as if we were its first discoverers.

November 2nd, Beyrout.—We closed with Joseph Mousali for an inland tour of thirty days. He was at work in an instant, and in a few hours reported all ready for a start to-morrow : our souls are now eager for the fray, and we start full of hope.

November 3rd.—Our course lay right through Beyrout, passing the scene of St. George's combat with the Dragon (?), and on through mulberry orchards. Sugar-cane and bananas are among the products of this district. The first point of special interest is the sculptured rock above Nahr el Kelb, or Dog river. Here you come successively on the records of four great nations, who have passed as conquerors by this spot : Egyptians, Assyrians, Romans, and French. The Assyrian tablets are the most striking, both figures and arrow-head inscriptions being quite distinct; they are rounded. at the top, while the other cartouches are square. Oddly enough the inscription of M. Aurelius, B. G. P., is more legible even now than that of Napoleon III. dated 1861, and commemorating the French occupation.

November 4th.—We suddenly found ourselves in front of a great amphitheatre of lofty cliffs, resembling the cirques of the Pyrenees ; descending we seemed to have reached the end of the world, the cliffs rising almost perpendicular on every side, while from a cave on their face rushes a beautiful clear stream, and leaps over the rocks in a series of cascades ; above these lie the massive ruins of a temple. This spot is Afka, the river Adonis and the temple of Venus,—a truly romantic and wonderful scene.

November 5th.—Our march to-day was a very stiff one, constantly up and down, crossing high passes, one about 5600 feet. Everywhere an energetic race wring a well-earned subsistence from the barren rock. There is at present a scarcity of fodder for their cattle, fat-tailed sheep, and diabolical looking black goats. We saw one of these last deliberately climb a mulberry-tree and devour the leaves, standing on the outmost branches. After seeing them one can appreciate their left-hand position in the parable. Nothing can be more friendly than the greetings of these free mountaineers, touching the forehead and breast successively, and looking you full in the face. I believe that for once the intervention of the Western Powers has been a real benefit to the subjects of the Porte.

November 7th, Baalbec.—The mighty pillars of Baalbec are visible a long way, and are dwarfed by the vast landscape much as are the cedars on Mount Lebanon ; very different is the effect when you actually stand in the acropolis, surrounded on all sides by the ruins of its vast and beautiful temples, amidst which our tents are now pitched. Such a sight has something melancholy and humiliating in it : we cannot now raise such buildings with all our modern science and power ; the Frank tent and the Arab hovel represent the existing generation in this half-desert country, among the wrecks of a past splendour and greatness of which no records, except such as these monuments furnish, could induce us to credit the reality. We wandered about, literally lost in amazement at the vast size of the scattered fragments, which lie in chaotic heaps everywhere around, as well as at the exquisite designs and execution of the ornamental work, which far surpasses in richness all ordinary specimens of Grecian art. There are three distinct periods and styles of architecture : first Cyclopean, or Phœnician, the foundation of all, composed of the largest blocks of stone ever moved by the hand of man, the three largest are each sixty-three to sixty-four feet long by thirteen high, and are raised twenty feet above the ground—how no one can even conjecture. Then comes the Roman, or Grecian period, to which belong the regular solid walls of lesser, but still very large blocks of stone, and the magnificent temples and courts, in fact all that is beautiful in Baalbec. Above these are the Saracenic fortifications, composed almost entirely of materials taken from Roman buildings, which have thus been mutilated and defaced in a twofold manner, as much almost by what has been added as by what has been subtracted. All the principal ruins are contained within the Acropolis, or Fort; it is no use attempting to describe them, but they make the Forum at Rome look very small; they are all of Corinthian order, colossal in size and exquisite in finish.

November 10th, Damascus.—On the crest of the hill Mahomet's view burst upon us, which the whole world cannot surpass. The sun was just sinking behind Mount Hermon, and lighted up the domes and minarets of Damascus, which shone like ivory against the dark green forest of orchards and gardens. Beyond them, again, on every side spreads the orange-tawny desert, like a golden frame, the hills of the Lejah and Hauran rising blue in the distance. This view of Damascus can only be compared with that of Constantinople; it is hard to say which city has it. In one case the sea, in the other the desert; one has nobler buildings, the other richer foliage and loftier mountains.

Two days sufficed them for the sights of Damascus, which they visited in company with Mr. T. Brassey, M.P., and his party, whom they had previously met at Baalbec. They made the acquaintance of Consul Burton, and learnt much about Syrian affairs from him, and made a pilgrimage to the grave of H. T. Buckle, in the Protestant cemetery. Their route now lay by the sources of the Jordan, near Banias, to the Sea of Tiberias.

November 19th.—Not far from Akka (Acre), we came to an open glade, and met a lot of regular negroes, somewhat to our astonishment. These coloured persons informed us that some large black tents in the forest to our right were tenanted by Sheikh Agheel, one of the greatest chiefs of the Bedawin, who can call several thousand men to his standard. We at once proceeded to pay our respects, and were received with much dignity

I

by the sheikh, who might have sat for a portrait of Abraham, and had at his right hand a young Ishmael of six years old. Carpets and silk cushions were spread for us, and we sat for about half an hour, Joseph being the chief spokesman, while the sheikh replied with a languid politeness, "which stamps the caste of Vere de Vere." He and his friends smoked their chibouks, but we were not offered pipes; swarthy attendants, however, pounded and prepared coffee for us, without sugar or milk, and the sheikh invited us to stay all night. The tent is very long and low, made of camel's-hair, and open at one side; in bad weather it affords shelter to his priceless Arab mares, a lot of whose foals were grazing close by; at one end of the tent were some very handsome Arab weapons, inlaid with silver. At parting we shook hands cordially, young Ishmael's hearty grasp much amusing his solemn parent.

November 21st, Khaifa, Mount Carmel. — Time, place, and weather were all suitable for a Sunday's rest, so we took matters very easy. Having made some inquiries as to chapels, a groom with two horses rode up to our tent with a couple of tracts from Rev. D. Hardegg, and the information that there was a German Protestant service at one o'clock. We made our way through the mud to his house, and were very kindly received; quite a number of excellent Germans, more than twenty, appeared, men, women, and children, and we had a primitive service : singing (two lines at a time), silent prayer, a chapter of the Bible, and any remarks which occurred to any " brother " present upon the chapter. Mr. Hardegg was the principal speaker, but one brother spoke, and of course all sang. They gave us coffee, bread and jam afterwards, and we had a very pleasant talk. They have come to Khaifa recently, and are apparently colonist missionaries. The Carmelite friars are said to class them along with locusts and cholera as judgments sent upon the land, but they seem to be very good fellows, as indeed are the holy fathers themselves.

November 22nd.—From El Muhrakah, the place of Elijah's sacrifice, we had a magnificent view, surpassing any we have seen in Palestine for extent, variety, and historical interest. It is truly vexatious to see how misgovernment and insecurity repress the energies of a frugal and industrious people. The Ottoman Government means simply taxation and conscription, it is otherwise a nonentity—no protection, no education, no public buildings except barracks, no irrigation; above all, no bridges nor roads. This is the system which we bolster up selfishly and ignorantly, but which has no strength to stand alone, and can be of no benefit in any way to England; fall it must ere long, and it will go hard, but something better will arise from its ruins.

November 26th, Jerusalem.—With the Church of the Holy Sepulchre we were much pleased; and whether any of the localities are genuine or not (they cannot all be), here, in any case, is the spot which Christendom for ages has held the most sacred on earth, and for which her blood has been poured out like water. Outwardly, at least, every Christian sect from Finland to Abyssinia meets on friendly ground common to all, and does reverence to the grave and memory of the great Founder, whom all profess equally to worship. The church is a vast building, and contains many chapels belonging to the various sects; of these the Greek is by far the largest and most splendid, a perfect mass of pictures and rich gilding. The sepulchre itself is in a sort of miniature church under a great new dome just completed by the Christian powers : you must stoop low to enter through two marble doors; in the inmost recess on the right are the marble slabs which are believed to cover the very spot where Christ's body lay. This little cell is scrupulously partitioned among the three principal sects, Latin, Greek, and Armenian, who seem at present here to dwell together in amity. Silence prevails, and the behaviour of all is reverential, altogether there is the stamp of genuine faith about the place.

November 29th.—Not long after leaving Bethlehem, olive groves and cultivation disappear, and you enter a desolate hilly wilderness. At last the lonely towers of Mar Saba convent appeared, a letter from the Greek Bishop gave us admission; and a queer place it certainly is, a perfect labyrinth of terraces, cells, chapels, and caves stuck anyhow about the face of the precipitous rocks, which overhang the glen of Kedron, as wild and desolate a ravine as can anywhere be found. A solitary date palm, a vine and a few pot herbs are the only signs of vegetable life; some ravens and seedy-looking garlicky monks represent the animal kingdom. The church of St. Saba is handsomely decorated in the Greek style, with gilding, painting, and a beautiful pavement of coloured marbles, but the cupola, as usual, is bare and shabby; there are some fine-toned bells also, from Russia. The excellent

fathers have an eye to the main chance, and even do a little trade
in walking-sticks on their own account; we partook of coffee, and
were not sorry to escape from the odour (of sanctity?) which
pervaded the place.

They returned to Jerusalem from the Dead Sea by
Jericho, and making their way to Jaffa, sailed from there
to Port Said. Passing down the recently opened Suez
canal as far as Ismailia, they went by rail to Cairo, where
the festivities after the opening of the Canal were still
going on. They attended a ball given by the Khedive in
honour of the Prince of Prussia.

December 7th, Cairo.—The Prince looked jolly and handsome,
the Khedive somewhat the reverse, but Monsieur and Madame
de Lesseps were after all the chief attraction, she very young, he a
handsome old man, dancing like a good one. A gorgeous supper
was spread, but we went home early, moralizing on the absurdity
and extravagance of all these entertainments of fizz and fireworks, in which the resources of Egypt are now being wasted.

December 8th.—We trotted gaily off to old Cairo, where we
crossed the mighty Nile to Ghizeh. A fine straight new road has
been made to the Pyramids, but it has not bridges enough, and
the Nile is apt to break holes in the dyke, which dams up the
river, thus causing much damage, that kings and kaisers may
have a carriage drive to the palace, which has been erected for
their convenience under the Pyramids. Wonderful to relate, the
Arabs actually allowed me to wander about in peace, and see the
Pyramids and Sphinx alone at sunset; this was an agreeable
change from the row and hurry of a former visit, and I wandered
all round them. I found Joseph installed in an airy cave, with
plenty of windows, through which the north wind blew freely. Our
couches were spread on the sand, and we consumed our frugal
meal by the light of a flickering candle. Just as we had finished,
a youth in knickerbockers with a gun appeared suddenly, and
offered us the shelter of his tent, speaking very disparagingly of
our cave. We declined his hospitable offer, and he partook of
the coffee, prepared with no little skill by the Bedouin at our
watch-fire. He has been encamped here for several weeks, is an
English lord, and his servant's name is Thomson. Before turning

in we sallied out with three Arabs to explore the tombs. In some of these are very fine paintings, the figures in relief on plaster, and the colouring quite bright. Men and animals in great variety are represented, but they sadly need protection from barbarians of all nations, who scribble on, and are rapidly destroying them. The effect of the moonlight was wonderful, the second Pyramid black and clear against the starlit sky, the Great Pyramid rising dim and huge like the grey spectre of a mountain.

December 9th.—Near the Pyramid of Sakkara, riding over the sand, you are suddenly aware of a door, a native opens it, and you enter what may truly be called the Mammoth Caves of Egypt—the Serapeum, or Catacombs of the sacred bulls. Vast galleries are cut in the rock ; and at regular intervals, on either side alternately, is a chamber containing a colossal sarcophagus of dark syenite, perfectly smooth and polished, large enough to hold the mummy of an elephant, let alone a bull. These sarcophagi are cut out of a solid block, and are covered with an immensely massive lid ; they are here by the dozen, each in its rock-cut niche, which in some cases it nearly fills up, but how they were ever brought here is indeed a mystery, probably the greatest in the way of engineering which we have yet encountered. A few are covered with hieroglyphics, but most are plain ; the syenite is exceedingly hard, and takes a beautiful polish, slippery as ice, we found on climbing inside, where we could not stand upright under the lid, although outside we could only just reach the lid with our hands. Altogether the Serapeum is in some respects a more wonderful work than the Pyramids, which are mere efforts of brute force and accumulated labour.

A lot of queer animals, lions, sphinxes, etc., have been found here, but they have a quasi-Grecian appearance, and far more interesting is a recently opened temple, the walls and pillars of which are covered with admirable paintings, as yet undamaged by the brutal tourist, and representing in most spirited style a great variety of scenes in agriculture, hunting, and domestic life ; the animals in particular being admirably drawn, perspective only defective. Artificial fattening of geese and cranes, in Strasbourg fashion, seems to have been a common practice ; monkeys and antelopes to have been extensively domesticated. In one scene a hippopotamus is being done to death with hooks and spears, while another calmly swallows a crocodile. In all pictures men are painted red and women yellow, and the figures are in slight relief; chopping up and slaughtering oxen is a favourite subject. Here we have the life of ancient Egypt depicted, uninjured by time or climate, but a few years exposure to the intelligent public will ruin all, if left unprotected.

December 17th, Bologna.—It is really delightful to experience the change from Egypt to Italy: here every one is civil and obliging, asking for nothing, and invariably thanking you for what you give; the accommodation is good, and the bills are moderate; you can get newspapers wherever you go, and no one bothers you when prowling about by yourself. The contrast is very marked, and not favourable to the shining Orient. I always liked the Italians, and their country, and the old love has revived as strong as ever.

December 18th, Chambéry.—At Susa the train starts upon the Fell railway to ascend Mont Cenis. On approaching the summit level, we had to turn out of the train, and betake ourselves to sledges, which were to convey us over the snow blocking up a portion of the line. These sledges are simply big boxes on runners, and are made to hold six—a very tight fit indeed, I found it, with three priests of various nationalities, an English colonel, and a young Frenchman; the windows are so small that you can with difficulty see out, and thus hardly realize the perils of the passage. For an hour and a half the mules were urged on, occasionally requiring human aid at bad places. We passed one or two inns along the shore of a mountain lake, and came upon our train in a long gallery with wooden sides and iron roof. We rattled down at a great pace to Modane, where are great works in connection with the tunnel being bored through the mountain. After that, however, matters were taken so easily, that we reached St. Michel two hours behind time, and our train was gone.

How much the charm of Sir David's company added to the pleasure of any tour, is shown by the expressions used by his fellow-traveller on this occasion.

"No man could possibly have had a pleasanter, more genial, more instructive travelling companion than I had. Possessed of a most wonderful memory, and of remarkable powers of observation, nothing, however trivial, escaped his notice ; and I have often known some slight occurrence awake in him a flood of memories, drawn both from former personal experiences, and from the vast fund of know-ledge he had in other ways acquired. This was, perhaps, especially noticeable in a tour such as ours was, through countries new to both of us, but full of glowing interests to a mind prepared, like his, to trace in almost everything the fading memorials of the past. He seemed incapable of fatigue, was thoroughly ready to enjoy everything as it came ; to find a bright side to any little accident, and to extract amusement or instruction from the most un-promising materials. But, perhaps, the most beautiful features in his character were his extreme tenderness with children, and his keen sympathy with all that was weak, helpless, or oppressed, and in lands ruled by the Turks such claims upon his sympathy were of frequent occurrence. The weeks spent at that time with him must ever remain among the very happiest memories of my life."

Shortly after his return, he delivered three popular lectures among his constituents in Ayrshire, on "The Turkish Empire and the Suez Canal ; " and from these the following is taken :—

Ever since the Crimean War the Turks have formed a very different idea of the treatment due to Franks—the name by which they designate Western Europeans generally. A short time ago it was not safe for a man in European dress to show himself in any Eastern city. But now a European in Constantinople is a sort of grandee, and, instead of being greeted with scowls, is treated by everybody with respect, so that one disagreeable feature that used to attend travelling in Turkey has now dis-appeared. The city is surrounded by an old wall, which dates back from the time of the Crusades, and I had pointed out to me the Golden Gate, by which the Turks believe that some day the infidel will once more enter the holy city of Stamboul. This shows that the Turks do not regard as permanent the hold they have upon Europe. They are prepared to be driven across the

Bosphorus, and it is a fact that all Turks who can afford it are buried at Scutari, on the Asiatic side of the water.

Coming down the Dardanelles, we passed close to the site of the ancient city of Troy. As we sailed along there was hardly a promontory, rock, or conspicuous object that did not remind one of some great classical author, or that was not associated with some tale of Grecian romance. Passing Troy, Mount Ida, and Lesbos, we entered the bay of Smyrna. This is the only one of the ancient cities that maintains its position—the only one of the seats of the seven Churches of Asia, and the only one of the twelve Ionian cities that now remains. From Smyrna we sailed amongst the numerous islands in the Ægean, every one of them famous in history, down as far as Rhodes. There is no point of the classical world that has more associations connected with it than this, and none which in modern times has more lost its ancient character. There is nothing now but the sun and the blue sea to remind you of the days of Homer, Æschylus, and Thucydides. It is impossible to describe the feelings which fill the breast in looking on a column, or a heap of stones that alone remains to tell of cities which were once as important as the leading cities of Europe now are.

These islands are inhabited by men of Greek descent, who retain somewhat of the character of their ancestors. They are Christian in religion, and several of them enjoy immunities from the Turkish government by treaty. I am afraid, however, that the absence of European Consuls causes frequent breaches of these treaties, and that the rights of the Christian inhabitants are very poorly respected. I am myself opposed to a policy of intervention in foreign affairs ; but I must say, that considering the amount of responsibility that rests on our shoulders for the presence of the Turks in Europe at all, I think it is our duty to see that the Christian populations ruled by the Turks have justice done to them, and that the treaties made with them are fulfilled. There can be no doubt that it is mainly the upholding hand of this country that maintains the Turks in Constantinople, and that but for the support of the Western Powers, they would have been driven across the Bosphorus ere this time ; and I for one do not think that any disaster would befall the human race were such a contingency to occur.

I have no hesitation in saying that along the southern shores of Asia Minor there is an inexhaustible field for the growth of cotton ; but at present that district has no inhabitants but a few wandering shepherds.   It has not always been so.   It is evident that in the days of the Romans this must have been a cultivated and populous province, and I have little doubt that, under a Government which would afford security for the fruits of their labours, the same state of matters might be again restored.   We hear a great deal about the capabilities of the Turkish Empire, and I am convinced that there are many districts under the sway of the Sultan, of which it would be difficult to exaggerate the capabilities of development.

Lebanon is a place of great interest, whether we regard it merely as a mountainous country peopled by an independent, freedom-loving race, or look upon its history in ancient times, or the events of which it has recently been the scene.   Lebanon is chiefly inhabited by Christians, and is, in fact, a sort of island in Syria, the inhabitants of which profess a different religion, and are derived from a different origin from the other inhabitants of the country.   They are divided into two great sects—the Maronites, who are Roman Catholics, and the Druses, who are neither Christians nor Mussulmans.   Some people believe them to be the descendants of the ancient Greek Pagans ; at all events, their religious rites are kept secret.   The probable explanation why there is not much known of them is, that there is not much to know, and that they have not much religion at all.   They are, however, more allied to the Mussulmans than to the Christians, and took an active part in the massacre of the Christians in 1860. Lebanon was covered at one time with magnificent forests, but now only one grove of the celebrated cedars remains.   There can be no reason, however, except want of protection for the young plants, why the whole mountain should not be covered with these trees, which for picturesqueness and value of timber can hardly be surpassed.   Certainly one of the objects which a wise paternal Government would aim at would be once more to cover Lebanon with those noble forests of which we read in the Old Testament, and of which the one remaining grove gives such a good idea.

The Romans are the only ancient people who have tried to make roads and bridges in Syria.   Even to the present day, if you find a piece of good road or a bridge in that country it is almost sure to be of Roman construction. If I have brought one idea more than another from my tour, it is that of the greatness and power of the Romans.

The first view of Jerusalem is of course striking, and on beholding it for the first time one shares, to a certain extent, the feelings of the Crusaders in days of old, or the pilgrims of the Middle Ages, when they looked upon it for the first time. The city still retains a great deal of its original splendour, and though a small place, containing only about ten thousand inhabitants, it has a magnificent appearance. Her walls are very complete, and the valleys which surround her are deep, and these circumstances give her a very animated aspect. The sites around are distinct, and are clearly and easily identified. The Valley of Jehoshaphat in particular, is a striking feature of the neighbourhood of the city, being filled entirely with stones, placed close together like mosaics : these are the memorial stones over the graves of innumerable Jews, who have come from all parts of the world to lay their bones beside those of their fathers. From the Mount of Olives the view of the city is very fine, the gilded dome and cupola of the Mosque of Omar from that point showing to great advantage. One cannot help feeling as he looks upon the city, that it is really to a great extent, in its external aspect, worthy to be the first holy city of the Christian and of the Jew, and the second holy city of the Mussulman, for it yields in sanctity only to Mecca, not even Damascus surpassing it.

The British Isles will not derive so marked an advantage from the Suez Canal as some other parts of the world. Vessels from Britain have to work their way through the Bay of Biscay, round by the Straits of Gibraltar, and up the Mediterranean. To the Italian and French Mediterranean ports, on the other hand, the advantage of the canal cannot possibly be over-estimated, and it will doubtless develop a traffic which does not now exist. I may say of this triumph of human energy and skill, that if it has in one sense separated the two continents, it has in a far wider sense united all the quarters of the globe, and those of the Old World in particular. The chief commerce of Europe and even North America, with India, China, Japan, Australia, New Zealand, and East Africa is destined to pass along this central throughfare of nations. It can hardly be doubted that the example set at Suez will be followed ere long at the Isthmus of Darien, which may present greater difficulties but where equal advantages will attend success.   Lesseps has been compared to Christopher Columbus, who discovered a new world.   He may be more aptly compared to Vasco de Gama, who first opened up a highway by water from Europe to the East.   Mainly by the indomitable perseverance and energy of one man, neither wealthy nor powerful, a geographical revolution was last year effected, and to commerce and industry a new doorway opened, which the civilized world will never suffer to be closed.

CHAPTER VIII.

1870.

VISITS HIS CONSTITUENTS IN AYRSHIRE—SECOND SESSION OF PARLIAMENT
—TOUR IN SPAIN—LECTURE ON " THE SOLAR ECLIPSE OF 1870."

EARLY in 1870 Sir David went down to Ayrshire, to visit his friends there, and at that time addressed a large meeting of the electors, held in the Corn Exchange at Ayr. In reviewing the events of the past session, the following were the points he chiefly touched upon :—

No doubt it has been a triumphant session for the Government and the Liberal party throughout the country; but as Scotchmen I must own that we are entitled to feel some disappointment, and in saying this I think it well to advert to a topic which I believe is intimately connected with the success or non-success of Scotch reforms—I mean as to the general administration of Scotch affairs in Parliament, and the appointment of a Secretary of State for Scotland. As long as Scotland is a country possessing distinct laws and institutions, and requiring distinct Acts of Parliament to affect these laws and institutions, she must not allow herself to be ignored by the Government and leave to free lances the redress of her grievances. I do not believe that there is the slightest necessity for creating a new office with a new salary. I merely consider, and would inculcate, if possible, the belief that the official who is ultimately responsible for the conduct of Scotch affairs must be a responsible member of the Cabinet.

With reference to the Irish Church Bill, I will only say that I have always considered that question to have been decided, not in the House of Commons, but on the hustings and at the polling booths in 1868. The bill which was placed before us was one that was admirably drawn, and I do not claim more for us as members of Parliament, than that we have gone pretty steadily through the drudgery which attended the passing of that bill.

I must allude to my having voted for the second reading of Sir Wilfrid Lawson's bill, commonly called the Permissive Liquor Bill. I was sensible of the gigantic nature of the evil at which it struck, and I could not shut my eyes to the fact that, while all admitted the evil more or less, none were prepared to bring forward a practical remedy except the advocates of the Permissive Liquor Bill. Believing the licensing laws required revision and amendment, believing that the management of the licensing system would be safer in the hands of the ratepayers than it is at present, believing also that the interests of the better class of those directly affected by the licensing system would be safer than they are now, and believing above all things that it was necessary to show our earnestness in desiring a reformation of those laws, I gave my vote very heartily for that bill.

The Scotch Education Bill was to me very unsatisfactory in its whole history, and in the shape in which it finally left the House of Commons; still I was very anxious that even in its mangled condition it should become law. I believe that, even as it stood when it went to the House of Lords, it would have secured a good education for a number of children, who have now at all events lost one more year; and I believe it introduced one very important principle—that of compulsory local rating for the purposes of education.

I must advert to the questions of Game Laws and Hypothec. Of course you know how they have fared. There were three Game Bills before us, and even those Scotch representatives who were most hearty in their wish to effect Game Law reform were not entirely decided as to which of these bills it was their duty to support. The discussions which took place on these bills were not altogether satisfactory, but I think a certain amount of advantage was derived from them, as having made the subject public and called the attention of many out of the House to it; I believe now that the great majority of the agriculturists of Scotland have definitely given in their adherence to the principle of Mr. Loch's bill.

Mr. Carnegie's bill abolishes hypothec altogether, both as to agricultural and urban subjects, and in consequence of its tenor it was opposed by a considerable number of the borough members. As far as principle goes, I am of opinion that there is no essential distinction, but believing that there has been no great cry for the abolition of the law as it affects urban subjects, I should have been prepared to separate the two, in order the more certainly to carry the bill affecting agricultural subjects.

With regard to the question of taxation, I think we have reason to congratulate ourselves. We have been relieved of a very considerable burden during the last session. I thought some of the taxes remitted were not very burdensome, and that we could have continued to bear them without suffering very greatly. I allude to such of the assessed taxes as fell upon carriages, men-servants, and other luxuries of the more wealthy classes, which I rather regretted to see reduced. On the other hand, we have had a reduction of income tax, the abolition of duty on fire insurance, and of the last remaining duties on corn, which is of course a boon to consumers all over the country. I think it is the duty of the great body of the people, who are relieved when taxes are taken off, to express clearly and distinctly their approbation of the Government which reduces taxation.

There is one measure to which I look forward with great hope during next session. My opinion is that we shall succeed in carrying the adoption of the ballot through the House of Commons—and I can scarcely suppose that the Upper House would so far interfere with the manner in which the people and their representatives think it proper to elect, or to be elected, as to throw out such a bill if it were sent up to their House. I think, without being unduly sanguine, we may by next session be able to pass a measure affecting the Land Laws of Ireland, which may, along with other remedial measures, go a long way to pacify that country. I believe that no measure which passes in one session will be likely to satisfy entirely the extreme men of either party. Of course a measure of justice never does satisfy the extreme men of either party, and I trust sincerely this will be a measure of justice.

The first occasion on which he spoke in this session was on the East India Bill. In his remarks on the sixth clause of the bill, which introduced into Indian administration a most important change, he said :—

It is now proposed to confer upon the Indian Government a discretionary power of promoting natives to the higher grades of the Civil Service. Ours is undoubtedly the wisest and most beneficent Government under which the Hindoos have ever lived, but it could not exist for a day without the presence of a powerful British force, nor can it be maintained without a staff of able, energetic, and faithful officials. It seems probable that we are about to try how far the spirit and prestige of British rule can be maintained by civil officials selected from the subject races. I, for one, regard this experiment with considerable apprehension. The general opinion of ourselves entertained by the people of India may be shortly expressed in the words of an intelligent native—"The sahebs do not understand us, and we do not love them ; but they endeavour to do justice, and they fear the face of no man." The interests of the people of India may be sacrificed to economize a few salaries, to gratify a few clever native subordinates, or to carry out the theoretical doctrine of an equality which has no real existence. I venture to point out what may be the possible results of the measure now before us.

Later in the session he moved for a select committee to inquire into the present system of conducting public prosecutions in Scotland, with the view of amending that system if necessary, and of extending to other parts of the United Kingdom the institution of public prosecutors. He spoke more than once on the truck system, complaining of the evasion of the existing law, and suggesting that weekly or daily payments would meet the difficulty :—

It is unnecessary for me to enter upon the details of the truck system, and the improvidence, recklessness, and intemperance produced by it among the working miners of Scotland. When we see a large body of intelligent and well-paid workmen unable to save money, and with their families and children verging on pauperism, instead of their being in that independent condition which ought to characterize the working men of that country, it is the duty of the Government and of the Legislature to institute an inquiry, whereby the opinions of those who are best qualified to judge may be obtained ; and therefore I trust that the Government will be prepared to grant this commission of inquiry.

He opposed the second reading of the Canada (Guarantee of Loan) Bill :—

I have ventured to oppose this bill, because I believe that the question is of the highest importance as regards, not merely our colonial policy, but our friendly relations in future with the United States—a most vital matter for the consideration of British states-men.   I believe one principal cause of the comparatively stationary appearance of Canada, frequently remarked by travellers from the States, to be the colonial policy of Great Britain.   This policy is now burdening the revenues of Canada by the construction of legislative palaces in the backwoods, of railroads which will not pay their working expenses, and of fortifications which are a futile menace to Canada's only neighbour.   The Act of Legisla-ture of Canada, which this bill is intended to confirm, authorizes the raising of money—£11,000,000—for defences of Montreal, Toronto, and other cities.   I believe it will be a great misfortune for all America if these proposed fortifications are ever constructed, and I maintain that neither British cash nor credit should be used for their construction.   We may be told that there is no risk, that by endorsing this bill we merely enable the Canadians to borrow at four instead of six per cent.   But, although the amount may not be great, our own credit is lowered just as much as theirs is raised. Believing the general principle of colonial guarantees to be per-nicious, while the special policy aimed at is useless, as well as dangerous, I now move the rejection of this bill.

This autumn, for the first time, he rented a Highland shooting—Rhifail, in Sutherlandshire, where he had been on a visit the previous year—and was joined in it by C. W. Bell, Bombay Civil Service, and W. E. Price, M.P.   He enjoyed the life there very much ; it is a beautiful Highland country, with good grouse-shooting and fair deer-stalking and salmon-fishing.   They lived in a little iron house close to the Naver.   He was a good shot and fond of sport, though in a rather different way to most men ; he never got wholly absorbed in it, whether shooting, hunting, or any other amusement.   While shooting he was always talking and thinking of all sorts of subjects, and observing natural objects; an instance of this is related by one of his fellow-sportsmen:—

"He was out on Ben na Grome, watching a herd of stag and some hinds, that were lying down. The keeper wanted to whistle, but he refused to disturb them, and preferred lying down in the heather and watching them from above. After an hour or so, the stag suddenly sprang to his feet, as though he had caught the stalkers' wind, but a roar announced the approach of a wandering stag, accompanied by a small number of hinds. Both stags immediately prepared for battle, the hinds withdrawing to a distance and watching the combat. The keeper, of course, was wild with excitement, and kept urging David to take the finest, being utterly incapable of comprehending the fact that he was with a naturalist, and not a deerslayer. After a while the fresh stag proved the victor, whereupon the vanquished one, with a roar of disappointment, turned tail and withdrew, and his hinds, with no apparent expression of sympathy for their former lord, quietly joined the herd of the conqueror, and commenced to browse. In spite of the expostulation of the keeper, David refused to fire at either stag, and returned home well satisfied with having been the spectator of so interesting a duel. He wrote an account of it to Darwin, who answered him promptly in his own handwriting, thanking him for the communication, and saying that he was glad of any notice as to the habits of animals, no matter how trivial it might seem to outsiders."

In the end. of November, Sir David and C. W. Bell sailed from Liverpool to Bordeaux, on their way to Spain, on board the Pacific Steam Navigation Company's fine vessel, *Araucania.* The Franco-German War was at its height, and they found Bordeaux much excited by reports from Paris, then in a state of siege.

December 2nd, Bordeaux.—The great Place was full of troops drilling, all classes being represented, from the shabby slouching little conscript, armed with chassepots, to the crack corps of young Bordeaux, whose only weapon was old Brown Bess. These last are in every respect like our volunteers, fine, tall young fellows, smartly dressed, and fairly well drilled, but shaky as to pivot men ; they seemed to enjoy their work, and were all in excellent spirits owing to the news from Paris of a successful sortie.

They spent a couple of days in a large country house ten miles from Bordeaux, owned by a rich wine merchant.

December 4th.—The life here is just that of the English squire, what with field sports and other country pursuits. Mons. C. is the local magnate, organizes night schools and benefit societies, acts as maire of the commune, until turned out by Gambetta, and serves as a simple soldier in the National Guard, under his own son. To-day there were in the house four young married ladies, all of whose husbands are serving in the army, or Garde Mobile ; the war monopolized our conversation, of course, as well as our time in picking lint.

December 8th, Madrid.—Matters here are in a very doubtful state, and the Duke of Aosta's election as king is far from being generally popular : his being a foreigner makes him many enemies ; his belonging to the House of Savoy sets the priests against him ; then there are the Carlists, and the Republicans, to say nothing of those who favour Montpensier, or the Prince of Asturias. My impression is that Amadeo I., if he comes, will have only a middling time, and that a majority of the deputies does not involve a majority of the people. Meanwhile all is very quiet, Prim and Serrano seem to govern successfully, and I only hope the new *régime* may not be inaugurated by a jolly row.

Of the Museum of paintings it is impossible to speak too highly ; the collection embraces specimens of all the great schools, and specimens which are not surpassed anywhere. The Spanish school of course takes precedence, with Murillo, Velasquez, Ribera and Juanez as its champions; but the various Italian schools are represented by pictures of Raffaelle, Guercino, Titian, Tintoretto, and others, which certainly cannot be equalled by any

---

* This forecast proved too true. General Prim was assassinated on the day of the king's entry into Madrid, and the reign of Amadeo I. was of very short duration.

gallery north of the Alps, while Van Dyck, Rubens, Memmeling, etc., well maintain the credit of the Low Countries. The equestrian portraits by Velasquez are really splendid. He is very successful with animals; a large dog in " Las Meniras " is worthy of Landseer, or Rosa Bonheur, and I think that this can be said of few mediæval masters. The family of Austria, with their Japanese faces, Philip IV. especially, appear in a variety of characters, and of all ages; and such pictures as " Jacob's Dream " and " Los Borrachos," show how thoroughly the Spanish peasantry have retained the type of face which they had in the days of Velasquez. The Murillos are of a much higher class than the little blackguard boys who abound at Munich, and are chiefly sacred subjects, including several beautiful Madonnas. Ribera excels chiefly in hideous old saints, so that his pictures are more powerful than pleasing. Juanez is a painter whose works I have seldom seen; he is somewhat stiff in his drawing, but his colouring has the depth, freshness, and brilliancy which characterize the older schools of painting in every country, and which their successors have never attained.

December 10*th.*—We sallied out to the Armoury, a most magnificent and beautifully arranged collection. The weapons and armour are as remarkable for the beauty of their workmanship as for the reputation of their former wearers—helmets, gorgets, and cuirasses, embossed and inlaid with silver and gold; rapiers of Toledo steel; Turkish and Moorish muskets, encrusted with coral, turquoises, ivory, and mother of pearl; complete suits of equestrian armour for horse and man, and all bearing famous names —Charles V., Philip II., Boabdil, El Gran Capitan, El Cid, Pizarro, Cortes. Most of these arms, however, seem to have been *de luxe,* and to have seen no service, being free from dint or fracture, except the helmet of Ali Pacha, the Turkish admiral at Lepanto. Several of the burgonets, or open helmets, are masterpieces of *repoussé* workmanship in the style of Benvenuto Cellini. Even if la Colada is not the sword of the Cid, it might have been possibly, and most of the other arms are undoubtedly, of the date ascribed to them, and almost as certainly they were worn by the men whose names they bear. Everything is kept in beautiful order, without a speck of rust or dirt; this is, I believe, the finest collection of armour in the world.

December 12*th.*—We travelled third-class to the Escurial, with crowds of Castilian peasantry, whose manners are certainly excellent. The landscape reminded us perpetually of the East, especially parts of Syria, the tone of colouring, the style of cultivation, the untidy tumble-down villages, the general absence of fences or roads. The eighth wonder of the world is certainly a wondrous edifice, representing so fitly the power, wealth, and bigotry of mediæval Spain. The church of St. Lawrence, which is, so to speak, the college chapel, is nearly as large as St. Paul's, and in its solid simple grandeur is a magnificent specimen of the Romanesque style. But perhaps the most interesting sight in the place is a small dark room, with plain wooden bureau and chairs, opening on one side upon a sort of lobby, on the other upon the church of St. Lawrence, close to the high altar. From this little den issued orders which spread more or less misery over half the globe, crushing civil and religious liberty; in this mean lobby waited the ambassadors of the great Powers, and in a dark recess between the bureau and the altar died the great Philip II., whose gloomy and monastic character, as well as his vast power, has been so well represented here in granite by his architect Juan de Herrera.

December 14*th, Toledo.*—Such is the variety of architecture and number of interesting buildings in Toledo, that it quite bewilders one to see them in so short a time; all over the city are scattered the remains of the various races, whose capital it has successively been—Roman, Visigoth, Saracen, and Castilian, to say nothing of the Jews, who flourished here exceedingly before their expulsion from Spain in 1492. The cathedral entirely beats my powers of description; the interior surpasses Burgos, and probably every other cathedral, in lavish richness of material and workmanship. There are two broad aisles on each side of the central nave, and these sweep all round the choir, meeting behind the copilla mayor, while beyond them in every direction extend large chapels, each one of which is a fine church. Owing to the double aisles there are three tiers of magnificent stained-glass windows, but the most beautiful are the rose windows of the nave and transepts, one of which is in fact a bouquet of Moorish soldiers and Christian saints. There are certain peculiarities in the method of celebrating mass in this cathedral, according to the Muzarabe ceremonial, the ringing of bells resounds like a mule team, while the floor is vigorously thumped with silver maces.

S. Juan de los Reyes, built by the Catholic sovereigns, and
covered with the ciphers F and I, is a perfect gem of Spanish
Gothic, the cloisters in particular, whose delicate tracery festooned
with creepers is enough to fascinate any artist. Jewish synagogues
converted into Christian churches are a peculiar feature of Toledo,
where now there is hardly a single Jew.   Roofs of Lebanon cedar,
inlaid with nacre ; brilliant encaustic tiles, richly coloured and
gilded stucco work with Hebrew inscriptions, still tell of the
wealthy and prosperous community whom Spanish bigotry sent
to enrich freer lands ; but whitewash has been laid on by barbarous
hands. " When I came back from the Alhambra, I could have
stuck a knife into the priest who whitewashed this place—but he is
dead already." So spake the solemn gentleman, like a broken-
down hidalgo, who escorted us through this most interesting
old city.

December 15th, Cordova.—By a night journey we found ourselves transferred, with startling suddenness, from a Northern to a
Southern climate, country, and vegetation.   Cordova surpassed
even Toledo in grandeur and renown under both Romans and
Moors ; now she hardly retains so many monuments of her former
greatness, but she has her Roman bridge, and Saracenic mosque,
and she is the birth-city of Seneca and El Gran Capitan.   Passing
through a small door in a dead wall, you find yourself in a
large court filled with olive trees, orange trees, and date palms,
fountains of clear cold water from the Sierra Morena, and crowds
of gaily dressed loafers smoking, chatting, and drawing water.
Inside this court is the Mezquita, or mosque, which in its turn
acts as a sort of court to the cathedral raised in its midst.   It
is simply a forest of columns, many hundreds in number, of all
colours and kinds of marble and granite, with Corinthian capitals,
and supporting horse-shoe arches.   The pillars are Roman, the
arches, of course, Moorish, and are painted red and white in
Oriental style.

December 17th, Granada.—The road from Archidona, where
we left the railway, is something too dreadful.   The team in our
diligence consisted of six mules and three horses, harnessed in
pairs, with an out-rider on the solitary leader ; the shouts, execra-
tions, and blows with which the wretched mules were urged on
were such as Spain only could produce.   An hour on the road
shows you more than days on the rail of the national peculiarities

and character, and I am afraid that kindness to dumb animals is not one of the Spaniard's strong points. " Pelegrina !" shrilly twice or thrice, with hand to ear like a huntsman ; " Carbonera ! " still more shrilly four or five times; " Lucera !" half coaxing, half hysterical ; then " Macho-o-o ! " with savage brutality, and whack, whack, whack, till the galled jade winces again.   An aide-de-camp on foot supplements the whipping, giving a widish berth to " Publia," who kicks.

December 18*th.*—Morning light showed that we were close to the Alhambra, and we entered the enchanted precincts, which to me, from Washington Irving's tales, have always had more romantic associations than probably any other spot.   One cannot look at " the two discreet statues " without thinking of pots of treasure, or at the massive Torre de las Infantas without re-membering Zorabayda, whose fate from my earliest childhood has always weighed upon my mind.   From the top of the bell-tower the view is really splendid, over city, plain, and mountain ; the Albaycin, or ancient Granada, is especially grand in its situation on a steep hill, between which and that of the Alhambra flows the Darro, a small stream in winter, but in summer, like the Xenil, it pours down abundantly the melted snows of the Sierra Nevada. These mountains glitter like a silver cloud over the vega of Granada, reminding one of the plain of Damascus with Mount Hermon.

December 20*th.*—At Loja we agreed with an *arriero*, at a high figure, for horses, and started before dawn to do upwards of forty miles to Cuesta la Reyna.   The horses had bits of rope with lots of knots to act both as bridle and whip, and shapeless sacks without stirrups for saddles, on which we were glad frequently to alter our attitudes.   We had received hints about robbers, but the road swarmed with Civil Guards, and very civil muleteers, so that we were quite tired of saluting and saying, " Vaya con Dios." We soon entered the mountains ; our guide says there is nothing in Spain to equal the scenery, and very grand and varied it is. We continued winding higher and higher ; the mountains, which are part of the Sierra de Alhama, becoming wilder and more precipitous, until, on approaching Colmenar, a most magnificent view burst upon us.   Towering high over all was the snowy summit of Sierra Tajeda, and through gaps in the lower ranges were visible the blue Mediterranean, and the fertile plain of Velez Malaga on the coast; on every side was a chaos of hills, rocks,

and valleys, with towns and villages perched and nestled in all
sorts of apparently inaccessible places.   At this great elevation,
several thousand feet above the sea, aloes grow freely, and vines
are cultivated to the very tops of the hills.

At last we began to descend, and after twelve hours' ride
reached the Venta of Cuesta la Reyna, and found it full, so had
to betake ourselves to a still humbler hostelry opposite.   Entering with our horses, we found the place occupied by many
quadrupeds and bipeds; the latter, who were seated round the
fire, at once made room for us, and a number of the former soon
joined the family circle, which was composed at one time of
some ten men, boys, and women, besides any number of dogs,
goats, and cats.   It would have made a fine subject for a painter:
when fresh branches of sweet-smelling shrubs were heaped on,
the smoke went curling up the great chimney, and the ruddy
light shone brightly on the group by the fire, and dimly on the
recesses of the background, where goats were being milked and
a casual pig was foraging.   We had an excellent dinner, with
good wine; after us the others all fed, and after the pipe of peace
we were shown into a sort of granary, where a couch was spread
upon the floor.

December 21*st.*—The usual rule in Spain held good here—
the more frugal the inn, the less frugal the bill; but we kicked
against the demand, and tendered two duros, which were accepted.
Travelling is dear in Spain, especially in out-of-the-way parts,
because Spaniards will treat strangers as rare exotic birds are
served by ornithologists—they skin them at once, instead of encouraging them to remain and multiply.

At Malaga they had a good view of the total eclipse of
the sun, on December 22nd (an account of which is given
farther on), and then left by rail for Seville.

December 24*th, Seville.*—The cathedral, with its famous Moorish
tower, the Giralda, is a magnificent building, not very striking
externally, but unrivalled in the grandeur of its interior.   On either
side of the central nave are twin aisles, each of which, though less
lofty than the centre, might form the nave of a great cathedral.
It surpasses both Toledo and Burgos in size, and in the imposing
effect of the general interior, the view of which is less impeded

by screens and such obstacles than in other great Spanish cathedrals.   Being Christmas Eve we attended midnight mass; the vast aisles, pillars, and arches looked very grand in the dim religious light, the roof being almost invisible from its great height.

Christmas Day.—The ascent of the Giralda might be performed by the puffiest old gentleman, as it is effected by a series of gentle slopes without steps, while the view of the city of Seville and its environs might recompense a much greater exertion.   The bells were being rung like mad: they are very numerous, of all sizes, and named after different saints; the heaviest of all are struck without swinging, but the others are so well hung that they turn over and over with great ease.   Just as the bell is on the point of turning, the ringer will allow himself to be lifted by the rope, and will perch like a bird upon the bell, or its balance weight, so as to check it, and bring it back the same way.   Soon there was a youngster swinging on every second bell, à la Quasimodo, one fellow actually flying out of the belfry with his rope into the open air, some 250 feet above the pavement.   The sight of this, and the sound of the bells between them, were almost enough to drive one mad, and we were glad to make our escape.

In the evening we attended the Spanish Protestant service, every word of which I could follow; the chapel was decorated with evergreens; the sermon was short and impressive, and we sang in Spanish the hymn, "There is a happy land."   It was a touching and pleasant thing to see these people worshipping according to their consciences, as freely and fearlessly as the Cardinal Archbishop himself.   Three years ago they were proscribed and persecuted, but Castelar's principles have triumphed so far at least.   *Viva la Republica !*

From Cadiz they sailed in a small steamer to Gibraltar, but, arriving after gun-fire, had to pass the night at Algesiras.   They spent four days at Gibraltar (where a few flakes of snow fell on New Year's Day, astonishing the oldest inhabitant), and returned to England by P. and O. steamer.

The following vivid description of " The Solar Eclipse of 1870 " formed part of a lecture delivered at Ayr :—

To the philosopher a total eclipse is productive of the highest pleasure and of the most eager interest, for in it he sees clear proofs of triumphs achieved, and brilliant prospects of triumphs yet to come. Such, indeed, is the grandeur and strangeness of the spectacle, that frequently its effect on those who see it for the first time is to incapacitate them from properly using the golden moments during which experiments and observations must be made. This I can well understand from my own sensations during these hundred seconds, which seemed to pass like five, but during which all nature seemed to be paralyzed, while silence, as well as darkness, descended upon the earth.

On the 22nd of December, 1870, the circumstances were in my case peculiarly favourable as to weather and position for seeing the eclipse. Unluckily, none of the expeditionary savants had selected Malaga as a station, so that the splendid spectacle was witnessed only by unskilled eyes, whose sole aids were field glasses and dark goggles. As soon as the eclipse was seen to have commenced, we made for the summit of Gibralfaro, the ancient Moorish fortress which overlooks the city of Malaga, and commands a magnificent prospect of mountain, plain, and sea. The officer of the guard at once accepted our explanation that we wished to observe the eclipse ; and being made free of the fortress, we posted ourselves on the highest battlement. During the progress of the eclipse, we had opportunities of observing its effects on the lower animals, as represented by a dog, some pigeons, and a few stolid Spanish recruits ; but we noticed nothing very particular in their behaviour. The swallows, however, which make Malaga a winter residence—almost the only one in Europe— gradually disappeared from the scene.

As the eclipse advanced, the blackness which came rapidly up from the north-west was not that of clouds, but the moon's shadow sweeping over land and sea. As the brilliant crescent of sunlight dwindled to a mere thread, the western sierras became black as ink, but overhead the diminution of light was by no means very striking, so long as any portion of the sun was visible. The "sickly glare of the sun's eye" had merely seemed like the light of a wintry afternoon. In another instant the black pall swept over us, "the stars rushed out," at one leap came the dark, the sun vanished, and in his place hung a black sphere, encircled by a number of ruby-coloured spots and by a silvery corona of divergent rays. These rays were unequal in length and brilliancy, even showing gaps here and there ; in particular one conspicuous notch on the south-eastern limb. Their general effect resembled the aureoles, or glories, with which mediæval painters encircle the heads of angels and saints. These brilliant appearances were most conspicuous round the moon's northern limb, as was natural from our position lying considerably to the north of the central line of shadow. Owing to the same cause the darkness was deepest towards the south, while in the east and west the horizon for a time was yellow, as if with the light of a double sunset or sunrise. In fact, day dawned rapidly in the west, while darkness settled down upon the east. Although, as it happened, three planets—Mercury, Venus, and Saturn—were all in proximity to the sun, we only observed one, which, from its size and brilliancy, must have been Venus. At no time was it too dark to see the hands of a watch with ease.

Just at the darkest moment noon tolled from the great bell of the cathedral. The grandeur and gloom of this " disastrous twilight " were sufficiently impressive, even when the eyes were directed downwards to earth and sea ; but, gazing at the eclipsed sun, almost made it possible to realize Campbell's poem of " The Last Man." The universe was darkened, Baldur the Good was dead. The only cheering sight was the fair planet, which smiled as it did upon Dante when he first emerged from the infernal regions. But in less time than that occupied by my very inadequate description, the wonderful vision was dissipated. A dazzling point of light flashed out, " scattering the rear of darkness," which swept away eastward over the sea, and in an instant planet, corona, and red prominences had entirely disappeared. The moon's shadow had no defined visible edge, owing probably to the presence of clouds in the sky, but it was drawn away like a curtain, and instinctively we gave a sigh of relief. It has been my good fortune to see many striking and beautiful sights, but none has made a deeper impression, and recurs more frequently and vividly to my memory, than this weird vision of the darkened sun and his ruby-studded crown.

CHAPTER IX.

1871.

ADDRESS TO THE ELECTORS AT AYR—TRIP TO SWITZERLAND—JOINS THE FAMILY AT SAN REMO—LECTURES ON "ITALY AND ROME."

IMMEDIATELY after his return from Spain, Sir David went to Scotland to redeem promises he had made to deliver lectures at Glasgow, as well as at several places in Ayrshire. He took the opportunity to address the electors at Ayr, and reviewed the legislation of the last session :—

After listening to the lengthy debates upon the Education Bill of last session, which we passed for England, I myself was convinced that without a compulsory clause any Education Bill would prove little more than a dead letter in those particular localities for which it was most specially required : I allude to the poorer districts of our large cities. Feeling strongly that we must have compulsion in any bill that is to deal satisfactorily with the mass of ignorance, of pauperism, and of crime with which we are now burdened, I also cannot help thinking myself that, if the poor are compelled to send their children to school, they ought to be relieved of all expenses, and protected against teaching of any kind which they may consider to be false or pernicious. I did certainly vote in the minority against many of the provisions of the English bill, which I thought gave scant justice to Nonconformists. Even allowing for that, I am prepared freely to admit it was a great step in the right direction, and I was very glad to see it made law. It was very nearly as good a bill as England is at present prepared for. I think, without undue pride, we may say that in Scotland we are all prepared for a more complete and comprehensive system ; and that mischief would result from adopting the English Act of last year either in Scotland or Ireland.

With regard to the question of University Tests, which is closely connected with what I have just been speaking of, a small measure of reform was passed last session by a large majority through the House of Commons.   Unfortunately the House seems determined to resist all compromise upon this important question, and I believe now that it will be necessary to pass a measure which will introduce into our great national Universities perfect religious equality between Churchmen and Dissenters, and which will sweep away all religious disabilities from academic and collegiate administration.

Government certainly did very little for Scotland, if we except the appointment of the Truck Commission, from whose labours I anticipate much benefit to the working-classes throughout the whole country, from the Shetland Isles to South Wales.

The Government Game Bill proved a failure, as all its pre-decessors had done, and as almost any bill is likely to do which has but few hearty supporters, and a great many determined oppo-nents.   Speaking for myself, I must frankly admit that a moderate measure of reform would have satisfied me, but when I saw the Government bill, and heard the Lord Advocate speaking in oppo-sition to Mr. Taylor's proposal for a total repeal of the Game Laws, I could not help feeling, as did many others, that it was our duty to vote for the second reading of Mr. Taylor's bill, in order to show that some of us, at least, were prepared even to accept so extreme a measure rather than endorse the doctrines propounded, and leave practically without reform of any kind the grievances which we had undertaken to do our very best to remedy.

It has been proposed to the House, and has received, to a certain extent, the sanction of the Ministry, to appoint this session a select committee to inquire into the government and finance of our great Eastern Empire.   This is a subject which, I think, receives far too little attention at present at the hands of Parlia-ment ; and we know that such an inquiry is earnestly desired by many, both in this country and in India, who take a warm interest in the affairs of that great empire.   I must anticipate much benefit from the inquiry which that committee will institute.

Probably the most important question before us is that of

Army Reform and Military Organization. We must amalgamate our three services, the Army, the Militia, and the Volunteers—we must make military qualifications, and not money, indispensable to promotion—and we must have one responsible head for all our defences, both of the Line and of the Reserves. And when we have accomplished these changes, the question will still remain as to the best method of filling the ranks up to a number requisite for safety. For my part, I have always considered that one of the first duties, if not the privileges, of a citizen was to serve in the defence of his country and of its institutions. I think too little attention has yet been paid to a system that has long been in operation in a free country; I mean that of general military service which is in force in Switzerland. One very important characteristic of the Swiss system is the amount of military training given to what may almost be called children—to boys at school, and to young men before they have attained to military age. Having been at school in Switzerland myself, I know something about that. I believe it works with very great effect; it is beneficial as a part of education in itself, besides rendering the subsequent acquirement of military knowledge comparatively easy.

We are told that there are four great objects for which Great Britain requires an army: first, the defence of the country at home; second, the protection of our colonies and possessions; third, the fulfilment of engagements under which we lie towards foreign Powers; and fourth, in order to intervene where we may consider our honour or our interests are concerned. Now, with regard to the fourth of these objects, I demur to it entirely. It has hitherto been used invariably as a pretext for involving us in ruinous and useless wars. With regard to the third, I am prepared to admit that there may be some outstanding engagements, incurred perhaps rashly, from which we cannot now withdraw in honour, but I hope that our statesmen will display very great caution and prudence in future, and not enter upon any such engagements. As for the second, the defence of our colonies and possessions, that seems to me to be quite a legitimate object, and one for which we are called upon to submit to a certain amount of burden and sacrifice. But it is for the first principally, as by far the most important, that I consider it necessary that our whole military system should be reorganized. This is in order that we may occupy a position of dignity, as well as of safety from everybody; from our enemies, if we have any, knowing in our intercourse with foreign States that we feel absolutely safe from all danger at home.

After the close of the session he started with his cousins, Lord and Lady Hopetoun, for Paris. The German troops were still in occupation of many parts of France, and at Creil they first found the "Pickel Haubes" in possession of the station, and the huge terminus at Paris was empty and silent. They put up at the Grand Hotel, which had recently been a hospital for wounded, and for four days examined the effects of the siege on the city, and suburbs for miles'round.

August 13*th, Paris.*—In the Rue Royale many houses have been burnt, and are still shells, and the statue of Lisle in the Place de la Concorde has been smashed, but the other cities of France, including Strasbourg, still sit proudly on their thrones. It is not until the grand façade of the Tuileries is seen, as complete a ruin as the Palace of the Cæsars, that the destruction wrought in Paris can be fully realized. The Hotel de Ville is another splendid ruin, which has not been touched, but almost everywhere else the hands of the restorer are busy. There can be little doubt that the main damage was done by shells, and not by deliberate incendiarism, as almost all the buildings which are burnt show numerous shell marks, and were, in fact, exposed to heavy bombardment.

August 15*th.*—We drove to Clamart, where we met Sir Charles Dilke, our cicerone for the day. He took us upon the railway embankment, to point out the scene of an action he had witnessed between the Versaillists and Communeux on the 4th of April. Houses and garden walls are riddled with shot, and the ground torn up by shell in every direction, Fort Issy having had it hot in both sieges; but, after all, the Prussians did little damage anywhere. Of the ruin and devastation to be seen on every hand, bridges blown up, houses smashed to atoms, trees and lamp-posts knocked down, walls turned into a mere series of holes, of all this the French themselves are the authors, either in their supposed defensive arrangements against the Prussians, or in their attack upon the Commune. The Versaillists are indeed responsible for nearly all, and the chief agent was Mont Valérien, which destroyed everything within a radius of three or four miles, without itself ever receiving a shot. As we approached the grim giant, his handiwork became more and more apparent, especially at St. Cloud, which is literally a pile of ruins.

From Paris he went to Geneva and Chamounix, and describes an excursion he made over the Mer de Glace to the Jardin.

August 19th, Chamounix.—In the centre of a vast amphi-theatre of snow, walled in by serrated ridges, appeared the Jardin, reminding me in its isolation of the famous group of cedars in the Lebanon. When it is finally reached, it proves to be a mass of rocks, quite free of snow, and literally a garden of Alpine plants, swarming with butterflies. It is difficult to understand how the seeds got here, unless they were brought by birds in days when there were such animals in Switzerland. Anyhow, here they are, bright and fragrant in a howling wilderness, remnants of an arctic flora, and even the bees manage to find their way to them, though nearly ten thousand feet above the sea, while no amount of snow seems to incommode the butterflies. Right in front are the dazzling snows of Mont Blanc, and in every direction rise the Aiguilles of every fantastic shape, and varying in colour from black to bright red. This was my first day fairly among the glaciers, and above them, and owing to the splendid weather it was every way most enjoyable.

August 28th, Hospice of St. Bernard.—In the inn at St. Rémy was a fine St. Bernard dog, whose portrait I proceeded to take, solacing myself by whistling the "Marseillaise" and "Wacht am Rhein," when I became aware of a gentleman, who proved to be none other than the late prime minister of France, Emille Ollivier. Being alone together, we were soon engaged in a very amicable and animated discussion upon English and French politics. He appears to understand our institutions and national character well, and on hearing that I am like his friend Grant Duff, Député Écossais, he became quite confidential. While professing thoroughly democratic opinions, he thinks highly of the advantages of an obstructive aristocracy. "You are slow in effecting reforms, but with you reforms are final; no one ever dreams of reverting to the ancient state of affairs, because the whole nation has time to understand and appreciate the reforms before they become law. With us nothing is final, every question is liable at any time to be reopened, because the people do not receive the political education afforded by debates and discussions in and out of Parliament, as well as by the press. The Peers have thrown out the Ballot Bill, and the result will be that you will address your electors, articles will appear in the journals, every one will inform himself of the advantages of secret voting, and next year you will carry a better bill, and you will never hear of the ballot in the British Parliament again. Time and labour will be saved in the long run. Do not think of abolishing the House of Lords; their action is really favourable to the cause of progress." I was much struck with this view of the matter, which was new to me, and came with great force from such a man as Ollivier. He went on to say: "The Emperor Napoleon is a man of advanced opinions; c'était l'esprit le plus élevé de la France, but the nation was not sufficiently instructed to appreciate his views." M. Ollivier was not without hopes that the commercial treaty with Great Britain would after all be renewed, its beneficial effects being so manifest, although free trade is not yet understood by the French. Of Richard Cobden he spoke in terms of unqualified admiration. I have seldom, if ever, had a more interesting conversation, and we parted on most friendly terms, when his frugal mule-cart was announced, he returning to Italy, while I set my face for Switzerland.

The fathers resident at the hospice are a set of very gentlemanly young men, about twenty in number, the older men living down at Martigny, after serving their time on the mountain. It is very trying to the constitution to live all the year round at this elevation of eight thousand feet, but the cheerful intelligent faces of the Bernardins show that a busy, useful life may be a happy one, even in a monastery among eternal snows. Their dress is black, with a cap like that worn by French *avocats*, whom they resemble in manner and appearance, having very little of the monk about them.

August 29th, Geneva.—So bright was the moonlight, that waking early I thought it was broad daylight and I had overslept myself. To my great satisfaction, "'twas not the morning's eye," merely the "pale reflex of Cynthia's brow," and I and my guide Charlet were off by five a.m. No vehicle of any kind was available on the road, and as the only chance of reaching Geneva to-night was to catch the midday train at Martigny, we had to step out. At one time hope was low, but all's well that ends well, though twenty-eight miles to catch a train before breakfast is too much of a good thing. I felt quite sad at parting with the honest Charlet, a good guide and a pleasant companion. It was, as usual, piping hot in the Rhone valley, and wasps swarmed to that extent in the railway carriage as nearly to frighten a good old Scotch lady into hysterics. The sight of the blue lake was most refreshing, and on board the steamer I at last got a meal, composed to a certain extent of ferras, the famous fish of Lake Leman. We had a charming sail, and when "day her sultry fires had wasted," the many lights of Geneva were seen glittering over the lake. The forced march of the morning had made my feet a little tender, and the last use of my alpenstock was "walked with to sustain uneasy steps" across the Pont des Alpes.

August 31st.—I was rewarded for turning out from the hotel at Bern at five a.m. by a splendid view of my old friends, the Alps of the Bernese Oberland. One returns to one's old love, and I must say that I have for the Jungfrau and her companions a different feeling from that with which I regard any other mountains. There they stood, glittering in the rising sun, just as I remember them twenty-seven years ago, not much in their existence certainly, but a large percentage of mine. Soon afterwards I was bowling along through familiar scenes ; I recognized at once the great house of Hofwyl with its bosquet, the little lakes on which we used to skate, and the wooded heights where we gathered blæberries.

On his way home he stopped at Strasbourg, to see the damage done to the grand old cathedral by the bombardment of the previous year, and found that it had suffered very severely, but was being restored at great cost by the German Government.

A few days after reaching home he went down to Scotland to shoot at Ben Hope, in Sutherlandshire, a moor which he and W. E. Price, M.P., had taken for three years.

They had a large house there, and were able to entertain many friends. He was very keen after ptarmigan, of which there were great numbers on Ben Hope, while old blackcock and black-headed gulls were his mortal enemies, the former because they were so cunning, the latter because they were supposed to kill young grouse in the breeding time. On the other hand, the true Raptores, the peregrine falcons, merlins, and eagles found in him a staunch friend, and he always protested against their destruction at the hands of the keepers. He was not dependent upon sport for his amusement : he read immensely, in one season reading the whole of Herbert Spencer's philosophical works ; he used to sketch specimens of all the birds and animals that were killed ; and with a good microscope, and games of chess and whist, time was fully occupied.

In November, he read a paper in Edinburgh, before the Scotch Law Amendment Society, on "Impediments to Scotch Legislation," which his experience of the last three sessions had impressed upon him. He described the difficulties of carrying purely Scotch measures through Parliament, and declared his intention of moving next session in the House of Commons for a committee of inquiry into the subject.

The state of his sister Margaret's health necessitated her going abroad for the winter, and Lady Wedderburn had taken a house at San Remo for the season. He started in December to join the family there, accompanied by A. H. Brown, M.P. They had a bitterly cold journey as far as Avignon, where they stayed two days, partly to pay a visit to John Stuart Mill, who had resided there for some years in a little country house.

December 12th, Avignon.—Mr. Mill received Brown and myself very kindly, and we had a long talk about affairs in general. He augurs favourably of the effect of decentralization in France, and the gradual creation of local independence, and public spirit.

Hitherto there has never been any sincere attempt made to break down the vast centralized organization which stifles personal and local action, because each party in turn hoped to wield in its own hands the mighty machine. Contrasting the national character and conduct of French and Italians, he said that the latter are perhaps the most prudent and practical people in Europe. This is hardly the conventional belief, but I have little doubt of its truth. He said also that he hoped a party would grow up in Great Britain favourable to the Federal system of government and legislation, although in the special case of Ireland great difficulties would be found in working it, owing to the chronic tendency which England and Ireland have to diverge upon questions of imperial interest. In the case of Scotland no such difficulties would arise, and the conditions would be specially favourable to local management of local matters. Mr. Mill is not a young man, but he looks a long way ahead, and accepts as readily as any impetuous youngster the organic changes which the future must bring, and which his political sagacity enables him to foresee.

The Musée Calvet is a very fine collection of paintings, sculpture, and antiquities. Its chief pride is a large ivory crucifix, a wonderful carving, all in one piece, except the arms; the expression of the face varies according to the position from which it is viewed. The Dutch paintings are particularly good, and some of them very humorous. There is an old bishop pushing back his mitre to scratch his head, in astonishment at seeing the infant Christ; his face is a model of stolid admiration, and fixed me the instant I entered the room. The colouring, as usual with Low Countries pictures, has been perfectly preserved, and the brilliancy of one by Fr. Floris, of Crœsus exhibiting his treasures to Solon, is a marvel; it is several centuries old, but no modern picture could surpass or even equal it. Certainly in oil paintings, as in stained glass, the colouring of the ancients has it easy. One end of the gallery is devoted to the Vernet family, which hails from Avignon, and numbers many painters among its members. Horace Vernet is of course the most famous, and his well-known picture of Mazeppa is here in duplicate, also a marble bust of him by Thorvaldsen. Several portraits of Petrarch's Laura resemble each other, inasmuch as they all represent a hard-featured young woman.

December 13th.—Nismes is a very cheerful and flourishing place, full of Roman antiquities, well preserved and utilized for modern purposes; but the great lion is the amphitheatre or "arènes," which is so perfect that it is regularly used for bull-fights during summer, when 8000 or 10,000 people are sometimes present. It will hold 25,000, being half the size of the Coliseum, but far more perfect, and built entirely of massive stone masonry. Arches, passages, stairs, and seats are all in complete order, up to the highest stage, where the marks of the supports for the awning are distinct in the stones. Considerable repairs have been made here of late, but the name of the restorer has been effaced from the commemorative inscription; it was no doubt Napoleon III. For such restorations as these, so perfectly done as hardly to be distinguishable even on careful examination, the ex-Emperor certainly deserves every credit; a stone put in judiciously here and there will preserve such monuments for as many centuries as they have already existed. In fact the Romans built so as to defy time, and it is as a rule only wilful injury that has to be repaired.

They drove along the Corniche road from Nice to San Remo, arriving there in the middle of December. He spent six weeks with his mother and sisters, and was much taken with the place, saying of it:—

As a winter residence San Remo combines more advantages than any other place that I have visited. The situation is perfect: in a sheltered bay facing S.S.E., with high hills rising immediately behind, protecting the place from all winds except the south, and even from the afternoon sun in the long summer days. Thus the warm winters of San Remo are not succeeded by very hot summers, which are tempered by the sea-breeze and the shadow of the mountains. The vegetation is scarcely European, as the date palm, aloe, prickly pear flourish along with lemons, oranges, pepper trees and loquats. None of these, however, appear to be indigenous, and while the hills are covered with lentisk, arbutus, and myrtle, there are no wild palms, as in the south of Spain. The swallows do not remain here during winter, and it is not so warm as Malaga, but then San Remo lies seven degrees further north. Animal life is not abundant; in all my rambles I have never encountered any beast of the chase, not even a squirrel, nor any game bird. All the real hard work is done by the women, with the usual result of converting in a very few years pretty graceful girls into haggard old women. In making the railroad, or in building houses, all the large stones are carried on the heads of women, even up ladders and on to scaffolding, where the men quietly await their arrival.

The land here is much subdivided, and the system of transferring and registering landed property is so rapid, simple, and cheap, as to afford a model to more barbarous nations. Of this we had practical experience when my sisters became "proprietarie;" for a matter of some twenty-seven francs covered all the legal expenses, including those of registration, the notary being bound under penalties to complete all formalities within a limited time; and for half a franc you may satisfy yourself, by a glance at the register, that the transfer has been duly recorded, or that the property is free of burdens. An *ad valorem* duty is payable to the State upon the agricultural value only of the land. The deed of transfer was written *currente calamo* in our presence, and was signed, witnessed, and disposed of in about half an hour.

· He left San Remo with the Vicomte de St. Jean, and went by steamer from Porto Maurizio to Genoa. Of the one day they spent there he has left a record covering nine pages of his journal, from which it is impossible to give more than a few lines. They were out early and on the move all day, visiting all the sights of "Genoa, which well deserves her epithet of Superb." In travelling nothing escaped his keen observation, and the impressions made on his mind were so permanent, that when he revisited a town years afterwards he could find his way about, and noticed the slightest changes, such as the new position or removal of a picture. A place did not lose its interest because he had seen it before; on the contrary, he enjoyed reviving earlier recollections, as well as finding new attractions.

February 1st, Genoa.—The ruinous brick exterior of the Church of the Annunciation renders the blaze of gold, of frescoes, of stained glass, and coloured marble perfectly dazzling, when you enter. Painting and gilding are in the richest and most brilliant style, but the marble and alabaster columns, altars, and pavement surpass anything that I have seen. All is of the finest material, and in perfect order and repair ; certain twisted pillars are solid blocks of a peculiar alabaster once quarried near Genoa, but now used up entirely. The roof is covered with frescoes as bright as when first painted, and altogether the church is simply gorgeous.

The gardens of the Villa Pallavicini have been laid out with a greater amount of expenditure than of good taste. Grecian temples, feudal towers, Chinese pagodas, Turkish mosques, rustic bowers are stuck about in the groves of ilex, arbutus and pine, as it might be " Neptune, Plutarch, and Nicodemus." Each group of tourists, and to-day they were in dozens, is accompanied by a stolid country bumpkin, who remorselessly trots his victims into every cave and moss-house, up to every tower and belle-vue, and has them ferried across every pond. It was very comical to see each lot going through the same performance in turn, and except ourselves all perfectly solemn.

A couple of miles outside the city is the new Campo Santo, which already contains hundreds of beautiful monuments by the best modern sculptors and of the finest Carrara marble, no other material being admitted. The Italians have not lost the art of sculpture, and the taste and execution of these monuments are very remarkable. Most of the statues and busts are portraits, evidently faithful, and the allegorical figures are many of great beauty. Here at least has been produced an object of admiration for posterity by the wealth, art, and " piety" of our own generation.

February 3rd, Milan.—When we climbed the Duomo, we found all clear, city, plain, and mountains, except to the south, where the Apennines were invisible, but northwards the Alps rose like a mighty wall, just as the Himalayas rise abruptly from the plains of Hindustan, and stretch away on either hand as far as the eye can reach. The huge mass of Monte Rosa overtops all other peaks, but many snowy towers and bastions vary the outline of the great range, which turns its precipitous side towards Italy, and presents a very different aspect to that which is seen from Switzerland. We wandered over acres of marble slabs, among a forest of exquisitely carved spires and pinnacles, each one of them a Scott monument with all its statues complete. The central spire is no doubt somewhat dwarfed by the number and height of those by which it is on every side surrounded, but it is four hundred feet high. The whole building, unlike most Gothic churches, has been completed upon one design, although the length of time taken to finish it is indicated by the various styles of the statuary, which fills every niche and crests every pinnacle, and by means of which the date of each portion might be determined as geological strata are recognized by their fossils. The awkward, sprawling renaissance saints look somewhat uncomfortable in their narrow Gothic niches, but the more modern statues seem quite at home ; among these are remarkable, three by Canova, in particular Napoleon I., who takes here a place among angels, patriarchs, and saints. Of Milan Cathedral, outside and inside, it may be truly said, " There is no deception," with one exception, the vaulted roof of nave and aisles is only painted, although it seems to be fretwork carving. Everywhere else the carving is of the richest, and the stained glass of the most brilliant. It seems to have been " raised by Titans, and finished by " carvers in ivory.

The admiration and affection for the country and people of Italy, which were first excited by his residence there as a boy, were constantly revived by his later visits to the country. Italy was the first subject on which he ever delivered a lecture, as early as 1860 ; in 1871 he selected it again for two popular lectures in Ayrshire, and from them the following is taken :—

Few things would give me greater pleasure than to be able, even in the smallest degree, to promote the friendly feeling towards Italy and the Italians, which a more intimate acquaintance with that noble nation is certain to produce in this country. The Italians can now command the respect and admiration of the whole civilized world ; but those who have travelled much in Italy, and lived among the people, feel more than this, and it has been most truly said, that whoever can step within the line of separation excluding foreigners, will be met with a warmth of heart, an originality and independence of character, and a picturesqueness of ideas, which will inspire him with a true affection for the nation, and make it no easy task for him to represent their faults clearly either to himself or others. Having had the good fortune to spend two years of my life in Italy, at an age when everything that attracts the attention makes an indelible impression on the memory, I can look back to many pleasant days spent in company with Italians, and I have not one disagreeable reminiscence of all my intercourse with them. Kindness, hospitality, and consideration were invariably displayed, especially by the country people, with whom a stranger is generally most brought into contact, and who may be considered as affording the fairest type of national character.

We are now so high among the nations, and sway regions Cæsar never knew: they have been of late so low. It was not so always, and Britain has been an Italian province, the most remote and unimportant of the mighty Roman Empire. We need not look far in order to discover traces of this ancient state of things; their camps are to be found on every commanding eminence, even under the very shadow of the Grampian Hills, the extreme northern limit which their eagles ever attained. They were, indeed, a great and terrible people, whose iron heel could leave such indelible marks even on the uttermost verge of their empire. Wise and liberal in their general policy towards their subjects, they gained their affection by administering equal laws at home, and protecting the frontier against external foes. It was therefore amid the tears and lamentations of the people, that the last Roman legions were withdrawn from Britain for the defence of Italy against the Huns.

The greatest blessings that a people can enjoy—liberty, plenty, commercial prosperity, and equitable laws—are not our own unless we are both able and willing to defend them ourselves, at all hazards and against all comers. We are taught again and again in the pages of Italian history, that it is madness to trust either to the protection or the forbearance of others, to pay others to defend us, or to let us alone. Apart from the national disgrace in such a course of conduct, we learn that the final catastrophe is merely delayed, since, eventually, he who has the steel will take the gold also. It was by pursuing this fatal policy that Rome lost the dominion of the world: while her own citizens fought her battles, no power on earth could stand against her; when she committed the protection of her frontier to mercenaries, the Goths soon thundered at her gates. Many centuries later arose the free cities and republics of mediæval Italy, under whose fostering care, art, science, and literature awoke from their long and death-like sleep; whose fleets were vehicles of commerce for all Europe, and the bulwark of Christendom against the Turk. They, too, fell in their turn under the power of strangers, and from what cause? because they were divided against themselves, and because they paid others to fight their battles; because public spirit and patriotism ceased to characterize their citizens, and none were found willing to sacrifice themselves and their selfish interest for the general good.

Italy is possessed of every advantage which can raise a nation to power and greatness—a delightful and healthy climate, commodious and safe harbours, a fertile and varied soil, capable of producing in abundance almost every plant which grows within the temperate zones, and containing a great store of mineral wealth beneath its surface. Her sons are brave, talented, energetic enough to compete successfully with any nation in the world; twice have they risen to the first and highest positions; twice have they lost the name of a nation altogether, while Italy became a mere battle-ground for strangers and barbarians, because the Italians had ceased to love their country more than themselves. This is indeed the greatest misfortune that can befall a nation, and no material prosperity can in any way counterbalance the decay of public spirit. Prosperity cannot long survive when that which alone creates and supports it becomes extinct.

The history and traditions of the Italians are as glorious as our own, and extend over a much longer period of time. While Britain was still a swampy forest, Italy was already the queen of nations, and had given birth to a host of warriors, statesmen, philosophers, and poets, such as might almost rival the ancient fame of Greece. When the Greeks had ceased to be a nation, and Athens had become a name; when England was still a semi-barbarous feudal kingdom; Italy was once more the mother of arts, and of all the greatest men whose names make the history of that period illustrious. There is hardly a building or a landscape throughout the length and breadth of the land which may not remind an Italian of the mighty dead upon whose dust he treads; and if the spirit of patriotism and union, which we have seen roused in our own day, resemble that which animated the Romans twenty-five centuries ago, we need not fear that the list of Italian worthies is now complete. Italian unity has been established by two of her own sons: the first of those was Count Cavour, who, however, did not live long enough to see the result for which he had wrought so hard, and had sacrificed so much to accomplish. There is still another man living to whom, next to Cavour, the unity of Italy is due. Garibaldi has been called the Washington of Italy, but he seems to resemble still more closely his own countryman Cincinnatus; he was a true Roman, and Garibaldi is such another as he. When work is to be done, or danger to be incurred, Garibaldi is everywhere, when the rewards of success are to be distributed, he is nowhere to be found; he has sacrificed himself freely in his country's cause, and has sought neither power, honours, nor riches for himself.

There is no country in Europe, except our own, which has been more clearly marked out by nature as the abode of one united people than Italy. The fair peninsula, "which Apennine parts, and the sea and the Alps surround," is almost as completely cut off from its neighbours as if it were an island. Throughout the whole of this singularly isolated country, we find a people of the same race, speaking the same language, loving the same literature, and acknowledging Italy as their common fatherland. With such natural bonds of union, it is hard to see what can so long have kept them asunder; but so it has been from the downfall of the Roman Empire to the present day, that Italy has been divided into a number of small states, whose boundaries appear almost as capricious as those of many counties and parishes in this country. These boundaries, drawn by the pen of the diplomatist, not by the hand of nature, are now all effaced, and the whole race of alien princes, Bourbons and Hapsburgs, are now swept away, and the old jealousies and hatreds forgotten. Until within the last few months was wanting the key-stone of Italian unity, and without Rome the fabric must always have been insecure. Now Italy is indeed free, "from the Alps to Mount Etna," and the Italian tricolour waves over the Capitol.

To a traveller from the north of Europe, the moment when he first descends from the snowy regions of Switzerland or Savoy, and finds himself in the classic land of Italy, is an epoch in his life which can never be forgotten. The charm of associations which history and poetry combine to throw around the people, and the landscape, whose deep azure blue is like nothing ever seen in this country, with the softness of the air and the brilliancy of all around, make it a sufficient happiness merely to live and breathe. We cannot wonder that an Italian should pine away in exile, or that no stranger should enter this "Garden of Europe" without longing to revisit it once more.

We have now every reason to hope that a new and glorious epoch is dawning for Rome, as well as for all Italy, and we may yet see Rome rise from her ruins, and the desolate Campagna become once more a fruitful cultivated plain. It is pleasing to know, that in spite of all disappointments, the Italians are still able to recognize in England a true friend, and to appreciate the sympathy felt with their cause by the great body of the British people. The union of Rome with Italy has not merely relieved a few hundred thousand Romans from an oppressive and hateful government; but it has at last accomplished the independence and consolidation of the whole Italian people. With Rome for the capital, the rivalries of Turin, Florence, and Naples disappear; the last foreign soldier has left Italian soil, and a united Italian people will take good care that the saying shall in future be verified, "L'Italia farà da se." The result of three great recent wars, in which Italians have been but secondary actors, or have taken no part at all, has been the rise of a liberated and united Italy; so true is it sometimes that—

> " Peace is wrought out of wrath by the swords of mankind,
> And the shout of free nations rolls forth on the wind ! "

"Beasts of Burden"
San Remo

CHAPTER X.

ADDRESS TO HIS CONSTITUENTS—SPEECHES IN PARLIAMENT—MEETS HIS
BROTHER IN THE TYROL.

IN addressing his constituents in Ayrshire after the session
of 1871, Sir David touched on the following points :—

The first important Government measure which we had to
discuss last year was that of Army Reform ; after debates protracted beyond almost all Parliamentary precedent, the policy of
the Government was affirmed in the most emphatic manner by
the House of Commons, and was subsequently as emphatically
negatived by the House of Peers. The subject appeared to me
to be an urgent one, involving the national safety and honour,
and the Government was bound to bring to an end this deadlock
of the legislature by the most rapid method which the Constitution afforded. No doubt the creation of peers would have had
this effect, but I venture to think that the Government adopted a
simpler and less violent method of carrying out the great military
reform of abolishing purchase by means of a Royal Warrant.

The next great measure, that of the Ballot, was met by the
Opposition with the same tactics which they employed against
the Army Organization Bill. It is clear that the result of such a
system can only end most disastrously ; if the Conservatives are
to abuse the forms of the Lower House, in order to delay measures,
and are then to use this as a pretext for the irresponsible majority
in the Upper House to reject those measures, they may indeed
prevent reform, but I think there is some danger that they may
cause revolution.

The third Government measure which was thrown out by these

unfortunate party struggles to which I have alluded, was the Scotch Education Bill. In this delay there are some compensating advantages ; we in Scotland know our own minds better than we did three years ago, and the experience afforded by the history of the same question in the sister kingdoms is most instructive. I believe now that the Scottish people are quite prepared for a really undenominational and compulsory system of education. If we do not adopt it, I feel satisfied that the Education Act will be a dead letter in those very places where it is now most required.

The cry of Home Rule is not one that British statesmen can afford to ignore or to neglect. The Irish people are in earnest about it, and we shall have to face it and to consider it. Self-preservation is undoubtedly the first of all laws, and it is quite clear that we cannot consent to the separation of Ireland from the empire, with the risk of her falling at some future time into the hands of a rival Power. There are, however, apart from such a contingency, many points in which a certain degree of home rule might possibly benefit Ireland, and would certainly benefit Great Britain. The principle of federation is quite in the ascendant now, not only in republics, kingdoms, and empires, but in our own colonies ; and it is possible that British statesmen may be called upon to consider, and even to adopt it, at no distant date, in these islands also.

The Treaty of Washington is to my mind one of the most satisfactory events of the past session. It has dispelled that bitter feeling which has prevailed in America against this country ever since the great civil war. This bitterness of feeling did not indeed involve any immediate danger, but it was clearly the duty of our Government to put an end to it if they possibly could. After repeated failures it has at last been accomplished. We have made some concessions indeed, but not more, I think, than justice demanded, to say nothing of the desirability of conciliating a high-spirited people smarting under a sense of injury, exaggerated perhaps, but not the less real. A permanent estrangement between the United Kingdom and the United States would produce far greater mischief than twenty *Alabamas*.

There is one more point to which I wish to refer, and that is the necessity, which has been so apparent during the past session, of revising the standing orders which regulate Parliamentary procedure, if the House of Commons is to transact the business

of the nation, and retain its character as the first deliberative
assembly in Europe, or in the world. A better division of labour,
and limitation of the powers now enjoyed by a few obstructives,
seem to me to be among the most urgent of the practical Parliamentary reforms at the present time.

In accordance with the notice he had given in the
previous session, Sir David, in March, 1872, moved for a
Select Committee to inquire and report on the best means
of promoting the despatch of Scotch Parliamentary business.
He made a long speech, in which he showed how little had
been done in three sessions for Scotland, by a Government
which numbered fifty-one out of sixty Scotch representatives among its supporters, and suggested the scheme of
Grand Committees. It may be noted that this is now, after
ten years, accepted as the best remedy for the delay of
business.

I might place the impediments which at present exist to
Scotch legislation under four heads, of which the last is certainly
the most important, and the one for which it seems the most
difficult to find a remedy. The first of these is, that Scotland is
at present without any official representation, either in the Cabinet
or in the House of Lords; the second is, that there exists, and
has existed since the Union, no efficient machinery for giving
Scotland the benefit of the United Kingdom legislation ; the third
impediment is, that the representatives of Scotland, a mere handful in this House, are liable to be outvoted, when tolerably
unanimous among themselves, by English and Irish members;
and the last is, that it is impossible for Parliament to give sufficient
time and attention to discuss in detail the measures which affect
Scotland only.

It seems to me that so long as the House of Commons takes
upon its shoulders to settle all the details of private legislation, as
well as all the details of public measures affecting only portions of
the United Kingdom, we shall fail in finding any remedy for the
evils of which we complain. If we could bring ourselves to treat
such public measures in somewhat the same manner in which mere
personal and local bills are treated now, a great deal of relief
would be afforded. When any measure has received the sanction

of this House, as not being contrary to the policy or the constitution of the empire, why should not the details of that measure be
referred to a public committee of those who are acquainted with
the subject, who are interested directly in it, and who are responsible to their constituents for the proper management and carrying
out of those details?   It seems to me, by some such change as
that, there would not only be economy of time and labour, but an
enhanced sense of responsibility in those concerned.   It is sometimes said now that the legislative machinery is choked with the
raw material, and requires relief.   If this be true, the wants of
Scotland deserve special consideration, as having been specially a
sufferer, partly owing no doubt to the patience and good temper
that the Scotch people have displayed.

In his visit to Gibraltar in the previous year, the abuses
connected with our position there attracted his notice, and
he took an opportunity of bringing the subject before the
House :—

In directing attention to the local revenue and expenditure of
Gibraltar, my object is to indicate that important reforms might
be effected in that military colony, if certain changes were made
in the method of raising the revenue, without either increasing or
diminishing its total amount.   There is one special matter in
which a great reform might be carried out, by the suppression of
the numerous low wine-shops, where drink of the worst quality
is obtained by the sailors and soldiers.   Licences have actually
been refused to regimental canteens on the ground that, "if
granted, a number of wine-shops licensed for the soldiers only
would be closed, and the revenue thereby diminished."   Those
who know the nature of these wine-shops, the company who
frequent them, and the quality of the liquor there furnished, will
no doubt consider any increase of revenue derived from their
maintenance as very dearly purchased at the expense of the
health and morals of our soldiers.   More than £5000 a year is
raised at Gibraltar from licences, but a Government financially so
prosperous has no excuse for maintaining such a system ; and,
even if the money is required, a reasonable duty on tobacco, now
free, will answer the twofold purpose of raising revenue, and
checking the contraband traffic now carried on with Spain.   The
present question is, whether, admitting the necessity of our retain-

ing this great fortress, we cannot prevent its being more than
a sentimental grievance to the proud, high-spirited people from
whom we wrested it, and against whom we have held it for more
than a century and a half. Spain has recently shown herself
worthy of the esteem and sympathy of free nations, and in no way
could we better prove our friendliness towards her and her
Government, than by exerting ourselves to repress smuggling, as
we are bound by treaty to do. If her Majesty's Government
would co-operate heartily with that of Spain in this matter, a great
injustice might be redressed, and much might be done towards
establishing a cordial understanding between two nations, who
have in common many great interests for the future, as well as
glorious traditions in the past.

In the discussion on Sir Wilfrid Lawson's resolution in
favour of this country withdrawing from all treaties of
guarantee, Sir David said :—

I wish to direct the attention of her Majesty's Government to
a particular class of guarantee treaties, which appears to me
exceedingly objectionable : they are conventions " for the protection of all routes of communication, natural or artificial, whether
by land or water, through the territories of the Republics of
Honduras and Nicaragua, between the Altantic and Pacific
Oceans." By the Honduras treaty, in return for certain concessions, of which two free ports are the chief, the strongest possible
guarantee is given by this country to the Republic, a guarantee
which can only be withdrawn upon six months' notice, and under
certain specified conditions. Considering the nature and position
of such a Republic as Honduras, its relations to its immediate
neighbours in Central America, and its past history, no incon-
siderable danger attaches to the signature of such a treaty, to say
nothing of the well-known Monroe doctrine, which might lead to
the most serious complications. The consideration of these
treaties has also an immediate practical bearing upon our present
policy ; a select committee of this House has been appointed to
consider the various projects for establishing railway communication between the Persian Gulf and the Mediterranean or Black
Sea. Should that committee report favourably of any one of
these schemes, it is only too probable that our Government will
be urged, and possibly induced, to contract with the Ottoman

Government a similar treaty to those with Honduras and Nicaragua. Against such a course the strongest protest should be entered beforehand ; we must, in fact, contract no more of these treaties, and we ought to take such steps as are consistent with honour to terminate those which already exist, especially in cases where it seems as if the national credit and safety were imperilled in order to promote the schemes of speculating capitalists.

His well-known interest in India, and his knowledge of the subject, led to his being appointed a member of the Committee, which sat during this session, to inquire into the Finances of India. As usual, he spoke in the debate on the Indian Budget of this year, taking up nearly the same line as Mr. Fawcett had done :—

There is no danger in India, either political or military, except such as is involved in the financial difficulty. There are changes rendered practicable by the progress of events, which would result in a considerable saving of expenditure, now that our dominion extends throughout India, and the various provinces are connected by telegraphs and railways. The existence of separate Commanders-in-chief, with their staffs in Bombay and Madras, seems to be productive of expense without any military advantage whatever. A saving could also be effected by a general employment of natives in the higher branches of the public service. A certain number of Europeans in the Indian Civil Service is essential in order to maintain the high tone for which that service has long been justly famous, and it is also essential for this purpose that the European element should be the very best obtainable. On the other hand, as Europeans are expensive, there should not be more than are absolutely necessary; at present there are a few native gentlemen in the Covenanted Civil Service, but these are paid at a needlessly high rate, as the best native talent can be secured on the spot at far lower rates. I would therefore suggest that a civil staff corps should be established, of limited numbers, and selected by competition as at present; that these civil officers should receive fixed rates of pay, according to their rank in the service, whether specially employed or not. Then all civil appointments should be thrown open, and be paid at such fair market rates as would secure the

M

services of good native officials.   When it was thought necessary to appoint a British official, he would draw the pay of the appointment, together with the staff pay of his own rank, while an outsider, native or European, would draw the pay of the appointment only.   A similar system prevails in the case of engineers in India : an officer of Royal Engineers drawing the pay of his rank in addition to that of any appointment which he may hold.   Under such a system economy might be combined with efficiency, and native officials might be amply paid without giving such salaries as would be objects of desire to influential, but ill-qualified Europeans.   At present the Indian Governments are subjected to considerable pressure on behalf of gentlemen from England, who are not members of the civil or military service, and are unacquainted with India.

His brother William came from India on furlough for two years in April, and joined the family at San Remo. In the Whitsuntide holidays Sir David went, by Harwich and Rotterdam, to meet them at Innsbruck on their way home.   Love of natural history made him visit every collection of animals, alive or dead, that he came near ; the enjoyment of watching their habits and making sketches of them never diminished.   He used to say that he had been to every zoological garden in Europe, and it was probably true ; he certainly went again and again to many of them, and knew their respective merits and peculiarities well.

May 12th, Rotterdam.—The most attractive sight of Rotterdam is the Zoological Garden.   It is kept up regardless of expense, and although there are not quite so many beasts as in Regent's Park, they look healthier and cleaner, with larger paddocks, in the case of the ruminants particularly.   Many rare species of animals are well represented, those from the Eastern Archipelago in particular, *e.g.* three fine specimens of the Anoa from Celebes, their horns carefully encased in leather.   A complete herd of huanacos, two huge Bactrian camels, and some splendid tigers and lions, all appeared to great advantage.   The aviaries are well constructed and of great size, so that the birds can fly about freely. A new sort of swan from Chili looked as if dipped in ink as to neck and head, and then topped off with red sealing-wax. A lot of ruffs were fully proving their title to be called "machetes pugnax," and were behaving in a most extraordinary manner. They seem to carry on their courtship, after the tournament is over, by standing motionless on one leg, their ruffs extended, their eyes half shut, and their long bills stuck upon the ground. They remain in this attitude during an indefinite period, the reeve looking complacently on, until another ruff approaches, when they at once begin fighting again. The variety of colouring in their plumage is very remarkable, if not unique in a wild bird. The axolotl is a very queer creature, a water salamander, with nostrils as well as gills. I spent several hours in the gardens.

May 16th, Innsbruck.—I found the little church, in which is the great lion of Innsbruck, the tomb of the Emperor Maximilian. It is indeed a splendid and unrivalled monument, for even the famous tombs of Burgos and Dijon do not equal it in elaborate detail and beauty of carving, nor indeed is their style similar. Here the marble alto and basso reliefs are carved with all the delicacy of Chinese ivory work, and represent the principal events in the life of Maximilian. Even to the minutest details the most scrupulous accuracy is observed, the dresses, the weapons, armorial bearings, architecture of buildings, and features of the principal personages, although on a Lilliputian scale. On the robe of a Pontiff the embroidered apostles are carefully sculptured, as are mythological frescoes on the walls of a palace. The number of faces is legion, and each has a characteristic expression, although it almost requires a magnifying-glass to observe it. The monument to Andreas Hofer, and his friends Speckbacher and Haspinger, is faced by another to the rest of the Tyrolese patriots, who fell in the war of independence. They certainly are fine fellows the Tyrolese, but the blind loyalty to the House of Austria, which mainly prompted their gallant efforts, was not the same ennobling influence, as the love of civil and religious liberty, by which their neighbours, the Swiss, were animated in their foreign contests. Although in many respects a similar people, the Tyrolese are far behind the Swiss in education, enterprise, and wealth.

May 24th, Berchtesgaden.—Willie and I were up long before any one else was stirring, and walked to the König See, a charming early march in the fresh morning. The scenery is quite

Norwegian, the surrounding "fields" being well wooded, and descending so precipitously into the water, that no space is left even for the passage of a chamois. We wandered into the forest in the direction of the great Watzmann, whose precipices frown over the lake. While botanizing under the shadow of a great cliff, the rattling of stones attracted our attention, and looking across the ravine we saw four chamois scrambling along a narrow ledge, while a patriarchal old buck looked down on them from above. At first they were within a hundred yards of us, and we watched them for a long distance, bounding and clambering over the rocks. We returned much pleased to have seen the gemsbok in his native wilds.

May 25th.—To avoid the extreme heat we made an early start to drive from Salzburg to Ischl. An ill-used animal is never seen in any vehicle; all fat and sleek, while the whips carried by drivers are a mere pretence, and have a gay-coloured tassel or two instead of knots. The wild flowers and butterflies were as beautiful and varied as ever, and the scenery diversified by forest, lake, and mountain, our old friend the Watzmann putting in a momentary appearance ; altogether it was a charming drive.

May 28th, Augsburg.—A portion of the city walls has been levelled into boulevards since we were here in 1858, but elsewhere the lofty brick fortifications, with their curious old gates, remain intact, and roe-deer feed peacefully in the grass-grown moat. Fugger's house is covered with new frescoes, and the old-fashioned houses, whose lofty gables all turn towards the street, are painted in various colours. Certainly Augsburg is a place, where "memories haunt the pointed gables as the rooks," or more accurately the storks, which may be seen calmly superintending their nests, and looking down amicably upon their fellow-citizens in the streets. The wine list of the "Drei Mohren" is as voluminous as ever, and the moderate samples, which we tried, are as good. In this very house the Emperor Charles V. was entertained by Fugger with a princely and lavish hospitality resembling that of Andrea Doria at Genoa, and, like Doria, Fugger, merely a private citizen, has left his name inseparably connected with the name and history of his native city. Long may it be before such interesting mediæval relics as old Augsburg are improved utterly off the face of the earth.

May 30th.—This morning Mayence was gaily decorated with

banners, the streets were strewed with daisies and peony petals, and crowded with spiked helmets and little girls in spotless white. All this in honour of Corpus Christi. The well-known scenery of the Rhine appeared to great advantage—the grey walls of the frequent feudal towers rising among the green leaves of May, the towns and villages decked with garlands and flags, guns firing, crowded steamers passing, long processions marching upon the banks; everything had a gay and holiday appearance. The island of Nonnenwerth in particular was overrun with girls in white, whose snowy robes seen through the trees gave the place quite a celestial appearance.

As soon as the Parliamentary session was over he joined the South Gloucester Militia, which were at Aldershot that year for their training, and he was with them during the autumn manœuvres on Salisbury Plain. He went down in September with his brother to their shooting at Ben Hope, in Sutherlandshire, but was not there long, as he hastened his return to Meredith in order to meet E. H. Percival, who had come home from India on short leave.

In December the brothers escorted their mother and youngest sister, with her two little children, an ayah, and other impedimenta, to San Remo. The previous winter their two unmarried sisters had bought a piece of land in one of the best situations there, and in the course of the summer a charming house, which they called Villa Speranza, had been built and finished. Thanks to the dryness of the climate, and the skill and industry of the Italian workmen, the prettily painted rooms were ready for occupation by the beginning of November. The family all liked the place, and began to feel quite at home there, laying out the garden and beautifying the house.

CHAPTER XI.

1873.

ALGERIA AND TUNIS — INDIAN FINANCE COMMITTEE — THE CHANNEL
ISLANDS — WOMAN'S SUFFRAGE MEETING — BATTLE-FIELDS OF THE
FRANCO-GERMAN WAR—DISSOLUTION OF PARLIAMENT.

SIR DAVID and his brother stayed only a fortnight at San Remo at this time, and started together for a tour in Algeria.

January 3rd, Nice.—The Douane on the Italian frontier caused very little delay, but the indignation of an Englishman was roused by being questioned as to his nationality, and he produced his passport exclaiming, "C'est le premier temps que j'ai jamais été demandé pour lui." Monte Carlo is perhaps the most picturesque spot on the whole Riviera, and now almost the last refuge of the gambler in Europe. People must be very short of ideas, who can find continuous amusement in losing five-franc pieces in this solemn, decorous manner, at a game devoid of skill, and where no relief is ever afforded to the feelings by either a laugh or an execration. The view is exquisite of the fortress rock of Monaco, over a "bay the peacock's neck in hue," and in spite of the gaming hells, it looks very like an earthly paradise.

January 4th, S.S. "Péluse."—We sailed from Marseilles on

board the *Péluse*, about the most comfortable vessel I was ever in; the saloon is on the main-deck, extending across from side to side, and the large ports alternate with elegant paintings.

January 7th, Algiers.—We were off at 7 a.m., and bowled along an excellent road to Staoueli; first-rate roads run in all directions from Algiers, well engineered as well as thoroughly kept up: the French, like the Romans, grudge neither labour nor expense in maintaining open means of communication, and utilize the military for that purpose. Staoueli is now occupied by a confraternity of Trappist monks, who possess 1100 hectares, and are engaged in converting a waste into a fruitful garden. At the convent we halted, and the excellent fathers at once admitted us, and invited us to partake of soup. Silence is preserved inside, except as regards Divine worship, but as soon as we emerged into the outer courts our guide became quite chatty. The monks are usefully employed in agricultural, pastoral, and mechanical labours, having orchards, vineyards, flocks and herds, besides workshops of every sort. They are 115 in number, and have a lot of military prisoners working under them, guarded by one or two armed sentries. Their library seems to contain but dull reading, chiefly sermons and hagiology; but, owing no doubt to an industrious and useful mode of life, the good fathers look cheerful enough, as they tramp along in broad-brimmed hats of the orthodox hermit shape, and with their gowns tucked up for work. "Soup" meant a most excellent *déjeûner*, without flesh meat indeed, but comprising a wonderful variety of delicious vegetables and fruit, as well as fish, omelette, macaroni cheese, and three sorts of wine. We "ravened" especially among the dried fruits and sweet wine, and staggered away, after making a little speech to the father on duty, and depositing our mite in the alms-box at the gate.

January 8th, Bougie. — The boatmen and porters give no trouble, and are kept in awe by the fierce official who finds himself on the quay. Altogether in Algeria one has the comfortable feeling that one is a "saheb," and an honorary member of the dominant race. "Picturesque," in the literal sense, is the epithet for the scenery of Bougie: there is an old Moorish arch, with a fine palm tree, which, with the boats in the harbour and the fort above, would furnish a perfect subject for Turner, Salvator Rosa, or Claude Lorraine.

Having despatched our portmanteaus by steamer to meet us

at Constantine, we only required two mules for ourselves ; a young
Frenchman, in a picturesque contrabandist costume and bristling
with weapons, was on a third, while a fourth was heaped with his
luggage, on the top of which perched a small and cheeky Arab.
With three dismounted natives in our train we started, and were
not long on our mules before we found that walking would be a
relief to ourselves, if not to them, as their pace was of the slowest.
No sooner, however, were we on foot, and striding along at nearly
double the former pace, than our Arabs were on the mules, keeping with us easily.   In fact, the only way to expedite our march,
as we soon discovered, was to toddle ourselves, and let our muleteers mount, using the beasts only to ford streams, of which a few
still remain unbridged.   The life of colonists here reminds one
partly of that of Indian officials, partly of that of settlers in the far
West.   The recent insurrection had some resemblance to the
Indian Mutiny, but it was even more like such outbreaks of the
Red Indians as have so frequently occurred in American frontier
history.   The Kabyles and Arabs, however, are not to be classed
with the Redskins for cruelty, or thirst of blood, and already the
colonists appear to have recovered complete confidence, while the
whole of Algeria is a model country as far as the safety and comfort of travellers are concerned.   In fact, Algeria is a land of
plenty, reminding one in this respect of America, only that the
food here is well cooked as well as abundant, which cannot
always be said of the Transatlantic cuisine.

January 12th.—Constantine is situated on a peninsula of rock,
cut off on three sides from the surrounding country by a deep
ravine with perpendicular sides, and so narrow that you do not see
it until you are close to the edge, and it is only here and there that
a glimpse can be obtained of the stream, to whose gradual operation, and not to any volcanic cataclysm this extraordinary chasm
is due.   We scrambled along a path on the face of the cliff, amid
masses of aloes and prickly pear, and were rewarded by a splendid
view.   The chasm is peopled by swarms of kestrels and jackdaws,
the latter somewhat resembling the Indian crow, both as to size
and marking, having grey heads and black foreheads, the reverse
of our common jackdaw.   We entered the gloomy gorge ; on each
side rise the cliffs for hundreds of feet, actually overhanging in
many places.   Passing under a mighty arch of travertine, a
second comes in sight, rather a tunnel than an arch, and its

gloomy blackness seems like the very gate of Hades. Nothing can be more thoroughly Dantesque and infernal, even to the smell, which, combined with the approach of darkness, deterred us from penetrating farther. It is a picture for Gustave Doré, quite unsurpassed in weird grandeur ; one or two Arabs, wrapped in their white burnouses, wandering across the foreground, enhanced the eerie effect, and peopled the scene with appropriate spectral figures.

January 15th, Batna.—We drove out to the Pic des Cèdres, 6500 feet. After a drive of ten miles we proceeded on foot, and found that the mountains are entirely covered with cedars of all ages and sizes, from grand old veterans, with gnarled trunks and broad-spreading branches, to healthy young seedlings a few feet high. Most of them exhibit on the upper surface of their foliage the silvery bluish tinge which characterizes the Lebanon cedars, but many of the younger trees are of a much yellower green, almost as if they were a different variety. The cones are similar to those of the Lebanon, but rather smaller, and the wood, when cut, has the same fragrant smell. The climb proved to be a pretty stiff one, as we soon got into deep snow, and the ascent is complicated by trees and rocks. The actual summit is bare of trees, and the view is magnificent, extending over the plains of Batna to the snowy ranges of the Aurès in one direction, in another over a great tract of mountainous country, beautifully timbered and watered, with open grassy glades ; to the north is an expanse of hill and plain, with occasional lakes, stretching away towards Constantine, to the south the view reaches to the margin of the Sahara. As on Mount Tabor, the game here consists of " panthers and partridges." We saw a lot of the latter, but they were wild; we also observed the familiar misselthrush, woodpeckers, and ravens.

January 16th.—We drove to the great Roman city of Lambaesis, the remains of which cover the country for miles. We wandered for hours among the ruins. No pains are taken to preserve these relics of Roman magnificence ; they are strewed about in glorious confusion, a fine head of Marcus Aurelius lying prostrate on the ground, recognizable at once from its resemblance to the great equestrian statue at the Capitol. This great city is now represented by a prison and a straggling village ; the convicts are employed in all kinds of useful and productive labour, making everything they require for themselves. In the prison dress the distinction between Europeans and Africans is not conspicuous, and the fellows look quite cheerful at their work. The climate at healthy, and a prisoner might be a good deal worse off than is Lambessa. The civil intelligent Deputy showed us a most beautiful mosaic of the Four Seasons and other devices, as fine a work of the sort as I have ever seen, the faces being very large and full of expression, and the colouring brilliant.

At Philippeville they separated, and while his brother returned to San Remo, Sir David went on to Tunis, changing steamers at Bône, where he landed.

January 18th, Bône.—It is remarkable how readily Christian, Mussulman, and Israelite amalgamate in these coast towns ; they live mixed up together in the same quarter, their children go to the same schools, and the barriers of race, language, and religion seem to a great extent broken down. A bare-legged Arab in a burnouse may be seen warmly grasping the hand of an official in gold lace cap, and wherever an Indigène can pay his way he is allowed to go without let or hindrance. It is different in India. In the Eastern portion of Algeria the Maltese, and in the Western the Spaniards, are the most numerous immigrants, and the latter are suspected of conspiring to restore Oran to Spain, only Spain is not such a fool. Poor, dear England is generally credited with all sorts of plots and schemes, of fomenting sedition, and instigating massacres, from her supposed jealousy of France. Probably a certain amount of foundation may exist for such exaggerated and absurd notions in the traditional policy still maintained in the Levant by a few consular officials of the old school. In the Western Mediterranean, moreover, the batteries of Gibraltar and Malta afford Great Britain a *locus standi*, and confer upon her an importance which makes it difficult to believe that she can abstain from "meddling and muddling."

We drove up to the site of ancient Hippo ; here in an orchard, pink with almond and peach blossom, is a monument to Augustine, the great bishop of Hippo. Storks' nests are conspicuous here, but an Indigène asserted that they had gone far to the south, to some desert lakes, where they assume the human form. This is a singular superstition, but if they breed here in

spring, why do they disappear now, when it is as warm as during
the summer of those northern countries, where they also breed?
There is no winter here, and frogs are croaking in every ditch;
where are the storks and the swallows?

January 20th, Tunis.—We started on horseback for the ruins
of Carthage; the enormous cisterns, which extend over many
acres of ground, are the only important remains now visible, but
they give a grand idea of the wealth and greatness of the city. In
the palmy days of Carthage, the province of Africa, corresponding
in extent very nearly to the Regency of Tunis, contained, it is
said, 17,000,000 inhabitants; its population is now about one-
twelfth of that number, having considerably diminished of late
years from cholera and famine. The soil has not lost its fertility,
for one good harvest, even imperfectly cultivated as it is, will
support the inhabitants for two or three years. But now two or
three foreign steamers, lying in the open roadstead, represent the
"dusky forest of Byrsa's thousand masts," which once almost
monopolized the commerce of the world. It is a far cry from
Hannibal to the present Bey of Tunis, a bankrupt broken-down
feudatory of the Turkish Empire; these shores indeed "obey the
stranger, slave and savage." We cantered home as fast as we
had come, the horses being quite fresh after a ride of some
twenty-four miles; altogether, what with the interest of the
locality, the pleasant company, good horses, and fine weather,
this ride to Carthage has been as agreeable an expedition as ever
I took part in. The whole affair reminded me of India, and
indeed there is much in the hospitable friendly mode of life of
the foreign residents at Tunis which resembles that of society at
a pleasant Indian station. Not even in the City of Palaces, however, are such handsome houses to be found as the British
consul's, which presents, with its marble halls, a fine specimen of
modern Moorish architecture.

He returned, after two days at Tunis, by the same
steamer to Bône, and thence to Marseilles, touching at
Ajaccio. In an hour or two of a dark rainy night, he
managed to see the house of the Bonapartes, where the
great Napoleon lived, and even to search out the Napo-
leonic statues, which adorn the town.

January 24th, S.S. " Oncle Joseph."—I found the commandant
excellent company; he is specially desirous of promoting pro-
vident and co-operative institutions among sailors and all classes
of working men.   The Swiss are regarded as models of prudence
in saving money, as in most other respects; in fact, Republican
institutions receive a general tribute of respect as exhibited in
Switzerland, "only we are not fit for them,"—a humiliating con-
fession for any people to make.

Whatever failings the French may display in their home-
politics, there can be little doubt that Algeria is prospering under
their rule, and in many respects their mode of governing a conquered people of alien race and religion will contrast favourably
with that of the British in India.   In Algeria neither trouble nor
expense has been grudged upon works of public utility; and in
developing the means of communication and irrigation, by roads,
bridges, lighthouses, and artesian wells, the French are worthy
successors of the Romans, who made Africa a garden from Nile
Delta to the Pillars of Hercules.   In carrying out this policy,
Algeria has not been crushed beneath a load of debt in order
that French capitalists might have a secure investment, but the
money of the French taxpayer has been spent freely for the protection and development of the struggling dependency.   Even
now the direct annual cost of Algeria to the French treasury is
estimated at fully a million sterling; at present Algeria certainly
derives greater benefit than France from the connection subsisting between the two countries.   As a colony, in the sense of a
field for French emigration, Algeria has not been a success; for
of the 300,000 Christian immigrants, who have been induced to
settle in the country, a large proportion are foreigners—Swiss,
Spaniards, Italians, Maltese.   It is somewhat strange that Frenchmen are not more disposed to settle in a country where they
would enjoy so much of what they value at home, along with a
fine climate and cheap living.   The history of Canada, Hayti,
the Mauritius, if fairly considered, prove the French to be, even
under adverse circumstances, very successful colonists; but
Algeria is not a true colony, any more than Java or Hindustan.

He returned to London in time for the opening of Parliament.   It does not appear that there were any subjects
taken up in this session that especially interested him,

except the Indian Finance Committee, which continued its
sittings. He was a most regular attendant at this committee, and always on the alert during the examination of
witnesses, but rather as a vigilant and intelligent observer
than as a questioner. The principal promoter of this
inquiry, Mr. Henry Fawcett, M.P., writes of him : "We sat
together during several sessions on the committee which
inquired into the financial condition and general administration of India, and I can well remember the keen unflagging
interest which he took in every question calculated to promote the welfare of the people of that country. During
the many years that we were in Parliament together, I had
frequent opportunities of observing that, in his political
actions, he was guided by the most unselfish motives : and,
never having any private aim of his own to promote, he
alone thought of advancing those political principles to
which he was so sincerely attached. Among the pleasantest
recollections of my life are those of the hours I spent in his
society, and there has been hardly any friendship which
I valued more highly than that of David Wedderburn.
I feel that any words that I can write will only give a
very feeble idea of the affection and respect I felt for him."

The Easter vacation of this year he spent in the
Channel Islands.

April 13th, St. Helier.—An air of general prosperity characterizes the country, which bears a considerable resemblance to
portions of Devonshire : the fences are partly banks, partly
hedges ; the trees are either in the lanes or hedgerows ; and the
only spots not arable or pasture are covered with golden gorse.
The town of St. Helier contains fully half the population of the
island, the other half being scattered broadcast over the country,
and there are hardly any villages. There is an appalling super-
fluity of women in Jersey, an excess of 5500 in a total population
of 56,000 ; as they are a handsome lot it is easy to see that this
must be a dangerous station for the British garrison.

Every little bay in the island seems to have its breakwater ;

two are in sight from Mont Orgueil : one of these is of great length, and must have been very costly, but appears to be quite unnecessary. Forts and barracks are sprinkled about freely, and the islands are full of armed men, British regulars and indigenous militia. It is really great nonsense keeping up this elaborate system of local defence, as the Channel Islands could only be seriously menaced in the event of a great disaster befalling the British Channel fleet. In any other case an occupying hostile force must infallibly be cut off, and the fate of the islands must depend upon the result of a struggle, which would certainly not be decided upon their shores. Against a mere raid the islanders ought to be able and willing to defend themselves. The militia are sturdy-looking fellows, but their drill is not continuous enough to give them great military smartness. Not merely natives, but foreign residents also are liable to military service ; exemption, however, can be obtained by a moderate payment. The town of St. Helier certainly contains capital shops, and you can get a glass of brandy and twelve pence for a shilling !

April 18th, St. Peter Port, Guernsey.—I chartered a small trap, and drove to Rocquaine Bay on the west coast. The " Creux es Fées " is a perfect dolmen, still covered with its mound, and forming a cave in which cattle find shelter. It is constructed in the same massive style as the Guernsey dolmens generally. Close by appears to be another, not excavated ; and, in fact, this small island probably contains more fine specimens than any other area of equal extent. Not far distant is also a Bauta stone, or menhir, of large size, standing by itself in the middle of a field. I was glad to observe Cornish choughs here, and I understand that the Wild Birds Protection Act has been adopted in the Channel Islands, where Acts of Parliament are valid only after registration by the local Legislature. In driving about Guernsey one is struck by the great number of elegant and comfortable houses, and the absence of anything like squalor and misery. There are no paupers in the country, and only a few in the town, and while there are not many rich, there are hardly any poor. The cause of this state of matters is industry combined with frugality, these qualities being greatly fostered by the subdivision of land. The quantity of glass in Guernsey is quite astonishing ; it is chiefly for the growth of grapes without artificial heat.

April 20th.—I went to Hauteville, where Victor Hugo had given me a rendezvous, and I had the pleasure of a long chat with the plucky old man, and his sister-in-law, Madame Chénay. He was surprised and pleased to find how "advanced" my political views are, not often meeting Englishmen who hold Republican opinions. He says that in twenty-five years continental Europe will be a great federal Republic, while England will cling to her antiquated institutions for a quarter of a century longer. As for kings and queens, he quotes the analogy of bees, and says he will admit the advantage of such functionaries when he can find a race of human beings of thrice the average stature, and monopolizing the power of propagating the human species ; queen bees, not drones, of course, were in his mind. He praised the prudence of the English governing classes, who have conceded liberty to the people, but have withheld power from them ; whose rule in fact is : "All for, nothing by, the people." This of course is only a very partial truth, but there is a good deal in it. When I rose to take leave Madame Chénay proposed to show me the house, and although Hugo maintained, "Ça ne vaut pas la peine d'être vue," I gladly accepted the proposal. It is furnished in a very peculiar style, or medley of styles, with tapestry, wood-carving, Dutch tiles, china of sorts, and some remarkable hangings of bead work and kincob, which once adorned the rooms of Queen Christina of Sweden. Among the most interesting relics is a table with the inkstands and manuscripts of Lamartine, Alexandre Dumas, George Sand, and Victor Hugo himself. Across a chair in the dining-room a chain is fastened, so that no mortal may occupy what is intended for the use of the great author's ancestors, when they assist at his repasts, as he believes them to do.

April 21st.—I took leave of Guernsey with regret, having been treated with much kindness and hospitality during my short stay.

While the House was sitting, he, as an officer of militia, attended the School of Instruction at Wellington Barracks, and for a month had to work hard. There was parade in the morning and in the afternoon, as well as book work ; he never missed a drill, and easily obtained his certificate of efficiency. At the close of the session he went down for a short time to the shooting in Sutherlandshire, and on his

way back visited friends in Ayrshire. After his return
home, he presided at a "Woman's Suffrage Meeting," held
on October 15th in Gloucester, at which he introduced his
friend, Mrs. Fawcett. She says of him, " I do not think he
ever missed a single opportunity, while he was in Parliament, of voting in favour of the removal of the electoral
disabilities of women; and, in all respects, he was a most consistent advocate of perfect justice and fair play to women."
In the course of his speech at the meeting, he said :—

I for one do not expect that when this bill becomes law any
additional strength will be given to the Liberal party in general, or
to the advanced section to which I have the honour to belong.   I
think reason, common sense, and judgment ought to be sufficient,
without any ulterior motives, to induce all to support this movement.   Ladies are by no means unanimous in their demands for
the suffrage, or no doubt they would be successful in getting it ;
the result is considerable apathy on the question.

There is one practical reform which I think may be carried
out in the present Parliament, and I intend during the ensuing
session to do what I can towards it by introducing a bill upon the
subject.   It is to obtain permission for women to study, and take
medical degrees at those Universities in Scotland, which have
hitherto been celebrated for their medical teaching.   There are, I
believe, a great many ladies, who, while they deprecate anything
like political privileges, object to the state of the law, which now
prevents young women from having their fair share of the great
endowments in this country for educational purposes, which ex-
cludes them from many honourable callings for which they are
well fitted, and which takes from married women the ownership of
their property, and the guardianship of their children.   I would
say to those ladies who wish to get these laws amended, that they
can only do so, first by obtaining the franchise, and then by
making use of it.   A very short experience of the working of Parliamentary questions proves to any one, that an unrepresented
class or individual find their interests neglected and ignored ; and
when ladies become electors they will receive from candidates for
Parliamentary honours, and full-blown legislators, that attention
which they have not yet been able to obtain.

In October Lady Wedderburn and her daughters started
for San Remo, and he went with them, to act as courier, as
far as Melun. ·From there he returned to see the principal
battle-fields of the Franco-German War.

October 23rd, Paris.—Pouring rain rendered the Louvre
Museum a most agreeable place for spending the day, and for
several hours I wandered through its endless galleries. The halls
of modern sculpture, which I now visited for the first time, possess
no doubt works of considerable merit, but the classical statues are
as superior to these as *they* are to Madame Tussaud's wax-works.
On one side are seen dignity, symmetry, and originality, on the
other contortions, sensationalism, and imitation. The art of
sculpture is now almost extinct as a creative and original art, and
even Thorvaldsen and Canova can but imitate classical models,
"such cunning they who dwell on high have given unto the
Greek."

October 25th.—The distant view from the heights of Mont-
martre is truly grand, embracing on one side the entire city of
Paris, on the other the great plain of St. Denis. Standing here
one can realize the gigantic nature of the task undertaken by the
Germans, who hemmed in this vast city, with all its surrounding
suburbs and forts, and closed it in as hermetically as the Romans
did with Jerusalem.

October 27th, Sedan.—The excellent Pasteur Gulden took me
over the battle-field, or rather the series of fields, lying all around
the town, where the great struggle of September 1, 1870, took
place. The fortifications of Sedan are picturesque, but old-
fashioned, and there are no outlying forts, so that no real protection could be afforded to the beaten troops, when they poured
into the town. The streets were full of demoralized soldiers,
wounded men, loose horses, ammunition waggons full of gunpowder and live shells, every element of misery and danger;
all around rose smoke, and the glare of burning villages, and even
of houses in the town, which the German shells had set on fire.
The Emperor then took the only course which could have prevented a most frightful catastrophe, in fact the utter destruction
of the town and all whom it contained; for his prompt and unconditional surrender the people of Sedan owe him a deep debt of
gratitude, for a little false pride must have involved their ruin.

N

As it was, the town hardly suffered any injury, but its resources were strained to the utmost by the charge of 16,000 wounded, equal to all its inhabitants, man, woman, and child.

October 29th, Metz.—The Germans are constructing an immense fortress here, which will be the key, not only of Metz, but of France or Germany, opening the way to the latter, closing it for ever to the former nation. A great many workmen at high wages are employed, and are making rapid progress; there could not be a greater contrast than that between the condition of the fortifications of Metz, in 1870, when about to become the base of operations in a gigantic war, and now, when the risk of war is indefinitely small. "Si vis pacem, para bellum," say my German friends here, and in this case I believe that they are right. The German Government, however, really seems to be forcing the pace a little too much, overworking its officers and its children.

October 31st, Luxemburg.—The political position of Luxemburg is most peculiar, of that portion at least of the duchy which is not Belgian. Nominally governed by a Regent in the name of the King of Holland, it is in reality quite as independent of Holland as it is of its neighbours, Germany, France, and Belgium; and governs itself much as the Channel Islands do. It belongs to the Zollverein, but its coinage consists of francs and centimes, and it has a mint of its own, at least for copper. The Dutch tricolour is in use, but hardly any Hollanders now reside here, except Prince Henry, the Regent. The language is a German *patois*, with a considerable admixture of Walloon words, and educated Luxemburghers prefer the use of French to that of German, although they speak both languages. The country people are bigoted Roman Catholics, and sympathized strongly with France in the late war.

The two brothers spent November and December alone together at Meredith, hunting, shooting, and enjoying each other's society. In January, Sir David, alarmed at the state of his sister Margaret's health, went to see her at San Remo, but had not been there many days before the news reached him of the sudden and unexpected dissolution of Parliament. He hurried back at once to Ayrshire to confer with his constituents. Unfortunately, several of his most influential supporters had recently died, and the register showed a considerable increase in the number of Conservative voters. The Liberal Party, and especially the tenant farmers, were however ready with their offers of support, and again agreed to guarantee the expenses. But although they declared that no one else would have so good a chance of success as Sir David, he was unwilling to give them the trouble and cost of a contest, the result of which was more than doubtful, giving as his reasons :—

The course which I felt it my duty to pursue upon the liquor licensing question has incurred the hostility of a numerous and powerful body—namely, those interested in maintaining the existing system. In addition to this, it has been intimated to me by constituents who were formerly supporters, that at a new election they could not vote for me. The reasons assigned were various, but mainly because of my holding the views of the more advanced section of the Liberal party.

It was ultimately decided not to contest the seat on this occasion, and Colonel Alexander was returned unopposed. The correctness of Sir David's judgment was shown by the result of the election in 1880, when the Hon. N. de C. Dalrymple, the Liberal candidate, was defeated by a majority of 247.

While still in Ayrshire, he heard the sad news of the death of his sister, on account of whose health the family had spent the last three winters at San Remo. This made him anxious to return to his mother, and after paying a visit to his sister and Colonel Hope, who now commanded the Brigade Depôt at Stirling, he again started for Italy.

Even on this occasion he, as usual, contrived to see something of interest by the way. He slept at Lyons, and in the course of a day, between there and Marseilles, stopped both at Avignon and Arles.

February 22nd, Avignon.—I proceeded on a pilgrimage to the cemetery, where John Stuart Mill is buried, close to the little house at which A. H. Brown and I visited him two years ago. On a broad marble slab are inscribed the virtues of Harriet Mill: "Were there even a few hearts and intellects like hers, this earth would already become the hoped-for heaven." The tomb is surrounded with flowers, and carefully tended, but there is not a word to tell that her husband has been laid beside her.

There is no doubt that, far from being disappointed at the decision that he should not then contest Ayrshire, Sir David hailed the release, at least for a time, from what he felt to be the drudgery and restraint of Parliamentary life. Instead of seeking a seat elsewhere, he was soon eagerly planning a lengthened tour to Australia and New Zealand.

Officer of Court Singhalese

Ratamahatmeya

District Court Kandy

Moorman

Kandian Chief

CHAPTER XII.

1874.

April 2nd, Venice.—When the day arrived I was very loth to leave Villa Speranza, and its inmates. In all my distant travels I shall not see any pleasanter sight than the face of the little "Rascal" [his nephew], who came to see me off at the San Remo station. It was a moonlit night when I reached Venice, and I had a charming row through the silent canals to the hotel. The black gondola gliding mysteriously through moonlight and shadow, no sound audible but the warning cry of the gondolier, as he rapidly turns a sharp corner with a dexterous twist of his oar, the almost total absence of apparent life stirring in the city at the hour of 11 p.m., all combine to give a romantic character to the very prosaic errand of hurrying to one's hotel in search of supper. Whatever places may have changed of late years, Venice has remained exactly as I remember her in 1847, and as she must have been long before then. She is quite unlike any other city, and retains her ancient characteristics in spite of railroads and steamers.

April 7th, S.S. " Ceylon."—We have a very pleasant company on board. I have got my little rubber, agreeable neighbours at dinner, and am gratified to find in Captain Orman, our skipper, a chess-player quite equal in force to myself.

April 17th.—Aden has increased and flourished since the canal was opened. We paid a visit to a large village inhabited by Africans, and were much struck with its peculiarities. The dwellings were framed and fenced with bamboos, and covered with mats, the streets were swarming with fat, pot-bellied children, gaunt cats, and tame buzzards, and there were plenty of women, but not a man was to be seen. We took the opportunity of ingratiating ourselves with these black ladies, some of whom were by no means ugly, having an Egyptian, not a negro cast of countenance, with intelligent and expressive eyes, and their hair made up à la Sphinx. A crowd of women and children soon collected round us, and seemed gratified at our examining and touching their ornaments, necklaces, and bracelets of silver, amber, and glass.

April 19th, S.S. " Khiva."—About sunset we saw, just ahead, a dhow lying becalmed with huge sail flapping, and a sort of flag hoisted half-mast high. There were crowds of people on board her, and they appeared to be endeavouring to attract our attention ; it was not, however, until they lowered a boat that this was fully realized, and the captain at once stopped the engines, while the *Khiva* came majestically round to meet the boat. Poor wretches ! it must have been a joyful sight for them, as the dhow proved to be from Bombay, with fifty-five persons on board, and without water for three days past. It is a shame that such a vessel should be allowed to go to sea, crammed with pilgrims, and without any possibility of affording them proper food or shelter.

April 27th, Colombo.—I started with two brother Scots for the drive from Galle of seventy-two miles. We had heard a good deal of the heat, the dust, the monotony of the road, the discomfort of the vehicles, and the badness of the horses. Perhaps our luck was exceptionally good, but I certainly never had a pleasanter drive. We were bowled along at a smart canter the whole way, and were charmed with the beauty and novelty of the scenes through which we passed. The road runs generally close to the sea through a continuous series of villages, embowered in the most luxuriant and varied foliage, the trees almost meeting overhead; it is crowded with bullock-carts and foot passengers, and the sea is covered with canoes, the whole district is evidently very populous. We met a marriage party, the bride crowned with flowers, and strings of Buddhist priests with shaven heads, in long yellow robes, and each carrying an umbrella and a fan. These articles are, or ought to be, all the property which they possess, but like priests of other denominations, they are not so rigid as they might be in keeping their vows of poverty.

April 29th, Peradeniya, Kandy.—I was met by A. C. Lawrie, and conveyed to his comfortable bungalow, both of us being much pleased at meeting. We took an early walk in the beautiful botanical gardens, where every tropical plant appears to flourish. Groups of palms of many different species, crowned by the mighty talipot, the handsomest of all; huge forest trees covered with brilliant blossom, either their own or that of immense creepers; bunches of bamboos with green and yellow stems, and feathery crests eighty or ninety feet high; ferns, orchids, and flowers of every sort grow in the greatest luxuriance, and are arranged rather with a view to picturesque effect than scientific order. In this *Paradiso terrestre* the evil principle is represented by swarms of leeches, which make at you even across the gravel walks, and fasten on your ankles, unless detected while ascending the boot. It is very comical to watch them peering about with their heads in the air, and then hastily proceeding by strides equal to their own length towards the intended victim.

I went with Lawrie to his court in Kandy, and sat for several hours listening to the cases, which are conducted through interpreters, and sketching the witnesses and officers of the court. The lawyers are a respectable body of men, most of them quite European looking, and the pleadings are in English. The dress of the Kandyan gentleman may be styled "low," as it begins at his waist, but when it does begin it is most voluminous, descending to his feet, with an enormous roll of stuff round his middle. His head is bare, as a rule, with short hair, and mutton-chop whiskers, quite unlike the low country Singhalese, with their tortoise-shell combs, long hair, and scanty beards. The chiefs wear circular flat hats of a peculiar shape, and every one carries a red and green talipot umbrella.

At the great Temple of the Tooth we found the lay incumbent, or chief officer, waiting to show us the interior. It was very hot inside, with an overpowering smell of various sacred flowers, of which great quantities are offered daily by the faithful. The unpretending exterior of the temple does not prepare one for the wealth of jewellery and gold, which is contained in the *sanctum sanctorum*, within the ivory doors. In a strong iron cage is the shrine of Buddha's tooth, covered with precious stones of all sorts, shapes, and sizes. The tooth itself is enclosed within seven cases, all of solid gold, except the outer which is silver-gilt, and all the sacred vessels are of gold encrusted with jewels. These are principally sapphires, rubies, cats'-eyes, pearls, and emeralds, all found in Ceylon; even the sand in the mortar of the temple is composed of precious stones. The place has never been looted, and is enormously rich.

May 11th, S.S. " Nubia."—It was with regret that I saw the lighthouse of Point de Galle disappear, and the Haycock become blue and dim in the distance, as I have had a very pleasant fortnight in Ceylon.

May 25th.—This morning we have been a fortnight at sea, without sighting land; the "wild sea birds that follow" are specially interesting, and all new to me. First, the stately Albatross, conspicuous from his white back, as well as his size, sailing about without ever flapping his wings, except after settling on the water. Then the Cape pigeon, a pretty little bird, barred and speckled with black and white, like a spotted woodpecker. Next, a large black-backed gull, called the Mollyhawk, resembling the Larus Marinus. The Sooty Albatross, a great brown bird with a light-coloured beak, and another called the Cape hen. All these, with a few ice birds or petrels, skimming like swallows or swifts over the waves, hovered in the wake of the ship, and greatly enlivened the scene; hitherto, during the voyage, we have scarcely seen a bird; not a living creature, in 'fact, except flying fish.

As it grew dark we reached the entrance to King George's Sound; here an unforeseen difficulty presented itself: on hearing that there had been a case of measles on board, the pilot refused to set foot on deck, but offered to guide us to the anchorage in his boat. Boats came about us, but did not dare to board us, and we were treated like lepers or pariahs. At last the health officer appeared, and, after much palaver, gave us leave to haul down the yellow flag to-morrow.   Australia appears to have carried the notion of quarantine to an absurd extent, but they have certainly contrived to keep all the worst epidemics out of the country.

May 26th, Albany.—We at last set foot on the great Australian continent; the "noble red man of the forest" soon made his appearance, and red he certainly was, smeared all over, head, face, and legs, with red ochre, the rest of his person being covered with kangaroo skins.   This colour denotes mourning, and a more hideous and forbidding specimen of the human race I never beheld, until a woman, or gin, appeared, and she was even uglier. Their hair is long, and done up in a sort of chignon, and they are armed with boomerangs and long javelins.   To obtain sixpence they threw the boomerang, one of the most dangerous amusements at which I ever assisted.   The boomerang, after skimming along near the ground, rises high into the air, and comes back twirling rapidly round.   The black fellows call, "Look out!" but it is almost impossible to dodge it, as it changes its course in the most capricious manner, and once it came whirling violently to the ground within a yard of me.

May 30th.—Adelaide presents an imposing appearance from its numerous towers and spires, as well as its wide streets and squares; but even to-day the sun was powerful enough to make us feel that there must be a sad lack of shade in summer.   We visited the museum, where any one may go and read any book that he pleases, and inspected with interest the collection of natural history; it is almost entirely limited to the fauna and other products of Australia.   Many of these we had an opportunity of seeing in a live state at the Botanical Gardens, where a number of animals are kept, both Australian and foreign.   These gardens are kept up at an annual cost to the Government of about £5000, not bad for a city of twenty thousand inhabitants, the whole population of South Australia being about two hundred thousand. Expense appears to be no object here, when public works, or buildings of any sort, are in question.

June 3rd, Melbourne.—There is a wonderful amount here of John-Bullism, and a desire to have everything as similar as possible to the pattern of the old country.   This was forcibly impressed upon me, when Mr. Bear took me to the Houses of Parliament, where everything is constructed on the model of Westminster, even to the red benches of the Legislative Council, and the green benches of the Assembly. The mace is a facsimile of the original "bauble," but the Speaker does not wear a wig; this omission is, I believe, accidental. I heard a debate in the Assembly on the Constitutional Amendment, or so-called "Norwegian Scheme," which is intended to obviate the difficulties of a deadlock between the two branches of the Legislature, by enabling them to vote collectively in certain emergencies. The speeches were very good, but I was astonished at the fine old Tory sentiments propounded: "No new-fangled notions from foreign countries! The wisdom of our ancestors, and the British Constitution. Nolumus leges Angliæ mutari. Save, oh save our old nobility! Precedent, privilege, dangerous innovation!"

June 8th.—I took the train for Sandhurst, better known as Bendigo, a hundred miles up country. I had a long tramp, under the auspices of Mr. Chumley, superintendent of police, about a city which boasts of being the most extensive in the world. It certainly covers an immense extent of ground, the houses and the mining machinery being scattered over an area of many square miles, although the population is only about twenty thousand. A very large amount of fixed capital is now invested here in machinery and other plant, and the miners get high and regular wages, so that the gold-digging has assumed the character of a steady industry. Mr. Chumley gives the miners a good character in his official capacity; energetic, industrious, peaceable, and sober. They are fine powerful fellows and very civil; they call each other "gentlemen," and behave as such.

June 14th, Hobart Town.—There can be no doubt that Tasmania still suffers in a variety of ways from her former condition as a convict settlement; a certain amount of dependence on extraneous assistance was created by the expenditure here of large sums of imperial money, and there is a lack of that vigorous self-reliant spirit which characterizes free colonies. Then the employment of convict labour has introduced the "Government stroke," whereby a minimum of exertion is undergone, and of work accomplished, and a lazy style of doing work has spread even to free labourers, very different from the style of Victorian miners working by the piece.

June 16th, New Norfolk.—Sir Robert Officer drove me to the fish-breeding ponds, in which he has long taken a great interest, and which have already stocked half Tasmania and New Zealand with trout. The experiment as regards salmon is still to a certain extent pending, but one salmon has been accidentally captured, having stranded itself on a mud-bank, and the reward of £30 for the first capture has been claimed and paid. Common trout are now abundant in many Tasmanian streams, and there are plenty of salmon-trout in the ponds. Various other sorts of English fish have been introduced into Tasmanian waters, and have thriven, especially perch, but sundry good native species are becoming scarce ; are they going to disappear like the human aboriginals ?

June 17th, Hobart Town.—The Tasmanian fauna is very peculiar, containing as it does several large quadrupeds, which do not exist on the continent of Australia : the " devil," " tiger " or " hyæna," and the brush kangaroo ; and of these there are good specimens in the museum. There are also portraits and photographs of the last surviving natives of the island, only one old woman being at this moment still left to represent the race. A moa skeleton has been set up alongside of a human skeleton, in order to contrast the size of the two bipeds : the former is almost as tall as a giraffe, with hardly any head worth speaking about ; it must have been quite idiotic. ·

Sir David took the coach for Launceston, but on his way across the island spent a week at different country houses, being made most welcome by hosts and hostesses, to whom he had no introduction, and who had never even heard his name. They showed him sport among the wattle-birds and wallabies, and he shot some beautiful specimens of parrots with brilliant plumage, which he transferred to his sketch-book.

June 22nd.—One is constantly struck in Tasmania by the English tastes and habits of the people, as well as their manners and language. The proprietors reside in their own country houses, go in for all sorts of country sports and games, and, whether well or ill off, are all given to hospitality as far as their means admit. Formerly the squatters here used to have convict labour on very favourable terms, and the loss of it is a' frequent subject of regret, when the backward condition of the colony is discussed ; but so idle and thriftless were the convicts, that they were dear at the money. It must be admitted that Tasmania is unable to obtain

free immigrants, owing to the stronger attractions of other neighbouring colonies, and that many even of her own young men
emigrate to Victoria and New Zealand, so that there are houses
full of young ladies only, just as in the old country.

After a couple of days at Melbourne, he started with
R. Farie, a Loretto school friend, by rail to Geelong, and
on by four-horse omnibus to Terang, to visit the estate of
Mount Noorat.

June 30th, Mount Noorat.—As the process of cattle mustering
was going on to-day, we were mounted to go and assist, but with
such fat well-bred bullocks as Mr. Black's, it was rather a tame
affair. Every fortnight a drove of splendid animals, such as we
now saw collected for departure, is sent off to Ballarat market,
more than a hundred at a time during the fat season. Those bred
on the station are all shorthorns, but many Herefords are bought
to be fattened on the fine pasture, which even at this midwinter
season is green and abundant, and will carry, on an average over
fourteen thousand acres, one bullock to four acres, besides sheep.
Of course in spring it will carry far more, but at present there
are 3200 in forty paddocks. Some of these enclosures present an
unbroken expanse of English grasses and clover, which plants
have raised the capabilities of the pasture from one or two to six
or eight sheep per acre. Although mainly a cattle station, there
are a lot of fine sheep at Mount Noorat, Lincolns and merinos ;
altogether it is a first-class specimen of a Victorian run, well
managed, and with every advantage of soil and climate, never
suffering from drought, and yet well drained, owing to the porous
volcanic subsoil.

July 1st.—With considerable difficulty a gun and ammunition
were rummaged out for me; although game of various sorts abound,
the managers seem to care very little either for killing or eating it,
contenting themselves with an unvarying diet of beef and bread,
without even butter. What different fare a French colonist would
have under similar circumstances! From the top of Mount
Noorat the view is extensive and striking; numerous lakes are
visible, as well as scattered townships and homesteads ; with
abundant wood and water, and a fertile soil, this district is the
garden of Victoria, or of all Australia.

July 3rd, Dunmore.—Round Belfast the country has a very
Irish appearance, devoid of trees, fenced with stone dykes, and in
many places somewhat boggy. We made for Dunmore, Farie's
domain, over stones and stumps, through creeks and quagmires.
Close to the homestead is a large lagoon, formed by damming
up the creek, and frequented by numbers of water-fowl, especially
black swans, which are here anything but *raræ aves*. Formerly
kangaroos were the chief product of this run, and it is said that
200,000 skins have been exported from it in a few years. There
are still plenty of them, both foresters and brush kangaroo, but
nothing to the vast mobs, which used to be driven into pits and
massacred. Almost the only plants to be seen besides eucalyptus,
or mimosa, are a few she-oaks and honeysuckles, native cherry
resembling a cypress, kangaroo apple, and tea-tree scrub.

July 9th.—Old Williams arrived soon after daybreak, accompanied by eight powerful hounds. In a huge oilskin coat,
high leather leggings, and a sou'-wester hat, he looked a queer sort
of huntsman, but he is a thoroughly sporting old fellow, and rides
furiously. Just as we were crossing a creek foresters were sighted
making off; with a yell the old boy started in pursuit, and before
the rest of us could get clear of the stream, huntsman, hounds,
and kangaroos had disappeared ; when we came up, two kangaroos
were already pulled down. Very soon another mob was sighted,
and scattered in all directions with the hounds in pursuit ; this
scurry ended in a few minutes with the death of three kangaroos.
There were too many hounds, as well as too many kangaroos, for
proper sport. Our horses displayed great aptitude for scrambling
after us over log fences, and for avoiding obstacles in galloping
through the bush, and it would have been great fun, but for the
feeling that it was butchery.

In taking leave of Dunmore, I could not help thinking that if
the specimens I have hitherto seen of Victorian managers and
book-keepers are not to be taken as altogether exceptional, it
would be difficult to speak too highly of such a class of men.
The five with whom I have been living for the last ten days, are
all young Scotchmen, active, intelligent, and trustworthy. They
are the very men whom absentee landlords can leave in charge
of large estates and important business. Absenteeism, unknown
in Tasmania, is evidently on the increase in Victoria, and is no
doubt promoted by the existence of such excellent lieutenants.

Nothing can be more polite and obliging than their manners, equally ready to act as host, as gamekeeper, or as groom, to play a game at chess or whist, or a tune on the fiddle.

July 12th, Woodlands.—From Ararat I had a very pleasant drive through hilly and wooded country, across the watershed of the Pyrenees, to Woodlands Station on the banks of the Wimmera. Many free selectors have tried their hands here at cultivation, but the only thoroughly successful culture appears to be that of the vine, conducted, strange to say, by Irishmen. The futility of legislative protection to agriculture, when pasture is the most profitable purpose to which land can be applied, is proved by deserted homesteads on every side. The selector picks out a desirable piece of crown land in the middle of a run, and after ringing a few trees, sticking up a few fences, and taking a crop or two off the ground, he sells it to the neighbouring squatter at a good profit. He pockets the money which the public might have got for the land, but the object of establishing an agricultural population is not attained, in spite of all the legal provisions as to residence and improvements.

July 13th.—My host, Mr. Wilson, is a most agreeable and well-read gentleman, the architect of his own fortunes, and a fine specimen of what a man may do for himself in this country, as regards education and breeding as well as wealth. We got on famously together, and it was quite a holiday to me, strolling about with him through his plantations of rare shrubs and trees, and being posted up in their names and qualities.

I was armed with an excellent breech-loader, and enjoyed myself thoroughly, mooning about the woods in pursuit of strange birds, of which I picked up a considerable variety, and drew the portraits of several. The bush is vocal with wattle-birds, a large species of honey-sucker; all the birds here appear to subsist upon honey, which must be very nourishing to judge by their plump appearance.

The sheep on this immense run, thirty or forty miles long, are all merinos, with faces that for sheep are quite pretty and intelligent. Whether for men or sheep, there is certainly no healthier country than Australia, and as regards the latter animal she stands unrivalled; the demand for wool may and will increase indefinitely, but nowhere on the face of the globe can be found another such land, without winter, wild animals, or wild men, a

land of settled government and boundless pastures, not too
tropical for wool to grow instead of hair, nor too cold for grass to
grow at all seasons.

July 21st, Melbourne.—The principal event of to-day was an
evening visit to the Observatory.   Mr. Turner explained in detail
the merits of the splendid telescope, one of the largest in existence,
and the pride of the southern hemisphere, where it reigns supreme.
Saturn with his rings and four satellites was very distinct, the belts
on his sphere being clearly visible.   But the most remarkable
sight presented to us was the nebula of Kappa Crucis in the
Southern Cross, which developed into a brilliant cluster of coloured
stars, like rubies, emeralds, and topazes.

July 26th, Sydney.—We passed the narrow, cliff-guarded
entrance, and found ourselves in Port Jackson, one of the most
beautiful land-locked bays in the world.   Promontories, inlets,
and islands, wooded to the water's edge, open out in picturesque
succession as the ship advances ; and the shores are everywhere
studded with charming villas and country houses, with gardens
and groves of varied foliage, among which towers conspicuous the
Norfolk Island pine.   On various commanding points batteries
have been erected, with guns grinning in all directions, and vessels
lie at anchor in every sheltered cove, their masts and cordage
apparently mingling with the branches of the trees.   Allowing for
difference of latitude, Sydney reminds me much of Stockholm in
its situation.   We anchored a good way from shore, and found it
an expensive business to be conveyed to land ; but it was the
sabbath day, and boatmen are robbers everywhere.

A bright afternoon showed the Botanic Gardens to great
advantage, and very charming they are : crowds of smartly dressed
people were strolling about, affectionate couples were seated on
every bench, pleasure-boats were splashing upon the water, while
overhead waved in profusion pines and palms, bamboos and tree
ferns, figs and eucalypti from all parts of the torrid and temperate
zones.

July 27th.—A friend took me to the Opera, where "Mosè in
Egitto" was performed very creditably to a well-filled house.   The
company is Italian, Dondi being the chief, and a mighty Moses
he was ; but our close proximity to the stage was very trying to
the scenery of Mount Sinai and the Red Sea.   My sympathies
throughout were entirely with Pharaoh, and the badgered Egyptians.

July 31*st.*—A learned professor had trysted me at the University, but on driving out there I found a couple of boys playing pegtop at the principal entrance, and was told that it was too wet a day for either students or professors to attend. I did however find, inside, one lecturer, without a class, employing himself in chemical research, and we laughed together over the wholesale defection on a day far above the average of an Edinburgh winter session. In fact a great mistake has been committed in locating the University where it now is, instead of in a central position, as formerly. Most of the students live in town with their families, and the attempt to introduce the English collegiate system has failed, as it deserved to fail, being utterly unsuited to all the conditions of the country. A very handsome building has indeed been erected, with a hall, which cannot be surpassed at Oxford or Cambridge ; library, museum, laboratory are there, only the students are wanting.

August 7*th.*—The Model School embraces about 1200 children of all ages, from mere babies up to young men and women. The senior classes of both sexes were put through their facings, and both did very well, but the girls were by far the most eager, jumping up and stretching out their hands with bright, intelligent faces which it was a pleasure to see. All learn singing and drawing, and the boys have regular military drill by an officer late of the British army. They receive religious teaching at certain hours, when any may absent themselves ; but very few, even of Jews and Roman Catholics, avail themselves of the privilege.

August 11*th.*—Louis [the Hon. Louis Hope, M.L.C.] and I had trysted Mr. Thomas Mort to show us his great meat-freezing establishment, and there we spent the morning, going carefully into the whole process—one of great interest, and certain ere long to develop into a very important industry. Mr. Mort has spent large sums of money and years of labour in trials, experiments, and improvements, and has certainly deserved success by his courage and perseverance.

It is very comfortable living in Sydney at the Australian Club, but it is too much like being at home : in the country, among kangaroos, and parrots, and gum-trees, one does feel that one is at the antipodes, and that one has got something new by the long voyage ; but not so in town.

August 17*th, Ormiston.*—The streets of Brisbane are full of excellent South Sea Islanders, about to return home, after a period of service, with their well-earned gains. They are busy completing their purchases before starting, and stowing them into capacious chests. They are almost as black as Australian natives, but are tidy-looking fellows, dressed like white men, only somewhat smarter, and particular as to protecting their heads with puggrees. We found Mrs. Hope and all her children expecting our arrival at Ormiston, and I was delighted with the situation and appearance of the house, garden, and shrubberies, which are neater and prettier than anything that I have seen on this side of the equator.

August 24th.—Sugar-cane cutting goes on actively, although there is a great scarcity of hands. Whites cut down the canes with adzes, while blacks trim them with short bill-hooks : they are industrious, cheerful, docile fellows, and without them sugar culti-vation could not be carried on ; they receive rations, clothing, and lodging, with £6 a year for their contract of three years. ·I had a crack with the Scotch gardener ; he has been here for eleven years, ever since he came out ; likes the climate, and feels as fit for work as he ever did at home. He cannot speak too highly of the islanders whom he has under him, and would not change them for any white men, who seem out here to be always looking "for the sun to set." I have had here the longest repose since leaving home, and am not likely to be so comfortable again for many a day.

Sir David accompanied Mr. Hope to his cattle-run of Kilcoy, and spent a pleasant week there, shooting and hunting.

August 29th, Kilcoy.—I was consigned to the care of Noggie, an aboriginal chief, for a visit to a distant "scrub," as all dense forest, whether high or low, is called in this country. As we rode along we dropped lighted matches into every tempting bunch of dry grass, and as a fresh breeze was blowing, we soon had an extensive conflagration. At this season there is no risk of the fire becoming unmanageable, especially if it is lighted in the afternoon, as the dew is certain to extinguish it. There are no sheep on Kilcoy, nor anywhere hereabouts ; they will not "do" here, and are supplanted by cattle, which seem to "do" anywhere. It was

O

like a chapter out of " Masterman Ready," Noggie being my guide,
philosopher, and friend, pointing out the nests of the mound-
making megapode, or brush turkey, the remains of a dingo's dinner,
a large carpet snake asleep, a wonga pigeon in an impenetrable
mass of foliage ; nothing could escape his piercing vision.   With
his tomahawk he soon cut out of a rotten tree enough large grubs
for a luncheon, and as we killed two black and yellow snakes
about six feet long, we should not have starved even had we been
gunless.

September 3rd.—I was despatched under the charge of " Constable," a black prince of sporting and idle habits, to ornithologize
in the scrub.   The black fellows in their tastes resemble strongly
the upper ten thousand at home, and used formerly in this district
to give battues in the most approved style, inviting their neighbours to join in the sport, and allotting the best places to their
guests.   Each chief had his own scrubs, or preserves, well stocked
with wallabies, paddy melons, and brush turkeys, and the laziest
would undergo any exertion in the way of sport.

September 6th, Darling Downs.—The run of Jondaryan at the
present moment carries 215,000 sheep.   Before breakfast I visited
the wool-shed, where shearing is now in full operation.   About
50 men are permanently employed, but at this busy time there are
160 employed in different ways.   Of these 52 are actually at work
shearing sheep, and they average about 65 head per diem ; being
paid by the piece they shear with greater speed than care, so that
the patient sheep receives frequent nips from the shears.   In this
country every one has a healthy, sunburnt, active appearance,
without an ounce of spare flesh, arguing hard work in a wholesome
climate. So numerous and troublesome have the wallabies become
in these parts that even dingoes are regarded with a friendly
eye, and the extreme remedy has been adopted of fencing in,
with wallaby-proof palings, a scrub of some ten miles in circumference at a cost of £100 a mile.   The remedy is cruel but
effectual, if the manager is correct in his estimate that fifty
thousand of his enemies have been starved to death.

He went by steamer to Rockhampton, and proceeded
by railway and coach to Wolfang on the Peak Downs, a
run of vast size, 256,000 acres already enclosed, belonging
to his friend Henry de Satgé.   In a week spent at Wolfang,

he had a good opportunity of seeing Australian bush life and sport under most favourable circumstances.

September 14th.—Emerging suddenly from the great scrub, through which we have travelled so long, we entered upon wide grassy plains of rich, black soil, varied with belts and patches of timber and stretching as far as the horizon. Here commence the famous Peak Downs, and we might have fancied ourselves in the happy hunting grounds, for the waving grass was alive with wild animals. Kangaroos were feeding in herds on every side, bronze-winged pigeons fluttering from tree to tree, huge bustards watching us in the most unconcerned manner within easy shot, and even three emus standing within a hundred yards of the track, and hardly deigning to notice us.

September 18th, Wolfang.—The Peak rises like a small Matter-horn out of the plain, and it is difficult to explain the existence of such a sharp isolated peak, composed as it is of stratified rock; doubtless it is of dolomite formation. When we reached home the sun had set, so that we had been riding, off and on, for some twelve hours, a most enjoyable day from first to last, and one which enabled us to do justice to the bustard, beautifully roasted, and about the best bird I ever eat. A possum in the kitchen caused great consternation among the maid-servants, and we were summoned to the rescue; it reminded me of rat hunts at Keith, but the game was larger, and even harder to kill, playing up old gooseberry among the pots and pans in the process. Five and twenty scalps and tails of poisoned dingoes had been brought in to-day in order to claim the proffered reward of £1 per head.

September 24th.—Henry having, in the kindest and most hospitable way, offered to speed the parting guest by driving me down to Broadsound himself, over 150 miles, we started in the buggy, accompanied by Teddy, who drove six extra horses before him. We pitched our tent near a water-hole, and made all snug for the night, hobbled the horses and lighted a fire. The heat was very oppressive, but lulled by the wail of the curlew and the importunate cry for "more pork!" we managed to get a little sleep.

September 25th.—At the first note of the laughing-jackass, and before the cockatoos had saluted the dawn with harsh scream, their snowy plumage and golden crests gleaming in the early light, we were astir. The kettle was soon boiling, the tent was struck, the horses, whose bell tinkled close by, were secured, and after breakfast our whole camp shrank up into one or two bundles, and was stowed away in the buggy. We reached our hostelry at dusk, the evening looking very stormy, and ere long lightning and thunder were succeeded by heavy rain, from which the bark roof afforded us a most inadequate shelter, but it was so warm that a shower-bath in bed was rather pleasant than otherwise.

September 26th.—To proceed upon wheels was clearly out of the question, so we requisitioned for saddles, and with the aid of our little landlady, we obtained all that was necessary, including a pack-saddle for the kit. We started on horseback, and soon found reason in the sticky condition of the track to congratulate ourselves on having left behind the "lumbering of the wheels." Nothing is more striking in this hot country than the way in which "sahebs" do everything for themselves, harnessing their traps, unsaddling their horses, carrying their kit, just as if they were niggers, or mean whites : in this respect the De Satgés are models of energy and self-help. Nobody here shoots, and the blacks are the sole purveyors of game and fish, such trifling work being only worthy of them, or of "new chums." Any one who does consider kangaroos, bustards, or ducks as worth pursuing, is regarded with a sort of good-natured contempt, as a man who shoots larks and blackbirds might be regarded at home.

October 9th, S.S. "Boomerang."—In bidding farewell to Queensland I must say that, much as I have enjoyed my visit, I should not like to live in the country. It has many of the drawbacks of a hot climate, without the compensating luxuries which may render existence tolerable even at Aden. The enjoyment of rude health will indeed make up for almost all deprivations, and all Queenslanders seem to be enviable in this respect, taking with impunity every sort of liberty with their constitutions, sleeping anywhere and anyhow, exposing themselves to the sun, and drinking dirty water or bad brandy, according to circumstances. On the other hand, a perpetual life of celibacy, in rough shanties, with bad cookery, and hardly any servants, can hardly be called luxurious, and this is normal bush life in Queensland. The young bushman is usually a bachelor, and is restless and unsettled, feeling "omne solum forti patria," and disposed to try changes of place and occupation. Station hands are well off in their way, a married couple receiving £90, and a single man £65 or £70 in wages, besides rations of meat, flour, and groceries, and free quarters.

October 11th.—In the afternoon we sighted Mount Warning, which told us we were now off the coast of New South Wales. After sunset the Zodiacal light, for which I have been lately on the look out, was particularly bright. Long observation has brought me to the conclusion that the southern heavens are grander than the northern, containing, as they do, so many stars of the first magnitude, and by far the brightest portion of the Milky Way, as well as the Clouds of Magellan. The Southern Cross, with the two brilliant "pointers" a and β Centauri, and the Coal-sack, forms the most striking object in the skies, except Orion, the brightest part of which constellation is southern.

October 14th, Sydney.—In the museum there is a very fine collection of Australian animals, the number and variety of which is quite astonishing, although a strong family resemblance runs through most of the Marsupials, which approximate more or less to the kangaroo type. The kangaroos themselves are far more numerous than I ever knew them to be, and very various both in size and colour, belonging to several distinct genera—Macropus, Osphranter, Halmaturus, Petrogale, etc. The birds are of course numerous and brilliant, the Scansores the most striking and peculiar, while the Grallatores present many forms resembling those of Europe. The venomous serpents may generally be recognized by the scales diminishing in size from the centre towards the extremities of the reptile. It appears from Gould's "Mammals of Australia," that it is a great mistake to suppose that the Marsupials have a monopoly of terrestrial quadrupeds in Australia, and that the dingo stands alone among them to represent the Placentals, as there are quite a number of true Rodents. Of the three volumes, embracing about 170 species, one is devoted to these, along with Chiropoda and Cetacea.

He finally left Australia on October 19th, sailing in the *Hero* for Auckland in New Zealand. After his return to England, he delivered two lectures, in November, 1875, upon Australia and New Zealand, before the Philosophical Institute in Edinburgh, and, in January, 1876, one on the same subject at Stroud, before the Liberal Association.   From these lectures some extracts are given.

From a political point of view few things are more desirable than that we at home should understand something of the manner in which is being carried out the grand and successful experiment of founding a new Britain at the antipodes. Nowhere on the face of the globe has greater success attended the working of popular institutions and local self-government, and nowhere has the development of material prosperity been more rapid and complete. Education and general enlightenment are as much characteristic of the colonies as industry and energy. It would be difficult to find a more law-abiding community ; the people themselves make the laws, and these are enforced by public opinion, frequently under conditions where no other power exists to enforce them. The high character borne by the magistracy in Australia contrasts favourably with that of similar officers in the United States, and proves sufficiently that popular institutions are not the necessary cause of judicial corruption.

Education, secular, gratuitous and compulsory, is provided by the colony of Victoria, and the other colonies have adopted an educational policy resembling this, almost in proportion to the strength of the popular element in their respective constitutions. It used to be believed that art, science, and letters received the highest encouragement under a cultivated and enlightened despot, whether Roman emperor or Arabian caliph, a Medici, or a Bourbon. But the city of Melbourne, not yet a generation old, can boast of scientific, literary, and artistic institutions, rivalling those of first-class European capitals, and supported by munificent grants of public money. The astronomical observatory, the museum of natural history, the botanic gardens, the gallery of arts, and above all the magnificent free library, are ample evidence that the rule of the people involves no niggardliness where knowledge and culture are concerned.

There was a time when a colony was regarded as a dependency to be governed for the exclusive benefit of the mother country, bound to take her manufactures whether it wanted them or not, to send all its produce into the home market, and to receive the offscourings of her criminal population. Such was the ancient theory of a sound colonial policy, and to this time succeeded a period when the principal colonies were permitted to enjoy the privileges, while relieved from the most serious burdens of self-government. During this period costly armaments were maintained at the expense of the British taxpayer, for the supposed protection of colonies, whose only danger of war arose from the very presence of Imperial troops. For putting an end to this state of affairs, which was justly stigmatized as tending to make the colonies a useless burden to the mother country, British statesmen have been accused of aiming at the disruption of the empire. But what has been the result? First, a cheerful recognition on the part of the colonists that prosperous self-governing communities ought to pay for their own defences; and, secondly, the discovery that the absence of standing armies was eminently conducive to peace.

Confederation under the Union Jack is the political destiny which their best friends desire for the Australian colonies, and in the mean time the adoption of a customs union would be an important step in the right direction. It is not realized in this country that each of the seven colonies has its own tariff, conceived in a spirit more or less hostile to its neighbours, and its own custom houses, through which everything entering the limits of the colony must pass. For this state of matters we are to a certain extent responsible. With the idea of discouraging the protective tendencies of the colonists, it has been declared by statute to be against the Imperial policy of free-trade for the colonies to make discriminative tariffs upon the imports or exports from or to particular countries. Thus, the colonists are prohibited from making tariffs of reciprocity among themselves as the first step to a complete customs union. In fact, it is hardly possible for the Colonial Office to interfere too little in Australian affairs, and a "masterly inaction" is the true policy. It is difficult to believe that the Australian colonies will long persist in maintaining a system of local transit duties, such as prevails in the worst administered countries of Asia, and tends to paralyze all inland traffic, except smuggling.

In the colonies there are, even among working men, many individuals of good birth and education, and all have that sense of personal dignity which springs from independent industry. At the diggings no one is a gentleman in the sense of being idle, but every one is a gentleman in the sense of being his own master.

Hence men, who in old countries are separated by a wide social gulf, meet in the colonies as equals, and will render or accept friendly services and hospitality without any idea of pecuniary remuneration.   It is even regarded as offensive to offer a gratuity in money ; but, on the other hand, no one ever declines if it comes in the form of a drink.   A pernicious and extravagant custom is this of "drinks," profitable to no one except the publicans.   Hospitality and good feeling are supposed to compel two acquaintances meeting casually, to stand drink to each other, whether it is wanted or not.   One man pays down a couple of shillings, two glasses of whisky are served out, each friend says, "Here's luck," and puts the glass to his lips.   Frequently the whisky is not drunk, but thrown quietly away, in which case the pocket only suffers, not the health.   It should be stated that habits of intemperance, the curse of our race in all countries, diminish sensibly among the new generation born in the colonies. Those who have had ample opportunities of observation maintained to me that the "cornstalk," or native-born Australian, is far more sober than the British immigrant, but that he is inferior in energy and perseverance.

Since returning from the southern hemisphere, I have frequently been asked, "To which colony would you recommend me to emigrate?"   I can only answer, that my advice would depend entirely upon the position and character of the intending emigrant. He may be an officer of the Indian service, with small means and a large family, in search of a healthy climate and cheap education, and in such a case Tasmania presents peculiar advantages.   A young man without encumbrances, willing to rough it, and eager to make his own way, had better try the interior of Queensland, or the north island of New Zealand, where he will be a pioneer of civilization.   A man possessed of some capital, who looks to improved agriculture and stock as a sure source of profit, and does not care to open up a new and wild country, will find good soil and climate, without leaving civilization behind him, in Western Victoria, sometimes called Australia Felix, or in Canterbury Province, N.Z.   If a man thinks of emigrating with a vague idea of improving his position in life, hoping to find "genteel" or "respectable" employment in some city, and is not ready to work with his hands at whatever may present itself—shearing, digging, or felling trees—my advice to him would be, "Don't !"

Even a new country at any given moment is nearly as full as an old one ; that is to say, there is little or no room for a new-comer who is neither a worker nor a capitalist. But the advantage of a new country is, that it presents a field of almost indefinite extent for the employment of labour and capital, and gives to both an equally hearty welcome. Strong arms are required as well as money ; hard labour alone can conquer the wilderness, and found a nation, even under the most favourable conditions of climate and soil. The class of emigrants who can take an active part in this work is what all the colonies require, and what many are eager to obtain by payments and concessions of the most favourable nature ; but of such a class there are not too many even in this country, and for those whom we would gladly get rid of, the colonies will not thank us.

It has been most justly said, that if, instead of being a vast hollow with raised edges, the centre of the Australian continent were traversed by a range of mountains, attaining to the permanent snow level, the continent would be the future home of a population to be counted by tens of millions. As it is, an insufficient and uncertain water supply, even after all possible improvements have taken place, must always limit to certain favoured districts the agricultural prosperity of Australia. On the whole it seems impossible that Australia can ever become the seat of such power and population as the countries occupying corresponding latitudes in Europe and America.

In March, 1876, he addressed a large meeting of the Gloucester Liberal Association, on " English Liberalism and Australasian Democracy," and contributed to the *Fortnightly Review*, in July of that year, a paper with the same title, in which he dwelt on the following points :—

While there is a great deal in common between the spirit of Liberalism (as understood in this country) and that of the democratic institutions prevailing in our colonies, there are also important points of distinction very striking to any observer imbued with Liberal opinions. Most of the objects for which English Liberals have struggled, more or less successfully, for so many arduous years, are to British colonists so much a matter of course, and have grown up so naturally as a part of their institutions, that they have hardly been regarded as questions of controversy. There are Conservatives so called in the colonies, no doubt, as well as here, but they have little or nothing that we call Conservative about them, and believe as little in hereditary legislators, privileged ecclesiastics, or entailed estates, as any Radical in England. They have been accustomed to think that free voting must be secret voting, that it is the duty of the community to educate the rising generation, and that the State should attach neither privileges nor disabilities to the profession of any form of religious belief. In countries where the feudal system has never prevailed, where there are no privileged classes, no privileged sects, and no standing armies, and where land passes readily and cheaply from hand to hand, it may seem as if little work were left to employ the Liberal reformer. But in these colonies the reformer can still find plenty of work, although the balance of power is so different, for he has ever to struggle against ignorance and selfishness from which a democracy is no more exempt than an aristocracy.

Upon the subject of Free Trade, Democracy in Australia shows itself to be thoroughly Conservative, and is as much disposed to employ its political power for its own protection against competition, as were ever the landlords of England in the old protectionist days. All things are said to be reversed at the antipodes, and free trade there finds its best friends among the up-country squatters, its greatest opponents among the population of the coast cities. The working man will tell you, "We do not wish to be swamped with cheap goods and pauper labour from Europe, or with heathen Chinese, who can flourish where a white man starves. We do not choose to lower the rate of wages by importing strangers at the expense of the colony: we are in no hurry to develop the country, that will come about in due time." The working classes at home cannot be expected to sympathize with such sentiments, but when they reach the antipodes they see things under a different light, and begin to realize the Conservative tendencies which the possession of a monopoly produces.

Perhaps the besetting political sin of the Australasian Democracies is that of extravagance, and in this respect they are more in sympathy with the Conservative than with the Liberal party at home. It is useless to disguise the fact that economy is not a popular virtue; in the colonies a ministry has little difficulty in obtaining money for any scheme that can be entitled "developing the country," even if it takes the form of an ironclad or a fortification.

Whether dreading or welcoming the steady advance of Democracy at home, we may equally watch with interest the working out of the political problem in our Southern colonies, where progress is swifter than it is here. Our colonists may be of service to us by affording alike examples and warnings; for prudent and prosperous as they undoubtedly are, their institutions still fail in various ways to satisfy impartial onlookers, or the most cautious and thinking among their own citizens. Australasian experience should teach advanced Liberals in this country that they must be prepared upon occasion to encounter popular opposition, and may also prove to timid Conservatives how much they have in common with the political instincts of the masses, when these are possessed of property as well as of power.

Since visiting the New World in the far South, I have been asked, "Has not your experience of Democratic institutions made you more Conservative in your opinions, and destroyed your faith in any benefit resulting to society from the political ascendency of the people?" To such a question I can only reply that a man must be hard to satisfy if he does not consider Australasia to be happy and flourishing. How much of this prosperity may be due to mere political institutions is, of course, open to dispute, but I am disposed to attribute a very large share to the successful working of local self-government by the people.

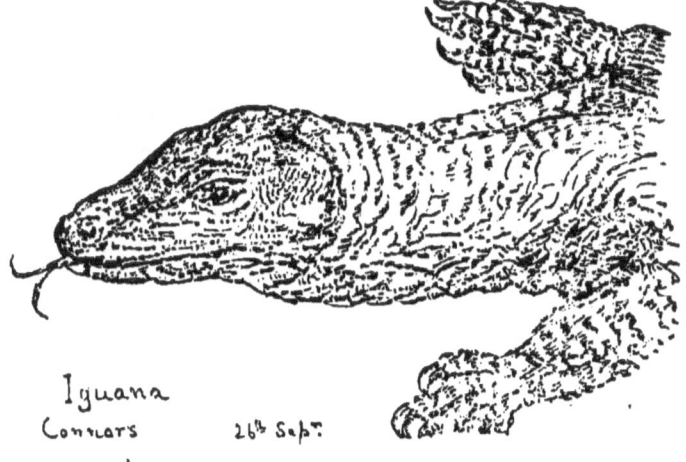

Iguana
Connors   26ᵗʰ Sept.

Tokano
Iretons and Naiads   Hot Springs   14th Nov 1874

CHAPTER XIII.

1874–1875.

NEW ZEALAND—HAWAII—CRUISE IN H.M.S. "REINDEER"—
"MAORIS AND KANAKAS."

October 25th, Auckland.—I was soon established in comfortable quarters at the Northern Club, where the meals are sociable and pleasant, and the fare is excellent. I was amused by the appearance of the first thoroughly civilized Maori whom I met: very fat, dressed in spotless black, with a white umbrella, and a face tattooed in the most elegant volutes and spirals. His name is Paul, and he has the reputation of being a capitalist—a rare case among Maoris, who usually live well up to their incomes.

October 27th.—To-day was a charming morning for a sail to Kawau, Sir George Grey's island kingdom. We steamed through an archipelago of islands, of which Kawau is the gem. The effect is quite startling, when, on rounding a steep wooded promontory, the sheltered bay appears, on the shore of which stands Sir George's large stone mansion, surrounded with gardens and shrubberies of all sorts of exotics. The "veteran Governor" was on the beach, with all his household, and I at once introduced myself as an old acquaintance, having met him at Sir C. Lyell's. I was very kindly received, and Sir George made the most of the short time at our disposal by trotting me over the garden and grounds, where almost every plant of the temperate, and many of the tropical regions flourish. All look healthy and well cared for, from the strawberries just ripening to the cinnamon and camphor. This happy island reminds one of the residence of the Swiss Family Robinson. It is in fact what Xenophon calls a παράδεισος, and though it does not much exceed five thousand acres in extent, it contains wild cattle and pigs, deer, kangaroos, opossums, wallabies, pheasant, turkeys, peafowl, and quail, in such numbers that it is difficult to understand how they can all find sustenance, as well as 1500 long-wooled sheep, and a lot of cows. This is one of the very few places in the Southern hemisphere where it is evident that money is being spent, rather than made.

October 28*th.*—In the early morning various species of kangaroo and wallaby were to be seen feeding, but by far the most conspicuous and attractive was the tree-kangaroo of New Guinea. These animals are about the size of a hare, and are beautifully marked with chestnut and black; they have long bushy tails, and look like large squirrels or lemurs, when perched, as they frequently are, on the broad branches or sloping stem of an old tree. Sir George has many literary curiosities, and showed me the Gospel of St. Luke illuminated, and written in an almost extinct Australian dialect; also letters of Cromwell's secretaries, Milton being one, and correspondence with the King of Sweden, referring to the assumption of a royal title by the Protector.

Sir David sent his luggage to Wellington by sea, and started overland across the North Island. He was advised to avoid the King's country, as matters between the English and Maoris were in a somewhat critical condition, partly owing to the railroad works approaching the boundary. On the way he visited farms in the neighbourhood of Cambridge, belonging to Mr. Leslie and Mr. Fergusson.

October 30*th.*—There is a certain analogy between our present position in New Zealand and that of the French in Algeria; life and property are safe, the law is obeyed, roads and bridges are

constructed, and the natives are treated with the respect and consideration earned by their courage and good faith. No one affects
to despise the Maoris any more than the Kabyles, and they enjoy
equality of position, whenever they choose to claim it, in public
conveyances, hotels, etc. At the same time there is, in this part
of the Northern Island at least, a certain sense of insecurity :
people here are living on the borders of an independent and
quasi-hostile country, and at any time the fears and jealousies of
the natives may bring about one more Maori war. It is possible
that this may be altogether avoided : the Pakehas do not behave
aggressively, and time is on the side of peace, gradually teaching
the natives the folly and hopelessness of an armed struggle, which
can only end in their final subjugation, although the colony might
be well-nigh ruined at the same time.

October 31st.—In every respect the Waikato country is a great
contrast to most parts of Australia, where comparatively little can
be done to improve the natural capabilities of the soil, and where,
for the present at least, nothing will pay unless done on a vast
scale. This is eminently a district suited for a man of moderate
capital, who can convert an absolutely barren waste into pastures
more productive by far than the choicest downs of Queensland, and
more profitable than the richest arable land can be in a country
of scanty population and imperfect communications. Richer
soil may easily be found, but none more grateful for moderate
outlay ; and if timber is somewhat scarce for fencing, this is a
trifling drawback compared with the ruinous cost of clearing
forest land. Lincoln sheep are the best adapted to this country,
and cattle are merely used as pioneers for them. The paddocks
are not very different in size from the enclosures in highly
farmed districts at home, and are chiefly fenced with earthen
dykes, upon which whins are sown; the creeks running through
the deep gullies form in many cases efficient boundaries, while
supplying abundant water at all seasons. In short, a practical
sheep-farmer cannot fail to do well here ; and if on a small scale,
he will soon be independent and prosperous, although it will
be long before he makes a fortune. Settlers are wanted here,
not squatters, in order to make the whole Waikato blossom as
the rose.

November 2nd.—On the way to Cambridge we visited two
flourishing farmers, whose comfortable houses, neat gates and

fences, blooming orchards, and fertile fields could hardly be
surpassed anywhere, and present an appearance of substantial
prosperity such as is rarely seen in a new country. But a very
few years ago these farms were a barren expanse of ferns and
tea-tree, identical with that which still surrounds them, and which
only requires similar enterprise and industry to render it equally
productive. We were regaled with cakes and wine in elegant
drawing-rooms, where the tones of the piano were hushed on
our arrival. The wine was home made from peach and cherry,
and was not quite so undeniable as the cakes. The magic of
property is already apparent in the planting, which these gallant
yeomen have commenced, and in which amenity, as well as profit,
has been kept in view.

Fergusson's house is just on the boundary of the King's
country, and his run extends into the territory of friendly natives,
from whom a large portion of it has been purchased. On the
opposite bank of the Waikato River the Maoris will not allow any
stock to be placed. There are beautiful sites for a Highland
castle on points overlooking the noble river, and on one of these
are the remains of a Maori pah, a ditch and rampart defending
the only assailable side of the position. The brown tints of the
general landscape are not unlike those of the Highland hills, when
the bloom of the heather has departed. The red deer are represented by wild pigs, which feed chiefly on fern roots, and so do
more good than harm ; and we highly approved of their flesh,
some of which we had for dinner. The establishment is gloriously
supplied with fresh eggs, milk, and cream ; this last assuming the
Devonshire form. Our young friend knows how to be comfortable.

November 5th.—I was sent by Fergusson on my way rejoicing,
mounted on a sturdy little grey mare, which carried me and the
provisions, in addition to a small valise and a waterproof blanket.
Captain Owen, in whose charge I had been placed, had a sack of
oats for the horses, as there is no feed at all to be found along our
route. As it grew dark a drizzling rain began to fall, and on
arrival at Te Whetu we found the settlement entirely deserted,
except by a poor old crone, too feeble to travel, whose moaning
and maundering alone disturbed the silence of the night. With
some difficulty a fire was lighted, by which we made our chocolate,
and eat our preserved meat and biscuits in considerable discomfort.
There was more smoke than light, but the form of our aged hostess,

"so withered and so wild in her attire," was just visible, squatting by the fire, and keeping up an incessant flow of very small talk, to which Owen good-naturedly replied. After supper we left her in possession, and retired to a smaller "whare;" here I lay down upon a mat, and slept soundly enough until daylight.

November 6th.—As it rained and blew a little during the night we were glad to have the shelter of the whare, which is a house built of reeds, fern stalks, and native flax closely woven together, and is perfectly weather-tight. The fire is lighted in the centre of the room, which has generally a door and a window, but is quite devoid of any furniture besides a mat. The gentleman, whose guests we were for the nonce, had left his stock-whip and two double-barrelled guns, such as have done deadly service against our troops; and has evidently perfect confidence in the honesty of his visitors.

Winding round the great wooded mass of Horohoro, for which we have been steering nearly two days, we finally left the land of mist, and entered a country which is a good deal warmer both below and above the surface. No sooner did we sight Lake Rotorua than a strong sulphurous smell was wafted to our nostrils, and jets of steam in various directions showed the presence of subterranean heat. By the road-side are numerous pools of fetid water and mud constantly bubbling and boiling, just as if some huge animal were floundering and snorting below the surface. These indications of volcanic action increase as Ohinemutu is approached, until one hardly knows where to tread, so rotten and hollow does the ground appear. Before turning in I was piloted down from the hotel with a lantern to the lake, and had a swim in its heated waters.

November 7th.—The native inhabitants are perpetually boiling themselves in the water or baking themselves upon hot stones, fuel being quite unnecessary either for warmth or for cooking. Domestic animals are very apt to scald themselves in the various holes and springs, with which the whole place is honeycombed, and horses may be seen limping about in a melancholy state. Europeans go in freely for bathing, and think that it does them good; most of those at Ohinemutu have adopted the Celtic garb, discarding breeks, and wearing a tartan shawl in the form of a kilt. We had a delightful ride in the morning to Taheki on Lake Roto Iti, fourteen miles distant; on our homeward ride we found

ourselves hemmed in by a raging fire, which was consuming the
tall withered fern on both sides of the narrow track, and almost
drove us into the lake. By watching our opportunity, and going
at it fast, we managed to dash through; but it was scorching hot,
and I did not think the horses would have faced the blaze. In
the evening we rode over to Wairoa by the light of Venus,
which cast distinct shadows; the bush was glittering high and
low with glow-worms, a fairy illumination, rivalling the stars, but
produced by a very minute worm.

November 8th.—Descending upon the Pink Terrace from
behind, you come first upon a deep pool of boiling water, the
reservoir from which the entire formation has arisen. A thick
crust of deposit has formed like ice round the edge of the pool,
and standing upon the overhanging verge of this you can look
straight down into the clear blue depths. Brimming over constantly the water flows down a series of steps or ledges, varying
in height from four or five feet to a few inches, the whole encrusted with enamel of snowy whiteness tinted with streaks of a
beautiful rosy pink, like the hue of a snowy mountain at sunset.
The horizontal surface of the terraces is as smooth as polished
marble; while the edges, over which the water trickles, are
adorned with pendent stalactites, and all foreign bodies, such as
twigs or insects, are encrusted with minute crystals, like hoar-
frost, and are gradually petrified. From the lowest terrace the
water falls into the lake, and seen from below the formation has
the appearance of a rosy glacier descending through the manuka
scrub. A succession of baths, in which nature surpasses art, are
formed upon the terraces, the temperature varying with the
height from boiling to tepid; they are four or five feet deep, with
smooth sloping sides, and floored with sand as soft as velvet, and
as white as snow. Several of us bathed, and we passed from a
warm to a warmer bath, but did not exceed 111°; the air felt very
cold on emerging, but the whole thing was thoroughly enjoyable. I could not help drawing a comparison favourable to the
former, between the wholesome brown of the Maori's skin and
the leprous-looking whiteness of the Pakeha.

Passing the White Terrace we came to a region where it was
eminently a case of "lightly tread," but the ground seemed anything rather than "hallowed;" in fact, a more unhallowed spot it
would be difficult to imagine. Everywhere steam and boiling

P

water are bursting forth with bubbling and roaring; a sulphurous odour pervades the atmosphere; little mud volcanoes have broken out, like so many pustules, all over the surface of the ground; and the stones are so hot that you might almost cook your dinner on them. From one cavernous hole proceeds a constant roar like that of a huge blast furnace, but no steam is visible; another much larger crater is known as the Witches' Cauldron, and is in a continual state of furious ebullition, the water leaping high into the air. Then there are regular geysers, which send up jets of boiling water at fixed intervals to a considerable height, and then suck it back with a gurgling noise into the depths of the earth. A curious pool of bright green water is quite cool, although steam is issuing from every crevice above and around it. It is hard to conjecture what can be the cause that produces a heat so constant in its amount, so local in its effects, and yet disseminated over so wide a surface. Anywhere throughout this region of "ever-burning sulphur unconsumed" one may come upon hot springs and traces of recent volcanic action, now at one level, now at another; while over large intervening spaces everything is quiet and cool.

November 11th.—We started amid heavy rain with thunder and lightning, my guide being George, an intelligent young Maori, and rode for a couple of hours through a rough country, where fallen logs added considerably to the difficulty of making progress, and my noble animal soon began to manifest symptoms of flagging energy. At a steep hill I accordingly dismounted, but the brute declined to follow, and on being remonstrated with at once fell down and remained there; we took off the saddle and tried again to raise it, but it simply turned on its back and began to roll down the hill. When at last it deigned to rise, I left the guide with his lame but plucky horse to bring on the sorry jade as best he might, and tramped away for Taupo. I had a weary trudge of three or four hours, without seeing a living creature, in drizzling rain, through an ugly country, which has the appearance of a bleak moor without heather, or grouse, or sheep. I arrived pretty well baked at the hotel, having had but slender fare for the last two days, chiefly sardines and bread. Walking upon this diet might not be considered as any great hardship, but it must be borne in mind that the cost of roughing it in this way amounts to more than £3 a day. George arrived in due time without my steed but he left it standing up.

November 12th.—The morning was magnificently bright and clear, and the view of the snowy peaks of Tongariro and Ruapehu glittering in the rising sun above the clear blue waters of the lake was sufficient to compensate one for all the troubles of the previous day's journey. Mr. Cross and I went off to have a warm bath, and a most amusing one it was. Between two large boiling cauldrons, and higher in level than either of them, is a deep hole in the tufa rock filled with water, which was at a perfect temperature. A great many black heads were bobbing about in it when we arrived, but by the time we had undressed and jumped in, there were about fifty men, women, and children, chiefly sitting round the edge, up to their necks in the water, regarding the Pakehas with amicable risibility of aspect. A number of these individuals were infants in arms, most comical little creatures, learning to swim before they could walk. In the evening I had an opportunity, under the auspices of Mr. Hull, as interpreter, of presenting Sir George Grey's letters to the two chiefs, Heu-Heu and Herekiekie, or "King Ezekiel." They were much gratified by the letters, but perplexed as to "how they could show me kindness when they had only potatoes and cabbage." On being asked to show us what a haka is like, we were taken to Paurini's whare, which was filled with a select society, and a small haka was performed; a little of it goes a long way, as it consists of queer contortions and discordant howls. King Ezekiel wore a handsome mat, ornamented with the feathers of the kiwi dexterously fastened all over so as to resemble a skin, and trimmed with green pigeon feathers. He expressed commendation of me for wearing moleskin trousers: "That is a man of sense; he knows that a Rangatira, such as Sir George Grey tells me he is, may wear what he likes."

November 15th.—Mr. Hull, Government road surveyor, is a great favourite with the natives, and like all who know the Maoris well, he is full of stories to their credit. For courage and generosity, tact and observation, few races, savage or civilized, can equal them. We lunched with Captain Gascoigne, who commands a detachment of armed constabulary stationed at Taupo. Mrs. Gascoigne gave us some very extraordinary entomological curios, in the shape of "vegetable caterpillars." These creatures bury themselves about six inches in the ground under the papanamu trees, and dry up to the consistency of pith, while a plant like the flower of a bulrush grows out of their heads, sometimes with two or three stems. The New Zealand armed constabulary resemble the Papal Zouaves in having many gentlemen in their ranks. They are a very fine body of men, some 750 in number; their pay is six shillings and sixpence a day, and their duties are not burdensome. They are, in fact, the only men of leisure in New Zealand, except the Maoris, and have time for pig-hunting, cricket, races, and other amusements characteristic of the " real gentleman."

November 18*th.*—The Criterion Hotel is a credit to the pretty little town of Napier, and is equal to any that I have seen in the Southern colonies, but I could not tarry to enjoy its luxuries more than one night, as the weekly coach for Wellington starts to-day. We breakfasted at Havelock; the place was full of Maori farmers, well dressed and well mounted, only to be distinguished with difficulty from swarthy sunburnt Europeans. The sights and sounds of feathered life are woefully rare in New Zealand, which thus presents a marked contrast to Australia.

November 23*rd, Wellington.*—I have been surprised at the amount of shipping in the harbour of Wellington, which is a flourishing and progressive place, not a mere political centre, and is likely to be not only the Washington, but the New York of New Zealand. It was selected as the capital by a mixed commission from Australia and Tasmania, in order to obviate local partialities, and will no doubt benefit by the projected abolition of provincial autonomy in the northern island, a measure which is certain ere long to extend to the southern also. New Zealand has been hitherto too much governed, and her public liabilities have developed themselves with alarming rapidity. It is observable that almost every one whom one meets in this country, has commenced his colonial experiences in some part of Australia; New Zealand is still very young.

November 28*th, Greymouth.*—The first rays of the rising sun illuminated a splendid sight: clear and brilliant the great chain of the Southern Alps seemed to rise immediately out of the sea, the mighty mass of Mount Cook towering above them all, a monarch of mountains. The snowy range stretched away to south-east, while the nearer and lower hills were covered with dense forest as far as the eye could reach. As the morning advanced the high mountains became less and less distinct, at last overclouding completely, so that I was fully rewarded for turning out at 4.30 a.m. We dropped anchor off Greymouth at six o'clock. By the advice of Mr. South, I resolved to land here and proceed overland to Hokitika, thus seeing more of the country. Mr. King took charge of me very kindly, and we drove out to Bonnerton coal-mines, where the future wealth of the district lies. The mines on the north side of the Grey River, owing to the dip of the strata, are by far the most favourably situated. You simply walk into a cave in the side of the hill, up a gentle incline, and you are soon in the heart of the coal-mine, where it is surprising to find the roof glittering with glow-worms, that never see the light, have apparently nothing to feed upon, and are perfectly transparent.

Education seems far from satisfactory in Westland, and it is very discouraging to find how indifferent parents in receipt of high wages are upon this subject, allowing their children to grow up into ignorant "larrikins." Combined with the present influx of uneducated immigrants, this may well cause some apprehension for the future of the country, politically and socially ; the material prospects of working men here are excellent, and domestic servants are at famine prices.

November 30th.—Hokitika is the offspring of the west-coast gold-diggings, and is only a few years of age. A Fenian riot here was one of the rare occasions when Irish disaffection has cropped up in the Southern colonies, and it brought out the genuine *loyalty*, or love of law and order, of the population generally ; numbers of gold-diggers left their claims to take care of themselves, marched down many miles to town, and enrolled themselves as special constables, doing duty until all was quiet. Such a demonstration pretty well snuffed out Fenianism, and enabled the Government to deal very leniently with the offenders.

December 2nd, Christchurch.—The coach from Hokitika was crowded. It contained eleven passengers, including a worthy Scotchwoman with three bairns, a rosy French priest, and a " heathen Chinee," who took his place on the top, and announced, amid shouts of laughter, that he was travelling, " not for business, but to see the country." The plain at the foot of the mountains is almost entirely natural pasture, which looks at present very parched and sterile, but further on there is a good deal of cultivation, and as Christchurch is approached the country assumes the appearance of a well-farmed district at home. Neat farm-houses, fields of corn and clover, enclosed by hedges of hawthorn and broom, are succeeded by elegant villas with gardens and shrubberies.

December 6th, Corwar.—J. C. Wason, son of my distinguished constituent in Ayrshire, being about to return home after a short visit to Christchurch, asked me to accompany him to his station, and I gladly accepted the invitation. A ride over the property revealed the sad havoc wrought among the merinos by the gale of the 4th. Recently shorn, and without any shelter, the wretched animals have "died like sheep," and the weather-side of one fence is strewed with their carcases, about two score in number ; the gulls, which seem to represent the birds of prey here, have picked out all their eyes. Cantering over these smooth plains, one cannot help regretting the utter absence of game, or animal life of any kind, except a sort of dotterel and very small lizards. Rain is the great want here, and it is wonderful how the sheep can find any sustenance on the unimproved plain ; but two acres will keep a sheep, which eats neither tussocks nor speargrass. Improvements can be made very cheaply : the plough is run through the tussocks, rape or turnips are sown and eaten off, a second crop is generally taken, when the land is fit for producing fine clover or rye-grass. Often this is done by men who own a team of horses, and who get the two years' crops for their labour. A man whose capital equals £1 an acre, after paying £2 for his land, can do very well here. Canterbury is a wealthy province, where literally they can hardly spend their income from the scarcity of labour. This wealth is due to their prudence in putting a good price upon land, which can be purchased at two pounds an acre all over the province, whereby the public, and not land speculators, have reaped the advantage, without any check to immigration.

December 8th.—At one station we visited there is a sheepwash, not a very common institution in these parts ; and although washing has not yet commenced, we went to inspect it, accompanied by a somewhat grumpy specimen of that New Zealand institution, "the married man ;" these Benedicks are always spoken of with the definite article, and are far scarcer than one would expect in a country where anybody can afford to marry. The sheep are first well soaked in hot water at 112° or so, and then played upon with jets of cold, until the dirt and the life are pretty well washed out of them. The native flax and cabbage-tree are now in blossom with red and white flowers respectively, and in many places the brown plain is yellow with native onions; the bracken and manuka, so characteristic of the north island, are scarcely to be seen here; flowers are as scarce as birds, and sweet scents as sweet notes.

December 15*th, Christchurch.*—Corwar has been made so pleasant to me, that I have lingered there fully as long as my remaining time in New Zealand permits, and to-day Wason drove me in his massive cariole to the railway station to return to Christchurch. The Canterbury museum is admirably arranged, and contains a collection of moa skeletons altogether unique; several species are here represented, and the largest, Dinornis maximus, looks like the anterior portion of a good-sized giraffe. There are of course good specimens of kiwis, kakapos, and other peculiar New Zealand birds, with their eggs. Dr. Haast, the director, showed me the bones of harpagornis, the great fossil harrier, which displays the shortness of wing characteristic of so many New Zealand birds. We discussed the evident tendency of New Zealand fauna and flora to be superseded by Northern forms, more thoroughly trained and adapted to fight the battle of life. He mentioned having visited a district in the interior a few years ago, finding three hundred species of plants, one-third of them new to science; at a recent visit he could not find above ten per cent., the rest have vanished. Snow never lies any time near Christchurch, and the climate is that of southern England, although the latitude is that of central Italy. In all respects Canterbury seems to be the most English of the colonies, and soon there will hardly be a plant or an animal throughout the province that is not a naturalized Britisher.

January 19*th, Honolulu.*—It was mid-day on December 30th before the *Cyphrenes* was fairly under way, and I bid a final adieu to the shores of New Zealand and of the Australasian colonies— long may they flourish! A long spell on the mighty Pacific, which ocean hardly treated us at the outset of our voyage so well as we might have expected. On January the 7th we sighted dimly the lofty island of Savaii, one of the Samoa, or Navigator group. It is very tantalizing to pass between these and the Fijis without touching at any of them. To-day we reached the island of

Oahu in the Sandwich group.   Nothing could be more attractive than the appearance of Honolulu, as seen by the "ivory moonlight" after a long sea-voyage; and the hotel, with its airy verandahs, and shady groves of bananas, papaws, tamarinds, and acacias, is by no means the least attractive place in the town.

January 20th.—The morning was delightful, and Honolulu looked charming with its bright flower gardens and bungalows embowered in palm trees and creepers.   The place is thoroughly well watered, and the grass springs as fresh and green as in old Ireland. We overtook the Royal Guards marching with their band and German bandmaster, and accompanied by two officers; they are quite a small corps, chiefly "pipers" in fact, and are attired in spotless white.   The people of Honolulu all wear straw hats, decorated with wreaths of flowers, natural or artificial, and the dress of the native ladies is both cool and becoming; a long, loose peignoir of some bright and pretty colour, gathered in a little above the waist, and flowing down to the bare feet.   They invariably ride à la Duchesse de Berri, and Mexican saddles with high pommel, and huge leather stirrups are in universal use.

January 23rd.—H.M.S. *Reindeer* left Honolulu for Waimea in the island of Kauai, and I was so fortunate as to be a passenger on board, as Captain Anson's guest.   Sailing, as such, on board a man-of-war is a very agreeable mode of locomotion; the officers of the *Reindeer* are a pleasant set of fellows, and the men a fine ship's company, all healthy and cheery looking, in spite of their recent service on the Mexican coast.   Our errand was to fetch away members of the Transit of Venus Expedition; we found them very comfortably lodged, and by no means anxious to have their exile terminated, as they are on excellent terms with the natives.

January 25th.—A hula-hula was commanded for our benefit; it strongly resembles nautches such as I have seen in Asia and Africa, but was rather more graceful and spirited.   First, two young girls, in short puffed skirts of yellow native cloth, with garlands of leaves on head and neck, and fringes of dry grass round the ankles, went through a series of chants, accompanied with balance movements, and clacking together of stones as castanets.   The songs were of the nature of laments for the late Kamehameha IV.   Then another young lady seated herself on the ground, and chanted at some length, beating time with a gourd, and swaying about with her eyes shut; she wore a large wreath and necklace of orange and yellow flowers, very becoming to a dark complexion. She was succeeded by several others, attired in the favourite yellow hue, whose performances were rather more lively; but a little of this sort of thing goes a long way, and after distributing largesse I left the scene of action. The whole population of the district assembled on the beach to see the last of the Transit Expedition, and as every man, woman, and child rides, there was a great show of horseflesh of sorts.

January 28th.—Coming on deck just at sunrise, we enjoyed a grand sight : four great mountains showed their summits high above the clouds enveloping their bases; two were covered with snow, being nearly 14,000 feet above the sea-level, and from the rounded dome of Mauna Loa a column of smoke arose, shining blood-red in the light of the rising sun. At 3 p.m. we were anchored in Kailua Bay; I strolled along the beach in the direction of the spot where Captain Cook was killed, about ten miles to the southward. At the extremity of the village I came to a swell native " Restauration," where lots of benches were placed under awnings in the open air, the ground was strewed with flowers and green leaves, and the whole place decorated with flags and crowded with people. My entrance evidently gave general satisfaction ; a chair was placed for me in the centre, and a table was soon covered with a variety of native delicacies by attendant handmaidens in yellow. I partook of poi, and another vegetable resembling maizena, but did not feel equal to a raw red mullet. The wreathed and garlanded attendants fanned away the flies, and the company at large regarded me with amicable risibility of aspect.

January 29th.—We steamed slowly down the north-east coast of Hawaii; the lofty cliffs, against which the sea breaks, are clothed with vegetation, and countless streams pour down their face in silvery cascades. It is, in fact, "a land of streams," and corresponds exactly to Tennyson's "Lotus-land ; " even the "pinnacles of aged snow" are there in the twentieth parallel of North latitude.

January 31st.—We were in the saddle at 6 a.m., and reached Volcano House about 5 p.m., at an elevation, by my aneroid, of 3650 feet. A warm bath of condensed steam proved so refreshing in combination with a good dinner, that I proposed a nocturnal visit to the great crater. This motion was at once seconded by Professor Forbes, and we started with two others. Three miles' tramping over rough lava, as well as a precipitous descent of 600 feet, must be gone through before reaching the active portion of the crater. On the recent lava our principal difficulty and danger were the cracks, which extend in every direction and through which may be seen the red-hot lava beneath. The light of our solitary lantern was quite insufficient, and once I fell into a crack, and, for a second, thought that I was "linking to Pele's pit," but the crack was a cool one, and I scrambled up. Our guide picked his way most cautiously, and after climbing a slope encumbered with fragmentary lava, very sharp and brittle, we saw before us one of those spectacles which engrave themselves indelibly on the memory, but which utterly overtax the powers of description.

Beneath us, with sides as precipitous as those of the great crater in which we stood, a "lower deep, threatening to devour us, opened wide." The main portion of its surface was black, but from three great depressions the molten lava leapt into the air in huge jets, falling back in fiery spray, and splashing high against the surrounding cliffs with a sound like that of a "melancholy ocean." We sat down for more than an hour, enjoying the grandest and most varied display of Nature's fireworks which can be seen at present on the face of the globe. Kilauea, the principal fiery lake, was at times almost crusted over with a black film of cooled lava, then a fiery crack would run rapidly across its surface, and the molten lava would come surging up in a mighty crimson fountain, the spray of which would be thrown a hundred feet into the air. Sometimes a series of concentric fiery rings would appear on the lake's surface, and gradually widening would convert a large portion into a sea of liquid fire, its edges "flaming with sulphur blue." We were so fortunate as actually to assist at the birth of a young crater, which broke forth without any warning just under the cliff where we sat. In a few seconds there was a circular orifice several yards wide, spirting liquid lava in every direction, and depositing fiery stalactites upon the surrounding surface. The young crater continued to increase slowly in size as long as we remained. Sitting on the windward side we were of course safe from the clouds of smoke and vapour, which rolled perpetually across the weird scene, and were illuminated by the ruddy glow from beneath. We returned faster than we had come, and without mischance, reaching the hotel after midnight, delighted with our expedition.

February 1st.—Wishing to see Kilauea by daylight I again descended into the great pit, after an interval of six hours only. Now for the first time I had an idea of the size of the main crater, walled in by precipitous cliffs 600 or 700 feet high, and many miles in circuit. Kilauea was far less active than yesterday, but the crimson waves were still surging and splashing against the cliffs, and as we watched it the fiery fountains broke out nearly at the same points. Very considerable changes take place from day to day, and even from hour to hour, in this great centre of volcanic energy, and last night we were specially fortunate.

February 14th, S.S. " City of Melbourne."—I share a very small cabin with two Frenchmen, members of the Transit Expedition to the Campbell Islands, of which, as to climate and productions, except sea-lions and albatrosses, they give a most dismal account. They are a party of four, all remarkably nice gentlemanly fellows, two of them naval officers. In all weathers, and under the most unfavourable conditions as to light and space, M. Bouquet daily tests the temperature and density of the sea-water, with the view of investigating the ocean currents. It is precisely through such patient and persevering experimenting that this complex subject will come finally to be understood. We have reached the Golden Gate, for which we have been steering so long, with the most perfect accuracy and punctuality.

In June, 1877, an article, entitled "Maoris and Kanakas," was contributed by Sir David to the *Fortnightly Review.* The threatened extinction of races of men and animals, as well as of many types of the vegetable kingdom, so noticeable in Polynesia, excited his keen interest and even regret. This was no doubt in some measure due to his belief in Darwin's theory of Evolution, which invested the study of natural history with a special charm for him. He never failed to examine, and record his impressions of every museum or collection of animals, alive or dead, to be found in the many countries he visited. From this article are taken some of his observations on the effects of civilization upon the inhabitants of Polynesia.

Nowhere has the destructive effect even of a peaceable European invasion been so marked as in Polynesia; nowhere have the robust invaders so rapidly established themselves to the extinction of feebler, if not inferior, breeds. The ultimate result might have been anticipated, but the rapidity with which it has been brought about is somewhat startling. In certain districts of New Zealand, settled a good many years ago, the native plants and animals have, with a few exceptions, already disappeared, and are replaced by those of Europe. In particular, the only conspicuous flowers and birds are those which make gay our own fields and hedgerows, while indigenous specimens must be sought for carefully, if they are to be found at all. Around Christchurch and Nelson the air rings with the song of skylarks and blackbirds, and is redolent with the scent of hawthorn and sweetbriar. The only gallinaceous bird indigenous in New Zealand is a species of quail, which was in many places very abundant a short time ago. It is now difficult to obtain a single living specimen, although the bird has undergone no severe persecution, and attempts have even been made to preserve it. Meanwhile the Californian quail has been introduced and flourishes, and Chinese pheasants have overspread the country.

The native rat, the only terrestrial mammal found in New Zealand by European discoverers, has so completely disappeared, that many naturalists are sceptical as to its having ever existed, and the little island in Lake Taupo is said to be its only remaining habitat. On the other hand, the common brown rat, the faithful companion of the white man in all his wanderings, has taken complete possession of the country, where its increase is restricted by no reptiles nor quadrupeds, and few birds of prey, and is encountered far beyond any settlements of its human fellow-colonists, close to the glaciers of the New Zealand Alps. The honey-bee of Europe has established itself as a very successful settler in the southern hemisphere, and has not merely suppressed the feeble insect rivals which it found there, but also in some parts appears to have caused a marked reduction in the number of honey-sucking birds.

Indeed it may be said that the indigenous animals and plants

of New Zealand succumb without a struggle, whether to the
domesticated varieties imported by the white man for his own
benefit, or to those noxious creatures and weeds of which he is
the involuntary introducer. Of the human aboriginals, however,
this does not hold true : in no sense are they a helpless or a feeble
folk ; to force they have never succumbed without a determined
resistance, and they have readily adapted themselves to such
peaceful changes as foreign civilization demands.

Nevertheless, the Maori race, gallant, vigorous, and intelligent
beyond any so-called savages with whom we have ever been
brought into collision, seems doomed to the same fate which is
overtaking the feeble short-winged birds characteristic of the
Polynesian fauna. Official statistics confirm the universal impression, among colonists and natives alike, that the Maoris are
dying out. In 1849, Sir George Grey estimated their numbers
at 120,000, and since then they have rapidly declined ; at the
census of 1874 there were 45,470 Maoris in the whole colony,
all except a couple of thousand being inhabitants of the north
island. If this rate of reduction continues, the " Maori difficulty "
will soon solve itself, and there will be room in the north island
for many more cattle and sheep ; but a brave, generous, intelligent race of men will disappear, and many, even of those who
will inherit their territory, cannot regard this disappearance without
regret.

The Maori is in truth as near an approach to the ideal of a
" noble savage " as has ever existed in modern times, and is a
worthy rival of the imaginary Delawares of romance :—

> " His valour, shown upon our crests,
> Hath taught us how to cherish such high deeds,
> Even in the bosom of our adversaries."

In attempting to account for the depopulation of Polynesia,
various causes are assigned by those who have considered the
question : intemperance, immorality, infantile epidemics, and
pulmonary diseases. Some persons lay stress upon one evil,
some upon another, the most careful observers being the least
ready with an answer. Although these may all be true causes of
diminished population, all combined appear inadequate to account
for the result. Thus much is clear, however, that civilization has
introduced in Polynesia causes of destruction more than counter-
balancing the advantages of education and good government, so

far as the natives are concerned. They are unable, even under the most favourable conditions, to resist evils which hardly affect the vitality and fecundity of the Indo-European or Mongolian, and those vices and diseases which merely scourge the individual of the stronger race, annihilate the less prolific breed.

When they are all gone there will be additional space in the world for a few Caucasians and a good many Mongolians, of whom there seem to be quite enough already; and no doubt the negro also would flourish and multiply in the tropical islands. On the whole, humanity will not profit greatly by the change. In frugality and industry the Kanaka is far inferior to the Chinaman, but not to the negro ; while courtesy, courage, docility, and generosity are not such common qualities that we can witness without regret the extinction of the Polynesians, who exhibit them in so marked a degree. Depopulation is not limited to Polynesia proper, but goes on all over the southern hemisphere as rapidly as in the kingdom of Hawaii, the only important insular group lying north of the equator in the Pacific Ocean. In the Fijis, since their annexation, the mortality has been appalling ; but these islands are inhabited by Melanesians, a black race very different to the brown Kanakas. The Tasmanian " black-fellow " is gone already, and his Australian brother is rapidly following him. We may pity even such irreclaimable savages as these are, and regret the mode of their extermination, but we must admit that for them there is no room within the pale of a truly civilized community, and that they are interesting only as ethnological curiosities, exhibiting in recent times a very early stage of human development. It will not take long to write their epitaph, although, in their keen love of sport and their invincible dislike to steady work, they bear a certain resemblance to some of the most exalted and highly favoured classes of mankind. With the polished Hawaiian and the chivalrous Maori it is different, and the loss caused to humanity by their disappearance is real.

For a quarter of a century the attempt to carry out a good government policy in Hawaii has been honestly made, under singularly favourable conditions and with very encouraging results, were it not for the well-grounded apprehension that the Hawaiian race, as it becomes civilized, is doomed to become extinct. No one who has passed any time among these happy lotos-eaters, can contemplate without sincere regret the consummation of so promising a political experiment. The statistics are, however, only too conclusive; and, as in the case of the Maoris, the diminution in numbers is so steady, that a limit at no remote date may be calculated beyond which the Hawaiian race will not survive.

The cause of this depopulation is certainly not political misgovernment. The theoretical excellence of the constitution has not been belied by its practical working. The political hardships of the Hawaiians, in fact, consist merely in being too much governed. Life and property are secure; the laws are just, and are well administered; the *quantity* not the *quality* of the government is in fault. The political machinery, with king, privy council, governors, judges, salaried ministers and legislators, is ludicrously in excess of the requirements of the dwindling population—less than sixty thousand, including all the foreigners.

Throughout Polynesia it is entirely due to the Christian missionaries that the natives are an educated people in the strictest sense of the word, for it is difficult to find anywhere within reach of mission influence a Polynesian, old or young, who cannot read and write. The missionaries began by creating a written language, simple as to orthography, and invariable as to pronunciation. Having reduced to writing, dialects which existed formerly as mere sounds, they ere long succeeded in converting warlike and indolent savages into lettered scholars, although many of their pupils had already attained a mature age. An achievement such as this reflects credit upon teachers and pupils alike. In Hawaii, Government schools have been everywhere established, eighty-seven per cent. of the children of school age are actually receiving instruction, and an Hawaiian unable to read and write is rarely to be found. The sale of intoxicating liquors to natives is forbidden by law, and the legal penalties are strictly enforced.

The Hawaiians have proved, in a most remarkable instance, their appreciation of a sanitary policy which places the welfare of the community above the prejudices and even the affections of the individual. A considerable and apparently increasing proportion of the Hawaiians is afflicted with a terrible disease known as leprosy, which has defied all available medical science, and is regarded as absolutely incurable. To prevent all risk of infection, and to stamp out the hereditary taint, which threatened to spread through the whole community, the Hawaiian Legislature about ten years ago took up the question in a spirit at once patriotic and scientific. Under the auspices of a board of health, a leper settlement was established in a secluded valley on the small island of Molokai, to which all persons known to be affected with leprosy were transported by officials appointed for the purpose. Examples of self-devotion were not wanting on the part of persons whose external symptoms of leprosy were so slight as to escape detection, but who surrendered themselves spontaneously in obedience to the law. Nothing can well be more touching than the story told by Miss Bird, in her book on the Hawaiian Archipelago, of poor "Bill Ragsdale," whose generous self-immolation savours rather of the antique Roman than of the Kanaka. This talented half-white, who had filled among other honourable offices that of interpreter to the Hawaiian Legislature, avowed himself to be a leper before any visible symptom betrayed him, and passed amid universal lamentation from the joyous society of Hilo to a living death at Kalawao. In that dismal valley of Molokai he is now a ruler, by virtue of his abilities ; but, perhaps, since the "Odyssey" was composed, the well-known words have never been so applicable to any living mortal :—

"Βουλοίμην κ' ἐπάρουρος ἐὼν θητευέμεν ἄλλῳ,
'Ανδρὶ παρ' ἀκλήρῳ, ᾧ μὴ βίοτος πολὺς εἴη,
Ἠ πᾶσιν νεκύεσσι καταφθιμένοισιν ἀνάσσειν."

Certainly the hardest life that a slave can lead elsewhere seems preferable to that of Governor Ragsdale, who now rules with beneficent and almost absolute authority over seven hundred lepers in every stage of a lingering but fatal disease. The last effort of his eloquence, when bidding farewell to his weeping friends, was to urge submission to the stringent measures taken by the Government for the purpose of stamping out leprosy. The law for the seclusion of lepers has been enforced without distinction of rank or nationality, and in the course of eight years more than eleven hundred persons have been transported to Molokai. The courage and liberality displayed in grappling with this national curse are worthy of the emulation of advanced European Governments.

Great as are the charms of scenery and climate—"where the golden Pacific round islands of paradise rolls "—the chief interest and romance of these regions are due to their aboriginal inhabitants, and will pass away with them. A country newly occupied by white settlers is neither romantic nor picturesque when the

primeval forest has been reduced to charred stumps, and a long
interval must elapse before the undefaced glories of the wilderness
can be replaced by the cultivated beauty of an old and prosperous
land. In time the fernland and bush of New Zealand will be
converted into a populous and productive country; but the
people and the products will be English and not Maori. Thus
the world becomes more prosperous and wealthy, but less interesting and varied, and the inducements to travel diminish as the
facilities increase. Even in older countries the variety of scenery,
of architecture, of costume, of social and political institutions, of
fauna and flora, so charming at the present moment, is tending to
become a thing of the past, and will be vainly sought for by the
travellers of another generation. An Eastern dragoman once said
to me, while we were gazing in admiration at a crumbling Saracenic
edifice, "We see these things, but our sons will not be able to see
them." The feeling to which his words gave expression was constantly in my mind when amongst the Maoris and Kanakas, whose
"tenakoe" and "aloha," their friendly greetings to the passing
stranger, have all the pathos of an eternal adieu.

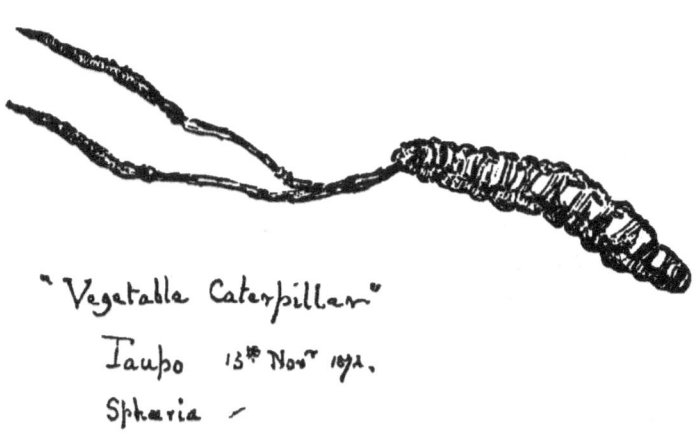

"Vegetable Caterpillar"
Taupo   13ᵗʰ Novʳ 1872.
Sphæria

CHAPTER XIV.

1875–1876.

February 15th, San Francisco.—We visited the Chinese quarter, and discovered a very elegant joss-house, or temple, high up in a many-storeyed house, and were much struck with the richness and beauty of its decorations, especially the carving and gilding of the altars, and the embroidery on the silken banners, which exactly resemble those used in modern ritualistic churches as to general style, although differing in detail. On what may be called the high altar is an image of Buddha, and the whole place is decorated with bronze ornaments, and artificial flowers, while little sticks of incense are burning everywhere. The Chinese wear usually a dark blouse and loose trousers, with a black wide-awake, and are as like one another as so many peas, all being short and nearly of a size; they adhere faithfully to their long pigtails. Occasionally a Chinawoman or a child may be seen, but they are not common. At night we attended the Chinese theatre, which was crowded with "Johns" to witness the performance of some Japanese acrobats, one of them a mere infant. A Chinese play followed, in which a highly rouged Dinah was driven off the stage by her enraged parent with a drawn sword.

February 16th.—I took my two French friends to see the wild beasts at Woodward's gardens, and we were quite pleased, especially with the indigenous animals, which include three magnificent grizzly bears, the first that I have seen alive, a pair of bisons, and a whole herd of sea-lions. It was an amusing sight to see the sea-lions fed;

their activity on land is quite astonishing, whether in climbing rocks, or galloping upon their paddles like ordinary quadrupeds. The afternoon was spent at the Union Club, where Mr. Booker, H.B.M. Consul, has inscribed my name, and where it was a real treat to get the English papers. The inferiority in news, style, printing, and every other respect, of the American journals to the English and Colonial is very marked; the comicalities are, in fact, the best things contained in them.

February 19*th.* — I accompanied Captain Lebon and Léon Weill to San Jose, where Weill gave us a capital dinner in a French hotel, and afterwards drove us by moonlight to the house of his friend M. Le Lièvre. It was a "surprise party," but he turned out and made us most welcome.

February 20*th.*—Nothing could be kinder than our host, his wife and daughter, to all of whom the surprise of our nocturnal visit seemed to be a real pleasure. At an early hour M. Le Lièvre drove us to the Almaden quicksilver mines; we did not enter the shafts, but inspected the smelting works. The ore is partly obtained in the form of brown argillaceous dust, without any apparent signs of mercury, partly in the form of rock, more or less scarlet from the presence of cinnabar. The discovery of the mine is attributed to the use of vermilion by the Red Indians in painting, which drew attention to the presence of mercury in the soil. The ore is heated in furnaces until all the mercury is driven off in vapour; this is condensed in a series of chambers, and settles down in the form of dew all over the surface of the condensers. As the metal accumulates it runs into little sloping troughs, and passes through siphons into larger troughs, down which it rushes, in the shape of silvery fish, or tadpoles, into a general receiver. Minute beads of quicksilver are to be seen all over the various apparatus, and a good deal of the metal must escape into the atmosphere, breathed by the workmen, as they "enjoy very indifferent health," and suffer especially in their teeth.

February 23*rd, San Francisco.*—After visiting an interesting museum of anatomical waxworks, and taking leave of those few who have shown me hospitality, I quitted the Golden City without a regret; it has proved the most disappointing place that I have yet visited. It is dusty, foggy, and dirty, but the fare there is good, after the monotonous cuisine of the southern hemisphere. Even the culinary comforts of these great hotels, however, are somewhat marred by the grimness and want of conviviality which prevails; everybody eats his or her food, and speaks to nobody.

In spite of the unsuitable time of year, Sir David and Mr. R. Johnson engaged horses and vehicles for the expedition to the Mariposa Grove, and Yosemite Valley.

February 27th.—We had a pleasant jog through splendid timber: sugar-pine, white and yellow firs, and "cedars," or rather cypresses. The sugar-pine is a magnificent tree, growing perfectly straight to a height of two hundred feet, with small symmetrical branches, and enormous cones; it produces a sweet resin-like manna. Soon, however, gigantic stems appear among the ordinary timber, conspicuous alike from their size and red colour; these are the Sequoias, or Wellingtonias, the far-famed Mariposa grove. The largest of all is the "Grizzly Giant," who has indeed lost his top, and most of his branches on the north side, but whose lower limbs would make large forest trees, and whose girth at the ground, as we measured it, is ninety-one feet. The cones are very small, and resemble those of a cedar; the seeds do not sprout so freely as those of the surrounding Conifers, and I looked vainly for an infant Wellingtonia. Some of the Sequoias grow as high up as six thousand feet, and here the snow was pretty deep; they flourish on the ridges as well as in the hollows.

February 28th.—We made an early start, with the same guide and horses, for the Yosemite Valley, a distance, by the winter trail, of twenty-five miles across the mountains. Twice we reached an elevation of 6000 feet, where the ponies had to flounder through snow; but little was to be seen in the way of a distant view, until suddenly the Yosemite Valley burst upon us in all its grandeur: el Capitan, the Three Graces, and the Bridal Veil Fall being the most conspicuous objects. As we rode up the valley, new and striking sights appear at every turn: the Cathedral Spires, exactly alike, two pinnacles of rock resembling the twin western towers of a Gothic church; three peaks, one above the other, called by the Indians with their usual felicity, "Mountains playing leap-frog," and numerous cascades of immense height, some of them now freezing up as the sun disappears, and being converted into gigantic icicles. The only hotel now open stands just under Sentinel Rock, a pinnacle resembling the Romsdalhorn, and from the cliffs opposite descends in three shoots, the highest 1600 feet, the great Yosemite Fall.

March 1st.—We walked some miles up to the head of the valley, where we were rewarded by the sight of the beautiful Vernal Fall, or "Cataract of Diamonds." One can see clearly here, that the difficulty experienced in realizing the dimensions of everything in the Yosemite valley is caused by the great height of the pine trees, which one takes naturally as a standard of measurement; it required the aid of my aneroid to convince me that the waterfall is at least 350 feet high.

March 7th, Salt Lake City.—We pushed on in order to reach Salt Lake City on Sunday, but were disappointed to find on arrival that the great Tabernacle is not used in winter. We proceeded to one of the meeting-rooms; the service commenced with hymns, after which the sacrament, in bread and water, was administered to all present, except ourselves. Mayor Daniel H. Wells then delivered a very lengthy harangue, touching upon many of the special Mormon doctrines, and the persecutions to which the Saints have been subjected at various times, but founding all his arguments and dogmas upon the authority of the Bible, to which the Mormon revelations claim to be additional, but in no sense contrary. We next had a very practical address from Mr. Cannon, exhorting to industry and sobriety, abstention from tobacco, also tea and coffee, and to the cultivation of all useful arts. These exhortations were mainly addressed to the juniors present, a saving clause being inserted for those elders who had borne the burden and heat of the evil days, and who, having now established this mountain refuge for the Saints, might require to "solace decaying nature" with an occasional pipe or other narcotic. The tone of both speakers was tolerant and rational; and the doctrines inculcated were simply those of a charitable form of Christianity. There was no allusion to the peculiar domestic institution which, for most Gentiles, sums up their entire notion of Mormonism.

The Tabernacle will be completely cut out in grandeur, if not in actual size, by the Temple of white granite now slowly rising beside it. The edifice is quite Egyptian in its solid magnificence, and will cost a vast sum of money, although a large proportion of the labour is contributed by the faithful without wages. The Tabernacle is an enormous building, elliptic in form, which will seat 14,000 people, all of whom can hear an ordinary speaker addressing them from a point near the focus of the ellipse. The roof is in unsupported span, one of the largest in the world; and the organ, a very fine one, was constructed here in Utah : proving that the Mormons are skilful artificers, as well as agriculturists. The Tabernacle is for public worship and assemblies only ; the Temple is intended for the various religious rites and ceremonies of marriage, baptism, and ordination. The mayor presented us with a lot of Mormon books, and took us to see President Brigham Young, who was very civil, and discussed a variety of subjects. He is a hale and hearty man, nearly seventy-four years of age, and whatever may be said of him, he has certainly founded a most prosperous commonwealth in the face of enormous difficulties, both moral and physical.

March 12th, Chicago.—A dense cloud of smoke overhung the city, and what with snow, slush, and fog, it had a very wintry and a very English aspect. The dismal grandeur, utterly devoid of real comfort, characteristic of a large American hotel, is well exemplified at the Sherman House. The " reading-room " is a dark, stuffy place without a single newspaper; while the guests all congregate in the marble hall, upon seats ranged along the walls, with their hats on, and do their conversation and expectoration in an atmosphere heated to suffocation. The drawing-rooms are handsomely carpeted and furnished, but do not seem to be intended for use, and as a rule they are entirely deserted, and the piano remains unopened. A few ladies appear at meals, then silently vanish, and conversation while feeding is a thing unknown. A drive through the principal streets and avenues enabled me to appreciate the extreme magnificence of the new buildings, which have been erected since the great fire of 1871, and which surpass anything to be seen in the business quarters of any other city. The style of architecture combines elegance with solidity, resembling that of modern Parisian houses ; rents are high, and those capitalists of the eastern cities who have rebuilt Chicago must be getting good interest for their money. At present, building is going on everywhere, especially in the way of churches, and all in the most costly and elegant style. This is certainly not pleasant weather : it is cold, but still thawing; everything outside is wet and dirty ; while all dwellings are kept as hot as forcing-houses, and as close.

March 17th.—At Memphis I found the *City of Helena* just

starting for Vicksburg. Although carrying nearly fifteen hundred tons she only draws seven feet and a half, and runs up to the bank at any point where two or three nigger huts are gathered together, to deposit mail bags, barrels of flour, sacks of corn, casks of pork, bales of hay. The niggers employed as porters on board the boat get the same wages as white men—a dollar a day and their board. They work well and cheerfully at jobs of this sort, involving short spells of severe work, but do not shine in steady continuous labour, like the "heathen Chinee." Not only are the quondam slaves illiterate, but the rising generation of blacks is growing up in equal ignorance, and without the habits of industry and obedience which slavery had taught their parents. They are thriftless and idle, spending their money as fast as they make it, and are as ragged as scarecrows, in spite of their high wages. The negro is, however, docile, and good-tempered, little disposed to crime, except petty larceny, and never riotous or aggressive. A black senator of Mississippi came on board, attired in store clothes and a stove-pipe hat ; but the dirtiest mean white would have scorned to sit at table with him, and he did not attempt to enforce his civil rights.

March 22nd, New Orleans.—Some of the streets are paved in Roman style with massive blocks of stone, others are still in the condition of a ploughed field ; but the local taxes are almost sufficient, if properly applied, to pave the streets with gold. The Crescent City lies on a great bend of the river, and reminds one of Bordeaux ; but although Bordeaux, with her grand bridge and large squares, is the handsomer city of the two, she can show nothing like the array of magnificent river steamers which throng the levees of New Orleans. They are quite a spectacle, lying close packed, with their bows touching the quay,—a street of floating palaces.

March 27th, Charlotte.—I visited the Military Institute, whose cadets in uniform enliven the streets of Charlotte. It contains about 110 cadets of various ages, from twelve years upwards. They are not destined for the army, except in one or two instances, but are sent here to acquire, along with book-learning, those habits of order, punctuality, and self-respect, which military discipline so well inculcates. Although the course of study is not specially military, the whole internal economy of the institute is that of a regiment, with parades, messes, bugle-calls, roll-calls,

and arrests; the cadets are all armed with Springfield rifles and
bayonets, have their officers and non-commissioned officers, and
are instructed in drill. If such a system were carried out generally
in public schools, physique and morale would alike benefit, and
every boy would be a potential soldier, without any cost either to
the state or to the individual. Habits of discipline and obedience
cannot be acquired too young, and are as useful to the citizen as
essential to the soldier; thus only can be satisfactorily carried out
universal military service.

April 2nd.—New York has not stood still since I saw it last,
and contains many fine buildings, public and private, sacred and
profane; but after all the bigness of the city is its main claim to
grandeur. Central Park is rather a resort for those who drive in
carriages than for the people at large; in fact the carriages monopolize almost all the available portion of the park, as the public is
not allowed to walk upon the grass, nor even in the drives, lest
they should get run over, forsooth! We were so frequently told
by policemen, "You must not walk there," that we began to
wonder what the park could be intended for, and what paternal
government we were living under. It was quite a relief to get
out of the place, without being taken into custody.

April 3rd, S.S. "L'Amérique."—Punctually at 3 p.m. we
quitted Pier 50 in the North River, and steamed away for the
wide Atlantic. Nothing can possibly be more comfortable than
L'Amérique in all its arrangements: luxurious saloons and cabins,
attentive stewards, polite officers, and excellent food. Now that
I am on the point of completing my periplus, one thing strikes
me forcibly, viz. those who wish to see new and strange things
in distant countries had better lose no time. All the influences
at work are tending to assimilate ancient differences, to extinguish
aboriginals of every sort, to establish everywhere the irrepressible
Caucasian, with his railroads and his grogshops. Everywhere I
have found the same process in active operation: in Egypt,
Ceylon, Australia, New Zealand, Hawaii, California. The romance
of the "Far West" has already been pretty well destroyed since
my last visit, now that it is traversed by Pullman's cars, and soon
the whole American continent will be reduced to the same level.
Levelling *up* it may be, but it *is* levelling, and a level country is
dull for a traveller. The early processes of reclaiming the wilderness are not conducive to the picturesque in nature, and art is

little thought of in a new country.   No doubt the earth supports
every day a larger number of human beings; and more spirits
and tobacco are being every day consumed, as well as corn and
wool, but "sweetness and light" do not increase in equal
proportion.

April 14th, Havre.—We had time for a drive through the city,
which is cheerful and busy, with very fine docks, handsome public
buildings, and wide streets.   There is an air of neatness and finish
about a flourishing town in Europe, which is looked for as vainly
in a new country as is the picturesqueness of antiquity and decay.

He rejoined his mother and sister at San Remo, on April
the 15th, and the party was completed, two days later,
by the arrival of the Percivals from India, with their second
boy.   A pleasant fortnight was spent in making excursions
in the lovely neighbourhood, but it was late in the season
for the Riviera, and early in May they started in two
carriages to drive to Genoa, sleeping at Alassio and Savona
by the way.   They went by rail to Pisa, and from there Sir
David spent a long day at the Baths of Lucca, where he
recalled every incident of the two summers he had passed
there thirty years before, and gladdened the heart of his old
Italian master, Signor Tolomei, by a visit.   He also diverged
to the grand old city of Siena ; and at Florence revisited
the galleries and churches, which he had known so well in
boyhood, generally accompanied by his little nephew, not
five years old, to whom he would patiently show and explain everything.   There he was obliged to leave the others,
and hurry home, to be in time for the militia training,
which was early that year.

In July the whole family went down to Stirling to spend
a month with Colonel Hope, C.B., who commanded the
Brigade Depôt there.   Excursions were made in the neighbourhood, among others one of two days to the Trossachs
and Loch Lomond.   He drove with the Percivals from
Tarbet to Oban on the way to visit friends in Mull and at

Ardtornish, and afterwards had some grouse-shooting with A. H. Brown, M.P., and others, and returned home by the end of September.

According to promise, he gave the first two lectures of the season before the Philosophical Institute in Edinburgh, in the beginning of November, but most of the winter was spent at Meredith.

He had been for some time a member both of the Cotteswold Naturalist Club and of the Gloucestershire Archæological Society, but was seldom able to attend the meetings. He was well up in general botany and geology, but was not a practical field geologist; while never tired of observing the habits of birds and animals, he cared more for the conclusions and inductions of geology than for its study in the field. However, in the spring of 1876, he gladly joined Sir W. Guise and Rev. W. Symonds, two Gloucestershire friends, in a geological expedition to the volcanic region of Auvergne.

May 11th, Clermont Ferrand.—The view of Nevers from the bridge across the Loire is very picturesque, and the country becomes prettier the farther one travels southward. Near Moulins it resembles the midland counties of England, very green with plenty of hedges and hedgerow timber, a capital hunting country, chiefly pasture, and level with good-sized fields full of white cattle. We found Mr. Lucy awaiting us at the Hotel de la Poste.

May 12th.—We ascended the Puy de Pariou, 4000 feet above the sea, one of the remarkable extinct volcanoes of Clermont. The crater is very perfect in shape, a complete circle, like an ant-lion's den, nearly 300 feet in depth. The interior of the funnel is thickly overgrown with heather and wild flowers in great variety; the place altogether is very like Mount Noorat, in Victoria, where extinct volcanoes are as common as in Auvergne. The charms of the day's ramble were greatly enhanced by the variety of investigations—geological, botanical, and entomological—which were carried on, and in which the whole party took equal interest, although not possessing equal knowledge.

May 14*th.*—The "Source pétrifiante" is a very curious estab-lishment, where a regular manufactory, or rather petrifactory, is carried on upon a large scale, every class of object being petrified, from a horse to a halfpenny.   The water, which is clear, is caused to trickle in a shallow stream over a succession of ledges covered with birds' nests, crayfish, shells, medals, mosses, etc., all of which are gradually encrusted with a fine calcareous deposit. When polished this substance resembles in its surface a fine cameo, and remarkably pretty brooches and tablets are made of it, as well as paper weights and such-like ornaments, containing the mummy of a lizard, a toad, or a prawn.   The process is carried on exactly in the same way as at the famous terraces of Rotomahana in New Zealand, where it is performed by nature on the grandest and most effective scale.

Everything valuable that is discovered in the provinces, whether in the shape of antiquities, fossils, or anything else, is carried off to Paris, and there engulfed in the vast collections of the Louvre and other museums.   In this way centralization acts mischievously, and objects, which would be examined with interest if exhibited near the spot where they were found, are lost in the mass and escape observation.   The museum to visit at Clermont is that of Dr. Le Coq, where local geology has had full justice done to it by the zeal and energy of a private individual.   A large room is devoted to the mineralogy and geology of the Puy de Dome alone, while other branches of natural history have not been neglected, and there is an excellent collection of the birds of France.

May 15*th.*—To-day the object of our excursion was the hill of Gergovie, interesting from its geological phenomena, as well as from being the scene of Cæsar's repulse by Vercingetorix and the Arverni, the only serious military check ever sustained by the great Julius.   It is easy to see how the Romans might have sus-tained a repulse after the exertion of rushing up so steep a hill in their armour, but the immediate and long-continued retreat of Cæsar, who was not given to that sort of thing, shows that he must have been very roughly handled by the gallant Arverni, whose name has passed almost unaltered to the province of Auvergne. Amid some general excitement we spotted a rare bird, the wood-shrike ; shrikes and other quasi-raptorial birds, as jays and mag-pies, are pretty common in Auvergne, and indeed birds in general are by no means scarce. This may be due to an awakening of the peasant mind on the subject ; the Government is wide awake, and has issued a circular dissuading from birds'-nesting and the slaying of hedgehogs and moles, and exhorting to the destruction of cockchafers. Moles certainly abound and some other burrowing animal, which our driver calls the " rat-taupe."

May 16*th*.—I started alone for the ascent of Puy de Dome, through groves of Spanish chestnuts, and orchards pink with apple-blossom, and knee-deep in fresh herbage. Everywhere are streams of clear water irrigating the pastures ; anything fresher, greener, and more agreeable on a sultry day can hardly be imagined. Very loth I was to leave behind me this wealth of waters, and emerge upon the bare parched plateau. As I approached the summit, I was suddenly aware of massive cornices and blocks of square-cut stone, such as could only have been shaped by the hands of the masters of the world—Roman masonry beyond a doubt. Sure enough, in digging the foundations of the new observatory here, they have come upon a grand temple of Mercury, the chief god of the Arverni. This temple must have been a splendid object, crowning the lofty Dome, but I would rather see there the comparatively humble observatory. My aneroid gave the top of the tower at 4850 feet above the sea ; it will be the second highest regular observatory in France, and, I think, in Europe also.

May 20*th*.—We started in a light carriage for a three days' driving expedition, with splendid weather. Our road to La Tour d'Auvergne lay chiefly through fine forests of silver firs, with occasional striking views of rock, snow, and open valley. In roads it must be admitted that the French rival the Romans, and no other nation rivals them ; the excellence and the abundance of roads throughout France, even in the wildest districts, must be regarded as a principal cause of her great material prosperity, and as a redeeming effect of her over-centralized government : free-trade, and roads, were two sound " Idées Napoléoniennes." The Auvergnats are a good-looking intelligent people, and thoroughly prosperous, even in the most sterile districts. They have an abundant supply of water, which they distribute by intricate channels all over the slopes of mountains and valleys, where the porous volcanic soil would otherwise be arid and barren, but where abundant pasture is now springing up, enamelled with oxlips, pansies, and marsh-marigolds. " Il n'y a pas ici de grandes fortunes, mais chacun vive bien chez soi," there is in fact little poverty and no pauperism among the mountains of Auvergne. The magnificent ruins of the Chateau de Murol tell of a very different period; it is one of the finest feudal castles in France, having escaped destruction in the Revolution, but it is now crumbling away. All the wealth and power of the surrounding hills and valleys was once in the hands of the Seigneur de Murol; now a prosperous peasantry has risen on their ruins.

May 24th, Bourges.—The impression produced by the magnificent western façade of the Cathedral of Bourges, with five richly sculptured archways, is calculated to prepare one for a grand interior, and the first view on entering enables one more rapidly to take in the full proportions of the building, than any other cathedral that I have seen. The result is a feeling of admiration, and astonishment, almost amounting to awe, even in the minds of some of our party a little deficient in the organ of veneration. We agreed that no cathedral had ever impressed us so strongly with the *genius loci*, as a place of religious worship. There are no transepts, but five complete aisles, each with its own splendid carved portico, and there is thus a double clerestory, as well as a double triforium. Most of the windows are filled with the finest old stained glass, such as cannot now be made or purchased anywhere. The building is of the thirteenth and fourteenth centuries, and has suffered little at the hands either of destroyers or restorers.

The party returned to England *viâ* Orléans and Paris. Sir David's companions on this occasion were a good deal older than himself, but he joined in all their pursuits, and they one and all speak of him as the life of the party; one of them saying, " He was a most cheery and genial companion, with a quick perception of the ludicrous, which betrayed itself in shouts of laughter, that was never ill-natured. He was easily pleased, and not easily displeased; quickly interested in anything new, keen in argument, and crowing with delight when he had floored his antagonist." He stayed a day in Paris behind the others to revisit the Louvre galleries, and the Jardin des Plantes, and to compare the Cathedral of Notre Dame with those of Bourges and Orléans. In his opinion it was intermediate between them, Bourges standing first.

In the summer of this year a camp of exercise was formed upon Minchinhampton Common, where the local militia were joined by regiments from London and elsewhere. He was present with the South Gloucester Militia during the whole of the time, and enjoyed the life in tents, although they suffered somewhat from the heat. He went down to Scotland for the 12th of August, and afterwards joined Mr. Sellar in a yachting cruise among the islands of the west coast. Whilst on this tour, he was summoned home by the sudden death of his sister Elizabeth. The loss of her last unmarried daughter left his mother alone, and more dependent upon his care and devotion than ever. It was therefore with some hesitation that he kept his promise to escort his youngest sister and her child to India, and return with his brother by China and Japan.

At this time indignation was strongly aroused in England by the recent atrocities committed by the Turks in the Balkan provinces. This feeling was fully shared in by Sir David, who had himself had opportunities of witnessing Turkish misgovernment, especially of the Christian communities, in different parts of their dominions. He wrote a letter to the *Gloucester Journal*, dated September 6th, on "England and Turkey," and addressed a public meeting convened by the Liberal Association at Nailsworth, on the same subject. He said :—

Whether we were or were not justified at the time of the Crimean War in fighting for the Turks may be a doubtful question, but I am certain that nothing would justify us in fighting for them now. The interval of twenty years has taught us to know them better, and to attach a true value to their promises of toleration and reform. In fact, the horrors which have recently electrified Europe afford merely an intensified example of the evils constantly impending over the Christian subjects of the Porte, evils which have goaded them again and again into despairing insurrection. During these twenty years, as previously, from every part of Turkey there has constantly been "steaming up a lamentation and an ancient tale of wrong," more especially from those parts where the inhabitants profess Christianity. Oppression, injustice, insurrection, and massacre, deficit and defalcation, pretty well sum up the history of Turkey for many years past. And this is the Power we have tried to bolster up, and to keep Russia from invading, lest she should attack our highways to the East.

Not only in Turkey, but throughout all Europe, we are regarded as the ally of the Sublime Porte, and as being in a great measure responsible for the outrages committed by the Turkish troops. That a grave responsibility does rest upon England in this matter cannot, I think, be denied; and we ought now at last to rise superior to the selfish and narrow considerations by which our policy has hitherto been influenced. Jealousy of Russia, and the fear of arousing Mussulman fanaticism in India appear to be those considerations. Since the creation of a united Germany, Russia has ceased to be formidable to Europe, and the risk of an outbreak in India, as the consequence of our leaving the Turks to fight their own battles, is not even worthy of consideration.

A letter was also written by him to the editor of the *Daily News*, and headed, "The Islands of Greece."

I should like to remind the British public, that the islands of the Archipelago belong all of them ethnologically to Europe, although geographically some of them appear to be Asiatic. They are the "Isles of Greece," inhabited chiefly by Greeks, who have proved by repeated insurrections against Turkey both their ancient love of liberty and the intolerable oppression which drove them to undertake so hopeless a struggle. If we, the English nation, are responsible, as I think we are, for the oppression and misgovernment of the Christians in the Turkish provinces of Europe, we are doubly responsible in the case of these islands, which we could so easily protect, but from which we have hitherto withheld, not only all material assistance, but even all tokens of moral sympathy. Feeling strongly that the case of the Bulgarians only differs from that of other Christian subjects of the Porte in having had the good fortune to find an eloquent exponent of their wrongs, I would fain arouse some sympathy for those whose sufferings have not been brought prominently before the eyes of Europe at this critical time.

An article by Sir David appeared in the *Fortnightly Review*, of October, 1876, entitled, "Mormonism from a Mormon Point of View." During his visit to Salt Lake City he had received, from one of the leading Mormons, several works containing an account of their religious doctrines, and a history of their Church. The paper, which he wrote after a careful study of these books, was considered by Mormons themselves to contain a fair account of their tenets, and he received more than one letter thanking him for his unprejudiced treatment of a subject which has been so often misrepresented. This fact gives a special interest to the article, from which the following is extracted :—

The admission into the Union of neighbouring territories with inferior population to Utah, appears to justify the assertion of the Mormons that the unpopularity of their religion is the sole cause of their exclusion. The fact is that, even in Protestant countries, complete religious toleration is limited to certain recognized persuasions, so that feeble and unpopular sects have still to unite in claiming for themselves the same liberty of conscience which has been conceded to all numerous and powerful dissenting bodies. Science now demands from theology absolute and unconditional freedom, and the day can hardly be far distant when theological heterodoxy will cease to involve any penalties in a free country. At present the Mormon refugees of the Rocky Mountains demand only that amount of civil and religious liberty which the Constitution professes to guarantee to every American citizen, and which the Pilgrim Fathers found for themselves "on the wild New England shore." They complain that their enemies have told their story, that their own statements have been ignored, and that no credit has been given to them for an honest attempt, in these latter days, to put in practice the doctrines of the early Church. Even their enemies will hardly deny that they displayed faith, courage, and endurance, when they resolved, after being expelled from one settlement after another, to plunge into the unknown wilderness, and to found a New Zion beyond the existing limits of the United States. In order to appreciate the tranquillity, sobriety, and steady industry of Deseret, it may be contrasted with Nevada, an adjoining State almost identical with Deseret as to soil, climate, and mineral products. The so-called Silver State stands now pre-eminent in the Union for its turbulent manners, for the number of its liquor-shops, and as being the only State which legalizes public gambling. Of course Nevada is merely passing through a certain rude stage of her existence, just as California has done before her, and she, too, will some day set her house in order; the remarkable point is that Utah should, alone among the young communities of the far West, have altogether escaped such a condition of things. To many persons this will appear to be sufficiently explained by the fact that the Mormons both preach and practice habits of extreme temperance, almost amounting to total abstinence from every sort of stimulant.

After all, it is upon "plural marriages" that the interest as well as the hostility of the outer world has always been concentrated; a Mormon has always been regarded as a man with a number of wives; and beyond this most people know little, and care less, as to the doctrines or customs of the Latter-day Saints. Were it not for their polygamy, it seems probable that the Mormons might now enjoy the same perfect toleration which is extended in America to other forms of religious eccentricity, and Deseret would long ere this have taken her place among the States of the Union. On the other hand, it must be borne in mind that polygamy is a comparatively recent innovation, condemned by the Book of Mormon in the strongest possible terms; but theologians can generally manage to explain away inconvenient texts and hard sayings, while in this case it may be held by the Saints that the previous injunctions were repealed by the subsequent Revelation on Celestial Marriage. With the Mormons, as with Mohammedans or Hindoos, polygamy is doubtless very much a question of expense, and I was informed on good authority that probably about one in four of the Saints is the husband of more than one wife.

Meanwhile, this Church of the nineteenth century possesses amazing vitality, and seems to carry us back to a bygone era of belief, exhibiting as it does the phenomenon of a religious sect

R

heartily convinced of its future mission and claiming the present for its own. While other Churches look to the past for all that is best and truest in religion, the Latter-day Saints regard the present also as a period of miracle and revelation. They expect, in the immediate future, the conversion of all who inhabit their vast continent with as serene a confidence as that with which the early Christians seem to have anticipated the evangelization of the Roman Empire.

The title of Parley P. Pratt's recent work, *Key to the Science of Theology*, indicates the desire of a distinguished Mormon theologian to keep abreast, if possible, of the scientific spirit of the age. Whether the attempt to do this may have proved successful or not, his policy is surely wiser than that which has frequently placed science and theology. in opposition so direct, that every conquest of knowledge over ignorance has appeared to be also a victory over religion. Indeed, Mr. Parley Pratt is entitled to a welcome from the lovers of free thought, considering how rarely theologians seek to identify the progress of their own tenets with that of humanity in every department of science and art, and how seldom it is that they do not—

> " Grow pale
> Lest their own judgments should become too bright,
> And their free thoughts be crimes, and earth have too much light."

It is hard to reconcile polygamy with "the progressive principles of the age," and with modern ideas as to the social position and dignity of women : but Mr. Parley Pratt is not without a scientific plea on behalf of his theological dogma. He maintains that—

" The principal object contemplated by this law is the multiplication of the children of good and worthy fathers, who will teach them the truth, and this is far preferable to sending them into the world in the lineage of an unworthy or ignorant parentage." " Our physical organization, health, vigour, strength of body, intellectual faculties, and inclinations are influenced very much by parentage. Hereditary disease, idiocy, weakness of mind or of constitution, deformity, tendency to violent and ungovernable passions, vicious appetites and desires, are engendered by parents ; and are bequeathed as a heritage from generation to generation."

These are the words of a leading apologist of polygamy, who

founds an argument in his own favour upon this truth, now generally admitted, but almost as generally ignored. It sounds plausible enough in theory, and perhaps the result of polygamy as practised in Utah is that a large proportion of offspring is born to the most energetic, intelligent, and industrious citizens.

The highest types of domestic animals have been developed under a system of breeding and selection, and the burden of proof seems to rest upon those who maintain that a high type of humanity cannot be developed after a similar fashion. Should the Mormons succeed in carrying out practically, for a few generations, any such ideas as are alleged to be the main objects contemplated in their law of polygamy, they would have fair grounds for the belief that they are destined to inherit the whole earth. A race of human beings developed (if such a thing were feasible) by strictly scientific selection and culture could not fail to gain the upper hand in the general struggle for dominion, but it remains to be seen whether any success in this direction will attend the system of the Mormons.

In a pamphlet by Orson Pratt on the "Divine Authenticity of the Book of Mormon" he compares the evidences of it and of the Bible, alleging that both alike have been confirmed by miracles, and that the prophecies of the Bible, especially those of Isaiah, have been fulfilled in the Book of Mormon and in the history of Mormonism. Throughout his elaborate arguments he assumes, the genuineness and authenticity of the Bible, and seeks to found thereon a revelation newer and more complete. It is somewhat disappointing, if the Book of Mormon is to be accepted as the new revelation, to find it so very inferior, both in matter and style, to its great predecessors. Nearly equal in bulk to the Old Testament, it lacks altogether the poetic grandeur and the graphic force of the Hebrew Scriptures, although the Biblical phraseology has been laboriously imitated throughout.

At the present day most of our religious creeds and systems resemble the great ecclesiastical edifices of the Middle Ages—relics of days when faith was stronger and zeal was warmer. These magnificent relics may indeed be renovated by modern hands, and upon a humble scale they can be reproduced, but the power of originating such buildings has passed away, and ecclesiastical architecture is no longer a living art. So it is with the chief accepted systems of religion; they have come down to us in their existing form from periods with which we have nothing else in common; they are not in harmony with the tone of modern life and thought, and could not have been established in modern times. Nevertheless they stand firmly on their ancient foundations, and will long continue to stand, more or less altered and repaired in accordance with modern exigencies.

But the Mormon Church is an exception; it has been founded in these latter days, and may be said to have introduced a new order of ecclesiastical architecture, although ancient materials have been largely employed. Hence the doctrines and history of this Church appear to deserve careful study, for it presents to us a living example of what its mightier predecessors must have been in their early career. Even those who have least sympathy with the peculiar doctrines of the Mormons may be willing to enter a protest in their favour, when the issue really lies between religious liberty and persecution. They are the only Christian sect that has suffered in our own days severe persecution at the hands of professing Christians, and their cause on that account demands especial sympathy from all who advocate absolute religious toleration.

Auvergnat Plough

Funeral Rites. Hansi 28th Dec 1876

CHAPTER XV.

1876-1877.

VOYAGE TO BOMBAY—THE DELHI DURBAR—BHÁVNAGAR AND PÁLITÁNA — " PROTECTED PRINCES IN INDIA " — " MODERN IMPERIALISM IN INDIA."

SIR DAVID started with his sister in the S.S. *Siam*, in November, 1876. They had an unusually rough and long voyage as far as Gibraltar; a life-boat was swept away, skylights were smashed, and the crockery and deck chairs suffered severely.

November 19th, Malta.—The Cathedral of St. John contains the tombs of all the most distinguished Knights Hospitallers of Malta : the pavement is entirely composed of coats-of-arms, inlaid in various coloured marbles, with long inscriptions relating the pedigree and character of knights belonging to the noble families of every country in Christendom. Although the dates of their tombstones extend over several centuries, there is a marked resemblance among them all, the style of the ancient being imitated in the modern, the most recent of which is dated in this year.

December 6th, Bombay.—While the baggage was being inspected, a careless fellow managed to let off a pistol, and shot an unfortunate old gentleman in the leg : the bullet was extracted in a flattened condition, but the bone was not broken. We drove to the High Court, Mazagon, where the ample airy rooms are in pleasing contrast to our confined cabins on board.

Bombay has vastly improved in every respect since my last visit, and is now quite a city of palaces : the trees planted in various places have grown well, the drives are broad and well kept, the streets are crowded with the most varied and picturesque population in the world, and altogether there is an appearance of stir and prosperity such as can be seen in few other cities. Even the secondary thoroughfares are so densely crowded that it is dangerous to drive at any speed, and the yellow-turbaned policemen seem to be more ornamental than useful, for they are so numerous as to encumber the streets.

December 9th.—Watt, Willie, and I went to pay our respects to the Thakore Saheb of Bhávnagar ; a guard of honour presented arms as we drove up, and the Thakore, with his courtiers, stood on the steps of the bungalow to receive us. We shook hands with him and a few of the native swells, after which we took our places on damask couches, arranged at the end of a long hall. I sat on the young chief's right, and he chatted a good deal in English ; while the other two sahebs discoursed the officials in Hindustani. They were all gorgeously attired, and beamed with good-nature and satisfaction. After sitting as long as good manners required, we rose to take leave, when the Raja sprinkled us with rosewater, stuffed our hands full of betel-nut neatly folded up in gilt leaves, and suspended large garlands round our necks. My garland was enormous, and formed of yellow chrysanthemums, the others were smaller and white, so that the Thakore evidently gives me credit for being the "big brother." We afterwards paid a visit to the Pinjrapole, that singular caricature of our poor-houses and asylums for incurables. It covers a considerable space in the heart of the city, containing several large yards and sheds crowded with animals of every sort in every stage of misery, such as "age, ache, penury, and imprisonment" can lay upon man or beast. On the whole, however, I was agreeably disappointed, as the creatures seemed to be kindly enough treated, to be more or less fed and watered, and even doctored to a certain limited extent. I could

not, however, bring myself to write in the visitors' book any praise
of an institution which ignores so completely the principles of
euthanasia, and happy despatch, although it is by no means súch
a den of horrors as I had imagined.

December 11th.—The swells of Bombay all inhabit the neighbourhood of Malabar Hill, and a warm job it is, driving up and
down among the volcanic rocks and the scattered palmyras from
one bungalow to another, in the heat of the day and one's best
clothes, in order to make calls, after the absurd etiquette of
Bombay. Why will people in India not adapt themselves to
natural conditions, get up at daybreak, dispense with tiffin, dine as
soon after dark as may be, and pay their visits either in the early
morning or after dinner, as in the happy isle of Oahu? After
tiffin, I took leave of my kind hosts, and made for the Byculla
station, arriving only just in time for the special train of our friend
the Thakore. Mr. Peile and I have a small saloon carriage
to ourselves, which is to be our home for the next four days.

December 15th, Delhi.—At last, out of the dull flat plain, above
the squalid mud villages rose the glittering domes and minarets
of the Jumma Musjid, and the imperial city of Delhi, the goal of
our long journey, appeared in view. The streets of Delhi, the
roads, the fields, the dusty camping-grounds, the whole place, in
fact, swarm with a motley multitude of men, horses, elephants,
camels, buffalo and bullock carts, through which a way is hastily
opened for the Saheb's carriage to pass, not without tremendous
shouting, great alarm, and a little danger. Everywhere are tents,
among which our own encampment, and that of the " Bombay
Chiefs," present by no means the least elegant and imposing
appearance.

December 18th.—The Bhávnagar elephants, in gala costume,
were paraded for inspection ; they are loaded with plates and
cloth of gold and silver, which conceal from view almost the
entire animal, except his trunk, and this is painted all manner of
colours. The howdahs are of silver and gold, decorated with
figures of tigers, antelope, fish, etc., and each elephant, as he stands
up, must be worth thousands of pounds. A very unanimous
opinion appears to prevail as to the folly of the present " Imperial
Assemblage," and the unwillingness of the Native princes to take
part in it. Times in India are bad, the expense is enormous,
and it is much too soon after the Prince of Wales' visit. Mean-

while, the affairs of the Empire, the famine, and frontier difficulties must take care of themselves; for all the high officials, British and Native, are engaged in boring each other, and playing with garlands, medals, atta of roses, and gunpowder.

December 20th.—Peile and I started early for the Kootub Minar. It was a very sharp morning and we drove furiously, our horses having plenty of excuses for shying at elephants and camels as they tore along; the road is good, and in an hour or there-abouts we accomplished the distance of thirteen miles from our camp. There is much to be seen around the Kootub in the way of mosques, tombs, and gateways; one of these last is a most beautiful specimen of Pathan architecture, and is covered with tracery and carving in white marble and red sandstone, as delicate as if it were a box of sandal-wood and ivory. But the grand monument of this place is the Minar itself, nearly 250 feet high, in five storeys, of sandstone and marble, a gracefully tapering spire covered with carving, the edge of which is as sharp now as on the day of its completion; the architecture is very ornate, although the date is early in the thirteenth century.

December 26th.—I took a ride through the camps, to observe the ever-varying stream of life which pours unceasingly through each artery and vein of their complex system. Owing to the crowded state of the roads, and the inveterate tendency of natives to tie up their heads, and then put a basket over them, it is difficult to get along at any pace without knocking some one down. The Sahebs like to rattle along fast, and natives will walk in the middle of the road: it is marvellous that serious accidents do not occur; none at least are ever reported. Endless strings of unladen camels were filing out into the country, doubtless in search of fodder; and wonderful it is that fodder sufficient, at moderate rates, should be found for the innumerable host of animals here, in-cluding several thousand elephants. Supplies for man and beast are indeed abundant and good, although the sudden influx of population might tax the resources of any market, and to Bombay folk everything appears cheap.

Having explored very thoroughly the antiquities and monuments of Delhi, and there being still some days to spare before the Durbar, he decided to spend the time in visiting Hansi and Hissar. At the latter place his brother

and family had been killed in the mutiny of 1857, and
he wished to see the spot, and, if possible, to hear some
particulars from survivors.

December 28th, Hansi.—It was strange to find myself alone,
the only white man in this fortress of Hansi, and to think how
different it was here not twenty years ago. The cantonments no
longer exist, and order is maintained by a native magistrate and a
few police. I followed a procession, bearing the remains of a
Hindoo out of the city, to a spot where Mussulman tombs were
surrounded with numerous little heaps of ashes, showing that here
was the last resting-place of Hindoo and Moslem alike. The
corpse, carefully wrapped up, was laid upon a few bricks and
potsherds; logs of wood were placed horizontally beneath and
around it; other sticks were heaped upon these, or interlaced
vertically, so as to form a pile of wood almost concealing the body.
Small sticks and bunches of thorn were then ignited on the windward side of this structure, and soon the whole was in a blaze. A
large concourse looked on during the process of cremation, which
had nothing disgusting about it; there was not much smoke nor
crackling, and in a short time nothing remained but the large
bones of the deceased, so fierce was the heat of the well-laid fire,
and when the operation is complete there ought to remain only
"two handfuls of white dust." When shall we be as wise and
civilized in this matter as our Aryan brothers of India?

December 29th, Hissar.—In front of the church is a plain obelisk
of sandstone: " In memory of John Wedderburn, his wife and child,
who fell victims near this spot to the Mutiny on 29th May, 1857."
Close by is another larger monument, erected by Government, in
memory of all those Europeans who were killed at Hissar and
Hansi in 1857. There are only the names of seven men, but
nine women and sixteen children perished here, rendering this
tragedy one of the saddest in the whole history of the great mutiny.
While reading the touching list of victims I could understand, if
not share, the feeling of the English soldiers who killed men
merely because their faces were dark, and because they were
found near the places where the poor little innocents were
slaughtered. Hissar is now again full of Christian women and
children, while there is not a British soldier within a hundred
miles, and all are living in the most perfect confidence of security.

Is this confidence misplaced? It is hard to say; but as matters stand at present, I think that it is not, while the generation still lives that remembers the swift and terrible retribution. Hissar was reoccupied by the British within a few days of the events which left not a single living Christian in the place. Those who escaped from the massacres were protected by the Native princes, whose territory adjoins the Hariana district; and it was here a conspicuous fact throughout, that the murders and plundering were the work of the Mussulman population, chiefly the butcher caste, while the Hindoos were friendly, or at least passive.

January 1, 1877, *Delhi.*—The general aspect of the Great Durbar was that of a very splendid circus, where everything was of the best material, and genuine, except the heraldry; and the glitter of jewels and gold, silken banners, and satin robes was certainly brilliant. Still there was a want of point and purpose about the whole affair: the house was full of a magnificent audience, but where were the actors? The gigantic herald, Barnes, read out, after a flourish of trumpets, the Imperial Proclamation; his voice is stentorian, but was lost in so vast a space: as for the Viceroy, who followed, his speech was a mere dumbshow. Even the one hundred and one *salvos* of artillery were dissipated in space, and the only effective performance was the *feu de joie* running up and down the ranks of the troops, whereby a stampede was caused of a few elephants.

January 5th.—The review has been undoubtedly *the* successful act of the whole pageant. First marched past the retinues of the Native princes, as varied in style, colouring, and costume as the host of Xerxes, those least Europeanized being by far the handsomest and most effective. Headed by their bands, playing out of tune, and marching out of time, infantry, cavalry, camels and elephants, with guns, litters, and led horses, went by successively. One feature was uniformly good throughout—the dear old elephants all looked stately and dignified, their trappings and housings were magnificent, and many of them trumpeted out a salute as they marched by; altogether there were 437 counted. The whole force, European and Native, numbered upwards of 16,000, and all looked well, especially the artillery in all its branches, which is exclusively British. Last, not least, came the 92nd Highlanders, whose costume rivals in picturesqueness any of the gay Orientals.

On the return journey from Delhi, he stopped at Jubbulpore long enough to see the marble rocks on the Nerbudda, and the School of Industry, where six hundred Thugs are peacefully employed in tent-making. At the holy city of Nassick he stayed for some days, with an old friend, H. B. Erskine; and from there made an excursion to Aurungabad, to visit the Caves of Ellora.

January 17th, Roza.—The caves worthy of being inspected are about thirty in number, the oldest being Buddhist, the next Brahminical, and the most recent Jaina. They are all nearly at the same level, and are cut out of the same layer of trap rock. The so-called Carpenter's Cave is shaped like a church with aisles, and a roof like the inverted hull of a ship; it is cut in imitation of wooden beams and rafters, and adorned with numerous seated figures of a distinctly Buddhist type. Then follow a series of five caves in triple storeys, like three-deckers, with colossal bas-reliefs, and numerous *viharas*, or cells for recluses. The Kylas is not a cave, but a magnificent temple cut out of the solid rock, a monolithic temple, in fact, about 100 feet in height. The rock has been cut in perpendicular scarps all round it, and galleries and colonnades have been excavated in the face of the cliffs thus artificially made. It is useless to attempt a description of the very elaborate carvings which adorn the temple inside and outside, as well as the surrounding galleries. The chief mass of the temple rests upon the backs of animals, principally elephants admirably represented, and two colossal elephants guard the entrance. It is singular to see the difference between these lifelike elephants, and the conventional lions (never any tigers) which are intermingled; many other animals appear in the sculptures, very rarely the horse. Plaster and paint still decorate the temple in many places, both internally and externally, and happily the hand of the Mussulman iconoclast has not been raised against these heathen works of art, of which the sculpture is in marvellous preservation. The style of Kylas is that which is so universally imitated in modern Hindoo temples, ornate in the highest degree, the surface of the stone being completely covered with sculpture in greater or less relief, of flowers, animals, and human beings; many of the female figures are very graceful, although somewhat conventional as to form, and all are more or less "draped."

He next went to Tanna, near Bombay, to stay with his brother, who was the judge there ; and then on by Surat, to visit the Percivals at Bhávnagar. For more than six years during the minority of the young chief, Mr. Percival had held the joint charge with the Native prime minister of this flourishing State. When Sir David arrived he learnt that, to the regret of all classes, his brother-in-law had suddenly been ordered away to take charge of Sholapur, one of the worst of the famine districts, and was preparing to start next day. He stayed with his sister for a week, till she was ready to follow, and during that time made an excursion to the Jain temples at Pálitána.

January 26th, Bhávnagar.—The great event to-day is the close of the Mohurrum, and we were invited to view it from the palace in the centre of the city. With difficulty the carriage made its way through the narrow streets, filled with a dense crowd of prosperous, well-dressed people : in all India I have not seen a population with a greater appearance of *bien être* than that of Bhávnagar. From the palace windows we looked down on a sea of brilliant turbans of every hue and shape, those of the country cultivators being very numerous, for the most part white with a twist of red or some other colour running through their innumerable folds. The large made-up turbans of Brahmin officials, and city Banias, usually scarlet or purple with a little gold, were also to be seen frequently, although the Mohurrum is of course a Mussulman festival, and the performers belong to that creed. There are a number of Moslems in Bhávnagar, but they belong mostly to the poorer classes ; they manage, however, to make a fine show with their *tabuts*, or shrines, and it is quite wonderful what effect is produced by the artistic use of a little talc, gold and silver tinsel, and coloured paper. The architecture of the tabuts is remarkable, somewhat in the style of the Lucknow palaces, with many domes and pinnacles ; they contain only a few cocoa-nuts and other fruits, and are borne very slowly through the surging crowd, to be thrown finally into the sea. The din of pipes and tomtoms is perfectly deafening ; a ring of men with musicians in the centre would form below us, yelling, jumping, and slapping the breast and arms,

somewhat like the howling dervishes of Scutari, until moved on
by the police, when their places were immediately taken by a fresh
lot. Hobby-horses; men painted yellow and black to represent
tigers, and led in chains by their keepers; men armed with wooden
swords and basket bucklers, engaging in terrific combats, passed,
along with the tabuts, and long poles with the rude representation
of a hand on the top. Cries of " Hassan ! Hosein ! " were occasionally audible, but there was no appearance of lamentation, all looked
as merry as mummers generally do, and I was strongly reminded
of the Carnival in Italy. Mohurrum, Huli, Carnival, Saturnalia,
Guisers, etc., are probably all derived from a common source in
the early history of the Aryan race, and have been modified only
by the religions with which they are now associated. The rickety-
looking roofs of the houses opposite us were loaded with spectators, including a few women and many children, who also mingled
in the crowd; but no accident occurred, and all were in good
humour, as well as sober.

January 29th, Pálitána.—The isolated mountain of Satrunji
rises just above Pálitána to the height of two thousand feet, and it
is upon its highest summit that the city of temples is perched. After
passing the gate of the fortification, you are requested to put on
slippers, and are at once admitted into the inner enclosures surrounding distinct groups of temples. The general effect is marvellous of this vast collection of elaborately carved and decorated
buildings, varying in size but uniform in style; all perfect as to
finish, repair, and cleanliness,—nothing mean, ruinous, or dirty
visible anywhere, to remind one of Asiatic incongruity. The
temples are constructed of stone from a distance, raised at great
cost to this almost inaccessible spot; the images which they contain
are of the purest white marble, covered with golden and jewelled
ornaments; all the figures are carved with artistic skill, and strongly
resemble each other. The flooring'of the temples is inlaid with
coloured marbles, and the interiors are brightly painted in various
colours, chiefly red. The exteriors vary little in design, although
several centuries have elapsed during which continuous building
has been going on here; the style appears to have become stereo-
typed at an early date, perhaps five hundred years ago, and all more
modern art has been merely imitative. Various sorts of trees
grow here and there, adding to the beauty of the general view,
which from certain points is quite fairy-like, a city of the genii,

perched high above the world, where the gods of Epicurus might "lie beside their nectar."

February 4th, Surat.—I visited the famous tombs of the early settlers, or residents in Surat, from England and Holland. The English tombs are in good preservation, and are in the same enclosure with the modern cemetery; they are indeed very different in style from anything of the present day, and tell of a time when Europeans in India affected Orientalism in everything, even in their graves. The people who were buried in tombs so like those of the Moguls, must have lived in Mogul fashion during their lives, and desired to leave permanent records behind them in the country of their adoption. As a rule English monuments, like English bungalows and cantonments in India, seem intended only to last about as long as one generation of the garrison of this great standing camp, and to be constructed with as little regard to appearance as to durability. Enough still remains of the Dutch tombs to prove that the old Netherlanders were merchant princes, and several Dutch inscriptions are legible enough; the work of native artists is made manifest by a nose-ring in the nose of an angel on one of the monuments.

February 11th.—A few days' stay at Matheran is a very agreeable change; climate, scenery, and mode of life are so different from what one is accustomed to in the plains. The hill, which is 2000 feet high, is nearly flat on the top, with precipitous sides, indented with deep ravines and running out in numerous promontories, known as "points." The whole of the top surface is covered with dense, evergreen forest, which presents a charming contrast to the brown withered vegetation of the low country. In the jungle are nestled numbers of jolly little bungalows, invisible until you are close to them, and frequently surrounded by nicely kept gardens on a very small scale. From the points are visible the sea, with the buildings of Bombay gleaming on the farther side of the harbour, the great ramparts of the Western Ghauts, the plains of the Konkan, and numerous deep ravines densely wooded. Altogether Matheran is a charming sylvan retreat, an apparently "boundless contiguity of shade;" the real extent is not great, but has been made the most of, so as to afford numerous walks and rides.

February 13th, Lanowlie.—We started on ponies for the caves of Karli and Badja; the latter is picturesquely situated under wooded hills, the flat tops of which are crowned with ancient forts. The Buddhist caves are very interesting, older even than those of Karli ; the style is similar, but everything is simpler and on a smaller scale. The cave temple is vaulted, and the roof is ostensibly supported by wooden arches of horse-shoe form, which resemble the ribs of a ship ; they are in perfect preservation, sheltered from wet, and impervious to white ants, and the ribs of teak appear to be as sound as they were when placed in their useless position twenty centuries ago. The wood dates back from the Buddhist architects, who not merely imitated wooden forms in stone, but treated the solid rock as if, like an ordinary roof, it required to be supported with wood.

In a letter, dated Bombay, February 8th, addressed to the editor of the *Daily News*, he says :—

There is no longer room between the Secretary of State for India and the Governors of Bombay or Madras for a Governor-General of India. A great saving might safely be effected here, but the question arises whether it is desirable to reduce Bombay and Madras to the rank of lieutenant-governorships, or to increase the powers of the two governors, to raise the three lieutenant-governors to a similar position, bringing them into direct communication with the Secretary of State, and to dispense altogether with the costly intermediate authority of the Governor-General and his council. The subject demands inquiry ; but I should be in favour of the second alternative, if the boundaries of the five great divisions of the Empire were so rectified as to be conterminous, as nearly as possible, with the boundaries of language and race. It is difficult to see why, in local matters, a Legislative Council sitting in Calcutta or Simla should be entitled to overrule one sitting in Bombay or Madras, when all alike are under the control of the Secretary of State in London. Retrenchment is more than ever essential now in India, with a depreciated currency, and an ever-recurring visitation of famine in one or other province of the Empire. I am convinced that financial collapse is the one serious danger that menaces our rule in India, and that, compared with this, the risk from disaffected chiefs, Mussulman fanaticism, or Russian intrigues is altogether a secondary consideration.

He contributed an article, entitled " Protected Princes of India," to the *Nineteenth Century*, in July, 1878. It is almost impossible, in a limited space, to give an idea of the way in which he treated large Indian subjects, but extracts from this, and other similar papers, will show the deep interest he took in them.

The authority possessed by the numerous chiefs, who rule collectively over a territory equal in area to France, Germany, and Spain, varies greatly in degree: some of them being wealthy princes, holding powers of life and death over populations equal to those of second-class European kingdoms; while others resemble feudal barons, exercising a limited jurisdiction over one or two villages.

The average life of an Indian prince is short, and the period of minority according to English law is long, so that Native States are frequently under a regency, and a large proportion of those seated upon the gadi, or cushion of State, are children. During the minority of young chiefs the paramount power claims a special right of intervention, and, like the Roman Senate and people in similar cases, assumes the office of guardian. The manner and degree of intervention have varied greatly from time to time; in some cases a British official has been appointed with large powers to govern the country; in the case of Baroda a distinguished Native statesman has been summoned from a distance, and placed in authority over the minor's dominions; in other instances a Native regency of local notables has been formed, and left to act mainly upon its own discretion. Perhaps the most successful of all arrangements has been that of "joint administrators," such as was adopted by the Bombay Government for the State of Bhávnagar. Here a member of the Civil Service was appointed to administer the State during a minority, in conjunction with a Brahmin of high character and great experience, the minister of a former chief. These two administrators exercised jointly the same powers as had been enjoyed by the late Thakore; a happy blending of European and Native ideas was accomplished, whereby local opinion was carried along with many reforms which appeared desirable from an English point of view, while in other cases the danger was avoided of injuring the people, as they are so frequently injured in India, by energetic endeavours to do them good against their will. The Native minister, thoroughly understanding his own countrymen, kept his European colleague clear of the besetting error of forcing on changes beneficial in themselves but premature. Among other merits, this arrangement has maintained a continuity of men and measures, and will leave the State in a condition fitted for the resumption of Native rule when the young Thakore attains his majority. Under the system of joint administrators the cheap and simple machinery of Native rule has been used to carry out the more enlightened principles of the British Government. How far is it possible to administer India generally in a similar manner and with similar results?

Meanwhile the young chief may be educated for his position, and the stifling atmosphere, moral and physical, of the zenana may be exchanged for the bracing influences of a college, such as has been established at Rajcote for the illustrious youths of Kathiawar. Here Rajpoot boys of the highest rank receive a liberal education, modelled upon that which, in English public schools, is deemed suitable for the rising generation of our statesmen and legislators. Manly games, including cricket, football, and gymnastics, are encouraged; and personal competition upon equal terms is developed among lads hitherto reared in haughty and indolent isolation.

In our relations with the Native States an important practical reform might easily be effected, which would remove one of the greatest blots upon our Indian administration. There exists at present no judicial tribunal for the decision of cases, civil or criminal, to which the protected princes of India are parties. In all such cases the British Government, as the paramount power, decides without appeal, inasmuch as the ultimate appeal lies to the Secretary of State for India, who is himself the highest executive officer of the Government. If the Secretary of State confirms the decision of his own subordinates, there remains, as a court of appeal, only the floor of the House of Commons, where a last effort may be made by a Native prince, if he is wealthy or influential enough, to force his grievances upon the attention of Parliament and of the public. In cases of dispute between rival chiefs the British Government may indeed act as an impartial arbiter, but even then the method of conducting the inquiry is very objectionable. The matter is investigated secretly by a Political Agent, through whom pass all communications between Government and the disputants, and upon whose confidentially expressed opinion the ultimate decision is based.

S

A most difficult and responsible duty devolves upon the so-called "Politicals," to whom has been entrusted hitherto the conduct of the peculiar relations subsisting between the British Government and Native chiefs. Ably and faithfully their arduous duties have been discharged, and no body of public servants can boast of more distinguished names than the Politicals, most of whom are soldiers. Had it been otherwise, and had our Indian political system been carried out by less worthy agents, it could hardly have survived until now. Open justice should be our mainstay on Native territory as well as in our own provinces ; and we have nothing to fear from publicity, even in the political department. A secret system affords opportunity for intrigue, corruption, and chicanery, in all of which the natives have the advantage ; our officers are hoodwinked and misled by diplomatists subtler and less honest than themselves. What is required is the substitution of the judicial for the diplomatic system in dealing with Native States. The mere existence of an impartial tribunal, however constituted, before which the Government might be compelled to assign publicly the reasons for their policy, would be a complete protection against any act of flagrant injustice. Possibly no existing tribunal would be competent to undertake such functions, and it may be necessary to create a special court for the purpose. Above all, it is desirable "to render it unnecessary for any man in India to cross the ocean to seek for justice," even from so competent a tribunal as the Privy Council affords. The principle of arbitration, which has been so successfully applied to the settlement of disputes between independent nations, might be difficult of application in India, when the paramount power is directly concerned, but it is in complete harmony with Native ideas and practice in ordinary life, and *punchayets*, or juries of Native chiefs, would command the confidence of their own countrymen.

The Native States are no longer to be looked upon as creating mere temporary difficulties and inconveniences, and as being certain to disappear sooner or later from the map of India. They constitute now a permanent and integral portion of the Imperial system, and the relations between them and the paramount power have assumed a new significance. Many suggestions have been made for utilizing the Indian princes as supporters of the Government, and for inspiring them with a genuine pride in their position as recognized feudatories of so mighty an Empire. The organization of an Imperial Diet has been proposed, and if such an assembly could be constituted, it is evident that many important questions would properly fall to be discussed and settled therein. For instance, the establishment of a Zollverein, or complete customs union, for the whole of India, including the Native States : to prevent smuggling of costly and portable articles, such as opium, is, with the existing frontiers, a simple impossibility ; and so great are the inconveniences at present experienced, that negotiations have been set on foot for the general abolition of inland customs duties. Evidently the proper method of conducting such negotiations would be to assemble a general congress for the whole Empire, where the Native chiefs could be represented by their *karbharies*, or appointed deputies.

The natives of India hardly appreciate the new-fangled merits of British rule ; they are genuine conservatives, and seem to prefer an ancient evil to a modern reform, liking to be misgoverned by their own people in the old-fashioned style. The very acts on which we rely for securing popular good-will, are frequently productive of bitter discontent, because we are out of sympathy with Native feelings, customs, and modes of thought. At the same time, our temperament and our motives of action are inscrutable to the natives, and the great gulf fixed between the two races remains unbridged. Then the costliness of our Government involves the necessity of perpetually trying to discover or invent new methods for raising money, and the inhabitants of the British provinces are kept in constant dread of some new turn of the fiscal screw. Looking back upon the good old times previous to annexation, they are apt to think of a former ruler as "a tyrant— but our masters then were still at least our countrymen."

The following is from a paper on "Modern Imperialism in India," read in June, 1879, before the East India Association, in which he expressed his disapproval of the policy then being pursued in India by Lord Lytton :—

The dangers and advantages of Parliamentary and popular English interference in the government of India have been fully discussed before this Association ; both the dangers and the advantages are doubtless real enough, but the latter greatly preponderate over the former, especially when such interference tends to counteract the tendency to substitute personal government for the reign of law.   In March, 1878, a bill was passed through the Legislative Council of the Government of India for the better regulation of the vernacular press.   Under the existing law libellous or seditious publications were liable to prosecution, and if, as alleged, the law was not adequate to punish them, it might properly have been made more stringent without any injury to true freedom of the press, which must, like other institutions, be subject to the law of the land.   The mischief of the "Gagging" Act is that it subjects the vernacular press of India to the arbitrary control of the Executive, introducing a system of warnings and confiscation utterly alien to English legislation.   It has been truly said of India that she is dumb before her rulers, as a sheep before her shearers is dumb ; but even a sheep will bleat feebly at times beneath the shears, when these bite deep into the flesh, and any attempt to silence such bleatings would be a wanton piece of cruelty.   Animals that bear cruelty in silence are liable to greater ill usage than those that give tongue, partly because much of cruelty results from the lack of imagination, partly because howling causes a public scandal.   Such of the Native newspapers as are printed partly in English are doubtless favourable specimens of their class, and can hardly be regarded as those most likely to offend ; but, having frequently perused them, I may venture to say that there are among them journals of so high a class, that any Government might well value their support and dread their censure. These journals, which would be creditable to any civilized community, are the growth of a full generation of liberty, and could only have been developed in a free atmosphere.   It is true that public opinion in this country has been so strongly expressed against the " Gagging " Act, as to place it almost in abeyance ; but even if it were repealed to-morrow, the mischievous effects of such crude and ill-considered legislation would remain, in a general sense of insecurity as to the best established rights and privileges of the natives.

There is one article in the Indian Imperialist programme which does not, in my opinion, deserve unqualified censure—viz. the employment of Native troops for Imperial purposes beyond the limits of Asia.   The position of the Native army, between a powerful British garrison, and a numerous quasi-military police, is

altogether anomalous ; and it may be fairly said, either make the
Native Infantry regiments thoroughly fit to take their places in
line of battle alongside their British comrades, or else, if distrust
and economy prevent this being done, convert them at once into
armed police, for the maintenance of internal order only.   The
classes from which we recruit the rank and file are excellent in
quality and inexhaustible in numbers ; courageous, docile, and
temperate, eager to enlist, and to serve upon slender pay.   The
martial races of India constitute as fine a nursery for soldiers as
any in the world.   India is already bowed down beneath her
military burdens, and is unable to pay for a great Native army,
requiring a corresponding British force to watch it ; but if Africa,
or any other portion of the Empire, needs soldiers, and if Imperial
funds are provided to pay for them, they can be furnished by
India to any amount, without serious difficulty or danger.   One
danger perhaps there may be—that of developing the aggressive
spirit of the " Imperial Englishman," and of encouraging annexation, if Indian soldiers, paid with British money, can always be
counted upon for service.   If a maritime rival should arise,
capable of interrupting our communications with India by sea,
then our Empire would indeed be menaced, and for such an
emergency we ought to reserve the strength which many in India,
as well as in England, wish to expend in fighting where our
national interests are not involved.   England and India united
are strong enough to defy all attack, and to wait in conscious
strength until they are attacked, of which there is at present no
chance whatever.

Is India a source of power and profit to the British Empire,
or have we no motive for retaining the country except that we
hold it in trust for the benefit of its inhabitants, and cannot in
honour repudiate the trust ?   This question is often asked and
discussed in England with a gravity which, to all except Englishmen, must appear sufficiently ludicrous, more especially to the
people of India themselves.   As regards India being a source of
power, it is certain that upon many occasions, seven times within
the last thirty-five years, England has borrowed troops from India
for Imperial exigencies, and so long as these are paid for out of
Imperial funds, such a proceeding confers strength on the Empire,
and is a relief rather than injury to India.   If England could
resolve to adopt a truly Imperial policy, and to support India

financially, by controlling her expenditure and guaranteeing her debt, she might draw from India an amount of military strength, which would render the British Empire as formidable on land as it is already on the seas. Unfortunately, the same policy which seems to have added a new element to our military strength, has saddled us with obligations and burdens, which may tax even the combined strength of Great Britain and India. The best friends of India cannot help feeling apprehensive that our new position in Cyprus and Asiatic Turkey will entail fresh burdens upon India, and that the resources which might have rendered our existing Eastern Empire impregnable, may be squandered in the attempt to make a new one. We cannot tell as yet what our liabilities in Asiatic Turkey really amount to, but that country may prove to us an exaggerated Algeria, and it is hard to see how territorial acquisition there can fail to weaken our military and financial position in India.

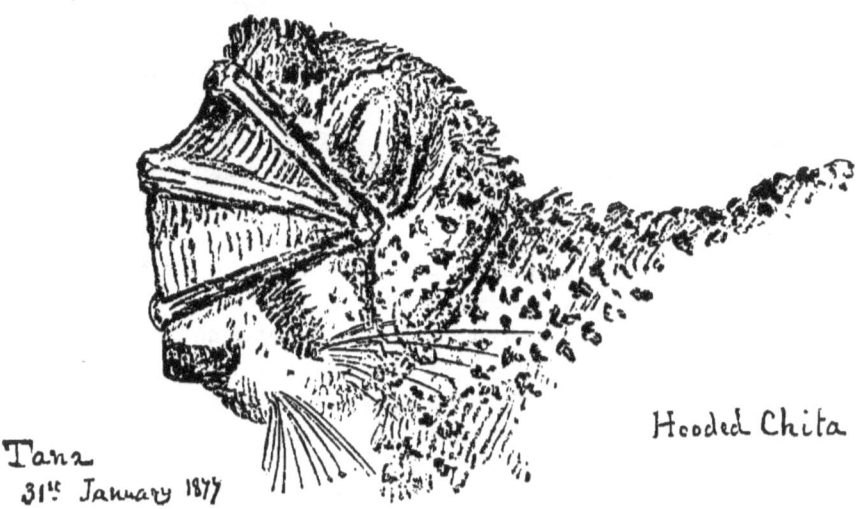

Tana
31st January 1877

Hooded Chita

Young Mahratta.
7 Feb. 1877
Sholapur Famine Districts

CHAPTER XVI.

1877.

THE FAMINE DISTRICTS—CANARA—CEYLON—SINGAPORE—"PARLIAMEN-
TARY DELEGATES FOR 'INDIA"—"POPULAR REPRESENTATION IN
INDIA"—"THE DECCAN."

February 14th, Sholapur.—The aspect of Sholapur is not particularly cheerful; the country is flat, bare, and dusty; the leafless
trees and the high winds are like February in the North, but the
heat is tropical enough. This country is certainly over-peopled,
its scanty and uncertain rainfall renders it almost as unfit for cultivation as the interior of Australia, and it could only become
prosperous through permanent depopulation. The inhabitants are
numerous, improvident, and dependent almost exclusively on
agriculture; they are thus subject to a chronic danger of famine,

which their low standard of comfort only renders more serious.
They have just sufficient in a favourable year, but nothing is laid
by for a dry day; making bad roads from village to village, and
digging tanks which will only hold water during the rains, are the
present make-shifts for employing the people; but their permanent
condition will not be thereby improved.   If half of them could be
evicted, or caused to emigrate, and the remaining half dissuaded
from recruiting their numbers up to the original mark, there would
be some hope for this poverty-stricken Deccan; as a pastoral
country it might even become rich, and would rapidly rally from
occasional droughts.

February 18*th, Bijapur.*—After no small difficulty, arrangements have been made for me to visit Bijapur, a distance of over
sixty miles.   There was little in the surrounding landscape to
induce one to linger on the road, neither wood nor water: a dark
brown desert stretches in every direction to the distant horizon.
No hills, except one stony ridge, break the monotony of a vast
plain; no rivers, only dry nullahs, with an occasional muddy pool;
no trees, except a few scraggy babuls along the roadside, and a
few stunted date palms marking the lines of empty water-courses.
At the present time this part of the Deccan is simply a desert, as
much as any part of Arabia; but it is not deserted, and villages
at frequent intervals show the only spots green in the landscape,
oases due to the existence of permanent wells.

The beautiful tomb of Ibrahim Shah is perhaps the most
perfect specimen of Bijapur architecture, and is in excellent preservation, only some of the most delicate tracery and pinnacles
having been injured.   The materials used for all parts of the
buildings, except the large domes, which are of brick, are hard
dark basalt, and cement almost as hard.   The stone admits of a
high polish, but retains the sharpness of its edges, and is well
adapted for carving the elaborate tracery which adorns windows,
parapets, minarets, and cornices.   The general rule in Indian
architecture holds good for Bijapur, the most modern of the great
Moslem cities now in ruins; and here the graceful style characteristic of the place is marked by the peculiar shape of the domes,
which have developed into complete spheres, and rest upon their
flower-shaped sockets, like a toy ball in its cup.   The walls of the
city proper are tolerably perfect, and enclose an extent nearly
equal to that of modern Delhi; the whole of this vast area is

covered with great tombs and mosques, most of them still in
excellent preservation, and some of them carefully repaired and
whitewashed. But the great sight of Bijapur is "the dome, the
wondrous dome" of Mohammed Adil Shah's tomb, second only
to St. Peter's in Rome. It is not much more than a hemisphere,
resembling in form Humayun's, but is of course much larger; it is
constructed of large flat bricks, excellent in quality, like all the
building materials here. Where did the fuel come from for
baking them? It is hard to realize that such a splendid city
should have arisen, and flourished, in this desolate and inaccessible country, and that a second-rate Indian kingdom should have
attained such wealth and prosperity in comparatively recent times,
and within comparatively narrow limits. It is not yet two centuries since Bijapur fell before the combined assaults of Moguls
and Mahrattas, and nothing to rival it has risen since its fall.

February 27th, Poona.—After a fortnight's stay in the famine
districts, where the Percivals are gradually reconciling themselves
to the disagreeable change from prosperous Bhávnagar, I regret-
fully took leave of them all, and proceeded by night train to Poona.
I drove out to the renowned and costly new palace of Ganeshkind, which is situated a few miles out of Poona, in a commanding but somewhat bleak and exposed condition. The whole
place is fitted up and maintained in first-class order; gardens,
grounds, offices are all got up regardless of expense, and the
interior is handsomely furnished. Ganeshkind might be the chief
palace of the Viceroy, instead of being the secondary residence of
a secondary Governor. From the top of the lofty tower the view
is very extensive, but there is nothing attractive at this dry season
in the brown plains of the Deccan.

He spent a week in the jungles of the Bassein district,
with W. B. Mulock, C.S., who hoped to have shown him
some tiger-shooting, but they were not lucky enough to bag
one while he was there. He, however, thoroughly enjoyed
the life in tents, which enabled him to see more of the
manners of the aborigines, and poorer classes, than could
have been done in any other way.

March 2nd, Bassein.—The interior of the fort is a wonderful
scene of architectural ruin and botanical luxuriance. Everywhere

towers and arches of churches and convents crumbling into decay are overgrown with parasites and creepers, and it is not easy to say whether this vegetation is doing more to uphold them, or to hasten their ruin.   Above the relics of Portuguese chivalry and monasticism, thoroughly European in style, it is strange to see the cocoa-nut and sago palm rearing their tall stems.   The principal churches have tunnel vaults, fretted and embossed somewhat in the style of Roslin chapel; here and there the embossed stone ribbing remains, while the rest of the masonry has fallen away, so as to leave an open fretwork of stone for a roof.   Every leading order of monks is here represented by a convent: Dominicans, Franciscans, Augustines, Jesuits, and when in power they vied with each other as proselytizers and persecutors.   The ecclesiasticism of the Portuguese was at least one important cause of the downfall of their Indian Empire, which must have attained a high degree of wealth and power when the city of Bassein was in its glory.   Coats of arms and inscriptions are still distinctly visible, the date on the cathedral being 1603, and the fortifications are almost as perfect as when besieged by the Mahrattas in 1739.

March 8th.—Nothing can well be pleasanter than the life of a revenue officer in districts such as those of Bassein.   If he is a sportsman, he has a practical monopoly of the large game; and although his expenses for sport are considerable in other ways, he pays no rent for his shooting.   Then he is not an idle man, whose sole business is the destruction of innocent animal life; he brings justice to every man's door, he protects the poor, he arranges revenue disputes, he collects Government dues, and tries prisoners in patriarchal fashion at the door of his tent.   If the "simple archon" sees approaching a shikari with news of a tiger or panther, he simply remands the prisoner, or adjourns the case in dispute, and is ready in a trice to sally forth to his "other duty" of slaying the ravager of the neighbouring villages, — pleasant duty and pleasant relaxation alike, for a hearty energetic fellow like my present host.

March 9th, Tanna.—A most business-like meeting was held in order to promote the establishment of arbitration, or "lawad" courts, in which unpaid Native juries, or "punchayats," are to act instead of judges or magistrates.   W. Wedderburn took the chair, and the room was crowded with a most respectable and intelligent assembly of Hindoos and Parsees, the former equipped in the

most brilliant variety of colour as to their cart-wheel turbans.
Speeches were made in Mahratti, resolutions were moved and
seconded, great unanimity and apparent zeal prevailing in favour
of the principle of arbitration, familiar to Hindoos.

March 15th, Bombay.—At the Framjee Cowasjee Hall I
addressed the Native notables of Bombay. My subject was
" Parliamentary Delegates for India," and my audience was large
and appreciative, consisting almost entirely of Natives, Sir M.
Nathoobhoy, C.S.I., in the chair. The chief fear is, that however
intelligent and clear-sighted these people may be, they have not
the power of combination necessary to obtain political concessions; in fact, the ability to sink personal disputes and jealousies,
when a grand common object is in view, seems to be precisely
what Hindoos lack, and is a most important cause for our
supremacy in India.

As his brother was unable to obtain leave of absence at
once, Sir David went on alone, down the coast to Carwar,
and from there made a run inland to the famous Gairsoppa
Falls.

March 21st.—The ruins of old Gairsoppa are buried in a
luxuriant jungle, with beautifully timbered hills rising one above
the other on every side, displaying the richest variety of evergreen
foliage. In the foreground the scarlet ixora and snow-white
karinda showed their starry blossoms, while in the distance the
young foliage of many forest trees looked like great bunches of
red, yellow, or purple flowers. We threaded our way through
lofty jungle, embowered in which are the Basti or Jaina temples;
the architecture and style of sculpture in these Canarese ruins
exactly resemble those of the modern temples of Kathiawar, the
largest being in the form of the Chaumukh, with four large figures
seated back to back in the centre. The carving is rich and
fantastic, with figures of men and animals (monkey, serpent and
fish); these last are not symmetrical, but are to be found here and
there, in the random fashion of Gothic grotesque sculptures. In a
small temple, constructed in the same style, is seated one colossal
statue, quite Egyptian in his appearance of solemn antiquity, but
being Jaina he is of course comparatively modern. In this lovely
spot the jungle has completely reasserted its supremacy, " satyrs "

dance, and bats swarm, and it must be a den of fever as well as that of wild beasts.

March 22nd.—On the top of the Devil's Peak, about 2300 feet above the sea, we had a splendid view over the hills and jungles of Canara and Mysore. A grand expanse of forest and mountain was visible, extending to the sea on the west, and in other directions apparently boundless, with few and feeble marks of human inhabitants. All around is green, but the variety of foliage prevents the view from being monotonous, and the young shoots have all the brilliancy of autumnal tints in Europe or America. Very pleasant it was in the shady aisles of the forest, the tall columns of teak, mango, boon spar, and numerous other trees, rising so high without a branch that it is difficult to make out their foliage and determine their species. Occasional glimpses, too rare indeed, are obtained of wooded hills and valleys, "breadths of tropic shade," rolling away in the distance, and occasionally a bare rock raises its summit above the trees ; altogether the scenery of the ghaut quite repays the ascent, apart from the waterfall.

March 25th.—I was escorted by the Patel to see the lions of Gokurn, one of the most sacred Hindoo places of pilgrimage. The real curiosities are the sacred cars, the largest of which is really a wonderful work of art. It is very lofty, running upon six huge solid wheels, and is richly carved in the style of Canarese sandal-wood boxes, with figures of gods and goddesses, men and monsters, birds and beasts of every sort. The car is of black-wood, and the whole would be in perfect taste, but for two shabby little painted hobby-horses stuck up in front, as if purposely to spoil the general effect of this handsome massive piece of carving. Some of the monsters have wooden balls larger than my two fists inside their mouths, carved along with the monster's head out of a solid block of wood. The car is dragged by human agency, and the ropes are still there by which it was recently hauled out for a great festival, thousands bearing a hand in dragging it along the street.

Proceeding by steamer from Carwar to Colombo, he determined, in the few days at his disposal, to ascend Adam's Peak, and went by rail to his friend Mr. Lawrie, at Peradeniya, who helped him on his way.

April 4th.—Our route lay for thirty-two miles through the heart

of the coffee districts, the elevation being generally from 3000 to
4000 feet above the sea. A valley devoted exclusively to the cultivation of coffee presents little variety either of colour or outline,
but many indications of comfort and prosperity. The houses of
the planters are dotted about upon commanding eminences, or
in sheltered nooks, with a frequency which proves that there is
nothing lonely or unsociable in the business of cultivating the
" fragrant bean." The coolie lines, or huts, are substantial buildings, and the Tamil population, by whom all the labour, except
felling timber, on the plantations is done, is numerous and well-
to-do. The roads are well made and bridged, and there are comfortable rest-houses for travellers at due intervals ; all this is the
work of coffee, which is the mainspring of Ceylon prosperity. An
estate of 250 acres will give sufficient employment to an assistant
superintendent, and will require at least one coolie to every two
acres, with additional hands during harvest. In some cases the
number permanently employed is much larger, but owing to the
gradual ripening of the crop extra labour may never be required.
The system of importing labour seems to work really well in
Ceylon, and the Tamils are by no means in the position of slaves.
There are certainly many worse trades than coffee-growing; it is
as healthy and independent as sheep or cattle breeding in the
colonies, but not so solitary, and the fellows all seem to like it.

April 5th.—We marched when the moon was supposed to
have risen, somewhere about midnight. It was a strange scene ;
the glare of the torches falling on the bright dresses of the Native
pilgrims, as they climbed slowly up the pathway, which winds
through jungle so thick as to meet close overhead. The effect
produced in the uncertain light is that of a steep staircase tunnelled
through a dense thicket of branches and leaves, as it might be the
" Hill of Difficulty " in " Pilgrim's Progress." We all felt more
or less like "pilgrims of the night," and certainly the conditions of
the ascent were altogether novel and striking. On the extreme
summit of the Peak is a large mass of granitic rock, ascended by
iron ladders ; and on the surface of this rock, sheltered by a small
temple, is the famous footprint, a shallow excavation several feet
long and a few inches deep, made in very rude imitation of the
human foot without toes. This footprint is sacred in the eyes of
all the religious sects of the country : the Buddhists claim it for
Buddha, the Hindoos for Siva, the Mussulmans for Adam, and the

Christians for St. Thomas. Their respective claims may be equally good, but the Buddhists have got possession, and a yellow-robed Singhalese priest, with his assistants, presides over the holy place. The pilgrims are principally Singhalese, with a sprinkling of women among them, and go through their devotións with a cheerful but apparently genuine piety, which doubtless causes them to descend the Peak with a sense of duty accomplished and merit achieved.

April 10th, S.S. "Zambesi."—Our principal fellow-passenger is Mr. Pope Hennessy, going to take possession of his new government at Hongkong. He is a very pleasant man, and thoroughly liberal, not only in his opinions, but in his acts. His sympathies are all with the weak against the strong, and the courageous way in which he has acted upon these sympathies, in Barbadoes and his other tropical colonies, has made him enemies among the whites; it is to be hoped that the gratitude of the blacks has made him amends. I can hardly imagine a more severe test of true courage than the constant clamour of all around you for securing their safety by arbitrary and violent measures, while you believe the danger to be chimerical, but stand alone in your opinion, and have the entire responsibility. Such was Pope Hennessy's position in Barbadoes; but he was bolder than Governor Eyre, as well as wiser, or the massacres there might have far surpassed those of Jamaica.

April 16th.—Singapore is certainly a very expensive place, where a dollar just about stands for a rupee. The Chinese are here completely in the ascendànt, forming the bulk of the population, making lots of money, and driving in their own carriages. They have evidently most of them no intention of returning to China, dead or alive, and they have their own cemetery, with little vaults sunk into the side of the hill, and closed by folding doors of stone. The most prominent Chinaman is the Hon. Hak Whampoa, M.L.C., to whom we paid a visit at his country residence. The garden, menagerie, and house are all worth seeing, especially the last, which is fitted up, regardless of expense, with very rare and valuable curios from China and Japan. The old gentleman takes pleasure in showing one round and pointing out the objects most worthy of admiration : a narwhal's ivory, nine feet long; the horn of a rhinoceros, most beautifully carved by a Chinese artist; an ivory ball containing fourteen concentric spherical shells, each carved with a different pattern. Jars, bowls, bronzes, and cabinets are all arranged very creditably to the taste of Mr. Hak Whampoa, who has risen, by his own talents and industry, from the foot of the social ladder, higher than any of his countrymen within the British dominions have yet done.

April 19*th, S.S.* "*Pateoah.*"—The little *Pateoah* is crowded with passengers, the cabins are not nearly large enough to allow of swinging a cat, and the stewards are a lot of newly caught Malay boys. We touched at Rhio, and a dark gentleman came on board with as many daughters as an English paterfamilias ; the young ladies embarked in European dress, but immediately disappeared, and I simply did not recognize them in the neat, becoming Javanese costume, in which they presently showed themselves on deck. A coloured skirt and a white jacket, slippers without stockings, and the raven hair tied in a knot at the back of the head, exactly suited their style of beauty, which is not of a strictly classical type. They have, however, pleasant, cheery faces, and an old Frenchman on board at once struck up a flirtation. He had a great advantage over the rest of us,—being deaf and dumb all languages are alike to him, and he can make himself understood by every one, keeping us in fits of laughter ; he has been travelling in Kamschatka among other places, also Siam, and requires no interpreter. At midday-eating we have a capital dish, the basis being rice, to which are added *à discrétion* about five and twenty different condiments and pickles, fish, flesh, fowl, vegetables, and spices ; " bouillabaisse " is a joke to it, so are hotch-potch and olla-podrida, but when compounded with discretion such as experience gives, this Malay pillau is most excellent. Just after sunset we entered the archipelago of a thousand isles, and anchored during the night a few miles from the roads of Batavia.

Allusion has been made to the address he delivered in Bombay on March the 15th : a few quotations will show the nature of his proposals.

I think you are all well aware of the fact that not only Parliament but British public opinion is beginning more and more to sway the councils of the Government of India ; and the effect of this powerful public opinion will be a blessing or a curse to the country exactly according as it is well or ill instructed. It is because I foresee the public opinion of England as expressed,

partly through Parliament and the Secretary of State, and partly
through the public press, will become a most powerful influence
in guiding and directing the Government of this country, that I
lay stress upon the necessity of your having fairly and truthfully
represented in England what you really want and what your
requirements really are.   Both sides of the House of Commons
are equally willing and ready, if they only understood how, to do
the best they can for this country; the only object they have in
view is its welfare.   The apparent indifference which the House
manifests to Indian affairs—I think it is more apparent than real—
results partly from the fact that the Indian constituencies are not
represented, and partly from the fact that the House feels and
acknowledges its own ignorance; and it is because of this that I
am so very desirous of seeing in the House of Commons some
persons from India.

It is on the example of the United States that I would
formulate what appears to me to be the most feasible plan, or at
least the most likely to be successful, and the most reasonable for
you to propose.   I advise you, without loss of time, to agitate and
move in all possible ways for the admission into Parliament of at
least six delegates to represent the different Presidencies and
Governments of India in the English·House of Commons.   I
think this Presidency ought to have two representatives; I am
certain that if two of the gentlemen I now see before me were to
take their seats in the House, they would be able, temperately
and clearly to set before the House the grievances and the wants
of their country; and I am perfectly certain from my experience
that they would receive a courteous hearing, and that their arguments and statements would be weighed with careful consideration.   The British Parliament's opinion I believe to be the
strongest political force in the civilized world; and there can be
no doubt that the opinion of the British public, as expressed
through the leading journals, echoes wherever the English language
is spoken, and, I may say, all over the world.   I want your efforts
to be directed to something simple and practical, to obtaining a
limited number of representative delegates to sit and speak in
Parliament, to have the power of joining in debates, and of presenting and supporting petitions, but not to have votes on general
subjects.   I would remind you of one thing—this country certainly
enjoys some privileges which have not yet been obtained by

independent nations in Europe; in fact, I know there are very few European countries where the right of free writing, free acting, and free speaking is as fully enjoyed as it is in this country. We have not had to ask leave of the Chief Commissary of Police to hold this meeting, as we should have had to do in some European countries. I think, as we are able to speak here as fairly and freely as we could do in London, Edinburgh, Manchester, or any other English town, it is the fault of the people themselves if they do not get their grievances remedied.

In March, 1880, he read a paper before the East India Association, in London, on "Popular Representation in India," in which he advocated a somewhat different scheme for obtaining the same object.

Three years ago I had the honour of addressing, in Bombay, a very large and influential public meeting upon representation for the people of India, and I then promised to do my best to bring the question before the British public and Parliament. As to the form which a scheme of representation ought to assume at the outset, on mature reflection I feel convinced that the Legislative Councils in India are the bodies into which an independent elective element, representing the Indian taxpayers, could be most advantageously introduced. The scheme of conferring seats in the House of Commons upon a few representatives, or delegates, from the great centres of population in India, so as to give the natives at least a hearing when Indian questions are discussed in Parliament, has much to recommend it in theory, but is beset with practical obstacles. The laws under which India is actually governed are made, not by the British Parliament, but by the Indian Legislative Councils; and without any startling or revolutionary change, the representative element can there be readily introduced.

In the Legislative Councils there are already certain gentlemen, Native as well as European, who, being non-officials, may be said to represent the general community, but who are nominated by the Government, and who are in a small minority as compared with the official members of council. In order to reform the Legislative Councils, by strengthening the non-official element, even now so serviceable, and in order to render them at least

T

partially representative, we have merely to introduce arrangements already in successful operation as regard the Indian municipalities. It appears that in the case of these municipalities there exist already constituencies, to whom might well be entrusted the privilege of electing representative members to the Legislative Councils. A commencement might at once be made by conferring this privilege upon the three Presidency cities, and a few other large centres of population. Upon financial questions the opinions and criticisms of members so elected would be of great practical value, so that it would be the interest, as well as the duty, of Government to give them ample opportunities for discussing the budget, and all measures affecting the incidence of taxation. Whether factories or forests, arbitration or irrigation, abolition of cotton duties or imposition of licence taxes, be the subject for discussion in the Indian Legislatures, it is desirable that natives of India should be permitted to explain their own views, and to receive explanations from the Government.

Doubtless it will be prudent to proceed gradually, and to be guided by experience, in extending the privileges of self-government to the Indian people. It is sometimes asserted that the grand object of British rule in India is to fit the people for ruling themselves, and that we shall be prepared, when this task has been accomplished, to leave India to work out her own destinies. Whether there be any truth in this assertion is extremely doubtful, but it is true that Englishmen desire to govern India with a due regard to the wishes and requirements of her people, and that it is knowledge, not good intentions, in which they are mainly deficient. The time seems now to have arrived for the Government of India to apply to Parliament for such powers as may be necessary to develop in India the principle of popular representation, already successfully introduced into the constitution of Indian municipalities, and sanctioned by the approval of many distinguished Indian administrators.

An article on " The Deccan " appeared in the *Fortnightly Review* of August, 1880. In this he discussed the famine policy of the Government, and some of the economic questions so perplexing to all who take an interest in India.

The economists who have recently taken upon themselves to

open English eyes to the real poverty of the " gorgeous East," have somewhat overshot their mark, for the statistics adduced by them to prove that India's poverty is due to over-taxation, would rather, if perfectly trustworthy, make it clear that no possible reduction of public expenditure can materially improve the miserable condition of the masses in India. Meanwhile we are assured by others that the Russians, still believing in the wealth of India, are guided in their Asiatic policy solely by the hope that, after forcing their way across the vast deserts and mountain ranges of Central Asia, they will be able to descend at last upon the fertile and defenceless plains of Hindostan, and repeat the plundering achievements of Timur Beg and Nadir Shah. The increased military strength of India under British rule is certain : she is now a great centralized military empire, the only one in Asia : a standing menace to all her Asiatic neighbours ; weak indeed financially, when judged by a Western standard, but, if backed by the credit of England, more than a match for all the Russias. What is the true state of the case as between the two opposite views : (1) that India is being steadily drained of her life-blood by the fiscal demands of a costly foreign Government ; (2) that she is decidedly a gainer in material wealth through the investment of British capital in her soil, and the importation of European skilled labour ? The first view is held by most of the educated natives who have written or spoken on this question, while the second finds favour with Englishmen both at home and in India.

For my own part, I believe that India has already derived great benefit, and will derive still more in the future, from the railroads constructed by British capital, although under the guarantee system there has been a want of due economy both in construction and in management. Railways and internal peace are two genuine boons conferred by England upon India, as all thoughtful natives readily admit ; but even these unquestionable benefits of our rule fail to touch the true causes of Indian poverty, which may even be too deep-seated to be greatly affected by such reductions in the public expenditure as can ever be effected by our most economical administrators. The Indian peasant is already so poor, that the slightest additional taxation is to him an intolerable burden ; and so great is his tendency to become poor, that even the remission of existing taxes would ameliorate his condition only for a very brief period. An increased salt duty and an agricultural cess aggravate his poverty, but they are not its cause, and he would be nearly as poor the day after their abolition, and perhaps quite as poor a few years later. He sinks habitually to a very low standard of comfort, in fact to a state of penury, which just enables him and those dependent upon him to subsist in ordinary years; in favourable years he has a transient gleam of prosperity, but when a bad year comes he has accumulated no reserve to fall back upon, and famine is the result.

The main cause of Indian poverty is over-population, an evil which British rule has aggravated by measures which must be characterized as just and humane, at least in intention. We have suppressed female infanticide, we protect the ryots against violence, and we endeavour to insure them against famine, the result of late years being an increase of their numbers, which, in Bengal especially, is almost appalling.

The French peasant usually postpones marriage until he has saved or inherited money enough to set up house; the Hindoo begins married life by plunging into debt, and considers himself fairly entitled to incur debt for so laudable an object. This distinction of custom and opinion is a vital one, and has more to do with the difference in their respective conditions, than soil, climate, and government. The Hindoo is industrious and frugal in the highest degree, but he is not prudent, and is willing to bequeath to his son no better portion than that of paying marriage debts incurred before his birth.

The land in the Deccan is held on the ryotwaree system, each peasant separately holding from the landlord, to whom he pays his rent, whether that landlord be the State or a private individual. The holder of land directly under Government cultivates it himself as a general rule, and the land-tax which he pays is a rent charge fixed for thirty years, after a careful survey and assessment. That this land-tax does not absorb the whole of the true rent is clear from various facts; the most conclusive one is that land subject to revenue assessment possesses a high saleable value, and is daily sold or pledged as security for large sums to the money-lenders, who are well qualified to estimate correctly the value of any security. Thus the British Government, by the revenue survey and settlement, has established a transferable and heritable tenant right at moderate rents, fixed for thirty years, and with liability to eviction for non-payment of rent only. With this

form of Ulster tenant right, under an all-powerful but just landlord, whose practice it is to grant remissions and allow outstanding
balances in specially bad years, the position of the Government
ryot is as favourable as that of any cultivator can be who does not
occupy a freehold of his own ; and whatever may be the hardships
of his lot, only a small portion of these are attributable to the rent
payable upon his land. If the land revenue were to be sacrificed
to-morrow throughout India, as it has been already sacrificed in
Bengal, a landlord class would doubtless be created and enriched,
but the actual cultivators of the soil would not reap a large share
of advantage.

Much of the Deccan is "unculturable waste," and the bringing
under cultivation of new land within the last few years is a
proceeding fraught with serious danger. The pressure of population causes poor grazing land to be broken up in favourable
years, and in dry years this lapses into "unculturable waste;"
while those who attempted its cultivation and trusted to it for
a livelihood are left without resource. There are districts of
India where the soil is fertile and the rain-fall abundant, as there
are districts which are not over-peopled ; but the Deccan is not
one of these, and its material improvement must be very slow
at the best. It is peopled far beyond the numbers which it can
properly maintain ; the rain-fall is scanty and uncertain ; the soil
is so unproductive that much of the cultivated land pays only
a few annas ($1\frac{1}{2}d$.) per acre of land-tax, and is even at that rate
sufficiently burdened ; many of the cultivators have no personal
property (except their bullocks) that would sell for ten rupees,
and many are hopelessly in debt. The same sort of land which
in the Deccan supports (in favourable years) a population of
cultivators numbered by thousands would, in Queensland, be
considered poor feeding for a flock of merino sheep, of which
numbers would perish in a season of drought. A country so
circumstanced cannot be rendered secure against famine by any
precautions Government can take; it is not possible to turn it
into a sheep-walk ; the inhabitants cannot be deported and will
not emigrate ; they can just wring a bare subsistence out of the
soil in ordinary times, and have, as a class, no reserve to fall
back upon. Railways have done, and will do, more than any
other public works to mitigate famines in India. In Northern
India grain was abundant in the spring of 1877, and nearly every

railway station between Delhi and the Deccan was encumbered with sacks of grain awaiting transport, which a single line with a limited rolling stock was unable to furnish.

After all, it is admitted on every side that the root of evil in the condition of the Indian cultivator is his indebtedness. The money-lender is essential to the cultivator, whom he supplies with capital, and without him a large proportion of the land could not be cultivated at all ; but our judicial system has given him unfair advantages over his client, and has exercised a depressing influence on agriculture. The evil is deeply rooted in the customs and traditions of an intensely conservative people ; but if we cannot convert the Indian cultivator to habits of forethought and saving, we can at least modify the mischief wrought by our own legislation.

It will take some time to pauperize the Hindoo in a strict sense, for, however poor he may be, he has not hitherto been a pauper looking to the Government to support him in bad times ; he has only been accustomed to receive help from more prosperous relatives, or from charitable and wealthy neighbours ; failing these resources, he has finally starved to death, and has whitened the way-side with his bones. The full horrors of former famines, such as men now living may recollect, have been averted in recent times in British territory; but this result has been obtained at a heavy cost. Many improvident and idle persons have been maintained at public charges in return for nominal labour at useless jobs, while the so-called " back-bone of the community," the industrious cultivator who has continued to " keep himself off the parish," is compelled to pay every pice of his old taxes, and to bear new burdens imposed upon him as a poor-rate for the future. Nay, more, the proceeds of this new poor-rate, or famine insurance, are no sooner collected than they are diverted to pay for a war, foreign alike to the territory and the interests of India.

It is matter for regret that the Commission appointed to examine into the causes producing the recurrence of famines in India, should have been composed almost entirely of distinguished European gentlemen, and should have included among its members only two Natives. It is not by sitting at Simla, or even at Ootacamund, receiving official reports and examining official witnesses, that any new evidence of value can be collected. The information necessary can only be obtained in each case upon the spot, from the mouths of local witnesses, and in such an inquiry the assistance of Native commissioners familiar with the inner life, with the habits, thoughts, and prejudices of their own countrymen, would have been invaluable. India will have to pay very dearly for these Famine Commissioners, and many persons are inclined to be sceptical as to whether India will get her money's worth in fresh information or independent criticism. Above all, it is desirable, before attempting agrarian legislation in India, to take the Natives into confidence ; and until something like genuine representation of the people has been introduced into the Legislature, the adminstrators of the executive can only ascertain the popular desires, grievances, and opinions through indirect means, such as general conversation and the columns of the vernacular press.

Bijapur
24th Feby. 1877

Boro Budor   Java
14ᵗʰ May 1877

CHAPTER XVII.

1877.

A MONTH IN JAVA—VOYAGE TO HONGKONG—ARTICLE ON "THE DUTCH IN JAVA."

April 21st, Batavia.—We soon made our way to the Hotel des Indes, a large establishment with an attentive and obliging manager, whose services as interpreter are in constant requisition. The Malay servants understand neither Dutch, English, nor French : luckily most Hollanders speak all three languages. The canals which traverse the streets of Batavia would remind one of Holland, but for the rapidity of their current, and the number of dark-skinned individuals bathing in them. In other respects the Dutch have truly left their country behind them, and seem to adapt themselves cheerfully to life under perfectly new conditions. The order of the day seems to be: early rising with a slight refection, business of all sorts until twelve o'clock, then "rijsttafel," or *déjeûner*,—a good solid meal followed by repose during the heat of the afternoon; when it gets cooler, people sally out for exercise or society, and the fashionable hour for calling is about sunset, dinner at 7 p.m. When the houses are lighted up the interiors are quite visible from the road, although each house stands in a neat little shady compound, and they look very comfortable and social with any number of rocking and lounging chairs. The appearance of cheerful and easy sociability reminded me of Honolulu on a far larger scale. When we came to penetrate within these elegant abodes, the reception we met with was most agreeable, and the letters of introduction we carried were thoroughly efficacious. The shops in Batavia are large and well-furnished, but the rate of profit seems to be too high, illustrating that—

> "In matters of commerce the fault of the Dutch
> Is giving too little and asking too much,"

and tending to deter customers.

April 22nd.—The whole country traversed on the way to Buitenzorg is fertile and populous, and the buffaloes rejoicing in damp pastures are as fat as pigs; many of them are of a bright pink colour, looking among their dark companions like Europeans alongside of Asiatics. The Belle Vue Hotel certainly merits its name, for the view from the verandah in the early morning is quite magnificent. The great volcanic mountain of Salak, clothed with dense forest to the summit, is the principal object in the picture, and in front flows a rapid river through luxuriant tropical vegetation. The most remarkable creatures here are the leaf and stick insects, of which there are many varieties, and vast numbers of all sizes and colours. Even when you know that a particular branch is covered with insects, it is difficult to distinguish them from the leaves, which they imitate in every respect as to colour, shape, reticulation, even spots and discolorations. Some are brilliant green, others bright red or yellow, like young or withered leaves. The stick insects are, if possible, more extraordinary still, and even when you hold them in your hand they seem to be merely bits of grey, brown, or white wood, or straw; they usually become

darker in colour as they grow older.   In the Botanic Gardens all
tropical plants flourish in a climate resembling that of a well-
watered hot-house : especially palms, ferns, orchids, and water-
lilies.   The variety and beauty of the palms surpass anything I
have seen in Ceylon ; birds are very scarce, even the ubiquitous
crow is not to be seen, but bats abound, and enter even into
the Viceroy's palaces. We dined with H.E. the Governor-General
and Madame van Lansberge, and had a very pleasant party ; every
one talked French, and almost every one English.   The rooms were
very large and airy, but no punkahs ; after dinner a reception, and
every one remained standing, many gentlemen smoked.

April 23rd.—We started, lightly equipped, in two small traps
of rickety construction, each drawn by two small ponies, for a hill
sanitarium nearly four thousand feet above the sea.   The drive
was through a most delightful country, over hill and dale, across
brawling mountain torrents, passing villages of picturesque native
houses, and crowds of picturesque natives, men, women, and
children, all of whom seem to be prosperous and contented.   The
hats worn by the Javanese are a caution : some of them are circular, and nearly as large as an archery target, painted moreover
in rings of red, white, blue, and gold ; others are shaped like inverted bowls, others again like mushrooms, or obtuse-angled cones.
The groundwork of all is light basket-work, which is covered with
numerous coatings of pitch, lac-varnish, and paint, until it affords
an equally good shelter against sun or rain.   They are chiefly
monopolized by the male sex, but occasionally a shabby old hat
may be seen on the head of a woman.   Before reaching the
summit, we left the high road and turned off through the virgin
forest to a little lake, apparently an old crater, which lies em-
bosomed among mountain slopes so steep as to be almost precipices ; but clothed from summit to base with luxuriant vegetation,
where in other climates there would be only the naked rock.   It
is quite the perfection of tropical scenery ; lofty trees festooned
with creepers, which in their turn are overgrown with an astonishing variety of parasites, orchids, ferns, etc. ; amidst this wealth
of vegetation, where the lower forms seem rather to enjoy an
advantage over the higher, tree-ferns are conspicuous for their
elegance, far surpassing any of the palms, which they resemble in
form and even in size.

April 24th.—We made an early start for the summit of the

extinct volcano of Pangerango, said to be ten thousand feet high; gradually as one ascends a certain number of plants indigenous to temperate climates appear, and at an elevation of nine thousand feet the beautiful Primula imperialis fills the path with its long leaves, lofty stem, and golden blossoms. It attains a height of three or four feet, and the deep yellow flowers grow in successive whorls several inches apart; it has very little scent, and is supposed to be peculiar to the summit of Pangerango. Our fainting strength was sustained by wild artichokes, strawberries, raspberries, and water-cress; and we recognized many familiar flowers, apparently identical with European species, *e.g.* great St. John's wort, common plantago, small yellow ranunculus. The presence of such plants on the summit of a volcano in the tropics, south of the equator, is a very astonishing fact. In one place we crossed a stream of water so hot as hardly to be bearable, and here the tree-ferns surpassed themselves in grandeur, mingling their graceful fronds with the foliage of lofty forest trees. A little further on, a spring of clear water, almost ice-cold, refreshed the weary climbers. Once the mist rolled away like a curtain, disclosing right opposite the vast crater of Gedé, walled in with perpendicular cliffs, and pouring forth a cloud of steam; the arid desolation of this active volcano is in startling contrast to the luxuriant verdure of Pange-rango, and the unexpected vision, for we had as yet seen nothing of Gedé, was grand in the extreme.

April 26th, Bandong.—The drive to Bandong was through a perfect garden, a rich plain waving with rice in various stages of growth, and densely sprinkled with groves of palms and fruit trees, beneath whose shade nestle *campongs*, or native villages. The houses are constructed of the lightest materials, and resemble in form the card houses built by children; bamboos furnish all the more solid portions in the way of rafters, posts, and flooring, the sides and roof are of bamboo, or palm matting and thatch. A great proportion of the houses by the road-side are places of refreshment, consisting of a large room surrounded on three sides with raised seats or divans of bamboo; the central one is covered with food and drink of sorts, the side ones are for the guests. Clean, cool, and comfortable these simple cafés are, and very convenient for a little refreshment and repose, during a long journey in the heat of the day. As in other tropical countries, wherever there is cultiva-tion there is the lantana, but nowhere have I seen it so beautiful

as here on the slopes above Bandong, every hue, from brilliant
orange, magenta, or purple to delicate pink, primrose, or white,
appearing not only on the same bush, but even in the same bunch
of flowers.

April 27th.—At the Residency, a large and handsome house,
Mons. and Madame Pahud de Mortanges received us most
kindly, and made us thoroughly at home.   Late in the evening,
when we expected all to retire, Madame called for the carriage,
and took us and her little daughter out for a moonlight drive.
The effect of a good siesta is to make the Dutch ladies fresh
and lively in the evening, nor do men display that tendency to
postprandial lethargy which is so characteristic of British India ;
freedom as to smoking also promotes sociability.   Except the
front-room and verandahs the houses are kept rather close, the
doors and windows being in European style, and frequently shut,
quite unlike the chicks and half-screens of Indian bungalows ;
moreover the punkah is a thing unknown among the Dutch, who
even here have a holy horror of draughts.   In this one particular
their notions are ill-adapted to the climate, which otherwise they
so well appreciate.

April 28th.—The Resident is now busy with the examination
of the Normal School.   One hundred young Sundanese are here
trained for the duty of teachers, and the whole system reminded us
of old Hofwyl: music, drawing, and gymnastics receive attention,
as well as mathematics and literature ; and the staff of European
teachers appears to be very strong.   The boys look somewhat
effeminate in their long skirts, but many have intelligent faces,
better in full than in profile, like Malay faces generally, which look
as if they had been sat upon.   Educational advantages here, as in
countries professing greater liberality, are almost exclusively limited
to the male sex.   The Regent had been warned of our intended
visit, and received us with a band of Native music, which surprised
us most agreeably with its melody ; it consisted of twelve performers, only one of whom played upon a stringed instrument,
a sort of rude fiddle.   The other instruments were either sets of
gongs, perfectly tuned, "each under each," or else "gamelongs,"
primitive pianofortes of metallic or wooden bars struck with small
drumsticks.   The effect of all these, played in excellent time, was
sweet and harmonious, something like a huge musical box ; a good
set of instruments costs a lot of money, containing as they do

so much fine bell-metal. As we drove through the town every one subsided into a squatting position in token of reverence: here people sit down and turn their backs when they wish to be very polite, so arbitrary are social customs; but after all, we are in the southern hemisphere, where all ordinary arrangements are reversed.

April 30th.—The hotel at Soekaboemi is kept by an Italian, who made us very comfortable; and if these houses kept by foreigners are a little dear, they are worth any money to travellers, who find in the interior of Java an interpreter as well as a host at every considerable town; these hotel-keepers receive a subsidy from the Government, otherwise they could hardly subsist on their few European visitors. Men, women, and children are constantly smoking, and it is a funny spectacle to see an imp of four years old, " mit nodings on," but a leaf cigarette between her infant lips; these cigarettes are shaped like cheroots, and resemble neatly made-up matches.

May 3rd, Sinagar.—Flower gardens and plantations round the house, the splendid distant views of the Gedé and Salak mountains, and the cheery hospitable manners of our hosts, make Sinagar a most charming location, and we are disposed to endorse the opinion of a former guest, who told Mr. Kerkhoven: "You have the prettiest place in the most beautiful scenery of the finest island in the world." Tea-planting seems, in Java at least, to be the pleasantest of all ways in which a man may earn his bread or make his fortune; it involves no lonely banishment, you are a ruler over many willing subjects, and all the processes with which you are concerned are agreeable and clean. There is absolutely no bad smell about tea in any stage of its manufacture; it is always sweet, and varies merely from the smell of fresh leaves to that of new-mown hay, until it attains the orthodox odour of tea. Mr. Kerkhoven has now under his own immediate charge about 520 acres planted with tea; he employs permanently several thousand coolies, men, women, and children; and in one month, January, he has made as much as 118,000 lbs. of dry tea. The elevation of Sinagar is only 1600 feet, more favourable to quantity than to quality of tea, which acquires a finer flavour at a greater height, but Java tea still rules low in the English market. Here tea-making goes on with slightly varying intensity all the year round, and the whole process may be completed within twenty-four hours, when the leaves are ready to be packed in lead-foil, and placed in the tea-chest. Of the blight insect there are few traces at Sinagar, as a price is set upon their heads, and every day the children bring in a lot, receiving one cent for a score; in one month as much as five hundred guilders has been spent here in this way, and the benefit resulting justified the outlay. Riding and walking about the estate one could not fail to be struck with the prosperous, contented appearance of the people, engaged in their picturesque and "pleasant labour." They encourage music and dancing in the evenings, and we assisted to-night at a savage minuet danced by a professional lady and an amateur gentleman. There are no European subordinates on the estate, the natives work under their own chiefs, and Chinamen are employed in the financial department; everything seems to work smoothly, and, in short, "this life is most jolly." It is pleasant to find that these planter gentlemen take a keen interest in the welfare of the Natives, and of the country generally, with which they identify themselves, like Colonials rather than Anglo-Indians, or even Ceylonese.

May 7th.—Samarang is the capital of Java proper, and ought from its central situation to be the capital of the whole island; it is apparently a flourishing place, with plenty of "Europe" stores. A drive through the fashionable European quarter showed us that Samarang, like Batavia, rejoices in shade, verdure, and flowers, pretty houses and muddy canals; in these last a large proportion of the Native and Chinese inhabitants are constantly bathing. At Soerakarta the difference of climate and country from the western provinces is quite apparent in many respects: it is much drier and a little hotter, the people are different in dress and appearance, bulls are used instead of buffaloes or horses to draw carts, women carry heavy burdens on their backs, and every man of any respectability has a kriss stuck into his belt. The gay varnished hats of Sunda have given place to queer things like exaggerated jockey-caps with the back part cut away, or to European sun-helmets. Courtiers and *employés* of the Emperor wear hats like truncated sugar-loaves, and officials are always accompanied by an umbrella-bearer, and a boy carrying a box for siri, or some such stuff for chewing.

May 12th, Magelang.—According to arrangement the officer commanding the household cavalry of the Sultan came to conduct us to the "kraton," within the extensive walls of which 3000 persons are said to dwell, the immediate dependents of the Sultan. Without any ceremony whatever, we proceeded straight to the royal presence, and found his Highness waiting to receive us in a small verandah, decorated with flower-pots and Dutch tricolors, and simply furnished in European style. The Sultan himself was dressed in the costume of a Javanese gentleman, with one or two orders on his breast, and is a pleasant, intelligent man, looking very young for his years, which he states at fifty-nine Javanese, or fifty-seven European ; the Dutch officer interpreted in French and Malay, and acted as M.C. His assistance was rendered all the more necessary by the presence of six blooming princesses, all seated in a row, who rose to receive us, and on seeing whom in a Mohammedan household, I began to think I must be dreaming. It required repeated instruction : " Shake hands with them, with *each* of them !" to give us courage to do so, lest our heads should be "immediately cut off." They seemed quite disposed for a chat over a friendly cup of tea, to which we all helped each other, no menials appearing, except one or two who crawled in with the tea-cups after a paralytic fashion, but unluckily we had no language in common.

Sounds of music proceeded from a large open pavilion close by, and his Highness invited us to go and see what was there taking place. Seated on the marble floor, at a low round table, we found the Queen, alternately playing a hand at cards with two pretty maids of honour, and superintending the instruction of more than twenty young ladies, who were practising the elements of Javanese dancing. They were prettily dressed, but somewhat too tightly for dancing ; and judging from their solemn and eager countenances all were doing their level best, keeping their eyes to the front, notwithstanding the unwonted spectators. Meanwhile music was discoursed on the gamelong, and several other young women lifted up their voices in song. We were introduced to the jolly fat lady, who seemed gratified by our visit, and invited us to examine the large room in front of which she was seated, and which was in fact the royal bed-chamber of state, and although handsomely fitted up as to walls, floor, and ceiling, contained little furniture, except a great bed or recess. On taking leave we again shook hands all round, the young ladies performing the ceremony in a very pleasing manner, half cordial and half demure ;

only one of them is the daughter of the recognized Queen, who has no son.   The Dutch Government has, however, extended its recognition to the second wife, whose son will succeed the present Crown Prince, a nephew of the Sultan.

Much gratified with our visit, we got out of our dress clothes, and started by post with four so-called horses for Magelang. The central square, with its emerald turf, its grand old waringins and tamarinds, its mosque and the handsome houses around, each in its own neat garden or compound, is thoroughly characteristic of Java, and is in striking contrast to the dust and desolation of an ordinary " station " in India.

May 13th, Boro Boedoer.—The great temple is within a stone's throw of the hotel, and the intervening space is adorned with fragments of statuary from the mighty mass: in one place lie forty-three heads of Buddha, of heroic dimensions ; the carvings may almost be estimated by the acre, and remind one in their varied details of Egyptian, Assyrian, Hindoo, and even of Christian art.   The temple is a vast rectangular pyramid, rising in successive stages to the central cupola, which crowns the whole ; round five of these stages run terraces, the walls on either side richly sculptured with a great variety of scenes, in which Buddha figures as the hero, whether as teacher, as ruler, as recluse, or as god.   The unity of design and of execution throughout the building seems to indicate rapidity of completion, and the middle of the fourteenth century is the date assigned to it.   Animals are particularly well represented : there are deer, sheep, apes, peacocks, fishes, tortoises, and many elephants; houses, ships, and trees are also skilfully executed. Horses, so rare in Indian sculptures, appear frequently, but not cows ; and harpies, half bird, half woman, recall the troubles of Æneas.   Seated in covered niches all over the temple are statues of Buddha, with long ears and short curly hair ; on the bas-reliefs a variety of human types are represented, many of them bearded, and none resembling the Malay or Javanese.   Except where intentional injury has been inflicted, the sculptures are remarkably perfect, and care is now taken to weed the building and protect it from farther damage.

May 15th.—We reached M. Chavannes' place in the evening, where we were most kindly received, and introduced to a large party of ladies and children. The coffee plantations are above the house and offices, at a height of four or five thousand feet,

and we ascended on horseback by steep zig-zag paths. A considerable fortune has been expended here in paths, roads, and bridges
alone, as the whole place was a trackless jungle a few years ago,
and the slopes are the steepest on which I have ever seen coffee
growing. The plantation extends over 650 acres, and has involved
already an outlay of £30,000. It requires about seven years for
the plants to produce full returns. Government gives the use of
the land, and releases the people employed on the plantation from
forced labour, in return for an annual rent of 6000 guilders : they
"give too little and ask too much." The labour of gathering
coffee, which is now in full swing, is certainly more severe than in
the case of tea, partly from the nature of the ground, partly from
the weight of the crop ; but it is almost equally clean and simple,
and if the work is harder during the harvest there are also slack
times.

May 19th, Batavia.—The General kindly sent his aide-de-
camp, a very pleasant and accomplished young officer of the
Colonial army, to lionize us and cart us about. The Military
Hospital would be an admirable institution if it were anywhere at
a respectable height above the sea, instead of in steamy Batavia.
General De Nève hopes in time to transfer more of his troops to
inland sanitaria, 3000 feet in this moist climate being considered
to be the best elevation. Meanwhile the clothing of the Colonial
troops leaves much to be desired, being in marked contrast to
that of the civil population—a purely European rig-out, and not
handsome at that. Heavy dark-blue uniforms, with black shakos,
form as ugly and unserviceable a costume for the tropics as can
well be imagined ; and here, as in the matter of hill stations, the
Dutch may well take a hint from the British. Money has not
been spared to make the hospital as good as its situation will
permit : it is airy, clean, and comparatively cool ; the patients,
many of whom are Europeans, look quite luxurious as to comfort.
There are at present about six hundred patients, for a large proportion of whom Acheen is responsible.

May 21st.—We spent the morning in the village of Tanah
Abang, watching the process of manufacturing "batik," the coloured
cloth so much affected by the natives for sarongs and handkerchiefs. We strolled through shady groves, from the abode of one
happy peasant to that of another, all delighted to see us, to exhibit
their manufactures, and to explain their processes. Combining,

U

as these people do, country and town occupations under their own cocoa-nut trees, in a delightful climate, what a contrast there is between their condition and that of English operatives or day labourers ! Even the compulsory cultivation of coffee, as it is now carried on, seems to involve no real hardship, and tends greatly to improve the material condition of the peasant. He is obliged to work, no doubt, when he would otherwise be dozing, but he obtains a crop with little trouble, which clears him of his Government dues. The fixed price on delivery may be too low; but were he allowed to sell it as he pleased, it would be made over beforehand to a Chinese money-lender, and the last state of the Javanese would be worse than the first. At present he has at least a sure market, and one which he cannot anticipate. As regards the other products, opium and salt are the only State monopolies, and the direct interest of Government in the sugar cultivation will cease and determine in a few years.

May 22nd, S.S. " W. Mackinnon."—Pangerango and the other mountains were all clear to bid us good-bye, and we leave Java with sincere regret, after a well-spent month, of which we have made the most, and during which all our undertakings have been thoroughly successful. The steamer was very crowded and dirty, for as usual this N.I.S.N. ship was full of troops. These gallant fellows were on their way to Acheen, and they certainly display one quality very valuable in soldiers, that of keeping up their spirits under discomfort. The decks were completely covered with them and their female camp-followers, Europeans and Asiatics mixed up together, without any of the discipline and organization supposed to be necessary in a troop-ship. The Europeans are stalwart-looking fellows, recruited from all parts of the continent, chiefly Belgium and Switzerland, besides the Netherlands proper, and all are armed with excellent breech-loaders and fixed bayonets, besides which they carry a sword available for cutting through the jungle; a great many of them wear medals, and Insulinde has certainly not been conquered without some hard bush fighting. The extent to which Dutchmen smoke is really astonishing; meals are not over before the cry is heard of " Spada ! Api ! " and fire is brought by a young Prometheus with a lighted cane, or "reed tipped with flame;" the same cry is heard incessantly, night and day, and there is no ceremony as to place, persons, or occasion when smoking is concerned. The

Malay boys are also constantly carrying round glasses of spirits, and cups of soup, coffee, or tea, so that one need never feel faint.

May 27th, Singapore.—A steam launch was in readiness to ferry us over to the mainland of the Malay peninsula, and the territory of H.H. Sir Abu Baker, Maharaja of Johore. We landed amid terraced gardens, and were conducted to the palace, where the Maharaja's nephews, two pleasant young fellows, dressed in European style, were waiting to receive us. The house and grounds have an Italian aspect, as it might be overlooking Lago Maggiore, but the smooth green turf is worthy of England, and the forest-clad shores of the strait remind one of rivers in the far West. We inspected the saw-mills, where an immense amount of timber is sawn, chiefly Johore cedar and teak ; and the dewan or court, where his Highness sits in judgment. Tiffin was served in a beautiful marble hall, adorned with magnificent vases from China and Japan. Our young hosts sat at table with us, and fed "like Christians." Pony carriages appeared to take us all to visit the plantations of pepper and gambier. The Chinamen were delighted to see us; entertained us with tea and a huge cocoa-nut, which furnished milk enough to satisfy the thirst of the whole party ; and showed us the process of manufacturing gambier. The shrub is about five feet high, when it is freely pruned, and the leaves are boiled in a large vat until the juice becomes thick and slab. The juice is then poured out and allowed to cool and harden into a yellowish gum, which is the gambier of commerce, is chiefly used for tanning, and is one of the principal exports from Singapore. The pepper plantations resemble hop gardens, as the vines are twined up long billets of wood, and are planted at regular intervals ; the plants are covered with peppercorns, which are being gathered, although quite green. The drive home was delightful : a good deal of virgin forest remains near the road still uninjured, the way-side is covered with the sensitive plant, and durians and mangostins hang in abundance on the trees— alas ! they are quite unripe.

May 28th.—Punctually at 6 a.m. the *Teheran* left the wharf, and steamed away past the city of Singapore, which looks quite grand with the numerous shipping, and the many handsome houses crowning the wooded hillocks around, conspicuous among them Government House itself. Certainly Singapore has a matchless position as an emporium of trade, and must have an important future.

June 2nd, Hongkong.—This afternoon we entered an archipelago of islands, and passed close to some gaily painted Chinese junks ; the island of Hongkong was next reached, the western point of which being rounded, the town of Victoria appeared, and we were alongside the wharf before dark.   The Governor's coolies were in attendance, and carried us up to Government House, where we were kindly welcomed.

In January, 1878, an article by Sir David, on "The Dutch in Java," was published in the *Fortnightly Review.* The following extract shows the impression made upon him by the different systems of government in India and Java.

In order to make a fair comparison between British and Dutch rule in Asia, we must pass over from continental India to the island of Ceylon, which, in climate, scenery, and products, is merely Java on a smaller scale.   Java and Ceylon were both taken by the British from the Dutch ; Java was restored, while Ceylon was retained : both islands are financially prosperous, and both owe their prosperity in a great measure to coffee ; but Java has progressed far more rapidly than Ceylon has done under similar natural conditions, and it seems fair to give some credit for this to political administration.   The superficial area of Ceylon is nearly one-half that of Java, but the population of Java was in 1871 just seven times that of Ceylon.   In Ceylon, great tracts of fertile land have relapsed into jungle, tanks constructed under former dynasties have fallen into ruins, large imports of rice are necessary to feed the scanty population, many of whom are not permanent residents, but immigrants from the mainland, working as coolies on the coffee plantations.   Java, although three or four times as densely peopled, is able to export rice, the staple food of the inhabitants, as well as the coffee, sugar, indigo, and tobacco, from which its European masters derive their wealth. In estimating the merits and demerits of the so-called "culture system" of Java, this comparison with Ceylon is not without significance, nor is it to the disadvantage of the former island.

Englishmen are disposed to believe that no other race except

their own understands the management of colonies, or the administration of a subject country, and in support of this belief
they contrast their own colossal Empire with the fragments now
alone remaining to those nations who were once their rivals in
maritime and colonial enterprise. The truth appears to be that
our colonial success is due mainly to our maritime supremacy,
which has gradually given us possession of all the most desirable
territory, either by conquest or colonization, while other nations
are obliged to content themselves with what has been left. But
twice in their short history the indomitable Dutch have established
a colonial empire : the first was due to their maritime power, and
passed into the hands of the English, their successful maritime
rivals ; while the existing Netherlands India has been created
within the last sixty years, almost unnoticed by the great Powers
of Europe. By far the most important and valuable part of
Netherlands India is Java, containing at the last census a population of nearly 18,000,000, four times as great as it had been in
1816, when it was restored by the British to the Netherlanders.
Many persons regard the surrender of this magnificent island as
a piece of reckless folly or quixotic generosity, but it was truly
nothing more than an act of simple justice, and one which
Englishmen may remember with unmixed satisfaction.

The modern Batavians possess certain imperial characteristics
in common with the two chief nations of conquerors and administrators, the Romans and the English ; in particular they practise
towards the religion of their subjects a policy of complete toleration, thereby obviating what is perhaps the most serious difficulty
in governing alien races. Wherever the Portuguese landed in the
East they at once proceeded to build a church ; when the Dutch
came they established a factory. The Portuguese churches are
now picturesque ruins, overgrown with tropical vegetation; but the
Dutch factories, like those of our own East India Company, have
developed into an Empire. It is true that a hard and fast line is
drawn between Europeans (and persons assimilated with them) on
one side, and Asiatics on the other. It may be said generally,
that the profession of Christianity is sufficient to acquire for any
one European privileges (with exemption from Native jurisdiction),
which are thus enjoyed even by persons of African blood. At
first sight this may appear inconsistent with the principle of
religious liberty and equality. It is, however, a necessary result

of carrying that principle into practice where law and religion are so completely intertwined as they are in the East. In Java a vast majority of the inhabitants are subject to Mohammedan law, of which the priest is the chief interpreter. If a Christian is to enjoy religious equality, it is clear that he must be withdrawn from the jurisdiction of the Mohammedan tribunals, and this, accordingly, has been done.

When comparisons are drawn between the modes of administration in British and Netherlands India, there is displayed on either side a certain disposition to believe that things are better managed beyond seas. If the Government of British India were to follow the example of the Dutch, and to send a few selected civilians to study minutely, on the spot, the working of the rival systems, as regards the collection of the revenues, the employment of natives in the public service, the construction of public works, etc., it would be found that we have quite as much to learn as to teach in the management of a great Asiatic dependency. There are in the world only two States which are constitutional at home and imperial abroad ; and those two are Great Britain and the Netherlands. The spectacle of a free European nation ruling with beneficent despotism over a subject Asiatic population, nearly seven times as numerous, is exhibited in the first place by England, and is repeated exactly by Holland upon a smaller scale. The United Kingdom has far outstripped the United Provinces in population and power, and the two countries have long ago ceased to be rivals, but Holland continues to play her part bravely on the world's stage, and, in proportion to her natural resources, administers possessions and bears burdens fully equal to those of England. The ease with which she does both (two-thirds of her debt are held at the rate of 2½ per cent.) shows still superabundant energy and credit, and leaves little sting in the taunt sometimes directed against England, that she is tending to become a second Holland.

Great Britain can feel neither alarm nor jealousy at the successful progress of the Netherlands, a smaller epitome of herself. The independence of the Netherlands is to Great Britain a matter of the deepest interest, and prosperous as the Belgian kingdom undoubtedly is, its establishment as a separate State may be regretted on the ground that it has rendered more difficult the future maintenance of that independence. If Belgium were now

able to share the benefits and the burdens of colonial empire with
her northern neighbours, a great additional security against foreign
aggression would be enjoyed by all, and the United Netherlands
would be a power capable of making its independence respected
and its alliance desired.   It is clearly to the interest of Englishmen that the splendid maritime resources of the Scandinavian
countries, or of the Netherlands, should not pass into the hands
of any nation likely to become a maritime rival.   Many Netherlanders apprehend that absorption in the Germanic Empire will be
their ultimate fate.   Such an event would confer upon a nation,
already possessing irresistible military strength, the elements of
naval power together with a ready-made Oriental empire.   It is at
least a possible event, and would threaten our Asiatic dominion
with the most serious danger to which it can be exposed—the
presence of a formidable maritime rival in Asiatic waters.

The culture system was established by General Van den Bosch,
in 1832, at a period of chronic deficit and threatened insolvency,
and resulted in a regular annual surplus.   During the generation
which witnessed the conversion of a heavy annual deficit into a
surplus of three millions sterling, the population of Java doubled
itself.   The system which produced these astonishing results required the compulsory cultivation by the people of certain valuable
products, to be delivered at a low fixed price to the Government,
who sold them in Europe at an enormous profit.   The products
so cultivated were those calculated to command the highest prices
in the home market, and included originally coffee, sugar, tea,
tobacco, indigo, pepper, and cochineal.   After a time, it was
found expedient to limit the employment of forced labour to the
cultivation of coffee and sugar only, and by a recent Act of the
Netherlands Legislature the compulsory production of sugar will
cease in 1890.   The profits made by the Government upon this
system are so great, that two-thirds of the Java revenue, *i.e.*
nearly £7,000,000, are annually derived from the sale of colonial
produce.

Another successful stroke of policy has been their maintenance
in working order of the whole machinery of internal administration, just as they found it under the Mussulmans; while they
secured, through the supervision of European officers, such checks
and amendments as were deemed sufficient.   The title of
Resident, which is borne by the principal Dutch official in each

province, remains unaltered from the time when it was used to denote a representative of the European paramount power at the court of a Native prince. The ruling princes, with a few exceptions, have disappeared, but the whole hierarchy of their subordinates remains, and all administrative functions, so far as natives are concerned, are intrusted to them only. A province, or residency, containing on an average nearly a million of inhabitants, is divided into several regencies, each of which is governed by a Native Regent, having under him a host of minor officials. The Regent invariably is a man of high birth, and frequently is a member of the princely family who once ruled over his district, so that he enjoys a large amount of prestige and influence apart from his authority as a Government officer. In each regency is stationed a European assistant-resident, whose instructions are to treat the Regent with the consideration due from an "elder brother" towards a "younger," and who has under him a certain number of European "kontroleurs." The duties of the assistant-resident and his young Dutch subordinates, are simply those of control and supervision, except where Europeans or quasi-Europeans are concerned.

The Dutch have been content to govern their subjects in accordance with Native ideas, and in making their Oriental conquests have talked very little about the duty of a great Christian nation to convert and civilize ignorant barbarians. They have made no attempt to introduce a national system of education; they even discourage the study of Dutch and other European languages, and they do not profess to regard a native as in any way a political equal. But if their ideal of government is not very exalted, they have fairly fulfilled it, such as it is. They have given to Java peace, prosperity, and religious toleration, with security of person and property; and after paying for the maintenance of all these blessings, they consider themselves entitled to appropriate to their own uses the surplus revenue. They do not pretend to govern Java for the benefit of the Javanese alone, and they claim for their own people a portion of the wealth which they have there created.

It is laid down in the constitution and regulations of Netherlands India that the special duty of European officials is the protection of the natives, and from the Governor-General downwards all are bound by oath to "protect the Native population against oppression, ill-treatment, and extortion." This oath is probably not kept by all to the very best of their ability, but at least the charge of pecuniary corruption is not brought against the Dutch Civil Service; this distinguished and honourable body of men being blamed only for lack of energy and courage in denouncing injustice in which they themselves have no share. Still it is the condemnation of the judge when the guilty are absolved, and an omnipotent Governor-General must be held responsible for the shortcomings of his subordinates as well as his own.

Without pretending to investigate the inward desires or aspirations of the Javanese, and judging solely by external facts, I believe that the Dutch sovereignty is about as popular and as secure as the rule of a few aliens over a great subject population can ever be made, and that the country flourishes under it as well as a subject country can ever be expected to do. Beyond all tropical countries Java seems to attract the love and admiration of strangers settling upon her shores, who speak of her as "nôtre Java bien-aimé," and are fond of describing her as "the finest island in the world." Swiss mountaineers are at one with low-landers of Holland upon this subject, and even islanders from Britain can hardly express dissent.

"Cursed Malayan Kriss"
Java   May/1877.

Canton 11ᵗ June 1877

CHAPTER XVIII.

1877.

CHINA AND JAPAN.

June 9th, Canton.—Archdeacon Gray volunteered to be our guide, and we set off for a real hard day of sightseeing, first crossing the river to visit the great monastery of Honam. It was at once apparent that we were in the best of hands: at a sign from the Archdeacon every door flew open; at sight of him every face was wreathed in smiles; priests, magistrates, and shopkeepers vied with each other in politeness and attention to a man who has been "long enough in Canton to learn civilized behaviour," who speaks Chinese, and does "chin-chin" in approved fashion with doubled fists. The Honam monastery is a very fine specimen of its kind, complete in all details, with which our guide is thoroughly familiar, and he led us from court to court, from temple to temple, explaining the life of a Buddhist priest to the last stage of his earthly career. Recrossing the river to Canton proper, we dived into the endless labyrinth of bazars, extending for miles in every direction, and making even those of Stamboul seem small in comparison; except London, indeed, no city that I know gives such a notion of immense population as Canton, said to contain, with

its suburbs, a couple of millions.   As we hurried along, our
procession of chairs was stopped again and again, in order that
Dr. Gray might call our attention to some interesting object : roast
dog, horse-flesh, or a notice that prime black cat was always to be
had on the premises.   Then he would dive suddenly into a close,
too narrow to admit chairs, to show us a native eating-house, a
pawn tower, or an opium divan, where besotted smokers lay in
their sleep of bliss, their heads resting on wooden pillows.   The
pawn towers are remarkable institutions, in which the business of
a pawnbroker is combined with that of a banker : they are lofty
edifices, half a dozen stories high, rendered fire-proof, as well as
impregnable to robbers, and are used as storehouses for all sorts
of valuables, placed here as pledges for pecuniary advances, or
merely for safe custody.   Climbing to the top by a series of
ladders, we had a bird's-eye view of Canton, a mass of roofs without
a single open space, the ground being nowhere visible ; evidently
the want of air is much felt in this solid conglomeration of houses,
and large windsails of matting are rigged up on every side.   The
monastery of five hundred Genii is a wonderful place ; in one of
the temples are the images of the five hundred saints, as large as
life, each one different from the others as to features and attitude,
and each supposed to be the portrait of an individual, to whom a
special story is attached.   The temple is modern and all the
statues are freshly gilt ; many of them have attendant animals,
and although ugly enough, their features are not by any means
Chinese, any more than their *chevelure*, which is short, a few
having blue beards.

About this period we were obliged to petition the indefatigable
Archdeacon to take us to a tea-house, where we had a thorough
"bouse out" of cakes and preserved fruits, washed down with
real Chinese tea, full of tea leaves and without sugar or milk.   The
cakes were in great variety, most of them excellent, and after our
schoolboy feast we hurried on again, like giants refreshed.   China
is certainly in many ways a highly civilized country, but nothing
can be more barbarous than the mode in which prisoners are
treated, even supposing them to be guilty as accused.   The
happiest are those permitted to work outside for their living, but
wearing perpetual chains ; more to be pitied are the wretched
creatures condemned to wear the *cangue*, or portable stocks,
not so much on account of the wooden collar itself, as of the

stifling dark den in which they are pent; on this sultry day their
dungeon was like a compartment in Dante's Inferno, but a dollar
made them quite happy for the moment. Outside the walls is the
city of the dead, a sort of temporary cemetery, where the remains
of distinguished strangers await conveyance to their ancestral
vaults: each junk-shaped coffin has a little house to itself, in the
back part of which it is placed with a screen in front, and an altar
to receive the offerings made by surviving friends to the manes of
the departed. Rent is, of course, payable for lodgings in this
gloomy city, and defaulting tenants are buried eventually at the
public expense with all due respect. The shades of eve were
falling fast, and we had to traverse the entire city of Canton from
east to west, in order to reach home, passing through a dark and
crowded labyrinth, to which Seven Dials are not a circumstance,
with a sense of security which could not be felt in the back slums
of London or Paris.

June 17th, Shanghai.—The boats here resemble those at
Penang rather than those of Southern China, being gaily painted,
and having two projecting points at the stern like an earwig's tail,
and an eye on each side of the bows; but we preferred a species
of land conveyance now seen for the first time. This is a
jinriksha, or light buggy on two wheels, drawn not by a horse
but by a man; on a smooth level road they run along right gaily,
and one has no fear of the animal bolting, when one is in the
vehicle, although he might do so if left with luggage only. These
" pretty tiny " rikshas are the aristocratic mode of conveyance,
humbler individuals making use of large wheelbarrows, on which
they sit sideways to the number of two or three, and are trundled
slowly along. In walking along the narrow thoroughfares one can
stop to watch ivory-cutting, silk or feather embroidering, wood-
carving, or any other of the delicate handicrafts here practised,
and there are no quadrupeds nor vehicles (except heavily laden
coolies) to disturb one's observations. The women are much given
to small feet, many of them having, in fact, almost got rid of their
feet, and they hobble along as if they had two wooden legs. This
fashion is the more to be regretted, as the loose trousers and
pelisse form a costume eminently suitable for action, and Chinese
women's dress is neither a badge nor a cause of social inferiority,
while their modes of wearing the hair are elegant and becoming,
which cannot be said for the men.

June 19th.—Having resolved to sail up the Yangtzekiang as far as Hankow, I had to go on board the great river steamer at night, and she sailed long before daylight, while Willie preferred going on ahead to Japan. The steamer is very large and powerful, making nearly ten miles an hour, even against the current, and as in ascending she keeps close to one bank or the other, one gets a good view of the country all the way. The Yangtze is indeed a noble river, and although not so large as usual at this season, it flows full "from bank to brim," through a verdant country, and shows to far greater advantage than it would do if in flood, converting the landscape into a waste of waters. A terrible enemy is descending upon the cultivators now in swarms of locusts, which literally darken the air, and at a distance appear like clouds of smoke rising from burning vegetation.

June 22nd, Hankow.—The quay of Hankow, shaded with willows, bordered with handsome European houses, and abutting on the mighty Yangtzekiang, quite astonished me with its grandeur. Mr. Clarke, a young Scotchman, a tea-taster in D. Sassoon's house, received me most hospitably, instructed me in the mystery of tea-tasting, and found for me a guide in the person of a Chinese custom-house official talking several European languages. We soon found that Italian was our best vehicle of communication, he having been educated in Rome; and crossing the river to Woochang, our first visit was to the Jesuit fathers, almost the only Europeans established there. Two pleasant Italians received me, and refreshed me with wine of their own manufacture, grown upon vines trellised in the Tuscan fashion. They are, of course, dressed in Chinese costume, and have about forty pupils under their care. Examinations are going on in the Hupei province, and the candidates, who seem as a rule to wear white, and to carry fans (so do coolies and prisoners for that matter), may be seen in considerable numbers about Woochang; these literati are frequently hostile to foreigners, but they treated me with civility. People crowded about me wherever I went, but cleared out of the way whenever I wished to move, and were quite respectful.* A Confucian temple, roofed with yellow and green tiles, the imperial and sacred colours, attracted my attention, and we dismounted from our chairs to inspect it; although by no means

* A few days later a murderous assault was made here on two Protestant missionaries.

ruinous, the courts have a very neglected appearance, being full
of weeds.   In the temple itself are no idols or images, merely
tablets with Chinese inscriptions in honour of Confucius.   The
population aggregated in the three cities around the junction of
the river Han with the Yangtze is really 'enormous, and is said
to exceed that of Canton; my guide calls it 3,000,000, but this
is manifestly an exaggeration.   We saw soldiers practising archery
by standing for an indefinite time bending a stiff bow, the left
arm supported by a rest.

June 23rd.—We were carried through flourishing and well-kept
market gardens, where the stinks were really sickening, as is usual
in Chinese agriculture, nothing being wasted.   At a considerable
distance outside the gates we reached a temple of horrors; all the
idols are thoroughly Chinese as to dress and appearance, and
wear an aspect of martial ferocity, quite unlike the placid Buddhas
of Hindoo origin.   This style characterizes the Tauist places of
worship, as distinguished from orthodox Buddhists, who are only
one of the three great Chinese denominations, the others being
Tauists, and Confucianists.   This temple has a shabby deserted
appearance, and few come to take warning from the groups of
clay figures, representing the torments of the wicked.   A horrible
ingenuity is displayed in these tortures, and it is to be feared that
they are not merely imaginary.   As women come in for their fair
share of the horrors, it was gratifying to find some female figures
among the divinities also, but this is contrary to orthodox doctrine
in China.   The fashion of small feet is almost universal here,
but the "tottering lilies" of Hupei manage somehow to hobble
through their household avocations; they discard none of their
garments in hot weather as the men and children do.   Hankow
is certainly a hot corner—it was 93° in the drawing-room just
before sunset, but people manage to do a little riding and lawn
tennis notwithstanding.

June 29th, Shanghai.—Here, as elsewhere in China, Europeans live even more apart from the natives than in India, having
no concern with them, except in the capacity of servants, and no
interest in country or people, except to make money out of them.
As servants they are above praise, surpassing, I think, even the
mild Hindoo, attentive, handy, and trustworthy.   Everything is
left in their hands as regards housekeeping and money matters,
and nothing seems ever to go wrong.   The "comprador" in

particular is a great institution, being house steward or major-
domo, and apparently the sole possessor of money in a well-
regulated establishment. The currency is a fearful nuisance in
China; there is, in fact, no currency; sums are reckoned in taels
of silver, worth now about 5*s.* 6*d.*, but non-existent as a coin.
The only genuine Chinese coin are "cash" of copper or brass,
with a hole in the centre, by means of which they are strung in
great coils. When one sees how absolutely Europeans are in the
hands of their shroffs and compradors, one ceases to wonder that
Chinese merchants are gradually buying out the barbarians, and
that the latter find it difficult to make fortunes. On the other
hand, Chinamen have little reason to complain of the demeanour
of Europeans, who doubtless realize that they are on Chinese soil,
and are very seldom bullying or violent, however much contempt
they may feel for Celestials, a contempt which is no doubt thoroughly mutual. As regards the great empire of Cathay, fifty
years of Europe *may* be preferable to a longer period of residence
there, but not on account of its being a barbarous land, still less a
savage one. It is rather a land of decaying civilization, like the
Lower Roman or Byzantine Empire. Internal wars and rebellions,
rather than foreign invasions, have brought ruin on China as on
the Roman Empire, and now the barbarians are upon them also.
But China has a great future before her. Geographically and
geologically, if not politically, she is the rival of the United States,
and it will be a sort of race between these two mighty nations,
the oldest and the youngest on the face of the earth, as to which
will first develop her almost boundless mineral wealth.

In a letter addressed to the *Scotsman*, dated Shanghai,
June 25th, he said :—

While sympathizing with the Russians in the struggle now
going on around the Black Sea, I wish to point out that there are
other parts of the globe where the aggrandisement of their empire
may menace British interests far more seriously than anything
which is likely to occur on the Danube or in Armenia. By a
series of recent treaties with China and Japan, Russia has, in the
far East, annexed territories greatly exceeding in value, if not in
extent, all that she has acquired by hard fighting during the same
few years in the deserts of Central Asia. The territories specially
referred to are in Manchooria and the Island of Saghalien, where

Russia has succeeded at last in obtaining harbours open to the ocean throughout the year, there being none elsewhere in her vast dominions. When it is borne in mind that these regions of North-eastern Asia are peculiarly rich in mineral resources; that coal and iron are found there and in the adjoining Chinese territory, it seems clear that any farther encroachment of Russia in that quarter will seriously menace our maritime and commercial supremacy, now completely undisputed in these seas. All legitimate means should be employed to maintain the position and influence enjoyed by Great Britain in the China seas, and it should be kept in view that the interests of India are far more closely connected with China than with any portion of the Turkish Empire, always excepting Egypt.

July 2nd, Nagasaki.—The beautiful land-locked harbour of Nagasaki is one of the safest and most picturesque in the world, with deep water and good anchorage for any amount of shipping. On the hills by which the city is surrounded stand temples; to one of these we ascended by a long flight of steps; magnificent trees of various species tower above, a portion of primeval forest preserved by piety and good taste combined. Adjoining the temple are tea-gardens, where we partook of delicious sweets, and drank as much tea as a dozen Japanese, calling for it in mugs, and creating much merriment thereby among the attendant damsels, who bring you a very small cup about half full, considered quite a liberal allowance. Archery with little toy bows of bamboo is a favourite sport among the young swells. They place the arrow on the right instead of the left of the bow, and thought it very funny that I did otherwise.

July 5th, Hiogo-Kobe.—I found Willie comfortably installed at the Hiogo hotel. We looked in at a good specimen of the Shinto temple, in a grove of noble old pines and cedars. A living white horse is kept here, also a monkey, and a wooden horse with stable and all accessories complete; in fact, horses, whether in the flesh, in statues, or in pictures, seem to be invariably found in Shinto places of worship, and usually associated with monkeys. Ropes of straw, with scraps of paper fluttering from them, and mirrors are also characteristic objects. In front of the shrine hangs a hollow brazen ball, answering the purpose of a bell, with a thick rope, which worshippers agitate violently before com-

mencing their prayers and making their little offerings, lest the
divinity should not be at attention.   In the evening we attended a
Japanese theatre, where two boys performed a variety of acrobatic
feats and jugglery.   The audience occupy squares marked out
with pieces of wood on the floor, and we were much struck with
the classical appearance of the men in their tunics and togas.
Short-clipped hair is the fashion of "young Japan," while conservatives adhere to the system of shaving the temples and crown of
the head, with short queue twisted coxcomb-like to the front.
Thus here, as in France and elsewhere, politics may be expressed
in the cut of the beard or hair of a man.   Ladies of all classes
apparently affect the same coiffure,—an elaborate affair, fastened
with pins of coral, metal, or glass, and stiffened, I fear, with grease ;
it is the only thing about their costume to which I object.   Nothing
can be nicer than their simple robe and skirt of blue, fastened
with a scarlet girdle tied in a great knot behind : this is worn by the
great majority, but occasionally the skirt may be red, the robe white,
or the sash purple.   Their feet are bare ; and if their wooden clogs
give them in the street the tottering gait of a Chinese lady, this is
laid aside at once on the threshold with the clogs themselves.

July 6th.—We started for Arima pulled by two men each ; and
if the leaders appeared to be a little skittish at first, it was no mere
flash in the pan, for they came in at night almost as fast, after
thirty miles of rough hilly roads, and would hardly allow us to walk
even at the steepest places.   The scenery throughout is charming.
After leaving the outskirts of the city the road at once enters a
gorge in the hills between steep green slopes, overgrown with
small white roses, "edible rubi," and campanula spotted like a
pale foxglove inside. Then succeed rich natural woods of krypto-
meria, cypress, and pine, intermingled with camellias, almost
attaining the dimensions of forest trees, not now, alas ! in flower.
Then rice-fields and picturesque villages, and tea-houses with
awnings of mats across the road, where our coolies paused at
intervals to partake of the crystal spring.   Arima has quite the
look of a Tyrolese village, and the inhabitants "gerne schwatzen,"
even when no common language exists between them and their
visitors.   A shaven bonze received us in a toy-house and garden
on the edge of a wooded ravine, where we refreshed and reposed.
The chief industry of Arima consists in fancy articles made of
bamboo, very tasteful and cheap, if not very serviceable.   There

X

are hot springs, in which the inhabitants were disporting themselves, ladies and gentlemen in separate compartments, but none
objecting to the presence of spectators.   Heavy rain came on as
we returned, soaking through our coverings of oil paper.

July 7th.—A very wet night was succeeded by a morning which
admitted of a trip by rail to Osaka, a free port, and the second
largest city in Japan.   The paddy-fields are now flooded with
water, and industrious agriculturists are busy rummaging and
weeding in the mud.   Although usually fond of working almost
naked, they clothe themselves very amply for this labour, in blue
tunics and leggings, with huge cane hats, and even grass cloaks
if it is raining ; as the job is both hot and wet, this is somewhat
remarkable, for a cooly's working costume is one rag round the
temples and another round the loins, and when wishing to be
respectful he removes the former of these.   The Shiro, or castle
of Osaka, is a mighty structure, strong even according to modern
notions, with deep moats, and lofty earthworks faced with granite
blocks.   Except at Baalbec or in Egypt, I have seen nothing to
equal in size many of these blocks; one which I measured roughly
is forty feet long and about sixteen high ; the masonry is polygonal,
and as neatly fitted as if each stone could be lifted in a man's
hand.

July 8th, Kioto.—A few hours of sightseeing at Kioto soon
convinced me that no temples which I had seen in Japan or China
were worthy of comparison with the noble edifices of this ancient
capital of the Mikado.   Our new interpreter, Maruda, is an
excellent guide, and put me through a very severe course of
Buddhist and Shinto places of worship.   All bear a certain resemblance to each other, with vast roofs sweeping down in
parabolic curves, gateways rivalling the main temple itself in
grandeur, innumerable lanterns in bronze and stone, fountains of
the same materials, broad flights of steps, and splendid old trees,
enormous bells, and an unrivalled profusion of timber in pillars,
roofs, and cornices.   The grandest of all is perhaps the Chioin
monastery : entirely constructed of wood, the enormous roof is
supported by pillars of kiaki wood, each one the solid trunk of a
very large tree ; the internal decorations are of gilding and bronze,
with fine lacquer-work in red and black.   The cemeteries are
situated on the shady slopes above the city ; they contain only
small plain monuments of stone with inscriptions, erected over

cinerary urns. Funerals appear to be cheaply and quietly managed in Japan, and I have as yet seen no sign of such a thing, except these tombstones in retired and picturesque spots. Cremation was recently prohibited for a short time, but an enlightened Government soon rescinded so mistaken an order, and the practice is again general.

July 9th.—At Nara, once the capital of the Mikado, there is much of interest, but the grand sight is the Dai Butz, or colossal bronze image of Buddha. This is by far the finest idol that I have ever seen, being of vast size, costly material, and majestic form. The seated Buddha is upwards of fifty feet in height, and displays the same calm impassive face and curly head as he does in Ceylon, Java, or China, but in this great statue the expression is truly majestic, and characteristic of Nirvana. He is seated on the lotus, and behind him is a golden glory of rays, forming a brilliant background to the dark solemn figure of bronze. Right and left are two colossal figures, far more ornate, but much smaller, and serving to render more impressive the size and simplicity of the central figure. The hill above Nara is covered with fine timber : notwithstanding the amount consumed in architecture, there is no denudation here, and the lofty conifers with their red stems and dark green foliage strongly resemble, on a smaller scale, the great sequoias of California. In these shady groves are numerous temples, shrines, and cemeteries; the rills of water descending from the hill are conducted into bronze fountains and lavatories, well supplied with little wooden ladles; deer come out of the forest, and will eat almost from your hand; and it is difficult to imagine a pleasanter place for a stroll on a warm afternoon. The young ladies of Nara seem partial to foreigners, and I had quite a flirtation with two, both very juvenile, and one speaking a little English, who had the pleasant ways of children, and came about me like bees, fanning me and examining my dress and accoutrements.

July 10th.—An early start brought us to Uji, the Greenwich of Kioto, in good time for a delicious breakfast of fresh-water fish, including trout, grayling, carp, eels, and crayfish. Here and there are mountain villages, where very rarely a European can have been seen, but where the well-dressed children bow to us with the solemn urbanity of courtiers, and where no dog thinks of barking at us. Everywhere the school is a conspicuous, generally a new

building, and in every sense the schoolmaster is abroad. We met
one followed by his flock of little ladies and gentlemen, from each
of whom we received a most gracious bow. Even mere babies
—old enough, however, to carry smaller babies on their backs—
salute us gravely ; the rising generation, who in other countries
would ridicule or insult us, being more punctilious than their
parents, although all are friendly. Women are engaged in sorting
and cleaning the tea, easy and pleasant work, especially when
performed as here in their own houses, not in a crowded godown.
Division and association of labour in cities may benefit the con-
sumer, and bring in larger profits to the capitalist, but they do not
promote the health or happiness of the actual workers, and sixpence earned in their villages is well worth a shilling in the town.
Here they are their own masters, with a variety of interests and
occupations ; there they are like a gang of slaves, toiling ever at
the same dull round. The substitution of factory for village
labour will be a very doubtful blessing to Japan : more stuff of
sorts will be produced, and the number of consumers will doubtless increase also ; the rate of wages will rise, but there will not
necessarily be a higher standard of comfort, and the average
prosperity of the people will not be increased. At present a
beggar or a ragged starving child may be looked for in vain, and
it will not be easy to find even a dirty and neglected child, either
in city or country. Plump, clean, and rosy, with their little heads
carefully shaven in a variety of fantastic fashions, the children
afford a certain indication of prosperity among the lower orders
in Japan.

July 12*th.*—Bulls and stallions are used as the beasts of burden,
men as those of traction, and it is rare to see a quadruped in
harness. The Japanese are kind to their animals, which are usually
fat and well-liking, shod with straw, and ill-used in no way, except
having their heads tied up too tightly, in bearing-rein fashion. The
scarcity of quadrupeds, except dogs and cats (the latter being
frequently tail-less), is very conspicuous, sheep, goats, and pigs
being non-existent. The total absence of these animals renders
plantations cheap and easy in Japan, as no fencing is required ;
and herein doubtless lies the secret of waste land being almost
invariably covered with luxuriant forest. At the theatre to-night
the performance was peculiar, the actors performed in dumb-show
merely, and an old gentleman seated on high with a book read

out the play in emphatic tones, a sort of Chorus or "Gower." When anything of importance occurs, attendants with candles on long sticks illuminate the features of the actors, the lighting in general being defective.

July 13*th.*—The pickling and packing of two giant salamanders, called here *San-shô uwo*, or "fish inhabiting mountains," and of five *imori*, or palace guardians (newts with scarlet stomachs), caused considerable trouble and anxiety to Maruda and self, as we had to hunt all over Kioto for bottle, box, spirits, wire, and cement. At last, however, they have been despatched, according to promise, *en route* to the museum at Oxford, and we started in four jinrikshas, one for kit, each drawn by two men, and chartered for the whole way to Tokio, *viâ* the Nakasendo, or central mountain road.

Hikone was, until quite recently, the seat of a great Daimio, and the castle remains deserted, but in almost perfect preservation. Fortified with a wide moat and double walls, and provided with numerous bridges and gateways, it forms a stronghold both formidable and picturesque. Not a sign of life, however, was visible, although we tried one gate after another ; all was silent as in the castle of the Sleeping Beauty, or the camp of the Assyrians. Wandering on we at last found an open wicket, and entered ; but now appeared a solitary warder, who politely but firmly declined to let us pass, and we did not feel justified in treating him as true knights-errant would doubtless have done, so that the Sleeping Beauty remains undisturbed. Outside the moat is a garden in genuine Japanese style, with ponds, bridges, rock-work, and plants fantastically trimmed or trained; but all is in a state of neglect and decay. Ten years ago this was the pleasure-ground of a great feudal chief, converted now with all his peers into an ordinary citizen, by a revolution to which no resistance was offered by the owners of fortresses almost impregnable even to modern artillery. It is hardly possible to realize how near we are in point of time to a feudal system, as perfect as that which existed in Europe five centuries ago, and which has now passed away as completely. Many of the Daimios are now in Tokio, and are endeavouring to patch their fallen fortunes by taking to business and starting companies. These feudal princes must be singularly ignorant of commercial matters, but possibly their names, as directors of joint-stock associations, may be of some use : in England, of course, they would be invaluable. The Daimio has vanished from the country, and the schoolmaster has come in his stead.

July 15th.—We were up very early, consumed our eggs and chocolate, and toddled on in the cool of the morning. When overtaken by the kit, we got into our rikshas, and were dragged manfully over very bad roads in very severe heat—88° in the shade. Our course lay chiefly through valleys and plains cultivated with rice, but we came for the first time on silk and jute culture also. Villages are numerous, and in each a different trade or manufacture is carried on—stone-carving, cotton-weaving, silk-winding, umbrella-making, mat-plaiting, etc. Trim little gardens, sometimes not much larger than a table-cloth, show the fondness of the Japanese for flowers, especially azaleas, gardenias, hydrangias, crysanthemums, and a shrub new to me, with a handsome orange flower. Wood-carts and other vehicles are propelled hereabouts by human labour, and women, dressed very much like men, do their full share of this severe work.

July 17th.—To-day our coolies entered a remonstrance against our rate of speed, admitting that they had under-estimated the labours of the journey, and begging for increased pay, or reduced work, or both. Their demands were not unreasonable, and would have been conceded had we not begun to regard our jinrikshas as an incumbrance ; so we paid them up to date, made them a present, and dismissed them. Crossing a pass upwards of three thousand feet high, we descended through lovely scenery to Medono. The steep hills on every side are clothed with beautiful hanging woods, displaying a wonderful variety of foliage, bamboo and pine, chestnut and arbor vitæ, walnut and hemlock yew. Everywhere is the sound of running water, with occasional cascades gleaming through the trees ; and although green is the prevailing hue, the shades are so various as to impart an exquisite colouring to the landscape. Our luggage was conveyed sometimes by coolies, sometimes on a pony, requiring at each stage the active efforts of Maruda to start it afresh. If this is not the best season for flowers, it certainly is for insects; butterflies, dragon-flies, beetles, and fire-flies in great variety and brilliancy, succeed each other perpetually, and immense spiders lie in wait for them on every side. Reptiles are not scarce, whether in the shape of snakes, lizards, or frogs, and fish are abundant wherever there is water; but warm-blooded animals, except human beings, are seldom visible in Japan. There is certainly a lack of music from birds, but tree-frogs and insects do their best to make up for this; and there is always in these lovely landscapes the sweet sound of running water.

July 28th, Tokio.—We caused a famous top-spinner to perform before us, and certainly the tops, which are of lacquered wood, weighted with lead at the circumference, seem quite indifferent to the attraction of the earth; they are set agoing with a mere twist of the hands, and go on spinning indefinitely in any position. The exhibitions of so-called "waxworks," which are figures almost life size, made of paper and wood, are quite amusing; they represent a variety of sensational scenes in Japanese domestic life, and reminded us of the "appalling nature of the murdering coffin." We also went to see fencing and wrestling in large booths erected for the purpose. The fencing somewhat resembles German "mensur," the combatants being equipped with cuirasses and other defensive armour; the weapons are long bamboos held in both hands, like quarterstaffs, and they rush at one another with loud howls, exchanging blows so rapidly that it is hard to say which has dealt the successful stroke. The wrestling is more interesting, and is very popular, judging by the crowded state of the booth, where it goes on nearly all day. In the centre is an open space where the earth is beaten smooth, on either side of this squat the wrestlers, powerful-looking men, naked, with the exception of a small loin-cloth; an umpire, with a fan, is in the centre. When he gives the signal, from each side arises a hero, and steps into the arena, slapping his thighs and stamping violently upon the ground. After glaring upon each other, both champions rinse out their mouths, take a little salt in their hands, and repeat the process of stamping and slapping, after which they take more water and salt. They then squat down, facing each other at very close range; the umpire asks if they are ready; one assents, the other objects, alternately, until at last by mutual consent the signal is given, and they leap up, each trying to get an advantageous grip of the other. When once they have tackled each other the struggle does not last long; "they tug, they strain, down, down they go," and the judge's fan indicates the victor. As a rule the award is received in silence, the rivals retire, and a fresh pair enters the arena; but once, in a doubtful case, the audience demurred with loud cries, and the decision was appealed to a referee. There is something very classical in the appearance of the naked athletes, and of the *gens togata* watching them so eagerly.

August 1st.—We set off again to-day on our travels, proceeding in jinrikshas through a very pretty country, with varied views of land and sea. Of pedestrian pilgrims, attired in white, with clean mats on their backs, large hats marked with the name of their village on their heads, chaplets of beads round their necks, and bells dangling at their sides, the name is legion.

August 3rd.—At Miyonoshita is a real hotel, with beds, tables, and European luxuries of all sorts, besides an elegant garden representing Fuji in a miniature of azaleas, a pond full of fish, red, white, and black, and delightful warm baths fed by natural springs. A young American, who has lived nearly all his life in Japan, gave us his views as to the present trying position of the Samurai class. They are now, many of them, in great pecuniary difficulties; their pensions have been reduced; in some instances they have received capitalized sums in lieu of pensions, and have lost these in their inexperienced attempts to carry on commercial business. Accustomed to be treated by all with deference and respect, to possess the monopoly of weapons, and to "keep the crown of the causeway," they suddenly find their occupation and their revenues gone, themselves and their families reduced to menial and dishonourable shifts for a livelihood, their swords taken from them, and the people disposed to regard them as stingless drones.

August 5th.—For the ascent of Fuji we did not reject the assistance of kagos; this mode of conveyance is only middling comfortable for a person with long legs, being merely a basket slung on a thick pole and carried by two men. When the ascent of the cone commenced, we proceeded on foot, at first through woods of mixed timber, like those of a gentleman's "policy" in Scotland, where flutter beautiful butterflies so tame that you may catch them with finger and thumb, examine and release them. Fleecy clouds began to collect around the middle portion of the mountain; and out of these, long strings of white-robed pilgrims with tinkling bells might be seen descending, while others toil like ourselves laboriously upwards—"ants upon Merapi." The signs of recent heat are everywhere, but the volcano appears to be quite extinct, at any rate it is very dormant. To the pilgrims night and day are pretty much alike, they seem to be always on the move, and at this season Fuji simply swarms with them; we must have seen many hundreds, if not thousands, on the mountain.

August 6th.—The pilgrims did not perch permanently, they came in a flight before daybreak, chattered like sparrows upon a housetop, took a cup of tea, and fluttered off again at the first streak of dawn, to explore the sacred places and drink of the sacred springs. Darkness came on as we descended on foot towards Sengoka. Making towards a light, we found the population assembled to witness a series of wrestling matches between the village youths, each champion holding the arena as long as he could overthrow his opponents, while women and boys acted as torchbearers, and the seniors officiated as judges. Seeing some foreigners comfortably seated at table in a house, we ventured to inquire where we could find accommodation. The reply was in French : " I think that you can sleep here. I know that you can have plenty to eat and drink. Please to come in." The party consisted of two ladies and two gentlemen ; they vied with each other in kindly hospitality, and an excellent supper was very soon placed before us, with red wine and absinthe *à discrétion.* Although the chase is not yet legally open, our French friends, who have a lot of sporting dogs, have commenced indulging in it, getting hares and pheasants, besides any number of little fishes taken with the rod.

August 7th.—In the early morning Fuji was clear as usual, and we had a beautiful walk down to Miyonoshita, through a country which reminded me of New Zealand, chiefly on account of the steam jets and solfatara visible here and there upon the hills. The hotel, with its warm baths, clean togas, and attentive damsels, was the lap of luxury after our fatigues, and I indulged in the process of being shampooed by a one-eyed amma, this function being a speciality of the blind. In the afternoon, I crossed the hills to Hakone, and took up my quarters in a teahouse for the last time. These houses consist of a series of small rooms, which may be separated from each other with partitions of paper on light wooden frames, or may be thrown all into one piece, coextensive with the whole floor of the house. The inner rooms are the most honourable, and we usually occupied those looking on the tiny garden, our coolies being equally well lodged in the outer; all are covered with clean matting, and are devoid of furniture, except a few ornaments, screens, or curios. On arriving and removing one's shoes, the first thing provided is a fire-pot, containing hot cinders for lighting pipes; then comes tea in very small cups, and perhaps little plates of sweetmeats with chopsticks, upon a lacquer table about six inches high. Clapping the hands is at once answered by a chirp, and brings a neat-handed little "wren," who ministers kneeling; this name we have given to the servant girls, on account of their rapid movements, cheerful voices, and sashes bunched up behind. The last sound at night, and the first in the morning, is their cheery "Hech ! hech !" in response to orders; and on arrival or departure you are overwhelmed with their chorus of "Ohaio !" or "Sayonara ! "

August 8th, Yokohama.—At Fuji-sawa, which takes its name from the "matchless" wisteria, common hereabouts, there is a fine temple, where a jovial old Buddhist bonze entertained us with tea, and in return obtained our signs manual, with a small contribution for a copper roof to the temple. To write one's name on a fan, or a piece of paper, is a favour frequently requested of a stranger in Japan. The road is an almost continuous succession of villages, whose brown thatched roofs are crowned with a green ridge of iris plants. In default of singing birds the villagers keep numbers of green crickets, in little wicker cages, to enliven them with chirruping. Our coolies insisted on being allowed to take us on the whole way to Yokohama, and kept up a steady trot, with rare pauses for drinking and washing their wearing apparel, consisting of a rag round the waist and another round the head. A trifle extra on arrival made them bow to the earth; certainly the Japs of all ranks are the least grasping and the most good-tempered, polite people that a traveller can have to do with. Their pluck and endurance would make first-class soldiers of them under European officers.

August 12th.—The *City of Pekin* came in during the night, and sails to-morrow at daybreak for San Francisco, so we must to-day make our adieus to bonnie Japan. Very few countries that I have ever visited can take rank with this in the number of pleasant impressions left on the memory by the land and its inhabitants. As regards the various minor tests which I am accustomed to apply in estimating the civilization of a people, the Japanese stand very high indeed, as well as regards some of the most important. Education is generally diffused; women and children are treated with the utmost kindness and consideration; dumb animals are better used than in any Asiatic and many European countries; cleanliness is carried almost to excess in the matter of bathing, while you may eat your dinner off the floor in the poorest houses; cremation is a common method of disposing of the dead, and all funerals are conducted with so little ostentation as rarely to be visible at all,—I saw only one, and that took place at 5 a.m. Then as to ornaments and gorgeous trappings, no nation dresses so simply as the Japanese; even women wear few or no ornaments, except for fastening up their hair, and do not pierce the cartilage of nose or ears in order to insert metallic rings! In political matters they are less advanced than in social, the Government hitherto having been everything and the citizen nothing; but already the south-eastern provinces, which have long taken the lead in politics, demand representative institutions, decentralization, and financial reform. Japan has her work cut out for her, but she is " mistress of herself, though China fall," and is determined at all costs to manage her own affairs.

The interest which China and Japan, especially the latter, aroused in Sir David's mind was shown by his writing five articles on subjects connected with these countries. In the spring of 1878, two articles on "Modern Japan" appeared in the *Fortnightly Review*, and a paper, "Girls in Japan," in *Every Girl's Magazine*. In October, 1878, and February, 1879, two interesting reviews followed, of " Two Fair Cousins," a Chinese romance, and " The Loyal League," a Japanese romance. From these stories, and the characters of their respective heroes, he brings out clearly the very different types of character which were admired by the two nations. In the former, a poor and unknown student, who has given proof of his talent by successful verse-making, is selected by the father of the wealthy and beautiful heroine, as a suitable husband for her, in preference to a suitor possessing rank and riches, but a plucked candidate for literary honours. In the latter, admiration is reserved for the courage and devotion of the

Samurai to their feudal chief, for whose sake they give up, not only life, but wives, sisters, parents, and children. He adds :—

John Albert de Mandelslo, who visited Japan and China, A.D. 1639, and gives many interesting details as to both countries, was much impressed with the want of resemblance between their respective inhabitants, and scouts the notion of their having a common origin : "There is so great a difference in their cloathing, their ceremonies, manner of life, language, and writing, that it is impossible that the same nation should have contracted, even in the sequel of many ages, such contrary habits." This accurate and observant traveller thus describes the Japanese—"They are so ambitious and highly conceited of themselves that it is seldom seen a Japonnese does anything wherewith he might be reproached, but, on the contrary, they would rather lose their lives than betray their honour."

The Samurai temper prevails among the Northmen of the sagas and early ballads; and the story of Rolf Krake's death, as told by Saxo and Evald, might almost, with a change of names, be told as a tale of Old Japan. The Danish armour-bearer of a more recent legend, who slays his fair young bride on the wedding night, has his exact counterpart among the fierce and faithful Ronins. The point of honour for which the Scandinavian and the Japanese are equally ready to sacrifice life and love, is almost identical in the mind of the European and the Asiatic warrior; and so great is the similarity of temperament between the two races that one is surprised not to find the Japanese playing conspicuously the part of Vikings in the history of Eastern Asia.

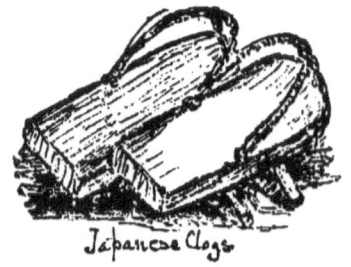

Japanese Clogs.

Icelandic
"Skin Socks"
June 1878

CHAPTER XIX.

1877-1878.

RETURN THROUGH AMERICA—ADDRESS TO THE ELECTORS OF DEVONPORT—
A MONTH IN ICELAND—VISITS IN DENMARK—ARTICLES ON "ICELAND"
AND "DENMARK."

August 30th, San Francisco.—The magnificent new Palace Hotel,
eight or nine storeys high, has been completed and opened since
my last visit, and is the largest hotel in the world. It is fitted
up with all modern improvements, and is a luxurious location,
its great height being compensated by numerous elevators in
constant action. The waiters are all coloured gentlemen, and are
quite kind and condescending for men of their haughty race;
they are marshalled and paraded like policemen. Everything
looks huge after Japan, horses and houses especially; but the

pavement is execrable, whether wood or stone, and we all miss the "pretty tiny riksha;" on the other hand, the fruit is quite delicious.   In the evening we saw a Polish lady act as Juliet, —Madame Modjeska, Countess Bozenta ; she did justice to her part, and had an excellent reception, with lots of bouquets.   A strange flag, intended apparently for the Polish, was presented to her, while "God save the Queen" was played—singularly inappropriate ; but she took the will for the deed, and was much affected by this blundering attempt to do honour to her unhappy country. The old nurse, Mrs. Judah, was excellent, but the men were hardly up to the mark.

On the 3rd of September his brother set off, with some of their fellow-passengers, to see the Yosemite Valley, and they agreed to meet again at Salt Lake City.   Sir David employed the time in a run to the geysers, and the petrified forest in the neighbourhood of Calistoga.   At Sacramento he joined Sir Joseph Hooker and Dr. Asa Gray of Cambridge, Massachusetts, and with these distinguished botanists made excursions to Castle Peak and Lake Tahoe in the Sierra Nevada.   After leaving them he drove down to Virginia City, where he visited the great Virginia consolidated silver mine, and noticed that in Nevada the eastern ranges of the great Sierra chiefly contain silver ore, whilst the western slopes of California contain gold.

September 17*th.*—This morning we started for the east by the Central Pacific Railway.   Nothing could be more brilliant than the colouring of the scenery throughout, the intense blue of the Salt Lake gleaming in the sun, the shores gold and yellow with sunflowers, the hills tinted with scarlet vegetation, and crested with silvery white.

September 18*th.*—To-night we were roused from our first sleep by a certain amount of excitement among the officials, and woke up to find that the train had been stopped and robbed by a band of men, armed and masked in melodramatic style.   The sleeping-cars were locked, and they had not time or inclination for a siege, as they had secured sixty thousand dollars in gold out of the express car, besides looting the passengers in the ordinary cars. Silver, of which there was a large amount in bars, they naturally despised, and behaved on the whole with consideration, stopping our train, and another immediately behind us, with the proper signals, and doing no injury to the track. They had previously taken possession of the station and telegraph office at Big Springs (the scene of action on the borders of Nebraska), and having drowned out the fire of our engine, they made off in the direction of the Black Hills, leaving us helpless, bewildered, angry, amused, and ashamed all at once. It was certainly humiliating for so many honest men to be robbed by so few rogues, but we were unarmed and unprepared in every sense of the word, and resistance was quite out of the question. No doubt there ought to have been a guard with so much treasure as we had on board, for stage robberies have been quite frequent of late in these parts, but it is long since a train has been ditched, or looted, as they used to be by Indians. The arrival of the emigrant train doubtless hastened the departure of our thirteen rogues " in buckram," and a delay of three hours in reaching our breakfast station was the only inconvenience sustained by the more aristocratic passengers.

September 23rd, Clifton House.—A day of real repose and enjoyment amid the glories of Niagara. A certain amount of caution must be exercised in the matter of towers, which have been erected at every possible point of view, and the ascent of which is both fatiguing and expensive, costing half a dollar a-piece. The burning spring well deserves a visit, being itself a natural curiosity, and being in a most beautiful situation, just above the Horseshoe Falls on the Canadian side. A marked change has taken place since I was here, eleven years ago, in the appearance of the mighty green curve, which is now broken by a deep indentation, only visible when the dense cloud of spray is blown aside. The Terrapin tower has disappeared since then; and so great are the forces here at work, that a very short time suffices to show practically how this deep gorge has been cut, and how the falls have assumed their present form.

September 24th.—From Oneida we drove out to visit the Perfectionist community, about four miles distant. We were very politely received by Miss Miller, a lady in neat and simple Bloomer costume, who took charge of us during the whole of our stay. The main industries of the community are canning fruit and vegetables, winding silk, and making traps for animals of all sorts, from a rat to a grizzly bear. These industries are conducted by hired labour, the community being now hardly in any sense a co-operative society, rather a joint-stock company employing labourers, and sharing profits among partners only. Some members' regret this falling off, and would fain see the work done by those within the pale of the community, but such is the deceitfulness of riches, that hired labour is on the increase. As regards the men there is no distinction in costume, but the ladies of the community are distinguished from their female helps by their Bloomer dress and simple coiffure. As all mess together, and the family numbers about three hundred, all told, an extensive kitchen is required, to say nothing of their numerous visitors, whom they undertake to feed at a moderate charge. To us, as English gentlemen of inquiring minds, their hospitality was unbounded and quite gratuitous; they ordered a late dinner for our special convenience, and gave us every rural luxury, cream and fruit in particular, such as I have never seen surpassed. In the evening there is a general gathering in the great hall, where ladies and gentlemen sit in easy-chairs to see and hear whatever may be brought before them in the way of music, theatricals, lectures, etc. To-night the proceedings were by no means lively: paragraphs were read out solemnly from the daily papers, in a dim light, by several of the leading swells; and I should have had to make a speech, had not our carriage been announced at the critical moment. *Sic me servavit Apollo !*

On their way to New York they stopped at Albany, and revisited the Shaker settlement at Watervliet, where he found all looking as peaceful and flourishing as it had done eleven years before. While at Boston he renewed his acquaintance with Dr. Wendell Holmes, and other friends, and spent a pleasant day at Concord with Ralph Waldo Emerson. The brothers sailed from Boston in the Cunard steamer *Marathon*, reaching England on the 19th of October, after a stormy passage, but found that the gale there had been worse than anything they had experienced in the Atlantic. In a letter, dated New York, October 1st, to the editor of the *Spectator*, he observed :—

This is the third visit which I have made to the United States since the close of the great civil war, and it is with great pleasure that I now at last perceive distinct indications of returning prosperity and fraternity throughout the Union. Early in 1875 the prospect was gloomier in the Southern States than it had been nearly nine years earlier; a policy of repression rather than one of conciliation was in favour at Washington, and the bitterest feeling prevailed between the two great political parties in the South. It was a discouraging time for all well-wishers of the Americans, but things were then at their worst, and have since been steadily mending. The conciliatory policy of President Hayes has been accepted with an astonishing unanimity of approval in the North as well as in the South, and Englishmen interested in America will certainly wish him all success.

Previous to his departure from England in 1876 on his lengthened tour, the Liberal party in more than one constituency had made proposals that he should come forward as their candidate at the next general election. He declined to give any promise, or to make any public appearance at that time, but his inclination was to stand for Devonport, where he hoped, with his friend Mr. J. D. Lewis as a colleague, to gain seats for the Liberal party. On his return from America, he consented to meet and address the electors of Devonport, and went there, with Mr. Lewis, early in December. He frankly laid before the meeting his own individual opinions on the most important questions of the day—a task easier to him than to many men, as, although his views expanded and developed with experience, he never wavered nor went back from any principle which he had once satisfied himself to be right and just. He said :—

I can hardly do better than begin by referring to the subject of the equalization of the franchise in counties and boroughs. The voice of the agricultural labourers and residents in counties has been but seldom heard, and the result has been apparently that their wants and requirements have been very much

Y

neglected. In a country governed as England is, those classes who are not represented actually suffer by any extension of the franchise from which they are excluded. By such extension a larger number have claims upon legislators and the ministry, and the chance of those who have no direct voice in public affairs being listened to is thereby considerably diminished. Therefore, I consider it to be essential to the interests of a large and important class of the community, that they should be admitted to that share in the government of the country, which their brethren who happen to reside within borough limits enjoy, and I confidently appeal to the electors of boroughs to assist them in attaining that equalization.

I am not one of those who cherish personal hostility to the Church of England; I do not consider that its disestablishment is a thing of the immediate future, but I believe that the principle of religious equality ought to be carried out thoroughly and completely in this Liberal country. Dissenters enjoy perfect toleration, but the very use of the word "toleration" implies that they do not enjoy religious equality. There ought to be no disabilities and no advantages, political or civil, that a man should either suffer, or enjoy, on account of his religious opinions. The opposition to the Burials Bill, a moderate and temperate measure, is one of the causes which has tended to promote the general feeling that disestablishment is not so very far off. There is another measure which was lost by the opposition of the Established Church. I refer to the bill for legalizing marriage with a deceased wife's sister. In every Protestant country, in the States of America, and in the English colonies, the object that bill sought to accomplish is already law.

In discussing reforms, I cannot help adverting to the Land Laws. In England it is a very tedious and expensive operation to purchase a piece of land. Some years ago, I was connected with the purchase of small properties in England and Italy; in the case of the English property, literally years passed, and I am afraid to say how much money was expended before the sale, upon which purchaser and seller were equally agreed, could take place, and have legal effect. In Italy a similar sale was carried out in about half an hour, at the expense of twenty-seven francs: that was simply owing to the satisfactory and distinct arrangements with regard to the register of title, and transfer of landed property; and the thing could be as easily done in England, if there were sufficient force to urge it on.

The question, which seems to arouse the most feeling of opposition and division in the Liberal party, is that of the Licensing Laws, and in particular the Permissive Bill. My own feelings and prejudices, if I may so call them, are strongly in favour of individual liberty; I am very loth to interfere with minorities, or with those who differ from me in their way of life; and I think a very strong case must always be shown before the majority interferes with the liberty of the minority. But in this particular case, it does appear to me that very strong argument is made out in favour of some interference. I cannot say that the Permissive Bill commanded my complete approbation, but upon the balance of argument it seemed to me my duty to vote for the second reading of that bill.

There is another question, the war in the East, on which I desire to say a few words. Many patriotic Englishmen, whose feelings and whose memories are still full of the recollections of the Crimean War, hardly consider this present war on its own merits; during the Crimean War I myself certainly regarded Russia in a very hostile spirit. Twenty years have elapsed, and we find that the excellent promises exacted by us from Turkey at the end of the war have not in a single instance been really kept. On the other hand, a great change has taken place in Russia; she has almost entirely ceased to take part or to interfere in the affairs of Western Europe, and has, under the present Emperor, emancipated her serfs—one of the grandest events in history. Besides this, there has sprung up upon her borders United Germany, now by far the greatest military power upon the Continent, and not a gun can be fired there without her consent. I do not believe that Russia will attempt to take possession of Constantinople, nor do I think the European Powers would let her do so. For my own part I rely for the maintenance of our Indian and Colonial Empire almost entirely upon England's maritime superiority. As we took possession of that Empire by the sea, so we must hold it by maritime supremacy; and as long as that is maintained, the Empire cannot be seriously affected. If we can only maintain our fleet at the proper degree of strength, and keep in full working order those institutions which are necessary for equipping, renovating, and completing the fleet, we need think

of no risk whatever from that honey-combed colossus—Russia—
with no money and no ships.

Most of the winter was spent at Meredith, taking care
of his mother, who was at that time living alone there,
with her two little grandsons, of seven and five years
old. He never was happier than when with her and his
nephews, of whom he made complete companions, talking
and explaining things to them, teaching them to repeat
poetry, and playing with them, both in and out of doors.
His love for all children was remarkable, and they seemed
thoroughly to believe in and reciprocate it ; he had a great
power of amusing and attracting even the shyest child.
The fact was, that in telling them stories and playing
games, he not only amused them but himself also, and
children soon found this out ; he often said, " Their conversation never bores me, which is more than I can say of
many people."   In the evenings, he used to read aloud to
his mother the wonderful journals he had kept of all his
travels, and which were written very much to give her
pleasure, as his letters home, although regular and frequent,
were always extremely short.

He would also brighten her evenings with games at
cards, euchre being their favourite ; fondness for games was
quite a distinctive feature in his character, and when playing he gave his whole mind and attention to what he was
doing.   On his travels he was always on the look-out for
any new game, which he would quickly acquire and remember ; in this way he brought home, and taught to the
rest of the family, such games as " Sancho Pedro," " ombre,"
" Russian whist," and others.   Gambling in any shape had
no attractions for him ; he neither liked to lose his own
money nor to win that of other people ; at home the
stakes were generally halfpenny cards, which he thoroughly
enjoyed winning, and always exacted full payment.   His
many voyages enabled him to keep up chess and whist,

and a good opponent at the former greatly added to his
pleasure on board ship, while at home four-chess was a
popular and more lively game.

In February, during his absence for a few days, Lady
Wedderburn met with an accident, dislocating her shoulder,
which at her age was a serious matter. As she did not
properly recover the use of her arm, her sons took her to
London in April, for further advice; after a month under
Mr. Hutton, the effects of the accident almost disappeared.

In May he went to Southampton to meet his youngest
sister, on her return from India, and feeling now that their
mother was in good hands, he found time for a month in
Iceland before the militia training in July.

June 3rd, S.S. "Phönix."—We went on shore to make the
most of a stay of about eight hours in the Faroe Islands. We
walked across the fells to Kirkeboe, where stand the unfinished
ruins of the Faroese cathedral, commenced in Roman Catholic
times, and left incomplete at the Reformation; it seems to be the
only stone building in the Faroe Islands.

June 5th.—Great whales gambolled freely around the vessel,
spouting their foam fountains, and as we approached the lofty cliffs
of the Vestmanna Islands we could see that they were literally
white with sea-fowl, which crowded every ledge of rock, and
swarmed upon the surface of the sea. Air, water, and land were
alive with guillemots, divers, puffins, auks, and gulls; but each
species keeps more or less together, and apart from the rest. The
sea-fowl here are strictly protected, and are a source of considerable profit, in eggs, feathers, and young birds, to the islanders,
who also feed a number of sheep upon the grassy summits of
their rocky isles.

June 7th, Reykjavik.—W. C. Krieger and I started by boat
at 10 p.m. Our first visit was to Engry, a flat grassy island;
and we were guided to the duckery, which occupies many acres
of hummocky grass land. The eider drake is a handsome conspicuous bird, black and white in plumage, with a curious green
mark on the back of his neck; and many drakes were visible,
swimming, flying, and standing about. Of the ducks, which are

of a mottled brown and grey, very few were at first to be seen, but on a nearer approach we found them squatting between the grassy hummocks, with a tameness almost shocking. Some allowed themselves to be stroked, lifted off their eggs, and replaced, with a few little grunts of remonstance; others, less tame, flopped slowly and heavily away for a few yards as we approached, waddling hastily back as soon as we had passed on. The eggs were usually four in number, but varied from two to five, and are of a fine olive green, long and elliptical in form, all resting upon neat little nests of the famous eider down, "so soft and brown." In one nest were newly hatched ducklings, apparently in no hurry to clear out of their comfortable abode; in another they were just chipping the egg, and the duck was very indignant at being disturbed at so critical a moment. The eder-fugl are protected all the year round under heavy penalties, the only birds enjoying legal protection in Iceland.

June 9th.—With a high barometer, splendid weather, and a very prepossessing young man as guide, I started under good auspices for Thingvalla and the Geysirs. Thorgrimur is a fine specimen of an Icelander, and looks quite up to his heroic name, tall, blue-eyed, and of most gentlemanly bearing. He treats me as a social equal when off duty, but when acting in his official capacity as guide and servant, he scorns no menial office, and will cheerfully pull off my boots. Said boots are of a peculiar nature, being Icelandic "skin socks," like loose jack-boots of untanned sheep-skin, green in hue and quite waterproof; they are worn over one pair of Icelandic shoes, or moccasins, with a second pair over them, and are fastened with various bands of leather, like the leggings of the orthodox brigand.

We have five ponies, two for each man, and one for the boxes, and the plucky willing little beasts pace away as cheerily as if they had not been more or less living on a straw a day for the last six months. Whether it be a ford or a snowdrift, a bog or a bare ridge of lava, the sense of security, as regards the Icelandic pony, is complete: he is as cautious as an elephant, snuffs every suspicious place, feels it with his fore foot, and, if left to himself, will never make a mistake. At present the country is wonderfully dry, and the only nuisance is the dust kicked up by the little caravan, the three loose horses requiring to be urged by Thorgrimur along the by no means flowery path, whenever a few blades of grass can

be picked up by the way-side. As a rule, there is no temptation
for the poor beasts to linger, and they jog along very contentedly.
It was nearly midnight when we reached the church and parsonage
of Thingvalla, but our arrival was taken as a matter of course,
and we were at once made welcome: I had the guest-chamber,
and Thorgrimur slept in the church, although doubts were expressed as to whether he might fear to do so alone; I was tired
enough to sleep anywhere.

June 10*th.*—I woke up thoroughly refreshed, and at once
sallied forth to inspect the classic ground on which we stood.
On the highest point of rock sat a raven, croaking "Nevermore"
for the departed greatness of the Icelandic Althing. The Lögberg,
or Hill of Laws, where the Althing used to meet, is a ridge of lava
with a chasm on either side; it is the greenest spot around, and
is enamelled with yellow dandelions and buttercups, while the
chasms contain water so clear as hardly to be visible. Somehow
Thingvalla Lake reminds me strongly of Lake Taupo, in New
Zealand: the lonely ride through a desolate land, the signs of
recent volcanic activity, the snowy mountains rising above the blue
lake and its brown shores, and the historical associations with a
departed national greatness, all combine to connect in the
imagination two places geographically so remote from each other.

June 11*th.*—The Geysirs were very quiet all day, and we gave
up hopes of seeing the big fellow exhibit, although his basin was
full to the brim of clear boiling water, welling up from the great
pipe in the centre. We set to work cutting turf to irritate Strokr,
the churn, who seemed tranquillity itself, and splashed in about
as much as one stout pony could carry. For five minutes there
was no change except that the water became muddy; then, after
a little bubbling, came a sudden furious rush of boiling water,
leaping high into the air in several jets, and throwing out the
sodden remnants of the turf. Again and again the boiling
fountain leaped up at irregular intervals, and without any warning,
until every fragment of turf had been ejected. The height of the
different explosions varied a good deal, some attaining, perhaps,
to fifty or sixty feet, but it is very difficult to estimate such
sudden spirts; for more than half an hour the spouting continued at intervals, and the young farmer said Strokr was in
specially good form to-day, as I am his first visitor this season,
and it is long since he has been disturbed. We paid for the turf

we had consumed, and took leave about 7 p.m., making for
Middalṛ, where there is a church, an important matter where
sleeping accommodation is scarce. It is a remarkably clean and
tidy one, with a chandelier, windows that will open, and no lack
of paint inside ; the people are obliging, and gave me dry hay,
clean sheets, and excellent dairy produce. Icelanders always
seem to have plenty to eat as regards quantity, although the
quality is often doubtful, and dried cods' heads take a deal of
gnawing.

June 14th, S.S. "Diana."—Men in Iceland wear no national
costume, but the women of all classes alike wear the "thufa," or
little cloth cap, with long silken tassel, and gold or silver ornament. The hair is plaited in many loops and tails around the
head, and the ladies generally have fair and florid complexions,
with a pleasing intelligent expression. The children have very
rosy faces, and are almost as polite and friendly as the Japanese,
coming up to shake hands with a " God dag ! " Shaking hands
is perpetual in Iceland, and when you have remunerated any one,
he first examines the coin carefully, and then warmly shakes hands.
It can hardly be said that there is any distinction of classes,
although the praest enjoys a certain rank and consideration ;
there are few countries where so thoroughly republican an equality
subsists in society.   Thorgrimur dined with me, and after a game
of chess, accompanied me on board the *Diana*, where I am the
only non-Icelandic passenger.

June 17th.—At Isafjördr fish-curing goes on to an immense
extent ; the sea-shore is neatly paved with large stones, on which
the bodies of the fish, cod and ling, are spread out to dry, and
are afterwards piled together in regular stacks, protected with
matting, roofed with planks, and pressed down with heavy stones.
These fish are sent principally to Spain, the heads only being
reserved for home consumption ; and, after all, the fisheries are
the only Icelandic resource capable of any great development :
at present, the lack of properly decked boats shuts out the
natives to a great extent from their principal source of wealth,
and exposes them to much additional hardship and danger.

June 18th.—Captain Wandel having made all arrangements for
an excursion to see Icelandic lignite *in situ*, he and I made an
early start, guided by the local pilot, a lively veteran of seventy-
two. The lignite is in thin layers, mixed with slaty rock, and

overlaid by vast masses of basalt ; it is partially carbonized and partially in the condition of ordinary wood, with its bark still adhering. It is difficult to understand how wood can underlie such masses of basalt, and hardly even be blackened or charred by the heat ; it is no doubt fairly combustible, but is not in sufficient quantities nor sufficiently accessible to be of any commercial importance. At a solitary farm we partook of lunch outside, surrounded by an admiring crowd of youngsters, Gisli, Hjalmar, Thora, Gudrun, etc., who displayed an intelligent delight at the pictures of the *Illustrated London News*, in which our food was packed, such as was both pleasing and pathetic to witness. We gave them both the papers and their contents, but they evidently preferred the pictures to the food, with the eager love of knowledge which characterizes the race. The interior of their dwelling was an extraordinary sight : on the ground floor is the kitchen, with one or two store or lumber rooms, all very dark and dirty ; but the family residence is in a low, dark, close little garret, where the whole clan, more than twenty souls, are housed. Round the sides of the room are half a dozen beds, and when our eyes became accustomed to the obscurity, increased by festoons of stockings hanging from the rafters to dry, we gradually discovered the inmates. On one bed sat an old blind woman knitting, with an old man, the patriarch of the family, beside her ; on the bed opposite, one of the younger women with maternal pride displayed a really pretty little baby girl, and in a cradle alongside lay another infant, apparently twins. Crowded, unwholesome dwellings, together with free "indulgence in alcoholic stimulants," are apparently insufficient in Iceland to shorten the lives of men constantly "exposed to the inclemency of the elements." These people might afford to live more comfortably, but they are conservative, and continue to build in a style which enables one to realize the domestic economy prevailing in a Sutherland " Pict's house."

June 20th.—Our passengers consist of lads going home for holidays from the Reykjavik College, rosy-faced daughters of parsons, aristocratic enough to travel in the first cabin, and deck passengers going to the fisheries on the east coast. At every place where we stop, the intelligent young ladies make a point of going ashore to see what there may be to see, and they take an interest in the machinery, compasses, telescopes, charts, etc., which does them great credit. I know no more certain proof of intelligence than admiration or astonishment at new things; stupid persons and stupid races are never astonished. The midnight sun, resting on the horizon like a mountain of glittering gold, and not hasting to go either down or up for so long a space of time, is really a strange and magnificent sight. He slides along the surface of the sea in an indefinitely prolonged sunset or sunrise, with all the brilliancy of colouring which in lower latitudes lasts only for a few minutes, but which here lasts literally for hours. We are here about forty-five miles south of the Arctic circle, but the effect of atmospheric refraction is to keep the sun from disappearing below the horizon. After enjoying this novel and gorgeous spectacle, I turned in for a little, and came on deck early, to find the vessel at the entrance to the Eyjafiordr completely surrounded with ice. · The aspect of affairs was thoroughly Arctic; the sea covered with floating ice as far as the eye could reach, and the land mainly covered with snow; the weather was brilliantly clear, and the sea perfectly calm, as usual when so much ice floats on its surface. In extricating ourselves from the ice, we had a mild experience of what an Arctic voyage is like; occasionally we struck a block, which craunched and crumbled at the blow, being now somewhat rotten, and much worn at the surface of the water, although very thick, and, of course, floating with about eight-ninths of its mass below the surface.

June 24th.—At Eskifjordr we were hospitably received by Fru Tulinius, who fed us, after which I mounted a noble little steed, and rode off along the edge of the fjord to visit the spot whence comes the famous double-refracting Iceland spar. Plenty of the spar lies scattered about in fragments of various size and transparency. The calcareous crystals are embedded in basaltic rock, which looks exactly similar to that of which half Iceland is composed, but the spar does not occur elsewhere in any known spot. The crystals, when quite transparent, are valuable for optical instruments, and a diamond-shaped piece about six inches long is valued at fifty kroner.

June 26th.—The lofty peaks of Iceland stood out above the haze against the clear sky, and I took a last farewell of Ultima Thule, the most western if not the most northern portion of Europe. After all, there is little to tempt a stranger to linger long in an island, which its inhabitants love so well; but the people are a good sort, and deserve every praise for their gallant struggle with a hostile sky and soil. The country combines the evils of every zone, volcanoes and glaciers, sandy deserts and swamps, lava and snow, furious rivers and inaccessible mountains ; no metals, no coal, only a little sulphur, lignite, and calcareous spar, no crops except a scanty and precarious hay crop, so that it is to the sea, rather than to the land, that they must look for increased prosperity. Fishes of various sorts are Iceland's best and most certain crop, and without their aid a country nearly as large as England could not even support its population of less than seventy thousand souls.

On his return he at once joined his militia regiment, which for the last time held their annual training at Gloucester, as their head-quarters were moved next year to Horfield, near Bristol. Owing perhaps to the unusual heat of this July, coming directly after his tour in Iceland, he suffered for some weeks from a slight but persistent attack of intermittent fever, which did not, however, prevent his attending the parades, even when hardly fit to do so. It continued to annoy him when at Paris, where he went in August to see the Exhibition ; and, on his return, he allowed his eldest sister to treat him with homeopathic medicines, with such complete success, that he used afterwards to recommend the system in similar cases. Although little addicted to doctoring in any shape, he always had a leaning towards homeopathy, as had his father before him ; in fact, all the family have had more or less faith in the system.

On his voyage to Iceland he had made the acquaintance of a young Danish gentleman, W. C. Krieger. Having many tastes in common, a friendship sprang up between them, and Sir David gladly accepted an invitation to accompany him to Denmark, in order to visit his relations there, and see something of the country life of the great Danish landowners. It was difficult to find a time which

suited them both, as Sir David was pledged to assist at his
brother's marriage to Miss Hoskyns, which was fixed to
take place on the 12th of September, in Somersetshire.
He escorted his mother there and back, and added much
to the cheerfulness of the occasion by the active part he
took in the festivities.   Soon afterwards he sailed, with
Mr. Krieger, from London to Hamburg, and in the next
ten days paid four most agreeable visits in different parts
of Denmark.

September 24th.—Frijsenborg Slot is a worthy seat for the
richest and most ancient family bearing the rank of Count in
Denmark, and is quite in keeping as to all details.   It is built in
the genuine Danish style of Christian IV., red brick with white
stone facings, and has lofty round towers with pointed roofs; it
is surrounded with a moat, which only leaves room for a few
small flower-beds close to the castle walls, and has an open
courtyard shaded by fine horse-chestnuts.   Deer of various sorts
abound in the park and woods, and there are extensive aviaries
of game birds, including Californian quail.   The laws as to forest
preservation are now very strict in Denmark, and trees may not
be cut down without the sanction of a Government inspector,
whose duty it is to see that young trees are not only planted to
replace the old, but are also taken care of.   We inspected one of
the many churches, which the Count, as owner of tiends, has
rebuilt and is rebuilding on his estates; there are thirty-six
altogether of these edifices.   The church contains an elaborately
carved wooden pulpit, and an old granite font, which looks as if
it dated from a period anterior to the introduction of Christianity
into Denmark.   The farm of Frijsendal is in every respect the
most magnificent establishment of the sort that I have ever seen :
the farmer's residence is a handsome mansion with an Italian
tower, and the farm buildings are simply palatial.   Each edifice
has over the door an artistically carved head of the quadruped
occupying it, whether horse, ox, or pig, and within are to be found
the animals themselves in multitudes; in the byre were 180 cows
in the act of being milked.   All the manure is collected under
cover in a vast building for the purpose, and the gentleman in
possession assured us that it pays to do so.   The presence of a

wealthy and liberal resident proprietor is everywhere manifest about Frijsenborg, in well-made private roads, well-built houses, well-kept plantations, and everything useful is to be found on the premises, including a telegraph office, a pharmacy, and a doctor.

September 27th.—At Maribo, I found Count Knuth waiting to convey me to Knuthenborg; here I am in most comfortable quarters, my young host devoting himself with the greatest zeal to my service and amusement. The farming on the estate is excellent, and a great deal of beet-root is grown for sugar ; all the farm-steadings are large and well built, such as can hardly be seen even in the best agricultural districts of Scotland. Expense is apparently no object at Knuthenborg, whatever may be the thing to be done, made, or built ; a church, a harbour, a road, a house, a wall, or a plantation. At the little town of Bandholm a really excellent harbour has been constructed at great expense, and a private line of railway made to connect the harbour with the main line at Maribo. The houses of the factor, forester, bailiff, and other functionaries, are all built in the handsomest style ; and numbers of choice trees, all carefully fenced, are dotted about in the park. The Count's ideal, and that of his brother before him, is to have his place kept in English style ; no money is spared, and the result is that it would be difficult to find in all England a place better kept. Judging from the appearance of the huge stacks of grain and hay, the harvest in these parts has been a very heavy one this season, but I am surprised to learn that the excellent land around Knuthenborg will hardly let for more than thirty-two kroner (thirty-five shillings) per tönde (an acre and three quarters). The young Lehnsgreve lives among his dependents in the most friendly and sociable manner, displaying no aristocratic pride whatever, hospitably entertaining parson, factor, skipper of yacht, head-forester, bailiff, and putting them all completely at their ease. Education and good-breeding are so widely diffused in Denmark as to render this sort of intercourse between persons of different social positions easy and pleasant, but I was not prepared to find so little exclusiveness in a Danish aristocrat, and it must be admitted that Knuth hardly follows English fashions in his extreme politeness to his social inferiors. Danes of all classes are more polite than Englishmen of a similar position, and it must be added that they are better educated. Knuth and his friend both speak English admirably, and it would not be easy to find a Danish lady or gentleman unable to converse in French.

That the pleasure which these visits gave him was also felt by his kind hosts, is proved by the remark of one of his Danish friends : " Although Sir David spent but little time among us, it was impossible but that his courteous demeanour, as well as his erudite conversations, should within a short space of time win him as many friends as people he met."

His interest in Scandinavia, which had never ceased since his visit in 1863, was again aroused by his tours in Iceland and Denmark, and, as usual, he gave to the public, in two articles, the lessons which he drew from his observations. The first, "Iceland," appeared in the *Nineteenth Century* of August, 1880, and the second, " Denmark," in the *Fortnightly Review* of July, 1881. The latter contained an able and exhaustive account of the system of land tenure in Denmark, with special reference to similar questions in England and Ireland. A mere outline can be given here :—

The recent history of Iceland—a poor outlying province of a distant metropolis—has been gloomy enough : misgovernment has combined with famine, pestilence, and volcanic eruptions to depress the condition of the inhabitants. Governed entirely by Danes, compelled to deal with Danes only in all commercial affairs, it is not surprising that the natives of Iceland should gradually have lost much of the energy and self-reliance which characterized their free forefathers. Six centuries of subjection have succeeded four centuries of independence, and now a third era is commencing in the history of Iceland, which is henceforth to experience the benefits of local self-government, and is in fact to enjoy a modified form of "Home Rule." The new constitution of Iceland is analogous to those of the Channel Islands, or the Isle of Man, and there is reason to hope that it may work as smoothly and favourably as in the case of those prosperous and loyal communities.

At the present time, when Italians and Germans display their readiness to sink all minor differences in order to build up one great nationality, it is disappointing to find among Scandinavians so little of the political wisdom which has made a United Italy, and has welded so many petty principalities in the mighty German Empire. When we are told of jealousies subsisting between Denmark and Sweden, or between Copenhagen and Stockholm, or of dynastic difficulties being insuperable, we cannot help feeling that Scandinavians either do not realize the perils of the situation, or that they are indifferent as to the continued existence of their own noble nationality. Unless Sweden is contented to become even as Finland, and unless Jutland wishes to follow Sleswig, the three Northern crowns must be again united upon one head, as they were upon that of Margaret, " Kong Volmers Datter prud."

The establishment of a united Scandinavian nation—a free, maritime, Protestant people of our own kindred—would seem to be a political event in all respects desirable from an English point of view, and calculated to frustrate territorial aggressions on the part of the two great military empires, by which the existence of the Scandinavian kingdoms is now menaced. The Northern question as well as the Eastern affects British interests; the Sound is a channel of commerce not less important than the Bosphorus; and a free Copenhagen is as essential to Europe as a free Constantinople.

The dynastic union of Sweden and Norway was accomplished by force, against the wishes of the Norwegian people; but both countries are now prosperous and contented, each enjoying self-government within its own borders, and being united for all purposes of external defence. It is difficult to discover any valid reason why the "United Kingdoms" should not be three instead of two, and why Denmark should not aspire to be the third kingdom of the league, which would unite all Scandinavians, 8,000,000 in number,—a nation strong enough with Western alliances to defend itself against its formidable neighbours on the east and on the south.

In many matters it is probable that " England will think to-morrow what Denmark thinks to-day." In carrying out the domestic reforms of which the United Kingdom stands so greatly in need, and to which of late years so little attention has been paid, certain valuable hints might be taken by British statesmen from the legislators and administrators of Denmark, which seems at present to have as little that is rotten in its state as any country in Europe. The history of agrarian reform in Denmark is of the highest interest to those who seek to reform the land system existing in Great Britain, and at the present crisis of the Irish land question that history is full alike of instruction and encouragement. By peaceful, constitutional methods, mainly within the experience of the present generation, as complete a change in the Danish land system has been carried out as that which was effected in France by the Revolution of 1789. During the last forty years the leasehold farms of Denmark have been converted into the freeholds of substantial yeomen, holding sixty or seventy acres of good land, or a larger extent where the land is poor. These yeomen and peasants have a majority in the Folkething, or popular Chamber, in which many of them sit; and the consciousness of their altered and independent position has exercised a salutary moral and social influence over the rural population in Denmark.

In recent times the Danish Legislature has consistently laboured to extinguish the reversionary right of the landlord, and to convert the tenant into a freeholder by purchase. The British Parliament has followed a different course : it has ignored the tenant right, which Irish public opinion and tradition have always recognized; it has presupposed an absolute and unrestricted right of property in the Irish landlord ; and it has acknowledged no interest in the soil on the part of the tenant, except such as he may derive from his contract with the all-powerful landlord. In 1870, for the first time in British legislation, it was admitted, in a somewhat grudging spirit, that the occupier has certain rights and claims beyond what may be derived from the mere good pleasure of the landlord.

The satisfactory working of the Danish land laws is doubtless largely due to the mode in which all titles to, and incumbrances upon, land are recorded in the public register. So perfect and so simple is the system that all necessary information as to a property about to change hands can be at once ascertained, and the process of conveyance and registration only costs between one and three per cent. on the purchase money.

. If Denmark were a mere dependency of a powerful and

prosperous neighbouring nation, whose ruling classes believed in the advantages of accumulating vast estates in a few hands, and invariably legislated with a view of bringing about such a result, then it is probable that Denmark would be at this moment a country of great landlords and pauper peasants, as it was a century ago.   Supported by the military force of the dominant nation, the Danish aristocracy could have resisted either constitutional reform or armed insurrection, and the Danish peasantry would now be in a condition resembling that of the peasantry in Ireland.   Happily the Danes have been able to make their own laws, and to carry into effect, by constitutional methods, those principles of land tenure which seemed good to them.   The privileged classes, knowing their inability to resist by force, accepted their change of condition with a wonderfully good grace, and the establishment of a landed democracy in Denmark took place without shock or convulsion, through gradual and spontaneous enfranchisement of the land.   The gloomy shade of feudalism has passed away for ever from Denmark, and the sun of freedom shines upon a prosperous and contented people, firmly rooted in the soil of their native land.

Arctic Fox.
S.S. "Diana"
June 1878.

CHAPTER XX.

1878–1879.

THROUGH GERMANY TO THE CRIMEA—TOUR IN GREECE AND ITALY—ELEC-
TION AS M.P. FOR HADDINGTON BOROUGHS—POLITICAL ADDRESSES.

October 3rd, Berlin.—At the Berlin station the cabmen are
drilled with the utmost rigour, and the whole place swarms with
military policemen, who evidently will stand no trifling, and one
feels that the political atmosphere is very different from that of
free little Denmark. In Prussia the helmeted bully "hides the
march of men from us," but education is not neglected, and the
sight of a young officer in full uniform and gold-rimmed spectacles
reminds one that book learning is combined with discipline in the
Prussian military system. Berlin is not to be recognized by those
who only knew it as the capital of Prussia; it is now a "Kaiser-
stadt," and has nearly a million of inhabitants. Grass does not
now grow in its wide thoroughfares; on every side handsome new
buildings have sprung up, or are even now rising, and statues of
marble and bronze adorn every square and every bridge. These,
like everything else, are military, and many of them commemorate heroes little known to the world outside Prussia, while one
looks vainly for names noted in art or science, such as may be
found in Munich, or any Italian city, inscribed upon the pedestal
of public statues.

October 5th, Cracow.—The cathedral contains inside some of
the handsomest and most interesting monuments to be found in
any church. They are the monuments of Polish kings and queens,
bishops and heroes, the most famous names being those of John
(Sobieski) III., Poniatowski, and Kosciusko. Many of the monuments are of a bright red marble, taking a very fine polish, and
are carved with a great deal of art and elaborate skill, affording

perfect models of the dress and armour of their period. In the vaults beneath the church are the actual sarcophagi of the Polish sovereigns and patriots, these above being mere cenotaphs; and into the dark recesses we were escorted not only by several very dirty ecclesiastical acolytes, but also by several still dirtier peasants, who seemed to take a real interest in the relics of their great compatriots. This cathedral is the Valhalla of Poland ; but after all, Poland has not produced many men of world-wide reputation.

October 11th, Sebastopol.—Porpoises gambolled alongside in the clear dark water as we entered the splendid harbour of Sebastopol, and approached a scene of ruin and desolation, which could hardly be more complete if the capture of the city had taken place yesterday, instead of twenty-three years ago. Not one stone remains upon another of the forts on the south, and on every side stretch the roofless walls and empty window-openings of what have once been vast public buildings. The harbour is perfect, being spacious and sheltered from every wind, with deep water close in shore, but there is evidently no trade ; all the former prosperity of Sebastopol was due to its military importance, and having been abandoned as the Russian naval head-quarters in the Black Sea, it has no recuperative power independent of Government funds. There has been no rebuilding ; there has not even been any pulling down ; Sebastopol is like a deserted city of India, Bijapur, or Fatipur Sikri, only the ruins are not so grand. We drove through almost continuous ruins to the hill on which stand the remains of the Malakhoff tower, the key of Sebastopol fortifications during the siege ; it is quite evident that after its capture the town was no longer tenable. From this point one obtains a fair notion of the way in which the principal attack was made ; it was a good big job, no doubt, but has been completely dwarfed by such sieges as those of Metz and Paris, where the area of operations is too vast to be taken in at any one point.

October 12th, Yalta.—We chartered a carriage and started for Yalta, a drive of eighty-two versts. The weather was splendid, and even the bleak uplands near Sebastopol looked cheerful. Yalta reminds one more of Mentone than of any other place, and to-day everything had a gay and festive appearance, church and market being alike crowded. Climbing to the top of a hill overhanging the sea, I lay down under a pine tree, and felt like a lotos-eater :

blue water, green trees, wild precipices, smiling orchards and vineyards, stately villas, and rude mountain villages, all lay around me
in a panorama, and although close to Yalta nobody came near me
except a solitary sportsman.   There is more variety here than in
the country around San Remo, especially in the colouring of the
trees ; instead of grey olives changing abruptly to dark pines on
the upper slopes, there are here many different hues of foliage,
passing gradually into each other, from the bright green of the
deciduous trees below to the sombre green of the pines higher up ;
while higher still the hardier sorts of deciduous trees reappear,
showing autumnal tints of red and gold.   We drove out to a
property of Prince Woronzoff, who seems to own everything hereabouts.   There are groves of cypress, plantations of sweet chestnut laden with fruit, and vineyards producing grapes in great
variety.   Vainly are Bordeaux wine-growers imported, as well as
Bordeaux vines ; the Crimean wine is not like claret, and resembles rather the product of similar attempts in Australia, California,
or Africa.

October 14th, S.S. " Czarevna."—The steamer was crowded with
passengers from stem to stern, ladies and officers aft, and a mass
of soldiers forward ; but the vessel was wonderfully comfortable,
in spite of crowding.   The mild manners of the Russian people
assist in rendering affairs easy to manage, and eventually every
one was well fed.   There is deep water close in shore along this
southern coast of the Crimea, and we steamed along so near the
land as to have a good view of Livadia, where the Czar is now
residing, and the far more splendid residence of Prince Woronzoff.
The indigenous vegetation clothes every part of the mountain
slopes, except where the rocks are actually perpendicular, and
except the summits, which are bare, and impart a wildness to the
charming landscape.   The moon shone bright, and the Euxine was
like the Indian Ocean on a fine night within the tropics.

October 21st, Constantinople.—A caïque is the pleasantest mode
of conveyance anywhere near the water's edge, but the rotten old
wooden landing stages are a scandal, as well as the utter absence
of any quays or piers for the numerous shipping.   Every natural
facility exists for a splendid range of quays, and when Constantinople gets into better hands they will soon be constructed, and
this splendid city will become what it ought to be, "the joy of
the whole earth."   Pera is a shabby place, although every second

doorway leads to an embassy; the whole place is crammed with
Turkish soldiers of every sort, and their tents whiten the surrounding country. A lot of loafing Circassians are to be seen in
the streets, with their bosoms stuffed full of cartridges, a fashion
adopted as a dress for page boys in Russia, instead of mere
buttons; these Circassians are the boys for committing atrocities,
if they get a chance of doing so, but they look quite tame in the
bazaars. A few Montenegrins were also visible, fine stalwart
mountaineers, in a showy dress, somewhat resembling that of
a Scottish Highlander in its general effect. The strong porters
of Pera turn out to be Armenians, not Turks, thereby depriving
the dominant race of the credit of doing at least one good turn
of work.

October 25th, Athens.—The Chamber of Deputies is now in
session, and I assisted at an afternoon discussion, being politely
seated in a place of honour in the gallery above the President,
who sits facing the Deputies, and occupies a common chair at
a table on a small platform, and possesses no badge of office
except a hand-bell. This he rings in order to obtain silence, but
not always with effect; in front of him is a sort of counter, and
any speaker who has given notice of his intention to address the
House, takes his place behind this. Other members speak from
their places, which are on semi-circular benches, like those in
a lecturing theatre. A good many members wear the national
Greek costume of white kilt, with coloured jacket and gaiters; but
the straw hat, which some indulge in, spoils the general effect,
and is a shabby substitute for the scarlet cap with blue tassel.

The temple of Jupiter Olympius is now represented by only
sixteen columns standing erect, one having recently fallen; they
are of the Corinthian order, very large, and resemble the columns
of Baalbec, but are of the finest white marble from Mount
Pentelicus. Of the same resplendent material are all the buildings
in the Acropolis, although time has stained their surface generally
with tints of yellow and brown. Although barbarians of every
sort, including Morosini the Venetian, and Elgin the Scot, have
aided the Turk in converting the fair temples into ruinous heaps,
they are still things of beauty, even in ruins, and nothing can
surpass the group of Propylæum, Parthenon, and Erechtheum,
standing, as they do, high above all other buildings, on the level
summit of the Acropolis rock. They exhibit in perfection the

stately and simple grandeur of the Doric order along with the grace and finish of the Ionic.

October 26th.—Extensive excavations have been recently made in the principal cemetery of ancient Athens, and many beautiful monuments have been discovered. They are chiefly bas-reliefs in white marble, and some of those now on the spot are finer than any in the museum ; most of them are in honour of ladies—the "love or pride" of Athenian husbands must have been great. Here, as everywhere in Athens, the inscriptions are perfectly clear and sharp, even when they have been long exposed to the weather ; the deep granite carvings of rainless Egypt are hardly more uninjured than these comparatively shallow Greek letters. The temple of Theseus is a wonderfully complete and uninjured Doric building; it is the Parthenon in miniature, and exhibits the mode in which these temples were roofed with large beams of marble, crossed by smaller ones, and finally covered in with marble tiles or shingles ; the whole affair, like Greek architecture generally, being a manifest imitation of wood.

In the afternoon Schliemann's museum was open, containing all the curiosities found by him at Mykenai, and a great show they make. They are exhibited at the Polytechnic, one of a series of beautiful marble buildings, now being erected by rich Greeks, resident abroad, to adorn the capital of their own country, a truly patriotic undertaking. Another of these is the University, built of dazzling white marble in Hellenic style, and adorned with gilding and painting in imitation of the ancients, in whose marble temples colour and gold undoubtedly were conspicuous.

October 27th.—Everywhere the names of streets, hotels, shops, and individuals are written in such classical Greek as might have befitted the time of Pericles, and to-day the first horse-races held here in modern times are advertised as ἱπποδρομοι. The Athenian ladies of the bourgeoisie wear very becoming little red caps, with long tassels of silk and gold fastened on the side of the head, almost exactly in the same style as the women of Iceland. The men, of course, appeared to-day in their cleanest kilts, and smartest embroidered jackets and gaiters. The so-called national costume of Greece seems to be really Albanian, but this is not surprising, when it is borne in mind that Albanian is still the common language throughout a large part of Greece, especially in Attica and Bœotia. As Greek only is taught in the public schools, and there is no Albanian literature, the latter language no doubt will die out ere long. A Greek civilian in his showy dress, with red cap well on one side, long moustaches, and upright carriage, is far more martial-looking than most of the professional soldiers in shabby European uniform.

October 30*th, Corinth.*—The summit of Acro-Corinthus, crowned with towers and battlements, rises grandly between the two blue gulfs, beyond which appear the crests of many famous mountains—Parnassus, Helicon, and others. The fortifications are of various dates, and the work of many nationalities, Greek, Frank, Turk, etc. They enclose a very large space on the summit, and Acro-Corinthus must have resembled one of the great Indian rock-fortresses, containing quite a large town within its limits. The ruins include the remains of heathen temples, Christian churches, and Mussulman mosques ; on the topmost point, " Venus heiterer Tempel stand " overlooking the " two bright harbours," and commanding one of the finest views in the world. There may be a more picturesque view elsewhere, but there is none with equal historical associations. It is not wonderful that successive races should have piled their fortifications and towers upon this great rock, the key of the Peloponnesus, for it possesses what is the great lack of so many hill forts, an abundant supply of excellent water. The famous spring of Pirene is now full of the clearest and coolest water at the driest season of the year ; where it comes from is a mystery.

October 31*st, Delphi.*—Suddenly, on turning the shoulder of the rocky hill, Delphi appears at the base of a grand precipice, overlooking a deep ravine, and enclosed by mountains on every side. The situation is truly grand, but the modern village is a mere collection of hovels, encumbering classic ground. Fragments of columns, and pieces of marble, with carvings and inscriptions, lie scattered about ; but no efficient excavations can be made at Delphi without abolishing the modern village. The mighty cliffs which overhang the place, and from which impious persons used to be thrown, look as if they would abolish it some day, and large masses of rock have fallen quite recently, but without doing much harm. We filled our water-skin at the fountain of Castalia, and noticed here and there a few traces of an ancient city, but it requires careful observation to detect them. Mount Parnassus himself remains, of course, much as he was in Apollo's time, but his forests have nearly disappeared, and his fountains have dwindled in consequence.

November 2nd.—Judging from appearances, most of the work hereabouts is done by the women, while the men lounge about with dog and gun, or discuss politics, and play cards in the village café. Notwithstanding their hard work, they are fine-looking women, with wonderfully good complexions ; it is to be regretted that such plucky industrious persons should condescend to wear false hair, as they do in a long plait, like a Chinaman's pigtail. Their condition, married or single, is known by the colour of a sort of zone or girdle, worn much lower than the waist ; the matrons wearing dark blue, and the maidens scarlet; here we have a Japanese custom ! Our house for the night was built of stone, large and solid, and contains no furniture whatever ; my bed is carried with us, a table was borrowed from the church, a stool from somewhere or other, and I had all I could wish for. My bedroom was heaped up with grain of every sort, and divided by a partition from the kitchen, the floor of which was heaped at night with human beings; below us the mules champed their food and rattled their bells. As I reposed with a book, a young woman suddenly entered, gave me a bunch of flowers, kissed my hand, and exit without a word. Before leaving I sent for her, found that she was unmarried, as her red belt betokened, but was engaged, so I gave her a wedding present, returning the kiss at the same time.

November 7th, Athens.—The red Parnes is the most successful imitation of Bordeaux that I have tasted in any part of the world, being, of course, free from resin, which is seldom put into red wine ; I have got quite accustomed now to resinous wine, and rather like it. The honey of Hymettus is quite worthy of its fame, and has such a clear golden colour, that it is placed in glass jars as a table ornament in the hotel. To-day is the feast of St. Demetrius, one of the too numerous holidays of the Greeks, among whom Demetrius is one of the commonest names, and to-day every one bearing that name receives visits of congratulation. Too much holiday, and too many Government functionaries keep Greece poor, the many well-educated young men preferring the public service to more independent work, which would really develop the resources of the country. The streets were crowded with bands playing, and everybody in gala dress, the women wearing their red caps. The resemblance between Greece and Iceland is noticeable in other things besides the female costume; in both cases the country is poor, and has seen better days; in both cases the people are intelligent, well-educated, and patriotic, lovers of social equality, familiar with their own literature and history, and proud of their glorious past. In one important respect the Greeks have recently set their house in order—they have completely suppressed brigandage in the districts where it was most prevalent a few years ago, and Greece is as safe a country for travellers as any with which I am acquainted.

November 12th, Naples.—The amphitheatre lies somewhat apart from the other excavated portions of Pompeii, and at once impresses one with the wealth and importance of the city which could build and utilize such an edifice, capable of containing twenty thousand persons. It is very perfect in all particulars, being built partly of bricks, partly of polygonal pieces of lava, and might now be used as a place of entertainment, if Italy, like Spain, had retained her ancient taste for combats of wild beasts. Within the last few days, some interesting discoveries have been made in what must have been a large hotel; and indeed everything seems to be worth digging out in this gem of a Roman city, where everybody seems to have been well off, and to have indulged more or less in frescoes and mosaics. The devices and designs are often of great artistic beauty, but it is evident, from the frequent repetition of the same groups and patterns, that Pompeian art had passed the creative, and was in the imitative or conventional stage.

November 16th, Salerno.—Pæstum has survived many more famous Greek cities, and its walls are still clearly to be traced throughout their whole extent upon the plain; they are built of large blocks of travertine, quite in Hellenic style. The three great temples of Pæstum have now no rivals in Greece, except in Athens itself, and the temple of Poseidon almost rivals the Parthenon in size, and the Theseion in its state of preservation. They are all more antique in style than the great Athenian buildings, the columns being shorter and less graceful, while the material is not saccharine marble, but travertine limestone, like pieces of stalactite, full of fossils and large holes. The effect of these grand ruins, standing solitary on the plain between the mountains and the sea, is certainly very striking; this almost unknown city of Magna Græcia has escaped the destruction which has overtaken so many more famous in Greek proper, and has left behind monuments such as we search for vainly at Argos, Corinth, and Thebes.

November 17th, Naples.—This was a day of great excitement on account of the arrival of the new King and Queen, with their little son, the Prince of Naples. The report of a murderous attack upon the King, near the railway station, proved to be correct ; Cairoli, the Prime Minister, was wounded by the assassin's dagger in defending his sovereign—a new form of ministerial responsibility.

November 18th.—The gala night at the San Carlo theatre in honour of the King and Queen was really a splendid sight ; the great house was crammed with some four thousand of the rank, beauty, and fashion of Naples, blazing in diamonds and uniforms. The opera was "Guarany," but the only music appreciated was "L'Inno," the hymn of Savoy, which was played again and again, the whole audience standing up, waving handkerchiefs, and shouting "Evviva il Rè !" as if they were mad. The King and Queen were obliged to rise and bow nearly a score of times in the course of the evening, until it seemed a regular persecution. I thought there should have been some cheering for poor wounded Cairoli. The Queen Margherita has a very sweet face ; Umberto himself looks as honest as the day, and is almost handsome in consequence.

In a letter to the *Scotsman*, dated Naples, November 18th, he describes the enthusiasm with which the King was received, attributing it, in great measure, to the fact that he and his house represent Italian unity and independence, and adding :—

In 1860 there was a great dread in the minds of all Italian patriots that their new liberties and the unity of the nation might be once more destroyed by European intervention. The four great Continental Powers had already intimated their serious displeasure at the course of events in Italy, and several of them had withdrawn their legations from Turin. England had still to speak, and it is pleasing to find that she then spoke as a great free nation ought to do when weaker nations are struggling to obtain the same liberty which she herself has so long enjoyed. Italy is now al o a great free nation, but she has not forgotten the support she then received from the only free power in Europe. Lord John Russell's despatch might, in my opinion, serve as a model for any British statesman charged with the direction of foreign affairs. After mentioning the action taken by the various Emperors in the matter, he says : " Her Majesty's Government must admit that the Italians themselves are the best judges of their own interests." This is a simple but most important admission ; the moral support of England was then of great value to Italy, and doubtless tended to prevent foreign intervention. The Italians are a generous and grateful people, and English good offices are still remembered. Why cannot we at the present time make friends among the races of the future in the East, as we have done in Italy? Even moral support would do much, but the moral support of England is given to the Turks, essentially a race of the past, and all our strong words are spoken on behalf of the tottering oppressors, not of the struggling oppressed. I am not one of those who wish Great Britain to abstain from intervention in European politics, but I wish her influence, and, in case of necessity, even her sword, to be cast into the scale of liberty and progress.

November 21st, Rome.—Thirty-one years have elapsed since I was in Rome, but my recollections are vivid, and, thanks to Signorina Baldassare, our parlatrice, I once knew Rome well. Setting off without guide or plan, and without asking any questions, I was pleased to be able to find my way wherever I wanted to go. I made first for the Piazza Colonna, where we used to live in 1847; then by the Arches of Titus and Constantine to the Colosseum, which shows no intention of falling ; then up to the Capitol, where the statue of Marcus Aurelius has made no apparent progress towards becoming entirely golden, so that the end of the world is not yet. Drove to the Baths of Caracalla, which are now completely excavated, and have proved the richest mine in Rome for statuary and mosaic. Their vast size, as well as the magnificence of their decorations, must have made them probably the most splendid building ever erected by human hands, either in Rome or anywhere else. These Thermæ are constructed with such solidity that they would still be almost perfect, but for the destroying hands of barbarous men ; the materials are all of the most enduring sorts, marble, brick, and Roman cement, so firmly bound together as not to crumble, even when the removal of pillars and supports has caused large masses to fall from the lofty roofs. A few torsos, with fragments of splendid porphyry columns, and richly carved capitals, in which the human figure is the principal ornament,—also plenty of mosaic, from walls as well as floors, —still remain to give a notion of what this palace of the Roman citizens must have been when entirely encased with the most precious marbles, and adorned with the finest statues.

November 28*th, Florence.*—The Pitti Palace is certainly a model of simple grandeur, with its huge blocks of rough-hewn stone, and entire absence of ornament externally. As a picture gallery it is unsurpassed : there is not a bad picture in the whole collection, and there are many of the highest class ; all are shown to advantage by their beautiful Florentine frames of carved and gilt wood, and the handsome rooms in which they are hung. The splendid tables of Florentine pietra dura excite my admiration, as they used to do of old. The long gallery, leading from the Pitti Palace across the Ponte Vecchio to the Uffizi, is completely filled with tapestry, engravings, and drawings by famous masters. The Medici chapels are splendid mausoleums, but the great recumbent statues of Michael Angelo give one a feeling of cramp to look at them, they are in such very uncomfortable attitudes, and in such unstable equilibrium ; it is never so with classical statues, which usually are equally expressive of power, grace, and repose. The arms of all the Tuscan cities which acknowledged the Medici supremacy, are beautifully executed in pietra dura around the walls of the domed building, which reminds one of the tombs of the great Mogul Emperors.

At Venice he had arranged to meet his brother, who was on the way to India with his wife. They spent a week together, thoroughly exploring the town and environs, and it was not till he had seen them on board the steamer that he started himself for England.

December 6*th.*—Padua is a city of arcades, in the old-fashioned Italian style, as mediæval perhaps as any now to be seen in Italy. She is proud of her ancient fame, and of the many great men to whom she has been Alma Mater : their statues have been placed in double row to adorn the Prato, a large piazza with trees and water; and although the individual merits of the statues are not great, the general effect is very fine. Amongst many of inferior mark appear Galileo, Petrarca, Ariosto, Tasso, John Sobieski, and, by themselves apart, Dante and Giotto. The grandest monument of Padua is the Palazzo della Ragione, or ancient palace of justice, built in the palmy days of the independent republic, and consisting of one vast hall, the largest in Europe, or perhaps in the world. Westminster Hall and the Imambarah of Lucknow are the only two I can think of to rival it, but it seems larger than either, and makes even the Sala del Gran Consiglio in Venice seem quite a snug little room.

December 7th, Verona.—The old castle with its battlemented bridge, under which rushes the rapid Adige, has a thoroughly mediæval appearance, while the splendid amphitheatre tells of Verona's greatness also in the classical past. This arena, or amphitheatre, is of course smaller than the Roman Colosseum, but it is far more perfect, and is constructed of finer materials, namely large blocks of marble, rough-hewn, and laid together without the use of cement. Take it altogether, there is hardly a finer Roman monument in existence, but its origin is veiled in obscurity; Galienus is the Emperor whose name is most associated with Verona, and various fragments of Roman workmanship are assigned to him. There are few cities, even in Italy, more famous, alike in history and in poetry, during both the eras of Italian greatness : the names of Theodoric, Catullus, Can Grande, and Dante are associated with Verona, as much as those of Montague and Capulet, Valentine and Sylvia.

He reached home, as usual, in time for his mother's birthday. On December the 29th a vacancy occurred in the representation of the Haddington Boroughs, in consequence of the death of the Marquis of Tweeddale, and the succession to the title of Lord William Hay, who was then member for the Boroughs. Sir David was startled by an unexpected invitation to come forward as the Liberal candidate for the seat. He replied that he could not accede to the proposal until he was released from his engagement to the Liberal electors at Devonport. The case having been laid before the chairman of the Liberal party there, Sir David was advised to accept the invitation of his friends at Haddington. Within a few days he presented himself before the constituency at Haddington, and, afterwards, on four successive days, delivered addresses at the scattered boroughs of Dunbar, North Berwick, Lauder, and Jedburgh.

It was probably partly owing to his connection with the county, that he was so immediately selected as a candidate. Keith House, where he had spent so many years of his early life, is only a few miles from Haddington, and although it was long since the family had left, the memory of his father was still fresh in the minds of many. At first it was expected that the election would take place shortly, and that there would be no opposition, but it was found that the seat did not legally become vacant until after the meeting of Parliament in February; and, meanwhile a somewhat formidable opponent came forward, in the person of Mr. Macdonald, the Solicitor-General for Scotland. Sir David's political opinions were well known in Scotland from his votes and speeches while representing South Ayrshire, in the previous Parliament; and there were few constituencies to which his advanced opinions were more likely to be acceptable than the Haddington Boroughs. Even here, however, there were, no doubt, questions on which he differed from some of his supporters, but how frankly and unhesitatingly he stated his views may be shown by a few extracts from his various addresses. With a strong Conservative Government at that time in power, his speeches were, of course, principally directed to criticism of their policy, especially with regard to foreign affairs. He complained that it was a policy of war and annexation in Asia and Africa, and of secret conventions in Europe, resulting in increased financial burdens on the tax-payers of both England and India, saying :—

I think that by far the most successful and brilliant foreign secretary of our times has been Lord Palmerston; he was one who upheld Liberal principles in all parts of Europe, and boldly advocated them when reaction was dominant in almost every other European country. His name was a name of terror to all the despots of Europe: now, I regret to say, the names of our representatives seem to strike terror into the hearts of those unfortunate Greeks and Bulgarians who have been making really heroic efforts to obtain liberty for themselves. Our insular position gives us security, and to a certain extent impartiality, but it does not deprive us of the right, nor exempt us from the duty, of interfering on occasion in Continental affairs. But if we do interfere, let it be upon the right side; do not let us endeavour to prevent others from obtaining that civil and religious liberty for which we ourselves have struggled, and which we prize so highly; and do not let us persuade ourselves that the interests of this country can in any way be identified with oppression and misgovernment in any other part of the world.

If I were a young man, asking for the first time to have senatorial honours conferred upon me, I should probably venture to make more promises than I now feel myself justified in making. The lapse of years has not made me less eager for reform; but it has certainly taken away some of that hopefulness which I once had of seeing many important reforms carried out in my own time.

The question of our licensing system is one of such great importance that it is impossible to pass it over; at the same time, I frankly confess that I have never yet seen my way to any thoroughly effective and satisfactory reform of that system. When I was in the House, I used to vote for the second reading of Sir Wilfrid Lawson's Permissive Bill, as being an honest attempt to deal with the evils of intemperance, and as recognizing the principles of popular control and of local option; and, if I were again in the House, I should feel it my duty to vote for it again.

The question of Disestablishment has not yet assumed, in my opinion, that practical importance which it undoubtedly will do some day; and as far as I am concerned, I am contented to wait till public opinion ripens upon the subject. There can be no doubt that it will do so with time and with discussion, but

I do not anticipate that this will take place immediately; if it does so in my time, I shall be ready to take my part, and do what I can for the cause of religious equality.

The name of Home Rule is thought by many to imply Irish disaffection, Parliamentary obstructiveness, and even disintegration of the United Kingdom. If that is the real meaning of Home Rule, I need hardly tell you I cannot be in favour of it, but that indeed I should give it as hearty opposition as the strongest Conservative could do. But it is clear to me that what has given strength to the movement for Home Rule is that, at the root of it, there exists a genuine grievance: this grievance is centralization; and I believe that a great many things, and a great deal of business conducted in London, might be managed better in Dublin or Edinburgh. I am quite satisfied that every part of the United Kingdom would benefit if we had a little less centralization, and a little more local self-government; and I am convinced that, if the people of Ireland could once come to terms among themselves, and let us know exactly what is the amount of local self-government that they require, we might find that their demands are not so very unreasonable; and I cannot see why a Parliamentary Committee should not be considered a proper method of elucidating this question.

The assimilation of the county franchise to that of the boroughs has been fairly adopted as an item in the programme of the Liberal party, but there are other particulars in connection with the franchise in which it is very desirable to assimilate the two. The expenses of contesting a county are much heavier than those of a borough constituency, and one reason of this is, that in counties it is legal for the candidate to pay the expenses of carrying voters to the poll, and that non-residents are entitled to vote at county elections. I hold that it ought to be made illegal for a candidate to spend money upon such object. When the Ballot Bill was under discussion it was urged that it would be most desirable to have a clause in the bill prohibiting the practice of having house-to-house canvassing, and more especially the employment of paid canvassers. By this means a great deal of undue pressure is put upon voters; and it would be a great relief to them, as well as to the pockets of the candidates, if such a process were made illegal. For my own part, I have always disliked the system of canvassing very much indeed; I hold that the candidate should meet those whom he hopes to make his constituents, publicly and openly, and that all the political communications between them should as far as possible be in public. It is, I suppose, a generally entertained idea that candidates very much dislike to be heckled ; and although the process is not altogether an agreeable one, still I am so anxious, upon occasions like this, to ascertain the wishes and feelings of the electors, and also that you should thoroughly understand my own views, that I feel I can cheerfully submit to the process if you think fit to inflict it upon me.   I hope, therefore, that if any elector wishes me to explain my views upon any political topic whatever, he will do me the honour to put such questions as he pleases.

Sir David did not object to a contest with a worthy antagonist, saying, that to make election speeches without one was like firing in the air.   The interest of the unexpected contest drew the following letter from his friend Sir Wilfrid Lawson, with whom he had so many feelings in common :—

> " On Wednesday, dear friend, when the poll is declared,
> Just ' wire ' the news to say how you have fared.
> I'm oppressed with alarm, and I'm troubled with doubt,
> For I don't like this Jingo who's raging about.
> The last time we met, I believed you in clover,
> And I felt pretty sure you would have a ' walk over.'
> When suddenly, down comes this Lawyer of note,
> And craftily touts for the publican's vote.
> ' Blood and thunder ' abroad, is the cause he will plead,—
> ' Drink and ruin ' at home ;—what a statesmanlike creed !
> He's sure to get votes, for since time first began,
> Such always has humbugged the natural man.
> But oh ! bitter will be the keen pang to my soul,
> If that Jingo should really be head of the poll.
> But just ' wire ' the news when the contest is done :
> I'll weep if you're beaten, I'll laugh if you've won.
> How I hope that the message will flash through the wire :
> ' Little David has slaughtered the Tory Goliath.'
>
> " BRAYTON, CARLISLE, *February* 23, 1879."

At the election, which took place in February, he was returned to Parliament by a majority of 198 votes.   He at once took his seat, and was regular in his attendance, but

found the position of affairs in the House much changed
since his previous experience. The system of obstruction
by the Irish members had begun to make itself felt, and he
soon made up his mind that, whether in opposition, as in
1879, or, later, as a follower of the Government, he served
his constituents and the country best by steady voting,
while seldom or never speaking in Parliament. He regretted the result for himself and for other independent
members, and believed, more than ever, that the public
were in future to be instructed rather through the medium
of the press, and out of doors, than by the debates in the
House of Commons.

For some years he had been a Vice-President of the
East India Association, and on more than one occasion
read papers before it, which have been noticed in the
chapters on India. The Farmers' Alliance was formed
during this summer, and he was one of the original
members and promoters of it, the objects aimed at being,
generally, such as he approved of, and was anxious to see
fairly discussed. He was a member of the Hellenic Society,
and took a great interest in the claims of the Greek nation,
feeling that as long as Thessaly, Epirus, and the Greek
islands remained under the yoke of Turkey, the permanent
peace of Eastern Europe could not be assured.

He was always willing to give to the public the benefit
of his wide experience and knowledge of the British
Colonies, a subject he considered to be particularly interesting to the working classes in this country. At the
request of his old friend, Mr. Nisbet, the Rector of St. Giles'
in London, he gave an address upon this subject at the
opening of a Working Men's Club in that parish. He also
accepted the invitation of the West Ham Liberal Association to deliver one of a series of political addresses, at
Stratford, in March, 1879, and again chose the Colonies as
his topic. On this, as on many other occasions, he entered

his protest against the policy of annexation, then being pursued by the British Government :—

For the annexation of the Transvaal it would be difficult to find a precedent. It may be freely conceded that the position of Great Britain is strengthened by the development of free communities under her flag ; but neither strength, honour, nor dignity can be derived from the compulsory subjection of the South African Boers. To acquire more possessions, whether in Zululand, or Afghanistan, or Asia Minor, simply means casting fresh burdens on the thirty-three millions of inhabitants of Great Britain and Ireland, who bear bravely the load on their own shoulders, but surely must now feel that they have as much weight as they can carry. Yet Englishmen continue to cry out for fresh burdens, more dusky subjects, more barren territory, more wars, and more debts. The Englishman who advocates an extension of our borders far from the sea, far into the heart of Africa, appears to me to be no true friend of his country.

During the Easter vacation he went down to Devonport with Mr. J. D. Lewis and Mr. Craig Sellar, who had been selected as the Liberal candidates at the next general election. He wished both to support them, and to take, what he termed, his " political farewell " of the Devonport electors, who had received him so kindly eighteen months before. His remarks turned very much on the prospects of the general election, in which he was already sanguine of a good Liberal majority. As to the Zulu War, he admitted that it was not the Government which had brought about the war, but attributed it rather to the action of the High Commissioner, saying :—

In South Africa our policy must be to a considerable extent directed by those who are on the spot, and whose lives and property are now at stake. I think the time is rapidly approaching when the British people will say that the relations which exist between this country and colonies like South Africa cannot be permanently maintained. It seems to me that British taxpayers reap little or no advantage from the connection with the South

African colony ; but when the Colonists find themselves in difficulties, they are called upon to furnish the soldiers and pay the
bill. I am quite sure that if these people were made to realize
that they must either keep the peace with their dark neighbours,
or that they must fight them and bear the·expense and the risk of
the contest, we should hear very much less about the necessity
of crushing Cetewayo. The real danger is, that feeling the whole
might of Great Britain at their backs, they fail to treat these
neighbours with that sense of justice and that consideration to
which savages are as fully alive as white men can possibly be. A
great deal of our policy, both foreign and colonial, is influenced
by persons who wish to draw fifteen per cent. upon dangerous or
insufficient security, and to have possible losses made good to
them by us, the British taxpayers. There are persons who lend
money to the Khedive, or who purchase frontier settlements, who
get a large nominal interest, or pay very little for their land, simply
because it is understood that the security of their capital is not
complete. After that, they attempt to influence the policy of this
country in such a way that they shall have absolute security for
their capital.

CHAPTER XXI.

TOUR IN HOLLAND AND BELGIUM —THE GENERAL ELECTION—BRITTANY—
THIRD VISIT TO IRELAND—ARTICLE ON "SECOND CHAMBERS."

EARLY in 1879, his brother-in-law, E. H. Percival, retired from the Bombay Civil Service, and joined his family at Meredith. They continued to reside there with Lady Wedderburn, and the presence of their three children gave an ever-increasing charm to the home life of Sir David and his mother. In September he joined the Percivals, and his cousin, Miss A. Hope, in a month's tour to Holland and Belgium, countries with which he was already well acquainted; but he liked places that he knew, and was glad to revisit them, and act as guide to others who could enjoy them with him.

September 6th.—I left the train at Gouda to see the famous stained glass, and found it well worth the trouble. The immense windows, about thirty in number, are filled with coloured glass of the sixteenth century, which has escaped destruction by Spaniards or Calvinists, and is quite unique in beauty and interest. The glass is the work of Gouda artists, but each window has been the gift of some great personage, or a province, or a city of the Netherlands, and among the donors appear the names of Philip of Spain and Mary of England; of Margaret, Duchess of Parma; William of Orange, the Silent; of Bishops, Abbots, and Lords; of the Burgermasters of Haarlem, Leyden, Amsterdam, Rotterdam, and the States of North and South Holland. The subjects are nearly all Scriptural, representing events appropriate to the occasion of the gift, the Leyden window *e.g.* depicting the relief of Samaria, and everywhere are figured the arms of the princes, knights, and cities to whose pious liberality these works of art are due.

September 9th, Leeuwarden.—Baron Rengers was able to give himself a holiday from his burgomagisterial functions, and drove me out into the country to visit some of his best farms in the neighbourhood.   Notwithstanding the law distributing land among brothers and sisters, there are many large estates in Friesland, and the ancient aristocracy still hold much landed property.   A higher rate of succession duty is payable when land is kept together by family arrangement, instead of being shared ; but, in spite of legal discouragement, this is often done, and what with marrying heiresses, and having small families, the Frisian nobility manage to maintain a respectable position.   There is, however, very little aristocratic exclusiveness in society, titles of nobility are almost ignored in conversation, and all ranks treat each other with civility, and without servility.   Socially the nation is quite democratic, but politically the feeling is rather conservative, the franchise is high, and no strong desire exists to have it lowered. Friesland seems to be the Scotland of the Netherlands : there are very few Roman Catholics here, and all the seven representatives are Liberals, the agriculture is excellent, and the people are industrious and educated.   A large proportion of the land is occupied by tenant farmers, who pay very high rents, in many cases from 120 to 150 guilders (1s. 8d.), or even more, per hectare (two acres and a half) for good land.   The farms are not large, forty hectares being above average, but the farmsteadings are first-rate, and the whole landscape is thickly studded, with huge barns, rising above the little plantation of trees which surround them.   One of the favourite crops here is chicory, and another is canary-seed, which is grown in few other localities and is almost a monopoly of the Frieslanders ; both crops are of a speculative nature.

September 10th.—Baron Rengers took me out into the country to dine with a neighbour of his ; it was a large family party, and we had a very pleasant evening, talking both French and English, there being a governess from England.   The young daughter of the house put on the Frisian golden casque, for my especial benefit, and very pretty she looked in it: the head-dress is very complicated, including a white cap (for washing), a black silk cap (for show), the golden helmet, and an elegant lace cap over all, to be topped out of doors with a bonnet.

September 12th, Amsterdam.—The grand old Stadhuis, with its traditions of Amsterdam's republican glory, seems to be desecrated by the name of palace, associated with the title of Napoleon's puppet king and brother. Its marble halls are defaced with the furniture and decorations necessary to render it habitable for a few days in the year by the present representative of the House of Orange, for whom the title of Stadtholder would be more appropriate and more dignified than that of King. The great hall is a magnificent apartment, worthy of the northern Venice, but differing in its proportions from the grand Venetian halls, being very lofty, nearly one hundred feet in height. Many Spanish banners hang here as trophies, along with Asiatic standards, and the great flag of Antwerp citadel. At the Van Der Hoop Museum, and at the Trippenhuis, especially the latter collection, the Dutch school of painting is seen to great advantage, and its many points of excellence are fully displayed. Fidelity to nature, variety of subjects, finish in details, and richness of colouring, all are combined in the paintings of the Dutch masters, whose period of artistic greatness coincided (as is usual) with the political supremacy of their country, and who are so numerous that scarcely any Dutch town cannot claim one or two as her citizens.

September 16th, the Hague.—Trees, water, open spaces, and handsome houses contribute to give the Hague a specially cheerful aspect, even among Dutch cities. In the museum, I found L. Courtney, M.P., who volunteered to "cicerone" me to Delft. In the old church at Delft (the tower of which leans almost like that of Pisa) is the monument of the gallant Van Tromp, who used to think nothing of fighting the English and French fleets combined; and in the new church are those of Grotius and William the Taciturn. A comic procession, with Bacchus, Silenus, and Cetewayo, paraded the town, to the great delight of the children, and to our considerable amusement, although a gentlemanly policeman, speaking excellent English, seemed to think little of it. We have all been impressed with the civil and friendly bearing of the Dutch people, as also with their linguistic

accomplishments. A beggar is never seen in Holland, but, on
the other hand, there is no display of riches, and the distinctions
between classes are faintly marked.   It is quite provoking to see
the cool assurance with which a Dutchman, aged under ten years,
will puff his cigar : this habit, combined with that of sleeping in
closed box-beds, must have an injurious effect on the national
health in Holland.   Men are always smoking at all ages, but
women apparently abstain from tobacco entirely ; and as regards
eating or drinking, the Dutch seem to be exceedingly moderate :
they are very rarely corpulent, and I have not seen a single drunk
person in this country.

  September 17*th, Antwerp.*—The *real lions* of Antwerp are
among its finest sights, and the Zoological gardens are the best
that I have ever seen, with capital quarters for all the beasts,
which are very numerous, healthy, and clean.   All sorts are well
represented, and the "grands carnassiers" are splendid ; the best
proof that they flourish is the number of young ones frisking all
about the place ; lions, camels, bisons, yaks, etc., with birds
innumerable.   The gardens are really kept up regardless of
expense, and are an institution of which Antwerp, a second-rate
city of a third-rate kingdom, may well be proud.   In the evening
there was an open-air concert at the Zoo ; the beasts were not
visible, but the place was alive with children, even of a very
tender age, playing about and enjoying themselves to a late hour,
à la Néerlandaise.

  September 27*th, Dinant.*—Steamers running on the Meuse
between Namur and Dinant afford an opportunity of seeing this
very fine piece of river scenery to full advantage.   The Meuse
winds between lofty cliffs of limestone, with numerous marble
quarries ; and at the base of these cliffs, now on one bank and now
on the other, extends a strip of green wood and meadow, with
handsome châteaux, of modern construction but ancient architecture, at frequent intervals.   Dinant is very picturesquely
situated, but is a good deal cramped for space between the rocks
and the river.   We were taken for a most charming drive, by the
Rocher de Bayard—an apparently inaccessible pinnacle, on which
an iron cross has been somehow planted,—to the summit of the
lofty cliffs above the Meuse, then down into the valley of the
Lesse, where in *einem kühlen Grunde* goes a mill-wheel, just
under a high rock, crowned with the old château (inhabited) of

Walzin. It is so retired. a spot that it looks like the "happy valley," and is almost inaccessible.

September 29th, Tournai.—Passing through the very cockpit of Europe, where the name of every village is associated with some "glorious victory," the five towers of Tournai cathedral appear in a cluster. It is a wonderful mixture of Romanesque and Gothic, the nave being in the former, the choir and transepts in the latter style, with a large tower in the centre surrounded by four smaller towers of equal height. The external effect is thus very striking and peculiar, while the interior is rich with stained glass and sculpture. In the sacristy are great stores of gorgeous ecclesiastical vestments, heavy with gold; and the jewels on the pyx and the bishop's mitre are of barbaric magnificence. Old tapestry and other curiosities of value are also kept here, and altogether Tournai cathedral has much to exhibit, the inevitable Rubens not being absent.

October 1st, Ghent.—I made my way to the Grand Béguinage, quite recently constructed upon the ancient model. The gates were open and I marched in, not without misgivings, as the only human figures visible were black-robed béguines, issuing in numbers from their abodes, and hurrying towards the church. They did not seem disposed to turn and rend me, however, so I ventured to follow them, and assisted at the ensuing vespers. As I was retreating, a lay female invited me to visit the interior of a house, and I was introduced to a pleasant old lady, who lays herself out to receive strangers, and seems to appreciate a visit. There are six hundred regular béguines and two hundred lay ladies resident in the establishment. My hostess is one of the latter, and is a swell, having half a house to herself, and two beautifully appointed little kitchens, one for winter and one for summer. Béguines surrender their private property while in residence, but they can claim it if they wish to leave, and it is restored to their heirs when they die. Altogether, they seem to be a very harmless, if not a highly beneficial, order of religious enthusiasts.

October 3rd.—Brussels is a very pleasant place to loaf in for a time, quite as much so as Paris, in my opinion. It is lively and cheerful, with good theatres, fine shops, capital restaurants, besides its attractions in the way of museums and orthodox sights. Every afternoon a good military band plays in the central park,

and is well attended by all classes of the community, young and
old. The trees are still as green as in June, and, with the sun
shining and fountains playing, the scene is very gay and pleasing.
From the top of the Congress Column there is an excellent view
of Brussels, and the Belgian lions who guard it are enough to
appal the stoutest heart; but there is something ludicrous, as
well as melancholy, in all these pompous monuments to Belgian
independence. For what does the whole thing amount to? The
Netherlands have been divided certainly, and thereby rendered
easy morsels for Germany or France to swallow; Belgium is
free, but not freer than Holland, in whose glorious history and
flourishing colonial empire the Belgians have now no share.

October 5th, Middelburg.—The good people of Middelburg, in
their best clothes, poured into the churches, which are filled with
pews all numbered and named. Even in the town, provincial
costumes are much affected by both sexes and all ages: the men
wear round jackets, with caps or high-crowned hats almost brim-
less; the women wear very bunchy skirts, straw bonnets placed
in a perpendicular way on their heads, gold corkscrews on their
temples, and large silver buckles on their shoes. In full dress the
ladies have bare arms, and are somewhat red about the elbows.
Each island or division of Zealand seems to have its special style
of ornament, and here a sort of earring is suspended on the cork-
screw. This beautiful morning I started for a good walk, and
proceeded along a regular Roman road, perfectly straight, paved
with stones and planted with trees. Suddenly appeared a huge
church, standing by itself amidst the remains of fortifications, and
I soon found myself within a splendid specimen of the Dutch
" Ville morte." The church is of immense size and handsome
Gothic style, but has apparently never been completed either as
to tower or choir. This grand edifice stands alone among gardens
and trees, with no houses near except a few cottages, but within
the lines of what must have been once a considerable fortified
city. In the principal square, which has dwindled away into the
condition of a tidy village green with flowers and grass, stands the
ancient Stadhuis in excellent repair, with a tall belfry and a façade
adorned with numerous statues. As there is no mention of this
place in the omniscient Bædeker, I was quite taken by surprise
at coming suddenly upon so interesting a spot, which I found to
be the ancient city of Veere.

At the end of October he went down to Scotland, where he delivered addresses to his constituents in the Haddington Boroughs, and paid many visits to his private and political friends. In the spring of the year, as a member of the Executive Committee of the Liberal Association of Midlothian, he had had the pleasure of being instrumental in obtaining Mr. Gladstone's consent to contest that county at the next general election. While he was in Scotland, towards the end of November, Mr. Gladstone came down and delivered the wonderful series of speeches known as the Midlothian campaign. Sir David was present at several of them, and on one occasion had the honour of introducing the great statesman to the meeting. He afterwards said that he should never forget the thunders of applause which greeted the utterances of Mr. Gladstone, from the vast assemblage of working men gathered in the Waverley Market of Edinburgh.

He was back at Meredith, as usual, for the 17th of December, and had a happy Christmas with the children, joining in charades and games for their amusement. He took an active share in the gaieties of the season, and assisted at private theatricals in neighbouring houses, once acting as the hero in Bishop Heber's "Bluebeard," and another time as Victor in "Ici on parle Français." While at home he wrote two letters to the *Gloucester Journal*, in both of which he quoted from speeches made by Sir James Mackintosh in Parliament, more than fifty years before, and expressed his admiration for the views of that distinguished Liberal. Sir James protested most strongly against new guarantees of foreign political arrangements, especially as regarded the Ottoman Empire, believing that such a guarantee could not be long enforced, but would shortly give rise to the very dangers against which it was intended to guard. Sir David said that the words he quoted required no alteration in order to express exactly the opinion which he, for one, held upon the recent Anglo-Turkish Convention.

As soon as Parliament met he went to London, but early in March the dissolution was suddenly announced. This was an event of which he had long been desirous, feeling sure that it would result in an immediate change of Government. His opinion was by no means shared by Liberals in general, who hardly hoped for a majority, much less a good working one, as he said it would be. He boasted that he won ten bets, of a shilling each, upon the subject from faint-hearted Liberals, and attributed their ignorance of the state of feeling in the country to the atmosphere of London clubs and drawing-rooms, in which so many of them lived. His faith in the good sense and true feeling of the bulk of the working classes never failed, and he felt that he could more safely propose a generous and disinterested course of political action to an audience composed of them, than to one composed of the richer and more highly educated classes.

At the general election in April, an unexpected and almost hopeless opposition was made to Sir David's return to Parliament for the Haddington Boroughs. Little need be given of his speeches on this occasion to the electors of the five boroughs, as no new subjects of special interest had arisen since his previous election, only thirteen months before :—

I did not expect that I should have been called upon to undertake a contest for the seat, partly on account of the two decisive elections which have so recently taken place, and partly on account of the tried character for faithfulness of the Haddington Boroughs. At the same time I have no complaint to make as far as I myself am concerned, and I cannot help admiring the courage and good temper which our opponents have displayed in various up-hill and hopeless contests throughout Scotland.

We are told by the Prime Minister that we are to seek for

ascendency in the Councils of Europe. Now, what does that mean? There is the ascendency enjoyed at this moment on the continent of Europe by the German Empire. That is an ascendency supported by a million of bayonets. We cannot aim at anything of that sort, I presume. But there is an ascendency to which, indeed, we may aspire, and which we possess, namely, that which is given to us, in all parts of the world, by our great naval supremacy. So far as the navy is concerned, I would grudge no sum that has ever yet been asked by Parliament to maintain the navy in an efficient and powerful condition. I say that, because I look on our navy as being that which enables us to maintain our Colonies and our external Empire, and because it neither menaces our neighbours nor our own liberties. There is a third kind of ascendency which I really should desire this country to possess. It is that pre-eminence which is given to a nation that is known always to support in a disinterested manner the cause of right and freedom.

We are asked if we wish to preserve the United Kingdom at home. We know that, unfortunately, there are within the limits of the United Kingdom a considerable number of fellow-subjects who are not friendly to the existing union. This is deeply to be regretted; but how are we to reconcile them to that union? I believe that if a policy of conciliation and justice is faithfully carried out—it cannot be done in a day, it cannot be done even in ten years—but if it were carried out consistently, the time would come within this generation, when the people of Ireland would be as faithful and as attached to the Union as the people of Scotland now are. I hold that those who tell us that we are to reply to the complaint and to the demand for redress that come to us from the other side of the Channel by new Coercion Bills, by silencing the press, and by enrolling more police—I say, those who counsel any such policy are the real enemies to the Union.

You have heard a good deal about the policy of obstruction in the House of Commons; I do not myself like at all what is sometimes called physical obstruction. I think it is very rarely justifiable to have recourse to such tactics; and it was with great pleasure I supported the Government—perhaps the only occasion on which I thoroughly and consistently supported them since I have been in the House—in their attempt so to alter the rules of the House as to put down this form of physical obstruction.

I have always thought that the House of Commons might intrust more power to the chairman of its own selection; and I not merely voted for that change, but would have supported a stronger change in the same direction.

I hope that the electors of the boroughs will return me by an increased majority, because I think it very important that the decision of the people of Scotland should be clearly given at the approaching election, and that those members who go to Westminster to vote against the present ministers, shall not merely represent a fair majority of the Scottish people, but an overwhelming majority.

His confidence in the electors was not misplaced. They returned him at the head of the poll, by 1019 to 607—a majority over his opponent, Captain Houston, more than double that obtained the previous year over Mr. Macdonald. Much the same results were obtained all over Scotland, where the Liberals carried all the seats but seven.

During the Whitsuntide holidays he made a run for a fortnight, to Brittany, in company with Mr. F. D. Finlay.

May 8th, Chartres.—Here we halted for a few hours, and strolled through the markets up to the cathedral. "Toutes les bourgeoises de Chartres" were doing business in the marketplace, which was a perfect sea of white caps, hardly a male person being visible. A very large business is done here in domestic rabbits, of which there were to-day many hutches full, while others were carried about by the ears; cheeses also, thin and flat, were exceedingly abundant. The choir of the cathedral is surrounded with marble carvings in high relief, and the stained glass is magnificent, all ancient and well preserved; the rose windows are particularly beautiful. An image of the Virgin Mary on a pillar is fearfully sacred, and was the object of worship to many while we stood by; kissing, bowing, kneeling, and lighting wax tapers seemed to afford genuine comfort to the worshippers, who were "lauter Frauenzimmer." Flowers, images, lights, and gaudily attired priests, all strongly resembled a Buddhist function.

May 9th.—The grand old castle at Angers remains almost intact; externally the lofty walls and massive round towers are in perfect preservation, resembling a great Mussulman or Mahratta fort in India. Internally, it has been utilized for modern purposes; but it reminds me of the great feudal fortresses of Japan, which were dismantled only a few years ago, and remain as yet uninjured monuments of a social state resembling that of France six centuries ago, when the castle of Angers was built. A bronze statue of King René, by David of Angers, occupies the place of honour in front of the castle, but Anjou has been mother of many kings, although not herself a kingdom, she has given kings to England and to Naples. The planta genista flourishes as brightly here as in the days of Henry Plantagenet, and its yellow tassels adorn every bank and hill-side.

May 11th, Auray.—The whole country south of Auray is dotted all over with so-called Druidical monuments; dolmens, menhirs, and tumuli. Among these we spent a long and pleasant day, driving and walking over a country of varied features, where the cultivated land is interspersed with woods and furzy knolls, and in which the inland sea of Morbihan is continually visible. The lines or avenues of Carnac are certainly disappointing, as the stones are most of them small, and, although the parallel lines of stones stretch across the country for nearly two miles, they are not conspicuous in the landscape. The mighty name of Julius Cæsar is associated with various mounds and monuments; he is alleged to have stood on Mont St. Michel to watch the fight between his galleys and those of the Veneti, but it was not his habit to stand afar off on such occasions. Near Locmariaquer are the longest dolmens of all, formed of vast flat stones such as could hardly be raised now, except by the aid of hydraulic pressure. They are large cells, with avenues or entrances formed of smaller stones, and resemble in all particulars the dolmens of the Channel Islands. Considerable respect has been shown to the ancient monuments, in leaving them undisturbed by cultivation amid thickets of broom and briars.

May 13th.—Dinan is a remarkably picturesque old town, with well-preserved and lofty walls. We walked out to the ruins of La Garaye castle, charmingly situated among woods and gardens, where every variety of bird was to be seen and heard, and where I found wild primroses of a purplish red, along with the common yellow. All around are shady lanes and avenues, and picturesque farm-houses; and as the day was delightfully bright and warm, while everything was looking green and fresh after the rain, we thought muchly of La Garaye.

May 17th, Avranches.—I took a long stroll into the country, which is charming, with deep shady lanes, and paths through fields, orchards, and woods. In fact, the whole country, as seen from an eminence, looks like a forest, so much is there of orchard and hedge-row timber, but it is both cultivated and populous, although the villages and farm-houses are invisible until you are close upon them. The rock of Mont St. Michel, crowned with its grand ecclesiastical fortress, is very striking indeed, as it is approached from the mainland. The architecture is so perfectly adapted to the form of the granitic mass, that the buildings, with their vast buttressed foundations, seem almost to grow out of the rock, with which they harmonize in material and colouring. It is a perfect labyrinth of vaulted and pillared halls, crypts, chapels, cloisters, dungeons, refectories, and dormitories, alike massive and elegant in structure, the material being granite.

He remained steadily in London through the whole of the session, which was unusually protracted, principally owing to the action of the House of Lords in connection with the Compensation for Disturbance Bill. Parliament at length rose, early in September, and he came down to Gloucester for the Festival of the Three Choirs, of which he was as usual a steward, and, as the family were in Scotland, he stayed with friends in the neighbourhood. Having previously arranged with L. Courtney, M.P., that they should go to the west of Ireland, to see for themselves something of the state of affairs there, they met at Limerick on the 18th of September.

September 25th, Cong.—The morning was splendid, and we had a delightful drive along the shores of Lough Corrib to Maam, and thence through a fine mountain glen to Leenane, little thinking of the terrible tragedy to be enacted on that road a few hours later, when Viscount Mountmorres was shot by unknown hands, near his own gate. All is peaceable and friendly to the passing stranger, but these mountainous wilds are in a state of siege, as regards landlord and tenant. Were it not for the presence of the black soldiers, nothing could appear more peaceful, but hidden fires burn beneath the surface of society.

September 28th, Achill.—The ordinary native villages are large and numerous, but are mere clusters of hovels, huddled together anyhow, and reminding one of Asia rather than of Europe. The population of Achill is far too large for the island to support, and (besides regular emigrants) many go to Great Britain during summer, returning with a few pounds of savings at the end of the season. Rarely does one meet man or woman in Ireland who has no near relatives in America, and there is no unwillingness to emigrate on the part of the rising generation. It is otherwise with their seniors, who have had little education, can hardly speak English, and naturally cling to the old country, having no idea of anything better in the way of soil, climate, or habitation. As for cultivation, it is impossible to detect any original advantage in the land now enclosed, over that which is still waste moor and bog. The labour of the cottier has made all the difference, and has given to the soil any value which it may now possess, beyond feeding for a few sheep or grouse. It is not surprising that these cottiers should resent the confiscation of their little crofts, because in bad times they fall in arrears with the rent, which would be reasonable for good land in England, including farm-buildings erected by the landlord. With security of tenure at a reasonable quit-rent, cultivation might spread indefinitely over these moorlands of Achill, until, as in County Clare, only the most barren mountains would remain as pasture, but this is not to be desired, unless the change were accompanied with an increased size of holdings and a higher standard of comfort.

He wrote a letter to the editor of the *Pall Mall Gazette*, dated, Westport, County Mayo, October 2nd.

Twelve years ago I visited this part of Ireland, and, on the whole, I certainly think that it has improved, although less than may have been hoped by many who have taken part in promoting remedial legislation for Ireland during the last ten years. The disestablishment of the Church seems to have been a complete success, and the Protestants, even where they are a small minority, as in Connaught, are flourishing and at peace with their Roman Catholic neighbours. The Land Act of 1870 has effected considerable benefit, but it does not go far enough to meet the

condition of this province, where a measure even more drastic
than the Compensation for Disturbance Bill seems to be urgently
required. Eviction for non-payment of rent, when non-payment
has been due to simple inability from failure of crops, is, in the
opinion of Irish occupiers, an act of confiscation on the part of
the landlord, with whom they claim to have a joint interest in the
land. In Connaught, eviction without any compensation is of
course legal, when the rent is not paid; and in numerous instances
it has recently taken place, arousing the bitterest sense of wrong
among the rural population. Apart from agrarian crime, there is
no country where person and property are safer than in Ireland,
and certainly none where I, a traveller of considerable experience,
feel more certain of receiving, as a stranger, amicable and kindly
treatment from all the inhabitants whom I may meet. Government must endeavour to maintain order and to repress crime in
Ireland, but this will not be done by proclaiming a state of siege,
which will only cause more bloodshed. If Parliament is called
together in winter it must be, not to pass a Coercion Bill for
Ireland, but a sweeping measure of land law reform. Even if the
land laws of Ireland were so completely reformed as to be in
consonance with the special conditions of the country, as well as
with abstract justice, all the existent evils in Ireland would not
be thereby removed. The poverty and over-population of the
country seem to be due to the miserably low standard of comfort
which prevails, rather than to any unwillingness either to work or
to emigrate. How to render Ireland rich and prosperous is one
problem; how to remove the causes of Irish disaffection and
agrarian crime is another. I venture to think that the second of
these problems at least is capable of solution, if the British
Government and Parliament will deal promptly and fearlessly
with the Irish land question.

An article by Sir David, entitled "Second Chambers,"
appeared in the *Nineteenth Century* of July, 1881, and
applies to this period. In it he drew an interesting comparison between the constitution of the British House of
Lords, and that of the Senates of other countries. The
following extract gives some slight idea of how strongly he
deprecated the action of the Peers in connection with the
remedial measures for Ireland—

The action taken by the House of Lords, in throwing out every important Irish measure sent up to them during the late session, has brought into strong prominence the peculiar and exceptional constitution of that illustrious assembly. The British House of Peers stands alone in the civilized world as a Legislative Chamber composed of members sitting by hereditary right. Nearly all the constitutional countries of Europe possess a senate, or second chamber, but beyond the United Kingdom the hereditary principle has been either entirely abandoned, or so greatly modified as to be of little importance.

The anomalous character and position of the House of Lords would perhaps escape observation if Great Britain alone. were concerned, so rarely does that House venture to reject, or even seriously to mutilate, any measure upon which British public opinion has been distinctly expressed, either by Parliamentary elections, or through the columns of the press, which almost wields the authority of a *plébiscite.* When Ireland is concerned it is altogether a different matter : the public opinion of that country exercises no influence over the House of Lords ; and upon Irish questions the conduct of the Peers has more than once well-nigh rendered the peaceable government of Ireland an impossibility, and the reform of the Upper House a necessity. The Liberal majority in the House of Commons, backed as it is by public opinion out of doors, knows well enough that it is quite unnecessary to accept Lords' amendments to popular measures, like the Burials, Employers' Liability, or Ground Game Bills, but there is a distinct unwillingness to coerce or humiliate the Upper House, and mischievous amendments are often agreed to, the plea being that the bill, even as it stands, is too good to be lost. On the other hand, upon all minor questions, affecting small sections of the community only, and upon all bills in the hands of independent members of Parliament, the House of Lords is supreme, and may postpone for an indefinite period the relief of Jews from religious disabilities, the legalization of marriage with a deceased wife's sister, the amendment of the laws affecting the property of married women, or the protection of ancient monuments from destruction. Members in charge of measures such as these in the House of Commons know, from sad experience, the perils of "another place," even when the bill has been modified so as to conciliate, as far as possible, the hostility of noble individuals, one or two of whom thus possess a practical veto on all legislation except first-class Government measures.

Hence occasional outbursts of irritation against the hereditary chamber may take place in the House of Commons, but the personal sympathy between members of the two Houses is so general, and so strong, that no serious proposal for the reform of the Upper House is ever likely to originate in the Lower. The impulse to Parliamentary reform must come from outside, whether Lords or Commons are concerned; and if the nation could be brought to understand the futility of dealing with one House, while leaving the other intact, the reform of the peerage would soon become a question of practical politics. The assimilation of the county and borough franchise, with a complete redistribution of seats, must shortly occupy the attention of Parliament, and the next Reform Act will doubtless produce a considerable change in the House of Commons, intensifying the political antagonism, and diminishing the personal sympathy between members of the two Houses. If the peerage is to continue as a political, not merely a social, institution in this country, it must, like all other political institutions, submit to modification. Most important questions affecting the ownership of land must ere long be dealt with by the Legislature, and upon such questions an hereditary legislative body, composed almost entirely of landowners, may find itself in a difficult and even dangerous position, considering the small proportion of landowners among the people of this country. Nomination by the responsible ministers of the Crown for life, or for a fixed period, seems to be the best method hitherto invented for recruiting a senate which shall be in general harmony with popular sentiments, but shall be superior to any transitory impulse.

CHAPTER XXII.

TOUR THROUGH RUSSIA—LETTERS ON THE TRANSVAAL WAR—HIS MOTHER'S
DEATH—TRIP TO THE PYRENEES—PAMPHLET ON "BRITISH COLONIAL
POLICY."

EARLY in October Sir David sailed from Hull for Russia,
reaching St. Petersburg after a cold, stormy and uncomfortable voyage of eight days.

October 11th.—The city of St. Petersburg certainly impresses
one with its great size, its wide thoroughfares, its large open
spaces, its huge buildings, and its mighty river spanned by bridges
both broad and long. At every door is seated a dvornik, or
porter, who never leaves his post apparently by night or day, but
may be seen at any hour, dozing in a huge sheepskin coat, and
protecting society from the Nihilists in some mysterious manner
known only to the authorities. Few policemen in uniform are
visible, and St. Petersburg has not nearly so much the appearance
of being dragooned as Berlin, or even Paris. Not even in
London is there a more bustling or gayer street than the Nevski
Prospect; public buildings are all on a grand scale, and imperial
residences are alarmingly numerous. For palaces, fortresses,
and churches, there seems to be always money in Russia; and
indeed everything in St. Petersburg indicates that the resources
of a great empire are squandered upon this centre of expenditure.
In fact the place literally glitters with gold, its splendour culmina-
ting in the cupola of St. Isaac's magnificent cathedral, the interior
of which is incrusted with mosaics, gold, and the richest marbles,
including in that term malachite and lapis-lazuli. These precious
materials have been so utilized as to give the impression that a

portion of the building is supported on mighty columns of malachite, but internally they are of a stronger substance, viz. iron. But the red granite pillars of the porches are solid enough, and most magnificent monoliths, hardly surpassed by Egyptian obelisks.

October 12th, Imatra.—The weather being fine for this time of year, we resolved to utilize it for an excursion into Finland; twenty miles from St. Petersburg the frontier is reached, and it is still a true frontier, although Finland is no longer Swedish. Finland has the most complete home rule, and prospers under it greatly, with perfect loyalty to the Imperial Government; it is the Scotland, Poland being the Ireland of the Russian Empire. In every detail the Grand Duchy retains its independence, even as regards the douane, and a visitation of baggage takes place on the frontier. Finland is not responsible for the Russian debt, and is herself thoroughly solvent; she is now subject to universal military service, but she has her own laws, language, religion, coinage, and budget. The ancient Swedish constitution still prevails in Finland, with four distinct estates of society, each having its own house—knights, priests, burghers, and peasants. The currency is silver, and instead of depreciated rubles and kopecks, there are marks and pennies, equivalent in value to francs and centimes. The names of the streets and public notices are written in three languages—Swedish, Finnish, and Russian, as different from each other as any three can well be, but the last is not spoken at all in the interior, and the first very little.

The environs of Wiborg are very pretty, with lots of ornamental villas, and a pleasing alternation of forest and lake. The posting arrangements are excellent, relays of stout little horses being obtained at stations about fifteen versts (ten miles) apart, with no loss of time, except for harnessing, and at very cheap rates. The country through which we passed in a drive of forty miles to Imatra, resembles Swedish scenery, with many lakes of all sizes and shapes. It was pleasant to arrive at an elegant hotel, resembling a large Swiss châlet, and to find that Imatra is not entirely deserted, although the season is over; it seemed as if we had been expected, for a warm bedroom and a warm supper were ready in a jiffy, and were most acceptable, as the night was cold and windy. The hotel stands within a few yards of the Imatra Falls, whose roaring reminds one of Clifton House at Niagara. In

summer the place is crowded; now all has been made snug for
the winter, and the space between the double windows is tastefully filled with moss, heather, and immortelles, instead of cotton
wool, and the windows cannot be opened; thus arranged, these
wooden houses are almost impervious to cold.

October 14th, Willmanstrand.—A good sprinkling of snow fell
during the night, and when the sun appeared, the landscape was
seen to great advantage. The blue lake of Saima, full of islands
(said to be one thousand in number), the woods, where the yellow
of the birches contrasted with the dark green of pines and firs, and
the silvery powdering of snow, all combined to form a characteristic
Northern picture with a few wooden houses painted red, after the
Swedish fashion. We feasted at the hotel on every variety of
smoked luxury, besides cooked dishes hot and cold, coming to
the conclusion that Finland is the country for cheap and good
living.   .

October 16th, St. Petersburg.—The grandeur and solidity of
everything here are in marked contrast to the style of arrangements in the other great Eastern capital of Europe. In Constantinople, nature has done everything and art nothing for the
development of a great city; here are no natural advantages, but
skill and labour have overcome all difficulties. The Russians
would make Constantinople the grandest city in the whole world,
if it were their capital. The collection of pictures in the Hermitage Museum is magnificent, every school of painting in Europe
is represented, and all are arranged in beautiful apartments, well
lighted and tastefully decorated. The vases, tazzas, candelabra,
and tables are in themselves a splendid collection, the materials
being malachite, lapis-lazuli, jasper, and a beautiful pink porphyry
(rhodonite) quite new to me. Peter the Great's gallery is simply
a grand curiosity shop, containing everything from a jewelled
snuff-box to an old turning-lathe; all the objects have either an
historical or an artistic interest, and the most interesting are those
associated with the name of the really great Peter, who created a
great empire, perhaps in a truer sense than any man in history,
except Alexander of Macedon.

October 18th.—The Hermitage is a place to which any number
of visits may be paid, and where any amount of time may be spent.
The rooms are magnificent, and beautifully arranged, with plenty
of space and light, and the monolithic pillars of granite are a sight

in themselves.   Here are antiquities of all sorts, including many fine classical statues, and splendid Etruscan vases in terra-cotta; but the most remarkable and unique collections are the Greek and Scythian from Kertch, and other parts of the Russian Empire. The objects found in the tombs near Kertch quite take the shine out of Schliemann's treasure-trove from Troy and Mykenai.   In artistic beauty, as well as in richness of material, the gold and silver ornaments are quite unsurpassed, and furnish beautiful models for the imitation of less tasteful generations.   The engraved gems are also remarkably fine, and if such art treasures have been discovered in a remote city of the Cimmerian Bosphorus, what must have existed in more important places, which have been less fortunate in escaping the spoilers of the dark ages? There is the greatest possible liberty of access to the public everywhere; mujiks, in high boots and sheepskin coats, may be seen strolling over the parquet floors, and among the gems and art treasures of the Hermitage Museum.   You may prowl about anywhere in public buildings without interference, policemen never tell you it is "verboten," and information is always given most politely, even by men in uniform.   In fact, the absence of official intervention is almost equal to what I recollect at Stockholm.

October 20th.—We drove across the great bridge of boats to visit the church containing the "Majesty of buried Russia." The imperial tombs are all alike, plain sarcophagi of pure white marble, without ornament, except a Russian cross of gold; from Peter the Great down to the late Empress there is nothing to mark date, rank, or sex.   All the sarcophagi are above ground, upon the floor of the church, and the simplicity and purity of these snow-white monuments are in pleasing contrast to the ostentatious magnificence, or the gloomy horror, of royal and imperial tombs in other parts of the world.   The church is decorated with banners, and other warlike trophies, with gold and precious stones galore, and with objects wrought by the hands of that most energetic and industrious individual, Peter the Great.   In an adjoining house is a large boat, built by the same mighty hands, and known as the "grandfather of the Russian navy."   The house inhabited by Peter himself, a very small one, is just outside; it is preserved with religious veneration, and may be called the "grandmother of St. Petersburg," being the oldest edifice in the city.

A small club of Britishers have a shooting-lodge, and a large tract of land, leased from its peasant proprietors for purposes of sport. We drove out thither in the evening, a distance of twenty-three versts. It was quite like a Highland lodge in the Lews, or Sutherland.

October 21*st.*—The frost was very sharp at night, and sledges were in readiness to convey us to our shooting-ground ; we found the entire population of the neighbourhood, men, boys, and women, collected to act as beaters. They were marshalled by Simeon, the Finnish gamekeeper, who, after posting the seven guns, and getting his fifty or sixty beaters into order, sounded a battered horn, when a shouting and yelling commenced, such as might strike terror to the stoutest heart. The female beaters con tributed their full share to this noise, and tramped right gallantly through the snow in high yellow boots, holding their skirts kilted (like Leezie Lindsay's) considerably above the knee. The cry indeed was great, but there was little wool, *i.e.* fur and feathers, our gross total only amounting to eleven head, including a big black woodpecker with red crest, who was mistaken for a black-cock. There were six large grey hares, beginning to turn white, but surprised by this premature winter ; two *riabchiks*, or hazel-grouse ; one willow-grouse, and one grey-hen. Although our bag was small for so large a party, we enjoyed ourselves thoroughly, and had a cheerful picnic luncheon in the snow. We returned to town in the evening, and found the roads somewhat slippery, one of our horses falling six or eight times.

October 22*nd.*—A snowstorm during the night, and this morning there was genuine winter in the streets of St. Petersburg.' In any Western city such a fall of snow would simply suspend traffic for an indefinite time, while here it is not even impeded, but greatly facilitated. The trottoirs are at once swept and scraped perfectly clean, and the snow is piled in great mounds on both sides of the wide streets. Meanwhile the rails of the tramways have been scraped clear of snow, and the tram-cars are the only wheeled vehicles which continue to run. Now the streets are as silent as the canals of Venice, and the sledges dart about in all directions, as smoothly and far more swiftly than gondolas. They carry no bells, and bear down upon you without a sound ; the drosky is metamorphosed into a small sleigh, barely holding two passengers, so that, if those two be a lady and gentleman, the latter is expected to place his arm round the waist of the former, in order to keep her from being jerked out in turning a corner. Private sleighs, drawn by two or three tall black horses with long tails, sweep by with alarming rapidity, the horses stepping out like American "pacers," and the vehicle behind them weighing a mere nothing. The coachmen wear large four-cornered caps of velvet, crimson, purple, or blue, and the horses' hind-quarters are covered with a long net, or cloth, to keep the powdery snow-dust from blinding the ladies, who of course enjoy furious driving, and can indulge in it here, without let or hindrance from the police. It is a good fault to be over-horsed, no doubt, but a waste of power is somewhat characteristic of this country, and too many servants, or *employés* generally, are to be found in all great establishments. In the Hotel Démouth the servants are quite too numerous, and Ivan helps Vassíli to do nothing; but it is an excellent and moderate hotel.

October 24th, Great Novgorod.—The Yuryef monastery presents an imposing appearance, yet cheerful withal, with its white walls, and numerous domes of green and gold. The interior of the churches far surpasses in splendour the exterior, which suggests rather a Mussulman mosque than a Christian place of worship. The floor of these churches is of bronze plates, and the ikonostas, or altar screen, is a blaze of silver and gold, the only portions not covered with the precious metals being the faces, hands, or feet of the saints, who are thereon depicted. Holy pictures in Orthodox churches are always so covered with embossed metal, except where the actual flesh or skin is represented. At 9 a.m. a grand function commenced, with infinite genuflexions, prostrations, waving of arms and candles, praying, reciting, and singing. The doors of the screen were opened and closed, priests and monks marched in and out; the abbot, as he appeared to be, took off and put on his globular mitre; little loaves of bread were brought to the front, and carried away by the faithful, and the censer was swung all over the church. The monks wear plain black gowns, with tall caps and black veil, but the garments of the officiating ecclesiastics are of bright colours, and stiff with gold embroidery. The chanting of the deep bass voices, and the smell of incense produced a soothing and soporific effect, and we fully intended to stay through the entire performance, but after two hours of varied services an old fellow settled down to steady droning, so we withdrew.

October 29th, St. Petersburg.—Mr. Lee kindly accompanied me to the Russian Versailles, viz. Tzarkoé Selo, and a splendid winter day we had for the excursion ; the trees were covered with glittering snow, and everything looked cheerful in the brilliant sun except the marble statues, which are not left "standing naked in the open air," but are shut up in wooden boxes. The great palace has at present a very deserted aspect, but we found some one to admit us, although we had no order, being strangers they took us in. The rooms are handsome, but comfortless, the decorations are generally in white and gold, but one room is entirely covered from floor to ceiling with amber. All the ornaments, including a set of chessmen, are also of amber, transparent as well as opaque, and displaying every hue from deep orange to pale gamboge yellow ; amber, like ivory, must be getting scarcer and more valuable daily. The bedroom of Alexander I. remains precisely as he left it for the last time, and a very uncomfortable apartment it is for any gentleman to inhabit ; the great Tzar was economical in small things, for his big boots are patched. There is a great deal in the present condition of Russia to remind one of France as it was a century ago, when a benevolent monarch reaped a bitter harvest sown by his despotic predecessors. How far will the parallel go ?

November 1st, Moscow.—It is at once apparent that Moscow is a city entirely *per se*, and is semi-Asiatic in its architecture and arrangements. The Kremlin is quite full of interesting objects : churches, palaces, towers, monasteries, museums. The Great Bell is, however, the most remarkable object of all ; it stands on the ground, like its big Japanese brother at Kioto, with a large fragment chipped out, and lying alongside ; the weight is about two hundred tons. Bronze guns of every size and shape, large and long, ancient and modern, encumber the whole place ; they are "rude presents that fortune has made" to Russia "in twenty victorious wars," especially in 1812. Fortune has certainly given victory to the Russians over nobler nations than themselves, notably the Swedes, but on the whole it is certain that Russian trophies commemorate the triumph of a progressive race over barbarians. Napoleon's visit, on the other hand, although his reception was not hospitable, seems to be regarded as a compliment : all relics connected with him are preserved as if they had belonged to Peter himself, and in this Treasury of Moscow the post of honour is occupied by a marble statue of Napoleon, in the robes of a Roman Emperor.

Mr. Leslie, the British Vice-Consul, took charge of me with the utmost kindness and hospitality. He is superintendent of the gas-works which supply Moscow; as usual in Russia, foreign capital and energy have carried out this great undertaking, and in this case (as indeed most often) Great Britain has supplied them. There is nothing more conclusive, as to the enterprise and organizing power of Englishmen, than the extent to which they succeed in monopolizing responsible and highly paid appointments, as regards industrial undertakings, in an independent country like Russia.

November 2nd.—The Sparrow Hills are a high bluff over the river Moskwa, which here winds in a very tortuous course, and forms with its wooded banks the foreground of a splendid panorama, rivalled by few and surpassed by none, as a view of a noble city. Moscow displays a variety of outline and colour quite special to itself, and sparkles with the precious metals like a vision of the Apocalypse; the prevailing blazons are or, argent, gules, and vert, and the architecture reminds one of China or India, rather than of Europe. On this bluff Napoleon's star culminated when the ancient Russian capital lay helpless at his feet, a splendid spectacle, but little better than a delusive mirage.

The Romanoff House is exhibited as the cradle of the reigning family, and a specimen of a boyar's residence in the sixteenth century; everything is on a very small scale, especially the door-ways, and the Romanoffs must have packed pretty closely when they inhabited this house. No contrast could well be stronger than that between so modest an abode and the gorgeous palace in the Kremlin, with its magnificent gilded halls, so lofty, so empty, and so uninhabitable; with polished floors, on which one can hardly walk; beds of silk, in which nobody sleeps; chairs of satin, on which nobody sits. Everything is in perfect order, as if an imperial coronation were an every-day affair, that being the occasion on which the Tzar is bound to visit his true capital. Cathedrals simply abound in Russia, and the Kremlin is full of them; three close together, used respectively for imperial corona-tions, baptisms or marriages, and burials. All are overlaid with gold and precious stones, and their wealth is steadily on the increase, as rich merchants and others compound for any sins committed in amassing riches by gifts to the church, and picture after picture is covered with gold, or adorned with jewels. In

Moscow the great name is not that of Peter I. but that of John IV., "Ivan the Terrible," and around his memory the Moscovite legends cluster, he being the first founder of the great monarchy.

November 5th.—The great theatre of Moscow is said to be second in size to the Scala of Milan only, and it is certainly a magnificent house with a very large stage. I saw it to special advantage, as in virtue of Mr. Leslie's gas functions he has the right to go anywhere at any time, and as a member of the Parliamentary committee on electric lighting I was made welcome to accompany him all over the place, while "Rigoletto" was being performed in Russian to a very demonstrative audience. We visited the great lustre at the top of the house, we went under the stage, behind the scenes, into the imperial boxes, the chief official himself doing the honours, and displaying the gorgeous furniture. The theatres form a distinct department of administration in Russia, and are managed in a very extravagant fashion, with suites of apartments always ready for the Emperor, who never comes, and crowds of officials with little or nothing to do.

November 9th, Kiev.—The great monastery of Kiev stands on the high bluffs above the Dnieper; it contains many churches with gilded domes and towers, and is the premier monastery of all Russia, and full, of course, of riches and relics. Although Kiev is a very ancient city, it does not contain many very ancient buildings, repeated fires causing a constant reconstruction of wooden houses. Now, however, the new houses are most of them built of fine yellow brick, in an elegant style of architecture quite characteristic of the city, which is gradually assuming a very handsome appearance. The place is rapidly increasing in population, and educational establishments are on a grand scale, from the University downwards. Kiev also deserves credit for erecting a monument to Count Bobrinsky, the man who introduced the cultivation of sugar-beet,—a benefactor, not a scourge, to humanity.

November 13th.—Warsaw flourishes and increases in population, while many handsome new buildings arise on all sides. There are more Jews in Warsaw than in any other city, nearly a hundred thousand, and doubtless some of this prosperity is due to their industry and economy. Colonel Maude, British Consul-General, being engaged to visit some country friends, took me out with him. Mons. and Madame Janasz welcomed us most heartily, and at once made me feel quite at home.

November 14th.—We drove out to visit the farm of their son, a pupil of Cirencester College; close to the farm is a great sugar-factory, which consumes all the beet-root grown in the neighbourhood. The beet (which is white in colour, and carefully selected for its sweetness, the sugar-factors furnishing the seed) is chopped up very small to begin with, then boiled, and the juice, or syrup, undergoes a long series of operations with lime, bones, alcohol, etc. The crystallized brown sugar is separated from the molasses in centrifugal machines; a recently discovered process has been patented by a Frenchman, and it is now possible to extract about fifty per cent. of sugar from a residuum of molasses, formerly almost useless. Women are employed in all sorts of labour (except, of course, such labour as is most highly paid), and, as usual, are found to work more steadily and conscientiously than men. Good land can be bought for some twenty years' purchase, and Colonel Maude is satisfied that British farmers, especially Scotch, would do better in Poland than in most British colonies, notwithstanding the admitted drawback of language. The peasants now possess many small properties, granted to them out of the confiscated estates of noble insurgents in 1863. We spent a very pleasant evening, with games and music, French, English, and German being spoken.

November 17th, Brussels.—The change in warming railway carriages is gradual as one proceeds westwards; in Poland stoves are still in use, although the carriages are divided into compartments, which are lighted with gas; in Germany hot water pipes run all through the train, and are always kept warm by the engine fire; in Belgium large tins of hot water are supplied and frequently changed; in England small tins of lukewarm water are grudgingly supplied. In Russia you are stifled with heat, in England you are frozen with cold on a winter railway journey. After crossing the Rhine at Cologne, and proceeding towards Belgium, I came to the first tunnel which I have passed during thousands of miles of railway travelling since landing in St. Petersburg, and the pretty scenery near Verviers was the only bit of hilly country traversed during the entire journey.

He spent Christmas at Meredith, but returned to London as soon as Parliament met, at the unusually early date of January the 6th. For the first time in his life, he was troubled by a slight cough this winter; whether it originated from the severe changes of temperature in Russia it is difficult to say, but from this time he was never quite free from it. It was not sufficient to alarm his friends generally, and he himself took little notice of it ; but his mother's fond eye detected a change, and her anxiety about him was aroused. There can be no doubt that the exceptionally cold weather of the winter and spring had a prejudicial effect upon his health, combined as it was with the worry and late hours of the session, during which there was more than one all-night sitting.

At the close of the year, the subject uppermost in his mind was the outbreak of war with the Boers of the Transvaal, a result which he had foreseen would follow, sooner or later, from the annexation of that country. Before the meeting of Parliament he wrote letters on the subject, both to the *Scotsman*, dated December 30, 1880, and to the *Gloucester Journal*, dated January 4, 1881.

We are now engaged in a struggle which may be protracted and murderous, in order to crush the independence of a free community, composed, not of heathen blacks, but of Christian whites. Since the American War of Independence there has been nothing in our history at all resembling the present crisis, and although the danger is not now so serious as it was a century ago, it is well that we should realize how serious it is. I, for one, am convinced that the people of England and Scotland, if fairly consulted, would protest alike against the policy of dragooning Dutchmen in South Africa, and of dragooning Irishmen in Ireland. In both countries remedial measures are required, not coercion, and the best remedial measure for the Transvaal is to restore its political independence, frankly acknowledging the error which was committed when it was annexed.

The question to be decided is this : Are the electors and taxpayers of Great Britain prepared to undertake a sanguinary and costly struggle, in order to crush the independence of a community composed of free-spirited, self-governing, Protestant Dutchmen, with whom the only cause of quarrel is a blunder committed by the British Colonial Office? Is South Africa to be drenched with

British and Dutch blood, because it is disagreeable for certain officials to admit their mistake in a practical manner by restitution and apology? The annexation of the Transvaal has never been approved by the British nation, whose honour will be tarnished by its retention, but who are not responsible for the original seizure. The powerful and generous people of England can well afford to do an act of justice without "being afraid of being thought afraid," and if the Government understand the feelings of those who so lately placed them in power, they will close their ears to the cry for more blood, and will seek, through mediation and inquiry, a peaceful and honourable retreat from an untenable position.

England is strong and the Boërs are weak, but they are determined; they have the sympathy of all Europeans in Africa who are not English, and they will have the sympathy of those who admire courage and love freedom in all parts of the world. We are familiar with the cry for coercion and punishment; we have heard it often enough, when India, or Jamaica, or Ireland has been concerned; and we know the class from whom it proceeds. The last general election proved that this class no longer constitutes a majority of the British electors, who ought now to make their voices heard upon a question of such vital importance as this new South African War.

One immediate response to his letter in the *Scotsman* was the following address, received by Sir David. It was drawn up and signed by forty-four South African students, then resident in Edinburgh, of whom only one was from the Transvaal, one from the Free State, four from Natal, and the rest from the Cape Colony, proving the strength of feeling on behalf of the Transvaal Boers among Afrikanders generally.

"Edinburgh, New Years' Day, 1881.

" SIR,

"The undersigned have read with much pleasure your manly letter, which appeared in to-day's issue of the *Scotsman*. They feel that as South Africans, united by ties of blood or of friendship, of religion or of sympathy, with their unfortunate but brave brethren in the Transvaal, it is

their duty to thank you heartily for such an expression of
opinion as you have given.

" Your name carries weight with it, and will bring conviction to the minds of many of the inhabitants of Great
Britain. We have step by step followed the doings of that
small section of brave Englishmen, who, in Parliament as
elsewhere, have not failed to make their voices heard in
favour of the Dutch Boers. We admire you, and are
convinced that the true honour of the British name, of the
British flag, is dearer to you than to many of those who,
while deeming themselves to be the only true patriots, by
their doings are bringing the time-honoured name of the
United Kingdom into disrepute abroad.

" And, finally, we beg to assure you that with our thanks
you also receive those of the majority of our countrymen,
both in Cape Colony and in the rest of South Africa.

" We are, sir, yours respectfully,

" G. A. DÖHNE."

(And forty-three others.)

These expressions of gratitude to himself, and appreciation of the efforts which he and others were making to
obtain justice for the Dutch Boers, were singularly gratifying to him. Such proofs of the value of his public labours
and independent position were felt by him to be the only
reward that he either sought or expected for the many
wearisome hours of Parliamentary life.

In March his mother went to London, to stay for two
or three weeks with her niece, Lady Mary Hope, in order
to meet her younger son, who came from India on a short
leave of absence. For a fortnight she thoroughly enjoyed
the almost daily society of both her sons, and was unusually
bright and active for her time of life. Although seventy-
seven years of age, she was as capable as ever, both in
mind and body, and her sympathy and interest in all

around her, and especially in anything connected with her sons, were wonderfully keen and unflagging. Her slight and fragile frame had always been more or less susceptible to changes of temperature, and, in spite of every care, the cold east wind, which set in while she was in London, brought on an attack of pleurisy. Although not serious in itself, it almost at once affected the action of the heart; and Sir David, whose devotion to her made him always watchful, was the first to take alarm, and to send for his youngest sister. The illness did indeed prove rapid, and on April the 7th, only five days from the first attack, she passed peacefully away, conscious and knowing her children to the last.

The shock of her death to Sir David was very great; she had been his one object and thought for many years, and, as he said, the light of his life went out with her. Now, for the first time, his singularly happy and boyish spirits seemed to fail, and he never again had the same perfect enjoyment of passing trifles, which had, till then, been so characteristic of him. It became obvious to all his friends that he was far from well, and the doctor, whom he reluctantly agreed to consult, advised rest, and change of scene and climate.

What he himself felt is shown by his answer to a letter of sympathy from a lady friend :—

Meredith, April 18, 1881.

It gives me pleasure that you should speak of the "love and devotion which I ever showed towards my sweet mother," for I certainly cherished those feelings as much as any son could do, and I fear only that I did not show them sufficiently. I can honestly say that all my actions and conduct were more guided by the desire to give her comfort and satisfaction than by any other consideration, and I now feel as if I had no particular motive of action at all. As you say, the strongest link binding us with the happy past is broken, and the future has, for me at least, lost most of its interest. Change of air and scene has been

recommended, and I leave to-morrow for the South of Europe with
a friend, meaning to remain away about a month. Willie has
returned to London ; his baby is a charming little thing, as is
Louisa's. The latter is my special pet, and always sits beside me
at meals.

He obtained a month's leave of absence from Parliament, and started with his old Australian friend, Henry
de Satgé, for the Eastern Pyrenees, to visit De Satgé's
brother, the Vicomte de St. Jean, at his château near
Perpignan.

April 24th.—The old château of Castellnou is a genuine fortress of the Middle Ages, and was a mere ruin until taken in hand
a few years ago by our host. He has restored the ramparts and
battlements, roofed in a large portion of the old castle, and is now
gradually furnishing it with antique articles and ornaments of all
sorts. The walls are of immense thickness and solidity, the cement
being as solid as the stones, and more so ; the castle is perched
on the summit of a rock, and can only be entered by means of
steps, although a carriage road has been recently made as far as
the entrance to the enceinte. The village nestles underneath the
château, and a battlemented wall with towers and gates encloses
both, and the fortress would be very strong were it not for a rocky
mountain which almost overhangs it. Huge balls, roughly cut
out of a sort of marble rock, have been found here in large numbers, and are used as ornaments ; they were intended originally
for the reception of besiegers. The view is grand and extensive
over mountain, plain, and sea, the snowy summit of the Canigou
being the most remarkable object. The valleys are full of cherry
and other fruit trees, and there are groves of cork trees, ilex, and
oak coppice, where nightingales abound. Yellow snapdragon,
purple and white cystus, and a small sort of gorse, very brilliant
but without sweet odour, are the most conspicuous flowers at
present.

May 1st.—Barcelona is a finer city than Madrid ; and the
flower market this morning in the Rambla was the most brilliant
I ever saw : roses and carnations, camellias and lilies were a perfect
blaze of colour. The public gardens, or Parque, are also a
splendid show of flowers, and are beautifully kept, with exotic

shrubs of every sort, many of them old friends of ours from the Southern hemisphere. The pond is "stiff" with gold-fish, nightingales sing in every bush, under the shade of araucaria, mimosa, and eucalyptus. The ladies wear black veils, or mantillas, which are very becoming, and make women in hats or bonnets look tawdry and vulgar. Barcelona is certainly a gay and festive place, with two Italian operas going on at the same time. We visited the Liseo, a splendid theatre, where "Hernani" was performed in excellent style, worthy of any capital city.

May 3rd, Montserrat.—Nothing can be more extraordinary than the outline of the Montserrat itself, as seen during the ascent, and it is not easy to comprehend how the action of meteorological causes alone can have cut the hard and solid conglomerate rock into such fantastic shapes. Although the monastery is deserted, the church is kept up, and is even now undergoing restoration ; a numerous choir of boys sing at vespers, airs which sound operatic rather than ecclesiastical. The hermitages, for which Montserrat was once famous, are now in ruins, and are perched all over the mountain upon pinnacles, apparently inaccessible to human foot. In old paintings of hermits in the wilderness, I have seen something like Montserrat depicted, and the scenery can hardly be exaggerated in any picture. The pinnacles of rock are curiously rounded at the top, looking like the fingers of a hand, or huge bunches of asparagus, while occasional pillars of rock stand quite isolated.

May 4th.—We bespoke a guide to lead us to the summit ; two or three points are about equal in height, but the hermitage of S. Geronimo has the credit of being upon the highest. The first part of the climb is very steep and somewhat *pénible*, up a narrow gully in the rocks, but higher up the path winds through pleasant thickets of evergreen oak, resonant with the song of nightingales. Out of these wooded ravines the naked peaks of conglomerate rise abrupt and inaccessible, their fantastic outlines glowing in the sun, upon a background of deep blue. Both the day and the season are perfect for Montserrat, this being the time of flowers, and a botanist could not wish for happier hunting-grounds. The variety of plants upon this one mountain is extraordinary, and the number of species here indigenous at different elevations must be very large. Flowers of every hue are at present in full bloom, growing in many instances upon the bare, hard rock, without a visible particle of soil or moisture; within a few feet of the summit, and there only, I found a small, yellow jonquil, quite new to me, as were many other plants. The four provinces of Catalonia, from the Pyrenees to the Mediterranean, lie spread like a map at one's feet, with the peculiar profile of the Montserrat alone interrupting the view in certain directions; the northern horizon is bounded by the Pyrenees, now crested with continuous snow.

May 5th.—Another heavenly morning, and, awakened very early by the roaring of the nightingales, I was able to admire the snowy range in the clear morning light, and to spend an hour or two more, wandering upon the rocky paths, among flowers of every colour and scent. Monserrat is the perfection of a hill sanitarium for the citizens of Barcelona, and on account of its sanctity, perhaps more than of its salubrity, it attracts many visitors of every social class. The diligence this morning was full of good folks belonging to the humbler orders, who were in the highest spirits, having evidently enjoyed their pious little "lark" to the full; they were of all ages, two being babes and sucklings.

He drove over the Pyrenees to Amélie les Bains, and, after another short visit to Castellnou, returned to London. The journal of this tour concludes with the remark, "We arrived late at Charing Cross, and agreed that the journey between the two capitals of civilization is about the most unpleasant on the face of the earth!"

During the remainder of the session, one of the longest and most arduous on record, he remained constantly in his place in the House. The heat of July was unusual, and he began to realize that the winter in England and the summer in London were almost equally trying to him. As he expressed it in a letter written to his brother at that time:—

Parliamentary life does not suit my tastes or constitution, with its late hours, big dinners, and residence in town. I have "had my whack" and am more than satiated. As I told you some time ago, doing an occasional little turn for the good of India is one of the few things that reconcile me at all to being in Parliament, but that occurs so rarely.

He had long wished to visit South Africa, and recent events had made him all the more desirous of seeing the country, and judging for himself of the state of affairs on the spot. His friends hoped that the dry climate of the Cape, and the long sea-voyage, would permanently improve his health, and his constituents gladly agreed to his absence from Parliament until Easter, rather than that he should resign his seat. After a short time at home in Gloucestershire, he went to Castle Howard, for the meeting of the British Association at York, and there met many scientific and political friends, but was hardly well enough to enjoy the pleasant social gathering. In Scotland, however, the air at North Berwick and Inveresk, and his favourite game of golf, seemed to revive him, and, although he did not make any public speeches, he met the Liberal Associations at three of the Haddington Boroughs, and in his addresses to them, said :—

I am glad indeed to have this opportunity of meeting you in a somewhat informal way. Owing, in some measure to the length of the exhausting session we have had, I have for the first time in my life been on the sick list, and have not felt myself equal to making what I might call an electioneering tour. I have endeavoured during this long session to give a consistent—or what I may call a consistent and independent—support to her Majesty's Government. I do not mean to pretend that everything that has been done has been exactly what I should have wished, but this I say with confidence, that my faith in the Ministry remains undiminished, while my admiration for the Prime Minister is greatly increased. There has been only one measure of first-class importance carried through the Commons. I hold that the Irish Land measure is in every sense of first-class importance, and that it will inaugurate a series of land reforms which will certainly not be limited to Ireland. There were two or three bills passed for Scotland, in which I took a good deal of interest and some little trouble. One of them was a measure which I thought exceedingly beneficial, intending to confer upon the property of married women belonging to the poorer classes some amount of the protection which is generally secured to the property of the wealthier sections of the community by means of trustees and marriage settlements.

As regards the future business of Parliament a very important matter is to come before us. It has become apparent, from the experience of not only this, but other recent sessions, that procedure and the forms of the House of Commons must undergo a very sweeping and wholesale reform. There are now in Parliament what there never have been before—a number of gentlemen who are hostile to the tone, we might almost say the character, of Parliament; who do not care for its reputation, but who rather pride themselves on desiring to lower that reputation, and who are not bound up to what used to be called "the general feeling of the House." To some extent, there have always been individuals of this class in the House, but never till within a few years has there been an entire and considerable section. Now, there is a distinct party, who honestly and openly profess that they do not care for the traditions of the House of Commons, and that they do not wish the House to do any business, at all events for their country; and who are willing to undergo any amount of opprobrium and any amount of fatigue in order to prevent measures, which a very small minority disapprove of becoming law. When it comes to that, it is clear that the rules that were intended merely to protect a minority and to insure that a subject shall be thoroughly discussed—that those rules must now be altered so that the majority shall be able to carry those measures, and make its will effective.

There is a difficulty looming ahead again in the next session which has troubled us a good deal in the past—I allude to the case of the member for Northampton. The Liberal party, I regret to say, have not been unanimous upon this point; but for my part, I never entertained any doubt as to the course that ought to be followed in this case. I always felt it was an example of a man who was duly, legally, and properly elected as a Parliamentary representative, and who, on account of his unpopular religious opinions, was by the majority of the House of Commons deprived of his civil and political rights. I regretted to see that various religious minorities were conspicuous in putting down the case of Mr. Bradlaugh. Roman Catholics, Jews, and Quakers all combined against him. I felt that we, the Liberal party, had in turn fought the battle of every one of those sects, and I regret to think that, now that they have attained civil and religious equality, they should endeavour to prevent a smaller and more unpopular minority from maintaining a similar equality. I do not know how you feel upon the matter, but I think it right to express my view, and say that I voted very heartily with Mr. Gladstone and Mr. Bright in support of Mr. Bradlaugh being allowed to take his seat.

It is only right to mention that I have an intention of going this winter to a Southern clime. My first object in going to South Africa is not for the sake of my health, but in order to see that important and interesting colony. That is my primary object in visiting South Africa. But, as I have said, I feel so much used up by the last session, and so thoroughly out of sorts, that I came to the conclusion it would be killing two birds with one stone— that I might obtain valuable information, and at the same time benefit my health; and I hope under these circumstances you will not think I am playing truant if I do not reappear when the House of Commons assembles. At the same time, I hope to be back before the session has gone far—say, probably, about Easter; and if, as I trust I shall be, strengthened and benefited by the sea-voyage and change of place and climate, of which we hear a great deal, then I shall do my best to serve you in Parliament and to see the session out. If, on the contrary, I should find it is not the case, I can assure you I will lose no time in giving you an opportunity of electing some one better qualified to do your work in Parliament.

When at home, before his departure for the Cape, his buoyancy of spirit in some measure returned, and he was almost like himself again, looking forward eagerly, as usual, to the new scenes he was about to visit.

In February, 1881, the National Liberal Federation issued a pamphlet by Sir David, entitled "British Colonial Policy," the fourth of a series on "Practical Politics." Although touching more or less upon all the British Colonies, the subject principally dwelt on was the position of affairs in South Africa. The pamphlet was written before the outbreak of the Transvaal War, which, however, occurred while it was going through the press. It is the longest paper of the kind written by him, and it is difficult to give even a summary of the contents.

The most serious error recently committed in colonial policy has been the annexation of the Transvaal territory; we have never before, in time of peace, appropriated forcibly the territory of an independent civilized community. Happily the blunder is not yet irreparable; it has caused as yet no bloodshed, and what has been destroyed by the stroke of a pen may be restored by the same agency. A certain amount of magnanimity is required to acknowledge in a practical manner that an injustice has been done, but, after all, we may fairly claim to be a magnanimous nation, and have repeatedly proved ourselves capable of similar acts of restitution.

Difficulties may from time to time arise in any one of the numerous and extensive colonies of Great Britain, but the prospect in general is full of hope, and the mother country finds herself gradually relieved of burdens and responsibilities as her colonial offspring become stronger and more independent. But South Africa is an *enfant terrible* in every sense of the word, and is likely in the immediate future to cause more trouble than all the others together. In most of our self-governing colonies the native population has either disappeared entirely, or has become peaceably merged in a preponderating mass of European descent. In the "Dark Continent" of Africa the natives do not recede before the white man, and the extent of country peopled with warlike savages is almost boundless; each new conquest or annexation brings us face to face with fresh complications, of which it is impossible to see the end. It would indeed be well for England if her territory at the Cape of Good Hope were limited, as at Gibraltar, Aden, or Singapore, to a coaling station, a fortress, and a free port.

The new panacea for African troubles is confederation, but none of the conditions favourable to confederation exist in South Africa. The English settlers are a mere handful among a numerous population of alien whites, and a far more numerous population of blacks, even within our own territory, while beyond those limits stretches a vast continent, more or less densely peopled with blacks. Confederation under such conditions is an absurdity, and can mean nothing more than the assumption, by the Cape colonists, of a task far beyond their powers, viz. that of administering unaided a territory which threatens to rival India in extent, if not in population. Such an undertaking can only result in disastrous failure, if attempted by a feeble and divided colony under the form of free institutions.

We cannot be too much upon our guard against that class of politicians who believe that the strength and resources of the British Empire necessarily increase with its territorial extension, and who regard all conquests or annexations of rival nations as affording just cause for alarm. They appear to think that every barbarous country, and especially every island, all over the globe, belongs, or ought to belong, to England. These "patriots" are frantic with jealousy, lest another great Power should do *once* what England has done over and over again, and should attempt to share the British monopoly in civilizing aboriginals off the face of the earth. If other great nations are willing to undertake a share in the task of civilizing Africa or Asia, a far-sighted policy dictates ready acquiescence on our part in what is really the imposition of a burden on the shoulders of a possible rival. Experience has taught us in many wars that remote colonies and possessions are a serious encumbrance to a belligerent of inferior maritime force ; and in particular it has been proved again and again, that all islands occupied by the rivals of Great Britain are simply hostages placed in the hands of that Power which so long has ruled the seas. Not without reason is the British navy popular, giving, as it does, security at home and empire abroad, without menacing liberty or unduly burdening the exchequer.

At the present period no portion of the empire, except India, would be seriously imperilled, if we did not possess any regular army at all, and if the defence of the whole were intrusted to a powerful navy, with a well-organized local militia in each colony, as well as in the United Kingdom. Even India, it must be remembered, was conquered from the seaboard, and our maritime supremacy alone enabled us there to crush our French rivals. Without that supremacy we could hardly hold the country for a year, while with the sea open to our transport vessels, and India garrisoned by a localized European force, no enemy exists that need alarm the most timid of patriots. For us the "gates of India" are on the Suez Canal, and Egypt is the only *land*, beyond the limits of India proper, the possession of which would strengthen our Eastern Empire.

The self-governing colonies of British origin have ceased to be a burden : they pay their own way, and might even become a support in any time of dire emergency ; but they contribute neither to the imperial forces nor to the imperial exchequer. The remainder of the Empire, including all the African possessions, must be regarded as entailing heavy responsibilities upon the people of the United Kingdom, without adding to the strength necessary for discharging those responsibilities. At the present time, Ireland is an additional burden on the military strength of the Empire, and, until Ireland is pacified by just legislation, England has only Scotland to assist her in sustaining "the too vast orb of her fate."

We possess already the most extensive empire that has ever existed on this globe, and a large proportion of this is still an unpeopled waste, requiring capital and labour to develop its splendid resources, and to support millions where now only thousands are found. There is an ample field for all our national energy within our own existing borders, and the Englishman who advocates the wider extension of those borders far from the sea, our own element, into the heart of Africa or Asia, is no true friend to his country.

The "forward" colonial policy has had a fair trial, and it has brought upon us, in Zululand and in Afghanistan, the two most serious military reverses ever sustained by the British arms in battle with a barbarian foe. These defeats have indeed been " avenged," but there is little glory or satisfaction to be gained in the punishment of men whose crime is to have fought bravely and successfully in defence of their native land against unprovoked invasion. If the Liberals really believe that rash and unjust acts have been committed by their predecessors in office, why can they not make manifest their belief by deeds as well as by words? How can those who condemn the seizure of the Transvaal, against the will of its inhabitants, treat the Boers as *rebels* for attempting to resist annexation? Is it impossible, or absurd, for a great nation to acknowledge a blunder, and make restitution for a wrong? If Liberal Ministers content themselves with censuring instead of altering the colonial policy of the Conservatives, they will have themselves only to thank when they reap the fruits of that policy.

Our future colonial policy must be to reform the institutions

and develop the resources of those countries for whose administration we are really responsible; to divest ourselves of all
liability for the action of those colonies over whose government
we exercise no power of control; and, above all, to put an end to
the system of "filibustering" by officials, traders, or missionaries
under shelter of the British flag.

CHAPTER XXIII.

1881–1882.

CAPE COLONY—NATAL—ORANGE FREE STATE—ARTICLE ON "SOUTH AFRICA."

October 28th.—The steamer *Conway Castle* was already lying in the beautiful harbour of Dartmouth when I arrived on the evening of the 27th. I put up at an old-fashioned hostelry, the Castle, quite in keeping with the general antiquity of Dartmouth, once a chief port of England, and always an excellent harbour. Large vessels, like the *Britannia*, can lie in perfect security anywhere near the town, and the river Dart expands here into a sort of narrow lake, enclosed with high picturesque banks. Numbers of nice villas and country-houses are scattered about upon these banks, which are well wooded, and altogether Dartmouth is a very pretty place.

November 18th, Capetown.—A stroll as far as the new reservoir gave me a very pleasing first impression of Capetown, which is beautifully situated, under the shadow of the great mountain, looking out upon the bay, the flats, and the distant ranges beyond. On the slopes, above the business quarter of the town, are numbers of pretty residences, embowered in oleanders, pomegranates, and myrtle, all in full blossom, and shaded by groves of dark umbrella pines. There are also shady avenues of oaks, and all the trees and plants appear to be exotic, including the familiar blue-gum. Every shade of colour, from pure ebony to rosy, may be seen in the faces of the population; the most picturesque are the so-called Malays, who have little or nothing of the Malay type, but are unmistakable Mussulmans. The men wear the red tarboosh, and, when in full dress, the flowing robes of the true believer; the women affect a costume peculiar to themselves, and' appear to have adopted the fashions of Holland, rather than those of Asia. Their skirts are enormous, trailing on the ground, and projecting very widely, with numberless undergarments, and high waists, quite in the old Dutch style. On their heads they wear a gay-coloured kerchief, usually yellow, folded so as to frame in closely the face, which is often not unpleasing, and by no means devoid of *cheek*, in any sense of the word. They affect brilliant colours in great variety, and are evidently fond of parading their clothes, the quantity of which indicates that the "Malays" in general are a prosperous community. Capetown altogether has an air of prosperity, as there are lots of good shops, and numbers of comfortable houses, great and small, with well-kept gardens.

November 20th.—I paid my respects to Sir Hercules and Lady Robinson, old acquaintances at Sydney, and dined at Government House. The Governor was most affable, and gave me his views on South African topics very freely : he *must* be an intelligent man, as we were quite agreed in the main ! The Robinsons do not like Capetown so well as Sydney, and Sir Hercules gives New Zealand the palm over all other colonies.

November 23rd, Wynberg.—I went out by train to Wynberg, where I had secured a room at Cogill's hotel, a very favourite resort. The place reminds me of Weybridge, with its extensive pine-woods, and numberless pleasant residences scattered about on every side, many quite concealed among the trees. The evenings here are delightful, there is no chill in the atmosphere at sunset, and in fact the temperature is singularly equable during the twenty-four hours. At Wynberg it is not so warm as in Capetown, and it is pleasant to stroll about the pine-woods and "sugar-bush" scrub, in search of birds, flowers, etc. With an air-gun, Percy, a fellow-passenger, shot several honey-suckers, which are abundant ; some have long tails, almost like birds of paradise, others are more like humming-birds.

November 24th.—Pniel is a mission station in the most picturesque situation, and presents a model of peaceful comfort and prosperity. The Rev. Dr. Stegmann received us most hospitably, and showed me with just pride his little principality, where he has ruled for forty years. The cottages of the coloured labourers might well excite the envy of a British working-man, so airy, well lighted, and well furnished are they, each with its garden. The people are of a mixed breed, and display many shades of colour; Hottentot, Malagasy, Negro, Kafir, and European blood runs in their veins. . One or two of the children in the school were quite white, with blue eyes and brown hair, having reverted to the type of an ancestor, the immediate parents being dark enough. Dr. Stegmann gives his pupils a high character for general intelligence, and they certainly look very happy and healthy. Among all the flourishing fruit trees, peaches, apricots, etc., the oranges present a melancholy contrast : the fatal dorthesia, deadliest of insect plagues, has penetrated into this remote valley, and has made a clean sweep of the splendid orange groves, of which stumps only remain, proving by their size how large the trees must have been. Its ravages are confined to the orange tree, and the Australian blackwood acacia, every twig of which is covered with bunches of their white and orange cocoons. In spite of all efforts at cleansing, the life is soon sucked out of the tree by some mysterious process, which is not apparent, as no life or movement is visible in the cocoons, which are full of minute scarlet eggs, and a nasty yellow fluid. Neither birds nor ants seem to touch the dorthesia, and its "enemy" has not yet been discovered.

November 25th, Capetown.—Mr. Justice Dwyer took me to inspect the public library, an institution of which the colony is justly proud. The most valuable portion was a gift from Sir George Grey, and is kept separate under the care of Dr. T. Hahn, fearfully learned in Hottentot dialects, which sound as if addressed to horses, being a series of encouraging clicks. Rare old editions of classical works in manuscript, and in print; fac-similes of Bushman drawings; photographs of the *indigènes*, ancient maps of Africa, and other interesting objects, were produced for inspection. As regards the geography of Central Africa some of these mediæval maps prove that modern explorers have only rediscovered most of the leading facts as to lakes, rivers, and mountains. The system of land registration and titles in Cape Colony is gloriously simple and cheap; mortgages are recorded on the title-deed, and must be cleared off when the property changes hands.

November 27th.—Mr. J. H. Hofmeyr, M.L.A., gave me a Dutch dinner, inviting several Dutch friends to meet me : Transvaal affairs were our main topic, the impolicy of the annexation, and the prudence of pacification being made clearly manifest by all that was said. The small numbers of the Boers engaged in the

various actions, and the remarkably small number of killed and
wounded on their side are facts of the greatest importance.   They
never had more than four or five thousand men in arms at any
one time, as they relieved each other repeatedly, and many of
their fighters were mere boys.   Their force was divided into nine
different detachments, the largest being at Lange Nek, about
1300 strong, and their total loss was about 70 killed or died of
wounds, half of the number having fallen at the action of Lange
Nek.   On Majuba Mountain they lost a couple of men, their force
was a mere handful, and their success was regarded as a fluke.

November 30*th.*—I drove out to visit the " ex-king " Cetewayo.   The "location for state prisoners," where he resides, is
in a somewhat bleak situation, and is reached by a rough road;
it is not in itself a bad sort of place.   Cetewayo was in good
spirits at the thought of going to England, and seemed quite
pleased to see me.   He was dressed in a blue serge suit, as if prepared for his voyage, and wore a smoking-cap.   He is fat and
well-liking, with small hands and long nails, of which he seems
proud; he is eager to start, and wishes the months could be cut
"like bread" for April to arrive.   He says his only hope of
restoration to his home is in the friends who in England have
interested themselves in his behalf, and that he would sleep comfortably to-night, after seeing me.   I told him I hoped that in a
few months he would be sent home to his own country, and that
I would help him whenever I could, so we shook hands very
cordially.

December 3*rd.*—I started by rail from Capetown with Mr.
Lawrence Van der Byl and some other friends, to spend a couple
of days at his place, Welmoed, in the Stellenbosch district.   His
house is surrounded by extensive offices, part of which is the old
slave quarters, and all around are orchards and vineyards.   The
trees are covered with all sorts of fruit, the apricots in particular
look most tempting, but are not quite ripe.   Ostriches are here in
all stages, and it is astonishing to see what a model husband and
father the cock bird is.   He sits upon the eggs, while the hen
struts idly about; he rushes open-mouthed at any intruder; the
chicks follow him rather than the hen, and he takes the greatest
care not to tread on them, of which there seems to be considerable danger.   He chooses his mate, and remains faithful to her
even after a long separation, when an attached couple will meet

with every sign of joyful recognition. The chicks just hatched present a very comical appearance : they are in size, colour, and shape exactly like hedgehogs as to their bodies, with heads and legs like large but feeble goslings. The old cocks are black and white, the hens and young birds are brown, but conspicuous colouring does not prevent paterfamilias from making himself domestically useful ; this is quite exceptional as regards birds, for he is very kenspeckle when sitting on the eggs, but then few animals care to meddle with him. Ostriches look very absurd when prancing, and waltzing, with their wings spread out, their thick bare legs exposed, and their long thin necks, topped with their diminutive heads. Cape farmers may say with Hiawatha—

> " ' Master of life ' he cried desponding,
> ' Must our lives depend on these things,' "

and on diamonds ?

December 4th.—My host took me in a Cape cart to visit some of his Dutch friends in Hottentot's Holland, now called Somerset West, with English snobbery and paucity of invention, after a certain noble Governor of the Beaufort family. We proceeded up a well-wooded valley to the farm of Mr. Morkel, a wealthy Dutch Boer, or Squire, for his house rather resembles that of a laird than of a farmer. The rooms are large and lofty, as in old Dutch houses generally, and the wood-work is of the finest timber, beams, flooring, and folding-doors, these last being of yellow wood. Near the house are grand old trees, planted by the early Dutch governors, the stone-pines being quite magnificent specimens ; everywhere is running water brought from the near river, so that Morgenstern has both shade and moisture, and is a model residence in this parched land. A little higher up the valley is another farm, where it pleased the prudent Dutchmen of yore to plant camphor trees ; these have attained enormous dimensions, and are without rivals in this country, being quite tropical in appearance. We were most hospitably entertained with every luxury by Mr. and Mrs. Morkel, and in the afternoon cart after cart arrived, heavily laden with brethren and their families, come for a Sunday visit, until the stoep was full of stalwart Morkels.

Lack of labour is the farmer's standing grievance : they have actually to labour with their own hands. This complaint is universal in this country, where coloured people abound, but

2 D

obtain easily all that they require, and, having obtained that, decline to work for the enrichment of others. Wages are very high in South Africa, and labourers are quite independent; white men will not work as farm servants, nor allow their children to do so. White immigration therefore will hardly solve the labour difficulty on large farms, perhaps Chinamen would.

December 6th.—Cordial invitations to return [when the grapes are ripe] were given me on my departure, when I took the train for Beaufort West. After ascending the mountains, the railroad crosses the Great Karroo, a vast level plain, bounded by distant ranges of dark, bare mountains, and apparently an arid desert, except where a few green mimosa bushes indicate water near the surface of the ground. The brown dry tufts of thorny scrub, which cover more or less the whole Karroo, contain a surprising amount of nourishment, however; and all sorts of animals, wild and tame, thrive here, with nothing, apparently, either to eat or to drink. At Beaufort there is a respectable inn, and the place is brilliant with oleander and pomegranate blossoms. After breakfast I took my seat in the post-cart, behind two capital little nags, and trundled away along a smooth and level track. It was rather warm during the day, but when the moon rose it was delightful, and we thoroughly enjoyed the drive as far as Aberdeen, where we arrived about midnight.

December 8th, Port Elizabeth.—The railway journey down to Port Elizabeth was quite agreeable after a scorching hot day at Graaff Reynet; the Karroo country, through which the line runs most of the way, is well stocked with animals of all sorts, especially Angora goats, which spot the brown plain with white, and apparently find plenty to eat. Ostriches also are numerous, and their owners in these parts are many of them in pecuniary difficulties, as they are worth just about one-tenth of the price they fetched a year ago. Feathers still command a good price, but birds are a drug in the market, a pair of good breeders fetching £23, instead of £230. At the terminus my old schoolfellow, Gilbert Farie, was waiting for me, and drove me up to his comfortable British residence; it is very pleasant meeting, after thirty years, once more.

December 12th.—Port Elizabeth is a busy flourishing place, with public buildings worthy of a much larger town. The surrounding country is grassy, and the short turf would be very suitable for golf. Not a single indigenous tree or bush grows in the neighbourhood, but public gardens have been planted, and are well kept with flowers in great beauty and variety. The harbour, or rather the lack of harbour at Port Elizabeth, which is only a "port" by courtesy, is a dreadful impediment to the progress and prosperity of the town. Algoa Bay is simply an open roadstead, exposed to the full force of the south-east gales, and all works undertaken for improving the anchorage have hitherto resulted in failure, causing sand to accumulate, and the harbour engineer is now gradually removing the old breakwater, and undertaking new operations. It is a treat to see the black navvies, chiefly Fingos, filling trucks with earth; Mr. Shield has taught them to work by the piece, and they send the shovelfuls flying in grand style. Strong, well-fed, and light-hearted, they are perfect navvies, when they will work, and in this climate can easily beat white men; they are also sober.

December 15th, Durban.—The first view of Natal at this season is charming after the arid shores of Cape Colony; the hills are all green, and well wooded, with many pleasant residences appearing among the trees. Mr. Andrew introduced me at the two clubs, and took me out for a very pleasant ride. We cantered along the beach and then turned inland, ascending the beautifully wooded hill of Berea, where the rich Durbanites have their abodes. Berea reminds me strongly of Matheran, although much lower,—the same verdant jungle, traversed by narrow rides, and studded with delightful bungalows and gardens.

December 17th.—Mr. Andrew and I proceeded by rail to Verulam, where we arrived after a two hours' run through a pretty country, reminding me of the hill districts of Ceylon. The resemblance is heightened by the frequent coolie huts, and by the bright-coloured dresses of the coolie women, who retain their Indian style in all respects, as the men retain their turbans, but do not despise a cast-off uniform. These coolies are mostly from Madras, and are a very thriving class of the community, being industrious and economical; when their term of compulsory service is completed, they become their own masters, and many settle in Natal, acquiring land and becoming masters of Kafirs also. They are now as numerous as the whites, and are exempt from the disabilities of the Native Africans, as to purchasing liquor, etc. Many of them rent small farms at very high figures, two or three pounds an acre, and are excellent paying tenants; indeed, it seems probable that the Indian coolies will become the chief population of the low country in Natal.

December 20th, Pietermaritzburg.—Started by early train for Pietermaritzburg. The line ascends rapidly from the coast, and traverses a very picturesque country, undulating and park-like, with large tracts of primeval forest, densely overgrown with creepers. Near Durban land sells for a very high price, much of it being held by speculators, who will not part with it at reasonable rates.

December 21st.—At Bishopstowe I was most kindly welcomed by Bishop Colenso and his family, who have been expecting me for some time, and I was installed as a resident in the pleasant old country house. Plantations of all sorts of trees, ornamental and fruit-bearing, with shrubs, especially raspberries, and flowers, grow luxuriantly at Bishopstowe, and pets in great variety abound. In fact, the place is a harbour of refuge for man, and bird, and beast; Bishop Colenso, a tall, handsome old gentleman, being a true "protector of the poor." Natives of all ranks and tribes infest the neighbourhood, each with his tale of wrong, and all are sure of a patient hearing, to be followed in all probability by a gallant effort at redress. The Bishop is a chivalrous "Ritter von dem Heiligen Geist," and his daughters support him zealously.

December 31st, Durban.—A demand was made for the despatch of a half-company of soldiers to the St. John's River in Pondoland, where one company is already stationed, and the steamer *Melrose* was chartered for transporting them. A number of excursionists, including Mrs. Andrew and myself, took advantage of this opportunity of visiting a picturesque and interesting place. It was late in the evening when we arrived off the St. John's River. During the night a change of wind laid the ship in the trough of the sea, and she rolled most unpleasantly. A steam-tender was in waiting to convey the troops across the bar, but it was announced that she could not come out again for twenty-four hours, the bar being only practicable by daylight and at high water. When the tender came alongside, it was so rough that the little vessel was washed from stem to stern at one instant, and then was lifted by the waves to a level with the deck of the *Melrose*. All who had a free choice elected not to attempt the shore, but the soldiers were hoisted one by one in a chair from the large steamer to the small, and bolted like rabbits into the cabin, where they were battened down. We watched the tender cross the bar in safety, and when she was in calm water, we steamed away homewards, considerably disappointed. The magnificent cliffs, and forest-clad slopes, enclosing the entrance to the river, had rendered us all anxious to have a peep inside, where hippopotami are still found.

January 2nd, Pietermaritzburg.—The Natalians are a peculiar people, with the ideas of an oligarchical society, being in fact a white oligarchy, grasping the control of a black nation, and having no sympathy with Liberal or popular impulses; in fact, "they are all bosses." Maritzburg may be described as a city with two bishops and no laundress. The perpetual and well-founded complaint is : "Labour, labour everywhere, and not a man to work !" The Kafirs merely work to pay their hut-tax, and then repose ; many whites think that they ought to be heavily taxed, and so compelled to work, as it seems hard that a white man should not be able to make as much as he wants to idle upon, because forsooth a black man is content to idle upon very little !

January 10th, Howick.—The important business of purchasing wagon, mules, etc., occupied a considerable amount of time, but we were most fortunate in coming across the very article required, in a light new wagon, built to order, but never claimed ; we also bought six mules. To-day I fairly got under way, and started at 3 p.m. for Howick. The wagonette is perfect, running very light, and easy on its springs. Charles, my driver, and his myrmidon, Derrick, however, found great difficulty in driving the mules, which tried to halt at every place of outspan.

January 11th.—We started early, but the ground was very sticky, and our progress was slow ; this was more the fault of the men than of the mules, as the myrmidon proved himself a fearful duffer, losing either his hat or the lash of his whip every few minutes, or entangling the same lash, like an awkward fly-fisher, in the harness. It was a dreary drive through thick mist and drizzle to Currie's Post, where I breakfasted. Hardly had I done so when General Leicester Smyth drove up, travelling with relays of excellent commissariat mules at a spanking pace. Gladly I availed myself of the vacant seat in his comfortable trap, and abandoned my own vehicle, with quadrupeds and bipeds, to follow as rapidly as might be. Two coloured boys urged on the eight mules at a furious rate, whenever the state of the road would permit. The day cleared up and we were able to see the scenery, which is pleasing and varied : there is a pretty piece of bush at Karkloof, and the mimosas are now a blaze of golden yellow blossoms, with a stray white bush here and there, looking like a hawthorn.

January 12th, Newcastle.—Storks abound, evidently our old friends from Europe, avoiding the Northern winter, and revelling in lizards and locusts.   At Colenso is a fine bridge over the Tugela, a large river even up here, but beyond this point there are as yet only drifts ; a genuine " Pontifex " is one of the greatest benefactors a country can have.   Stalwart Kafirs, working under a white "boss," are not unfrequently to be seen filling up some of the worst holes along the road ; they have a wonderful mode of threading beads in their woolly hair, while their wives draw their crisp locks back into a sort of knot, like Canova's Venus, and stain them with red pigment.   The laws regulating the right of outspan, and the pounding of animals, furnish a very pretty quarrel between two important interests : those of farming and transport-riding.   The mounted police of Natal seem to fail as preventive of crime, having too much of the military element, and being above their proper work.   At the camp at Ingagane River a gorgeous apparition in scarlet and gold presented itself suddenly in the bare wilderness : it was a young officer of the Enniskillen Dragoons, got up as if for the Faynix, and ready to act as orderly to the General.

January 15th.—To-day the General took a holiday, and we started in a couple of ambulance wagons, with six mules each, everything being done in style under the auspices of the chief Commissariat officer.   When we reached the top of Schain's Hoogte we alighted, and went carefully over the battle-field, Captain Essex acting as guide.   He bears a charmed life, having escaped unhurt from Isandhlwana, Schain's Hoogte, and Lange's Nek !   It is an awkward double drift at the Ingogo River, but to-day we crossed without any difficulty, and arrived at a little hotel kept by an ex-officer of the British army : for a gentleman to keep an inn is not uncommon in Natal.   The evening closed over as fine a view as this colony affords, extending from Amajuba across the Buffalo Valley into Transvaal.

January 16th.—At 8 a.m. we were all in the saddle, and rode across the veld to the site of the camp on Prospect Hill ; nothing can be pleasanter for riding than this veld, where it is at all level, but for the blessed ant-bears, which dig the most insidious pitfalls, descending into the bowels of the earth, and well concealed with long grass and other vegetation. The scene of Brownlow's charge is, however, very steep, and was not too easy of ascent, even in the absence of the Boers, whose slight breast-works lie a little way beyond the crest of the hill, quite invisible from beneath. We rode along the ridge of the hill to the obelisk, which marks the point assaulted by the 58th Regiment, and bears inscribed the names of those who fell. Here we planted a few flowers on the graves, and satisfied ourselves that the Boer position might have been turned easily on their extreme left, where the ground is comparatively level, between Lange's Nek and the Buffalo River. The Boer force during the action was only about thirteen hundred strong, but was soon afterwards largely reinforced, when additional and stronger breast-works were made at the Nek, and on the side nearest to Amajuba. Along this line of defences we rode up towards the mountain, which towers over the whole position, a huge truncated cone ; we followed the Boers' line of ascent, which is by far the easiest side of the mountain, and rode as far as a spring of water, a few hundred feet below the top. A short but steep climb brought us to the top of the rocky rim, which surrounds the cup or crater, about a mile in circumference. This is no volcanic crater, but simply a grassy hollow, enamelled with beautiful wild flowers ; and in the centre are the monuments erected to the 92nd Highlanders, sailors, and others killed in action. Ensconced snugly in this hollow, safe from the enemy's distant fire, Sir G. Colley seems to have remained, like the proverbial ostrich with his head concealed, until the Boers suddenly appeared upon the edge of the crater, and rushed down upon the British, with whom it was *sauve qui peut* over the opposite edge, almost a sheer precipice. Certainly the Boers must have been as much astonished as their enemies were, when they reached the summit without any resistance, and it is almost certain that they could have had no expectation beforehand of ever getting there. They seem to have crept on and on, wondering how far they would be allowed to come, until they saw their unprepared foes at their feet, and charged at once. They were a mere handful, and even if it was a sort of fluke, one feels inclined to say with Lars Porsena : "Such a gallant deed of arms was never done before." From the crater nothing is visible except the sky, but from the

edge of the "krans," or "wreath" of rocks, the view is grand,
extending from the Orange Free State to the Transvaal territory,
a wide expanse of mountainous country.

January 19th.—We ascended the Drakensberg this morning,
and it was a very heavy stage : one serious obstacle was the
number of wagons met and passed on the road; some of these
were quite remarkable for the beauty of their teams, each lot of
sixteen or eighteen oxen being of the same colour, red, black, red
and white, black and white, matched with as much care as the
horses of a smart battery. My own mules went well to-day,
Charlie having got used to them, but his myrmidon is absolutely
inefficient, and lazy, very good indeed at eating and sleeping, but
not at anything else.

January 21st.—The stony road having worn the hoofs of the
mules considerably, at Harrismith four of them were shod, on the
fore feet only, at a price which would almost purchase silver shoes
in England. Storks are so numerous by the road-side, that there
must be myriads in the country, if they are at all equally distributed
over its surface; they do not affect marshy ground, and seem to
find abundant prey in the long grass. Long-tailed black finches,
with red throats, are also numerous, and it is very amusing to see
the other birds teazing them; they pursue their tormentors with
great vigour, but their tails are far too large for them, and they can
only flutter along with great difficulty, rising and falling as they go.

January 22nd, Bethlehem.—The "Sandown" hotel is kept by
two gentlemanly young Englishmen, and is very comfortable; it
has been recently built, at a considerable outlay, and will succeed,
I trust, but the word "home" is too often in the mouths of
the proprietors, as is customary with Britishers in South Africa.
"When were you last at home?" "When are you going home
again?" Such phrases savour rather of India than of a true
colony.

January 24th.—The inn and farm at Zand River are kept by a
lady of cockney origin, who has been here for twenty years, and
has not yet lost her pristine energy. She actually works in the
garden, as if she were a German, the only sort of white woman
(according to Charlie) who ever works in the open air out here.
The results of her energy are manifest in abundance of fruit and
vegetables, milk and butter, besides black Berkshire pigs, and
plenty of cattle, not without shorthorn blood. The garden con-

tains a small forest of peach trees, bent down and overladen with fruit, to which we were made heartily welcome; the ground was covered with fallen fruit, making a grand display of abundance, and our hostess preserves and dries fruit on a large scale.

January 25th.—Senekal certainly bears away the palm for ugliness and discomfort from any village that I have seen in this or perhaps any country. Although only a few years old, it has already an appearance of premature decay, and the wretched little group of houses and hovels seem to have been thrown down anyhow, with a fine northerly exposure to the baking sun, while a wall of rock on the south reflects the heat, and keeps off any cool breezes. Of course, it is not always so hot as at present, but we were glad to leave Senekal very early, with a long day of forty-two miles before us, without a single accommodation house anywhere on the road.

January 31st, Bloemfontein.—The little town is quite pleasing in its general aspect, as there are many gardens, with well-laden fruit trees, and many comfortable-looking houses. The principal church is large and handsome, with twin spires; in this edifice I attended a service of the Dutch Reformed faith, which reminded me rather of Scotland than of Holland. The army of the Free State was present, in the person of some soldierly-looking young men in neat dark uniforms with yellow facings, the officer richly bedizened with gold lace. They are really a sort of cadet corps, sons of farmers, who receive a military education; they number between thirty and forty, and remain three years in the corps, so that a good many available officers exist, should an emergency arise, and the Free State should be drawn into war with the Basutos, or anybody else. The Bishop of Bloemfontein took me over all the Anglican schools, homes, and cottage hospital, which seem to be admirably managed, and are on a very large scale for the size of Bloemfontein. The children pay £60 per annum each, but so expensive is living here that this merely defrays the cost of board, and tuition is therefore given gratis: deficiencies are made up partly through funds from England, partly through the gratuitous services of pious ladies and gentlemen of High Church proclivities. President Brand gave a big dinner in my honour, and invited all the notables of the place to meet me: my opinions on Transvaal affairs are well known here, and insure me a friendly reception from German as well as Dutch residents.

February 1st.—Drove out of Bloemfontein *au grand trot* of the six mules, but the unspeakable Derrick, having received his ill-earned wages this morning, could hardly even sit humped up in his usual corner, holding the reins loosely in his hands. Luckily he is not my slave, or I would have him flogged! Soon one of the mules showed most alarming symptoms of collapse, and when outspanned, lay down, declining to eat. We therefore proceeded with four mules harnessed, two running alongside, and the brute's indisposition proved to be only temporary. Mules are irritating animals in many ways, but they are so hardy, and so much indisposed to overdo the thing, that they pull through better than any other beast of burden. The country is very flat, its surface being only diversified by ant-heaps in the foreground, and a few stony kopjes on the horizon. Ants are in great variety and numbers, but are timid and uninteresting in their behaviour.

February 4th, Kimberley.—Under the auspices of Mr. Josephs, chairman of the "Gem" Company, I was taken down to the famous diamond mine, proceeding, at my own request, in one of the flying buckets. The bucket is said to be a dangerous mode of conveyance, and bad accidents do occur now and then, but it is rapid and agreeable, giving a capital view of the mine above and below. Working in the mine does seem horribly dangerous, perched as the men are on narrow ledges of crumbling soil, with a precipice beneath, and big lumps of rock constantly rattling down from above. Each gang of niggers, from six to a dozen, is watched by a white man, who sits there in the blazing sun under an umbrella, and must occasionally nod. Then is the black man's chance, for at this stage of picking and shovelling the largest diamonds are usually found; or else he raises an unearthly yell, as if the whole mine were crumbling in, the overseer looks up for an instant, and he has the stone in his mouth at once. After all the diamondiferous soil, brought out of the claim during the day, has been washed and sifted, the result is represented by a moderate collection of small stones. A director, or some other responsible man scrapes away heap after heap, until he suddenly pounces on a crystal, picks it out with the point of his scraper, and deposits it in the palm of his left hand. When the last sieves have been emptied, and the contents searched, the hollow of that hand may contain a teaspoonful of little white and yellow crystals, which pay for the wages, salaries, machinery, fuel, taxation, profits, and general outlay of a large company. It seems incredible and absurd, but so it is. Such a vast expenditure of capital and labour, and such a paltry result ! The most wonderful fact to be borne in mind is that the whole of this vast accumulation of machinery, with all the tramways, cars, and iron articles of all sorts in enormous quantities, has been dragged in bullock wagons for hundreds of miles, and has cost, for this land carriage alone, about £35 per ton.

February 6th.—Dust and flies have their head-quarters at Kimberley, and never was I better pleased to turn my back on any place, especially as I left behind the drunken lout Derrick, getting a new boy, John Steijn, of a yellowish complexion.

February 19th, Port Elizabeth.—With joy I found myself once more in G. Farie's hospitable house, able to repose indefinitely, and to eat and drink abundantly at regular hours. Charlie and his myrmidon were duly despatched by steamer to Natal, and a great sense of relief succeeded this final winding up of my travelling arrangements. Whether a driving tour in the interior of South Africa be a game worth the candle of expense and bother is at least doubtful, but certainly when it is completed one feels relieved. On the whole it is somewhat disappointing : there is so little variety, so little that is pleasing to the eye ; beasts and birds, trees and flowers, all are alike scarce ; while the common objects of the way-side are broken bottles, empty tins, and skeletons of beasts.

February 28th, Grahamstown.—Much refreshed by a week of complete rest, I started once more on my wanderings, in order to see something of the Eastern Province, and the so-called frontier. Grahamstown is quite a pretty town, well planted up with trees of all sorts, including some fine kafirbooms, an indigenous flowering tree, very handsome in every way. The Botanic Gardens are very charming, well laid out and well kept, by far the best that I have seen in South Africa. The private gardens also are many of them pretty, and maintain the character of the English as a " gardening nation," for Grahamstown is essentially an English settlement ; the houses are built of stone, and have an appearance of solidity, as well as neatness, unlike what is usual in a new country. Lunched with Mr. J. Ayliff, M.L.A., who is a member of the Native commission, now sitting here. The evidence of the natives is given in an admirable manner, clear and consistent as to their own laws and customs, polygamy, dowry arrangements, etc., and they are never at a loss for a reply.   In many respects their unwritten laws, enforced by the authority of the chiefs, are remarkable for equity and good sense; they have little to gain by coming under European magistrates, and English or even Roman-Dutch law.   Their evidence is strongly in favour of prohibition as to the sale of spirits to natives; even their own Kafir beer is denounced by them as the cause of great evils.   This is the most thoroughly English district in the colony, even as to the language spoken by natives.

March 9th, King William Town.—The drive out to the range of mountains, on whose slopes grow the primeval forest visible from King William Town, is one of the most pleasing and varied in all South Africa.   Hill and valley, pasture and cultivation, dense wood and open mimosa bush alternate in the landscape, while there are abundant human habitations visible, from the prettily situated town of " King," to the numerous farm-houses and Kafir kraals with which the country is dotted.   The bush at present is bright with two flowering shrubs, one scarlet, the other pale blue; the weather was perfection, and company agreeable. The frugal German peasant, who so unwillingly left Pomerania for "heisse Afrika," has thriven here, as he deserves to thrive.   On the very edge of the forest we saw one of them, himself holding a plough drawn by four oxen, while his wife acted as driver with the whip, and his boy as voorlooper.   No other white people in the colony will work in the fields after this fashion; while the country around swarms with natives, neither British nor Dutch will condescend to cultivate the soil with their own hands.   It remains to be seen whether the Afrikander descendants of the German farmers will be as industrious and frugal.

March 14th, Port Elizabeth.—A pleasant trip was organized to St. Croix Island, the spot where Bernardo Diaz first landed, when he had doubled the Cape of Storms without sighting land.   A rabbit, two cats, a cock and a hen are the visible colonists of St. Croix, but the aboriginal inhabitants are the penguins, which we came on purpose to see.   At first only a few of these singular birds were visible, seated on the rocks, near the sea, and regarding us with stolid indifference.   We soon discovered, however that there was a penguin, or a pair of penguins, in every crevice of the rocks large enough for the bird to squeeze its body inside. They are perfectly fearless, defending themselves and their eggs with desperate bites of powerful beaks, and they are most difficult to dislodge from their intrenchments. When poked at with a stick they utter pathetic grunts of remonstrance; at other times they yell defiance in notes like the braying of an ass. Penguins are to be found ensconced even on the summit of the island, some two hundred feet above the sea, but how they get up and down in the course of the day is a mystery, so slow and awkward are their movements on land. When driven hastily downwards, they tumble and slip on their backs in the most ludicrous manner, sliding into the water anyhow; once there, they are in their element, and are no longer awkward, but swim like fishes. A large number of eggs were collected, notwithstanding the gallant resistance of the penguins, which have an absurd way of twisting their heads and necks, as if trying to get a better sight of you. In stepping from rock to rock one has to keep a bright look-out, lest, like Achilles, one should receive a deadly wound on the heel from an unseen beak.

March 20th, Capetown.—Mr. Gie drove me out to the famous vineyard of High Constantia; it is the property of Mr. Van Reenen, who has, besides vineyards, excellent orchards of various fruits, especially loquats. A large amount of wine has been already pressed, but the finest grapes remain still ungathered, and the vines are covered with bunches of splendid Haneputs, both purple and green, the latter quite brown on "the side that's next the sun." It is impossible to find a mouldy or rotten grape, the overripe merely become raisins, and the flavour is delicious, but these grapes are so solid as to be both meat and drink. A large, round, black sort in particular resembles a plum, rather than a grape. The Pontac grape is black, and very small, like a currant, and grows upon vines, the leaves of which turn red, in conspicuous contrast with the green of the vineyard generally. The area of valuable vine-land does not exceed a few acres, being mysteriously limited, as there is a good deal of ground in the neighbourhood that looks similar in quality. Cape people boast (justly) of their grapes, but apologize (needlessly) for their wines, which only require good names to rival those of Spain and Portugal.

April 7th, Madeira.—I went on shore with Major and Mrs.

Reeves, to visit their quinta and garden; we were received with genuine demonstrations of pleasure by their Portuguese servants, who have been their own masters for two months, during the Reeves' trip to St. Helena. The quinta is a charming villa in a garden, which is now a perfect blaze of scarlet from the magnificent geraniums, although roses, verbenas, and many other flowers grow in almost equal profusion. The variety of trees which flourish here, and bear fruit, is very remarkable: mangoes, date-palms, loquats, oranges, oaks, besides vines, sugar-canes, bananas, etc., all within the limits of a small garden. Every prospect pleases, but man, at least official man, is vile; and it seems as if most Portuguese institutions were about as efficient and as trustworthy as the "men-of-war" styled "Portuguese," which abound in these seas. Madeira, with all its natural resources, is reduced to poverty, by misrule and taxation, while Teneriffe flourishes as a free port.

While he was in South Africa, he wrote several letters to the *Daily News* and the *Scotsman*, on different political questions. In the first, he advocated the withdrawal of all Imperial troops from the Cape Colony, as the most likely way to insure peace in future; in another, he spoke of the so-called settlement of the Zulu territory as clearly a failure, considering that there was no intermediate course between annexation and the restoration of Cetewayo, the latter alternative being the one he naturally preferred. He thus concludes the last of these letters :—

After a somewhat prolonged journey through the interior, I am satisfied that there is no country (as yet visited by me) where money may be made by steady industry so easily and so rapidly as in South Africa. Having visited all the greater British Colonies, I would recommend South Africa as the best for money-making, although, perhaps, the least agreeable generally as a residence. Wages in every trade and occupation are high, and the demand for labour of all sorts is far greater than the supply. The profits of business are also high, and a few years of industry and self-denial will convert a working artisan into a small capitalist. A country where this is the case must have a prosperous future, notwithstanding the numerous difficulties with which South African colonists have to contend.

The following is taken from an article on "South Africa," which appeared in the *Contemporary Review* of July, 1882. In it are clearly expressed the opinions which he held after his long visit to the Cape, during which he had unusually favourable opportunities of hearing all sides of the important questions then agitating the colony :—

The political future of South Africa is a hard problem, and it must be admitted to be a country very heavily handicapped in the race of colonial progress. Even setting aside the great "Native Difficulty," there is quite enough to exonerate the Cape Colony from the reproach sometimes directed against her, that she has suffered so many younger colonies to pass her in this race.

South Africa is a country without harbours, without navigable rivers, without certain rainfall. Where pasture is abundant it is, as a rule, unsuitable for sheep, and the good wool-producing districts of this vast area are comparatively limited. The lack of sufficient moisture prevents the wide extension of wheat cultivation, even upon soil which is eminently fertile in cereals wherever water is obtainable. The result is that the colony imports wheat, as indeed it imports nearly every article of food except fresh meat. In return for all these imports the colony exports wool, hides, mohair, ostrich feathers, and diamonds. Most of these may be described as fancy articles, liable to depreciation from a mere change of fashion, although they continue as yet to maintain their price with surprising firmness.

Among the causes impeding the progress and darkening the future of South Africa, a prominent place must be given to the antagonism existing between the two nationalities to which nearly all the white settlers belong, the British and the Dutch. The treatment of the Dutch colonists by the British Government in former days is "an ancient tale of wrong," upon which no candid Englishman can reflect without shame and regret. The natural feeling of resentment entertained by the Dutch against the English, and the arrogance of the latter, as the dominant race, long prevented anything like hearty co-operation or friendly intercourse between the two nationalities. Equal and just government, however, in course of time produced its natural effects, and a few

years ago the bitterness of feeling between English and Dutch
colonists was almost a thing of the past; at all events it was
dormant and quite unobtrusive. All at once the annexation of
the Transvaal Republic, and the war which ensued, aroused the
ancient animosity in full vigour, and many old colonists, of both
races, have assured me that they have known nothing similar to
it in their time. Of all the disasters resulting from that act of
"fraud, force, and folly," the Transvaal annexation, the greatest,
probably, is the stirring up of old race hatred among the white
colonists, whose heartily united strength would be by no means
too great for the task which devolves upon the white man in
Africa.

Throughout South Africa (to a great extent, even in the Dutch
States) the population of the towns and large villages is mainly
English, the banks are sustained by English capital, the stores
and hotels are owned and managed by Englishmen. On the
other hand, the English farmer is comparatively rare, and is only
found in a few districts, while Dutchmen are spread all over the
country from Table Mountain to the Limpopo, chiefly as owners of
flocks and herds, and many thrifty Germans make a comfortable
living by cultivating small farms. Many of the Englishmen who
come out to South Africa are in a hurry to make money and to
leave the country as soon as possible. They have not patience to
labour, like the German cultivator, for small and certain returns;
nor will they settle like the Dutch Boer, in the remote pastoral
wilderness, where few comforts and no luxuries can be enjoyed.
A store, or, better still, a canteen, brings in profit more rapidly
than a farm, and successful speculation in shares at the Diamond
Fields is best of all.

The religious census gives a fair idea as to the relative proportions of the different white nationalities in the Cape Colony, and
the overwhelming preponderance of the Dutch Reformed is very
striking, outnumbering all the other denominations together by
nearly three to one. Hitherto this great majority has never
exerted its constitutional power, and has allowed the minority to
govern and legislate almost unchallenged: a British ascendency,
less oppressive, but not less complete than in Ireland, has hitherto
existed in the Cape Colony. Happily, there is a simple constitutional remedy for this anomaly, and the Dutch need only take the
trouble of going to the poll, and of recording their votes, in order

to secure a Parliamentary majority, and the practical government of the colony, and in any case we shall not have an African Ireland on our hands. The Cape Colony is Dutch almost as completely as the province of Quebec is French, and with genuine home rule the former country may easily become as loyal and contented as the latter. The remedy of home rule, or the power of legislating and administering in all internal affairs according to the wants, feelings, and prejudices of the community, has never yet failed in reconciling any discontented dependency of the empire, and each successful experiment will render us bolder in the application of the remedy, until even the name of "Irish Home Rule" will lose its terrors for British statesmen.

In one matter South African politicians of all opinions are agreed—all alike deprecate Downing Street interference in their local affairs ; and, indeed, the record of Colonial Office intervention in Africa presents an almost unbroken series of well-meaning but disastrous blunders, even down to the latest phase of the Basuto difficulty. How can it be otherwise, when the Colonial Secretary and his immediate advisers have no personal knowledge of the countries and communities over which they seek to exercise control? In this matter there is little to choose between Liberal and Conservative : both are alike desirous of acting for the best ; both are alike ignorant as to the special conditions with which they have to deal, and to both alike may be recommended, at least in South Africa, a policy of masterly inactivity.

Public-spirited men, desirous of serving their country in the Cape Legislature, must needs make heavy sacrifices as to emolu- ments and personal comforts, leaving professional practice, farms, and stock to take care of themselves for months together, while they travel many weary miles, over land and sea, to distant Capetown. Happily, public spirit is not wanting in South Africa, and many leading men of all professions and pursuits are found quite willing to make such sacrifices. In the Parliament of Cape Colony there are many thoughtful and prudent politicians, men who would do credit to any legislative assembly, and most of these know well that their constituents are determined to have no more native wars under present circumstances. The first want of Cape Colony is peace, and such is the present temper of the people that peace may be regarded as secure, except in the very improbable contingency of a genuine Native aggression. At the same time, it would help to promote peace if every red coat were withdrawn from the colony, leaving only a small garrison to occupy the naval station at Simon's Bay.

It is evident to all who have seen anything of South Africa that the " nigger " in that country has, on the whole, a very good time, and might well be an object of envy to many of his white brethren in Europe.   Unjust wars have undoubtedly been forced upon the African natives, and they have been deprived of much land upon flimsy pretexts, but cruelty and injustice have ceased when peace has been again established, and the natives have found the yoke imposed upon them to be easy and light.   In the Cape Colony a black man enjoys all the rights of citizenship on terms of perfect equality with the white man ; he possesses the Parliamentary franchise, if otherwise qualified, and is under no legal disability whatever on account of his colour.   Europeans, Malays, Hindoos, Hottentots, Fingos, Kafirs, all have a fair field and no favour, and prosper according to their industry and sobriety.   In no country is equality in the eye of the law, irrespective of race or colour, more thoroughly established ; but the social separation of races is as complete as their legal equality, and Afrikanders (whites born in Africa) are more exclusive than European immigrants.

Afrikanders generally are of Dutch origin.   For centuries this sturdy unpliable race has retained in exile its peculiar characteristics, ever ready to abandon home and country for the sake of freedom and independence.   Their motto has been, " Ubi libertas ibi patria."   A hard task is before the Boers in their vast frontier territory beyond the Vaal, surrounded on all sides by warlike native tribes, and their immediate future can hardly be peaceful ; but they are genuine frontier men, and perfectly adapted to their position.   Let us hope that *their* difficulties and *our* responsibilities will not be increased by officious officials, seeking to enforce the unknown rights involved in the mysterious phrase, " British Suzerainty."

SIR DAVID landed at Plymouth on April 11th, and went to Meredith for the few remaining days of the Easter vacation. His friends were disappointed to find that he had not derived so much benefit as they had hoped, from his visit to South Africa. For the first few weeks, and while he remained near the sea, he had written very cheerfully about himself, praising the climate, and apparently equal to a good deal of exertion. But the heat and discomfort of the inland journey, through the Free State to the Diamond diggings, were more than he was fit for, and before he returned to his friends at Port Elizabeth, he had lost all the good that he had previously gained.

Although he was manifestly not in a state to take up again his Parliamentary duties, he was determined to keep what he considered his promise to his constituents to persevere through this session. He continued regular in his attendance at the House, but avoided very late hours as much as possible. On the first night of his return to Parliament there was a debate on the subject of Cetewayo's visit to England, in which he took part, expressing his approval of the plan. He thought that the King's presence would arouse a feeling in this country in his favour, which would facilitate restoration to his kingdom.

In July he was once more moved to write to the *Daily News* on the subject of Zululand, by the publication of a letter from the Governor of Natal to Bishop Colenso, in which the Governor said that the intervention of the Bishop in the political affairs of Zululand added greatly to the difficulties of the situation. He wrote :—

" Further correspondence respecting the affairs of Zululand " has just been presented to Parliament, and I have read with indignation the rebuke addressed by the Governor to the Bishop of Natal. Sir Henry Bulwer seems to find the difficulties of his task enhanced because Bishop Colenso has taken steps compelling him to hear all sides of the great question on which he has to decide, viz. the future government of Zululand. There is a very powerful party in Zululand having something to say, which the Governor does not seem to care about hearing. Not having been listened to when they first asked for the restoration of their King, these Zulus have been guilty of " agitation," and they have appealed for assistance to Bishop Colenso, in whom they have confidence, and who understands them and their language. And here is the real offence committed by the Bishop. To acquire the confidence of native races, to understand their wishes and fearlessly to proclaim these when ignored by men in power, will always be offences in the eyes of certain officials ; but Bishop Colenso is not likely to be deterred from committing such offences even by the arrogant letter which he has recently received.

In the course of this session he felt himself constrained on more than one occasion to vote against the party which he generally so warmly supported. It was painful to him to assist in passing another Coercion Bill for Ireland, and he absented himself from the principal division, saying, " There are always plenty of men ready to vote away the lives and liberties of Irishmen." He even opposed some of the more stringent clauses in committee.

He could not bring himself to agree with the policy of intervention pursued by the Government, which resulted in the Egyptian War. It astonished and disappointed him to find that the admiration of the country for their great leader, blinded them to the inconsistency of the course Government was pursuing. Even his own constituents, whom he regarded as the embodiment of common sense, were, he found, inclined to prefer men to measures. He thus wrote to the *Scotsman*, on July 1st :—

It now seems as if we were on the very verge of war in order to impose a foreign rule upon an unwilling people in Égypt, and there is not a word of remonstrance from Parliament, or from the nation. The Turks are to be reinstated in Egypt by force, and burdens will be imposed upon British and Indian tax-payers in order that the uttermost farthing may be wrung from the Egyptian peasantry for the benefit of wealthy stock-jobbers and speculators in Western Europe. Of course we are told, as usual in such cases, that British interests are involved, and that British influence must be maintained. In particular the Suez Canal must be pro-tected. Now, I venture to think that British interests and influence will be most effectually promoted by identifying England in the minds of the Egyptians with a just and non-aggressive policy, and by permitting them to be governed by a man of their own selection. They do not wish for rulers from London, Paris, or Constantinople, and why should they be compelled to accept any such ? Above all, why must they submit to the Turks ? The Turk in Africa is scarcely more acceptable as a ruler than he is in Europe. As for the Canal, it is menaced by no danger except such as may arise from hostility to European aggression, and from a dread that the same Power which recently filched Cyprus may seize upon Egypt also. In Egypt, as in so many other countries, the present British Government received an evil inheritance from their predecessors, and the present Secretary of State for Foreign Affairs has shown neither courage nor decision in dealing with his inherited difficulties ; so that now we are drifting into war and isolation from other Powers. No Liberal can suppose that our Egyptian policy has been dictated by Mr. Gladstone, but the Prime Minister cannot be expected to direct the policy of every great department of State in every detail, otherwise we might have heard something of the doctrine that " Egypt is for the Egyptians," and not for the Jews.

A few days afterwards he said, in a letter to the Rev. James Dodds :—

> In writing to the *Scotsman* "liberavi animum meum," but I expected no sympathy in that quarter.   When asked, as I am sometimes, "What will the Scotch electors say to this or that proceeding?" I always answer, "The Scotch will accept whatever Mr. Gladstone proposes, or whatever is proposed in his name." Nine times out of ten they may be right in so doing, but even Mr. Gladstone is not infallible.   In the Egyptian business the Government are carrying out the Jingo policy, and they will be allowed to do this by the Liberals, who would have at once protested against a similar course had the Tories been in power.   In India, on the other hand, they have reversed that policy, and never in my day have Indian affairs looked so promising.   A strong, united, and friendly Egypt would be as desirable a creation as a ditto Afghanistan, but is that Lord Granville's idea? or has he any definite idea?   Is Arabi to have the fate of Shere Ali and Cetewayo?   It looks rather like it.

How conscious he was that the line he was taking was likely to risk his own popularity, is shown by another letter, written to Major Carmichael.

> House of Commons, July 17, 1882.
>
> With gratitude I receive your designation of myself as a "Knight of the Holy Ghost."   Heine's description of the Order is exactly what I should aspire to ; and it is the only order of knighthood worthy of acceptance, in my opinion.   I know well enough that, in spite of your trade, you are really Liberal and democratic at heart.   As for courage, very little is required when nothing valuable is risked.   My seat and position in Parliament have no value for me, and I am longing to get free from this place, and to do exactly as I like,—going to bed early, and spending summer in the country.

Feeling strongly that those who disapproved of the war were bound to declare themselves, he attended a public meeting held in London to protest against it.   By that time his state of health was such that he himself said afterwards, " I do not suppose that I shall ever speak at a public meeting again."

Some of the causes which led, in his opinion, to what may be considered the failure of the session as regards any satisfactory legislation, were noted in an unfinished article left among his papers. Being the last thing that he ever wrote, it has a special interest, and some extracts are therefore given, although it is, no doubt, a mere fragment of what he intended it to be.

Twice Mr. Gladstone has been placed in power by splendid majorities, at the general elections of 1868 and of 1880. After five sessions of arduous and successful labour, the Parliament of 1868 was dissolved, having almost without an exception redeemed every pledge, and performed every promise given by the Liberal Ministry; having consistently carried out a policy of peace, retrenchment, and reform ; having reduced taxation and, at the same time, having accumulated a magnificent surplus.

Nothing could be more promising and hopeful for ardent reformers than the appearance of the political horizon in this country when the present Government took office in the spring of 1880, but hitherto the career of the present Parliament, very different from that of its Liberal predecessor, has been marked with failure and disappointment. The results of its labours have been : Coercion Acts for Ireland, war in Egypt, and enhanced taxation.

Mr. Gladstone can do as he pleases—he has the British people at his back ; the masses not only find themselves possessed of political power, but also of a leader imbued with the true popular fibre, eager, earnest, and democratic. Opposed to him there is now no great name, no powerful personality. Since Disraeli passed away from the political arena only two names, those of Gladstone and Bright, have been universally known to the populace, and the Tories have had no name to shout as their rallying cry. Even those who strongly condemn the armed intervention in Egypt cannot withhold a tribute of admiration to the vigorous and prompt manner in which that intervention has been carried out. England has invaded Egypt in order to protect British interests and to restore the authority of the Khedive. But the maintenance of that authority implies the permanent occupation of Egypt with British troops, and many in this country will consider such an occupation to be inconsistent with British interests.

At the present moment the ruling political sentiment in society is a bitter personal hatred of Mr. Gladstone. The masses hear their chosen leader denounced in malignant language by members of the privileged classes, and they naturally think : " These men denounce Gladstone because he is on our side, because his sympathies are with the people, and against privilege." The result is that the Prime Minister can now do no wrong in the eyes of the multitude, and that the conduct of his enemies has made him dictator. Such a result is not altogether pleasing to many independent Liberals, who have been accustomed to think rather of measures than of men. The fact that we have now a " one man " Government is exemplified by the successive retirement from the Cabinet of several most prominent members, without any loss of power or popularity being thereby caused to the Ministry. The Thanes fly from him, it is true, but the same causes which produce the disaffection of the privileged, have rallied to him the mass of the nation. They love Mr. Gladstone, because they think that he is upon their side, as against the rich and powerful, and because they believe that he is always ready in their cause to "forbear his own advantage." The power of Garibaldi over the hearts of the Italian people was founded upon a similar belief.

It is possible, however, for a great man to have many attached personal friends and to be the idol of the multitude, and yet to fail in securing anything like personal devotion among his immediate subordinates and supporters. To be in continual proximity to the chief, without receiving the slightest indication that one is known to him, by name, or even by sight, must chill the ardour even of the most zealous follower :—

> " And if his name be George, I'll call him Peter ;
> For new-made honour doth forget men's names."

Even when there is not the faintest suspicion that the mistake is intentional, there is a mortification for the follower in the discovery that he has no personal identity in the memory of his great leader, a memory which is almost preternatural in its retentiveness and grasp. The most successful leaders of Parliamentary majorities have always cultivated a knowledge of their supporters, as to character, opinions, and prejudices. Such a knowledge Mr. Gladstone does not possess, and the lack of it weakens him not a little in his capacity of Parliamentary leader; but it is perhaps natural in a man of his earnest and conscientious temperament that he should despise what may seem petty and insincere methods of acquiring personal influence in Parliament.

The strength of the present Prime Minister in the House of Commons is by no means so great as it is out of doors, and constant remonstrances are addressed by Liberal constituencies to members for alleged failure in their duty to give the Government a cordial and uniform support. In this respect little distinction is made between half-hearted Liberals, who join the Conservatives upon critical occasions, and extreme Liberals, who endeavour to prevent ministers from leaning upon Tory support, and from pursuing what they regard as a Tory policy. All alike are apt to be reminded plainly enough that those who sent them to Parliament expect them to have confidence in their chief, and to sink their individual opinions.

A newly elected House of Commons is very different in character from the same House after it has existed for several sessions, and in the Liberal section the change produced by the mere lapse of time is far more rapid and more conspicuous than it is among Conservatives or Home Rulers. Indeed the influences, chiefly social, which in London perpetually tend to disintegrate the Liberal party, all tend to consolidate the Parliamentary Tories. As for the Home Rulers, they have, partly from choice, partly from necessity, held themselves completely aloof, and English society exercises over them no influence whatever. These social influences produce, of course, no effect upon the mass of Liberal electors out of doors, but they are very real, and upon most men their effect is nearly irresistible. A Radical member of Parliament is, for the time being, a privileged aristocrat, admitted by virtue of his position to social circles otherwise closed to him, and perpetually brought into contact with persons of extreme Conservative views. At the same time he is made to feel that his political opinions are vulgar, and hardly those of a gentleman, or of a man worthy to join a respectable club. In clubs professedly Liberal these influences are at work to a certain extent; Radicalism is there also at a discount, even if it is not regarded as a positive disqualification.

It is well that the difficult task of reforming the rules of Parliamentary procedure has fallen upon so powerful a Government as that of Mr. Gladstone. The changes actually proposed will hardly meet the urgency of the case, which involves the very existence of Parliamentary institutions. If the forms of debate are such as to enable a small minority to monopolize the time of the House, to protract discussion indefinitely by mere iteration, and to take division after division upon the dilatory motion for adjournment, thus preventing the House from voting upon the real question at issue, there is no practical meaning or effect in a Parliamentary majority. Of course the "clôture" is stigmatized by its opponents as calculated to stifle free debate, but many who have had considerable Parliamentary experience will be inclined to hope from its adoption something more like free debate than the endless flow of one-sided talk with which for several sessions we have been familiar.

The change which has taken place in the character and composition of the House of Commons, within the last few years, is perhaps greater than any resulting from an Act of Parliamentary reform. Until recent times the two great political parties, differing indeed widely in opinions and principles of policy, have been practically identical in education, in manners, and in social feeling. Rank, wealth, and social status were not unequally divided between the two sides of the House, and all members of Parliament were disposed to acknowledge the same standard of good breeding and gentlemanly conduct. To act in any way contrary to "the feeling of the House" involved a degree of courage, or temerity, such as few possessed, even in a good cause ; and the awe thus inspired did more to preserve order and amenity in debate than any rules of procedure, or even the authority of the chair.

Now all is changed, and it has become clearly apparent that it is impossible any longer to legislate, or to conduct public business in an orderly manner, under the antiquated rules of procedure, and the restricted powers hitherto exercised by the Speaker. The House, fettered by its own rules, has learnt its own helplessness, and submits sullenly to be talked at indefinitely by the dominant minority. The power of the majority has been paralysed, and individuals composing the majority have been silenced, because the forms of the House have favoured the action of an unscrupulous minority. Unless these forms are changed it is idle to talk about government by Parliamentary majorities; and if the Conservatives really expect to regain office at no very distant date, they must feel it to be their interest to aid the Government in an honest attempt to emancipate Parliament from the thraldom of the obstructionists.

It was not until the close of the session that he agreed to consult a doctor, and the verdict was so unfavourable as to leave no doubt that he must at once resign his seat in Parliament. The news of his resignation was received in the Haddington Boroughs with much regret. The feeling there entertained for him is thus described by one of his most trusted constituents :—

"Sir David Wedderburn struck one at the very first as a man of quiet and unpretending candour. Alike in his private conversation and public addresses, he gave the impression of calm straightforward sincerity in the expression of his opinions. He never attempted to garble any of his political convictions to serve a selfish end—neither withholding views which he guessed might be unacceptable to the electorate, nor exaggerating and colouring others in hope of fanning the enthusiasm of friends. His ideas with respect to legislative work had been carefully matured in his own mind; and when he came to ask the suffrages of the community, he simply told his audience, in frank and ungarnished terms, what he believed concerning the various questions that were trying the wits of the statesmen. He never courted popularity, either by word or act. In the spirit of a true gentleman, manly and honourable in all his bearings, he expected those who concurred with the general tenour of his views to rally around him on principle as their 'fit and proper' representative—without ado on their part or the need of self-interested attention on his. While kind and courteous to all with whom he came into contact, and singularly obliging to any he could conscien-

tiously serve, he never tried to sway the feelings of the
electors by flattery or fuss of any sort. He had travelled
too widely and thought too deeply to get into a gush or
flurry over the shifting movements and uncertain issues of
political life ; and he seemed contented to perform his
duties to his constituents in a cool and dignified manner—
leaving them to judge him purely by his quiet fidelity to
public engagements, by the fulfilment of his promises and
the consistency of his career as a Parliamentary representative. A man of this type is not so likely to excite
enthusiasm as to command respect and inspire confidence.
Although his representation of the Haddington Burghs
lasted but for a very few years, his political work and
views and victories will not be readily forgotten by those
who were proud to acknowledge him as, for the time being,
their Parliamentary representative."

It is difficult to say to what extent he was prepared for
the serious view of his case taken by the doctor ; but
certainly for a short time it had a depressing effect on him,
as he expressed it himself, " not so much on account of the
immediate danger, although there may be that too, but
the prospect of being an invalid and giving up one by one
the things that make life pleasant." At the same time, how
calmly he faced the prospect before him appears from a
letter to the Rev. J. Dodds, in which, with characteristic
simplicity he speaks of his retirement from Parliament.

House of Commons, August 3rd.

By this time you know that you are to have an election in
the Haddington Burghs, if not a general election. The doctor
whom I consulted a few days ago about a bad cough, at once
said that I must spend the winter abroad, and that I ought to
give up Parliament. I fear that the case is serious, and that my
active life is at an end, even if my actual life is prolonged. However, I must try what care and repose will do. I read with great
interest your letter about Keith, especially about old Scarlett.

Probably I may yet pay you a visit at Dunbar if I go to Scotland, and I see nothing at present to prevent it, as I am feeling pretty well, in spite of the doctor.   I shall retain my seat until the Arrears Bill is passed.

The announcement that he had resigned his seat in Parliament called forth expressions of sympathy and regret from so many friends in and out of the House, that he was quite touched by them, and said, " I had no idea that so many people cared about me."   As usual, when he came down to Meredith he began to brighten up under the influence of country air and quiet, and to discuss with some interest plans for the winter, as he had been ordered on no account to stay in England beyond September.   His scheme finally was to spend two months at Constantinople with his Danish friend Krieger, and then go on to Bombay to stay for the rest of the winter with his brother at Poona. But he determined first to go to Scotland for a fortnight, principally to visit his sister and General Hope, who were occupying Inveresk Lodge, his own house near Musselburgh.

After a week with them, he went for a couple of days to Dunbar, to stay with the Rev. James Dodds ; and on his return, wrote cheerfully to his youngest sister—the last letter she ever received from him.

Inveresk Lodge, September 7, 1882.

Just a line to say that I am prospering here, having returned from a couple of days' visit to the Dodds, at Dunbar.   The opinion there was that I was looking better than on the occasion of my last visit, but I took care to explain that any apparent improvement was due to my release from Parliamentary worries ! A still more conclusive evidence of this is the gain of several pounds' weight, which I discovered on weighing at the New Club, and which must have taken place in the last few weeks. We have had some nice drives to Arniston, Whitehill, Edmonstone, etc., and the Dodds took me to Dunglas, a charming place. We have only had one game of golf, but to-day we are to play again.   The weather is now perfect for harvest.   I believe you are

right, and that Poona, all things considered, would be my best
bargain for the winter; it would be so jolly being with Willie,
and, after all, it is my "native air." How many birds on the 1st?
Love to Edward and the Brats. I enclose stamps for Johnnie.

The particulars of his last illness, which came on a few
days afterwards, are given by his sister, Mrs. Hope, who
was with him the whole time.

"When he came to us for a farewell visit before going
abroad, there was a marked change in his appearance since
the spring. Still his calm and cheerful manner, and the
pleasure he took in seeing old friends, in a quiet game
at golf, and especially in long country drives, somewhat
reassured us. He selected each day's drive to see places
and views in the neighbourhood that he remembered when
riding on 'Sunbeam '—the last was by Duddingstone and
Wardie. On Saturday, the 9th of September, he played
golf—' Almost in my old form ;' staying out too long, we
thought, but he said, ' It did me good.' On Sunday he
wrote letters, and several pages of an article for the *Fortnightly*, intending to go out in the afternoon, but as rain
came on he remained at home, conversing more brilliantly
than usual. At nine in the evening, a slight but strange
cough startled us. He sprang up and said, 'I did not
think it would have come so soon—it is like a dream,' and
instantly the life-blood welled out, and he became unconscious for a time.

"There was no return of hemorrhage, and when Dr.
Balfour, from Edinburgh, saw him next day, he considered
him convalescent, at least for a time. When his youngest
sister arrived on Tuesday morning, she was relieved to find
him apparently going on well, reading to himself, and
taking an interest in everything. On Thursday, however,
the disease suddenly spread to the good lung, and the
failing strength and terribly rapid pulse showed that the
brilliant life was fast ebbing away. He was the first to

realize that there was no hope of recovery, and expressed thankfulness that his mother had been spared this trial, and that the attack had come upon him in the old house, and surrounded by those he cared for most. 'The old traveller has come home for the end,' was his remark; 'this might have been in the centre of Africa.'

"The chief thought in his mind was to spare the feelings of the watchers by his side, assuring them that he was free from pain, and enjoying their presence. Love for each member of the family was shown in many ways; one of his kind thoughts was for his little nephews and niece, and he dictated a letter to his brother, asking him to increase some legacies he had left them. He looked back calmly and without any regret, alluding to his past life as having been a very happy one, that he would gladly live over again. Many little things that he wished to have done were thought of, and he arranged for his funeral to be as simple as possible. His mind remained clear and acute, and his memory as strong as ever; he seemed surprised himself that there was no failure of his mental power, saying, 'I could give you my opinion of Arabi Bey now.' When tired of talking he would ask to be read to; indeed, we read aloud to him almost constantly.

"On Sunday morning he was very faint, and said, 'I shall not see Edward [his brother-in-law]. Tell him I waited for him as long as I could;' but when, soon after, his brother came, he revived, and in answer to his sorrowful greeting, said, 'It is not so bad as it looks.' The day and night passed without much change, and he continued listening and speaking a little, till near midday on Monday, when he looked up, saying, 'It is a beautiful day. What o'clock?' 'A quarter to twelve.' 'Ah, twelve o'clock, Monday, 18th September.' And a few moments after, his breathing suddenly changed, and his pure and noble spirit passed away without a sigh."

The funeral, which was quite private, took place at the Inveresk churchyard, so near the house that all were able to walk, as he had wished. He was laid in the family burying-ground, where Sir David and Lady Wedderburn, his uncle and aunt, and other members of the family are buried.

Among the many notices which appeared in the papers at the time, the following was written by a friend who had known him well for many years, both in Parliament and in his home life :—

" Sir David Wedderburn was a man of large capacity, varied attainment, and liberal culture. To the usual accomplishments of English university education, he added a familiar acquaintance with the languages and literature of modern Europe ; and endowed with a naturally inquiring mind, great love of travel, and unusual aptitude in the mastery of any subject, however new to him, he possessed a large fund of interesting information, with the gift of communicating with facility what it had cost him no great effort to acquire. He was therefore an instructive as he was also a most genial and attractive companion.

" In politics he belonged to the advanced section of the Liberal party, to what may be called the Philosophical School of Liberalism. He was distinguished by a natural tendency to regard political questions from the point of view of abstract principles, and had great difficulty in subordinating principles to the claims of expediency in the necessities of compromise. He was therefore more of the Politician (in the English and not the American sense) than the Statesman ; and never could have reconciled the restraints of official life with the irrepressible utterance of any strong conviction with which his mind was charged. He was thus wanting alike in aptitude as in ambition for office, and his resolution to accept no official responsibility was well known to his more intimate friends. Nor could it ever be to them a matter of surprise that, with a strong feeling of loyalty to the party with which he was in general sympathy, he was nevertheless often incapable of following its lead.   The apparent eccentricity of such men may well be pardoned ; for if the current of political action must sometimes diverge from the line of principle along which its course should run, it is to be desired that the line itself should, *by some one*, be clearly traced, that the angle of divergence, however necessary, may not fail to be observed.

" For Parliament itself, as an institution, he had the greatest reverence, believing it to be the most perfect of governing machines ; but in the languor and weariness of declining strength he was somewhat despondent of its future, and the state of demoralization into which it had fallen in the last session, and the unbridled spirit of faction which was fast sapping the foundations of its moral force, aroused his most righteous indignation and contempt.

" In private life his habits were simple and his manner somewhat reserved ; but in his intercourse with friends he displayed the most genial nature, and a disposition which attracted towards him the confidence of all classes and conditions, covering the whole wide interval between infancy and age."

No tribute to his memory was more touching than that which came from India.   The gratitude felt by the natives for the interest he had taken in the affairs of that country, was shown by the notices in the Native papers, and by the many letters of sympathy which poured in on his brother. A few sentences are quoted from two of these letters.

" We have received with deepest sorrow and regret the sad intelligence of the untimely death of your distinguished brother, and India's disinterested friend and well-wisher.   His powerful advocacy of Indian interests, both in and out of Parliament, has made his name known in India as one of those few English statesmen who take genuine interest in this land and its people. We are, therefore, certain that the whole of India bewails with us the sudden and premature loss of one who exerted his great powers to secure for us a hearing from the English nation. The great attention that he gave to all Indian questions can never be forgotten by a grateful people ; and the whole country will bless, for ever, the memory of one who per- haps risked his own popularity among his countrymen by pleading the cause of the dumb millions of a country about which so little is yet known in England.

"(Signed) ABBAJEE NANAJEE."

(And others.)

"I am quite at a loss to express, myself, in adequate terms our deep sympathy for the great loss you have sustained in the death of a brother who has been always so dear to you. In your present bereavement it must be some consolation to know and to feel that your loss is shared in throughout the length and breadth of India ; for we believe that in him we have lost a most sincere friend and a well- wisher, who had made India's cause his own, and who was competent to do this self-imposed task with an ability and strength of character as but a few could command. With these few expressions of sympathy for the loss of one who was as dear to us as he was to you,

"I am yours very sincerely,

"ATMARAM PANDURANG."

These expressions of regret and admiration fitly close the record of a life begun in India, and in many ways so closely connected with that country, which he was fond of calling his " native land."

INDEX.

THE END.

PRINTED BY WILLIAM CLOWES AND SONS, LIMITED, LONDON AND BECCLES.

A LIST OF

KEGAN PAUL, TRENCH, & CO.'S

PUBLICATIONS.

.

10.83

1 Paternoster Square,
London.

A LIST OF

KEGAN PAUL, TRENCH, & CO.'S PUBLICATIONS.

ADAMSON (H. T.) B.D.—THE TRUTH AS IT IS IN JESUS. Crown 8vo. cloth, price 8s. 6d.

THE THREE SEVENS. Crown 8vo. cloth, price 5s. 6d.

THE MILLENNIUM ; OR, THE MYSTERY OF GOD FINISHED. Crown 8vo. cloth, price 6s.

A. K. H. B.—FROM A QUIET PLACE. A New Volume of Sermons. Crown 8vo. cloth, price 5s.

ALLEN (Rev. R.) M.A.—ABRAHAM ; HIS LIFE, TIMES, AND TRAVELS, 3,800 years ago. With Map. Second Edition. Post 8vo. price 6s.

ALLIES (T. W.) M.A.—PER CRUCEM AD LUCEM. The Result of a Life. 2 vols. Demy 8vo. cloth, price 25s.

A LIFE'S DECISION. Crown 8vo. cloth, price 7s. 6d.

AMOS (Prof. Sheldon)—THE HISTORY AND PRINCIPLES OF THE CIVIL LAW OF ROME. An aid to the study of Scientific and Comparative Jurisprudence. Demy 8vo. cloth, price 16s.

ANDERDON (Rev. W. H.)—FASTI APOSTOLICI. A Chronology of the Years between the Ascension of Our Lord and the Martyrdom of SS. Peter and Paul. Second Edition. Crown 8vo. cloth.

EVENINGS WITH THE SAINTS. Crown 8vo. cloth, price 5s.

ARMSTRONG (Richard A.) B.A. — LATTER-DAY TEACHERS. Six Lectures. Small crown 8vo. cloth, price 2s. 6d.

AUBERTIN (J. J.)—A FLIGHT TO MEXICO. With 7 full-page Illustrations and a Railway Map of Mexico. Crown 8vo. cloth, price 7s. 6d.

BADGER (George Percy) D.C.L.—AN ENGLISH-ARABIC LEXICON. In which the equivalents for English Words and Idiomatic Sentences are rendered into literary and colloquial Arabic. Royal 4to. cloth, price £9. 9s.

BAGEHOT (Walter)—THE ENGLISH CONSTITUTION. Third Edition, Crown 8vo. price 7s. 6d.

LOMBARD STREET. A Description of the Money Market. Eighth Edition. Crown 8vo. price 7s. 6d.

SOME ARTICLES ON THE DEPRECIATION OF SILVER, AND TOPICS CONNECTED WITH IT. Demy 8vo. price 5s.

BAGENAL (Philip H.)—THE AMERICAN-IRISH AND THEIR INFLUENCE ON IRISH POLITICS. Crown 8vo. cloth, price 5s.

BAGOT (Alan) C.E.—ACCIDENTS IN MINES : Their Causes and Prevention. Crown 8vo. price 6s.

THE PRINCIPLES OF COLLIERY VENTILATION. Second Edition, greatly enlarged, crown 8vo. cloth, price 5s.

BAKER (Sir Sherston, Bart.)—THE LAWS RELATING TO QUARANTINE. Crown 8vo. cloth, price 12s. 6d.

BALDWIN (Capt. J. H.)—THE LARGE AND SMALL GAME OF BENGAL AND THE NORTH-WESTERN PROVINCES OF INDIA. Small 4to. With eighteen Illustrations. New and Cheaper Edition. Price 10s. 6d.

BALLIN (Ada S. and F. L.)—A HEBREW GRAMMAR. With Exercises selected from the Bible. Crown 8vo. cloth, price 7s. 6d.

BARCLAY (Edgar) — MOUNTAIN LIFE IN ALGERIA. Crown 4to. With numerous Illustrations by Photogravure. Cloth, price 16s.

BARLOW (J. W.) M.A.—THE ULTIMATUM OF PESSIMISM. An Ethical Study. Demy 8vo. cloth, price 6s.

BARNES (William)—OUTLINES OF REDECRAFT (LOGIC). With English Wording. Crown 8vo. cloth, price 3s.

BAUR (Ferdinand) Dr. Ph., Professor in Maulbronn.—A PHILOLOGICAL INTRODUCTION TO GREEK AND LATIN FOR STUDENTS. Translated and adapted from the German by C. KEGAN PAUL, M.A., and the Rev. E. D. STONE, M.A. Third Edition. Crown 8vo. price 6s.

BELLARS (Rev. W.)—THE TESTIMONY OF CONSCIENCE TO THE TRUTH AND DIVINE ORIGIN OF THE CHRISTIAN REVELATION. Burney Prize Essay. Small crown 8vo. cloth, price 3s. 6d.

BELLINGHAM (Henry) M.P.—SOCIAL ASPECTS OF CATHOLICISM AND PROTESTANTISM IN THEIR CIVIL BEARING UPON NATIONS. Translated and adapted from the French of M. le Baron de Haulleville. With a Preface by his Eminence Cardinal Manning. Second and Cheaper Edition. Crown 8vo. price 3s. 6d.

BELLINGHAM (H. Belsches Graham)—UPS AND DOWNS OF SPANISH TRAVEL. Second Edition. Crown 8vo. cloth, price 5s.

BENN (Alfred W.)—THE GREEK PHILOSOPHERS. 2 vols. Demy 8vo. cloth, price 28s.

BENT (J. Theodore)—GENOA : How the Republic Rose and Fell. With 18 Illustrations. Demy 8vo. cloth, price 18s.

BLOOMFIELD (The Lady)—REMINISCENCES OF COURT AND DIPLO-MATIC LIFE. New and Cheaper Edition. With Frontispiece. Crown 8vo. cloth, 6s.

BLUNT (The Ven. Archdeacon)—THE DIVINE PATRIOT, AND OTHER SERMONS, Preached in Scarborough and in Cannes. New and Cheaper Edition. Crown 8vo. cloth, 4s. 6d.

BLUNT (Wilfrid S.)—THE FUTURE OF ISLAM. Crown 8vo. cloth, 6s.

BONWICK (J.) F.R.G.S.—PYRAMID FACTS AND FANCIES. Crown 8vo. price 5s.

BOUVERIE-PUSEY (S. E. B.)—PERMANENCE AND EVOLUTION. An Inquiry into the supposed Mutability of Animal Types. Crown 8vo. cloth, 5s.

BOWEN (H. C.) M.A.—STUDIES IN ENGLISH, for the use of Modern Schools. Third Edition. Small crown 8vo. price 1s. 6d.

ENGLISH GRAMMAR FOR BEGINNERS. Fcp. 8vo. cloth, price 1s.

BRADLEY (F. H.)—THE PRINCIPLES OF LOGIC. Demy 8vo. cloth, 16s.

A 2

BRIDGETT (*Rev. T. E.*)— HISTORY OF THE HOLY EUCHARIST IN GREAT BRITAIN. 2 vols. Demy 8vo. cloth, price 18s.

BRODRICK (*The Hon. G. C.*)—POLITICAL STUDIES. Demy 8vo. cloth, price 14s.

BROOKE (*Rev. S. A.*)—LIFE AND LETTERS OF THE LATE REV. F. W. ROBERTSON, M.A. Edited by.
  I. Uniform with Robertson's Sermons. 2 vols. With Steel Portrait. Price 7s. 6d.
  II. Library Edition. 8vo. With Portrait. Price 12s.
  III. A Popular Edition. In 1 vol. 8vo. price 6s.

  THE FIGHT OF FAITH. Sermons preached on various occasions. Fifth Edition. Crown 8vo. price 7s. 6d.

  THE SPIRIT OF THE CHRISTIAN LIFE. New and Cheaper Edition. Crown 8vo. cloth, price 5s.

  THEOLOGY IN THE ENGLISH POETS.—Cowper, Coleridge, Wordsworth, and Burns. Fifth and Cheaper Edition. Post 8vo. price 5s.

  CHRIST IN MODERN LIFE. Sixteenth and Cheaper Edition. Crown 8vo. price 5s.

  SERMONS. First Series. Thirteenth and Cheaper Edition. Crown 8vo. price 5s.

  SERMONS. Second Series. Sixth and Cheaper Edition. Crown 8vo. price 5s.

BROWN (*Rev. J. Baldwin*) B.A.—THE HIGHER LIFE: its Reality, Experience, and Destiny. Fifth Edition. Crown 8vo. price 5s.

  DOCTRINE OF ANNIHILATION IN THE LIGHT OF THE GOSPEL OF LOVE. Five Discourses. Fourth Edition. Crown 8vo. price 2s. 6d.

  THE CHRISTIAN POLICY OF LIFE. A Book for Young Men of Business. Third Edition. Crown 8vo. cloth, price 3s. 6d.

BROWN (*S. Borton*) B.A.—THE FIRE BAPTISM OF ALL FLESH; or, the Coming Spiritual Crisis of the Dispensation. Crown 8vo. cloth, price 6s.

BROWNBILL (*John*)—PRINCIPLES OF ENGLISH CANON LAW. Part I. General Introduction. Crown 8vo. cloth, price 6s.

BROWNE (*W. R.*)—THE INSPIRATION OF THE NEW TESTAMENT. With a Preface by the Rev. J. P. NORRIS, D.D. Fcp. 8vo. cloth, price 2s. 6d.

BURTON (*Mrs. Richard*)—THE INNER LIFE OF SYRIA, PALESTINE, AND THE HOLY LAND. Cheaper Edition in one volume. Large post 8vo. cloth, price 7s. 6d.

BUSBECQ (*Ogier Ghiselin de*)—HIS LIFE AND LETTERS. By CHARLES THORNTON FORSTER, M.A., and F. H. BLACKBURNE DANIELL, M.A. 2 vols. With Frontispieces. Demy 8vo. cloth, price 24s.

CARPENTER (*W. B.*) LL.D., M.D., F.R.S., &c.—THE PRINCIPLES OF MENTAL PHYSIOLOGY. With their Applications to the Training and Discipline of the Mind, and the Study of its Morbid Conditions. Illustrated. Sixth Edition. 8vo. price 12s.

CERVANTES—THE INGENIOUS KNIGHT DON QUIXOTE DE LA MANCHA. A New Translation from the Originals of 1605 and 1608. By A. J. DUFFIELD. With Notes. 3 vols. Demy 8vo. price 42s.

  JOURNEY TO PARNASSUS. Spanish Text, with Translation by JAMES Y. GIBSON. Crown 8vo. cloth, price 12s.

CHEYNE (Rev. T. K.)—THE PROPHECIES OF ISAIAH. Translated with Critical Notes and Dissertations. 2 vols. Second Edition. Demy 8vo. cloth, price 25s.

CLAIRAUT—ELEMENTS OF GEOMETRY. Translated by Dr. KAINES. With 145 Figures. Crown 8vo. cloth, price 4s. 6d.

CLAYDEN (P. W.)—ENGLAND UNDER LORD BEACONSFIELD. The Political History of the Last Six Years, from the end of 1873 to the beginning of 1880. Second Edition, with Index and continuation to March 1880. Demy 8vo. cloth, price 16s.

SAMUEL SHARPE—EGYPTOLOGIST AND TRANSLATOR OF THE BIBLE. Crown 8vo. cloth, price 6s.

CLIFFORD (Samuel)—WHAT THINK YE OF THE CHRIST? Crown 8vo. cloth, price 6s.

CLODD (Edward) F.R.A.S.—THE CHILDHOOD OF THE WORLD : a Simple Account of Man in Early Times. Seventh Edition. Crown 8vo. price 3s.
    A Special Edition for Schools. Price 1s.

THE CHILDHOOD OF RELIGIONS. Including a Simple Account of the Birth and Growth of Myths and Legends. Eighth Thousand. Crown 8vo. price 5s.
    A Special Edition for Schools. Price 1s. 6d.

JESUS OF NAZARETH. With a brief sketch of Jewish History to the Time of His Birth. Small crown 8vo. cloth, price 6s.

COGHLAN (J. Cole) D.D.—THE MODERN PHARISEE, AND OTHER SERMONS. Edited by the Very Rev. H. H. DICKINSON, D.D., Dean of Chapel Royal, Dublin. New and Cheaper Edition. Crown 8vo. cloth, 7s. 6d.

COLERIDGE (Sara)—MEMOIR AND LETTERS OF SARA COLERIDGE. Edited by her Daughter. With Index. Cheap Edition. With one Portrait. Price 7s. 6d.

COLLECTS EXEMPLIFIED (The)— Being Illustrations from the Old and New Testaments of the Collects for the Sundays after Trinity. By the Author of ' A Commentary on the Epistles and Gospels.' Edited by the Rev. JOSEPH JACKSON. Crown 8vo. cloth, price 5s.

CONNELL (A. K.)—DISCONTENT AND DANGER IN INDIA. Small crown 8vo. cloth, price 3s. 6d.

THE ECONOMIC REVOLUTION OF INDIA. Crown 8vo. cloth, price 5s.

CORY (William)—A GUIDE TO MODERN ENGLISH HISTORY. Part I.— MDCCCXV.-MDCCCXXX. Demy 8vo. cloth, price 9s. Part II.— MDCCCXXX.-MDCCCXXXV. Price 15s.

COTTERILL (H. B.)—AN INTRODUCTION TO THE STUDY OF POETRY. Crown 8vo. cloth, price 7s. 6d.

COX (Rev. Sir George W.) M.A., Bart.—A HISTORY OF GREECE FROM THE EARLIEST PERIOD TO THE END OF THE PERSIAN WAR. New Edition. 2 vols. Demy 8vo. price 36s.

THE MYTHOLOGY OF THE ARYAN NATIONS. New Edition. Demy 8vo. price 16s.

TALES OF ANCIENT GREECE. New Edition. Small crown 8vo. price 6s.

A MANUAL OF MYTHOLOGY IN THE FORM OF QUESTION AND ANSWER. New Edition. Fcp. 8vo. price 3s.

AN INTRODUCTION TO THE SCIENCE OF COMPARATIVE MYTHOLOGY AND FOLK-LORE. Second Edition. Crown 8vo. cloth, price 7s. 6d.

COX (Rev. Sir G. W.) M.A., Bart., and JONES (Eustace Hinton)—
POPULAR ROMANCES OF THE MIDDLE AGES. Second Edition, in 1 vol.
Crown 8vo. cloth, price 6s.

COX (Rev. Samuel)—SALVATOR MUNDI ; or, Is Christ the Saviour of all
Men ? Eighth Edition. Crown 8vo. price 5s.

THE GENESIS OF EVIL, AND OTHER SERMONS, mainly expository.
Third Edition. Crown 8vo. cloth, price 6s.

A COMMENTARY ON THE BOOK OF JOB. With a Translation. Demy
8vo. cloth, price 15s.

THE LARGER HOPE : a Sequel to 'SALVATOR MUNDI.' 16mo. cloth,
price 1s.

CRAVEN (Mrs.)—A YEAR'S MEDITATIONS. Crown 8vo. cloth, price 6s.

CRAWFURD (Oswald)—PORTUGAL, OLD AND NEW. With Illustrations
and Maps. New and Cheaper Edition. Crown 8vo. cloth, price 6s.

CROZIER (John Beattie) M.B.—THE RELIGION OF THE FUTURE.
Crown 8vo. cloth, price 6s.

CYCLOPÆDIA OF COMMON THINGS. Edited by the Rev. Sir GEORGE
W. COX, Bart., M.A. With 500 Illustrations. Third Edition. Large post
8vo. cloth, price 7s. 6d.

DAVIDSON (Thomas)—THE PARTHENON FRIEZE, and other Essays.
Crown 8vo. cloth, price 6s.

DAVIDSON (Rev. Samuel) D.D., LL.D.—CANON OF THE BIBLE : Its
Formation, History, and Fluctuations. Third and revised Edition. Small
crown 8vo. price 5s.

THE DOCTRINE OF LAST THINGS, contained in the New Testament,
compared with the Notions of the Jews and the Statements of Church Creeds.
Small crown 8vo. cloth, price 3s. 6d.

DAWSON (Geo.) M.A.—PRAYERS, WITH A DISCOURSE ON PRAYER.
Edited by his Wife. Eighth Edition. Crown 8vo. price 6s.

SERMONS ON DISPUTED POINTS AND SPECIAL OCCASIONS. Edited by
his Wife. Fourth Edition. Crown 8vo. price 6s.

SERMONS ON DAILY LIFE AND DUTY. Edited by his Wife. Fourth
Edition. Crown 8vo. price 6s.

THE AUTHENTIC GOSPEL. A New Volume of Sermons. Edited by
GEORGE ST. CLAIR. Third Edition. Crown 8vo. cloth, price 6s.

THREE BOOKS OF GOD. Nature, History, and Scripture. Sermons,
Edited by GEORGE ST. CLAIR. Crown 8vo. cloth, price 6s.

DE JONCOURT (Madame Marie)—WHOLESOME COOKERY. Crown
8vo. cloth, price 3s. 6d.

DE LONG (Lieut.-Com. G. W.)—THE VOYAGE OF THE 'JEANNETTE.' The
Ship and Ice Journals of. Edited by his Wife, EMMA DE LONG. With
Portraits, Maps, and many Illustrations on wood and stone. 2 vols. Demy 8vo.
cloth, price 36s.

DESPREZ (Philip S.) B.D.—DANIEL AND JOHN ; or, the Apocalypse of
the Old and that of the New Testament. Demy 8vo. cloth, price 12s.

DOWDEN (Edward) LL.D.—SHAKSPERE: a Critical Study of his Mind
and Art. Sixth Edition. Post 8vo. price 12s.

STUDIES IN LITERATURE, 1789-1877. Second Edition. Large post
8vo. price 6s.

DUFFIELD (A. J.)—DON QUIXOTE : HIS CRITICS AND COMMENTATORS. With a brief account of the minor works of MIGUEL DE CERVANTES SAAVEDRA, and a statement of the aim and end of the greatest of them all. A handy book for general readers. Crown 8vo. cloth, price 3*s. 6d.*

DU MONCEL (Count)—THE TELEPHONE, THE MICROPHONE, AND THE PHONOGRAPH. With 74 Illustrations. Second Edition. Small crown 8vo. cloth, price 5*s.*

EDGEWORTH (F. Y.)—MATHEMATICAL PSYCHICS. An Essay on the Application of Mathematics to Social Science. Demy 8vo. cloth, 7*s. 6d.*

EDUCATIONAL CODE OF THE PRUSSIAN NATION, IN ITS PRESENT FORM. In accordance with the Decisions of the Common Provincial Law, and with those of Recent Legislation. Crown 8vo. cloth, price 2*s. 6d.*

EDUCATION LIBRARY. Edited by PHILIP MAGNUS :—

> AN INTRODUCTION TO THE HISTORY OF EDUCATIONAL THEORIES. By OSCAR BROWNING, M.A. Second Edition. Cloth, price 3*s. 6d.*

> OLD GREEK EDUCATION. By the Rev. Prof. MAHAFFY, M.A. Cloth, price 3*s. 6d.*

> SCHOOL MANAGEMENT ; including a General View of the Work of Education, Organization, and Discipline. By JOSEPH LANDON. Second Edition. Crown 8vo. cloth, 6*s.*

ELSDALE (Henry)—STUDIES IN TENNYSON'S IDYLLS. Crown 8vo. price 5*s.*

ELYOT (Sir Thomas)—THE BOKE NAMED THE GOUERNOUR. Edited from the First Edition of 1531 by HENRY HERBERT STEPHEN CROFT, M.A., Barrister-at-Law. With Portraits of Sir Thomas and Lady Elyot, copied by permission of her Majesty from Holbein's Original Drawings at Windsor Castle. 2 vols. Fcp. 4to. cloth, price 50*s.*

ENOCH, THE PROPHET. The Book of. Archbishop Laurence's Translation. With an Introduction by the Author of the 'Evolution of Christianity.' Crown 8vo. cloth, price 5*s.*

ERANUS. A COLLECTION OF EXERCISES IN THE ALCAIC AND SAPPHIC METRES. Edited by F. W. CORNISH, Assistant Master at Eton. Crown 8vo. cloth, 2*s.*

EVANS (Mark)—THE STORY OF OUR FATHER'S LOVE, told to Children. Sixth and Cheaper Edition. With Four Illustrations. Fcp. 8vo. price 1*s. 6d.*

> A BOOK OF COMMON PRAYER AND WORSHIP FOR HOUSEHOLD USE, compiled exclusively from the Holy Scriptures. Second Edition. Fcp. 8vo. price 1*s.*

> THE GOSPEL OF HOME LIFE. Crown 8vo. cloth, price 4*s. 6d.*

> THE KING'S STORY-BOOK. In Three Parts. Fcp. 8vo. cloth, price 1*s. 6d.* each.

> *** Parts I. and II. with Eight Illustrations and Two Picture Maps, now ready.

'*FAN KWAE*' AT CANTON BEFORE TREATY DAYS, 1825–1844. By AN OLD RESIDENT. With Frontispieces. Crown 8vo. price 5*s.*

FLECKER (Rev. Eliezer)—SCRIPTURE ONOMATOLOGY. Being Critical Notes on the Septuagint and other versions. Crown 8vo. cloth, price 3*s. 6d.*

FLOREDICE (W. H.)—A MONTH AMONG THE MERE IRISH. Small crown 8vo. cloth, price 5*s.*

GARDINER (*Samuel R.*) *and J. BASS MULLINGER, M.A.—*Introduction to the Study of English History. Large crown 8vo. cloth, price 9*s*.

GARDNER (*Dorsey*) — Quatre Bras, Ligny, and Waterloo. A Narrative of the Campaign in Belgium, 1815. With Maps and Plans. Demy 8vo. cloth, 16*s*.

Genesis in Advance of Present Science. A Critical Investigation of Chapters I. to IX. By a Septuagenarian Beneficed Presbyter. Demy 8vo. cloth, price 10*s*. 6*d*.

GENNA (*E.*)—Irresponsible Philanthropists. Being some Chapters on the Employment of Gentlewomen. Small crown 8vo. cloth, price, 2*s*.6*d*.

GEORGE (*Henry*)—Progress and Poverty: an Inquiry into the Causes of Industrial Depressions, and of Increase of Want with Increase of Wealth. The Remedy. Second Edition. Post 8vo. cloth, price 7*s*. 6*d*.

   * Also a Cheap Edition, limp cloth, 1*s*. 6*d*.; paper covers, 1*s*.

GIBSON (*James Y.*)—Journey to Parnassus. Composed by Miguel de Cervantes Saavedra. Spanish Text, with Translation into English Tercets, Preface, and Illustrative Notes by. Crown 8vo. cloth, price 12*s*.

Glossary of Terms and Phrases. Edited by the Rev. H. Percy Smith and others. Medium 8vo. cloth, price 12*s*.

GLOVER (*F.*) *M.A.*—Exempla Latina. A First Construing Book, with Short Notes, Lexicon, and an Introduction to the Analysis of Sentences. Fcp. 8vo. cloth, price 2*s*.

GOLDSMID (*Sir Francis Henry*) *Bart., Q.C., M.P.*—Memoir of. Second Edition, revised, with Portrait. Crown 8vo. cloth, price 6*s*.

GOODENOUGH (*Commodore J. G.*)—Memoir of, with Extracts from his Letters and Journals. Edited by his Widow. With Steel Engraved Portrait. Square 8vo. cloth, price 5*s*.

   * Also a Library Edition with Maps, Woodcuts, and Steel Engraved Portrait. Square post 8vo. price 14*s*.

GOSSE (*Edmund W.*)—Studies in the Literature of Northern Europe. With a Frontispiece designed and etched by Alma Tadema. New and Cheaper Edition. Large post 8vo. cloth, price 6*s*.

   Seventeenth Century Studies. A Contribution to the History of English Poetry. Demy 8vo. cloth, price 10*s*. 6*d*.

GOULD (*Rev. S. Baring*) *M.A.*—Germany, Present and Past. New and Cheaper Edition. Large crown 8vo. cloth, price 7*s*. 6*d*.

GOWAN (*Major Walter E.*) — A. Ivanoff's Russian Grammar. (16th Edition). Translated, enlarged, and arranged for use of Students of the Russian Language. Demy 8vo. cloth, price 6*s*.

GOWER (*Lord Ronald*)—My Reminiscences. Second Edition. 2 vols. With Frontispieces. Demy 8vo. cloth, price 30*s*.

GRAHAM (*William*) *M.A.*—The Creed of Science, Religious, Moral, and Social. Demy 8vo. cloth, price 6*s*.

GRIFFITH (*Thomas*) *A.M.*—The Gospel of the Divine Life: a Study of the Fourth Evangelist. Demy 8vo. cloth, price 14*s*.

GRIMLEY (Rev. H. N.) M.A.—TREMADOC SERMONS, CHIEFLY ON THE SPIRITUAL BODY, THE UNSEEN WORLD, AND THE DIVINE HUMANITY. Third Edition. Crown 8vo. price 6s.

HAECKEL (Prof. Ernst)—THE HISTORY OF CREATION. Translation revised by Professor E. RAY LANKESTER, M.A., F.R.S. With Coloured Plates and Genealogical Trees of the various groups of both plants and animals. 2 vols. Third Edition. Post 8vo. cloth, price 32s.

THE HISTORY OF THE EVOLUTION OF MAN. With numerous Illustrations. 2 vols. Post 8vo. price 32s.

A VISIT TO CEYLON. Post 8vo. cloth, price 7s. 6d.

FREEDOM IN SCIENCE AND TEACHING. With a Prefatory Note by T. H. HUXLEY, F.R.S. Crown 8vo. cloth, price 5s.

HALF-CROWN SERIES :—

. A LOST LOVE. By ANNA C. OGLE (Ashford Owen).

SISTER DORA : a Biography. By MARGARET LONSDALE.

TRUE WORDS FOR BRAVE MEN : a Book for Soldiers and Sailors. By the late CHARLES KINGSLEY.

AN INLAND VOYAGE. By R. L. STEVENSON.

TRAVELS WITH A DONKEY. By R. L. STEVENSON.

NOTES OF TRAVEL : being Extracts from the Journals of Count VON MOLTKE.

ENGLISH SONNETS. Collected and Arranged by J. DENNIS.

LONDON LYRICS. By F. LOCKER.

HOME SONGS FOR QUIET HOURS. By the Rev. Canon R. H. BAYNES.

HAWEIS (Rev. H. R.) M.A.—CURRENT COIN. Materialism—The Devil — Crime — Drunkenness — Pauperism — Emotion — Recreation — The Sabbath. Fifth and Cheaper Edition. Crown 8vo. price 5s.

ARROWS IN THE AIR. Fifth and Cheaper Edition. Crown 8vo. cloth, price 5s.

SPEECH IN SEASON. Fifth and Cheaper Edition. Crown 8vo. price 5s.

THOUGHTS FOR THE TIMES. Thirteenth and Cheaper Edition. Crown 8vo. price 5s.

UNSECTARIAN FAMILY PRAYERS. New and Cheaper Edition. Fcp. 8vo. price 1s. 6d.

HAWKINS (Edwards Comerford) — SPIRIT AND FORM. Sermons preached in the Parish Church of Leatherhead. Crown 8vo. cloth, price 6s.

HAWTHORNE (Nathaniel)—WORKS. Complete in 12 vols. Large post 8vo. each vol. 7s. 6d.

VOL. I. TWICE-TOLD TALES.
II. MOSSES FROM AN OLD MANSE.
III. THE HOUSE OF THE SEVEN GABLES, and THE SNOW IMAGE.
IV. THE WONDER BOOK, TANGLEWOOD TALES, and GRANDFATHER'S CHAIR.
V. THE SCARLET LETTER, and THE BLITHEDALE ROMANCE.
VI. THE MARBLE FAUN. (Transformation.)
VII. & VIII. OUR OLD HOME, and ENGLISH NOTE-BOOKS.
IX. AMERICAN NOTE-BOOKS.
X. FRENCH AND ITALIAN NOTE-BOOKS.
XI. SEPTIMIUS FELTON, THE DOLLIVER ROMANCE, FANSHAWE, and, in an appendix, THE ANCESTRAL FOOTSTEP.
XII. TALES AND ESSAYS, AND OTHER PAPERS, WITH A BIOGRAPHICAL SKETCH OF HAWTHORNE.

HAYES (A. H.) Jun.—NEW COLORADO AND THE SANTA FÉ TRAIL. With Map and 60 Illustrations. Crown 8vo. cloth, price 9s.

HENNESSY (Sir John Pope)—RALEGH IN IRELAND, WITH HIS LETTERS ON IRISH AFFAIRS AND SOME CONTEMPORARY DOCUMENTS. Large crown 8vo. printed on hand-made paper, parchment, price 10s. 6d.

HENRY (Philip)—DIARIES AND LETTERS. Edited by MATTHEW HENRY LEE. Large crown 8vo. cloth, 7s. 6d.

HIDE (Albert)—THE AGE TO COME. Small crown 8vo. cloth, 2s. 6d.

HIME (Major H. W. L.) R.A.—WAGNERISM : a Protest. Crown 8vo. cloth, 2s. 6d.

HINTON (J.)—THE MYSTERY OF PAIN. New Edition. Fcp. 8vo. cloth limp, 1s.

LIFE AND LETTERS. Edited by ELLICE HOPKINS, with an Introduction by Sir W. W. GULL, Bart., and Portrait engraved on Steel by C. H. JEENS. Fourth Edition. Crown 8vo. price 8s. 6d.

HOLTHAM (E. G.)—EIGHT YEARS IN JAPAN, 1873–1881. Work, Travel, and Recreation. With 3 Maps. Large crown 8vo. cloth, price 9s.

HOOPER (Mary)—LITTLE DINNERS : HOW TO SERVE THEM WITH ELEGANCE AND ECONOMY. Seventeenth Edition. Crown 8vo. price 2s. 6d.

COOKERY FOR INVALIDS, PERSONS OF DELICATE DIGESTION, AND CHILDREN. Third Edition. Crown 8vo. price 2s. 6d.

EVERY-DAY MEALS. Being Economical and Wholesome Recipes for Breakfast, Luncheon, and Supper. Sixth Edition. Crown 8vo. cloth, price 2s. 6d.

HOPKINS (Ellice)—LIFE AND LETTERS OF JAMES HINTON, with an Introduction by Sir W. W. GULL, Bart., and Portrait engraved on Steel by C. H. JEENS. Fourth Edition. Crown 8vo. price 8s. 6d.

WORK AMONGST WORKING MEN. Fourth Edition. Crown 8vo. cloth, 3s. 6d.

HOSPITALIER (E.)—THE MODERN APPLICATIONS OF ELECTRICITY. Translated and Enlarged by JULIUS MAIER, Ph.D. 2 vols. With numerous Illustrations. Demy 8vo. cloth, 12s. 6d. each volume.

VOL. I.—Electric Generators, Electric Light.
II.—Telephone : Various Applications : Electrical Transmission of Energy.

HOUSEHOLD READINGS ON PROPHECY. By A LAYMAN. Small crown 8vo. cloth, price 3s. 6d.

HUGHES (Henry)—THE REDEMPTION OF THE WORLD. Crown 8vo. cloth, price 3s. 6d.

HUNTINGFORD (Rev. E.) D.C.L. — THE APOCALYPSE. With a Commentary and Introductory Essay. Demy 8vo. cloth, 9s.

HUTTON (Arthur) M.A.—THE ANGLICAN MINISTRY: its Nature and Value in relation to the Catholic Priesthood. With a Preface by his Eminence Cardinal Newman. Demy 8vo. cloth, price 14s.

HUTTON (Charles F.) — Unconscious Testimony; or, the Silent Witness of the Hebrew to the Truth of the Historical Scriptures. Crown 8vo. cloth, 2s. 6d.

IM THURN (Everard F.) — Among the Indians of British Guiana. Being Sketches, chiefly Anthropologic, from the Interior of British Guiana. With numerous Illustrations. Demy 8vo. cloth.

JENKINS (E.) and *RAYMOND (J.)* — The Architect's Legal Handbook. Third Edition, Revised. Crown 8vo. price 6s.

JENKINS (Rev. R. C.) M.A. — The Privilege of Peter and the Claims of the Roman Church confronted with the Scriptures, the Councils, and the Testimony of the Popes themselves. Fcp. 8vo. price 3s. 6d.

JERVIS (Rev. W. Henley) — The Gallican Church and the Revolution. A Sequel to the History of the Church of France, from the Concordat of Bologna to the Revolution. Demy 8vo. cloth, price 18s.

JOEL (L.) — A Consul's Manual and Shipowner's and Shipmaster's Practical Guide in their Transactions Abroad. With Definitions of Nautical, Mercantile, and Legal Terms; a Glossary of Mercantile Terms in English, French, German, Italian, and Spanish; Tables of the Money, Weights, and Measures of the Principal Commercial Nations and their Equivalents in British Standards; and Forms of Consular and Notarial Acts. Demy 8vo. cloth, price 12s.

JOHNSTONE (C. F.) M.A. — Historical Abstracts: being Outlines of the History of some of the less known States of Europe. Crown 8vo. cloth, price 7s. 6d.

JOLLY (William) F.R.S.E. — John Duncan, Scotch Weaver and Botanist. With Sketches of his Friends and Notices of his Times. With Portrait. Second Edition. Large crown 8vo. cloth, price 9s.

JONES (C. A.) — The Foreign Freaks of Five Friends. With 30 Illustrations. Crown 8vo. cloth, 6s.

JOYCE (P. W.) LL.D. &c. — Old Celtic Romances. Translated from the Gaelic. Crown 8vo. cloth, price 7s. 6d.

JOYNES (J. L.) — The Adventures of a Tourist in Ireland. Small crown 8vo. cloth, price 2s. 6d.

KAUFMANN (Rev. M.) B.A. — Socialism: its Nature, its Dangers, and its Remedies considered. Crown 8vo. price 7s. 6d.

Utopias; or, Schemes of Social Improvement, from Sir Thomas More to Karl Marx. Crown 8vo. cloth, price 5s.

KAY (Joseph) — Free Trade in Land. Edited by his Widow. With Preface by the Right Hon. John Bright, M.P. Sixth Edition. Crown 8vo. cloth, price 5s.

KEMPIS (Thomas à) — Of the Imitation of Christ. Parchment Library Edition, 6s.; or vellum, 7s. 6d. The Red Line Edition, fcp. 8vo. cloth, red edges, price 2s. 6d. The Cabinet Edition, small 8vo. cloth, red edges, price 1s. 6d. The Miniature Edition, 32mo. cloth, red edges, price 1s.

*** All the above Editions may be had in various extra bindings.

KENT (C.)—Corona Catholica ad Petri successoris Pedes Oblata. De Summi Pontificis Leonis XIII. Assumptione Epigramma. In Quinquaginta Linguis. Fcp. 4to. cloth, price 15s.

KETTLEWELL (Rev. S.)—Thomas à Kempis and the Brothers of Common Life. 2 vols. With Frontispieces. Demy 8vo. cloth, 30s.

KIDD (Joseph) M.D.—The Laws of Therapeutics ; or, the Science and Art of Medicine. Second Edition. Crown 8vo. price 6s.

KINGSFORD (Anna) M.D.—The Perfect Way in Diet. A Treatise advocating a Return to the Natural and Ancient Food of Race. Small crown 8vo. cloth, price 2s.

KINGSLEY (Charles) M.A.—Letters and Memories of his Life. Edited by his Wife. With Two Steel Engraved Portraits and Vignettes. Thirteenth Cabinet Edition, in 2 vols. Crown 8vo. cloth, price 12s.
*** Also a new and condensed edition in 1 vol. With Portrait. Crown 8vo. cloth, price 6s.

All Saints' Day, and other Sermons. Edited by the Rev. W. Harrison. Third Edition. Crown 8vo. price 7s. 6d.

True Words for Brave Men. A Book for Soldiers' and Sailors' Libraries. Tenth Edition. Crown 8vo. price 2s. 6d.

KNOX (Alexander A.)—The New Playground ; or, Wanderings in Algeria. New and Cheaper Edition. Large crown 8vo. cloth, price 6s.

LANDON (Joseph)—School Management ; including a General View of the Work of Education, Organisation, and Discipline. Second Edition. Crown 8vo. cloth, price 6s.

LAURIE (S. S.)—The Training of Teachers, and other Educational Papers. Crown 8vo. cloth, price 7s. 6d.

LEE (Rev. F. G.) D.C.L.—The Other World; or, Glimpses of the Supernatural. 2 vols. A New Edition. Crown 8vo. price 15s.

Letters from a Young Emigrant in Manitoba. Second Edition. Small crown 8vo. cloth, price 3s. 6d.

LEWIS (Edward Dillon)—A Draft Code of Criminal Law and Procedure. Demy 8vo. cloth, price 21s.

LILLIE (Arthur) M.R.A.S.—The Popular Life of Buddha. Containing an Answer to the Hibbert Lectures of 1881. With Illustrations. Crown 8vo. cloth.

LINDSAY (W. Lauder) M.D., F.R.S.E., &c.—Mind in the Lower Animals in Health and Disease. 2 vols. Demy 8vo. cloth, price 32s. Vol. I.—Mind in Health. Vol. II.—Mind in Disease.

LLOYD (Walter)—The Hope of the World : An Essay on Universal Redemption. Crown 8vo. cloth, 5s.

LONSDALE (Margaret)—Sister Dora : a Biography. With Portrait. Twenty-fifth Edition. Crown 8vo. cloth, price 2s. 6d.

LOWDER (Charles)—A Biography. By the Author of 'St. Teresa.' New and Cheaper Edition. Large crown 8vo. With Portrait. Cloth, price 3s. 6d.

LYTTON (Edward Bulwer, Lord)—Life, Letters, and Literary Remains. By his Son the Earl of Lytton. With Portraits, Illustrations, and Facsimiles. Demy 8vo. cloth. [Vols. I. and II. just ready.

MACHIAVELLI (*Niccolò*)—DISCOURSE ON THE FIRST DECADE OF TITUS LIVIUS. Translated from the Italian by NINIAN HILL THOMSON, M.A. Large crown 8vo. cloth, price 12s.

THE PRINCE. Translated from the Italian by N. H. T. Small crown 8vo. printed on hand-made paper, cloth, bevelled boards, 6s.

MACKENZIE (*Alexander*)—HOW INDIA IS GOVERNED. Being an Account of England's work in India. Small crown 8vo. cloth, 2s.

MACNAUGHT (*Rev. John*)—CŒNA DOMINI : An Essay on the Lord's Supper, its Primitive Institution, Apostolic Uses, and Subsequent History. Demy 8vo. price 14s.

MACWALTER (*Rev. G. S.*)—LIFE OF ANTONIO ROSMINI SERBATI (Founder of the Institute of Charity). 2 vols. Demy 8vo. cloth.
[Vol. I. now ready, price 12s.

MAGNUS (*Mrs.*)—ABOUT THE JEWS SINCE BIBLE TIMES. From the Babylonian Exile till the English Exodus. Small crown 8vo. cloth, price 6s.

MAIR (*R. S.*) *M.D., F.R.C.S.E.*—THE MEDICAL GUIDE FOR ANGLO-INDIANS. Being a Compendium of Advice to Europeans in India, relating to the Preservation and Regulation of Health. With a Supplement on the Management of Children in India. Second Edition. Crown 8vo. limp cloth, price 3s. 6d.

MALDEN (*Henry Elliot*)—VIENNA, 1683. The History and Consequences of the Defeat of the Turks before Vienna, September 12, 1683, by John Sobieski, King of Poland, and Charles Leopold, Duke of Lorraine. Crown 8vo. cloth, price 4s. 6d.

MANY VOICES.—A Volume of Extracts from the Religious Writers of Christendom, from the First to the Sixteenth Century. With Biographical Sketches. Crown 8vo. cloth extra, red edges, price 6s.

MARKHAM (*Capt. Albert Hastings*) *R.N.*—THE GREAT FROZEN SEA : a Personal Narrative of the Voyage of the *Alert* during the Arctic Expedition of 1875-6. With Six Full-page Illustrations, Two Maps, and Twenty-seven Woodcuts. Sixth and Cheaper Edition. Crown 8vo. cloth, price 6s.

A POLAR RECONNAISSANCE: being the Voyage of the *Isbjörn* to Novaya Zemlya in 1879. With 10 Illustrations. Demy 8vo. cloth, price 16s.

MARRIAGE AND MATERNITY; or, Scripture Wives and Mothers. Small crown 8vo. cloth, price 4s. 6d.

MARTINEAU (*Gertrude*)—OUTLINE LESSONS ON MORALS. Small crown 8vo. cloth, price 3s. 6d.

MAUDSLEY (*H.*) *M.D.*—BODY AND WILL. Being an Essay Concerning Will, in its Metaphysical, Physiological, and Pathological Aspects. 8vo. cloth, price 12s.

McGRATH (*Terence*)—PICTURES FROM IRELAND. New and Cheaper Edition. Crown 8vo. cloth, price 2s.

MEREDITH (*M. A.*) — THEOTOKOS, THE EXAMPLE FOR WOMAN. Dedicated, by permission, to Lady AGNES WOOD. Revised by the Venerable Archdeacon DENISON. 32mo. limp cloth, 1s. 6d.

MILLER (Edward)—THE HISTORY AND DOCTRINES OF IRVINGISM; or, the so-called Catholic and Apostolic Church. 2 vols. Large post 8vo. price 25s.

THE CHURCH IN RELATION TO THE STATE. Large crown 8vo. cloth, price 7s. 6d.

MINCHIN (J. G.)—BULGARIA SINCE THE WAR: Notes of a Tour in the Autumn of 1879. Small crown 8vo. cloth, price 3s. 6d.

MITFORD (Bertram)—THROUGH THE ZULU COUNTRY. Its Battlefields and its People. With five Illustrations. Demy 8vo. cloth, price 14s.

MIVART (St. George)—NATURE AND THOUGHT. An Introduction to a Natural Philosophy. Demy 8vo. cloth, price 10s. 6d.

MOCKLER (E.)—A GRAMMAR OF THE BALOOCHEE LANGUAGE, as it is spoken in Makran (Ancient Gedrosia), in the Persia-Arabic and Roman characters. Fcp. 8vo. price 5s.

MOLESWORTH (W. Nassau)—HISTORY OF THE CHURCH OF ENGLAND FROM 1660. Large crown 8vo. cloth, price 7s. 6d.

MORELL (J. R.)—EUCLID SIMPLIFIED IN METHOD AND LANGUAGE. Being a Manual of Geometry. Compiled from the most important French Works, approved by the University of Paris and the Minister of Public Instruction. Fcp. 8vo. price 2s. 6d.

MORSE (E. S.) Ph.D.—FIRST BOOK OF ZOOLOGY. With numerous Illustrations. New and Cheaper Edition. Crown 8vo. price 2s. 6d.

MURPHY (J. N.)—THE CHAIR OF PETER; or, the Papacy Considered in its Institution, Development, and Organization, and in the Benefits which for over Eighteen Centuries it has conferred on Mankind. Demy 8vo. cloth, 18s.

NELSON (J. H.) M.A.—A PROSPECTUS OF THE SCIENTIFIC STUDY OF THE HINDÛ LAW. Demy 8vo. cloth, price 9s.

NEWMAN (J. H.) D.D.—CHARACTERISTICS FROM THE WRITINGS OF. Being Selections from his various Works. Arranged with the Author's personal Approval. Sixth Edition. With Portrait. Crown 8vo. price 6s.
₊ A Portrait of Cardinal Newman, mounted for framing, can be had, price 2s. 6d.

NEWMAN (Francis William)—ESSAYS ON DIET. Small crown 8vo. cloth limp, price 2s.

NEW WERTHER. By LOKI. Small crown 8vo. cloth, price 2s. 6d.

NICHOLSON (Edward Byron)—THE GOSPEL ACCORDING TO THE HEBREWS. Its Fragments Translated and Annotated with a Critical Analysis of the External and Internal Evidence relating to it. Demy 8vo. cloth, price 9s. 6d.

A NEW COMMENTARY ON THE GOSPEL ACCORDING TO MATTHEW. Demy 8vo. cloth, price 12s.

NICOLS (Arthur) F.G.S., F.R.G.S.—CHAPTERS FROM THE PHYSICAL HISTORY OF THE EARTH: an Introduction to Geology and Palæontology. With numerous Illustrations. Crown 8vo. cloth, price 5s.

NOPS (Marianne)—CLASS LESSONS ON EUCLID. Part I. containing the First Two Books of the Elements. Crown 8vo. cloth, price 2s. 6d.

NOTES ON ST. PAUL'S EPISTLE TO THE GALATIANS. For Readers of the Authorised Version or the Original Greek. Demy 8vo. cloth, price 2s. 6d.

NUCES: EXERCISES ON THE SYNTAX OF THE PUBLIC SCHOOL LATIN PRIMER.
New Edition in Three Parts. Crown 8vo. each 1s.
。 The Three Parts can also be had bound together in cloth, price 3s.

OATES (Frank) F.R.G.S.—MATABELE LAND AND THE VICTORIA FALLS.
A Naturalist's Wanderings in the Interior of South Africa. Edited by C. G.
OATES, B.A. With numerous Illustrations and 4 Maps. Demy 8vo. cloth,
price 21s.

OGLE (W.) M.D., F.R.C.P.—ARISTOTLE ON THE PARTS OF ANIMALS.
Translated, with Introduction and Notes. Royal 8vo. cloth, 12s. 6d.

OKEN (Lorenz) Life of.—By ALEXANDER ECKER. With Explanatory
Notes, Selections from Oken's Correspondence, and Portrait of the Professor.
From the German by ALFRED TULK. Crown 8vo. cloth, price 6s.

O'MEARA (Kathleen)—FREDERIC OZANAM, Professor of the Sorbonne:
his Life and Work. Second Edition. Crown 8vo. cloth, price 7s. 6d.

HENRI PERREYVE AND HIS COUNSELS TO THE SICK. Small crown
8vo. cloth, price 5s.

OSBORNE (Rev. W. A.)—THE REVISED VERSION OF THE NEW TESTA-
MENT. A Critical Commentary, with Notes upon the Text. Crown 8vo.
cloth, price 5s.

OTTLEY (Henry Bickersteth)—THE GREAT DILEMMA: Christ His own
Witness or His own Accuser. Six Lectures. Second Edition. Crown 8vo.
cloth, price 3s. 6d.

OUR PUBLIC SCHOOLS—ETON, HARROW, WINCHESTER, RUGBY, WEST-
MINSTER, MARLBOROUGH, THE CHARTERHOUSE. Crown 8vo. cloth, price 6s.

OWEN (F. M.)—JOHN KEATS: a Study. Crown 8vo. cloth, price 6s.

OWEN (Rev. Robert) B.D.—SANCTORALE CATHOLICUM; or, Book of
Saints. With Notes, Critical, Exegetical, and Historical. Demy 8vo. cloth,
price 18s.

OXENHAM (Rev. F. Nutcombe)—WHAT IS THE TRUTH AS TO EVER-
LASTING PUNISHMENT? Part II. Being an Historical Enquiry into the
Witness and Weight of certain Anti-Origenist Councils. Crown 8vo. cloth,
2s. 6d.

OXONIENSIS—ROMANISM, PROTESTANTISM, ANGLICANISM. Being a
Layman's View of some Questions of the Day. Together with Remarks on
Dr. Littledale's 'Plain Reasons against Joining the Church of Rome.' Small
crown 8vo. cloth, 3s. 6d.

PALMER (the late William)—NOTES OF A VISIT TO RUSSIA IN 1840–41.
Selected and arranged by JOHN H. CARDINAL NEWMAN. With Portrait. Crown
8vo. cloth, 8s. 6d.

PARCHMENT LIBRARY. Choicely printed on hand-made paper, limp parchment antique, 6s.; vellum, 7s. 6d. each volume.

ENGLISH LYRICS.

THE SONNETS OF JOHN MILTON. Edited by MARK PATTISON.
With Portrait after Vertue.

POEMS BY ALFRED TENNYSON. 2 vols. With Miniature Frontispieces
by W. B. RICHMOND.

FRENCH LYRICS. Selected and Annotated by GEORGE SAINTSBURY.
With miniature Frontispiece, designed and etched by H. G. Glindoni.

PARCHMENT LIBRARY—continued.

THE FABLES OF MR. JOHN GAY. With Memoir by AUSTIN DOBSON, and an etched Portrait from an unfinished Oil-sketch by Sir Godfrey Kneller.

SELECT LETTERS OF PERCY BYSSHE SHELLEY. Edited, with an Introtion, by RICHARD GARNETT.

THE CHRISTIAN YEAR; Thoughts in Verse for the Sundays and Holy Days throughout the Year. With etched Portrait of the Rev. J. Keble, after the Drawing by G. Richmond, R.A.

SHAKSPERE'S WORKS. Complete in Twelve Volumes.

EIGHTEENTH CENTURY ESSAYS. Selected and Edited by AUSTIN DOBSON. With a Miniature Frontispiece by R. Caldecott.

Q. HORATI FLACCI OPERA. Edited by F. A. CORNISH, Assistant Master at Eton. With a Frontispiece after a design by L. ALMA TADEMA. Etched by LEOPOLD LOWENSTAM.

EDGAR ALLAN POE'S POEMS. With an Essay on his Poetry by ANDREW LANG, and a Frontispiece by Linley Sambourne.

SHAKSPERE'S SONNETS. Edited by EDWARD DOWDEN. With a Frontispiece etched by Leopold Lowenstam, after the Death Mask.

ENGLISH ODES. Selected by EDMUND W. GOSSE. With Frontispiece on India paper by Hamo Thornycroft, A.R.A.

OF THE IMITATION OF CHRIST. By THOMAS À KEMPIS. A revised Translation. With Frontispiece on India paper, from a Design by W. B. Richmond.

TENNYSON'S THE PRINCESS : a Medley. With a Miniature Frontispiece by H. M. Paget, and a Tailpiece in Outline by Gordon Browne.

POEMS : Selected from PERCY BYSSHE SHELLEY. Dedicated to Lady Shelley. With Preface by RICHARD GARNET and a Miniature Frontispiece.

TENNYSON'S 'IN MEMORIAM.' With a Miniature Portrait in *eau-forte* by Le Rat, after a Photograph by the late Mrs. Cameron.

*** The above Volumes may also be had in a variety of leather bindings.

PARSLOE (Joseph) — OUR RAILWAYS. Sketches, Historical and Descriptive. With Practical Information as to Fares and Rates, &c., and a Chapter on Railway Reform. Crown 8vo. price 6s.

PAUL (C. Kegan)—BIOGRAPHICAL SKETCHES. Printed on hand-made paper, bound in buckram. Second Edition. Crown 8vo. price 7s. 6d.

PAUL (Alexander)—SHORT PARLIAMENTS. A History of the National Demand for Frequent General Elections. Small crown 8vo. cloth, price 3s. 6d.

PEARSON (Rev. S.)—WEEK-DAY LIVING. A Book for Young Men and Women. Second Edition. Crown 8vo. cloth, 5s.

PENRICE (Maj. J.) B.A.—A DICTIONARY AND GLOSSARY OF THE KO-RAN. With Copious Grammatical References and Explanations of the Text. 4to. price 21s.

PESCHEL (Dr. Oscar)—THE RACES OF MAN AND THEIR GEOGRAPHICAL DISTRIBUTION. Large crown 8vo. price 9s.

PETERS (F. H.)—THE NICOMACHEAN ETHICS OF ARISTOTLE. Translated by. Crown 8vo. cloth, price 6s.

PHIPSON (E.)—THE ANIMAL LORE OF SHAKSPEARE'S TIME. Including Quadrupeds, Birds, Reptiles, Fish, and Insects. Large post 8vo. cloth, price 9s.

PIDGEON (D.)—AN ENGINEER'S HOLIDAY; or, Notes of a Round Trip from Long. 0° to 0°. New and Cheaper Edition. Large crown 8vo. cloth, price 7s. 6d.

PRICE (Prof. Bonamy)—CURRENCY AND BANKING. Crown 8vo. Price 6s.

CHAPTERS ON PRACTICAL POLITICAL ECONOMY. Being the Substance of Lectures delivered before the University of Oxford. New and Cheaper Edition. Large post 8vo. price 5s.

PULPIT COMMENTARY (THE). Old Testament Series. Edited by the Rev. J. S. EXELL and the Rev. Canon H. D. M. SPENCE.

GENESIS. By Rev. T. WHITELAW, M.A. With Homilies by the Very Rev. J. F. MONTGOMERY, D.D., Rev. Prof. R. A. REDFORD, M.A., LL.B., Rev. F. HASTINGS, Rev. W. ROBERTS, M.A.; an Introduction to the Study of the Old Testament by the Venerable Archdeacon FARRAR, D.D., F.R.S.; and Introductions to the Pentateuch by the Right Rev. H. COTTERILL, D.D., and Rev. T. WHITELAW, M.A. Seventh Edition. One vol. price 15s.

EXODUS. By the Rev. GEORGE RAWLINSON. With Homilies by Rev. J. ORR, Rev. D. YOUNG, Rev. C. A. GOODHART, Rev. J. URQUHART, and Rev. H. T. ROBJOHNS. Third Edition. Two vols. price 18s.

LEVITICUS. By the Rev. Prebendary MEYRICK, M.A. With Introductions by Rev. R. COLLINS, Rev. Professor A. CAVE, and Homilies by Rev. Prof. REDFORD, LL.B., Rev. J. A. MACDONALD, Rev. W. CLARKSON, Rev. S. R. ALDRIDGE, LL.B., and Rev. MCCHEYNE EDGAR. Fourth Edition. Price 15s.

NUMBERS. By the Rev R. WINTERBOTHAM, LL.B. With Homilies by the Rev. Professor W. BINNIE, D.D., Rev. E. S. PROUT, M.A., Rev. D. YOUNG, Rev. J. WAITE; and an Introduction by the Rev. THOMAS WHITELAW, M.A. Fourth Edition. Price 15s.

DEUTERONOMY. By Rev. W. L. ALEXANDER, D.D. With Homilies by Rev. D. DAVIES, M.A., Rev. C. CLEMANCE, D.D., Rev. J. ORR, B.D., and Rev. R. M. EDGAR, M.A. Third Edition. Price 15s.

JOSHUA. By Rev. J. J. LIAS, M.A. With Homilies by Rev. S. R. ALDRIDGE, LL.B., Rev. R. GLOVER, Rev. E. DE PRESSENSÉ, D.D., Rev. J. WAITE, B.A., Rev. F. W. ADENEY, M.A.; and an Introduction by the Rev. A. PLUMMER, M.A. Fifth Edition. Price 12s. 6d.

JUDGES AND RUTH. By the Bishop of Bath and Wells and Rev. J. MORRISON, D.D. With Homilies by Rev. A. F. MUIR, M.A., Rev. W. F. ADENEY, M.A., Rev. W. M. STATHAM, and Rev. Professor J. THOMSON, M.A. Fourth Edition. Price 10s. 6d.

1 SAMUEL. By the Very Rev. R. P. SMITH, D.D. With Homilies by Rev. DONALD FRASER, D.D., Rev. Prof. CHAPMAN, and Rev. B. DALE. Sixth Edition. Price 15s.

1 KINGS. By the Rev. JOSEPH HAMMOND, LL.B. With Homilies by the Rev. E DE PRESSENSÉ, D.D., Rev. J. WAITE, B.A., Rev. A. ROWLAND, LL.B., Rev. J. A. MACDONALD, and Rev. J. URQUHART. Fourth Edition. Price 15s.

B

PULPIT COMMENTARY (THE). Old Testament Series—continued.

EZRA, NEHEMIAH, AND ESTHER. By Rev. Canon G. RAWLINSON, M.A. With Homilies by Rev. Prof. J. R. THOMSON, M.A., Rev. Prof. R. A. REDFORD, LL.B., M.A., Rev. W. S. LEWIS, M.A., Rev. J. A. MACDONALD, Rev. A. MACKENNAL, B.A., Rev. W. CLARKSON, B.A., Rev. F. HASTINGS, Rev. W. DINWIDDIE, LL.B., Rev. Prof. ROWLANDS, B.A., Rev. G. WOOD, B.A., Rev. Prof. P. C. BARKER, LL.B., M.A., and Rev. J. S. EXELL. Sixth Edition. One vol. price 12s. 6d.

JEREMIAH. By the Rev. T. K. CHEYNE, M.A. With Homilies by the Rev. F. W. ADENEY, M.A., Rev. A. F. MUIR, M.A., Rev. S. CONWAY, B.A., Rev. J. WAITE, B.A., and Rev. D. YOUNG, B.A. Vol. I. Price 15s.

PULPIT COMMENTARY (THE). New Testament Series. Edited by the Rev. J. S. EXELL and the Rev. Canon H. D. M. SPENCE.

ST. MARK. By the Very Rev. E. BICKERSTETH, D.D., Dean of Lichfield. With Homilies by the Rev. Prof. THOMSON, M.A., Rev. Prof. GIVEN, M.A., Rev. Prof. JOHNSON, M.A., Rev. A. ROWLAND, LL.B., Rev. A. MUIR, M.A., and Rev. R. GREEN. Third Edition. 2 Vols. 21s.

PUSEY (Dr.)—SERMONS FOR THE CHURCH'S SEASONS FROM ADVENT TO TRINITY. Selected from the published Sermons of the late EDWARD BOUVERIE PUSEY, D.D. Crown 8vo. cloth, price 5s.

QUILTER (Harry)—THE ACADEMY, 1872–1882.

RADCLIFFE (Frank R. Y.)—THE NEW POLITICUS. Small crown 8vo. Cloth, price 2s. 6d.

REALITIES OF THE FUTURE LIFE. Small crown 8vo. cloth, price 1s. 6d.

RENDELL (J. M.)—CONCISE HANDBOOK OF THE ISLAND OF MADEIRA. With Plan of Funchal and Map of the Island. Fcp. 8vo. cloth, 1s. 6d.

REYNOLDS (Rev. J. W.)—THE SUPERNATURAL IN NATURE. A Verification by Free Use of Science. Third Edition, revised and enlarged. Demy 8vo. cloth, price 14s.

THE MYSTERY OF MIRACLES. Third and Enlarged Edition. Crown 8vo. cloth, price 6s.

RIBOT (Prof. Th.)—HEREDITY: a Psychological Study on its Phenomena, its Laws, its Causes, and its Consequences. Large crown 8vo. price 9s.

ROBERTSON (The late Rev. F. W.) M.A.—LIFE AND LETTERS OF. Edited by the Rev. Stopford Brooke, M.A.

    I. Two vols., uniform with the Sermons. With Steel Portrait. Crown 8vo. price 7s. 6d.

    II. Library Edition, in demy 8vo. with Portrait. Price 12s.

    III. A Popular Edition, in 1 vol. Crown 8vo. price 6s.

SERMONS. Four Series. Small crown 8vo. price 3s. 6d. each.

THE HUMAN RACE, and other Sermons. Preached at Cheltenham, Oxford, and Brighton. New and Cheaper Edition. Crown 8vo. cloth, price 3s. 6d.

NOTES ON GENESIS. New and Cheaper Edition. Crown 8vo. price 3s. 6d.

ROBERTSON—continued.

EXPOSITORY LECTURES ON ST. PAUL'S EPISTLES TO THE CORINTHIANS. A New Edition. Small crown 8vo. price 5*s.*

LECTURES AND ADDRESSES, with other Literary Remains. A New Edition. Crown 8vo. price 5*s.*

AN ANALYSIS OF MR. TENNYSON'S 'IN MEMORIAM.' (Dedicated by Permission to the Poet-Laureate.) Fcp. 8vo. price 2*s.*

THE EDUCATION OF THE HUMAN RACE. Translated from the German of Gotthold Ephraim Lessing. Fcp. 8vo. price 2*s. 6d.*

The above Works can also be had bound in half-morocco.

*** A Portrait of the late Rev. F. W. Robertson, mounted for framing, can be had, price 2*s. 6d.*

ROSMINI SERBATI (LIFE OF). By G. STUART MACWALTER. 2 vols. 8vo. [Vol. I. now ready, price 12*s.*

ROSMINI'S ORIGIN OF IDEAS. Translated from the Fifth Italian Edition of the Nuovo Saggio. *Sull' origine delle idee.* 3 vols. Demy 8vo. cloth. [Vols. I. and II. now ready, price 16*s.* each.

ROSMINI'S PHILOSOPHICAL SYSTEM. Translated, with a Sketch of the Author's Life, Bibliography, Introduction, and Notes, by THOMAS DAVIDSON. Demy 8vo. cloth, 16*s.*

RULE (Martin) M.A.—THE LIFE AND TIMES OF ST. ANSELM, ARCH-BISHOP OF CANTERBURY AND PRIMATE OF THE BRITAINS. 2 vols. Demy 8vo. cloth, 32*s.*

SALVATOR (Archduke Ludwig)—LEVKOSIA, THE CAPITAL OF CYPRUS. Crown 4to. cloth, price 10*s. 6d.*

SAMUEL (Sydney M.)—JEWISH LIFE IN THE EAST. Small crown 8vo. cloth, price 3*s. 6d.*

SAYCE (Rev. Archibald Henry)—INTRODUCTION TO THE SCIENCE OF LANGUAGE. 2 vols. Second Edition. Large post 8vo. cloth, price 25*s.*

SCIENTIFIC LAYMAN. The New Truth and the Old Faith : are they Incompatible ? Demy 8vo. cloth, price 10*s. 6d.*

SCOONES (W. Baptiste)—FOUR CENTURIES OF ENGLISH LETTERS : A Selection of 350 Letters by 150 Writers, from the Period of the Paston Letters to the Present Time. Third Edition. Large crown 8vo. cloth, price 6*s.*

SHILLITO (Rev. Joseph)—WOMANHOOD : its Duties, Temptations, and Privileges. A Book for Young Women. Third Edition. Crown 8vo. price 3*s. 6d.*

SHIPLEY (Rev. Orby) M.A.—PRINCIPLES OF THE FAITH IN RELATION TO SIN. Topics for Thought in Times of Retreat. Eleven Addresses delivered during a Retreat of Three Days to Persons living in the World. Demy 8vo. cloth, price 12*s.*

SISTER AUGUSTINE, Superior of the Sisters of Charity at the St. Johannis Hospital at Bonn. Authorised Translation by HANS THARAU, from the German 'Memorials of AMALIE VON LASAULX.' Cheap Edition. Large crown 8vo. cloth, price 4*s. 6d.*

SMITH (Edward) M.D., LL.B., F.R.S.—TUBERCULAR CONSUMPTION IN ITS EARLY AND REMEDIABLE STAGES. Second Edition. Crown 8vo. price 6*s.*

B 2

SPEDDING (*James*)—REVIEWS AND DISCUSSIONS, LITERARY, POLITICAL, AND HISTORICAL NOT RELATING TO BACON. Demy 8vo. cloth, price 12*s*. 6*d*.

EVENINGS WITH A REVIEWER; or, Bacon and Macaulay. With a Prefatory Notice by G. S. VENABLES, Q.C. 2 vols. Demy 8vo. cloth, price 18*s*.

STAPFER (*Paul*)—SHAKSPEARE AND CLASSICAL ANTIQUITY: Greek and Latin Antiquity as presented in Shakspeare's Plays. Translated by EMILY J. CAREY. Large post 8vo. cloth, price 12*s*.

STEVENSON (*Rev. W. F.*)—HYMNS FOR THE CHURCH AND HOME. Selected and Edited by the Rev. W. Fleming Stevenson.·

The most complete Hymn Book published.

The Hymn Book consists of Three Parts :—I. For Public Worship.— II. For Family and Private Worship.—III. For Children.

*** Published in various forms and prices, the latter ranging from 8*d*. to 6*s*. Lists and full particulars will be furnished on application to the Publishers.

STEVENSON (*Robert Louis*)—VIRGINIBUS PUERISQUE, and other Papers. Crown 8vo. cloth, price 6*s*.

STRAY PAPERS ON EDUCATION AND SCENES FROM SCHOOL LIFE. By B. H. Small crown 8vo. cloth, price 3*s*. 6*d*.

STRECKER-WISLICENUS—ORGANIC CHEMISTRY. Translated and Edited, with Extensive Additions, by W. R. HODGKINSON, Ph.D., and A. J. GREENAWAY, F.I.C. Demy 8vo. cloth, price 21*s*.

SULLY (*James*) *M.A.*—PESSIMISM: a History and a Criticism. Second Edition. Demy 8vo. price 14*s*.

SWEDENBORG (*Eman.*)—DE CULTU ET AMORE DEI, UBI AGITUR DE TELLURIS ORTU, PARADISO ET VIVARIO, TUM DE PRIMOGENITI SEU ADAMI NATIVITATE, INFANTIA, ET AMORE. Crown 8vo. cloth, price 6*s*.

SYME (*David*)—REPRESENTATIVE GOVERNMENT IN ENGLAND: its Faults and Failures. Second Edition. Large crown 8vo. cloth, 6*s*.

TAYLOR (*Rev. Isaac*)—THE ALPHABET. An Account of the Origin and Development of Letters. With numerous Tables and Facsimiles. 2 vols. Demy 8vo. cloth, price 36*s*.

THIRTY THOUSAND THOUGHTS. Edited by the Rev. Canon SPENCE, Rev. J. S. EXELL, Rev. CHARLES NEIL, and Rev. JACOB STEPHENSON. 6 vols. Super-royal 8vo. cloth.   [Vol. I. now ready, price 16*s*.

THOM (*John Hamilton*)—LAWS OF LIFE AFTER THE MIND OF CHRIST. Second Edition. Crown 8vo. cloth, price 7*s*. 6*d*.

THOMSON (*J. Turnbull*)—SOCIAL PROBLEMS; OR, AN INQUIRY INTO THE LAWS OF INFLUENCE. With Diagrams. Demy 8vo. cloth, price 10*s*. 6*d*.

TIDMAN (*Paul F.*)—GOLD AND SILVER MONEY. Part I.—A Plain Statement. Part II.—Objections Answered. Third Edition. Crown 8vo. cloth, 1*s*.

TIPPLE (*Rev. S. A.*)—SUNDAY MORNINGS AT NORWOOD. Prayers and Sermons. Crown 8vo. cloth, 6*s*.

TODHUNTER (*Dr. J.*)—A STUDY OF SHELLEY. Crown 8vo. cloth, price 7*s*.

TREMENHEERE (*H. Seymour*) *C.B.*—A MANUAL OF THE PRINCIPLES OF GOVERNMENT AS SET FORTH BY THE AUTHORITIES OF ANCIENT AND MODERN TIMES. New and enlarged Edition. Crown 8vo. cloth, 5*s*.

TUKE (Daniel Hack) M.D.—CHAPTERS IN THE HISTORY OF THE IN-SANE IN THE BRITISH ISLES. With Four Illustrations. Large crown 8vo. cloth, 12s.

TWINING (Louisa)—WORKHOUSE VISITING AND MANAGEMENT DURING TWENTY-FIVE YEARS. Small crown 8vo. cloth, price 3s. 6d.

TYLER (J.)—THE MYSTERY OF BEING; OR, WHAT DO WE KNOW? Small crown 8vo. cloth, price 3s. 6d.

UPTON (Major R. D.)—GLEANINGS FROM THE DESERT OF ARABIA. Large post 8vo. cloth, price 10s. 6d.

VAUGHAN (H. Halford)—NEW READINGS AND RENDERINGS OF SHAKESPEARE'S TRAGEDIES. 2 vols. Demy 8vo. cloth, price 25s.

VIATOR (Vacuus)—FLYING SOUTH. Recollections of France and its Littoral. Small crown 8vo. cloth, price 3s. 6d.

VILLARI (Professor)—NICCOLÒ MACHIAVELLI AND HIS TIMES. Translated by Linda Villari. 4 vols. Large crown 8vo. price 48s.

VILLIERS (The Right Hon. C. P.)—FREE TRADE SPEECHES OF. With Political Memoir. Edited by a Member of the Cobden Club. 2 vols. With Portrait. Demy 8vo. cloth, price 25s.

VOGT (Lieut.-Col. Hermann)—THE EGYPTIAN WAR OF 1882. A Translation. With Map and Plans. Large crown 8vo. cloth, price 6s.

VOLCKXSOM (E. W. V.)—CATECHISM OF ELEMENTARY MODERN CHEMISTRY. Small crown 8vo. cloth, 3s.

VYNER (Lady Mary)—EVERY DAY A PORTION. Adapted from the Bible and the Prayer Book, for the Private Devotions of those living in Widowhood. Collected and Edited by Lady Mary Vyner. Square crown 8vo. extra, price 5s.

WALDSTEIN (Charles) Ph.D.—THE BALANCE OF EMOTION AND INTELLECT; an Introductory Essay to the Study of Philosophy. Crown 8vo. cloth, price 6s.

WALLER (Rev. C. B.)—THE APOCALYPSE, reviewed under the Light of the Doctrine of the Unfolding Ages, and the Restitution of All Things. Demy 8vo. price 12s.

WALPOLE (Chas. George)—HISTORY OF IRELAND FROM THE EARLIEST TIMES TO THE UNION WITH GREAT BRITAIN. With 5 Maps and Appendices. Crown 8vo. cloth, 10s. 6d.

WALSHE (Walter Hayle) M.D.—DRAMATIC SINGING PHYSIOLOGICALLY ESTIMATED. Crown 8vo. cloth, price 3s. 6d.

WEDMORE (Frederick)—THE MASTERS OF GENRE PAINTING. With Sixteen Illustrations. Crown 8vo. cloth, price 7s. 6d.

WHEWELL (William) D.D.—HIS LIFE AND SELECTIONS FROM HIS CORRESPONDENCE. By Mrs. STAIR DOUGLAS. With a Portrait from a Painting by SAMUEL LAURENCE. Demy 8vo. cloth, price 21s.

WHITNEY (Prof. William Dwight)—ESSENTIALS OF ENGLISH GRAMMAR, for the Use of Schools. Crown 8vo. price 3s. 6d.

WILLIAMS (*Rowland*) D.D.—Psalms, Litanies, Counsels, and Collects for Devout Persons. Edited by his Widow. New and Popular Edition. Crown 8vo. price 3*s*. 6*d*.

Stray Thoughts Collected from the Writings of the late Rowland Williams, D.D. Edited by his Widow. Crown 8vo. cloth, price 3*s*. 6*d*.

WILLIS (*R.*) M.D.—William Harvey. A History of the Discovery of the Circulation of the Blood : with a Portrait of Harvey after Faithorne. Demy 8vo. cloth, price 14*s*.

WILSON (*Sir Erasmus*)—Egypt of the Past. With Chromo-lithograph and numerous Illustrations in the text. Second Edition, Revised. Crown 8vo. cloth, price 12*s*.

The Recent Archaic Discovery of Ancient Egyptian Mummies at Thebes. A Lecture. Crown 8vo. cloth, price 1*s*. 6*d*.

WILSON (*Lieut.-Col. C. T.*)—The Duke of Berwick, Marshal of France, 1702–1734. Demy 8vo. cloth, price 15*s*.

WOLTMANN (*Dr. Alfred*), *and* **WOERMANN** (*Dr. Karl*)—History of Painting. Edited by Sidney Colvin. Vol. I. Painting in Antiquity and the Middle Ages. With numerous Illustrations. Medium 8vo. cloth, price 28*s*. ; bevelled boards, gilt leaves, price 30*s*.

Word was Made Flesh. Short Family Readings on the Epistles for each Sunday of the Christian Year. Demy 8vo. cloth, price 10*s*. 6*d*.

WREN (*Sir Christopher*)—His Family and his Times. With Original Letters, and a Discourse on Architecture hitherto unpublished. By Lucy Phillimore. Demy 8vo. With Portrait. Price 14*s*.

YOUMANS (*Eliza A.*)—First Book of Botany. Designed to cultivate the Observing Powers of Children. With 300 Engravings. New and Cheaper Edition. Crown 8vo. price 2*s*. 6*d*.

YOUMANS (*Edward L.*) M.D.—A Class Book of Chemistry, on the Basis of the New System. With 200 Illustrations. Crown 8vo. price 5*s*.

THE INTERNATIONAL SCIENTIFIC SERIES.

I. FORMS OF WATER : a Familiar Exposition of the Origin and Phenomena of Glaciers. By J. Tyndall, LL.D., F.R.S. With 25 Illustrations. Eighth Edition. Crown 8vo. price 5s.

II. PHYSICS AND POLITICS; or, Thoughts on the Application of the Principles of 'Natural Selection' and 'Inheritance' to Political Society. By Walter Bagehot. Sixth Edition. Crown 8vo. price 4s.

III. FOODS. By Edward Smith, M.D., LL.B., F.R.S. With numerous Illustrations. Eighth Edition. Crown 8vo. price 5s.

IV. MIND AND BODY : the Theories of their Relation. By Alexander Bain, LL.D. With Four Illustrations. Seventh Edition. Crown 8vo. price 4s.

V. THE STUDY OF SOCIOLOGY. By Herbert Spencer. Eleventh Edition. Crown 8vo. price 5s.

VI. ON THE CONSERVATION OF ENERGY. By Balfour Stewart, M.A., LL.D., F.R.S. With 14 Illustrations. Sixth Edition. Crown 8vo. price 5s.

VII. ANIMAL LOCOMOTION ; or, Walking, Swimming, and Flying. By J. B. Pettigrew, M.D., F.R.S., &c. With 130 Illustrations. Third Edition. Crown 8vo. price 5s.

VIII. RESPONSIBILITY IN MENTAL DISEASE. By Henry Maudsley, M.D. Fourth Edition. Crown 8vo. price 5s.

IX. THE NEW CHEMISTRY. By Professor J. P. Cooke. With 31 Illustrations. Seventh Edition. Crown 8vo. price 5s.

X. THE SCIENCE OF LAW. By Professor Sheldon Amos. Fifth Edition. Crown 8vo. price 5s.

XI. ANIMAL MECHANISM: a Treatise on Terrestrial and Aërial Locomotion. By Professor E. J. Marey. With 117 Illustrations. Third Edition. Crown 8vo. price 5s.

XII. THE DOCTRINE OF DESCENT AND DARWINISM. By Professor Oscar Schmidt. With 26 Illustrations. Fifth Edition. Crown 8vo. price 5s.

XIII. THE HISTORY OF THE CONFLICT BETWEEN RELIGION AND SCIENCE. By J. W. Draper, M.D., LL.D. Seventeenth Edition. Crown 8vo. price 5s.

XIV. FUNGI: their Nature, Influences, Uses, &c. By M. C. Cooke, M.D., LL.D. Edited by the Rev. M. J. Berkeley, M.A., F.L.S. With numerous Illustrations. Third Edition. Crown 8vo. price 5s.

XV. THE CHEMICAL EFFECTS OF LIGHT AND PHOTOGRAPHY. By Dr. Hermann Vogel. Translation thoroughly revised. With 100 Illustrations. Fourth Edition. Crown 8vo. price 5s.

XVI. THE LIFE AND GROWTH OF LANGUAGE. By Professor William Dwight Whitney. Fourth Edition. Crown 8vo. price 5s.

XVII. MONEY AND THE MECHANISM OF EXCHANGE. By W. Stanley Jevons, M.A., F.R.S. Sixth Edition. Crown 8vo. price 5s.

XVIII. THE NATURE OF LIGHT. With a General Account of Physical Optics. By Dr. Eugene Lommel. With 188 Illustrations and a Table of Spectra in Chromo-lithography. Third Edit. Crown 8vo. price 5s.

XIX. ANIMAL PARASITES AND MESSMATES. By Monsieur Van Beneden. With 83 Illustrations. Third Edition. Crown 8vo. price 5s.

XX. FERMENTATION. By Professor Schützenberger. With 28 Illustrations. Third Edition. Crown 8vo. price 5s.

XXI. THE FIVE SENSES OF MAN. By Professor Bernstein. With 91 Illustrations. Fourth Edition. Crown 8vo. price 5s.

XXII. THE THEORY OF SOUND IN ITS RELATION TO MUSIC. By Professor Pietro Blaserna. With numerous Illustrations. Third Edition. Crown 8vo. price 5s.

XXIII. STUDIES IN SPECTRUM ANALYSIS. By J. Norman Lockyer, F.R.S. With six Photographic Illustrations of Spectra, and numerous Engravings on Wood. Crown 8vo. Third Edition. Price 6s. 6d.

XXIV. A HISTORY OF THE GROWTH OF THE STEAM ENGINE. By Professor R. H. Thurston. With numerous Illustrations. Third Edition. Crown 8vo. cloth, price 6s. 6d.

XXV. EDUCATION AS A SCIENCE. By Alexander Bain, LL.D. Fourth Edition. Crown 8vo. cloth, price 5s.

XXVI. THE HUMAN SPECIES. By Prof. A. De Quatrefages. Third Edition. Crown 8vo. cloth, price 5s.

XXVII. MODERN CHROMATICS. With Applications to Art and Industry. By Ogden N. Rood. With 130 original Illustrations. Second Edition. Crown 8vo. cloth, price 5s.

XXVIII. THE CRAYFISH: an Introduction to the Study of Zoology. By Professor T. H. Huxley. With 82 Illustrations. Third Edition. Crown 8vo. cloth, price 5s.

XXIX. THE BRAIN AS AN ORGAN OF MIND. By H. Charlton Bastian, M.D. With numerous Illustrations. Third Edition. Crown 8vo. cloth, price 5s.

XXX. THE ATOMIC THEORY. By Prof. Wurtz. Translated by G. Cleminshaw, F.C.S. Third Edition. Crown 8vo. cloth, price 5s.

XXXI. THE NATURAL CONDITIONS OF EXISTENCE AS THEY AFFECT ANIMAL LIFE. By Karl Semper. With 2 Maps and 106 Woodcuts. Third Edition. Crown 8vo. cloth, price 5s.

XXXII. GENERAL PHYSIOLOGY OF MUSCLES AND NERVES. By Prof. J. Rosenthal. Third Edition. With Illustrations. Crown 8vo. cloth, price 5s.

XXXIII. SIGHT: an Exposition of the Principles of Monocular and Binocular Vision. By Joseph Le Conte, LL.D. Second Edition. With 132 Illustrations. Crown 8vo. cloth, price 5s.

XXXIV. ILLUSIONS: a Psychological Study. By James Sully. Second Edition. Crown 8vo. cloth, price 5s.

XXXV. VOLCANOES: WHAT THEY ARE AND WHAT THEY TEACH. By Professor J. W. Judd, F.R.S. With 92 Illustrations on Wood. Second Edition. Crown 8vo. cloth, price 5s.

XXXVI. SUICIDE: an Essay in Comparative Moral Statistics. By Prof. E. Morselli. Second Edition. With Diagrams. Crown 8vo. cloth, price 5s.

XXXVII. THE BRAIN AND ITS FUNCTIONS. By J. Luys. Second Edition. With Illustrations. Crown 8vo. cloth, price 5s.

XXXVIII. MYTH AND SCIENCE: an Essay. By Tito Vignoli. Crown 8vo. cloth, price 5s.

XXXIX. THE SUN. By Professor Young. With Illustrations. Second Edition. Crown 8vo. cloth, price 5s.

XL. ANTS, BEES, AND WASPS: a Record of Observations on the Habits of the Social Hymenoptera. By Sir John Lubbock, Bart., M.P. With 5 Chromolithographic Illustrations. Sixth Edit. Crown 8vo. cloth, price 5s.

XLI. ANIMAL INTELLIGENCE. By G. J. Romanes, LL.D., F.R.S. Third Edition. Crown 8vo. cloth, price 5s.

XLII. THE CONCEPTS AND THEORIES OF MODERN PHYSICS. By J. B. Stallo. Second Edition. Crown 8vo. cloth, price 5s.

XLIII. DISEASES OF MEMORY: an Essay in the Positive Pyschology. By Prof. Th. Ribot. Second Edition. Crown 8vo. 5s.

XLIV. MAN BEFORE METALS. By N. Joly. Third Edition. Crown 8vo. cloth, price 5s.

XLV. THE SCIENCE OF POLITICS. By Prof. Sheldon Amos. Second Edit. Crown. 8vo. cloth, price 5s.

XLVI. ELEMENTARY METEOROLOGY. By Robert H. Scott. Second Edition. With numerous Illustrations. Crown 8vo. cloth, price 5s.

XLVII. THE ORGANS OF SPEECH AND THEIR APPLICATION IN THE FORMATION OF ARTICULATE SOUNDS. By Georg Hermann von Meyer. With 47 Woodcuts. Crown 8vo. cloth, price 5s.

XLVIII. FALLACIES: a View of Logic from the Practical Side. By Alfred Sidgwick. Crown 8vo. cloth.

MILITARY WORKS.

BARRINGTON (Capt. J. T.)—ENGLAND ON THE DEFENSIVE; or, the Problem of Invasion Critically Examined. Large crown 8vo. with Map, cloth, price 7*s.* 6*d.*

BRACKENBURY (Col. C. B.) R.A., C.B.—MILITARY HANDBOOKS FOR REGIMENTAL OFFICERS:

I. MILITARY SKETCHING AND RE-CONNAISSANCE. By Colonel F. J. Hutchison and Major H. G. Mac-Gregor. Fourth Edition. With 15 Plates. Small 8vo. cloth, price 6*s.*

II. THE ELEMENTS OF MODERN TACTICS PRACTICALLY APPLIED TO ENGLISH FORMATIONS. By Lieut.-Col. Wilkinson Shaw. Fourth Edit. With 25 Plates and Maps. Small crown 8vo. cloth, price 9*s.*

III. FIELD ARTILLERY: its Equip-ment, Organisation, and Tactics. By Major Sisson C. Pratt, R.A. With 12 Plates. Second Edition. Small crown 8vo. cloth, price 6*s.*

IV. THE ELEMENTS OF MILITARY ADMINISTRATION. First Part: Per-manent System of Administration. By Major J. W. Buxton. Small crown 8vo. cloth, price 7*s.* 6*d.*

V. MILITARY LAW: its Procedure and Practice. By Major Sisson C. Pratt, R.A. Small crown 8vo.

BROOKE (Major C. K.)—A SYSTEM OF FIELD TRAINING. Small crown 8vo. cloth limp, price 2*s.*

CLERY (C.) Lieut.-Col.—MINOR TAC-TICS. With 26 Maps and Plans. Sixth and cheaper Edition, revised. Crown 8vo. cloth, price 9*s.*

COLVILLE (Lieut.-Col. C. F.)—MILI-TARY TRIBUNALS. Sewed, price 2*s.* 6*d.*

HARRISON (Lieut.-Col. R.) — THE OFFICER'S MEMORANDUM BOOK FOR PEACE AND WAR. Third Edition. Oblong 32mo. roan, with pencil, price 3*s.* 6*d.*

NOTES ON CAVALRY TACTICS, ORGANI-SATION, &c. By a Cavalry Officer. With Diagrams. Demy 8vo. cloth, price 12*s.*

PARR (Capt. H. Hallam) C.M.G.—THE DRESS, HORSES, AND EQUIPMENT OF INFANTRY AND STAFF OFFICERS. Crown 8vo. cloth, price 1*s.*

SCHAW (Col. H.)—THE DEFENCE AND ATTACK OF POSITIONS AND LOCALI-TIES. Second Edition, revised and corrected. Crown 8vo. cloth, price 3*s.* 6*d.*

SHADWELL (Maj.-Gen.) C.B.—MOUN-TAIN WARFARE. Illustrated by the Campaign of 1799 in Switzerland. Being a Translation of the Swiss Narrative compiled from the Works of the Archduke Charles, Jomini, and others. Also of Notes by General H. Dufour on the Campaign of the Valtelline in 1635. With Appendix, Maps, and Introductory Remarks. Demy 8vo. price 16*s.*

STUBBS (Lieut.-Col. F. W.) — THE REGIMENT OF BENGAL ARTILLERY: the History of its Organisation, Equip-ment, and War Services. Compiled from Published Works, Official Re-cords, and various Private Sources. With numerous Maps and Illustrations. 2 vols. Demy 8vo. price 32*s.*

POETRY.

ADAM OF ST. VICTOR—THE LITUR-GICAL POETRY OF ADAM OF ST. VICTOR. From the text of Gautier. With Translations into English in the Original Metres, and Short Explana-tory Notes. By Digby S. Wrangham, M.A. 3 vols. Crown 8vo. printed on hand-made paper, boards, price 21*s.*

AUCHMUTY (A. C.)—POEMS OF ENG-LISH HEROISM: From Brunanburgh to Lucknow; from Athelstan to Albert. Small crown 8vo. cloth, price 1*s.* 6*d.*

AVIA—THE ODYSSEY OF HOMER. Done into English Verse by. Fcp. 4to. cloth, price 15*s.*

BANKS (*Mrs. G. L.*)—RIPPLES AND BREAKERS : Poems. Square 8vo. cloth, price 5*s.*

BARNES (*William*)—POEMS OF RURAL LIFE, IN THE DORSET DIALECT. New Edition, complete in one vol. Crown 8vo. cloth, price 8*s. 6d.*

BAYNES (*Rev. Canon H. R.*)—HOME SONGS FOR QUIET HOURS. Fourth and cheaper Edition. Fcp. 8vo. cloth, price 2*s. 6d.*

*** This may also be had handsomely bound in morocco with gilt edges.

BENNETT (*C. F.*)—LIFE THOUGHTS. A New Volume of Poems. With Frontispiece. Small crown 8vo. cloth.

BEVINGTON (*L. S.*)—KEY NOTES. Small crown 8vo. cloth, price 5*s.*

BILLSON (*C. J.*)—THE ACHARNIANS OF ARISTOPHANES. Crown 8vo. cloth, price 3*s. 6d.*

BOWEN (*H. C.*) *M.A.*—SIMPLE ENGLISH POEMS. English Literature for Junior Classes. In Four Parts. Parts I. II. and III. price 6*d.* each, and Part IV. price 1*s.*

BRYANT (*W. C.*) — POEMS. Red-line Edition. With 24 Illustrations and Portrait of the Author. Crown 8vo. cloth extra, price 7*s. 6d.*
A Cheap Edition, with Frontispiece. Small crown 8vo. price 3*s. 6d.*

BYRNNE (*E. Fairfax*)—MILICENT : a Poem. Small crown 8vo. cloth, price 6*s.*

CALDERON'S DRAMAS : the Wonder-working Magician—Life is a Dream —the Purgatory of St. Patrick. Translated by Denis Florence MacCarthy. Post 8vo. price 10*s.*

CASTILIAN BROTHERS (*The*)—CHATEAU-BRIANT, WALDEMAR, THREE TRAGEDIES, AND THE ROSE OF SICILY. A Drama. By the Author of 'Ginevra,' &c. Crown 8vo. cloth, price 6*s.*

CHRONICLES OF CHRISTOPHER COLUMBUS : a Poem in Twelve Cantos. By M. D. C. Crown 8vo. cloth, price 7*s. 6d.*

CLARKE (*Mary Cowden*)—HONEY FROM THE WEED. Verses. Crown 8vo. cloth, 7*s.*

COLOMB (*Colonel*) — THE CARDINAL ARCHBISHOP : a Spanish Legend. In 29 Cancions. Small crown 8vo. cloth, price 5*s.*

CONWAY (*Hugh*)—A LIFE'S IDYLLS. Small crown 8vo. cloth, price 3*s. 6d.*

COPPÉE (*François*)—L'EXILÉE. Done into English Verse, with the sanction of the Author, by I. O. L. Crown 8vo. vellum, price 5*s.*

COXHEAD (*Ethel*)—BIRDS AND BABIES. Imp. 16mo. With 33 Illustrations. Cloth gilt, 2*s. 6d.*

DAVID RIZZIO, BOTHWELL, AND THE WITCH LADY. Three Tragedies. By the Author of 'Ginevra,' &c. Crown 8vo. cloth, 6*s.*

DAVIE (*G. S.*) *M.D.*—THE GARDEN OF FRAGRANCE. Being a complete Translation of the Bóstan of Sádi, from the original Persian into English Verse. Crown 8vo. cloth, 7*s. 6d.*

DAVIES (*T. Hart*)—CATULLUS. Translated into English Verse. Crown 8vo. cloth, price 6*s.*

DE VERE (*Aubrey*)—THE FORAY OF QUEEN MEAVE, and other Legends of Ireland's Heroic Age. Small crown 8vo. cloth, 5*s.*

LEGENDS OF THE SAXON SAINTS. Small crown 8vo. cloth, price 6*s.*

DILLON (*Arthur*)—RIVER SONGS and other Poems. With 13 Autotype Illustrations from designs by Margery May. Fcp. 4to. cloth extra, gilt leaves, 10*s. 6d.*

DOBELL (*Mrs. Horace*)—ETHELSTONE, EVELINE, and other Poems. Crown 8vo. cloth, 6*s.*

DOBSON (*Austin*)—OLD WORLD IDYLLS, and other Poems. 18mo. cloth, extra gilt.

DOMET (*Alfred*)—RANOLF AND AMOHIA : a Dream of Two Lives. New Edition revised. 2 vols. Crown 8vo. cloth, price 12*s.*

DOROTHY: a Country Story in Elegiac Verse. With Preface. Demy 8vo. cloth, price 5*s.*

DOWDEN (Edward) LL.D.—SHAKSPERE'S SONNETS. With Introduction. Large post 8vo. cloth, price 7*s. 6d.*

DOWNTON (Rev. H.) M.A.—HYMNS AND VERSES. Original and Translated. Small crown 8vo. cloth, price 3*s. 6d.*

DUTT (Toru)—A SHEAF GLEANED IN FRENCH FIELDS. New Edition. Demy 8vo. cloth, 10*s. 6d.*

EDMONDS (E. W.) — HESPERAS. Rhythm and Rhyme. Crown 8vo. cloth, price 4*s.*

ELDRYTH (Maud)—MARGARET, and other Poems. Small crown 8vo. cloth, price 3*s. 6d.*

ELLIOT (Lady Charlotte)—MEDUSA, and other Poems. Crown 8vo. cloth, price 6*s.*

ELLIOTT (Ebenezer), The Corn Law Rhymer—POEMS. Edited by his Son, the Rev. Edwin Elliott, of St. John's, Antigua. 2 vols. crown 8vo. price 18*s.*

ENGLISH ODES. Selected, with a Critical Introduction by EDMUND W. GOSSE, and a miniature Frontispiece by Hamo Thornycroft, A.R.A. Elzevir 8vo. limp parchment antique, price 6*s.* ; vellum, 7*s. 6d.*

EVANS (Anne)—POEMS AND MUSIC. With Memorial Preface by ANN THACKERAY RITCHIE. Large crown 8vo. cloth, price 7*s.*

GOSSE (Edmund W.)—NEW POEMS. Crown 8vo. cloth, price 7*s. 6d.*

GRAHAM (William) — TWO FANCIES, and other Poems. Crown 8vo. cloth, price 5*s.*

GRINDROD (Charles) — PLAYS FROM ENGLISH HISTORY. Crown 8vo. cloth, price 7*s. 6d.*

GURNEY (Rev. Alfred)—THE VISION OF THE EUCHARIST, and other Poems. Crown 8vo. cloth, price 5*s.*

HELLON (H. G.)—DAPHNIS: a Pastoral Poem. Small crown 8vo. cloth, price 3*s. 6d.*

HERMAN WALDGRAVE: a Life's Drama. By the Author of 'Ginevra,' &c. Crown 8vo. cloth, 6*s.*

HICKEY (E. H.)—A SCULPTOR, and other Poems. Small crown 8vo. cloth, price 5*s.*

INGHAM (Sarson C. J.)—CÆDMON'S VISION, and other Poems. Small crown 8vo. cloth, 5*s.*

JENKINS (Rev. Canon) — ALFONSO PETRUCCI, Cardinal and Conspirator : an Historical Tragedy in Five Acts. Small crown 8vo. cloth, price 3*s. 6d.*

KING (Edward)—ECHOES FROM THE ORIENT. With Miscellaneous Poems. Small crown 8vo. cloth, price 3*s. 6d.*

KING (Mrs. Hamilton)—THE DISCIPLES. Fifth Edition, with Portrait and Notes. Crown 8vo. price 5*s.*

A BOOK OF DREAMS. Crown 8vo. cloth, price 5*s.*

LANG (A.)—XXXII BALLADES IN BLUE CHINA. Elzevir 8vo. parchment, price 5*s.*

LAWSON (Right Hon. Mr. Justice)— HYMNI USITATI LATINE REDDITI, with other Verses. Small 8vo. parchment, price 5*s.*

LEIGH (Arran and Isla) — BELLEROPHÔN. Small crown 8vo. cloth, price 5*s.*

LEIGHTON (Robert)—RECORDS AND OTHER POEMS. With Portrait. Small crown 8vo. cloth, price 7*s. 6d.*

LESSING'S NATHAN THE WISE. Translated by Eustace K. Corbett. Crown 8vo. cloth. 6*s.*

LIVING ENGLISH POETS. MDCCCLXXXII. With Frontispiece by Walter Crane. Second Edition. Large crown 8vo. printed on hand-made paper. Parchment, 12*s.* ; vellum, 15*s.*

LOCKER (F.)—LONDON LYRICS. A Cheap Edition, price 2*s. 6d.*

LOVE IN IDLENESS. A Volume of Poems. With an etching by W. B. Scott. Small crown 8vo. cloth, price 5*s.*

LOVE SONNETS OF PROTEUS. With Frontispiece by the Author. Elzevir 8vo. cloth, price 5*s.*

LOWNDES (*Henry*) — POEMS AND TRANSLATIONS. Crown 8vo. cloth, 6s.

LUMSDEN (*Lieut.-Col. H. W.*) — BEOWULF: an Old English Poem. Translated into Modern Rhymes. Second and revised Edition. Small crown 8vo. cloth, price 5s.

LYRE AND STAR. Poems by the Author of 'Ginevra,' &c. Crown 8vo. cloth, price 5s.

MACLEAN (*Charles Donald*) — LATIN AND GREEK VERSE TRANSLATIONS. Small crown 8vo. cloth, 2s.

MAGNUSSON (*Eirikr*) *M.A.*, and PALMER (*E. H.*) *M.A.* — JOHAN LUDVIG RUNEBERG'S LYRICAL SONGS, IDYLLS, AND EPIGRAMS. Fcp. 8vo. cloth, price 5s.

MDC. Chronicles of Christopher Columbus. A Poem in Twelve Cantos. Small crown 8vo. cloth, 7s. 6d.

MEREDITH (*Owen*) [*The Earl of Lytton*] LUCILE. With 32 Illustrations. 16mo. cloth, price 3s. 6d.; cloth extra, gilt edges, price 4s. 6d.

MIDDLETON (*The Lady*) — BALLADS. Square 16mo. cloth, price 3s. 6d.

MORICE (*Rev. F. D.*) *M.A.* — THE OLYMPIAN AND PYTHIAN ODES OF PINDAR. A New Translation in English Verse. Crown 8vo. price 7s. 6d.

MORRIS (*Lewis*) — POETICAL WORKS. Vol. I. contains Songs of Two Worlds. Vol. II. contains The Epic of Hades. Vol. III. contains Gwen and the Ode of Life. New and Cheaper Editions, with Portrait, complete in 3 vols. 5s. each.

THE EPIC OF HADES. With 16 Autotype Illustrations after the drawings by the late George R. Chapman. 4to. cloth extra, gilt leaves, price 21s.

THE EPIC OF HADES. Presentation Edition. 4to. cloth extra, gilt leaves, price 10s. 6d.

DAY AND NIGHT. A Volume of Verses. Fcp. 8vo.

MORSHEAD (*E. D. A.*) — THE HOUSE ATREUS. Being the Agamemnon, Libation-Bearers, and Furies of Æschylus. Translated into English Verse. Crown 8vo. cloth, price 7s.

THE SUPPLIANT MAIDENS OF ÆSCHYLUS. Crown 8vo. cloth, price 3s. 6d.

NADEN (*Constance W.*) — SONGS AND SONNETS OF SPRING TIME. Small crown 8vo. cloth, price 5s.

NEWELL (*E. J.*) — THE SORROW OF SIMONA, and Lyrical Verses. Small crown 8vo. cloth, 3s. 6d.

NOAKE (*Major R. Compton*) — THE BIVOUAC; or, Martial Lyrist. With an Appendix: Advice to the Soldier. Fcp. 8vo. price 5s. 6d.

NOEL (*The Hon. Roden*) — A LITTLE CHILD'S MONUMENT. Second Edition. Small crown 8vo. cloth, 3s. 6d.

NORRIS (*Rev. Alfred*) — THE INNER AND OUTER LIFE. Poems. Fcp. 8vo. cloth, price 6s.

ODE OF LIFE (THE). By the Author of 'The Epic of Hades,' &c. Fourth Edition. Crown 8vo. cloth, price 5s.

O'HAGAN (*John*) — THE SONG OF ROLAND. Translated into English Verse. New and Cheaper Edition. Crown 8vo. cloth, price 5s.

PFEIFFER (*Emily*) — GLAN ALARCH: his Silence and Song. A Poem. Second Edition. Crown 8vo. price 6s.

GERARD'S MONUMENT, and other Poems. Second Edition. Crown 8vo. cloth, price 6s.

QUARTERMAN'S GRACE, and other Poems. Crown 8vo. cloth, price 5s.

POEMS. Second Edition. Crown 8vo. cloth, price 6s.

SONNETS AND SONGS. New Edition. 16mo. handsomely printed and bound in cloth, gilt edges, price 4s.

UNDER THE ASPENS: Lyrical and Dramatic. Crown 8vo. with Portrait, cloth, price 6s.

PIKE (*Warburton*) — THE INFERNO OF DANTE ALIGHIERI. Demy 8vo. cloth, price 5s.

RARE POEMS OF THE 16TH AND 17TH CENTURIES. Edited by W. J. Linton. Crown 8vo. cloth, price 5s.

RHOADES (*James*) — THE GEORGICS OF VIRGIL. Translated into English Verse. Small crown 8vo. cloth, price 5s.

ROBINSON (A. Mary F.)—A HANDFUL OF HONEYSUCKLE. Fcp. 8vo. cloth, price 3s. 6d.

THE CROWNED HIPPOLYTUS. Translated from Euripides. With New Poems. Small crown 8vo. cloth, price 5s.

SAUNDERS (John)—LOVE'S MARTYRDOM : a Play and Poem. Small crown 8vo. cloth, 5s.

SCHILLER'S MARY STUART. German Text with English Translation on opposite page. By Leedham White. Crown 8vo. cloth, 6s.

SCOTT (George F. E.)—THEODORA, and other Poems. Small crown 8vo. cloth, price 3s. 6d.

SELKIRK (J. B.)—POEMS. Crown 8vo. cloth, price 7s. 6d.

SHAW (W. F.) M.A.—JUVENAL, PERSIUS, MARTIAL, AND CATULLUS : an Experiment in Translation. Crown 8vo. cloth, 5s.

SHELLEY (Percy Bysshe) — POEMS SELECTED FROM. Dedicated to Lady Shelley. With Preface by Richard Garnett. Printed on hand-made paper, with miniature Frontispiece, Elzevir 8vo. limp parchment antique, price 6s. ; vellum, price 7s. 6d.

SIX BALLADS ABOUT KING ARTHUR. Crown 8vo. cloth extra, gilt edges, price 3s. 6d.

SLADEN (Douglas B. W.)—FRITHJOF AND INGEBJORG, and other Poems. Small crown 8vo. cloth, 5s.

SOPHOCLES : The Seven Plays in English Verse. Translated by Lewis Campbell. Crown 8vo. cloth, price 7s. 6d.

TAYLOR (Sir H.)—Works Complete in Five Volumes. Crown 8vo. cloth, price 30s.

PHILIP VAN ARTEVELDE. Fcp. 8vo. price 3s. 6d.

THE VIRGIN WIDOW, &c. Fcp. 8vo. price 3s. 6d.

THE STATESMAN. Fcp. 8vo. price 3s. 6d.

TENNYSON (Alfred) — Works Complete :

THE IMPERIAL LIBRARY EDITION. Complete in 7 vols. Demy 8vo. price 10s. 6d. each; in Roxburgh binding, 12s. 6d. each.

AUTHOR'S EDITION. In 7 vols. Post 8vo. cloth gilt, 43s. 6d. ; or half-morocco, Roxburgh style, price 54s.

CABINET EDITION. 13 vols. Each with Frontispiece. Fcp. 8vo. price 2s. 6d. each.

CABINET EDITION. 13 vols. Complete in handsome Ornamental Case, 35s.

THE ROYAL EDITION. In 1 vol. With 26 Illustrations and Portrait. Cloth extra, bevelled boards, gilt leaves, price 21s.

THE GUINEA EDITION. Complete in 13 vols. neatly bound and enclosed in box. Cloth, price 21s.; French morocco or parchment, price 31s. 6d.

SHILLING EDITION. In 13 vols. pocket size, 1s. each, sewed.

THE CROWN EDITION. Complete in 1 vol. strongly bound in cloth, price 6s. ; cloth, extra gilt leaves, price 7s. 6d.; Roxburgh, half-morocco, price 8s. 6d.

*** Can also be had in a variety of other bindings.

Original Editions :—

POEMS. Small 8vo. price 6s.

MAUD, and other Poems. Small 8vo. price 3s. 6d.

THE PRINCESS. Small 8vo. price 3s. 6d.

IDYLLS OF THE KING. Small 8vo. price 5s.

IDYLLS OF THE KING. Complete. Small 8vo. price 6s.

THE HOLY GRAIL, and other Poems. Small 8vo. price 4s. 6d.

GARETH AND LYNETTE. Small 8vo. price 3s.

TENNYSON (Alfred)—continued.

ENOCH ARDEN, &c., Small 8vo. price 3*s*. 6*d*.

IN MEMORIAM. Small 8vo. price 4*s*.

HAROLD : a Drama. New Edition. Crown 8vo. price 6*s*.

QUEEN MARY : a Drama. New Edition. Crown 8vo. price 6*s*.

THE LOVER'S TALE. Fcp. 8vo. cloth, 3*s*. 6*d*.

BALLADS, and other Poems. Small 8vo. cloth, price 5*s*

SELECTIONS FROM THE ABOVE WORKS. Super-royal 16mo. price 3*s*. 6*d*. ; cloth gilt extra, price 4*s*.

SONGS FROM THE ABOVE WORKS. 16mo. cloth, price 2*s*. 6*d*.

TENNYSON FOR THE YOUNG AND FOR RECITATION. Specially arranged. Fcp. 8vo. 1*s*. 6*d*.

THE TENNYSON BIRTHDAY BOOK. Edited by Emily Shakespear. 32mo. cloth limp, 2*s*. ; cloth extra, 3*s*.

*** A superior Edition, printed in red and black, on antique paper, specially prepared. Small crown 8vo. cloth, extra gilt leaves, price 5*s*.; and in various calf and morocco bindings.

THORNTON (L. M.)—THE SON OF SHELOMITH. Small crown 8vo. cloth, price 3*s*. 6*d*.

TODHUNTER (Dr. J.) — LAURELLA, and other Poems. Crown 8vo. 6*s*. 6*d*.

FOREST SONGS. Small crown 8vo. cloth, price 3*s*. 6*d*.

THE TRUE TRAGEDY OF RIENZI : a Drama. Cloth, price 3*s*. 6*d*.

TODHNUTER—continued.

ALCESTIS : a Dramatic Poem. Extra fcp. 8vo. cloth, price 5*s*.

A STUDY OF SHELLEY. Crown 8vo. cloth, price 7*s*.

TRANSLATIONS FROM DANTE, PETRARCH, MICHAEL ANGELO, AND VITTORIA COLONNA. Fcp. 8vo. cloth, price 7*s*.6*d*.

TURNER (Rev. C. Tennyson)—SONNETS, LYRICS, AND TRANSLATIONS. Crown 8vo. cloth, price 4*s*. 6*d*.

COLLECTED SONNETS, Old and New. With Prefatory Poem by ALFRED TENNYSON ; also some Marginal Notes by S. T. COLERIDGE, and a Critical Essay by JAMES SPEDDING. Fcp. 8vo cloth, price 7*s*. 6*d*.

WALTERS (Sophia Lydia) — A DREAMER'S SKETCH BOOK. With 21 Illustrations by Percival Skelton, R. P. Leitch, W. H. J. Boot, and T. R. Pritchett. Engraved by J. D. Cooper. Fcp. 4to. cloth, price 12*s*. 6*d*.

WEBSTER (Augusta)—IN A DAY : a Drama. Small crown 8vo. cloth, price 2*s*. 6*d*.

WET DAYS. By a Farmer. Small crown 8vo. cloth, price 6*s*.

WILKINS (William)—SONGS OF STUDY. Crown 8vo. cloth, price 6*s*.

WILLIAMS (J.)—A STORY OF THREE YEARS, and other Poems. Small crown 8vo. cloth, price 3*s*. 6*d*.

YOUNGS (Ella Sharpe)—PAPHUS, and other Poems. Small crown 8vo. cloth, price 3*s*. 6*d*.

WORKS OF FICTION IN ONE VOLUME.

BANKS (Mrs. G. L.)—GOD'S PROVIDENCE HOUSE. New Edition. Crown 8vo. cloth, price 3*s*. 6*d*.

HARDY (Thomas)—A PAIR OF BLUE EYES. Author of ' Far from the Madding Crowd.' New Edition. Crown 8vo. price 6*s*.

HARDY (Thomas)—continued.

THE RETURN OF THE NATIVE. New Edition. With Frontispiece. Crown 8vo. cloth, price 6*s*.

INGELOW (Jean)—OFF THE SKELLIGS. A Novel. With Frontispiece. Second Edition. Crown 8vo. cloth, price 6*s*.

MACDONALD (G.) — CASTLE WAR- LOCK. A Novel. New and Cheaper Edition. Crown 8vo. cloth, price 6s.

MALCOLM. With Portrait of the Author engraved on Steel. Sixth Edition. Crown 8vo. price 6s.

THE MARQUIS OF LOSSIE. Fourth Edition. With Frontispiece. Crown 8vo. cloth, price 6s.

ST. GEORGE AND ST. MICHAEL. Third Edition. With Frontispiece. Crown 8vo. cloth, 6s.

PALGRAVE (W. Gifford)—HERMANN AGHA : an Eastern Narrative. Third Edition. Crown 8vo. cloth, price 6s.

SHAW (Flora L.)—CASTLE BLAIR; a Story of Youthful Days. New and Cheaper Edition. Crown 8vo. price 3s. 6d.

STRETTON (Hesba) — THROUGH A NEEDLE'S EYE. A Story. New and Cheaper Edition, with Frontispiece. Crown 8vo. cloth, price 6s.

TAYLOR (Col. Meadows) C.S.I., M.R.I.A. SEETA. A Novel. New and Cheaper Edition. With Frontispiece. Crown 8vo. cloth, price 6s.

TIPPOO SULTAUN : a Tale of the Mysore War. New Edition, with Frontispiece. Crown 8vo. cloth, price 6s.

RALPH DARNELL. New and Cheaper Edition. With Frontispiece. Crown 8vo. cloth, price 6s.

A NOBLE QUEEN. New and Cheaper Edition. With Frontispiece. Crown 8vo. cloth, price 6s.

THE CONFESSIONS OF A THUG. Crown 8vo. price 6s.

TARA : a Mahratta Tale. Crown 8vo. price 6s.

WITHIN SOUND OF THE SEA. New and Cheaper Edition, with Frontispiece. Crown 8vo. cloth, price 6s.

BOOKS FOR THE YOUNG.

BRAVE MEN'S FOOTSTEPS. A Book of Example and Anecdote for Young People. By the Editor of 'Men who have Risen.' With Four Illustrations by C. Doyle. Eighth Edition. Crown 8vo. price 3s. 6d.

COXHEAD (Ethel)—BIRDS AND BABIES. With 33 Illustrations. Imp. 16mo. cloth gilt, price 2s. 6d.

DAVIES (G. Christopher) — RAMBLES AND ADVENTURES OF OUR SCHOOL FIELD CLUB. With Four Illustrations. New and Cheaper Edition. Crown 8vo. price 3s. 6d.

EDMONDS (Herbert) — WELL-SPENT LIVES : a Series of Modern Biographies. New and Cheaper Edition. Crown 8vo. price 3s. 6d.

EVANS (Mark)—THE STORY OF OUR FATHER'S LOVE, told to Children. Fourth and Cheaper Edition of Theology for Children. With Four Illustrations. Fcp. 8vo. price 1s. 6d.

JOHNSON (Virginia W.)—THE CATSKILL FAIRIES. Illustrated by ALFRED FREDERICKS. Cloth, price 5s.

MAC KENNA (S. J.)—PLUCKY FEL- LOWS. A Book for Boys. With Six Illustrations. Fifth Edition. Crown 8vo. price 3s. 6d.

REANEY (Mrs. G. S.)—WAKING AND WORKING; or, From Girlhood to Womanhood. New and Cheaper Edition. With a Frontispiece. Cr. 8vo. price 3s. 6d.

BLESSING AND BLESSED : a Sketch of Girl Life. New and Cheaper Edition. Crown 8vo. cloth, price 3s. 6d.

ROSE GURNEY'S DISCOVERY. A Book for Girls. Dedicated to their Mothers. Crown 8vo. cloth, price 3s. 6d.

ENGLISH GIRLS: Their Place and Power. With Preface by the Rev. R. W. Dale. Fourth Edition. Fcp. 8vo. cloth, price 2s. 6d.

REANEY (Mrs. G. S.)—continued.

JUST ANYONE, and other Stories. Three Illustrations. Royal 16mo. cloth, price 1s. 6d.

SUNBEAM WILLIE, and other Stories. Three Illustrations. Royal 16mo. price 1s. 6d.

SUNSHINE JENNY, and other Stories. Three Illustrations. Royal 16mo. cloth, price 1s. 6d.

STOCKTON (Frank R.)—A JOLLY FELLOWSHIP. With 20 Illustrations. Crown 8vo. cloth, price 5s.

STORR (Francis) and TURNER (Hawes). CANTERBURY CHIMES; or, Chaucer Tales Re-told to Children. With Six Illustrations from the Ellesmere MS. Second Edition. Fcp. 8vo. cloth, price 3s. 6d.

STRETTON (Hesba)—DAVID LLOYD'S LAST WILL. With Four Illustrations. New Edition. Royal 16mo. price 2s. 6d.

TALES FROM ARIOSTO RE-TOLD FOR CHILDREN. By a Lady. With Three Illustrations. Crown 8vo. cloth, price 4s. 6d.

LONDON : PRINTED BY
SPOTTISWOODE AND CO., NEW-STREET SQUARE
AND PARLIAMENT STREET

www.ingramcontent.com/pod-product-compliance
Lightning Source LLC
Chambersburg PA
CBHW052333110726
47901CB00005B/1219